Rowan stared down into her glass. In the last few days she had thought about the future a lot, but in very general terms, never confronting the next hour, the next day, the next week. Time had passed and she had taken not one positive decision.

'I want to be the one to see to the firm,' she said suddenly. 'I mean, I'm the only one who knows even vaguely what's going on. I'll talk to the bank manager and sell things and so on.'

The words were automatic. To Rowan's surprise she was feeling a great and delicious relief. She swallowed and felt her head spin, probably because of the sherry. She would be alone, for the first time in her life. No one to care for, no one to worry about – it was as if she was laying down a heavy burden. She tried to concentrate her thoughts, for of course there would still be the mill, which despite everything was still her responsibility. Somehow that never weighed heavy. It intrigued and demanded, and in the end gave you back exactly what you deserved. None of the others knew how important it was, they didn't care, they didn't understand.

Rowan turned her face away from her mother. At last, at long last, she could have the mill to herself.

Also by Elizabeth Walker

Dark Sunrise
A Summer Frost
Wild Honey
Voyage

Rowan's Mill

Elizabeth Walker

HEADLINE

First published in 1988
by Judy Piatkus (Publishers) Ltd

First published in paperback in 1989
by HEADLINE BOOK PUBLISHING PLC

Printed and bound in Great Britain by
Collins, Glasgow

HEADLINE BOOK PUBLISHING PLC
Headline House
79 Great Titchfield Street
London W1P 7FN

Acknowledgements

Whilst the characters and organisations described in this book are entirely fictitious, I have nonetheless tried to depict Yorkshire and the textile industry as accurately as I can. The research was enormous fun, because the West Riding is full of larger than life people and places. I was able in the space of a morning to go from wild moorland to twenty-first century technology and then into a vast mill built over a hundred years ago where the past seems to be nudging at your shoulder. Many people were very kind and patient, taking the time to describe what are often complex processes in terms that I could understand. In particular I must thank Abraham Moons of Guiseley, Parkland Textiles of Apperley Bridge, Woolcombers, the Wool Marketing Board and the International Wool Secretariat. Let me stress that any disasters and inefficiencies I describe are the product of my imagination, with no reflection on the realities of life in these firms.

In addition I should like to express my gratitude to the many textile men who were kind enough to tell me what it is really like travelling to far-flung places buying and selling, although to them it is so everyday that they really couldn't work out why I wanted to know. I hope this book explains all.

Chapter One

The warehouse roof was leaking. At some time during the storms of the past winter, rain had come in and soaked four or five bales of scoured wool. Since then they had sat and mouldered. Now, broken open on the floor, they spilled out their contents. The smell was disgusting, like sour dish-cloths, and it was somebody's fault.

Andrew turned to the warehouseman. 'Which is it? Do we know?'

'Oh aye. It's the good stuff.'

Of course, it would be. Though why good wool had stood unused in the warehouse for months was beyond him, they might as well leave pound notes to go sodden in the rain. Did he have to do everything himself, from counting bales of wool to watching for leaks in the roof? 'Somebody should have told me,' he said loudly. 'Surely someone noticed?' The warehouseman eyed him inscrutably.

Andrew sighed. There was no point in making it worse. But what in God's name did they do now? Sinking his hands into his pockets, he said tightly: 'Can we send it back to the scourer? It might wash out.'

The warehouseman seemed almost insulted to be asked about something so far outside his experience. He said frostily, 'Buggered if I know. Might never get rid of the stink.'

For a minute Andrew thought about sending the wool through the mill as it was, if they could dye it navy blue they would almost match the mould. God knows what the workers would say though. Besides, they didn't need navy blue yarn, they needed piece-dyed orange cloth and they needed this wool to make it.

Stamping back through the warehouse, his feet splashing

in other, less damaging, puddles, he let the problem slip from his mind. Tomorrow, when he felt fresh, the solution would present itself. Pity they couldn't start on the order but there was just no telling when this sort of thing might happen and disrupt everything, especially with a firm like Judge's housed in a vast old mill that crumbled about them. Sometimes he dreamed of letting the whole shooting match burn down. Sometimes he dreamed of lighting the fire himself.

The clack of high heels sounded on the slate floor. He looked up expectantly, a smile already brightening his thin, serious face. He could always tell Diana's step, long and unhurried. She came in from the yard, holding her fur jacket close to her neck against the chill spring wind. He thought how lovely she was.

'Oh, there you are, Andrew, Frances said you were in here. Lunch. Don't say you've forgotten.'

His wife put up her cheek for him to kiss, a sure sign that she was still irritated with him. With a sense of glum horror he realised that he had forgotten to ask Frances to book a table, the morning's crisis had put it quite out of his mind. This lunch, intended as a peace-offering, might well degenerate into another squabble.

'Go and sit in the car, darling, I must wash my hands,' he said hurriedly. 'I won't be a tic, I promise.'

Diana sighed gustily.

He was gone a good ten minutes, because Frances couldn't find the number of the restaurant, and then couldn't get through. But there was a table, for which Andrew felt a profound relief. He ran across to his Jaguar and climbed in beside his wife.

'Sorry. Telephone call.' He reversed out of his parking space and swept through the high, wrought-iron gates that bore the inscription 'Isaac Judge Ltd.' in gold letters, into the narrow road where now and then the cobbles pushed their way back up through the tarmac. Within the space of this one road were two more mills, both empty, their chimneys pointing uselessly at the sky. They'd both gone down in the last ten years, beaten by shrinking markets supplied at give-away prices by Far Eastern sweatshops. Throughout it all, Judge's had held on. Their chimney still smoked, the orders dribbled in: for old lady skirtings, drab overcoats, sometimes a cheap grey flannel. Hanging on, waiting for the upturn that never seemed to come.

The car lifted its nose and sped up the hill, at once deserting the confines of the town and plunging into the country. That was the thing about Bradford, it was industry lapped all about by hills, moors, the cold blue Yorkshire air. The wind whistled in the rough grass. Sheep ran across the road in front of them.

Andrew opened the window and took in great gouts of air. Diana shuddered pointedly. He wound the window up again. 'Sorry, darling. I'll put the heater up.' Before he could reach the controls Diana did it, her long, thin fingers neat and precise. The silence in the car became almost solid.

Suddenly Andrew pulled the car hard on to the grass at the side of the road. Diana squeaked with fright, choking the sound off as they jerked to a halt.

'I'm sorry,' he said. 'You know I'm sorry.'

'You're always bloody sorry,' said Diana bitterly.

Andrew swallowed. 'I hate to hear you swear.'

'Well, I hate feeling so – let down.'

He reached across and put his hand over both of hers, where they twisted in her lap. 'Does it mean that much to you?' he asked, and her eyes blazed at him, amazed that he should even ask.

'You know it does! Honestly, Andrew, it isn't even as if I hadn't given up things to have it. My car's falling apart, I have to make up excuses every time Linda suggests we go clothes shopping, but I don't mind that! I just want my music room.'

'And a new violin for Andy,' muttered Andrew.

'Well of course! You weren't going back on that, were you? Not as well? He's got talent, he *has* to have a decent violin!'

His face worked desperately. 'Darling, I know he needs it, if I had the money do you think I wouldn't buy it today? And Rowan needs her skiing holiday with the school, and Sally needs a new bike – but with the firm as it is, there just isn't the spare cash.'

'Except for this nice new car.' A voice of cut glass.

'I've told you! If I don't have a new car, people will think we're going down,' insisted Andrew. 'We have to look as if we're doing well. No one's going to place orders if they think we're about to go out of business.'

'Well, build the music room and impress them,' snarled his wife. 'I've heard the same excuses ever since we moved into the blasted house, when the truth is you're jealous of my music and of Andy! You promised me and I've waited years and years, it isn't fair to spoil it now!'

She began to cry, angry tears of frustration and pain. A headache thumped at Andrew's brain. She was right, of course she was right, he did resent the love affair she had with her music, but not enough to deny her this. His mistake had been in letting her think the music room would be this year. She had rushed ahead with the plans, found a builder, talked to the gardener about moving the plants from the bed next to the house, everything. Like the craven he was, he had put off doing the sums, put off discussing it with her, until it was all much too late. And he couldn't bear to see her cry.

'Darling – if we changed the plans a little,' he ventured. 'Suppose we put up the basic structure and then did the inside as we can afford it?'

Her head came up. 'You mean – just the outside walls and things? I could still have my floor-length windows, couldn't I? And the vaulted ceiling?'

'Well, I suppose so.' Andrew was hurrying down his escape route. 'We'll do what we can, anyway. Perhaps Andy wouldn't mind waiting a few months for his new violin, his old one's not that bad – '

'He'll never win competitions with it,' interposed Diana, but her husband rushed on regardless.

'– and then we can finish if off gradually. I know it's not quite as you wanted, darling, but since you want it so much . . .'

Diana's eyes were brilliant in her pale face. She put out her arms and hugged her husband, enveloping him in her scent, her softness, her warmth. 'I'm sorry I was such a beast,' she whispered. 'I know it will cost a lot, but I want it desperately! I've waited so long, Andrew, I couldn't bear to be put off now. We can afford it, can't we?'

A brief vision of the bales of mouldy wool flashed into his head; half the weaving shed was standing idle waiting for the yarn to be spun from it, and with so thin an order book he ought to be travelling, ought to be getting business. Still, if he lied about a new order he should get a few bales of wool from the merchant, and some money might come in before he had to pay. And the mouldy wool would be worth something – but his wife didn't want to hear it. He bent his head and kissed her. 'You have just what you want.'

James Barton ran his fingers down the grain of panelled oak. It had come from a once prosperous mill and he had saved it, snatched it from under the noses of the liquidators, to line his office. The pleasure it gave him was undiminished, partly because of its beauty, mostly because of his acumen.

Below, in the yard, they were unloading dyed yarn, and he considered going down to have a look at it. But he would soon hear if there was anything wrong, he had good men checking. It was just that he was restless today; there were things to be done and they needed doing, but nothing was urgent or unpredictable. When he had first grabbed Bardsey's from his father's incapable fingers, every day had been filled with knife-edge decisions that had to be right. He hadn't been able to sleep, he remembered, not through fear, because he had never feared anything, but excitement. They had been good times, stretching, growing times, when he had even managed to surprise himself.

Not that he slept very well nowadays. He supposed he was bored, though that was a slight word for what seemed like lead in his soul. Was it a year since he had first noticed it, first woken up and thought of the day and felt – bored? At night now he lay beside Marjorie as she murmured and snored, and wondered about the point of it all; all that striving and energy, struggle and brilliance, just to come to this. A plump wife, her lips shiny with nightcream; a house heavy with affluence, a son well established at a good school. In the dark of the small hours he asked himself, 'What now? Here you are, James Barton, you made it. What next?'

There was a perfunctory knock on the door and Saul came into the office. James at once transferred his irritation to him.

'What the hell do you want?'

Saul paused, but with his usual insouciance said cheerfully, 'God, you must have a hangover. I've brought the samples for you to look at.'

'So you have. Put them on the side table.'

James watched irritably as Saul went to obey. It was an interesting game, to see how much his brother would take before he acknowledged James's hostility, and fought back. Two or three times there had been monumental rows, but in the end Saul always came to heel. It was as if he hadn't the energy to spare for trivial things like position and power, preferring fast cars, fast women and amusement. Which, if nothing else, proved that very little of the same blood flowed in their veins.

They weren't even much alike in looks, for Saul was thicker, more muscled, his eyes a soft liquid brown that could turn the colour of autumn leaves. The two men were of a height though, well over six feet, but leaving that aside James wondered, not for the first time, if Saul was indeed his own father's son. Where was the pale skin and carrot hair that were James's legacy? Perhaps in the matter of paternity, as in so much else, old man Barton had been mistaken. Still, though he had accepted and provided for this late-born son, he hadn't made the even bigger mistake of marrying the mother.

'How was Spain? I see you managed to fit in your sunbathing.' James took a swipe at the tan he could never achieve and Saul managed almost all year round.

'I did some good business,' said Saul casually. 'And like a fool I made the mistake of going to see a bullfight, a real local *corrida*. I don't say the bloke wasn't brave, but when they skewered the poor beast I was an inch from throwing up. The lady I was with wasn't amused.'

'Who was she? A contact, I hope.'

'A daughter of one of the customers. Pretty as anything but the soul of Lucrezia Borgia. I ruined my chances by suggesting she start a campaign to abolish the bullfight – which seems to be tantamount to a call for the compulsory castration of all Spanish men. Don't look so alarmed! I sent her a leather handbag the next day. At the moment she wants to marry me.'

James snorted. An endless queue of ladies wanted to marry Saul, but he seemed to be able to avoid it and keep them happy. It was one of his major talents.

'If we could talk about work?' he said patiently.

'Anything you like, brother mine. Thought you were more interested in rending my living flesh, but even you must get bored with it.'

He was right. Today nothing could lighten James's mood.

Saul began expertly spreading out the sample cloth on the table. Clearly it was something he had done many times before, but the colours themselves were startlingly fresh: purple and orange and bright green. Saul set them out in interesting combinations, filling the centre with a matt-black coat material, dense and flat. They had produced it on a hunch of James's because he had seen a calf-length black coat at a tacky London fashion event and for him it had rung bells.

'Looks good,' said James, shining a torch on the orange.

The shade changed, taking on a bluish tint: 'Couldn't we get this better?' he demanded. 'Women's suiting, isn't it? You know how the bloody shops complain, all those housewives and typists bringing things back because they thought it would match the blouse and now it doesn't seem to. You did notice it, I suppose?'

'Not exactly my department,' retorted Saul. 'All I do is sell the stuff. I mean, if you want me to pop back from New York, or even Tokyo, and check the dye then I'll be delighted. Of course you're just round the corner, and an innocent might think it would be easier for you, but anything to oblige.'

'Oh, you're so bloody funny,' said James sourly. He knew perfectly well that they had settled on the inferior dye because not only did it cost less but thankfully did not come off on the skin, as did the more expensive stuff whatever they tried. They needed to put some real money into researching dyes; he would have to brace himself and do it despite the unprofitable time it would take.

The thought depressed him still further. Determined to rile Saul he said, 'You should consider letting someone else do some of the long trips; I've mentioned it to you before.'

The brown eyes fixed on him, but for once Saul was silent. They both knew that James was threatening him with the loss of his job, and if there was one single thing in the world Saul cared about it was that. A brilliant, inspired salesman, his biggest thrill was using the world as his backyard. He was that rare and almost extinct species, a natural traveller. Luxury hotel or mud-floored hovel, it was all the same to him.

He spoke six languages, knew personally most of the stewardesses on the long-haul routes and could just as easily chat up the lady owner of a Chinese junk. He went to China nowadays to buy raw silk, and to sell cloth, but unless specifically requested he wouldn't bore you with tales of silk farms where the worms hung for weeks in humid sheds and women sat all day unravelling the cocoons. The satisfaction was for himself alone, and for James to hurt him irrevocably he had only to take away his job. Thankfully not even James could afford to lose him – yet.

They went through the samples, comparing weights and prices, discussing lead times on orders.

'It's all very new,' said Saul doubtfully. 'It's a risk. Perhaps we should play safe and combine it with some of the old range.'

'I think not.' It was James's turn to be adventurous. 'After all, we're selling a look, not a ragbag of styles. We'll push the new range first, we can send someone else out with the old faithfuls.'

'When I've fallen flat on my face with this,' retorted Saul. But he knew he wouldn't. It was good and it was of the times, and as usual James was right. How he hated to admit it.

Unexpectedly, James went to the drinks cabinet and poured them both a whisky. Surprised and somewhat mollified, Saul took his. An uncomfortable silence fell and Saul hunted about for something to say. James's threat had rattled him badly. Finally he said, 'I met Joss Wainwright for lunch; he's trying to tempt us with South African tops again.' Every now and then someone who didn't understand the situation at Bardsey's lunched Saul under the mistaken impression that he had something to do with the running of the firm.

'Tell him to get his quality right, then we'll talk,' commented James.

'That's what I said to him. Andrew Judge was there – wife in a fur coat, new Jag in the car park.'

'Good God!' James was honestly surprised. 'And I thought they were starving to death. That firm's gone downhill ever since the old man died.'

'In such marked contrast to Bardsey's,' said Saul thinly. It could not be said that his fortunes had improved since the death of Frederick Barton. At least while he was alive Saul could believe in the fiction that the firm would one day be shared between the two sons, disregarding the small matter of his illegitimacy. Afterwards Saul saw exactly where he stood, which was in the same place as his mother, the housekeeper, on an unmarked spot between the Promised Land and the Wilderness.

'Would you say Judge's was a sound firm?' asked James suddenly.

Saul shrugged. 'Produces good cloth of its type. At least it did. These days it's falling apart. I wouldn't have thought we need concern ourselves.'

'Supplies the cheaper end though, doesn't it? Undercuts us by pounds per yard.'

'If that's what you like. We're a quality firm, James, Bardsey's quality worsted, and Judge's is a little woollen outfit paddling around in a pond. They don't compete with us!' He watched his brother closely. 'What are you after?'

Draining the dregs of whisky, James said, 'Whatever it is, it has nothing to do with you. Are you going to stand around here drinking all day or can I expect to see your usual ridiculous expenses claim some time this year? I must be paying for half the champagne in France!'

Saul allowed himself a slight grin and gathered up his samples. 'I never drink French wine in Spain, it upsets the natives. Tact, James, tact. Not that I need to tell you about that!'

The door closed behind him, and despite himself James felt himself grinning. Thoughtfully he chewed the inside of his cheek. Suddenly he felt restricted and enclosed, he couldn't breathe. The office was too hot; outside in the yard a fork lift truck was whining with the persistence of a drill. He had to get out into the air, to clear his head of whisky and dullness. Grabbing his coat from the cupboard, he strode from the room.

Chapter Two

James took the Mercedes up to Shipley Glen. Nobody was there on such a brisk weekday, and he parked and wandered amongst the stiff, barely sprouting bilberry. He wanted to walk but not alone; he wouldn't have minded taking his son Richard with him, except that he was away at school. He wanted – something. What a curse had fallen upon him, to have the world offered to him on a plate and to desire none of it. He supposed he could travel, but unlike Saul he loathed the planes and the food, the hotel bedrooms and the stench of street markets. His mind turned back to what had so often been his consolation in the past, his only consolation: work, deals, money. He thought of Judge's.

It was doing better than might be expected, it seemed, and he could almost envy Andrew Judge, a man he knew but slightly. For him the struggle was still before him, the battle yet to be won. Each day would bring its own new challenges, the hours rushing by on a charge of adrenaline. How he would like to be running that firm!

He thought about the two concerns. Bardsey's was essentially in worsteds, using the long flat fibres of fine wools to make smooth, quality cloth. In the past they had prospered on men's suiting, but the advent of casual wear had put a dent in that market. They were more versatile now.

Judge's was a woollen firm, taking the lesser quality, short fibres of a fleece and spinning them into fluffy yarn for tweeds and cheaper stuff. Unlike Bardsey's, who designed and wove the cloth, leaving almost everything else to outside firms, Judge's did everything, from the raw wool to the dyeing and finishing of the fabric, all under the same roof. It was both a strength and a weakness. If you had everything under your own control, you didn't rely on others to meet your deadlines. But if times were hard, you had capacity, and people, you couldn't use. James had been thinking about diversification for a long time. That yarn today had arrived late from a commission spinner. Bardsey's didn't have enough control at that end, they were left apologising for late deliveries that were nothing to do with them. Suppose they owned the spinner? And the dye-house, and the finishing plant, perhaps even the firm that took the sheared wool and combed it, the whole damned shooting match? Suppose they owned even a little woollen concern to mop up the other end of the market? Research needed a spread of applications to make it worthwhile, so in a way he would be justifying that investment. The risks were considerable, it would be difficult and expensive, but surely it would not be boring. That had to be the first consideration.

He turned and began to stride back to his car, his heavy coat whirling around him. A crow, hopping about on the grass, shrieked and flapped slowly into the air. James picked up a pebble and threw it after the bird, sending the stone high into the cold blue sky. Today, without wasting time, he would go and look at Judge's and see for himself.

Although they didn't finish lunch until half-past three, Andrew insisted that he must go back to work, for half an hour at least. Diana decided to wait for him; she hated to see the harassed look that came upon him when she was difficult and work was difficult, and in general she tried not to add to his problems. Sometimes, though, he had to be pushed. Andrew wasn't a very positive person and on occasion she had to insist on things. He could be too kind and gentle for anyone's good.

Andy would be on his way to his music lesson now. When the music room was built she would insist that his teacher came to the house, it was too exhausting for the child to trail around here, there and everywhere. One thing she wouldn't compromise on was adequate sound-proofing; she could not bear Rowan and Sally to intrude with their blaring television, and then to complain about Andy's scales. Girls were awkward beings, Rowan especially. Diana clashed with her elder daughter almost daily, about clothes or tidiness, and mostly Rowan's impossible jealousy of Andy. Undoubtedly he received a great deal of time and attention, but he was the one with the talent. Rowan must learn to accept it.

To pass the time, she strolled up and down the long oak-floored corridor that overlooked the yard. When she first met Andrew it was lined with paintings, there was silver in the boardroom and Crown Derby on the tea tray. All that had been swallowed up, poured down the throat of the mill because at all costs the creature must be kept alive. Why? Why hadn't they sold out years ago, when they still had money, when Andrew was young and drove a two-seater and made jokes that delighted her?

A Mercedes drove into the yard, the numberplate JB.1. Everyone in Bradford knew that number, it was the whiz kid of Bardsey's, the man they called lucky because no one knew how he did it. She watched him step from the car. Tall, with carroty hair and pale, almost white, skin. The men in the yard wiped their hands on their trousers and sent messages, while James Barton put his hands in his pockets and stared up at the windows. He had rather prominent grey eyes. Diana stepped back.

Andrew, obviously flustered, came hurrying out of his office. Diana turned to him. 'Darling, isn't that James Barton?'

'Seems so. Wonder what he wants.' Andrew straightened his tie nervously, clearing his throat with his habitual tense cough.

'Is he coming up?'

'I said I'd go down. Come on, darling, you can meet him too.'

They went down the wide staircase, once polished daily but now dull and cobwebbed. Andrew hurried across to greet Barton but Diana, with some instinct of pride, took her leisurely time.

'Andrew!' Barton was holding out his hand. 'Good to see you after so long.'

'Good to see you too, James.' Andrew had hardly been aware that Barton even knew him. 'May I introduce my wife – Diana, James Barton.' Barton automatically extended his hand, only to find it ignored. Diana inclined her head graciously, remaining at some distance. Andrew almost hiccupped.

'What can I do for you, James?'

He was too eager. It would have been better to let Barton make the approach. James said, 'To be honest, Andrew, I really wanted to have a look round. Please, say no if you'd rather I didn't, but I just felt – well, there might be some business in it. There's a future for your type of cloth.'

The colour came and went in Andrew's face and he glanced towards his wife, as if for reassurance. Diana stared at Barton. 'It's hardly convenient today, Andrew,' she said thinly.

'Well – let's make it convenient,' said Andrew. 'You don't mind, do you, darling? Go and wait upstairs if you'd rather.' He ushered Barton towards the buildings, but for some reason James stopped.

He turned to Diana and said in an odd voice; 'I hope I'm not spoiling your day. Forgive me if I am.'

They looked at each other. She could see a pulse beating under the pale skin of his forehead. In a softer tone she murmured, 'Perhaps we can spare half an hour.'

As the men went into the warehouse, James said, 'What a beautiful woman your wife is.'

'Yes.' In that one word Andrew encapsulated all the surprise that had never abated, despite three children and years of marriage, in his capture of a woman as beautiful and talented as Diana. As the years went by and she acquired elegance and style, he found himself marvelling more and more. At dinner parties he looked at her white neck and glossy auburn hair, echoed in huge gold-flecked eyes, and wondered how on earth he had come to be married to her.

'Odd smell you have in here,' said James.

'Nothing serious,' replied Andrew quickly, rushing him past the mouldy bales. He had forgotten them, or he would have brought the visitor another way.

All at once he saw the place through a stranger's eye: the disorder, the odd parcel of camel or deer hair that had been left over from a job and never used since, the puddles, and above all the stink. Yet Barton said nothing.

They passed the boiler-room, where the monolithic coal-eating monster that supplied the mill's needs rumbled and coughed. Barton stopped for an unscheduled look, though Andrew couldn't imagine why. 'We're not very up to date in here, I'm afraid,' he apologised. 'But it works.' A fine film of dust lay over everything, the boilermen looked like miners at the end of a shift. Andrew almost dragged his visitor on into the mill.

Inevitably one of the cards was stopped. Judge's carding machines, designed to bring order to the tangled mass of fibres in a fleece so that it could be spun, were getting on in years. So was the man who cared for them, and heaven knows who would keep them going once he retired.

'All right, Nobby?' he yelled.

Nobby, long since deafened and as always armed with screwdriver and oily rag, scanned the visitor. 'Oh aye, sir. We'll have it going soon, sir, that we will.' Word of the visitor had travelled and he was on best behaviour. Throughout the mill figures could be seen suddenly sweeping up and getting on. Judge's was doing its best to look presentable, but nothing could give work to idle looms. In the old days it was impossible to talk in here with the roar of hundreds of sheds clattering up and down.

'We're about to start a big new order,' hastened Andrew. 'We want to keep clear for it.'

'Very wise,' said Barton. Was there a hint of irony there? Hard to tell.

They went on, through the dye-house where a cauldron of grey cloth bubbled and foamed, and overflowed on to the floor, into the burling and mending department where women sat in a north light all day, mending faults in the weave. Perhaps the light made it seem drabber than need be. Rolls and rolls of dull fabrics, most of it quite well made but old-fashioned and uninspired.

Andrew stopped at a coarse green cloth. 'One of our new designs,' he said doubtfully. Even he didn't think it looked very new. Judge's had been making a variation on that pattern since his father took over.

Barton suddenly seemed impatient. He pulled his hands from his pockets and made for the door. 'Sorry to have taken up so much of your time. Good to see you're doing well, Andrew.'

Andrew, long legs loping beside him, said, 'I suppose we're lucky to have made it through the last ten years really. That must say something.'

James almost laughed. Yes, he thought to himself, it says that your father was a damn sight better at this job than you are. The only thing that's kept you going these last ten years is the money he made, and there should have been better ways of spending it. Aloud he said, 'I'll just say goodbye to your wife, if I may? I should apologise for disrupting your afternoon.'

Diana was in Andrew's office, idly leafing through an old copy of *Country Life*. The desk was disordered, the open shelves behind cluttered with papers and unread magazines. Wool samples gathered dust on top of a filing cabinet. 'God,' thought James. 'God Almighty.'

He turned and met Diana's large tawny eyes and suddenly he didn't know what to say. They looked at each other with complete understanding. She put the magazine back on the table and idly ran her finger through the dust. He swallowed. 'I just came to say – goodbye.'

She spread her hands. 'Well then – goodbye.' It was tempered with a slight smile and, encouraged, he said: 'Don't be too cross with me. I know I ruined your day.'

'Oh no.' Diana folded her magazine and got up, moving to stand beside her husband. She took his upper arm in both her hands and James thought, 'She knows that's annoying me.' She smiled back at him and said coolly, 'Today couldn't be spoiled. Andrew's agreed to build my music room. That may not sound much to you but I've waited for it for years.'

'Diana plays the violin,' explained Andrew. 'She's quite brilliant.'

Diana wrinkled her nose, the one slightly imperfect feature in her face. It had a slight hook to it. 'Not at all,' she murmured. 'My son is the one with the brilliance.'

James said, 'I wish I could hear you both play.'

Back in his car and driving out of the narrow gate, James looked in his mirror and saw Andrew standing uncertainly, watching him. He felt suddenly drunk, though he had only had the one whisky with Saul. He was almost glad to get away, out of that sour-smelling, doomed mill, away from the cool sensuality of Judge's wife. She disturbed him.

He drove on for a while and then stopped next to a row of derelict shops. Judge's was a mess, out of date, overmanned, disorganised. They would survive only as long as their flimsy facade of prosperity remained intact. He could destroy it and them tomorrow if he wished, just by a few casual words. 'Judge's? On their knees, old boy. Went round the other day, place is a bloody shambles. Might have a new car but he sodding well can't afford it.'

If it had been a fraction less bad he might have bought them out. As it was he would leave them to stew and in a few months, perhaps a year or two, Judge's would be on the scrap heap and that would be that.

'It's all so bloody unfair.' He spoke out loud, bitterly. Because tonight Andrew Judge, that long lanky incompetent, was going home with his beautiful wife. She knew what her husband was but today she was delighted with him because he was spending money she knew he couldn't afford. Those pale legs, that she crossed and uncrossed so seductively, would be well and truly open tonight, and it seemed to James, suddenly, that Andrew Judge had the one thing that he, James Barton, wanted.

Chapter Three

Diana put on her old woollen jacket and stepped out into the garden. The daffodils were waving gaily in the breeze, in other years she had picked them, brought them into every room in the house, called the children to see how pretty they were. Not this year, not in her present mood. She felt a rising tide of bitterness. She walked quickly down the path, stopped under the beech tree and turned to look at the house. Now she could see exactly how bad things were.

In her mind's eye she had pictured an octagonal building linked to the main house by a narrow spur of brickwork, and that was what she had planned and the architect had drawn. It would have been gracious, sunny and beautiful. This rectangle, still mercifully only three feet high, was nothing like her intention. She felt unreasoning rage.

Marching back up the garden, she cursed the builder, the workmen, and most of all Andrew. He was the one who had demanded the changes, and presumably agreed this emasculation of the project. How on earth could he permit this monstrosity to be fixed to the house, like a pimple, like a ghastly suburban garage? She aimed a spiteful kick at one of the walls, and to her surprise it wobbled. The mortar was still damp, it was only an hour or two since the bricklayer left, driven away by her fierce complaints.

'Right,' she muttered and looked round for an implement. One of the pieces of timber they used for shuttering concrete was lying on the ground. She picked it up, wielded it like a cricket bat and hit the wall. Only two bricks fell off, so she hit it twice more, and then leaned against the house and pushed with her feet. That was very effective. She breached an entire hole and what was left tilted crazily.

'That's making a terrible mess of your shoe.'

She spun round, scarlet with surprise and shock. James Barton stood at the French windows, watching her.

'How did you get in ?'

'The front door was open. I'm sorry, I thought something might be wrong.'

Diana snorted and turned back to the mess of bricks around her. 'You were right. God, but I hate it,' she said unnecessarily.

James stood in silence and Diana aimed another vicious kick at the wall, then another, and another. He reached out quickly, and grabbed her arms. 'Don't. Please – don't.'

Diana pulled free and brushed away angry tears. 'Just come and look,' she hissed and pulled herself free. She started back down the garden and James followed, thinking that he was in the presence of a mad woman. But how he loved to touch her.

When she stopped, he turned obediently and looked back at the house. Even he, who lived in a house she would certainly despise, could see how unsuitable the embryo building would be. Non-committal, James said, 'Not at all what I would have chosen.'

'Don't think *I* chose it,' snapped Diana. 'The plan was for an octagon, with a vaulted roof and floor-length windows leading out on to the lawn. I'd rather not have anything than – this!' Her gesture encompassed everything, all her frustration and anger.

'Shall I knock it down for you?' asked James.

The tawny eyes turned on him like twin cannon. 'Yes.'

He tore the wall down with his bare hands, brick by brick. Diana stood and watched him, her face as set as that of an angry goddess. When he had finished and the bricks lay in a jumble of half-set mortar, James panted: 'Will that do?'

'Yes. Thank you.'

He was breathing hard, there was mud on his trousers and

a graze on one hand. Was that all she would say: 'thank you'?

They went into the house. Diana put the kettle on, saying, 'I suppose you're looking for Andrew. He's in London this week.'

'Is he? Damn.'

'Didn't his secretary tell you that?'

'No, she didn't.' Although she might have done had he asked her. He was only here because someone had mentioned that Judge was going to town for a few days. He hadn't intended to come really. Somehow he just had.

While she waited for the kettle, Diana took off her shoe and studied the heel. The leather was badly scratched. 'What a mistake it is to let temper get the better of you,' she said ruefully.

To her surprise, James reached out and took the shoe from her. 'I'll see to it for you.'

'We can still afford shoe repairs, I can assure you.'

'Really, I have some shoes to take in myself. I'll bring it back tomorrow. We can lunch.'

Diana shook her head. 'I couldn't.'

'Please.' James came a little closer, bending his head to her confidingly. 'I'd like to talk about Judge's. I'm sure you can tell me as much as Andrew, if not more. He's too close to it.'

Glancing up with a long-necked flick of her hair she said, 'I may as well admit it, I hate the place. It's a great big fly that needs feeding all the time. All that grubbing and struggling. Why do you men bother with it?'

She fixed him with her clear gaze and he stared back. 'I don't know,' he said with sudden honesty. 'It used to excite me.'

'But not any more.'

'No.'

She moved away and made the tea, her stockinged foot balanced on the toes.

James felt a surge of emotion for that poised, slender foot. He said, 'I'll pick you up at twelve.'

'Oh God, if you must. How I hate talking about that damned firm.' She passed him a mug of tea. Marjorie always presented a visitor with a cup, she didn't know how to be casual. She put on her pearls just to go down to the supermarket and she kept her house, too, on permanent best behaviour. Here there was attractive disorder. Misty flowered wallpaper, and on the polished wood of the hall floor a couple of worn Persian rugs. Marjorie woud have got rid of those years ago.

They said nothing, but Diana seemed unconcerned by the silence. At last James finished his tea and put the mug down. 'Don't mention this to Andrew just yet,' he said briskly. 'We don't want to raise his hopes.'

'All right' said Diana. 'Look, I must go and change my shoes, I have to collect my son in half an hour. Can you see yourself out?'

'I saw myself in,' said James.

'So you did.'

She was gone, and he stood alone in the kitchen, holding the shoe. He ran his fingers over the torn leather.

He arrived at the house twenty minutes early the next day, the shoe on the seat beside him. Switching off the engine, he stared at the building, or at least all he could see through the thick screen of laurel and conifer, elm and beech. Like Judge himself it was restrained and out of its time. A good house to live in, though.

After ten minutes he started the car again and drove the last twenty yards up to the front door. It was shut this time, and there was no sign of life within. The sharp thud of disappointment in his gut took him by surprise, he almost grunted. Instead he went to the door and rapped on it forcefully, and in a few moments he heard soft footfalls in the hall. Diana stood there, in stockinged feet, wearing a silk blouse and the pencil skirt of what was probably a suit if she had had time to put on the jacket.

'You're far too early. I've hardly begun to get dressed.'

'Come as you are.' He laughed, but choked it off as her face stiffened. She wasn't ready for that sort of informality. Quickly he added, 'We're only going to talk business.'

'I think at least I should brush my hair,' she said.

Leaving him there, she went quickly back through the hall and up the wide staircase. James had a vision of following her, rushing after her into the bedroom. The urge was so strong he actually took the first step. He circled his wrist with the fingers of his other hand and squeezed. What was he doing here, why was he making such a fool of himself? Suppose she told Judge all about this when he came home?

So far there was nothing to tell. Besides, Judge was a nobody on the road to nowhere who had nothing to recommend him but his beautiful – so beautiful – wife.

Diana descended the stairs again at twenty past twelve. James had booked the restaurant for half-past. 'Do you always take so long?' he asked, because he never allowed himself to be kept waiting.

Diana confounded him by replying. 'I really couldn't say,' she said. 'I take as long as I need. It would be silly otherwise, because if I wasn't dressed properly I shouldn't enjoy my lunch. Would you rush out half-shaved because the clock said eight o'clock, and then spend the whole day looking ridiculous?'

James was taken aback. He moved mentally into a higher gear, even then could think of nothing to say and fell back on a compliment. 'Beautiful women don't need to spend hours getting ready.' She cast him a sideways look out of her wide tawny eyes. 'I cannot agree. Beauty is a fragile plant and it dies without nourishment.'

In the car she picked up the shoe and studied it briefly. 'Why, thank you. Where did you take it?'

He grinned. 'A man I know.' He hadn't known him

before yesterday, a little Pakistani cobbler working from a rundown shop in the Asian district of Bradford. No one else had been open at that time. Diana tossed the shoe on to the back seat of the car and waited for James to drive away. He forced himself to stop watching her and do so.

They lunched at a country pub, on steak and kidney pie. James had never been there before but the smart places were all frequented by textile men and they would have been seen. To make up, he bought a half bottle of champagne. Diana put her elegant elbow on the table, rested her chin on her hand and stared at him. 'Why are you doing this? You don't give a damn about Judge's.'

He held her glass under her chin for the bubbles to tickle her. 'I don't know if that's true. At the moment I'm just enjoying your company.'

'What do you mean?'

She disconcerted him every time she opened her mouth. He heard himself say, 'You excite me. You make me feel alive.'

And she nodded, understanding him. 'It's terrible to go through life half-asleep. Most people do, you know, most of the time.'

'Do you?'

'I have my music.'

She hadn't mentioned Andrew Judge. Did he bore her the way Marjorie bored him? When she lay beneath him at night was it the reverse of him and Marjorie, he dutifully poking a weak erection in and out of her flab?

Diana said, 'You're very rich, aren't you?'

'No. I've made money, I'm good at it. I could be very rich if I went on. But when I talk to you I realise I haven't done anything else, there isn't anything else to me. I'm ashamed of that.'

'Why?' Diana smiled at him. It was a soft, open smile that she only allowed herself when she knew she was the victor. She felt this man bowing down to her.

'I'm ashamed of not making more of my life.'

Her smile disappeared. She said, 'I feel that, too, you know. There are so many things I want to do, but I can't let myself do them. I feel cooped up here, I feel trapped!'

'You mean your music, don't you? You could have been famous.'

She flared at him, almost vicious. 'You don't know anything about it! I could be terrible, you don't know that I'm not. Everybody always wants genius. They don't want to live next door to a quite good player, they don't want to know if someone's just a hundred times better than most, they want them to be the best ever, the only talent, the new Mozart! I'm not that wonderful. I'm just very good.'

James swallowed. Flattery wasn't the way to Diana's heart – if that was where he wanted to go. Where was he going? 'You're right,' he admitted. 'But I don't know a damn thing about music, it's one of the things I never got round to. Your son's good though, isn't he? Didn't you say that?'

He watched her anger dissolve away. 'Oh yes. Andy's wonderful. Much better than I was at his age. One day he just might be the best, but people never understand how much it costs, not in money but in dedication! And it's got to be worth it. I mean, suppose he was giving up his childhood, giving up football and carpentry and just the luxury of doing nothing, to devote himself to playing an instrument he's never going to be brilliant at? That would be such a waste, there'd be nothing to make up for it. Andrew doesn't understand that whatever it costs financially it isn't anything. He never sees the more important thing, he gets sidetracked by the girls wanting holidays and the bloody, bloody bank! God, I get sick of it all. It's hard enough without all these other things.'

She fell silent, twirling her glass, and James watched her intently. He could see that some inner spring had unwound a few turns, easing her temper and her nerves. 'This is important to me, you know,' he said.

She shook her head. 'It's one of the things we're not allowed. Important people come in clearly labelled boxes, and you haven't got a box for me.' Then she looked at him. 'But we can be unimportant to each other.'

The waitress came and asked if they would like pudding, and they shook their heads without looking at her. 'The bill, please,' said James. 'We must be going.'

Outside in the car he said, 'We could go somewhere. If you wanted.'

She sat with her hands braced against the dashboard, long slender hands with hard strength in the fingers. 'I don't know what I want. Have you got a wife? You have, haven't you?'

'Oh yes. And a son, I've got a son, Richard. I've never done this sort of thing before, I want you to know that. But, my God, Diana, you make me feel so alive!'

She breathed deeply through her nose. 'As long as you remember that we aren't important. That is what I want, James.'

He drove the quiet car into the quiet lane, taking it softly up the tree-lined drive. 'Nobody here,' he murmured.

'Not today, no.'

James said, 'I'm coming in.' He got out of the car and went round to her side, pulling open the door. She stared up at him. After a moment he reached across and unfastened her seat belt, smelling her perfume, the scent of her hair. He grabbed her arm and pulled her out of the car and she came, long-legged and unresisting. But when he tried to kiss her she turned away. He let her go.

She walked to the house, fumbling in her bag for her key and leaving the door swinging when she had opened it. James followed her inside, thinking, 'How can she do this to me, how can she be so bloody cruel?' He would do anything if she would just – could just – it would be enough to caress her bare feet!

She threw down her bag on a chair, her coat on the floor, walking through the house as if she were alone. James, hating himself for his subservience, followed. She entered a small, cluttered room, piled high with music, a piano crammed against one wall, a collapsing sofa against another and music stands like spiked insects in the centre of the floor. As James watched, she opened a violin case, took out the instrument and tuned it briefly.

'I don't need a damned music lesson!' he cried, but she didn't look at him. Her long arms in their silk blouse moved with heartbreaking grace, her head tilted to send her shining hair in a fall against her cheek. The music began.

He was assailed by it. The notes crashed out at him, rivers of them, torrents foaming against the walls of the room. She wrenched chords from the depths, plucked shrieks from the heavens, built a wall of sound within which she stood, exposed. Her teeth were clenched. There were tears glistening at the corners of her eyes. James took off his jacket and threw it down, pulled off his tie and discarded it. He went to her. He knelt on the worn carpet and embraced her, pushed his face into the fabric of her skirt, caressing her narrow bottom, feeling her knees shaking against his chest. She played on, harder, desperately. His fingers unfastened her skirt. He drew it down, exposing her white lace slip. He hooked his fingers in at her waist and stripped her.

The playing faltered and went on. He put his nose into wiry auburn hair, grunting with the pleasure of it. The smell of her, the heat. He placed his hands flat against her belly, reaching his square thumbs out to probe. Her bow slid wildly, she played a last wild screeching note. 'No! For God's sake no!' But she stood there for him. His two thumbs padded gently against her. It was so, so quiet. When she screamed it was like an animal in pain.

She took no part in what came after. He pushed her

down, mounted her, and she watched him as if in shock. Afterwards, too, when his head was spinning, when pleasure drugged him, she said nothing, did nothing. When he went, he left her lying on the old sofa.

Chapter Four

Perhaps it would have been better if Andrew had been furious about the demolished music room. As it was, when he came back from his trip, his understanding, his sorrow, his apologies, all increased Diana's irritation. She deserved anger, she wasn't the paragon he imagined, she was a wilful, faithless woman aware of nothing but her selfish needs.

In a fit of temper she declared, 'I don't want the music room! Not like this! Why do you always try and keep everyone happy? In the end you make everyone miserable. God, Andrew, you can be so indecisive.'

'Darling, please!' But it was said to her retreating back. Did that mean he should recall the builders, or not? It was just one amidst many problems.

But, unaccountably, business was improving. One or two unexpected orders had come his way, from people he had never done business with before, which was very encouraging. At tea he said to Diana, 'Let's have another go at the music room with another builder. If we get the orders out on time we should have some spare cash.'

Rowan, pert and cheeky at fifteen, said, 'You should put the money back in the firm, Dad, you know you should. We don't need a music room.'

'Jealous,' said Andy unemotionally. He was a plump thirteen year old, calm and sensible, capable of getting himself up at six to practise, voluntarily forgoing the school trip because it clashed with a music lesson.

'Your mother wants the music room,' said Andrew firmly. 'It's decided.'

'No it isn't,' snapped Diana, putting her fingers to her

head. 'If the money should go into the business, then it should. At least then we wouldn't have to flinch every time there's a letter from the bank.'

'Please, darling, not in front of the children,' murmured her husband.

'It's all right, Dad,' chipped in Sally, the youngest at ten. 'We understand all about it. Miss Rogers says that all the mills that ought to go out of business have gone out of business. Everybody else is going to be O.K.'

'Not just because Miss Rogers says so,' sneered Rowan. 'Honestly, you don't understand anything. All those foreign peasants are working away in the Far East making things much cheaper than we can and putting us out of business. It isn't fair!'

Andrew took a scone and buttered it enthusiastically. 'Well, it depends on how you look at it, Rowan. Just think, when the mills here were built we were flooding the market with cheap goods and putting everyone else out of business. How can we complain now?'

'Because it's us!' declared his daughter. 'Besides, they don't make things nearly as well as we do.'

'Darling, people don't want wonderfully made things any more,' broke in Diana. 'They used to wear heavy suits and coats and trousers, but now it's all jeans and T-shirts. Look at your own clothes, hardly a wool dress to be seen.'

'I'll buy one tomorrow,' said Rowan, flinging her arms wide dramatically. She had her mother's long arms, but her father's dark colouring. 'Made in Britain!'

'We can't afford it,' said Andrew, looking comically lugubrious. Everyone laughed.

Returning home after the morning chaos of the school run, Diana wandered round the garden. The wreck of the music room kept catching her eye, but she knew she had been right to cause it. Ugliness proliferated when you let down your guard; it had to be fought against, resisted, even when you were too tired and preoccupied almost to notice. The sound of the vacuum came from inside the house, the daily doing her usual inadequate best. Restlessness nagged, and Diana refused to consider why. Guilt lurked in a corner of her mind and she hated it, because she did not feel it was justified. She had needed James Barton for herself, it had nothing to do with the family or Andrew or indeed Judge's. Although it was passing strange that the orders had come in just when Barton most wanted to impress her . . . She liked the way he looked at her, as if he was stalking a deer, trying this way, then that, never diverted from his purpose.

There was the sound of a car in the drive and she went through to see who it was. Glancing out of the window she saw James Barton standing before the door, her shoe held in his hand.

'I'll get it,' called Diana quickly as the vacuum droned to silence. She waited until it had begun again and then confronted her visitor.

'I've been meaning to bring this round,' said James. 'You left it in the car.'

'Thank you.' She did not ask him in.

'I wouldn't mind some coffee.'

'My daily's here. Besides, I don't want to see you again.'

He grimaced. 'I hope that's not true. I know we ought not to see each other again, but that's not the same thing at all.'

The daily woman switched off her machine and came clumping downstairs with her head swivelled in curiosity towards the visitor.

'I did hope your husband would be home, Mrs. Judge,' said James. 'But I'm sure I can explain the problem to you if you have the time.'

'Not really,' said Diana. Then, as the daily stood and James stood, she gave in. 'Perhaps I can spare ten minutes.'

In the kitchen James said, 'I hear things are a bit better at Judge's.'

She gave him a cold stare. 'I knew it was you. I didn't need paying.'

'Don't be stupid, please! I wanted to give you the world that afternoon, more than the world, but I couldn't even send you flowers. So I tried to give you your music room. I keep hearing your music in my head, it was – such an experience! All of it, the music, you –' He tailed off, shaking his head inadequately.

Suddenly fervent, she turned to him. 'I know! For me, too, I think. We should leave it at that, one afternoon we'll never forget. Somehow, I don't know why, I'd lost my sensuality. You gave it back to me.'

James put his hand on her arm, a hot hard touch. 'Not for him I didn't! For me! I've been dead half my life, I didn't understand feeling! I need more, Diana. I've never had it. I thought I knew what there was and I hadn't begun to explore. You've got to take me further. Don't give it to him!'

She turned her head and caught sight of the daily standing in the doorway.

'Shall I do the lounge?' asked the woman quickly.

'The drawing-room? Yes, please,' said Diana in the dismissive tone of one who has always employed help in the house. James wondered if he would like Marjorie better if she too had no lounge, but a drawing-room instead. As the woman went off he said, 'We can't talk here. Let's lunch. We can go to the same pub.'

'Don't be silly, you know we can't. We mustn't.'

'We have once, what difference would it make? We're both adults, we know it won't stay like this forever. I wake at night thinking about your breasts, I've never seen your breasts! Just once more. Something fantastic. On the moors, naked in the heather.'

She said slowly, 'Last night I dreamed you were making love to me. I knew I should stop you but I couldn't.'

James said, 'What time does the woman go?' Diana cast her eyes down. 'Twelve.'

When he had gone, she went upstairs to her room and closed the door. Last night when she had dreamed of James, Andrew had woken her. They had made love, in the gentle, respectful way that was typical of her husband, and it had satisfied her, gently. Why was she now burning for this other man? He pretended kindness but he wasn't kind. But then, neither was she. Each responded to the other's selfishness.

She put on a cream wool dress that fell high-necked from shoulder to knee. Underneath she wore nothing and her nipples stood out against the cloth. Twelve o'clock came and the daily went. Minutes later the Mercedes drew up at the door.

'I watched to see her go,' said James. 'I couldn't wait.' He was wearing jeans and an open-necked shirt. His grey eyes gleamed with excitement. Already his erection bulged stiffly beneath his belt. On the back seat of the car rested a bottle of champagne, two glasses, several packs of salmon and prawn sandwiches and two large rugs.

'You're very organised,' said Diana, settling herself into the car.

'Everything runs better with organisation,' said James, and grinned wolfishly.

They drove high on to the moors and then down a very rough track that led to one still rougher. 'Suppose we get stuck?' said Diana.

'Then we get stuck,' said James. 'I've got money enough to buy us out of most situations. I know that sounds bloody mercenary but it happens to be true.'

They stopped at last. They were very high up, on a track never used except during the shooting season. Away to the left was a crumbling stone hut, long since abandoned, all around was the circle of wide blue sky.

Stiff heather crunched beneath their feet and a grouse flew up, cackling noisily. James took the rugs from the car and moved to a slight depression in the ground. He laid one rug down. 'The other goes on top,' he explained. 'We don't want to freeze to death.'

Diana smiled. 'No.' She bent and took the hem of her dress in her crossed hands, then peeled it off over her head. James let out his breath in a gasp. Her breasts had begun to sag a little, hanging heavily like oranges in a net. They aroused him unbearably, as her abandon aroused him, the way she spread wide her arms to the wind and the sun. He had not intended to be naked himself until the last minute, had shrunk from the thought of his white body with its scant carrot hair and erotic protuberance exposed to her critical gaze. But to hell with caution, to hell with responsibility, to hell with everything. He ripped off his shirt, dragged off his jeans. He was going to make the most of every sweet, sweat-smelling second.

Andy was playing a gentle, lilting sonata, full of peace and harmony. Diana listened tenderly, her judgment marking the points that required improvement, her senses utterly bewitched. After a while and a couple of jarring passages she stood up and waved him silent. Taking up her own instrument she began to play the same piece, sending the music into every room in the house. Rowan, doing her homework in the kitchen, lifted up her head. Sally left her jigsaw and Andrew, working in the study, felt tears come to his eyes. The playing held everything there was of happiness, and beneath it, whispering, regret.

Chapter Five

There was an air of bustle about Judge's that Andrew found most heartening. Some of it was the result of the new orders, but there was also the rush of optimism to be taken into account. People who were despairing of Judge's suddenly began to wonder if it might be all right after all, if Mr. Andrew really did have his head screwed on. Weren't they a quality mill, couldn't their work be relied on? Not recently no, I grant you, but it takes a long time to ruin a reputation like Judge's. Let's make a go of it, they said to each other, let's all turn to and make this a success!

It was good to see the men busy, the girls smiling and planning their holidays. It had been a long time since Andrew asked anyone where they were going on holiday because the answer would probably be 'We thought we'd better not this year. We'll wait and see how things turn out.' And, amazingly, he thought it might all be due to James Barton. He must have put in a good word for them, he was the only man with the power to do it. Andrew made a mental note to speak to him at the Textile Dinner later in the week. It was only right that if it had been James Barton, Andrew should show proper gratitude.

Nobby was at his elbow. 'Sorry, Mr. Andrew. Card's gone again. We need a new bearing for the swift.'

Andrew hurried across. The safety guards were swung clear away from the machine and the whole dusty interior was revealed to be nothing more than a procession of spiked rollers, the wool passing from one to the other until it emerged at the end like a transparent carpet and was condensed into a fragile rope of sliver. The main roller, the swift, had been lifted out on a block and tackle.

'See here,' said Nobby. 'You can see what's to do.'

Even Andrew could see the marks of abnormal wear. 'Nobby, we need this card,' he said firmly. 'It'll take too long for a new bearing. It has to run.'

'I'm telling you, Mr. Andrew, it won't.'

'And I'm saying it must!' An inrush of panic made him curt. He tried to sound reasonable. 'Please, Nobby. We cannot afford to deliver this order late. Just get it working, as best you can.'

He turned on his heel and left Nobby looking helplessly at the machine. Andrew's mind raced. What ought he to do? Should he chase the bearing or try and find some other firm to card the wool? Suppose he sent the wool off and then Nobby did get the card to run? Suppose he didn't and the machine stood idle for weeks? Suppose they could after all manage on one card and he was worrying needlessly? All his peace of mind vanished like sunshine in the face of winter.

In his father's day they'd run twenty-four-hour shifts, putting Asians on at night. Nowadays there were no night shifts, and besides, if he ran one exceptionally, the remaining carding machine might crack under the strain. It too was no longer in its first youth. There seemed nothing to do but keep on hoping for the best. Nobby so often fixed things that looked impossible, surely he would do so now?

The Textile Dinner was held in a Bradford hotel, a non-descript place where the food was no more than mediocre and the surroundings uninspired. All the dinners were held there, yet the food never improved and the décor never changed. Like so much else, it had been different in the old days.

Andrew was glad to be out in dinner jacket and bow tie, it avoided another evening of worry. A little socialising might put things in a better perspective, there were sure to be others in a worse mess than himself. Nobby had not repaired the card, and in trying to run it with the bearing gone had sheared a holding pin for another roller. There was a three month wait for the parts, which were out of stock and out of date. After wasting days, Andrew was now trying to find someone who would either card the wool for him, or sell him carded sliver of similar quality. All of it was uncalled for expense and all of it delayed the order. There was no way it could go out on time.

He saw someone he knew, a man who had been at school with him. Rodney Lewis, that was his name, scion of a mohair spinner. 'Hello, Rodney. How are things?'

The other man was florid, running to seed. He was also rather drunk. 'Not so bad, my son. Market's been unstable for so long I'm beginning to get to like it. Got a new machine in though, an absolute bugger. Latest thing and no one knows how to work it. Chewed up stuff all over the shop. Sometimes I wonder why in God's name we don't stick to the old bangers we know and hate.' Delivered of his boasting, Rodney shifted his paunch more comfortably over his trousers and added, 'You through your bad patch, are you? Heard things weren't so good.'

'We're over the worst,' said Andrew quickly. 'I just wish the mill wasn't so old. It's damned hard to run efficiently in a great tomb of a place on five floors. We don't use half of it.'

Rodney nodded sympathetically. Andrew remembered that at school he had been everybody's friend until everybody discovered his little habit of stabbing you in the back. He rushed to put up more of a front. 'We've some very big orders on at the moment. Very big. Thinking about a night shift. Terrible strain for everyone, of course – ' but Rodney had seen someone he liked better, or at least thought could do him more good. He drifted away to drop hints of an imminent Isaac Judge collapse. It might be true, as for so many before.

Andrew had a bad taste in his mouth. He looked around

for a familiar face, but those he saw seemed to be engaged in parties of their own. Then James Barton came in, taller than most, his skin stained with freckles, the carrot hair receding to give him an intellectual look. His dinner suit had the fresh sheen of recent make, noticeable amongst all the let out and retextured models around him. Heads turned to glance surreptitiously, but no one went to speak to him. Andrew seized his chance and bustled across.

'Hello, James. Good to see you. Can I get you a drink?'

For a moment Barton seemed taken aback. A laugh hovered around his mouth. 'Thanks,' he said at last. 'Er – Scotch, I think.'

Andrew caught a waiter and delivered the order. Barton said, 'How's business?' rather quizzically Andrew thought.

'Fine. Just fine. I imagine you put in a good word for me – well, I feel it must have been you. I wanted to thank you. I mean, it's difficult with old machines but I always say it's quality that counts with our market and that we try and achieve – '

Barton cut him off abruptly. 'How's your wife? Have you built her that music room yet?'

They were interrupted by the waiter with the drinks and Andrew paid for them clumsily, counting out silver instead of simply handing over notes.

'Good heavens,' he said as he finished. 'What a memory you must have. We haven't agreed a design yet – it's proving rather dificult. Diana is so particular, you see. I suppose all women are.'

'Yes.' Barton watched him, grey eyes unblinking. 'I hear you're having machinery trouble,' he said suddenly. 'What are you going to do about it?'

His pride stung, Andrew said stiffly, 'I can't imagine why you think it's any concern of yours, James. I assure you everything is under control. I don't have to – I mean it's very kind of you to take such an interest but Judge's has managed very well on its own for a good many years.'

James snorted. 'You really ought to get your finger out. People don't accept late orders these days. They're not interested in your reasons, only your results. Get your business sorted and Diana can have a dozen music rooms!'

'I'm well able to take care of my own wife, thank you,' retorted Andrew. 'And my own business.'

'Glad to hear it. Thanks for the drink.' Barton sauntered off across the room.

Trying to gather his wits, Andrew went out into the foyer. He didn't understand Barton. What made him think he had the right to interfere in Judge's affairs? If one gesture of goodwill meant sacrificing all privacy and independence, then he'd be damned – except, of course, he would be damned. When men like Barton paid the piper, lesser mortals danced.

It was time to go in to dinner. His appetite had fled, he wanted nothing more than to go home and tell Diana about it, to go back into the one safe haven of his home. Instead, he went to his place, made small talk about golf and chewed his way through tough lamb cutlets.

James Barton had indulged himself in attacking Andrew. It was a small revenge for Diana's treatment, for her wilful refusal to need James as much as he needed her. He felt that he had inspired not the least degree of commitment in her, and he was galled that Andrew, so inadequate, should have what he was denied. He had an urge to wreck the neat pattern of Andrew's life, to seize its prizes for himself. In the evenings when he went home to Marjorie and the television, he sat in his airless lounge and thought about Diana.

He took to looking at his wife, assessing her. She was a short woman who had thickened, not excessively but she lacked the height to carry it. And she dressed in dowdy tweeds, neat jumpers, always with a diamond and pearl brooch fastened to the shoulder. No mane of auburn hair for her, but a tidy mid-brown perm. There was nothing vulgar or pretentious about her. She was comfortable with money, sensible with it, living as modestly, sensibly and downright boringly as her mother had done before her. No wonder, she had always been nicely off, and had she not, then James would not have married her. It was a bargain he had kept for many years, fidelity in exchange for hard cash. A bargain he had kept for too long, he now believed. He hadn't known what he was missing. Sometimes James thought he would stifle.

The day after the Textile Dinner he sent Diana a diamond hairclip. The special messenger arrived mid-morning, and as he roared up on his motorbike Diana felt a surge of mingled panic and rage. She knew what was coming. James didn't care if people found out. He wanted them to find out.

She took the box up to her bedroom and opened it well away from the daily's gaze. Her heart turned over. It was an exquisite spray of flowers, perfectly understated. She swept her hair up and tried the clip in it, knowing she could not keep it, that even if she did there would be nowhere it could be worn. Besides, what would Andrew say? She picked up the bedside 'phone.

'Bardsey Textiles? Mr. Barton please. A personal call. Mrs. Judge.'

James came on the line. 'Diana? Darling.'

'James, how dare you? I won't have it. If you do anything like this again then it's all over. I warn you, I won't let you wreck my life. I thought we understood each other.'

'Darling, it's only a present. I can't resist giving you things. I wanted to give you pleasure.'

Diana pressed her fingers to the bony bridge of her nose. 'That's very sweet of you. But you know I couldn't wear it, it's so obviously expensive. Are you trying to trap me, James? Is that it?'

'Look –' he paused and could be heard murmuring to someone in the room – 'darling, I can't talk now. Tomorrow. Please.'

'No.' She replaced the receiver, hard. How dare he talk to her with someone else listening?

Later that day, when the children were home from school, the special messenger roared up to the door once again. He had another package.

'What on earth is it?' demanded Rowan, green eyes sparkling.

'Can I open it? Let me!' squeaked Sally.

Even Andy, who was studying a score, looked up with interest.

'It's probably come to the wrong house,' said Diana desperately. 'I'll take it back tomorrow. It isn't mine.'

'It says you,' said Rowan. 'Anyway, how can you know what it is before you've opened it?'

'Rowan, it's none of your business!' flared Diana. She rushed from the room, the package clutched in her hand. When she opened it, she froze. It was a diamond heart-shaped brooch, and within it were smaller hearts, until in the centre was a large, solitaire diamond. Underneath was a card, and in James's scrawled handwriting she read: 'I love you.'

At dinner, the children were full of the mystery parcel. 'What is it, dear?' asked Andrew curiously.

'A brooch. I think it's for another Mrs. Judge. I certainly don't know anyone likely to send me brooches.'

'Can we see it? Why can't we see it?' Sally bounced up and down, as usual giving her enthusiasm physical expression. When she was happy she bounced, when she was sad she rocked, when she was bored she bit her nails. Stillness, with Sally, probably meant coma.

'I've already wrapped it up to go back,' said Diana firmly. She was only too aware that Andrew was watching her.

When they were alone and drinking coffee, he said, 'Has someone sent you a present?'

Not looking at him, she said, 'There was no name. I really don't know.'

'But the children said it was the right address.'

'No, it was just Mrs. Judge.'

'Diana Judge, they said.'

'Really, Andrew, it isn't for me! I shall go to the shop tomorrow and make some enquiries, there's no point in subjecting me to this inquisition. What is it you suspect me of? A clandestine affair?'

'Darling, of course not!' But he looked away.

James drove up at half-past twelve the next day. Diana flung the door open before he reached it. 'How could you! You bastard, get out of here, get away from me!'

James reached out and pushed her back into the hall. She went back hard and hit out at him, bruising her knuckles on his teeth.

'Stop it! Stop it!' He caught her wrist and twisted her arm up behind her back. His lip was bleeding.

'You're hurting. Let me go.' Her eyes were huge, the pupils black with pain. He twisted her arm some more, enjoying it. She cried out and he let go.

'I don't want you any more,' hissed Diana. 'Get out.'

'I won't get out. I love you, and I think you love me. I want us to be together.'

'No, you don't! You just want to win, that's all. You want everything your own way.'

James came close to her, cupping her breasts. 'Why shouldn't I? Why shouldn't you? We're so alike, we want the same things. If I could just see you more often, twice a week, that's all. I don't want to make you unhappy. I want to love you, I *have* to love you!'

When he kissed her she tasted salty blood. When he made love to her on the hard floor it was as violent as a battle.

Chapter Six

James came to the house on Mondays and Thursdays. Any scruples that Diana felt about betraying her husband in his own house she forced herself to ignore. It was safer here, they were less likely to be seen. James was dangerous, James was prepared to assault her marriage to get what he wanted. Giving in to him, and to her own needs, was the best way out.

People began to say how well she looked, there was a glow about her, a fine shining edge. Odd new items of clothing started appearing. A jacket that Andrew was sure was new but which Diana claimed she had had for ages. A new handbag. And in her handkerchief drawer, found by Andrew and carefully put back, the heart-shaped brooch.

He didn't think about it. He didn't dare think about it. If it was anybody it was James Barton, but of course he was imagining things. They had a life together, they had a family, three wonderful children. But he couldn't help noticing how much less intense she was about Andy's training, how much less short with the girls. If it wasn't for work he would go mad, he knew it. He went to the doctor about loss of appetite.

As for Diana, she was alive! Before James she had been sliding into acid middle-age, years before she was ready for it. It occurred to her that she had been putting too much of herself into Andy's music, because her own music had failed her, through no one's fault but her own. In those valuable years of the late teens Diana had lost her dedication; she had dated and gone to parties, skimping practice and trying to bluff her way through lessons. She had paid for it a thousand times, mourned by her teachers as one of the girls who might have but didn't. Only when it was too late did she regret it, only when she was married to Andrew and the gloss was wearing off. For Diana could have been better than her son, if she had wanted to be. The knowledge gnawed at her soul.

Of course she told herself that with James it was only sex, and in part it was true. They were switched on to each other, they had only to touch to be aroused. Wild, adult sexuality was their own personal discovery, as far from dull marital duty as the earth from the sun. But it was also that, with James, she was herself. There was no need to hold back and be kind, and besides, the enslavement of a man at the top of his particular tree was an achievement which delighted her. She almost wished people knew about it.

Then one day her friend Linda came by for coffee and said excitedly, 'You'll never guess! James Barton's having an affair!'

Diana swallowed. 'How do you know?'

'Well, Gillian is very thick with his wife, Marjorie, and though she doesn't look it – I mean she's a real Mrs. Rabbit, all warm fires and crumpets – she's got her head screwed on. And Marjorie Barton's been finding bills for presents, like diamonds! I thought that went out with the Ark! How I wish someone would send me diamonds.'

Diana's legs felt weak. She knew she should get up and pour more coffee but couldn't. 'Well, the woman can't be married then,' she said desperately. 'A married woman couldn't have diamonds, her husband would notice.'

Linda wrinkled her nose. 'If it was me, I'd keep them and hide them. Then I could drool over them in my old age, and remember when I was being screwed by a rich old man!'

'James Barton isn't old!' snapped Diana.

'Not really, no. I quite fancy him actually,' added Linda thoughtfully. 'He's got that wonderful streak of cruelty – you just know he's the sort that enjoys squashing flies. Probably got some woman he can tie to the bed and flog. If you did that to Marjorie Barton she'd witter away about the best type of whip and don't mark the wallpaper.'

Diana laughed. It amazed her how much she liked to hear James's wife being slated.

The next afternoon she let James take her to bed straight away, something she didn't usually permit. She liked him to suffer. As he reached out for her, she caught hold of his erection and gripped hard.

'Your wife knows about us.'

He grunted. She looked for the expression of alarm, but there was none. He flexed against her hand. 'You want her to know,' she whispered.

In answer James ducked his head and fastened his teeth on her breast, biting hard and leaving a clear crescent, like a brand. Diana shrieked and tried to get free of him, but he pushed her down and somehow, in the struggle, got inside. They lay together, staring and angry.

'This is the end,' said Diana. 'I won't leave Andrew.'

'He'll kick you out when he knows,' said James.

'Will he?' She laughed up at him, in control even now. 'I'll tell him I was mad, I'll tell him I'm sorry. He'll forgive me.'

'God, but you think you're so clever!' He bucked into her and she gasped; he knew that he was exciting her, that soon she would be satisfied. And he couldn't bring himself really to hurt her. 'I love you, Diana!' he panted, watching the sweat form in the hollow of her throat, seeing her eyes close to exclude him. He would never let her go!

Nothing more was said about ending it. But the next Thursday, when James called, she was out. There was a letter lying on the step.

Dear James,

I meant what I said. If you really want to hurt me, then I suppose you will tell Andrew, but you'll gain nothing by it. I don't like being threatened. Please don't try and get in touch with me, because I think we both know we should stop now, before we get ourselves in a real mess. Don't think I'm not grateful for what we've had. You are a very remarkable person.

Love, Diana

He started to laugh. The letter seemed to epitomise all that she did not know about him. The depth of her ignorance, in thinking that she could so easily just stop when it pleased her, was a challenge. It was time she learned what had got him where he was today, time she saw some part of the tenacity that had dragged a tired firm to the pinnacle of success. The battle to come delighted him, he was grateful to her for adding this twist to the story. At the same time, denied her, he wanted her more than ever. It seemed nothing could make up for what he could not now have.

He slammed back into his car, seeing a child's bicycle lying by the path to the front door. Quickly he turned the Mercedes and crushed it under his wheels.

In the evening Sally was in tears over her bicycle. 'I'm sure we'll get you a new one,' said Diana distractedly. 'Just stop making such a fuss, Sally!' She was trying to listen to Andy practise, and Rowan had the television turned up again, and she had a splitting headache and a feeling as if her skin was being attacked by insects. He might have gone straight round to Andrew, in which case this evening's chaos could only get worse.

But when Andrew came in he seemed much as usual. He flared when he heard about the bicycle though. 'Sally, it's entirely your own fault, you left the blasted thing there! We can't afford a new one, there's no question of it. Diana, why didn't you make her put it away? Who was it anyway?'

'How should I know, I was out,' shrieked Diana. 'God, Rowan, will you turn off that damned television!'

Andrew went stonily upstairs to get changed, and

afterwards everyone sat down to supper. It was soon clear that Andrew had no appetite.

'Is something the matter?' Diana forced herself to ask the question.

Andrew cleared his throat. 'Not really. Well, yes. The new order's been cancelled. It should have been going out next week and we were going to be late, but it seems they heard and cancelled it.'

'Couldn't you do a deal?' demanded Diana. 'You can pay a forfeit, can't you?'

'I did suggest it, yes. They wouldn't listen.'

Into the silence piped Sally's voice. 'I can't have a new bike, then?'

'Shut up, Sally,' said Rowan. She was staring at her father out of intense green eyes. 'We're not finished, are we?'

He tried to smile. 'Of course not, darling.'

Andy, as usual self-absorbed, said, 'I've been asked to do three pieces for the school concert. But I'll only do two, I don't want to practise lollipop music all the time.'

'Just about your level,' snapped Rowan. 'Can't you see this is important?'

'And it's nothing to do with you,' rebuked Diana. 'Honestly, Andrew, why do you have to worry the children? That firm is always in trouble: if it isn't late orders it's wrong dyes or faults in the weave or poor quality or something! Why can't you for once get to grips with it?'

The outburst surprised even her. Andrew said, 'It may well be my fault. I do my best, that's all I can say.'

'Of course you do,' said Diana frostily. 'I'm sorry.'

In the bedroom that night, he said, 'I am sorry, you know.'

'What about?' Diana was distracted, hoping very much that he would not want to make love to her, because her breast was still so bruised.

'About making such a mess of things. I know I'm not making you happy.'

She couldn't meet his eyes. Yet at the same time she hated him for making her feel so terribly, damnably guilty! If he was more like James, she found herself thinking, if he fought back instead of meekly going under, then there would be no need to apologise. James was striking at Andrew, and at her, and it was what she would have done in his place.

'I am happy,' she said distantly.

'Diana – are you sure? It's just I've wondered – I mean, you're an attractive woman, a beautiful woman. I wouldn't be surprised if –'

As he tailed off, Diana's mind raced. Had James told him or was he guessing? Trust Andrew to beat about the bush in this cowardly way!

'I don't know what you're talking about, Andrew,' she announced, flinging back the sheets and getting into bed. 'Stop worrying about me and get on with running the firm. If you've lost this order you can get others, but no one's going to do if for you!'

She lay down and determinedly turned off her bedside light, her position in the bed making it clear that she did not want him to touch her. Andrew knew he wouldn't be able to sleep, the thoughts were buzzing in his head. Why had the order been cancelled like that? A brief message to say they had been informed by Bardsey that the delivery was likely to be late, and that Bardsey were arranging for the order to be fulfilled from elsewhere. What in God's name did it have to do with Bardsey, and why had they given the order in the first place, only to take it away now? Was it a plot to destroy him? Did it have everything to do with Diana or nothing at all?

He lay down and closed his eyes, trying to calm himself. He was almost crying. Suddenly, painfully, he longed for his father, he wanted to cry out to him for help and guidance, the unfailing wisdom that had been his prop for so long. But he was quite, quite alone.

Chapter Seven

The Summer Ball was an event the Judges seldom missed, and now with rumours flying they were compelled to go. The Bartons did not normally attend, but for some reason this year James told his wife that they would. And attend they did, he immaculate in his dinner jacket, she frumpy in an expensive but unsuitable tulle frock. James and Majorie were standing together when the Judges entered. Diana was wearing tawny shot taffeta, long-sleeved, high-necked and infinitely seductive. Marjorie Barton felt the electricity in her husband, it leaped the space between them. 'So,' she thought, 'that's her.'

James took hold of his wife's arm and bore her across to be introduced. Andrew's face turned to stone but Diana's cool never faltered.

'Good heavens, Mr. Barton,' she said lightly.

'How nice to see you, Mrs. Judge. Andrew. May I introduce my wife, Marjorie?'

They were polite to each other. Andrew was intent on moving away, the very presence of Barton made him feel shaky. But James would have none of it. Working with absolute determination he insisted they all go to the same table, ordered champagne, chatted as if they were all firm friends. The band was playing a quickstep.

'Do you dance, Diana?' said James. 'Come on, Andrew, let's show the ladies a good time.' He took hold of Diana's arm, a determined clasp. She could have resisted, she almost did, but when she saw his roguish smile it was matched with her own. 'All right,' she said and stood up. Andrew and Marjorie were left looking at one another.

On the floor James said, 'Thanks for the letter.'

'Bastard,' said Diana dispassionately. 'We're nearly ruined.'

'Oh no, I give you at least three months. I should have done for you by then, I think.'

She looked him full in the face. 'What does it take to make you stop? Do you want me to sleep with you again?'

He grinned, like a wolf with an empty belly. 'That was what the price used to be. But it's gone up. If you leave him and come to me, he can keep his business. I'll pull out all the stops for him, help him all the way. If you stay, then it goes down.'

She gasped. 'You're not serious!'

'Absolutely. Have you missed me, Diana?'

'No.' But they both knew it wasn't true. They were dancing very close, and it was as much her doing as his. He could feel her trembling.

She put her lips to his ear. 'Please, James, don't be so cruel. I've my children to think of. Please, can't it be like it was?'

Andrew and Marjorie danced by. Two anxious faces watching them. James murmured, 'I'm going to marry you,' almost loud enough for them to hear. And suddenly he meant it. He danced Diana to the open floor-length window, and pushed her out on to the terrace. Below stretched the gardens, dark and mysterious. He caught Diana's hand and pulled her down the steps and across the damp grass. Hidden in the shadow of a tree he began to kiss her. 'Say you love me! Say it!'

'I love you! I love you!' She responded wildly, tasting the skin of his face, the sting of aftershave, the dregs of his champagne. At least here, in these few moments, she could let go, have an end to the tensions of home, the unspoken accusations, the failures. This man matched and exceeded her. She didn't have to be kind for he wasn't kind, any more than she.

In the ballroom, Marjorie clutched at Andrew's arm. 'They've gone outside. I wonder why.'

'It is hot in here,' said Andrew, looking like an ostrich as he watched the hem of his wife's dress slip out of sight.

'But you know what's been going on, don't you?' She stared up at him, plain, frightened, someone he didn't know who wanted to talk about things he dared not think of.

'Going on? I'm sure it isn't – I trust my wife. Of course I do – ' His feet faltered in the rhythm of the dance and he crushed Marjorie's toes, but she didn't seem to notice.

'If we go, then we'll know, won't we? I've got to know.' She pulled insistently at his arm and reluctantly he went with her, although he didn't want to know, could not bear to know.

It was dark in the garden, and with relief he thought they wouldn't find them. But Marjorie, in sensible shoes, hurried unerringly across the grass. And in the darkness, there was the gleam of shot taffeta, the animal sounds of people locked in passion. Let her not be naked, prayed Andrew. Spare me that. But still, when he saw her neck stretched back for James to mouth the skin, the neck that she had passed on to Rowan and which drooped so diffidently in their daughter, he thought he would be sick. He let out a cry, like a creature gripped in a snare. They froze. Their heads turned towards him.

Andrew was sobbing, open-mouthed. 'Why? Why did you have to?'

Diana tried to move out of James's arms, but he held on. Andrew embarrassed her, she wished he would control himself. Why was it that he never ever responded to crisis in a way that impressed her? 'I'm sorry, Andrew,' she said grittily. 'I didn't mean you to know.'

'But you did, didn't you, James,' said Marjorie bitterly. 'That's why I'm here, to be shown, isn't it? Well, I've decided. I'm not going to put up with you. I'm not going to let you humiliate me. You can have what you bloody well like, but I'm not going to give up my house or one single thing in it.'

James laughed. He was enjoying every minute of this, because he had constructed the scene, and he was the one coming out best. 'Well done, Marjorie,' he said cheerfully. 'I always did like your good sense, if very little else. You never keep on with a losing streak, I suppose you learned that from your father, unlike Andrew here. He never seems to know when to quit.'

'You bastard!' Andrew launched himself at James, fingers clawed. In one continuous movement James put Diana to one side, ducked and hit Andrew in the balls. He fell in motionless agony.

'Oh my God,' moaned Diana, and knelt at his side, her hair in her eyes. 'Andrew, I'm sorry, I'm sorry. Let's go home, Andrew. I won't leave you, I promise, let's go home.' Then looking up at James she screamed, 'Why did you have to hurt him? I hate you!'

Marjorie snorted and said, 'It's a fine time to find that out. Oh, you go to him, Mrs. Judge, and see how long it is before he's bored with you.'

A crowd was gathering, and James decided that enough was enough. He gestured to Marjorie. 'Go to the car. I'll drive you home, then I'll go to the club. Diana, let's get Andrew up, you'd better take him home.'

'Don't touch him,' sobbed Diana, but obediently took one arm while James took the other. People parted to let them stagger through, Andrew coughing with pain.

They put him in the back and then Diana flung herself behind the wheel. James caught the door and held it open. 'I'll come round tomorrow. I won't let it go on, I know what it's like for you.'

'It isn't going to happen, James.' She glared up at him, and they both knew she didn't mean it, that they weren't turning back, either of them. He bent his head and kissed her, knowing that he had won. He felt a massive upsurge of exhilaration.

Diana drove away fast. By the time they reached home Andrew could speak, but he wasn't speaking, he was crying. 'Please, Andrew, stop it,' begged Diana. 'I didn't want it to be like this!' She got him out of the car and pushed him towards the house. 'We'll talk about it later, tomorrow, we'll feel better then.'

'Tomorrow!' he shrieked. 'You won't even be here tomorrow! Is it the money, is it that? What do you want, Diana, what do you want me to give you?'

Rowan appeared at the top of the stairs. 'Mummy? What's the matter?'

Diana tried to pull herself together. Andrew was ranting at the top of his voice. 'Nothing, darling. Daddy's not well.'

He rushed up the stairs towards Rowan. 'That's right, yes, I'm not well. I can't stomach the sight of her and her lover. Your mother's been fucking another man, how do you like that, Rowan? Even tonight, there they were, pawing each other! Where did you do it, Diana? In the car, in his big flash car, or in some sleazy motel?'

'In our bed, actually,' said Diana. It was an impulse of cruelty she was beyond repressing. 'Go to bed, Rowan.'

The girl's shocked face retreated. Andrew seized hold of Diana's shoulders and shook her, shouting: 'Bitch! Prostitute! If you don't care about me, then what about them? All right, go to him, leave us all and go, I don't want you here!' But then he let her go. He couldn't bear it if she left him.

In the end he slept on the sofa, and Diana went upstairs. All the children were awake, woken by the smashing of plates and the screaming. Diana had a swelling bruise on the side of her face but she was controlled.

'Is it true?' demanded Rowan, fierce in a white nightie. She had her arm around Sally, who was very frightened.

'Of course it isn't,' said Andy. 'Dad's drunk.'

'I'll explain in the morning,' said Diana. 'You must all go to bed.'

'It is true then,' said Rowan. 'It's the man that sent you the brooch.'

Diana paused. At that instant she deeply disliked her eldest child, who at fifteen sat there and judged her with as little sympathy as a lump of marble. 'You can think what you like, Rowan,' she said stiffly. 'If you want to think that I would do things I should be ashamed of, then you may.'

'Of course you wouldn't do anything bad,' declared Andy loyally. 'It's the firm, that's the trouble.'

Diana smiled at him, tapping the deep well of her love for her son. 'That's right, Andy. Mostly it's because of the firm.'

At dawn Andrew could be heard downstairs, definitely drunk this time, and breaking things with a hammer. Diana remained behind closed doors, so Rowan went down. She stood and watched her father breaking a china cabinet, smashing the little cups and figurines with drunken precision.

'Please don't, Daddy,' she said tremulously. He turned and saw her, and his face crumpled.

'She doesn't love me any more,' he said mournfully. 'She loves him. She's going to leave us and go to him.'

'Would you like a hanky?' asked Rowan. She held out a tissue and Andrew took it, mopping his streaming face. 'We still love you,' said Rowan. Her father's face twisted again, he fought against grief and gave in to it. Rowan put out her arms and held him.

It was a week before Diana left, a week of horrors. In every hour Andrew swung from rage to wild grief; from begging her to stay to threatening to throw her out, then and there. If James Barton appeared he threatened to knife him and once Rowan, who had not dared go to school, stood in the kitchen with her back to the door to prevent her father from going out and stabbing both James and Diana. In the end he slashed the door inches above her head, while she stood too terrified even to close her eyes. And afterwards, awash with guilt, he talked about killing himself.

'I've got to go,' Diana said to her, in an attempt at explanation. 'He'll be better once I've gone, he'll come to terms with it. I never thought he'd take it so hard.'

'Why don't you say you're sorry? He'd make up. You know he can't stay cross for long.'

'I'm afraid I can't,' said Diana. 'James – Mr. Barton – he has a lot of power. I don't think the firm would survive if he didn't – if I didn't.'

'Daddy would still rather you stayed,' said Rowan implacably.

Diana struggled for honesty. 'Perhaps I don't want to stay. I think we've both changed, your father and me. We don't seem to know each other very well. Or we might know each other too well, I don't really understand it. I – need – somebody like Mr. Barton.'

'I won't live with him,' said Rowan.

'Well – ' Diana had not even considered this possibility. But now she did she put forward the conventional solution. 'Of course, when we're settled you will, and see Daddy at weekends. The children always go with the mother.'

'Well, I won't,' said Rowan. 'And I'll tell Sally not to either.'

'God, Rowan, you can be a little beast!' snarled her mother, and slapped her, hard, on the leg.

When James came finally to take Diana, Rowan tried to keep her father away. But he stormed out of the house, unshaven, his clothes a mess, raving like a maniac. James feared him not at all. 'What in God's name do you think you look like?' he said.

Andrew stood there, shaking, unable even to frame a coherent response. He rubbed his hand against his face, saying confusedly, 'You mustn't take her. You can't.'

Rowan ran out of the house, prepared to do battle where her father would not. There had to be something she could do to stop this, there had to be some way of putting it right. James Barton stared at her calmly. She wanted to kill him. She stood before him, fists clenched, and screamed: 'You're spoiling our home! It's your fault we're all so sad, we all hate you. We'll hate you forever.' The words weren't enough, but she had nothing else. If she had a gun she would shoot him and her mother, dent that terrible, calm control.

'Will you now?' For once James was slightly nonplussed. She was so boyishly tall, and so clearly enraged. 'You'll feel better when things have settled down,' he managed.

'I am never going into a house with you in it,' sneered Rowan. 'I would choke to breathe the same air. You're disgusting, ugly and old and perverted. Both of you are.' She included her mother in a searing glance of contempt.

'Rowan! At least you can be polite,' snapped Diana. 'I'm sorry, James, she's upset. I should have made sure she went to school with Sally and Andy.'

'Then who would take care of Dad?' demanded Rowan. 'You don't care about him at all, all you care about is you, you, you!'

'Don't go away,' begged Andrew. 'Diana, my darling, you know how I love you!'

'No, you don't,' screamed Rowan in a voice that sounded years too young for her. 'You hate her, we all do! Daddy, don't talk like that in front of *him*!'

Andrew slumped on to the low wall that bordered the drive. He dropped his head into his hands and wailed.

'Daddy! Daddy, don't!' hissed his daughter.

'Goodbye,' said Diana. 'I'll be in touch.' She got into the car. James got in too, but on a sudden impulse leaned out of the window to wink triumphantly full in the face of Rowan's rage.

She threw stones as the car drove away, but they all missed. 'Oh God,' said Andrew. 'Oh God, I want to die.'

'We should be glad she's gone,' declared Rowan. 'She's horrible. We don't want her here.'

Wrung out with emotion, Andrew said dully: 'It was all my fault, you see. I failed her so terribly.'

'Of course you didn't!' Although he seemed not to listen to anything she said, Rowan tried to bolster him. She was hoarse with screaming, her throat hurt. She coughed and said bitterly, 'She's the real failure. She hasn't done anything herself, but she wants other people to do things. And she's wicked, she'll go to hell and burn and I wish she was there now. I hate her!'

Andrew sighed, again close to tears. 'I don't. Oh, Rowan, how are we to manage without her?' He looked about him at the lovely old house, the garden in full summer bloom, and it seemed to him that he was faced with a barren moonscape, without any of the essentials for life. He couldn't think of any way of going on.

Chapter Eight

Rowan sat in the windowseat and bit her nails. Andy was practising again, endless runs of scales, oblivious to the anguish around him. Rowan hated the sound of the violin; in a moment she would go and hit him till he stopped.

It was three weeks since Diana had left, and Andrew had hardly been out of the house once. Sometimes someone from the mill telephoned, but he wouldn't talk to them. Today Rowan's form mistress had called and Rowan had lied, saying she had been ill with 'flu and would be back next week. She hadn't dared let Miss Perkins see Andrew; she'd send him to a mental home and put all three children into care.

Sally wandered in, the collar of her school blouse black with dirt. 'What are we going to eat, Rowan?'

'There isn't anything. And there isn't any money.'

Sally watched her with huge eyes. 'Then what are we going to do?'

And that indeed was the question Rowan had been pondering for hours. Where did money come from? How did you eat when you didn't have any? For as long as she could remember they had been poor, in so far as they didn't have a Porsche or foreign holidays, but they went to private schools and had tennis lessons. No money for food was more than poor, it was destitute.

'Why don't we ask Mummy?' said Sally.

'No! And don't you dare try and get in touch with her, I'd rather we all died.' Every time Diana 'phoned, Rowan made sure she answered and hung up as soon as she realised who it was. Because it was no use pretending she cared now; if she had really cared she wouldn't have gone.

Sally sat down on the carpet and started making a jigsaw with some of the broken pieces of china that still lay there, not cleared away. The daily had abandoned them in the first week, she wouldn't work for nothing. 'I wish Daddy would get up,' said Sally mournfully.

Rowan unwound her long legs from the window seat. She went slowly upstairs to the spare room, where her father now slept because he would not lie down in a bed 'Where your mother fornicated with that bastard!' as he kept on saying. When she knocked on the door, there was no response, so she turned the handle and went in.

Andrew was lying on top of the bed, staring blindly at the ceiling. He had lain like that for days and days, stirring only to go to the bathroom and occasionally to eat what Rowan provided for him. 'Daddy,' she said anxiously, 'we haven't any money.'

His head turned. 'We never have any money.'

'But – we can't buy food. I don't know what to do.'

His face quivered. 'And now you're hungry. Now my children are going hungry! Oh God, I can't bear it.' He put his hands over his face and Rowan suppressed an urge to hit him. Why wouldn't he get up and do something, instead of lying there not bearing it? If he didn't, who would?

She left him and went back downstairs. Money, they had to have money. The place to get money was the bank, and she would go there tomorrow and see how you got some. For tonight she might be able to steal some food perhaps – though she didn't think she'd be very good at it and would probably get caught. Borrowing, then. Humiliating as it would certainly be, she would have to ask someone if she could borrow some money.

Briefly she considered asking the neighbours, but they lived as the Judges did, in the isolation of their acres of gardens, and they didn't know them well. Besides, such people wouldn't just lend you five pounds. They would call down officialdom in all its horrible forms and the children would certainly end up in care. Rowan went into the utility room and put on her scuffed trainers. She had long, thin feet that she felt to be unfemininely large, and she often went around barefoot because they seemed more attractive that way. They didn't look so big somehow, and the long toes might have been elegant. The violin scales still persisted, so she called out to Sally, 'I'm just going out, Sal. I'll be back with some shopping.'

She had no money for the bus, so she had a long walk to the mill, and no time to waste if she was to be there before it closed. Rowan wasn't sure what time it did close, perhaps seven? Someone was sure to be there who would help her. They would have money to give her. But when, at last, she trudged wearily down the narrow street, the gates to Isaac Judge were closed.

She refused to believe she had come all this way for nothing. If she could get into the mill, then she could take a typewriter or something and sell it. After all, it was her father's firm, it was all theirs really. She went round to the little side gate that the watchman used, and to her relief it was unlocked, and so too was the side door into the mill itself. But in the cavernous, echoing interior she was engulfed by a wave of loneliness and fear. Hunger made her weak. She would have liked to curl up on the hard stone floor and give up the struggle, but here, in the ghostly mill, she dared not.

Water was dripping somewhere, an eerie, echoing sound, and in the half light every shadow might have been a monster. When she was little Rowan had had nightmares about wolves eating her, and even now shadows made her heart stutter. If she could get to her father's office there would at least be familiar things to comfort her.

Somehow, alone, she couldn't quite work out where she was in the mill. When she came here with her father she simply followed him around, she didn't navigate for herself.

So in the twilight she blundered into the dye-house and soaked her feet in the orange puddles on the floor, then she trailed her orange footsteps through into the weaving shed. It was unnaturally quiet, when always before there had been the clatter of looms. But then she had never been in the mill when it wasn't working. As she tried to find the door to the offices, she couldn't help noticing how few looms were actually in use, and perhaps more significantly, how few of the great wooden balloons, on which the warp threads of each piece of cloth were laboriously set out prior to weaving, had anything on them at all.

Real fear touched her. Suppose the firm went under and her father hadn't even that to keep him going? All her life Isaac Judge had been a name that filled her with a sense of security, of times past leading on to times to come. The difficulties had always been there, but it was understood that things would pick up, as so many times before. Now, when everything else was crumbling, it was unthinkable that this should go as well. Fate couldn't let it happen all at once.

Her eye lighted on the narrow door that led up to her father's office and she slipped through it thankfully. The stone back stairs led directly into the main corridor, and received ten times more wear than the posh wooden staircase because of the continual dashing up and down to see how things were going where it counted, in the mill. That was the way things had always been: keep an eye on the product and the selling will do itself.

Just as she reached out to open the door of her father's office, Rowan froze. There was a noise. Someone – something – was inside. Her impulse was to turn and run, as fast as she could, away and out. But who could it be in there? It was her father's office, no one had any right! Reaching out with terrified determination, she pushed open the door and confronted – the cleaner, Elsie, who had been at Judge's forever.

'Hello, Rowan love. How are you?' Elsie's squinting

gaze focused on her kindly. Rowan, faced with the impossibility of making a suitable reply, twisted her hands together.

'Heard your dad wasn't well,' said Elsie diplomatically. She knew, as did all Bradford, that Diana Judge had done a flit with James Barton, and they were even now set up in luxury in the Midland Hotel, buying a bottle of champagne every night and getting up to no good at all in a four-poster bed. But it wasn't something to talk about with the daughter, who was only fifteen and a beanpole that blushed. 'Fancy a cup of tea?' added Elsie. 'I always make one about this time. Breaks the night up.'

'Thanks.'

They went off to the little kitchen that served the offices, and Elsie brewed tea and added condensed milk. Rowan almost gagged on it, because she was so terribly hungry. She had eaten nothing all day. 'You all right, love?' asked Elsie. It was hard to tell if she was looking intently at you or not, because her squint made it seem as if she could be staring at a point over your left shoulder.

Rowan took a deep breath. 'I wondered, Elsie – I know this must seem a bit odd – but, well, I'm in a bit of trouble.'

'Oh, yes?' said Elsie cautiously, because her own daughter's trouble was now two years old and a right handful. 'What sort of trouble?'

Rowan looked her more or less in the eyes. 'I haven't got any money. And I need some because there isn't anything to eat, and my sister's only ten and she didn't eat her school lunch today, because it was liver. Andy ate his, but he's thirteen and he gets awfully hungry. I mean, it's only for tonight really because tomorrow I'll go and see the bank manager and he'll give me some money, but for now – well. I haven't any.'

Elsie did not show the least sign of surprise. 'Where's your dad then?' she asked.

'At home, in bed. He's not well. I can't – he doesn't – I

don't think he understands.'

Elsie, who did understand, asked no further questions. She reached for her handbag, a dusty brown affair crammed with papers. In a plastic bag at the back she kept her Christmas savings, four ten-pound notes at this time of year. She took them all and gave them to Rowan.

'I'm sure I don't need that much,' said Rowan in embarrassment. 'I will pay you back, I promise.'

'Let's not talk about that now,' said Elsie firmly. 'But you'll have to speak to your mother and get something sorted out. This is no way for children to live, no way at all. I've known your father a long time, and he isn't a man who can cope, he never has been. It's for your mother to see to you.'

'I am never going to talk to her again,' said Rowan, and she looked so fierce that Elsie paused in her homily.

'Well, that's as may be, but she's the one with the money now, and you children need it. I'll tell you something. One of my lads works here in the finishing, and he says the place is on its knees. Matter of weeks he says, the secretary doesn't even know where the wages is to come from. So your dad can't help you, only your mum. And if it isn't either of them, then it'll be the social, and that's not what you're used to, I'm sure!'

Rowan pushed the money into the pocket of her jeans. One of the first rules she had ever learned was never to talk the firm down. 'I'm sure he's wrong,' she recited automatically. 'My father will soon be back at work, putting everything in order. And of course I'll pay you back, Elsie, I really do promise. Thank you so much.'

She trudged home, half-dead with weariness. The fish and chip shop was open, and she ordered four lots of haddock and chips, knowing that they would be lukewarm by the time she walked home. And when she got there Andrew didn't want his and Andy gobbled it, complaining that he would have preferred a pie.

'Why don't you help? All you do is play that beastly violin!' flared Rowan.

'That's because I have to. It doesn't mean I don't care.' Andy's eyes, so like his mother's, stared at her. Then he said, 'By the way, I put the washing in the machine, all the shirts and blouses and things. If we don't go to school looking decent, people will know.'

'They know anyway,' said Sally. 'They just stop talking about it when I come in.'

'I hate Mummy,' said Rowan shakily. 'It's all her fault.'

'It's that man,' said Andy. 'They should put him in prison with rats.'

Without saying anything, Sally began to cry.

In the morning Rowan went out early and bought bread and cereal from a little shop run by an Asian who survived by being open forever. The shop always smelled strange and usually she only ever bought sweets there. Now, standing in the early morning queue of people buying cigarettes, she felt conspicuous and pushed the money over defiantly. It seemed to be going so fast, and it was all she had.

The post brought a final demand from the electricity board, but she said nothing to anyone and hid it behind the clock. Once Andy and Sally had left on the school bus, she tried to gather her courage. Dad's bank was in Bradford, so she would have to go in on the bus, dressed up in the horrible suit Diana had bought her for Christmas. The sleeves were two inches too short by now but it would have to do, she couldn't wear her favourite jeans and Sitting Bull T-shirt. And she would have to look older than she was.

Her few experiments with make-up had brought derision from her schoolfriends as well as her brother, so she normally didn't wear any. Now, though, she struggled with mascara, avoiding the eye-shadow that always seemed to be her downfall. Colours looked garish on her, because her eyes were so very green. Just at the tricky bit, the telephone rang. It was Diana.

'Rowan! Please, please don't hang up. How is everyone?'

'I don't know why you bother to ask.'

'Because I care about you. Darling, how are you managing? Why aren't you at school, I thought your father would answer.'

'I've got a cold,' lied Rowan.

'Oh dear. Is Andy all right? And Sally?'

'They're at school,' said Rowan non-committally.

'That's good, I am glad. Darling, James and I have been talking. We're moving into a new house at the end of the month . . . actually it's an old house, very old, with wonderful gardens and a trout pond with a fountain. You children will absolutely love it. You can have your rooms done just exactly as you like, and there's a turret room with a clock – '

'I'm not coming. I'm staying here.'

Diana's almost panicky recital stopped. 'I wish you wouldn't hate me,' she said.

'And we wish you hadn't gone. I can't talk now, I'm busy.' She put the 'phone down and then viciously ripped up the telephone notepad, throwing the pieces on the floor to add to the general mire of neglect. She went up to see her father.

The room smelled stale and dirty. Andrew was sitting up, reading through old letters. 'That was her,' said Rowan.

'Did she ask about me? What did she say?'

'She wants me and Andy and Sal to go and live with her,' said Rowan, and watched her father's face.

It dropped just a little more. 'I suppose that's generally the way things go, isn't it?' he murmured.

'Well, I won't go!' declared his daughter. 'But, Daddy, what's going to happen? You ought to be at work, you can't stay home forever!'

'Why not? I tried my best with Judge's and I couldn't get

it right. Perhaps things will be better if I don't try at all. I don't know what else to do, Rowan, I don't know the answers.'

'We've got to do something. How are we going to live?'

He seemed to be giving it some thought. Then, without warning, he picked up a letter and said, 'You know, she used to like me. See what she says here. "I loved you last weekend, you were wonderful." I mean, she felt that once, it wasn't a lie.'

Rowan sighed. She couldn't expect her father to help her.

When she arrived at the bank she didn't know who to ask for, and consequently they kept her standing at the Enquiry desk for ten minutes while the staff cast curious glances in her direction. She could feel the gossip flying about her like winged insects. At last they took her upstairs and into the presence of a large, craggy man in a battered suit.

'My name's Blood,' he said jovially. 'A pretty dreadful name but there it is. And you are Miss Judge, I understand?'

'I'm Rowan Judge, yes.' She was tense and unsmiling, miserable in the outgrown suit and unglamorous flat shoes, chosen to make her feel shorter. She sat down before the desk and they eyed each other. He was going to try and put her at ease, she knew, making little jokes and so on, and she couldn't bear it.

'I've come to ask for money,' she burst out. 'My mother's left home, my father's having some sort of breakdown and the business is going to collapse. So I need some money. Please.'

Mr. Blood blinked. He had seen some customers in his time, but they weren't usually quite so tall, so pale or so desperate. He had the feeling that one word out of place would cause all that brittle control to snap into pieces. 'Why exactly do you want the money?' he asked cautiously.

'To live, of course!' said Rowan. 'To buy food and pay the bills – since my mother left it's been nothing but bills –

and they're going to turn off the electricity next week. I mean, I know you're not a charity but this is where Dad has his account, isn't it? There is money in it?'

Mr. Blood grunted, as if at a blow in the solar plexus. The one thing the Judge account never had in it was money. It was full of anguish, hopes, promises and despair, but not money. The Judge family had been living on overdraft for so long that he had ceased to look for a day when they were in credit. And the worst of it was, if things were as bad as the girl said, she was going to have to lose her home as well, to at least in part pay the debt.

'I really shouldn't talk about the family's affairs with you at all,' he prevaricated.

'Well, there isn't anyone else,' said Rowan. 'And I'm the one that needs the money.'

'Yes. Yes, I can see your point. How old are you?'

'Seventeen,' she lied, knowing that at her height no one ever knew her age. Eighteen would have been better, but she didn't think she'd get away with it.

The answer seemed to satisfy Mr. Blood because he rang through for the Isaac Judge file. While it came, they sat and stared at each other, Mr. Blood trying to make conversation and Rowan saying nothing. At last the file arrived and Mr. Blood said jovially, 'Well now, let's see if we can explain a thing or two, shall we?' reminding Rowan somehow of visits to Father Christmas, when you came out of the grotto clutching a disappointingly cheap plastic doll. She tried to concentrate on what he was saying, because he was trying to explain the firm's entanglements and it was not easy to understand.

'Is it all Dad's fault?' she asked suddenly.

Mr. Blood paused. 'It isn't easy running a business. It's the hardest thing there is.'

Rowan's clear green gaze remained fixed on the columns of figures he drew for her, because at least no one could pretend things about sums, they were as they were and deceived no one. 'This is the limit of the mill's credit,' explained Mr. Blood. 'Now, unless someone pays in some money next week, we shan't be able to let anyone at Judge's have the money to pay the wages. You can see that, can't you?'

'Yes. But if we don't pay the wages I can have some for us to live on, can't I? I could have some now.'

'Well – you could,' said Mr. Blood carefully. 'But then the firm would be out of business and there would be no way of paying off this overdraft. We should have to sell your house.'

'Is it worth all this?' demanded Rowan.

'No. We should still be owed an awful lot of money. We should have to sell the mill, the stock, the machinery, everything.'

'Oh.'

Rowan sat peering down at the figures. Mr. Blood reflected on what a strange-looking girl she was, with her long thin extremities, her small, short-haired head on a long thin neck. What a pity her clothes didn't fit her. Rowan said, 'I'd better just have fifty pounds, I think. I've got to talk to my father. We have to get some money in. He's always talking about people who owe him money.'

Mr. Blood looked pained. For how long had he too been talking to Andrew Judge about the people who owed money, begging him to get tough. At least his daughter realised the urgency. 'Can you do that, do you think?' he asked.

'I don't know,' she said. 'I can have the fifty pounds, though, can't I?'

'Oh yes,' said Mr. Blood. 'I think you deserve it.'

Rowan felt calmer on the way home. When you faced problems, when you knew what it was that was frightening you, although you still felt scared, you weren't paralysed any more. If, when all her money was gone, they were still in this mess, then she would go to her mother and ask for help, if not for her then for Sally and Andy. But until then she had a breathing space in which to try, and it was worth it because being paid for by James Barton would choke her. She passed a hamburger place and bought herself the cheapest take-away. The electricity board would have to be staved off; she would ring them up and say they'd already paid, it would take a while to sort out. Eventually no doubt the telephone would be cut off, and the gas and everything. And even after the hamburger she was still hungry.

When she got home, Andrew was sleeping. She stood looking down at him, wondering why he looked so much more handsome when asleep. There was none of the anxious hesitation of his waking hours, just a clear, calm face. She was overwhelmed with protective love for him.

'Dad. Dad, please wake up.'

He did so slowly, recollection of his whereabouts, his situation, sweeping back into him. Wrinkles formed on his brow. 'What is it?'

'Dad, I've been to see the bank. You've got to get dressed now and go back to work, it's really important. We don't have to worry about orders or anything, we've got to get the money that's owed. I'll come with you, I'll help.'

'What do you mean?'

'We've got to go and see the people that owe money. We've got to ask for it.'

At another time, Andrew would have laughed. 'But, darling, it isn't that simple. They are old established firms, you can't chase them like crooks! They won't do business with you again if you do.'

'Well, they won't anyway if Judge's goes bankrupt! Don't worry, I'll do the asking.'

He wrestled with this unlikely vision for a moment and then rejected it. He made as if to lie down again. 'You're being silly.'

'No, I'm not, Dad. Dad! You've got to get up, please! I

don't care if you never do anything for us again, but you've got to do this. If you don't, we'll have to go to that horrible man James Barton, we won't have any choice!'

Turning his face away from her, he said, 'Perhaps you should go there. I can't look after you.'

Rowan hit the mattress with her fists. 'I can see why Mummy left you, you don't try! I've done all this and you won't help at all. Mummy won't ever come back if the firm collapses. She might get tired of him and come back, you don't know she won't, and then what happens if Judge's has gone?'

'Will she come back, Rowan? Might she?'

Sullen, Rowan muttered, 'She might. But not if the firm goes down.'

Some vestige of interest kindled in him. Motivated by Rowan's fierce determination, he bathed, shaved, changed into business clothes. He staggered a little as they went out to the shiny new Jaguar.

Rowan said, 'I'd forgotten about the car. We can sell that.'

'It's bought on instalments,' said Andrew.

Rowan went very quiet. As they drove to the mill, she said, 'Has it been like this always? Pretending?'

Her father sighed. 'Not when I was a boy, no. We had more money than we knew what to do with . . . a Rolls-Royce, silver. We had a yacht for a while but my mother, your Grandma Rose, was seasick. We went on holiday to Switzerland twice a year. Once in the summer and again to ski.'

'I was going to learn to ski,' said Rowan dismally. It seemed a long time ago, in the days of her childhood.

'When I met your mother,' went on Andrew, 'I had a lovely little sports car, British racing green and the bonnet held down with a leather strap. We went everywhere in it, driving like the wind. Diana loved it.'

Rowan gave a snort of contempt.

'We were so happy,' said Andrew, his voice cracking.

'Look, we're nearly here,' declared Rowan. 'Come on, Dad, let's hurry.'

Almost nothing was happening in the mill. One or two looms were going, but apart from that people stood around in groups, talking. When Andrew arrived, a flutter went through the place, a shudder of hope, of expectation. He went straight up to his office, looking at no one. 'We've got to go through the books,' said Rowan. 'You tell me who owes the money and I'll write it down.'

'There's a list somewhere,' said Andrew vaguely.

Rowan blinked at him. If there was a list, why had it not been acted upon? She didn't understand.

The secretary came hurrying into the room, a neat lady in a brown cardigan. 'Oh, Mr. Andrew! Thank goodness you're back. On behalf of everyone at Judge's I should like to say how sorry, how very sorry we were to hear about – well – '

'Hello, Frances,' said Rowan clearly. 'My father wants the list of the people that owe the firm money. We're going to go round and see them.'

Frances looked from Rowan to her father and back again. 'Is that right, Mr. Andrew?' she asked. He said nothing. He was fingering the photograph of Diana on his desk.

'Please get it, Frances,' said Rowan. 'It really is urgent.'

Frances pulled down her cardigan, because she was not the sort of woman to put up with being bossed around by children. Then, because Andrew had still said nothing, she went and got the list.

Rowan was shocked by the names, and the amounts. Thousands and thousands of pounds on which Judge's were paying interest. 'It shouldn't be allowed,' she declared. 'They ought to know what happens when they don't pay.'

'Half of them can't pay,' said Andrew wearily. 'I'll mark the ones we needn't bother with. And the really big boys won't pay up either, not unless we summons them.'

'Then we should do it,' said Rowan. 'They shouldn't get away with it, even if it does cost us money.'

'But then we'd lose their business,' said Andrew. 'We need them more than they need us. It's a cruel world, my darling.'

But Rowan wouldn't be put off. Finally they had a list of ten names. 'I'll write to them,' said Andrew vaguely.

'Oh no! We're going today, to see them.'

'But, darling – then they'll know we're desperate. It could finish us.'

'Daddy, if we don't go we're finished anyway. Can't you see, we have to? I'll go in, you can stay in the car if you like.'

And suddenly Andrew couldn't bear it. Her competence, her determination, completely unmanned him. He turned away, racked by dry sobs.

Chapter Nine

In the end it was Rowan who stayed in the car while Andrew went round asking for money. The experience was a surprise to him, because he had expected contempt and ridicule, and instead received kindness. Everyone knew what had happened and few people imagined that they, let alone Andrew, would have come off best in an encounter with James Barton. They felt sorry for him, knowing how bad things were and that if they didn't pay up then they would certainly bear some of the guilt of Judge's collapse.

Back in the car, after the third successful visit, Andrew said to Rowan, 'I thought they'd think I was weak, letting the business go like this. But they're trying to help.'

'Everybody hates that man,' said Rowan.

'Do they?' said Andrew. 'They have no reason to like him, anyway. They might think it could happen to them, you know how these wool men travel. Never home, really.'

'You didn't travel much,' said Rowan. 'I mean, she'd have had an excuse then.'

Andrew held the steering wheel tightly, though he hadn't as yet started the engine. 'Perhaps I should travel more. I always feel I can't leave the mill, there's so much to go wrong. But the order book's so thin – '

'When I'm sixteen, I shall leave school and run the mill,' said Rowan. 'They you can do the travelling and get the orders.'

Andrew laughed. A warm bubble of love for his gangly daughter exploded inside him, momentarily obscuring his misery. 'Darling Rowan,' he murmured, 'you stay at school and get your exams, a mill is no place for a girl. I want you to go to university. You could be a barrister, anything. The wool business is just so messy and dirty and difficult. It's on its knees in this country. When you three are grown and off our – my – hands, there won't be any need for Isaac Judge any more.'

'But what about all the jobs?' asked Rowan. 'There's always been the mill, it's a good mill, you can't let it go!'

Andrew lifted his shoulders in a weary shrug. Then he started the engine.

Diana sat in the hotel room and watched James work. She had no objection to him working if she herself had anything to do, but for almost the first time in her life she was idle. James complained if she played her violin because it affected his concentration, there were no children to supervise, no meals to cook, no telephone calls to make. Her friends had deserted her one and all, because although it might be permissible to leave one's husband, abandoning the children was something else again.

And yet she hadn't abandoned them! Just today she had gone over to the new house and instructed the decorator on a scheme for Andy's room, a striking mixture of green and ruby red. Sally was to have a little girl bedroom, all lace and pink roses, but as for Rowan – well. Would she even come? Diana had no illusions about her elder daughter, she had set her face against Barton and nothing would bring her round. She had influence over the others, too. Diana bit her lip. Perhaps Rowan ought to stay with her father, they were very close. After all, Andrew ought to have somebody.

Thinking about Andrew was unpleasant, because it meant thinking about how she had treated him. There ought to have been a way of extricating herself without hurting him so much, but in the end there hadn't been a choice. James hadn't given her one.

She glanced across at him, carrot head bent over his papers. 'James.'

'Ummmm? Yes?' He briefly glanced up.

'Are you going to do something for Judge's? You said you would.'

'I know I did. I will, when I get the opportunity.'

'That isn't what you promised. Have you heard how they're doing? Things were bad, you know, and it would be too much for the firm to go bust as well as everything else.'

James looked up properly. 'Too much for whom?'

'Andrew, of course. I was married to him for over sixteen years, James. I don't want to live with him any more but that doesn't mean I hate him! Though I imagine he hates me.'

James came across to her and knelt at the side of her chair. 'You know he doesn't. You know he loves you to distraction and always will.'

She eyed him thoughtfully. 'Will I get that from you?'

'I'm no lapdog.' He kissed the skin of her neck, but she wasn't about to respond.

'That's not what I asked.'

'Wasn't it? The trouble with poor old Andrew was that he knew he wasn't up to you, he had to buy you off with his devotion. Now, that isn't what I'm giving.' He dropped his hand to her skirt, reaching up under the hem.

Diana gasped as he touched her. 'I don't need you just to get laid, James. I can have that anywhere.'

'So you can, my darling. But don't forget I'm not Andrew, I don't let go of things. I only throw them away.'

He groped between her legs, finding the warm folds within her clothes, watching her face register slight irritation that he should arouse her when she wasn't really in the mood. 'Oh God,' she said crossly. 'I suppose we might as well, there isn't anything else to do around here.'

In one of those unexpected gestures that so excited him about her, she stood up and languidly stripped off her skirt and pants. All his sophistication died as he looked at her, naked from the waist but for stockings and suspenders, her pubic hair an auburn cloud, her legs as long and slender as any gazelle's. Lust was suddenly choking him, but as he reached out for her she pushed him back on to the floor, expertly unzipping his trousers. The initiative well and truly lost, he lay back stunned as she straddled him and then lowered herself carefully on to him.

'Oh God. Oh God,' he moaned.

'Shut up,' said Diana distantly. 'I'm sick of things always going your way.'

He was going to come, it was like an express train. Desperately he fought it, because in this he had to satisfy her. She was watching him, riding him, her eyes cool and determined, and he couldn't stop himself. The explosion of feeling engulfed him.

Diana rolled away from him. 'Thanks a lot,' she murmured.

'I'm sorry. I couldn't help it,' said James.

She wiped herself with a tissue. 'Then I think you'd better learn to help it,' she said nastily, and smiled at him with an angry glitter. Ye gods, sometimes he felt like a seal jumping through hoops. For a second, quite unexpectedly, James felt a stab of longing for his wife.

Diana called at the house when the children were home from school. This had always been her time, with Andrew at work and the day's happenings to be traded, hot off the press. As she got out of the car she could hear Andy playing the violin and she closed her eyes and stood, savouring it. Was he really better, or was it only that she hadn't heard him in weeks? Such power, at thirteen years old!

She went into the house without knocking. Sally was sitting at the kitchen table, still in rumpled school clothes, while Rowan inexpertly chopped an onion, wiping the tears from her cheeks with the back of her hand. They both looked up, startled.

'Mummy! Mummy!' Sally flung herself towards her mother, but Rowan reached out one long arm and caught her.

'Don't, Sally! Remember what she did to Daddy! And she left us!'

'Don't be so silly, Rowan,' said Diana, and came over to gather Sally into her arms. 'Have you missed me, darling? I've missed you terribly. And look at your hair, birds could nest in it. What has happened to your brush?'

'That's right, bother about the important things,' sneered Rowan.

'Oh, Mummy, it's been awful,' burst out Sally. 'We didn't have anything to eat.'

'What?' Diana stared at Sally, shocked.

'Don't be silly, Sal,' said Rowan quickly. 'She means I forgot to shop one day, that's all.'

'No, I don't,' said Sally. 'There wasn't any money. We were starving.'

'Oh my God!' Diana looked up and met Rowan's defiant gaze. 'Why didn't you tell me?'

'I'd rather we starved to death!' Rowan picked up the chopping board, onion and all and hurled it at her mother. She ran from the room, thundered up the stairs and banged into her bedroom.

Later Diana came upstairs. She knocked on the door, then went in. Rowan was lying face down on the bed.

'Darling, talk to me,' she said gently. 'We must talk.'

'No.'

'Sally's been telling me what happened. I know how you feel but you should have told me! There was no need for it. Daddy might have been better in a hospital, I could have arranged that, had you properly looked after – '

Rowan rolled over, her face red and puffy. But she was coherent. 'You'd have put him in some mental home and he'd never have got better. He's OK now really, just sort of miserable.'

'Sally says the electricity's going to be cut off.'

'Course not, I've paid the bill,' lied Rowan. She was rather worried about that actually. Dad said if they wrote any more cheques the bank would bounce them, but they were due some money at the end of next week and might only be cut off for four days, if they would put it back on as soon as you asked. On the other hand it might be four weeks, and the cooker was electric and so was the heating.

'Don't you think I know when you're lying,' said Diana flatly. Rowan bit her thumbnail.

Suddenly Diana was fighting tears. 'Oh God, Rowan,' she sobbed. 'Do you have to make things so hard? I can provide for you, I *want* to provide for you, I'm not a wicked woman! James isn't a wicked man! People get divorced all the time, it isn't a crime!'

'Not officially, I don't suppose,' said Rowan thoughtfully. 'But it's worse than robbing a bank or something. I mean, if you went in with a gun and threatened to shoot people and then didn't and stole the money, well, it would only be money. Everybody would be over it in a week. But Dad won't ever get over it.'

'Oh, of course he will!' flared her mother. 'You wait, he'll have some girl in here not two years older than you, and then see how glad you are to live with him! Whereas I can give you a lovely house and James and – '

'He doesn't want us,' said Rowan. 'He won't stand us for a minute.'

'He knows you have to come to me, and anyway you haven't a choice.'

They glared at each other.

Diana went downstairs to make a cup of tea and the children, seduced by the old order, sat round and drank it. Andy was very quiet.

'Will you go?' Rowan asked him at last.

He looked from her to Diana. 'No.'

'Oh, Andy! Whyever not?'

'Because I won't live with that man. Rowan and me have done our best to keep things going and look after Dad, you and him didn't help at all.'

'But you wouldn't let me, you didn't tell me! Did she tell you I was 'phoning, did she say she wouldn't let me speak to any of you?'

Andy gulped his tea. He knew he was betraying his mother. 'I think I should stay with Rowan.'

Diana, white-faced, swung round on Sally. 'And what about you?'

Sally looked desperate. 'I don't know. Rowan!'

'I can't tell you what to do,' said Rowan. 'If you can leave Dad just because things have been tough, and go and live with that man with all his money and his evil ways – '

'Rowan, you're being ridiculous! Anybody would think he was a murderer or something,' shrieked Diana. 'Go upstairs and get your things, Sally, you at least are coming with me tonight. This house is filthy, freezing cold and you're living on baked beans and mince. You can't stay here, any of you.'

'I don't want to leave Daddy,' sobbed Sally. 'Why can't you come home and make things right again?'

'Because I can't,' said Diana grittily, putting her hands to her head. 'Just come as you are, Sally, right now. I shall be back to see about you two.'

She grabbed the child's arm and marched her out to the car. Rowan and Andy sat looking at each other.

'What's going to happen, Rowan?' asked Andy.

'I don't think she can make us go, not without going to court or something. And we can't leave here, Dad wouldn't stand it.'

'No.' Andy shivered and looked around at the disaster that was the kitchen. 'Think we can turn the heating up?'

Rowan wrinkled her nose. 'I suppose we could. After all, they're going to cut us off anyway.' She went to the thermostat and turned it up full, but somehow even when the room was at last warm it still didn't seem homely.

They didn't want to tell Andrew about Diana's visit, but

even he eventually realised Sally was missing. 'She's gone with her,' said Andy gruffly. 'Rowan and me wouldn't.'

Andrew said nothing for a moment. He looked at his two set-faced children. 'You might be happier with her, you know. She's your mother, she can take proper care of you. If you want to go I shall be quite all right, I promise you.'

'That's silly,' said Rowan. 'You'd be on your own.'

Andrew sighed. 'I went to see Mr. Blood today, at the bank. He was very impressed with you, Rowan. And – there are one or two problems. School fees for one.'

'That's all right,' said Rowan. 'We'll go to the comprehensive, won't we, Andy?'

But Andy said slowly, 'I don't mind that, but – my music lessons. We've got to afford those.'

'Yes, of course, we must,' said Andrew. 'I just don't see how at the moment. And your mother could afford them. But there is another thing.'

Rowan's heart sank. 'Mr. Blood wants us to sell the house,' she said mournfully. 'He said we might have to.'

They sat in dreadful silence, until Andy said, 'This is so awful it's like a horror film.'

'It's not really that bad,' said Andrew in an attempt at cheer. 'You two could go to your mother and I could live at the mill in one of the terraced houses. A lot cheaper, a lot more convenient and the bank balance would look a great deal healthier with the money from this place in it.'

'We'll come and live in the mill house, then,' said Rowan.

'It's a wreck,' said Andrew. 'I'll get it done up, of course, but just now – well, I'll be living in my office.'

Eventually Andy and Rowan went off to bed. The awfulness of everything drew them together as never before. They sat side by side on Rowan's bed and talked about it.

'They stab people at the comprehensive,' said Andy. 'They'd stab me if I went there, they shout when I go by in my cap.'

'I'd look after you,' said Rowan.

'I don't want to be looked after by my sister! Why can't we have that man's money and not go and live with him?'

'Because nothing's ever fair!' said Rowan. 'Something horrible ought to happen to him, to pay him out for what he's done to us. But it won't. He'll go on and on, getting more and more beastly.'

'But why did she go with him?' asked Andy, puzzled.

'Because of the diamond brooches,' said his sister. But at fifteen, she knew what it really was. When she saw James Barton she understood, as did her mother, that here was the herd leader, the stag to whom all females should submit. The attraction, felt even by Rowan who hated him, was entirely to do with power.

James was feeling rather bad-tempered. He was tired, and as he got older he noticed the below par days more and more. Living at the hotel had been bad enough, with the departing revellers late at night and clattering chambermaids early in the morning, but he had expected an improvement when they moved into Aspley Manor, especially considering what it was costing him. Sadly, things were worse. The newly installed central heating had air in it or something, and the autumn chill was striking very cold in the huge rooms and long corridors. To help things along, teams of workmen still arrived at crack of dawn. And that damned child Sally had nightmares!

He could never remember Marjorie indulging Richard as Diana did her daughter. Whatever the hour, and however many times an hour, she would respond at once to the shrieking and sit with the brat, calming her and offering to make her cocoa or something. Anyone with half an eye could see she was trying it on.

'I wish you'd stay here, Mummy, and not go to bed with him!' Sally had begged last night, so appealing in her expensive French nightgown, paid for by him. It was ridiculous and he didn't intend to tolerate it a moment longer, he would speak to Diana about it that evening.

There was a perfunctory knock on the door and Saul entered. He was wearing a cream linen suit that would not have been out of place on the Riviera. James growled, 'What the hell do you want?'

Saul studied him briefly. 'You look ill,' he commented. 'The glamorous Mrs. Judge is proving too much for you, I suppose. She won't like it if you can't get your leg over twice a night. Oysters and champagne, James, they're your only hope.'

'Mind your own damned business,' muttered James, surprisingly mildly for him.

Saul threw a folder on to the desk. 'Sales figures.'

'Up or down?'

'Up. Fantastically up, it's the new range. But, everybody wants everything yesterday, and if we don't get our fingers out the Italians will. I hate to be so businesslike but we've got to shorten lead time.'

James leaned back in his chair and stared at his half-brother. 'You're just too bloody soft, you couldn't negotiate for a sandwich. If they want what we've got to sell, you tell them to wait till we deliver.'

Saul considered. 'I know when to back off, if that's what you mean. You don't know what it's like outside, there are wolves prowling in the streets! In New York I was being followed round by the Italians. They're sending out teams. Admittedly they're so bloody snooty they alienate most Yanks but we're talking pressure here. And their stuff is good, take a look at this.' He reached into his pocket and brought out a small pack of samples, the type that salesmen distribute to customers.

James unfastened the binding and spread the materials out on the desk to study them. Even in these small pieces it was obvious that they were new designs and weaves, richly coloured and subtly blended. 'They look very expensive,' he commented.

'Nothing in it,' said Saul. 'Except lead time. If we want to hang on in there, we've got to smarten up.'

James grumbled and grunted, but production was his department and not Saul's. So, to vent his spleen, he savaged Saul about the cost of the stolen samples. 'Your expense account is an absolute fucking disaster and I want it halved!' he snarled. Then he became aware that Saul, far from listening, was looking towards the door. Diana stood there, a slightly pained expression on her face. She looked mesmeric, dressed in soft black with a little black hat on the back of her auburn hair. There was a diamond brooch on the hat and another on the dress. James almost groaned as he looked at her.

Clearing his throat, Saul said hoarsely: 'Mrs. Judge. Saul Barton, I don't think we've been introduced.'

'How do you do. I've seen your photograph in gossip columns.' She extended her gloved hand to him.

'You shouldn't believe everything you read,' murmured Saul. She smiled and then nodded coolly at James. 'James.'

'Darling.' He got up and went to her, but as he reached out to put his arms round her she moved away. 'We were having a business discussion,' he said feebly.

'So I heard. Do you always scream obscenities in the office?'

'Only at me,' said Saul. He was amazed to see James without the initiative, having assumed, as did everyone, that James had seen, grabbed and tamed the beautiful Mrs. Judge.

Diana seemed to relent. She put her hand on James's shoulder and said confidingly, 'James, dear, Rowan telephoned. She and Andy will be coming tonight and I'm in town to get some things for their rooms. We'll have a celebration meal this evening. What time will you be home?'

'Er – about seven-thirty. But they're not coming for good, are they?'

'Yes, thank God. They've been having a terrible time, I'm just so relieved.'

'But why the hell can't they live with Andrew? They said they wanted to, and quite honestly I'd rather they did.'

In clipped tones, Diana retorted, 'I daresay you would, dear, and if you hadn't reneged on your promise to help the firm, they might be there yet. Andrew has had to sell the house and move into one of the mill cottages. It needs a lot of work, and the children can't stay there. I'm sure you wouldn't wish them to.'

'Yes, I'm sure you wouldn't, James,' interposed Saul. 'I well remember how much you like children, playing with them, getting up to jokes. He locked me in the cellar once for about six hours. I was four, he was nineteen.'

'Good God,' said Diana. She didn't know if she should believe him. He spoke as if it were a joke but there was a grim undercurrent somewhere.

'Get out of here, Saul,' said James viciously.

'By all means, brother mine.'

When he had gone James went to Diana, took her in his arms and kissed her hard. She returned the kiss, almost losing her hat.

'Stop it!' she murmured. 'You're wrecking me.'

'Am I? Diana, if the children are there we won't be able to do this, you know. Send them back. I'll buy out Andrew.'

'There's nowhere to send them back to, the electricity's been cut off. Besides, it won't be as bad as you think. They'll come round, you'll like them.'

'Even Rowan?'

'Well – it's a difficult age. You must know that from your son, and he'll want to come and stay in the holidays, won't he?'

James hadn't even considered it. On reflection he supposed he might come, though he hadn't even seen Richard since the split with Marjorie. It wasn't that he hadn't wanted to – again and again he had been on the verge of arranging something, but then he thought of the conversation. How did you explain abandonment? How did you excuse lust? Not even he could tell his own son he had left home because his mother was a boring cow and useless in bed. It was a reason and a justification, but Richard wasn't old enough to understand.

'I don't want that girl screaming at me in my own house,' he said pugnaciously.

'She won't,' soothed Diana.

James was late for the celebratory meal. Diana was edgy, Sally over-excited and Andy was determinedly practising the violin in the dining- room, though they had a perfectly good music room acres away from everyone. As for Rowan, she was in her jeans and would not change, any more than she would alter her expression of sullen and fulminating resentment.

'Just don't get at him, Rowan,' her mother warned.

'Why not? Are you frightened he'll go off you?'

The violin played wildly, adding a manic background to everything that was said. Sally did a handstand, came over hard and crashed against the table. Two glasses fell over and one of them broke.

'Oh, for God's sake, Sally!' yelled Diana.

Andy played wrenching chords, one after the other, Sally burst into tears, and in the midst of it all James arrived.

Andy stopped playing. They cleared away the glass and sat down to the meal. 'Come and help carry things, Rowan, please,' said Diana.

Rowan went, absolutely silent. James turned to Andy. 'How's the playing coming?'

Andy sighed, letting it be known that this sort of inane comment was one he suffered endlessly. 'OK, thanks,' he muttered.

'Is that all you can say? I asked how it was, I expect to be told how it was,' snarled James. He would not be bullied by these children, he refused.

Andy eyed him belligerently from beneath a fringe that

needed cutting. 'Well,' he began, 'the concerto is coming along well though I'm having trouble with the scherzo, partly because of my age, my hands haven't developed fully. I'm disappointed in my progress this year, my mother used to teach me a lot and she's been doing other things. I was hoping to have begun some Rachmaninoff but my practice hasn't been going too well and I haven't, so I've a lot of catching up to do. And if you don't know much classical music you soon will because I play it all the time. And scales.'

'Thank you,' said James. They sat in silence until Rowan and Diana came in with the food.

Rowan had to hand round the warm plates and she did so sensibly, until she came to James's. She banged his down hard.

'Rowan!' Diana glared at her.

'It was hot,' lied Rowan. She passed round a dish of peas, managing to spill a sizeable portion into James's lap.

'Oh God! James – I'm sorry – just let them go on the carpet and I'll sweep up later,' apologised Diana.

'No, you won't,' said James. His face, always pale, had twin blotches of high colour on the cheekbones. Rowan, watching him, felt her stomach twitter with fright. What had she done? 'Get up to your room, Rowan,' rapped James. 'The rest of you eat up and shut up. This is my house and I insist on politeness and respect, even though I don't want you to like me and I don't have to like you. I will not pay for brats who think it's funny to be rude!'

'We didn't ask you to pay for us,' said Rowan tremulously. 'If you hadn't wrecked our lives you wouldn't even have to know us. You should have thought about us when you decided to – to do it with my mother. You ought to have known what we'd think of it, you filthy old bastard!'

James leaped from his place and came at her. Diana screamed 'James!', Andy dived to rescue his violin and Sally shrieked 'Rowan!' and threw herself at her sister's legs.

With Sally holding her, Rowan couldn't even run and James grabbed her long arm. But he hadn't expected to catch her and didn't know what to do now he had. Her frightened, green-eyed face was inches from his own.

'I'm warning you,' he said softly, 'I won't have you spreading your own special brand of nastiness in this house. One more outburst like that and I'll pack you back to that weak-kneed, mewling man you call a father – whether he's got a rathole for you or not.'

'Mummy, Mummy, stop him!' wailed Sally. 'He's going to kill Rowan!'

'Will you kill me?' asked Rowan shrilly. 'Because I won't be quiet. I hate you, Mr. Barton.'

Diana pulled Sally upright and then held James's shoulders. 'We'll all sit down now and eat our meal,' she said with studied calm. 'You too, Rowan. We're all upset and it will be better when we've eaten. James, I've poured you some champagne.'

James allowed himself to be somewhat mollified. 'I mean it, Rowan,' he said grimly. He had yet to learn that with Rowan he never had the last word.

'You can mean what you like, you don't own me,' she snapped. But she sat down at the table. The meal that was to have been a celebration was eaten in stony silence.

Chapter Ten

The leaves were being blown from the trees in clouds, and the rooks shrieked as they were tossed on the wind. Aspley Manor was on an exposed rise of hill and took the worst of the weather, particularly on a day such as this, when winter was rushing in like a wild grey hag. Twigs rattled on the roof of Saul's beloved Aston Martin as he passed along the drive. He glanced anxiously up at the ancient trees that might decide to crash down to earth on any one of these days. There could be no greater contrast to James's cosy, suburban house than this.

He could see why James had bought it, though. The Manor proclaimed what he had become, it was a testament to his achievements, and the same could be said about the new woman in his life. Diana was a woman to be proud of.

Saul ran quickly up the stone steps and jangled the bell on the massive front door. The house seemed very quiet, and he had expected everyone to be at home. He rang the bell again, and after a few minutes, when his blood was congealing in his veins, Diana answered. She was very pale and there was a scratch on her forehead.

'Good God, are you all right?'

'What? Oh, my head. Yes, I'm fine. I'm sorry, we'd forgotten you were coming.'

Saul went into the hall, a magnificent entrance in panelled oak with Turkish rugs on the parquet and a marble table Diana had found in a shop in Harrogate. 'James did ask me to come,' Saul ventured. It had in fact been a command, to attend at the house as soon as he returned from his exploratory trip to South Africa. And here he was. From somewhere upstairs there was the sound of sobbing.

'Look, if it isn't convenient I can come another time,' he said. His brown eyes gazed at Diana with real concern. Some of the tension went out of her. He was younger than she yet so admiring, it restored some measure of her control. 'There's been an upset,' she explained. 'James became very angry about Andy playing the violin, and he should have been in the music room but wasn't. I yelled at James, and of course Rowan got involved, as she would, and then – well, Andy's violin has been broken. James blames Rowan, Rowan blames James, Andy's distraught and I – I think I'm going to have a total nervous breakdown.'

She laughed unhappily and Saul somehow couldn't help himself putting his hands on her shoulders. James's voice cut across them. 'What in God's name do you think you're doing, Saul? Let go of her!'

Saul did not immediately comply. James's hair was on end and his face bore the clear imprint of a handslap. 'Was that Rowan?' Saul asked, grinning.

James rasped, 'Will you let go of Diana? I know what you're like with women! Don't think you can come sniffing around while I'm out, hoping to get in her bed.'

'Oh, James! We don't have to have that sort of paranoia, do we?' Diana stepped away from Saul and put her hands to her head, and James, struggling for control, burst out, 'All right, all right. It's just – let's have a drink, God knows I need it.'

They went into the drawing-room, and the fire was dying. Cold air hung in the room as substantially as curtains. 'The bloody heating never works,' growled James. 'Why don't you ever get on to them, Diana?'

'I do, every two days,' she intoned. 'I want straight Scotch.' She went and revived the fire, throwing coal on with a vicious disregard for smoke and dust. Saul felt a deep and delighted pleasure at such disarray, it satisfied him utterly to see James backing a loser. As if sensing his thoughts, James said, 'This is as far as I'm going, Diana. I'm no martyr and I won't stand for this sort of thing, it's not doing anyone any good. Rowan goes back to her father today.'

'I thought it was Andy's violin you couldn't stand,' said Diana tightly.

'She leads him on, he's as weak as his father. Rowan's the one, an absolute bloody hellcat, she is.'

'And what about Sally? Haven't you got something awful to say about her as well?'

'She's a mewling brat. Why in God's name can't a child of nearly eleven sleep through the night?'

There was a long silence, in which they could hear the coal burning on the fire, the clink of unnecessary ice in Saul's drink. Saul said, 'Judge's is nearly broke. Andrew can't afford the children, I'm sure.'

James drained his glass and poured himself another. The booze was calming him, he was looking more like his old self. 'I'll pay him to have them,' he said with a hint of humour. 'I'll send Rowan gift-wrapped in five-pound notes. Honestly, Diana, did you ever see anything like it?'

She grinned. 'Frankly, no. Well, I suppose it's an opportunity to get Andy a decent violin at last. I'd better go and see to him, he's so shocked. It's like smashing a part of his body.'

'Poor kid,' said Saul. As Diana went out he said to James, 'Rowan must be in a state too, isn't she?'

'Save your sympathy there,' replied James wryly. 'She damn nigh knocked my teeth out. I bet you've been hoping someone would do that for years, eh, Saul?'

'I never thought it would be a girl of – how old is she now?'

'Sixteen,' said James. 'For her birthday last week I bought her a gold watch and she left it floating in the bidet in my bathroom. She makes a viper look lovable.'

It was unusual for James to talk openly to anyone. The two men sipped their drinks. Saul said, 'Are you going to get a divorce?'

'Yes,' said James violently. 'I know everyone wants to see me crawling back to Marjorie with my tail between my legs but I'm going to disappoint you. Rowan is doing her childish best to upset things and she won't get away with it. Will you take her back with you? Judge's isn't too far out of your way.'

Saul couldn't restrain himself. 'Be reasonable, James! The kid's had a terrible time, you can't treat her like some sort of parcel. You must have expected trouble. Naturally they blame you for breaking up their home, people can't be ordered to like you.'

'I don't want her to like me,' said James. 'But I will not have her spitting poison every minute of the day. Anyway, she's making Diana miserable.'

His brother eyed him ruefully. 'If that's genuine, I'm impressed. I didn't think you could care about anyone except yourself.'

He got up and went without asking out into the hall. A fair-haired girl was sitting hunched up on the stairs. Her pretty face was puffed from crying. 'Are you Sally?' he asked. 'I'm Saul.'

'Hello,' she said dismally. 'Rowan says she won't go unless he gives her five hundred pounds.'

'Well, she'll probably get it. Are you going too?'

'We'll all go if Daddy can look after us. That man's really mean.'

Saul considered. 'Yes, he is a bit of a shit. Won't you miss your mum, though?'

Sally sighed gustily. 'She likes Andy best. And I'd have Rowan, she lets me get in bed with her when I have nightmares.'

'I wouldn't think it was much fun getting into bed with James, I admit,' grinned Saul.

'Mummy likes it,' said Sally enigmatically.

Saul felt a rush of hot embarrassment. Diana appeared at the bend of the great staircase, accompanied by a tall, gangling girl carrying a suitcase. The antagonism between the girl and her mother made the air hum.

'I must ring your father and warn him to expect you,' said Diana distantly.

'I'm surprised you give him that much consideration,' retorted Rowan. The two exchanged fulminating glances before Diana stalked off to telephone.

Saul said, 'I'm going to drop you off, if that's all right. I'm Saul, James's half-brother. On the wrong side of the blanket,' he added.

'What does that mean?' demanded Rowan, fixing him with her fierce green eyes.

'My father, mine and James's mutual father, never got around to marrying my mother,' he said easily. He had given up being embarrassed about it at school, when James had made sure everyone, but everyone, knew.

'Runs in the family, I suppose,' said Rowan. 'Look, he's got to buy Andy a new violin, can you make him? If he doesn't, Andy will just die. It really is important.'

'I can't make him do a damned thing,' said Saul. All at once he very much wished that he could. The girl was so young and so strung out, the spirit within blazed with an intensity that seemed to threaten her thin body. He found her immensely touching.

James came out and Rowan at once stiffened. 'I'll buy the sodding violin as long as he doesn't play it where I can hear it.'

'I bet Mother didn't know you were a Philistine,' remarked Rowan. 'I'd watch it if I were you, she won't like it at all if you're mean to Andy.'

Since James had already realised this about Diana, he was not best pleased. 'If you'll take your brother and sister with you I'll buy him a bloody Stradivarius,' he promised wildly.

'Oh, he won't go yet,' said Rowan. 'Buy it first and then we'll see. We know all about your sort of promises.'

Saul started to laugh. James was having his nose tweaked

and for the first time in his life could do nothing at all about it. 'And you can stop braying like a hyena,' yelled his brother. 'Get in the car, Rowan.'

'I'm coming, too,' said Sally and got to her feet.

'That just leaves one,' said Saul. 'And it's the one that makes the most noise. I think I believe in God, James, this is your personalised Day of Judgment.'

'Go to hell!'

Saul grinned. 'I think you've got the ticket, actually. Come on, girls, we'll leave him frying.' He ushered his little flock out to the car.

Rowan sat in the worn leather front seat, restless with tension. In the back Sally gazed dreamily out of the window, lost in her world of childhood, into which adult storms and troubles were an unwelcome intrusion.

Saul said, 'You girls haven't brought much.'

'I suppose Mother will send it on,' said Rowan. Her fingers twisted together, long slim fingers with surprisingly clean nails. 'This is a nice car,' she added. 'Have you had it long?'

'Five years. I mortgaged my soul to buy it and I wouldn't sell it for anything in the world. Fortunately I'm away so much it doesn't do many miles, I spend as much time underneath as I do inside.'

'You don't look the mechanical sort,' commented Rowan, casting him a sideways glance under her long, dark lashes.

Saul realised he was making an impression. He allowed himself to admire the long legs coming together in the tightest of tight jeans, and felt ashamed of himself. The child was barely sixteen. 'Do you like cars?' he asked ingenuously.

She nodded. 'A lot more than I used to. It comes from using public transport, I never realised you can wait whole days for a bus.'

'It's not that bad, is it?'

She sighed. 'Men grow old in bus queues. And all you car drivers zoom past and never see us at all, you're too busy worrying about your overhead cams and turbo chargers.'

'I haven't got a turbo charger. The Aston would fall apart screaming if you showed her one. We think they're vulgar and unnecessary.'

'So this doesn't go very fast then?' queried Rowan and Saul conceded the point. 'Not any more, no. She's beautiful but frail and I have to cherish her.'

'Do you like cherishing things?'

Saul suppressed a grin. He was the subject of an experimental flirtation, and he wasn't in the habit of disappointing people. He changed gear, leered suggestively, and murmured, 'Very much.' To his amazement Rowan blushed scarlet, sat up rigidly straight and stared fixedly out of the window. It forced him to chuckle. 'You innocent,' he said. 'You sweet little girl.'

'I beg your pardon?'

She was looking at him out of frightened eyes, quite out of her depth. He thought of the woman he slept with at the moment, divorced from a peer and more knowledgeable in her cradle than this girl right now. 'Will your father be able to look after you?' he asked suddenly. 'I mean, if he can't you must let me know. I wouldn't want to think you were in trouble.'

It was a bad choice of words. Her cheeks flamed again. 'Thank you. We'll be quite all right,' she said stiffly.

When they reached the mill she made him stop outside the gates, saying goodbye as if giving formal thanks for a jelly and blancmange party. When he looked back in his driving mirror he saw her watching him go, a child not quite a woman, wand-thin and shivering in the cold.

The Bradford hamburger joint was run down, the seats slashed and the glass of the windows murky. It was due for revamping, when the prices would go up and the customers would change, but for the moment it catered for the lesser, poorer end of the market: the tramps, the unemployed, the flabby women with endless children and no winter shoes. Andy, Sally and Rowan sat grim-faced at a corner table.

'I still think I should leave,' said Andy. 'I mean, if Mum spends five minutes teaching me, he's yelling. They fight about it.'

'All the more reason for you to stay,' said Rowan implacably. 'They deserve to be miserable.'

'I wish we could go back to the way we were,' said Sally, but the others took no notice. It was a sentiment she frequently expressed and they had tried all sorts of answers, but still she kept on saying it.

'If they split up, there's no one to pay for my training,' said Andy.

Rowan was taken aback. This single-mindedness of her brother, often encountered, was nonetheless still shocking, like meeting a brick wall when you had thought you were stepping into the garden. 'There'd be some way,' she blustered.

'No there wouldn't. How's the house?'

'All right.'

There was no point in telling him the half of it: damp plaster they couldn't afford to hack off, ill-fitting curtains, five plugs on one dangerous socket, the strange and devious wiles of the poor that she was being forced to learn. 'I'm leaving school at the end of term,' she volunteered.

'Won't *he* pay?'

'I don't want him to. I'm going to help Dad, there's no way he's managing. He just blunders from one disaster to the next. We had a loom go up in flames last week. Dad said they shouldn't have put it out, they should have let it all burn. Except the mill isn't insured any more, the premium was huge.'

Sally sucked up the last of her watery, additive-rich milk shake. 'Dad won't let you leave school,' she commented.

Neither Rowan nor Andy said anything. They both knew that if Rowan set her mind to something, Andrew wasn't the man to stop her.

'Well, I'm not letting Beastly Barton off the hook,' said Andy. 'I'm going to make him pay for me to go to music college in London. I can board, it'll be super. If I can get through the audition.'

'You'll walk it, you know you will,' said Rowan.

He shrugged. Worms of doubt wriggled at the back of his mind. They were never far away, he could never really believe he was as good as people said. When he performed and was acclaimed he believed it, briefly, but a day, two days, later he was anxious again. He was quite serious in thinking that the audition might be beyond him. As he saw it, a year ago he would have walked it, but recently he had lost hours of practice, his mother had been distracted from his lessons, he had even found his mind wandering when always before he had possessed total concentration. He had to pass! Escape was the only, the inevitable, answer. If he was to follow that shining star, treading a cold road upward, everything else had to be left behind.

'Did you bring anything?' asked Rowan.

Andy reached into his pocket and handed over three silver teaspoons. At that moment he felt a sudden, fierce resentment of Rowan for involving him in something that took time and energy and bravado and lies. He wanted to be on his own, to be rid, finally, of his obligations. He said: 'You know you don't really have to pinch things. Mum said to ask if you needed anything, clothes and so on. She'll buy it and put in on her credit card, he'll never notice.'

'A Sindy doll!' said Sally. 'The one with the wedding dress. And Rowan needs some new jeans, hers are awful.'

'I'll buy what I need myself,' said Rowan haughtily, knowing that Andy would ensure that the jeans arrived.

It was all money. She thought about it endlessly, it even haunted her dreams. Husbanding pennies, thinking twice and three times before spending a pound, always aware that James Barton had buckets of the stuff and all she had to do to gain access to it was swallow her pride. To be tempted was worse than to be deprived. How she hated this bitter, endless dependency!

Chapter Eleven

Life had always been difficult for Andrew Judge. He was aware that other men found it easier, at times, and were therefore always optimistic about things picking up soon. In the past he too had believed that one day he would stop being anxious and would become the calm, resourceful, successful man he knew he should be. But in the end he had to face it. Some people were doomed to miss out.

Not even when he and Diana were together had he been really happy. The difficulty of sustaining life as she wished it to be had been an ever-present cloud in the sky. Looking back he realised that this had been the best part, the part he should have enjoyed most, but at the time he had worried. It was as if all along he had been anticipating what was to come.

He shivered in the chill evening air. Winter was officially at an end, as his marriage was officially over, but there was still sleet in the falling rain. The mill loomed darkly above him, and darker still were the hills around, punctuated here and there by the lights of houses. The lights of his own house gleamed behind him and there at least it was warm, but he didn't want to go inside. For the sake of the girls, who wanted to believe he was all right, he put on a pretence of contentment. Tonight, with black misery whirling behind his eyelids, he couldn't stand the strain.

So he went into the mill. He thought he might make himself a cup of tea, but the sight of Elsie's tin of condensed milk, with yellow blobs congealed on the lid, put paid to that idea. It seemed even colder inside, and because there seemed no reason to fight it he went and sat on the cold stone steps that led from his office to the weaving shed. They epitomised Judge's for him. Cold, dirty, smelling of decay, and leading down, down, down. He didn't look up, for him there was no up, it was all downhill for him and Judge's and everyone. God, how tired he was of it.

The thought came again. He had considered it four times before, and each time there had been a reason for its rejection. Because of course, something would turn up. Finally, inevitably, he realised that nothing was ever going to change, that for some reason to do with the turning of the world and the fortunes of people like James Barton, people like him had to be losers. And wasn't it typical of him that it was taking so long to decide to do something so obvious? Couldn't he at last decide something, do it and do it well?

There was a rope in the warehouse, thin nylon that would not break, for the final indignity would be to bungle it. The stone stairs had an iron handrail, and the stairwell fell straight for about twenty feet, more than enough. He tied the rope on carefully, suddenly remembering how he had been taught those same knots as a wolf-cub and had barely used them since. He felt a tremendous lightening of his spirit, as if the pressure building inside him was at last being released. This was clearly and honestly the only thing to do.

As he straddled the rail, the rope looped neatly around his neck, he wondered if he should leave a note. But what could he say that would not sound trite and obvious? That he was sorry? He had always been sorry, he was truly sorry now to be leaving the girls in that mucky little house and the mill workers out of their jobs and everybody in the lurch, but for once he was doing what was right, for him and no one else. He laughed. And slipped over the rail.

Rowan said, 'Dad said he was coming in, didn't he, Sal?'

Sally, sitting on the moth-eaten rug before the fire, her knees clasped to her chin and a copy of *Black Beauty* balanced on them, said, 'He was going to wander round a bit. He had a fit of the dismals.'

The girls exchanged glances. They were used to his moods and had their own techniques for handling them. 'He hasn't had anything to eat,' said Rowan.

Sally unravelled herself and stood up. 'I'll go and fetch him, tell him his supper's spoiling and you're upset.'

'Don't forget your coat,' said Rowan.

Sally slipped out of the little house and stood waiting for her eyes to accustom themselves to the dark. She expected to see her father in the yard, staring at things, but it was raining and he wasn't there. Sally pulled her coat round her and scampered across the puddles. High on the black face of the mill was the glimmer of a light. He was in his office.

The mill at night was scary, and usually she didn't go in, but if Dad was there, cold and miserable, she had to fetch him. She switched on the strip lights and ran through the weaving shed, calling, 'Dad! Dad! Supper's ready!' Her voice echoed in the cavernous room and she ran faster, to get to Dad and safety. The door to the stairs was half-open. She slipped through it, reaching for the light-switch she knew to be close by. Something hit her in the face. She lost her breath, found it, and in the same moment her reaching fingers switched on the light.

The scream she had been mustering turned to a ball of ice in her lungs. Her father's feet swung inches from her face, the heel of his shoe worn down on one side as it always was. There were his hands, helpless at his sides, swinging forward of the body in an unreal way. Above, suffused with dark blood, the green eyes bulging in a look of horrific surprise, was her father's face.

She reached out and touched the foot lightly. It set the whole body swinging on the end of its twenty-foot pendulum. It came at her, she couldn't get away. She thrust at it and back it swung, hitting her in the face. Somehow, when she tried to get back into the weaving shed, it wouldn't let her. It hung on to her, the legs tangling up and dragging in her way, catching on the heavy door. The scream came out, a cry of raw panic, and she was through the door and running, screaming.

She didn't stop, she couldn't stop, even when she was back in the house and Rowan was there she couldn't stop screaming. When, at last, her throat closed and she screamed no more, the noise in her head went on. It went on for years.

At the funeral, the three children stood together, wanting no-one near them. Diana came and stood apart, dressed so strikingly in black that Rowan hated her for it. She imagined her mother trying this and then that, determined to look her elegant best even at Andrew's funeral. When, at the graveside, Diana dissolved into shuddering, graceless sobs, Rowan was amazed. Sally watched with her expression of frozen fear that had stayed with her night and day. Rowan put her arm round her and it was left to Andy to go to Diana. Rooks flew from the tall, thin trees beside the gate. The hills rose up like a purple backcloth beyond them, Bradford's hills, enmeshing the city in their folds and undulations. In the graveyard the silence smothered even the cackles of the birds.

Few people came, because it was one of those messy, tragic affairs that make attendance at the funeral almost like a reproach. Life had failed Andrew, they had failed Andrew, there should have been something they could have done. As they were leaving the graveyard, Diana supported by her son, a dark-red Rolls-Royce was waiting. James stood beside it.

Normally Rowan would have savaged him, but now she was filled to the brim with tears and dared not open her mouth. Nonetheless when James saw her, he said, 'Don't think you can blame this on me. He'd have done it anyway in the end.' Rowan said nothing. She simply stared at him with wide green eyes, her face pale and anguished, almost matching that of her sister. James swallowed. Why had he said that? Surely he need not have been so brutal. Yet he could never let an enemy pass without a blow struck, and Rowan was certainly an enemy.

Diana pushed past him into the car. She said, 'Why did you bring the Rolls today? It's such bad taste.'

James sucked in air through his nose, sharply angry. Whatever it cost him in taste he had been determined to show this pauper's funeral why it was that he had won, the impossibility of letting the meek and the incompetent take the prizes. At least Diana could try to understand him instead of joining the chorus of accusation. Andy was staring.

'Are you coming?' demanded James aggressively.

'No.'

Suddenly James had to say it. 'I didn't mean this to happen, I never expected it. Perhaps I didn't know him very well. I wanted to tell you – that I'm sorry. Tell the girls for me.'

When he had gone, Andy joined the girls in the funeral car. He sighed. 'He said he's sorry. I think he is, really.'

'Like hell,' snorted Rowan. 'He can afford to be sorry now Dad's out of the way.'

'But he didn't mean it to happen. He's not all bad, Rowan, I mean he's paying for my music college and Sal's school fees and things.'

'You're going over to his side,' she accused. She had a sudden vision of how it would be. Andy, who liked anyone who helped him with his training, seduced into the Barton camp. Sally too young to fight back, drawn into the opulence and order of Barton ways. And Rowan herself, left alone, the only one truly to know what James Barton was like. She would never get over hating that man.

There was a period of limbo after the funeral, during which everything hung fire. The mill was lurching on from one payday to the next, but no one expected it to last. Rowan and

Sally remained in the mill cottage, rejecting out of hand Diana's plea that they should go to Aspley Manor. The future seemed a confused mess. They had no idea what was to happen to them but they would not go over to James before their father was even cold. Sally went like an automaton to school but Rowan simply sat at home, helpless. One evening about a week after the funeral Diana paid them a visit. Rowan let her in.

Diana said, 'You look a wreck, darling. Your hair needs cutting.'

'I'm letting it grow,' said Rowan in a sullen voice. She wasn't, particularly, but somehow she and her mother never agreed on her appearance. Diana tried to impose her style on Rowan and it did not suit, they were such totally different physical types. Next to Diana's hard-edged elegance, she always felt hugely out of proportion.

She was surprised to see that there were shadows beneath her mother's eyes and fine lines from thin nose to mouth.

'Are you all right, Sally?' asked Diana, as the younger girl remained curled up in her chair. 'I've been worried.'

'I'm all right,' said Sally in a small voice. Rowan and Diana exchanged glances. Sally was clearly not all right, but what were they to do? An experience such as hers could not be erased, however much they should like to do so.

'Go upstairs for a moment, please, darling,' said Diana, and Rowan added, 'Yes, Sally, you go on up. I'll call you.'

When she had gone, Diana said, 'I've been to the solicitor. I wanted to tell you what's in the will.'

'I didn't think there was anything to leave,' said Rowan jerkily.

'Well, there isn't really, I suppose, not if you do the sums. But the mill's still here, and this cottage and so on. He's left everything to you three, with me as guardian. Andy gets half, you and Sally a quarter each.'

Rowan found that she couldn't speak. In all her life she did not think she had ever been so sharply hurt, it was a dagger between the ribs. After all she had done, after all the love and care and effort – he preferred Andy! He had left the most to Andy.

'Why?' It was a grunt, all she could manage if she was not to howl.

'Don't be upset, darling,' said Diana with forced lightness. 'You know what these wool men are like: it's the boys who should be in the business, the girls shouldn't get their hands dirty. And of course it isn't anything really, because it will all have to be sold. There isn't any future for it.'

'But – but I was working here. I was the one involved.' Her voice shook dreadfully. She couldn't hide the pain, it wasn't possible.

'You can't have expected him to give it all to you, can you?'

'No, of course not. Just to divide it fairly. A third for each of us, that would have been fair.'

Diana sat down in one of the easy chairs, a sagging but comfortable thing they had brought from the old house. She looked very tired, Rowan realised, and rather unhappy. 'It isn't fair. I was surprised when I found out, but when I think about it I suppose I should have expected something like this from Andrew. It was what his father would have done, you see – but then you can't see, you never knew the old man well. He didn't think much of girls.'

Rowan said, 'Why couldn't Dad understand? After all, he killed himself, he wasn't run down by a bus or anything, he knew how things stood. Andy has his music, Sally's still at school, but all I've got is the mill. I mean, even if it does have to be sold, at least I wouldn't have felt so – I thought he loved me!' she burst out.

Diana went to put her arms around her, but Rowan shook her off. She addressed her daughter's bent head. 'He did love you! I think he loved you best, if the truth were known, but Andrew was never his own man. He did what other people expected – me, his father, everyone. If he'd known you'd feel like this he might just as easily have left it all to you and slighted the others. He never did have any backbone!'

'Don't talk about him like that,' sobbed Rowan.

'Why not? That's the way he was.'

Diana went into the crowded little kitchen with its second-hand units and battered fridge. A half bottle of sherry was there, probably left over from the funeral when all right-minded people had sherry in the house. She found two glasses and sloshed a measure for herself and Rowan. The girl took hers and sipped at it, making a face at the taste.

'I didn't think you were still that naive,' said Diana testily. 'It's only sherry.'

'Yes, but it's bad sherry,' retorted Rowan. 'Thick as glue.'

Diana giggled. 'Well, what are you going to do?' she demanded. 'I know better than to suggest anything, you'll only throw it in my face.'

'Only to be expected.' Rowan stared down into her glass. In the last few days she had thought about the future a lot, but in very general terms, never confronting the next hour, the next day, the next week. Time had passed and she had taken not one positive decision.

'I want to be the one to see to the firm,' she said suddenly. 'I mean, I'm the only one who knows even vaguely what's going on. I'll talk to the bank manager and sell things and so on.'

'Well, I certainly don't want to do it,' replied Diana. 'Look, I know you won't like me saying this, but James is the man to help. When I see the way he handles his business, I realise just where Andrew went wrong.'

Rowan bristled. 'He can keep his stinking nose out of it! He'd only try and get his greedy paws on anything good. I wouldn't trust him as far as I can spit.'

'Don't be so bitter, Rowan. All right, see how you get on.

But what about Sally? She looks dreadful, I thought I might take her for a holiday. Bermuda perhaps, just me and her. She'd be missing school, of course. I'd take Andy if he wasn't starting college. You don't want to come, do you, Rowan?'

'Me? No thanks. I'll have to get on here.'

The words were automatic. To Rowan's surprise she was feeling a great and delicious relief. She swallowed and felt her head spin, probably because of the sherry. She would be alone, for the first time in her life. No one to care for, no one to worry about – it was as if she was laying down a heavy burden. She tried to concentrate her thoughts, for of course there would still be the mill, which despite everything was still her responsibility. Somehow that never weighed heavy. It intrigued and demanded, and in the end gave you back just exactly what you deserved. None of the others knew how important it was, they didn't care, they didn't understand.

Rowan turned her face away from her mother. At last, at long last, she could have the mill to herself.

Chapter Twelve

The mill began working at eight, so Rowan went into the weaving shed five minutes before the hour. To mark her changed position she was wearing the hated suit, knowing full well that it made her look gawky. Some instinct told her that if she wanted to be taken seriously it was better to look plain, but again, vanity made her tie her hair back in a big black ribbon. It didn't suit her very well because her elfin face looked peaked against such severity, but at least it was better than shaggy untidiness.

Her heart bounced a little inside her chest, not from fear but excitement. No Andrew dithering around, unsure if they should do this or that, taking everyone's opinion before his own. Now she could get on with things, without having to ask permission or justify herself, and she had nothing, so there was nothing to lose. A sudden thought came to her: would they know about the will, had they heard that it had been left to Andy? A small flame of unquenched anger licked again inside her, because of course it was not Andy's, that was merely the foible of a distraught mind. Really, she didn't think it was anyone's. The mill was the mill, and it was up to her, Rowan, to see to it.

One of the lads saw her and started to sidle away, but she called to him. 'Tony, would you go and tell everyone I want to see them, please? We'll have a meeting in the canteen, everyone's to come.'

He looked wary. 'All right, Miss Rowan. If that's what you want.'

She went through to the spinners, setting up their banks of spindles for the day in the desultory fashion of men who know they are really wasting their time. Two men nowadays where once there had been fifty. It was automation, progress and decay, all wrapped into one. They too listened to her with fatalistic apprehension, for they all expected to be out of a job by the end of the day.

She could feel eyes watching her as she went up the stairs to the canteen, deliberately choosing the route that took her past the place where Andrew had dangled. Her father hadn't frightened her, alive or dead, and his ghost would never haunt her. She thought briefly of Sally and raged inside. Who had he thought would find him?

As she went into the high, cold room that was now the canteen and in the prosperous days had housed looms and spindles, bales and bundles of wool she felt suddenly as if she wasn't in charge of herself any more. She was afraid and yet quite sure of what she must do. She could no more have turned back now than flown down the stairs and away across the frosty valley. The low buzz of conversation died away. She turned to confront them.

'I hope you can all hear me,' she croaked, her throat tight with nerves. A rumble of assent came back to her. Without a note, folding her thin hands in front of her, she began: 'I'm sure you all realise that things have been difficult with Isaac Judge for some time now, and my father's death hasn't made things any easier. For the moment, I am in charge.'

Somebody laughed, but rapidly choked it off when it wasn't taken up by others. Rowan lifted her chin. 'I assure you I'm taking it seriously,' she said clearly. 'It seems to me that we're all going to have to work very hard if we're to save anything out of the business, and we mightn't be able to save anything at all. There are just six orders to fill, and they are short runs from some of our old customers. If we got them out on time, and we never do, we'd be idle in ten days.'

'Card's gone again, miss,' said Nobby lugubriously.

'I know,' said Rowan. 'We'll send it for scrap, it takes up

far too much time and effort. We're also scrapping the oldest looms. And I'm going to try and sell the land at the back for building, someone might want to put an office block there.'

'We use that land for the vehicles!' someone complained.

'Oh yes, I should have mentioned that the wagons are going too,' said Rowan. 'We can't afford our own transport any more. So of course we can't keep the drivers on, or some of the weavers, and there's some others that have got to go. I've made a list.'

One of the drivers, a young and belligerent man with tattoos on both arms, pushed his way to the front. 'This isn't fair,' he said, looming with Saturday night menace.

Rowan wondered if he was going to hit her. 'It's all on the list,' she said levelly. 'This is just the people out today, there's no saying anyone will have a job soon. I'm going to see the bank manager and he might insist we close down right away, and if people want to complain and make a fuss all that will happen is they get sacked quicker.' She forced herself to look the driver in the face. 'Like now instead of tonight. Get your coat, I'm not stopping you.'

'You don't bloody care, do you?' he said. 'You just want to keep your well-feathered nest, you don't give a damn about us jobs! Living off the fat of the workers, that's you!'

Rowan bit her lip. She was scared and enraged at one and the same time. 'That's not true,' she managed. 'I'm doing my best to keep as many jobs as possible. And if I didn't care about Judge's and – and everything, I'd just let it all collapse, I don't have to bother about it!'

One of the menders, a fat woman in a wrap-over apron, shouted: 'Leave the lass alone! She's doing her best, just like her grandad!'

Rowan's head came up. 'He didn't think women ought to be in business,' she said loudly. 'You might think that as well. But there's only me that's prepared to try and make a go of the mill, so if you don't back me we've had it. Please try and understand.'

The driver, still a foot away from her, said, 'What are you going to do for transport then? One of them posh carriers?'

'I don't know,' said Rowan cautiously. 'I haven't decided what to do.'

'Well, you don't want to use them big firms,' said the driver emphatically. 'They don't give a shit about small loads, take my word for it.' He turned on his heel and went back into the throng amidst a buzz of discussion. Rowan tried to swallow but her mouth was dry.

That night she sat in the quiet little house and tried to get used to being alone. All her life she had craved solitude yet now that she had it she felt vulnerable and lonely. Still, it was good to be able to mull over the events of the day in peace, and bad to have no one to comment on them. Mr. Blood had been gloomy. If she didn't get orders she had no business; if she got them her machinery was barely up to fulfilling them; and unless some miracle happened he could see no way in which they could make it past six months. He was, however, impressed with her actions thus far. It seemed that Judge's was almost fortunate in being so far down the tube, because it made difficult decisions that much easier to carry out. There was no choosing between this or that option, it was do this or die.

Exhilaration filled her for a wild, heady moment. Such power as she had, to say to this man, 'Get your coat', to that one 'Set this up right now.' Her father had never seemed at home with it. He had been embarrassed at having it. She, on the other hand, was all too likely to let it go to her head. How hard it was to keep your eye on the point of it all, and not to become bogged down in the endless needs of the people and machines. Orders, money, profit, those were what she must pursue. But how did you get orders when you had no new sample range, when you could not even fulfil the commissions you did have? She pondered and fretted, curled up in all her long length on the frayed carpet.

There was a knock at the door. She sat on the carpet, quite

still. The knock came again, but who could it be at the mill so late at night? 'Who is it?' she called out anxiously. The front door led straight into this room, the caller was separated from her by a scant two inches of wood.

'Joe Partridge,' the voice came back. 'I wanted to talk to you.'

Her heart thundered a tattoo inside her. It was the driver she had sacked that morning. What had he come for, revenge? 'I'm – busy,' she called. 'I'll see you in the morning.'

'It's all right,' said Joe. 'I just wanted to talk about something, I won't be five minutes.'

Suppose she opened the door and he raped her? She would have no one to blame but herself. He might even stab her, although among her contemporaries rape was held to be the worse of the two, since everyone would undoubtedly say it was your own fault or think it even if it wasn't said. Of course if he did attack her he'd be arrested and surely he wasn't so stupid. He was one of the workers after all. The knock came again. She got up and opened the door.

On this chill evening the tattoos were covered with a flash motorbike jacket. Rowan noticed his face, wide with high cheekbones and a rather mashed nose. 'It's cold out here,' he said nervously, jigging from one foot to another.

'Come in,' she said, and stood aside to let him enter.

He looked wonderingly around the shabby mill cottage. Rowan was not in the least houseproud and there were books and papers spread on the thin carpet, the remains of her tea still on the table. Joe said, 'You've come down in the world.'

'I never did live in a palace,' snapped Rowan. 'Look, if you've come to ask for your job back, it isn't any use, I can't do anything.'

'Oh, I know that,' said Joe, and hovered, not saying more. Rowan folded her arms and waited until at last he was driven to speak. 'It's like this,' he began, forcing his hands into his jeans pockets. 'I want to set up doing freelance driving. I've got a van, like, and I've meant to have a go for a bit, and seeing as I'm out of a job and it's your fault – '

'Oh no it isn't!' cried Rowan.

'I didn't run Judge's into the floor,' retorted Joe.

'And neither did I!' flung back Rowan. 'Things are as they are, and blame doesn't pay bills, so stop bleating and get on with it!'

He looked nonplussed. Rowan knew that as usual she was being far too aggressive. 'I'm sorry,' she said more gently. 'You want to do carrying for Judge's, is that it?'

'Yes. Yes, miss, it is,' said Joe thankfully. 'I mean, you know I'm honest and reliable, and I'd be dead cheap. You'll have to use someone.'

'If we were doing any business, we would,' agreed Rowan. 'It's a good idea. Have you got a card or something with your address on?'

'Well, I haven't got anything proper done yet,' he admitted, drawing from his pocket a crumpled piece of paper. Rowan took it and scanned it.

'You'll have to get something printed,' she advised. 'If you want to go into it seriously. Look, I'll get in touch when we've some work, OK?'

She waited for him to go, but he stayed put. He was a couple of inches shorter than she but feet wider, the sort of man who played Rugby League and regularly spat out teeth on to muddy pitches. 'Come for a drink?' he said hopefully.

Rowan felt herself blushing. It was the first time in her life anyone had ever asked her out. Her immediate impulse was to refuse, but then, Joe had had a difficult day. So in fact had she. 'All right,' she said. 'Have you got a car?'

'Bike.'

She dusted her hands on the jeans which she wore so much more comfortably than the suit and put on her anorak. As she shut the front door, Joe said, 'Bit miserable all by yourself, isn't it?'

'I haven't had time to find out,' said Rowan, and

suddenly realised that he had asked her out because he felt sorry for her, all alone in her dismal house. But it was too late, he was handing her a helmet and stamping on the kickstart of his bike. She buckled her head into its bucket and climbed on behind him. She had never been on a bike before.

When they started she intended to hold on to the underside of her seat, but at the first corner she clutched Joe's waist and hung on. Wet road flashed past inches away, he opened the throttle and overtook two buses and a taxi. 'You all right?' he yelled back to her.

'Yes. Fine. It's fantastic!'

The wind froze her lungs when she spoke, it lashed her bare hands until they were ice. When they drew up at the pub she was gasping. It seemed impossible that something so thrilling and dangerous could be legal.

'Do you ever come off?' she asked as they went inside.

'Broke me leg once,' he said enigmatically. 'When I was young and daft.'

'What are you now?' she queried.

He paused and looked at her. 'You're too bloody clever for me. What'll you have?'

She didn't know what to choose. It had to be cheap because he was paying, but she had never bought a drink in her life and didn't know how much they cost. 'Er – beer,' she decided.

He ordered her half a pint. When he saw her determined sipping he said, 'You don't like that, do you? I can afford to pay, you know.'

Deciding on honesty, Rowan said, 'I don't know how on Judge's wages. I'd like a glass of white wine really, but I don't know how much things cost. Is it expensive?'

'Dunno, never bought it,' he confessed. 'Bit posh for me, like.'

He drank her beer as well as his own and she sipped her wine. They talked in short staccato bursts. He did indeed play Rugby League, he was good and his nose had been trodden on in a much publicised incident she had never heard of. In his own eyes Joe was a man going somewhere. Rowan wondered if she should see him like that too, because to her he looked like just a nice, energetic bloke that she wouldn't have sacked if she had known him better. 'What's your van like?' she asked.

'Beat up. But now I'm out of Judge's I'll paint it a bit. You won't be ashamed to use me, I promise. Partridge Carriers, that's me.'

Abruptly Rowan stood up and asked to be taken home. He didn't seem to mind her lack of finesse, he was equally gauche himself. In silence they mounted the bike and blasted off back to the mill, terrorising a learner driver into gibbering incompetence. Joe whizzed past contemptuously, swinging into the mill yard in one long, smooth slide.

He walked her to the door of her cottage and she turned, saying firmly, 'Thanks for the drink, Joe. I'll be in touch if there's any work.'

'Right you are.' Then, almost as an obligatory end to the evening, he put his arms round her and kissed her. Rowan felt his tongue glide between her lips, his mouth very warm and soft. Revulsion battled with pulsating waves of feeling, coursing through her body from that strange, probing tongue. She wondered if she ought to hit him. 'You got right cold from that bike,' he commented, letting her go. 'Night, miss.'

She fell through the door of the cottage. Her skin was tingling all over. So much for her superiority over Joe Partridge! He at least knew how to kiss. It was her very first, so for her it held an importance she was sure it didn't for him. He was one of those men who didn't know how to treat women if they weren't matrons or girlfriends. She sat in the old, battered armchair, drawing her knees up to her chin. It was an extraordinary end to an extraordinary day.

* * *

At some time during the night, Rowan was seized with inspiration. She couldn't believe that she hadn't thought of it before. The whole thing sat in her head, perfect and organised.

Judge's would contract out all their existing orders to firms who could and would fulfil them, devoting themselves meanwhile to sorting out the mill and doing sample runs on a new range. It would mean, of course, that they would have to do a lot of running about, taking the wool they already had to be dyed, carded, then spun, woven, and finished wherever there was capacity at a fair price. Joe Partridge could do the carrying and he'd better be as cheap as he promised. The only loser would be Judge's pride, but that paid no bills. And as for the sample range . . . the best thing to do would be to get a look at someone else's and copy it.

They would make no money on the orders but would lose none either, and in the meantime they would have a breathing space to plan. Machinery failure had to stop; they couldn't afford any more lost time on that stony road. Discipline had to improve as well. It was no use making a beautiful cloth if some cretin dropped it in a puddle before it was packed. People had come to accept a sloppy mill, and made no effort to keep it smart. There was no doubt but that was going to change.

She turned her mind to what seemed to her a far more difficult task. A new range and new orders. Whose samples could she copy? The only ones close at hand were Bardsey's, who of course had a lovely range of worsteds, far beyond what Judge's could produce. She had seen some pieces lying around at Aspley Manor, delicious orange and green and heavily woven black.

Of course they couldn't match that. But if – just supposing if – Judge's copied it in their own inimitable woollen way? Suppose she found out whom Bardsey's supplied and followed them round with her own, much cheaper but very similar range? You got what you paid for, in cloth as much as anything, but in an age of throwaway fashion nobody wanted things to last forever.

There was just one problem. She would have to be nice to bloody James Barton.

Chapter Thirteen

Rowan stood in James Barton's office, her hands in front of her, her whole demeanour redolent of an interview with the headmistress. James stared at her sourly. 'Why in God's name do you look so terrible? I can't believe Diana doesn't buy you clothes, she spends a fortune.'

'I didn't come to talk about fashion,' said Rowan clearly. 'I suppose you know that Judge's is in terrible trouble?'

'I'm not lending you any money, your brother and sister are costing enough,' said James.

'It's not that.' Moving hesitantly Rowan sat herself down in front of his desk, deliberately settling her legs in a gawky schoolgirl pose. Her whole manner declared, 'This is a child, don't bother about her, she is very, very young.'

'I'm going to have to get a job,' she said meekly. 'And I wouldn't want one here because of everything, but I thought – well, I thought if I looked round, at the design side and things, I might see something I'd like to do. Something I could train for.'

'You! In design! If you've got talent in that direction, I'll eat my hat.' He leaned back in his chair, surveying Rowan as scornfully as if she were a rusty car. James, with what he believed was the complete upper hand, was enjoying himself. At last he had Miss High and Mighty where she belonged, sitting like a badly-dressed little girl asking for sweeties. He allowed himself a brief moment of gloating.

Her head drooped on that long, thin neck, like a swan with lead poisoning. It disarmed him, he felt he was being unnecessarily mean. 'But of course you can look round,' he said, covering the impulse with an offhand air. 'I'll get Saul to show you the design end, you might have some flair for it. God knows, it's hard enough to find even in the obvious places.'

Rowan looked up at him, her eyes intensely green. 'That's most awfully kind,' she said sweetly. Later James remembered that sweetness and raged at himself for an absolute gullible fool.

Saul came to the office and collected her. For a moment he couldn't relate this meek and drooping girl with the termagent he had ferried to the mill. Her hair had grown but was scraped back with an elastic band in an unbecoming ponytail.

'Good to see you again, Rowan,' he said.

'Yes. And you,' said Rowan breathily. Saul had haunted her dreams for many a night. She had imagined his hands, his deep brown eyes. Now that he was there she felt almost dizzy.

'I was so sorry about your father,' he said.

Rowan had difficulty swallowing. 'Were you? That was kind.'

'Look, I haven't time to waste on drawing-room chatter so would you please get out of here and show her the design side?' said James testily. 'She's going to look for a job in textiles, and needless to say Judge's had about as much design input as your average camel. Dullest range I ever saw.'

Saul saw Rowan stiffen and said quickly, 'Then she'll be interested in what we've got to show. Come along, Rowan.'

He hustled her out of the office. After a few strides Rowan stopped and took several deep breaths. 'If you knew what it costs me to be civil to that man!' she said fiercely.

'I think it was sensible of you to approach him, though,' said Saul.

'Do you?' He was surprised by the laughter that bubbled up into her eyes, by the look of naughty secrecy. But the next instant she had gone inside herself again.

Somehow the considered stroll round the desks of Bardsey's four designers was over more quickly than Saul was used to. He was patiently explaining what each one did and how they worked out the number of threads per centimetre and it was as if Rowan, who professed to want to know, was barely listening. She was pushing him on, looking about her, always wanting to go on to the next and the next department. He was telling her about dye selection when she said, 'Look, I know all this. Can we go and look at the samples? I want to see the range.'

There was a pause. Saul said, 'Have I been teaching my grandmother to suck eggs?'

'You have rather,' said Rowan. 'Judge's used to be a very big firm, you know. It's only recently it's been so creaky. I could have worked out pics per centimetre when I was three.'

His warm brown eyes watched her. They were the colour of syrup, heaped on the spoon. 'Are you spying?' he asked bluntly.

'Of course not.' But she didn't look him in the face. 'You don't usually show the range to people, do you? People who aren't buying.'

'No. No, we don't.'

'That's what I thought. Can I see it, please?' For a terrible moment she thought she had guessed wrongly, that he would turn on his heel and go and confront James with this latest evidence of her perfidy.

'Why do you want to see it?' he asked with surprising lack of heat.

'To see what I should be aiming at. We may never even get it out, we're in such trouble. We're so far behind the times it isn't true. Nothing we can do at Judge's will hurt Bardsey's, so it isn't wrong at all. May I see?'

Saul looked hard into her face and then away. He had an irresistible urge to help Rowan, she seemed so young and vulnerable. On the other hand, if James found out what he had been doing he would most certainly be out on his ear with no job, and the one good thing about the family firm was his job. It was fun and it was lucrative, which were things James never seemed to regard as in any way essential for his younger brother. He was coming to wonder if James thought his living at all was an unnecessary indulgence.

'Please help,' said Rowan softly. 'There isn't anyone else I can ask.' Her young mouth, so pink and curved, seemed tantalisingly available. Close to she wasn't at all plain. He could admire each separate part, she could only be faulted when you observed them all together. He wondered what she thought of him, if she considered him James's creature or merely took James's view – that he was a playboy, good in a limited field. Suddenly he wanted to impress her, and more than that, to kiss her. Girls were never tall enough for him, he always got a crick in his neck kissing them, but to kiss her now he would only have to bend his head . . . .

But this girl, this child, was thinking of quite different things. He pulled himself up short. 'Just don't tell anyone I showed you,' he said gruffly.

They went together to his office. Saul pulled the heavy sample cases up on to the display table at the side and started to spread the fabrics out. 'These have sold very well recently, the orange and the black. I always display them together, they look stunning, and I show them first. Never build when selling cloth. If you bore them at the start you've had it. Show your best right off and don't let them tell you it's bad. If they say it's bad, tell them they're out of date and go on to something else. They might come back to it.' He couldn't resist resting his hand on her knee as he spoke. She seemed barely to be aware of it.

'Can you tell me who you sell to? I mean, how do you get orders?'

With an effort of will he took his hand away. It would have been so easy to slide it up towards her crotch. He imagined her squeal, her falling back, his fingers miraculously finding her tight, wet opening. He said hoarsely, 'I've a list of people I visit. There'll be one at Judge's somewhere, but I don't think your father was trying very hard the last couple of years. Too many refusals get you down, there's no escaping it. You add to the list all the time, you have to have ears like a bat, listening all the time for names. Overseas you use the trade missions and the embassies, agents and people. There's a track, you just have to find it. Some people won't see you, so you try and get an introduction through a back door, someone who knows someone, or use a backhander if you're anywhere in the Middle East. It helps to speak the language.'

'What do you speak?' asked Rowan, who had just scraped French 'O' level.

'French, Spanish, Italian, some Japanese, better Arabic,' said Saul. 'I've an ear for it.'

'Good heavens!' Rowan was impressed.

Saul squashed her against the table as he reached for some more samples, plain white this time in an interesting weave. The heat of his leg could be felt through his trousers. He embarrassed her. As she leant over the table his hand rested on her back, in a brotherly fashion.

Rowan said shrilly, 'Who have you sold the orange to? And the black?'

He rattled off some names that meant nothing to her, and the one or two that she recognised were far too large for her to tackle – yet. She looked down at the floor and nibbled her lip, a habit her mother hated.

Saul paused in his listing. 'What's the matter?' he asked gently.

'Could you write down some names for me?' she asked. 'I don't want it to be your customers, though of course we wouldn't ever compete with you. I wouldn't bring you into it at all. Just some people I could visit. I know Dad had the firms he usually went to, but if they'd been going places they wouldn't have bought from us. Our cloth is really dreary, you know. By the way, are you getting a lot of burr in the wool?'

Saul blinked. 'I don't know – I suppose our combing plant could tell you.' He almost felt like lying, it was so satisfying to please her.

Rowan sighed. 'Oh yes, I forgot. You don't have anything to do with it until it's all nice and neat.'

Saul picked up the scorn in her voice. 'We don't have such an easy life, you know. And actually James is buying the comber's.'

'Whatever for?'

'Power, I should think. Bardsey Combers will be supplying quite a few of the competition, we shall know exactly what they're doing and how much they're paying in material cost. And he's getting it cheap, they're making a loss right now.'

'He's so bloody conceited,' she said bitterly. 'James Barton's magic touch.'

'What about Rowan Judge's?' teased Saul. But she didn't take him up on it.

Instead she edged back towards the subject that really interested her. 'It is difficult to know which firms really deserve your attention,' she ventured. 'After all, I might go to a firm that you know is making a loss and I'd get an order, but they wouldn't ever pay. That would be dreadful, wouldn't it?'

'Terrible,' said Saul. 'You're very persistent, aren't you?'

She drooped again. 'It occupies my mind,' she said sadly.

Half an hour later Rowan emerged from Bardsey's with the vital list of names folded into a small square in her pocket. Saul had been amazingly easy to lead. They began with firms he knew about, progressed to firms he visited, and finally he told her which ones had bought what. She was in a hurry now, to get home and make notes next to each name before she forgot it.

A voice interrupted her frenzied mental recital of facts

and figures. 'Hey! Miss!' A battered transit van drew up next to her. Inscribed in professional letters on the side were the words 'Partridge Carriers'.

Rowan hurried across and pulled open the passenger door. 'Take me back, Joe. And shut up, I've got to write things down.' She climbed up and pulled out her list, sitting crouched over it, scribbling with a pencil.

'Is that important?' asked Joe.

'Shut up!'

Obediently he drove in silence back to the mill. The road twisted and turned, at one point winding round the steep corner of a hill to reveal half the city spread breathtakingly below. The ground seemed to fall away in front of them so that they might almost have been about to plunge into the black ribbons of terraced houses, or down amongst the pin-dot cows in luminous green fields. Against the blackened stone, all the greens seemed to gain something.

'Grand view,' said Joe conversationally. Rowan barely grunted. Even when they were in the yard she did not look up but scribbled on, furiously. Joe sat beside her, stolidly silent, until at last she let out a sigh. 'Got it. Thank goodness I saw you, I'd have forgotten half before I had a chance to write it down. Right, how's the work going?'

'That's what I wanted to tell you. I don't think they're busting a gut at the spinner's. Took the wool there this morning, they didn't look at it. Just told me to sling it in a corner and they'd see to it when they had time. Place is groaning with big lots from posh firms, they won't do us on time.'

Rowan added her groans to those of the spinners. 'OK, go and get it back,' she said. 'I'll 'phone and tell them we didn't like their attitude. I'll put the men on tonight and they can spin it here.'

'That'll cost a bit,' said Joe. 'Double time, I shouldn't wonder.'

She shrugged. 'I just feel we shouldn't ever deliver late,

whatever it costs us. Never, never, never. So they can do the spinning when everyone else has gone home. People won't get in the way then, moving things.'

'What things?'

For answer Rowan slid her list carefully into her pocket and got out of the van. She marched into the mill, Joe following at her heels.

They confronted a scene of turmoil. The offending card was being dismantled, bit by bit, and the dust of generations was covering everything. Several looms were also on the way out and others were being stripped down to bare metal. Industrial vacuum cleaners were roaring importantly and when they ceased there was a clatter from the roof, where men crawled about nailing on felt and repairing skylights.

'This'll cost a bit,' said Joe, and it struck a raw nerve.

'Don't keep saying that!' exploded Rowan. 'Look, the house brought in quite a lot and all this machinery's being sold off to Africa and places, the agent said. It won't be easy doing the spinning because everything's being cleaned and mended, but it's got to be done.'

'If you say so, miss,' said Joe doubtfully. 'Just so long as I get paid.'

'Just so long as you do the job right,' retorted Rowan. 'I can't stand here gossiping. You go and get the wool, at standard rate, and I'll ring up and square it with them.'

When Rowan was older she cringed to think of herself at almost seventeen. She barged in where angels feared to tread, ringing people up and telling them she hated them, confronting aged workers to say that if they didn't stop bleating about the old days and do things her way, then they were out. It seemed to her quite sensible to ask to speak to the managing director of the spinning company and to tell him straight that they were a lousy firm, inefficient, probably without morals, and that her wool was being removed before it became corrupted.

The net result was an explosion in the spinning firm, the

Judge wool was found and dragged from under the very nose of Joe Partridge, and went through the mill at breakneck speed. The managing director accompanied it on its travels like an outrider at a royal engagement; he was not going to be told by a slip of a girl that they couldn't do their job. Major customers had their orders set aside without apology while the little parcel of wool went through. Thirty-six hours later it was back, spun, at Judge's, and before thirty-seven hours had elapsed it was off again to a commission weaver.

Rowan judged that they could be allowed all of five days to produce the woven cloth, and again she rang the company to speak to the managing director and explain that if this couldn't be done she didn't want excuses but hard cash. It was the courage of seventeen that drove her, the inexperience that made her see all things in black and white. At sixteen she would have lacked the confidence, at eighteen she knew too much. But at seventeen she had the fire and the morals of an avenging fury.

But then a problem cropped up which caused her much anxiety. It was her appearance. If it was all right, and advantageous, to look dowdy in some circumstances, it was all wrong and self-defeating to look anything other than glamorous when trying to sell things. What was she going to wear? The problem seemed to her so important that she took time off work and tramped the streets trying on clothes in shop after shop. She even went to Harrogate, which she couldn't afford, to see what was there, because Diana often shopped in Harrogate, especially since James had put his coffers at her disposal. How Rowan wished her mother was at hand to be tapped for one expensive present.

When at last she admitted defeat she was so depressed she spent an uncharacteristic pound on a coffee and a cream cake in Betty's. It seemed a trivial sum when set against the hundreds it would need to kit her out in executive style. She did not dare look cheap, and yet cheap was all she could afford, with her arms protruding from nylon sleeves and skirts that seated in a week. On the train back to Bradford she even considered making something herself, although her only construction thus far in life had been a cookery apron that had caused the domestic science teacher to write on her report: 'Rowan lacks that dexterity so necessary to successful needlework. She would be advised to practise sewing on buttons.' Rowan had not sewn on buttons and was presumably as hamfisted as ever.

Wandering hopelessly back through Bradford's streets to catch the bus, she passed her father's old tailor's. As a little girl she had gone with him to have suits fitted, or a camel coat made. The window was dark and filled with dark material, but inside there was a light. They had talked and laughed, her father and his tailor, exchanging gossip and still having time for her. She pushed open the door and went in.

The tailor was sitting at his worn desk, surrounded by bolts of cloth, half-made suits on a rail beside him. The room was shabby but, as Rowan knew well, in Bradford that was no guide to prosperity. 'Hello, Mr. Suzman,' she said shyly.

He looked up, taking off his half-moon glasses. 'Good heavens. Is it – Rowan Judge? My dear, I was so sorry about your father.'

'I didn't think you'd remember me.' She stood shyly twisting her hands. He waved at her. 'You always were a very tall child, with such wonderful green eyes, and you are still much the same. How can I help?'

Now that it came to it she was embarrassed. He brought out a chair, its collapsing bottom covered by a worn cushion, and patted it invitingly. 'Is there something I can do for you, my dear? Be quick, my wife will be waiting with my dinner. I can't tell her I've been chatting to a pretty girl!'

She smiled obediently. 'It's just – I need some clothes, Mr. Suzman. I know you're a man's tailor, but I'm so tall I can't get anything to fit. And – I'm in the firm now. We're not doing very well. I wanted a dress so I could go out selling, and I can't afford the sort of thing I need.'

The expected amused rejection did not come. 'What sort of dress, my dear?'

'Something in wool. Plum-coloured wool, very plain. Everybody always thinks that sort of thing is expensive.'

'But isn't that a little old for you, Rowan? You must be – well, no more than seventeen.'

'No, I'm not. I need to look older, Mr. Suzman, ten years older at least.'

He laughed. 'Impossible! I can give you five at most, I think. Of course I shall make for you, I make for all my four daughters! I have no such wool now but if you come back in two days, I shall measure you and we will begin. All right, my dear?'

She blinked at him. 'I was so sure you'd say no.'

He tapped her nose with a long finger. 'As I say, you are still very young. We will make you a beautiful lady!'

Two days went by and Rowan presented herself to be measured. She had feared it might be embarrassing, but Mr. Suzman's impersonal flicking of a tape across her shoulders and down her back was entirely functional. He wrinkled his nose at her bust measurement. 'We shall give you curves you do not have. Eat more and worry less, that's my advice.'

'I eat like a horse,' she complained, and he retorted, 'If you were a horse of mine, I would shoot you! Entirely out of kindness, you understand.'

They laughed. 'Can I see the material?' asked Rowan diffidently.

He was already engrossed in jotting down figures. 'At your fitting. A week, all right?'

'Yes – yes, thank you.'

She was out in the street, task completed, and half an hour to wait for a bus. Impatient as always, she started to walk home and after a few minutes Joe Partridge's van passed her, travelling the same way. She waved frantically and shouted. He pulled up a hundred yards ahead.

'Hello, Ro. Missed the bus, did you?'

'Yes. It takes me ages to get around, I just wish I could drive.'

He sniffed and looked thoughtful, barely waiting until she had scrambled up before driving off. 'Teach you, if you like,' he said diffidently. 'I mean, you could get yourself an old banger on the firm, couldn't you? Teach you in that.'

For a second Rowan thought her heart would explode with gratitude. To drive was her truest wish, she longed to be able to do it. No more trains and buses, no more hanging around waiting on others' convenience. She had thought her whole selling career would have to be conducted by expensive and hard to come by taxis.

'I shall never forget this, Joe,' she said fervently. 'It's the most wonderful thing anybody could ever do for me.'

He sniffed. 'Righto then. Glad you're pleased. I'll look out for something cheap, OK?'

They bumped along the road, quite silent. Rowan felt immensely and precariously happy.

The dress, her tailored dress, was all that she had requested and more. She had asked for plum, and instead she had deep, purplish burgundy. Against the wool her hair gleamed like a raven's wing, her green eyes sparkled and her skin came to life. Somehow Mr. Suzman had created bust and hip where there was very little of the real thing, darting in to her narrow waist and lightly padding the shoulders. The length was an inch above the knee, which seemed chic and elegant.

'At least twenty-five,' said Mr. Suzman. Rowan was beyond speech, she merely nodded, helplessly staring at her reflection in his pock-marked mirror. 'And I said to myself,' he went on, 'what is the use of being a tailor if you cannot make jackets? So, I make you a jacket.' A conjuror's flourish and he brought out the jacket, the same plum wool, braided in black.

'It's just perfect,' gasped Rowan. For the first time in her life she was wearing clothes that fitted. She had never seen herself look like this; to stare into a mirror and see a svelte and elegant lady cast her into confusion. All her preconceived notions of who she was and how she should behave seemed cast in the dust, because this lady was calm and well-spoken, she almost certainly played the piano and had spent a lifetime practising sewing on buttons. She wasn't Rowan at all.

Mr. Suzman let out a cry and ripped the sleeve off the jacket. Rowan gaped at him, helpless. 'What are you doing? You're ruining it.'

'I ruin my reputation if I let you walk the streets in that. Such a crease – my girls are fools! Take the dress, come back in a week for the jacket. It is a disaster, useless! My career's at an end, I am losing my touch!'

'I'm sure you're not,' she said hastily, and saw that he was laughing at her. 'I'm sorry, my dear, I'm teasing you. You are so serious! Life is a game of snakes and ladders, up so high and down again, bump! But there is a crease in the jacket, so off with you, off with you.'

Her dignity was a little damaged. 'I must pay you for the dress,' she said stiffly. 'It's so lovely, it must cost a lot. How much?'

He intended to wave it away, but he saw that would not amuse her. The girl bristled with pride. 'I had the material anyway, it isn't the best quality. Twenty-five pounds for dress and jacket.'

'My father used to pay far more for a suit!'

'Well, yes, a man's suit is much more work. This is a great deal easier.'

She beamed because she had been in agony about the cost from the moment she tried on the dress. The notes were pulled at once from her bag and thrust in handfuls at Mr. Suzman. 'I want to see you again,' he said as she left. 'Next time, we shall make something a little more amusing. Time enough to look twenty-five when you last saw fifty!'

Chapter Fourteen

James was rather bored. With Diana away there seemed to be endless hours in which to work, and when all the work was done, as it was this evening,there was nothing to do. Another two weeks before she came home, and filled the house with her own sharp mixture of wit and sex and determination. The latter had surprised him. When she set her mind to something, not he nor anyone else could divert her from it. James didn't mind on anyone else's behalf but he did where he was concerned. He preferred to think that he held sway over her.

He went to the window and looked out into the dull, dank evening. God, but this house was a barn when you were the only one in it. If Diana was here what would they do? Have a drink, go to the theatre, go to bed and screw each other stupid. He felt a shudder of desire, and anger at Diana for swanning off and leaving him like this. What was he supposed to do with her gone? Find a prostitute or something?

He toyed with the idea, making a fantasy of what he would do if he was with a prostitute. Of course he would never go, you'd catch something unless you used one of those rubber johnnies – which he could do. After all, every man ought to find out what was on offer just once in his life. His youth had been spent working hard and being scared of women, he must have missed more opportunities than anyone alive! The years had flicked past faster than he would have believed. If he didn't enjoy himself now, there wasn't going to be much chance later. Everybody paid for it at some time or another.

He laughed, and felt himself good and hard in his pants, as if he was a boy again. What did you do, just drive up to a girl, get her in the car and screw her? He had a vision of some whore, probably chewing gum, chatting boredly about the weather while he shoved at her. Somehow the thought of it excited him further. Before he knew it he was picking up his keys and going out to the Mercedes.

But he was only going to look. He would drive along Lumb Lane and see how grotty they were and he'd come back and have a whisky and go to bed. He might even tease Diana by saying he'd gone to one, that should frighten her. He'd tell her after they'd made love, and tease her all the way to the special clinic. There was more than one way to revenge yourself on someone you thought deserved it.

The car was warm and comfortable, a haven in which he felt totally in charge and at home. An all night chemist was open, and he stopped, hopped out and bought a packet of sheaths from the girl assistant. She handed them over without a blink, which in some way made him think that he was being left behind, that everyone else, at least all her customers and perhaps the girl herself, really was indulging in some wild sexual free for all. Why should he be the one to miss it? He'd wasted all those years being faithful to Marjorie and she, the cow, had waved goodbye to him with barely a tear shed. She didn't give a damn about him when it came down to it, all she was interested in was her knitting and her garden. What price fidelity then? And what was Diana doing all these weeks in Bermuda?

The turret and portcullis gates of the park showed up as white ghosts, monument to extravagant days when these suburbs had been stuffed with wool barons and their money. As he drove further into the city he began to weave his way through streets of narrow terraces, gathered round the mills like the tracks of snails.

The long nose of the car swung smoothly into Lumb Lane. By day it was seedy and unappetising, dotted with unwholesome Asian takeaway cafés with barred windows. At night it took on a different air, of seductive shadows and dim lights. Groups of girls stood around, and some were on their own, standing on the kerb as if waiting to cross the road. They all had the same stance, weight on the back leg, the other thrust out in front. They all wore very short skirts, some wore stockings.

One or two were revolting, fat old women in tight tops, but others were very young. They watched the cars drive slowly on, and they waited, and waited. The car in front of James drew in to the side of the road. A girl with dirty blonde hair leaned down, spoke for a few seconds, then got in. 'Damn,' thought James. 'She was OK, that one.'

He passed a short one with a plump, full figure. As he drew near she stuck out her breasts and threw her head back, pouting at him in a kiss. Without intending to stop, James put his foot on the brake. He pressed the button for the electric window. 'How much?'

She leaned in, businesslike. 'Ten quid to you. Ought to be twice as much, flash car like this.'

'Don't be greedy. OK then, get in.'

She opened the door and got into the passenger seat. She turned and smiled at him, pulling down the neck of her tight nylon top so he could see her cleavage. 'Drive up the end here and turn left,' she instructed. 'There's a place round the back.' Following her instructions they came to a long blank wall, that bordered a canal or an institution or something. The street light had been broken and it was in darkness. One other car was parked there.

The girl wriggled and pulled her skirt up round her waist. She wore stockings and suspenders but no knickers. Her pubic hair was a sparse brown matt and she smelled all right, not of soap but of animal sweat and, faintly, semen. 'Give us the money,' she said matter-of-factly. He pulled out ten pounds and gave it to her.

'How many have you had today?' he asked.

'You're the first,' she lied glibly. 'I've only been doing it two weeks.'

'Don't give me that! I don't mind how long you've been

doing it. But how many today?'

'You a journalist or does it turn you on?'

'Turns me on,' admitted James. And it did, he was as hard now as he would ever be.

'Then you'll be the tenth,' she said. 'And if you take much longer you'll have to pay double, I can't waste all night. Does this seat tip back? I get terrible backache sometimes.'

James touched the switch that put the seat back. Then, as the girl lay and watched him, he unzipped his trousers and tried to fit a condom on to his erection. 'Another fiver and I'll do it for you,' she offered. He gave her five pounds. Her hands on him were warm and slightly sticky.

When he got on top of her, he didn't immediately go inside. 'For fifteen quid I ought to see your tits,' he demanded. Sighing, she pulled them free, her top and her bra cutting into the underside, forcing them up like an obscene cartoon. He grabbed them hard and she said, 'Oh Christ, steady on!' But when he touched her nipples she laughed and said, 'Go on, give 'em a lick,' like a nanny letting her charge have an ice lolly. He thought how many other men had licked her, and he hung on at the entrance to her body, prolonging the moment. But she had her living to earn. Lifting her hips she expertly slotted herself on to his penis, rocking herself up and down on him.

'I like your arse,' she said chattily, holding it in a vicelike grip. She closed her legs a little and bore down on him. All his experience in marriage was that women tried to prolong it, but she wanted him out as fast as possible. Her hand slipped between them and gripped him, he couldn't help but come!

As he tried to subside on her, panting, she slid away from him and neatly removed thc condom, flinging it out on to the road. 'Right, smashing,' she said.'Drive me back, will you, love?' Head spinning, he took a few deep breaths but she was tutting impatiently. He started the engine and drove carefully back the way they had come. Was that all of it, all there was to it? He felt pleased and vaguely disappointed. As she made to get out, he said, 'Look, suppose I wanted two of you together?'

She pushed her shoulder up, easing her bra. 'Right little raver you are. Tomorrow OK? I'll get my friend Marje, she's got a place. Be here about ten. Cost a lot though, sixty quid.'

It thrilled him to think that a prostitute had the same name as his ex-wife.

'I'll give you more if you give me a good time,' he said, grinning.

'We are going up in the world,' said the girl, infinitely bored by it all.

Once home, James scrubbed himself to get rid of any taint then slid between cool sheets. It had on the whole been better than expected: no false enthusiasm, no criticism, just a businesslike opening of the legs. If that was professionalism, he was all for it.

A thought occurred to him. If he had discovered prostitutes earlier, would he ever have gone with Diana? For once he felt uncomfortable. She should never have left him for so long, that was all it was. He pictured her at his side, so beautiful and stylish, encapsulating talent and femininity. But prostitutes came with no strings attached, while Diana, whom he had expected to leave everything for him, was encumbered with those blasted kids. It was just the kids that got in the way. When the two of them were alone they wanted for nothing.

'Here, have you seen this?' demanded James, barging into Saul's office, the *Yorkshire Post* waving in his hand.

'What?' asked Saul, squinting painfully. He had been at a party last night and could remember very little after dancing the conga in and out of some house or other. Had the house-owner even been at the party? He seemed to remember some rather annoyed onlookers.

'This bloody article! Listen: "Isaac Judge Ltd., thought by many to be on the verge of collapse following the tragic death of chief executive Andrew Judge, has landed a huge new order. L. G. Knowles & Son, who supply many of the top retail names in the High Street, has asked Judge's to provide woollens for several of their ranges. 'We were most impressed by the firm's approach and presentation,' said Mr. Samuel Knowles yesterday. 'They knew just what we wanted and were prepared to provide it at a most competitive price. We are all very pleased.' This order should ensure there are no further sackings at Judge's, where fifty jobs went only last month."'

Saul looked down at his blotter. God Almighty, she'd got Knowles. It had taken him nearly a year to crack that particular nut. But, of course, Rowan had a head start. 'Aren't you pleased?' he asked. 'She's doing OK.'

'And what in all Hades was she doing here bleating about wanting a job? My God, if Diana was here I'd make her bust that firm! One minute the girl's in here sniffing about, the next she's got in with one of our best customers! I mean, they'll fall flat on their faces because Judge's hasn't got the machines to cope with much, but she got it. How?'

'I've really got no idea,' said Saul patiently.

'What did she offer you? A quick screw down a back alley?'

Saul was on his feet and at him. James wasn't expecting it, he had flung the insult automatically. Saul's first blow caught him in the chest, his second grazed the point of his jaw. He stumbled back against a cabinet, ducking sideways out of some animal survival instinct. Saul was blazing mad, murderous!

'Mr. Saul! Mr. James!' Saul's secretary stood frozen in the doorway, clutching a tray of coffee. As another fist hit him in the ribs James dived to the floor at her side. Heroically the secretary stood her ground, holding her tray and wailing, 'Please, Mr. Saul! Do please stop!'

Saul fell back. He swallowed down thick, gluey saliva. His loss of control shocked him. He had often thought about hitting James but had never before been driven to it. Somehow James had put his finger right on the sensitive spot.

'You bastard,' said James bitterly. He was upright now, leaning against the doorpost to catch his breath. His face was unmarked except for a graze on his jaw, but he was dusty and dishevelled. 'Don't think you're getting away with it.'

'With what exactly? Selling the firm's secrets, hitting you, or screwing your family?'

'You're welcome to the girl, I wouldn't fancy it,' said James.

Saul turned away, not trusting himself.

The secretary spoke up, full of irony. 'Can I consider it safe to go now?'

'Thank you, my dear, you may,' said James. 'A timely entrance, if I may say so.'

After she had gone the two men still stood, wondering where this latest development placed them. 'I could sack you,' said James.

'You wouldn't get anyone who could do the job half as well,' said Saul.

'I concede that. But I might be prepared to lose efficiency to lose you as well. Have you thought of that?'

'Oh yes,' said Saul.

'Well then.' James was surprisingly rattled, he wanted to sit down and drink a cup of hot sweet tea. 'Let's say I'll keep my own counsel on the Judge affair, for now. I know what I think, whatever you say. But as far as I'm concerned, you're on borrowed time. Understood?'

'I always understand you, James,' said Saul bitterly. 'And you have never once surprised me.'

If the cacophony of present day looms was less than in days gone by, reflected Diana, then in the past it must have deafened within hours. The noise was constant, a steady thrumming that you became used to until you tried to speak to someone and realised that only a bellow inches from the ear would suffice. All the workers should have worn ear muffs or plugs, but the older ones never bothered. If someone enquired about it, they produced the stock excuse. 'Just popped outside for a minute, I haven't had time, sir.' And a lot of comfort fooling the factory inspectorate would be when they were stone deaf at sixty!

Although she was largely unfamiliar with the details of the weaving shed, even Diana could see that things were different. Looms had been moved, and there were three new Sulzers, grouped together. They weren't the latest type but they were revolutionary by Judge's standards, regulated by punched cards fed in on a roller. What was more, there seemed to have been a sudden infusion of colour to the place. Every shunt of the nearest loom produced another half inch of vivid green cloth, the one next to it glaring orange.

Wearied by the noise, Diana slipped out of the side door and up the stairs to what had been Andrew's office. When she reached the top corridor, she paused in surprise. There was a smell of polish in the air, and on one side table a vase of flowers, ineptly arranged but present nonetheless. Rowan was certainly making herself at home, then. Rapping on the door with a peremptory hand, she did not wait for a reply before entering.

'Good heavens, Rowan! What are you doing?'

Her daughter, wearing a superb plum wool dress, her hair a gleaming black cap, was standing before a side table, grinning into thin air, casting down pieces of cloth like a conjuror. Rowan jumped, turned and went pink.

'I was practising. I've got an appointment today.'

'For the Magic Circle, I presume?'

Rowan gathered up her samples almost protectively. 'It's a big firm, I've got to do it right.'

Diana sat herself down in the chair before the desk and surveyed the room. 'You've certainly cleaned this place up. But I need hardly say, Rowan, that this wasn't the idea. You were to wind the business up, remember?'

'It – wasn't possible,' said Rowan airily. 'The bank manager didn't want me to, he was really keen for me to carry on. We wouldn't have got anything if we'd folded it. And, actually, we're making a remarkable recovery.'

'So James tells me,' said Diana meaningfully.

'I don't know how he should know.' Some of Rowan's confidence ebbed away. She hunched one shoulder, all at once vulnerable. 'You won't let him get at Judge's, will you?' she asked worriedly. 'I know he's saying horrid things about us. He told one firm that we can't deliver, they rang up and said so.'

Diana's eyebrows lifted a millimetre. She looked delicious this morning, her auburn hair glowing against her biscuit tan, a gold clip holding a white and tan silk scarf at her throat. 'You've been spying, Rowan,' she said in a sing-song voice.

'No, I haven't! I've just been using my intelligence. And we're doing really well, Mr. Blood at the bank keeps boasting about me at meetings.'

'You're certainly dressing better,' remarked Diana. 'What a superb dress. You look at least twenty-five, and nowhere near as plain as usual.'

'Thank you,' said Rowan grimly. Her mother never paid a real compliment, she was incapable of it. Still, half a loaf was better than no bread.

'Aren't people a little surprised to find that you are in charge of Judge's?' asked Diana with feigned innocence. Rowan was getting far too entrenched here, a position based on a falsehood.

'Nobody knows,' retorted Rowan. 'And I would rather Dirty Jim didn't go around telling them. When I go for orders everyone thinks I'm just the daughter of the family who's gone into selling. If they want a price reduction they think I have to go back and ask someone, some professional, if that's OK.'

'And do you?' asked Diana, amazed.

'I come back, sit in the office for five minutes, and 'phone them,' grinned Rowan. 'It's quite simple really. All I have to do is work out what making something costs us; Mr. Blood helps me with that; and if necessary I sell it at that price. We've got to get in with them, you see. We'll make the profit next year.'

'I see.' Diana folded her gloves.

Suddenly Rowan realised that her need to boast had taken her beyond caution. 'You won't tell James, will you?' she begged. 'Please don't let him get at me.'

'Honestly, Rowan, he is not an ogre!' snapped her mother. 'Anyway, I didn't come to talk business. I came about Sally.'

A grin split Rowan's pale face, paler than usual these days from hours spent indoors. 'He wants her out of the house,' she declared. 'You've only been back a week! Now tell me he isn't an ogre.'

'It's just – Sally isn't very – she doesn't fit in. I feel it myself, she can hardly make a remark without mentioning her father. And of course she is at a difficult age, very moody. I've discussed it with her and she wants to come back to you. I shall take care of her financially, of course. It might be best, Rowan –'

'He's threatening to stop Andy's college fees,' said Rowan shrewdly.

Diana flared. 'He wouldn't dare! Oh, Rowan, you're an adult, you understand about sex! The moment we try to make love, and we've been apart for weeks, she's hammering on the door. If we forget to lock it she walks straight in and stands by the bed, demanding a drink of water or something. I absolutely cannot bear it.'

Rowan felt choked with hot rage, and hotter embarrassment. That her mother should think her the proper recipient for such confidences! Had she no sense of shame at all? But all she said was a prim, 'You're not even married to him.'

'Do be your age!'

Her daughter turned away, tears pricking her eyelids. Why

did she have to come here, bringing it all back, bringing with her memories of how it used to be, in a warm, safe childhood when if you went into Mummy's bedroom Daddy was there too, with a hug and a kiss and an invitation to snuggle down between them. Why did she have to smash that mirror, to overlay the image with one of her and James Barton, obscenely linked, in an act of which Rowan knew nothing?

She swung round. 'I'll have Sally back, today, right now. She shouldn't stay with you.'

'Thank goodness! Of course, we can all still go on holiday together -'

'No, thank you,' said Rowan. 'By the way, I'd rather you didn't visit us here. After all, I'm not sure that I can trust you not to tell him more than he should know.'

Diana stared at her. 'Don't forget, Rowan dear, that although you are nominally in charge, the power is mine,' she said thinly.

Rowan was silent. Her gaze was fixed on the floor, where the worn carpet had been taken up and the wood floor polished, even though it was draughty. It was all a front, everything in it was pretend, she wasn't really in charge, the firm wasn't really doing well, the range wasn't original and the new looms were only new to them. But, if it was a lie, it was one she had to live, because one day it might be true.

Diana drifted to the door with that long, cool stride that in Rowan was giraffe ranginess.

''Scuse me.' Joe Partridge barged past her into the room, a navy T-shirt showing his tattoos to advantage, a clutch of dockets in his mechanic's hand. 'Here Rowan,' he said forcefully. 'We can't have them buggers in the warehouse taking delivery without checking. Took one look and I could see they'd got half a load of t'wrong wool! Carpet stuff it is, Herdwick or sommat.'

Rowan sighed. 'I'm going to give him the push, you know, the one that tells you it can't be done before you've finished telling him what you want. He's been working here thirty years too many already .'

'Right,' said Joe. 'OK for a driving lesson tonight?'

''Bout seven? Oh – I can't! My little sister's coming. I could bring her too though, couldn't I?'

Joe looked dubious. 'Thought we might go for a drink after.'

'Well, you come at seven and we'll see what's happening.'

Joe nodded and left, giving Diana a cursory grunt in passing. She came back into the room. 'Rowan dear – '

Rowan looked up from perusing the dockets Joe had brought. 'I thought you'd gone, Mother,' she said distantly.

'Are you taking up with that man?'

Rowan shrugged. Her hackles were even now starting to rise. 'I don't quite know what you mean.'

'He is greasy, he has tattoos, your father would die if he knew you were selling yourself so cheap. I at least gave you credit for some discrimination.'

Her daughter's fingers closed on the dockets, crushing them. 'My father's already dead,' she flamed. 'At least I don't do things in front of people! He's kind, he's energetic, he's considerate and he isn't anyone else's husband. In my book that makes him a thousand times better than bloody James Barton!'

Diana let out her breath in a weary sigh. 'You'll never be told, will you, Rowan?' She turned on her heel and left.

On her own, Rowan seethed. Why had she gone on like that about Joe? He was a good friend, but no more than that. They kissed a bit, he sometimes had to be restrained from putting his hand on the crotch of her jeans, but that was just his idea of a proper end to an evening. What really interested him, both of them, was getting Judge's back on its feet, and with it Partridge Carriers. They wrangled over his rates and the number of trips he did. But now, because of Diana's shocked and hypocritical reaction, she had an urge to take Joe and flaunt him, tattoos and all.

Chapter Fifteen

Driving down the familiar suburban street set up in James a flurry of sensation. He had passed this way at least twice a day for years and years, you couldn't rub out history. He remembered the day he and Marjorie had first taken Richard to boarding school, at the tender age of eight, driving down this road with everyone talking tensely about school and how they would be sure to take care of Richard's rabbit.

There was the day Marjorie's mother had died and he had driven this route with her, sobbing wearily into her handkerchief as he tried to sympathise, and instead fought impatience. And in the last years, the heavy homeward trips to what seemed to him a stifling and joyless house. He spun the wheel and swung automatically into the drive.

The sameness was almost shocking. He could believe that he had only to walk in, as he used to do, and call peremptorily 'Marjorie! Marjorie, I'm home!' for her to emerge from the lounge and set about getting his dinner. She had always been very good about that, he remembered. As soon as he had changed, the dinner would be there, on the table, waiting for him.

At Aspley Manor they often had guests, or were dining out. There were long hungry waits before food, and if he went into the kitchen there weren't any biscuits or anything, just avocados and apples. He went up to his old front door, and there was the key, still on his ring, next to those for the car. He slipped it into the lock.

'Marjorie! Marjorie, it's me.'

The hall was just the same: thick carpet, pictures of

Richard on the walls, revolting floral wallpaper. It had all the hallmarks of suburban affluence from the brass barometer to a dozen limited edition prints of birds. In the past he had regarded Marjorie's lack of taste as a major crime, but standing there, waiting, it seemed familiar and comforting.

She came out of the lounge and said, 'Hello, James.' She was just the same, short and dumpy, wearing one of the endless house cardigans she knitted for herself. 'Fancy a cup of tea?' she asked.

'Wouldn't mind,' said James. They went through to the kitchen, dripping with Georgian oak and latticed windows. He noticed how warm the house was, in stark contrast to Aspley Manor where the wind blew outside the house and inside the carpets lifted in the draught. 'I thought Richard was going to be here,' he said.

Marjorie made a quizzical face. 'He's angry with you still. He might come in later, we'll just have to see.'

'Are you still angry with me?'

She met his eyes. 'I never was, James, or at least not for long. You left me behind. Perhaps I should have tried to keep up, but I didn't. It was both our faults.'

He swallowed. 'That's very decent of you.'

She set a tray with dainty china cups and twee tea spoons and took it through to the gas fire in the lounge. James felt familiar irritation as he sat there, the ghosts of too many leaden evenings rising up to haunt him.

'Diana and I are getting married next month,' he said aggressively.

'I trust you're not giving me an invitation,' said Marjorie.

'Not you, no. Richard though. I would like him to be there and meet Diana. He might understand a bit more.'

Marjorie let out a hoot of laughter. 'See what a classy bit of stuff you got on top of!'

'God, Marjorie, I'd forgotten how vulgar you can be sometimes.' James put down his cup angrily. Suddenly everything about her angered him, but most of all her lack of feeling.

'You didn't give a damn whether I left you or not, did you?' he snapped.

She met his eyes fair and square. 'Not a lot, no. When I did care you were working. Years and years I never saw you, except in bed. Richard hardly knew you at all, I had to show him pictures! I made a life for myself, I had to.'

James said nothing. Marjorie reached down the side of her chair and got out her knitting, clicking up and down the rows as efficiently as a machine.

They heard the front door open. James got to his feet and went out into the hall, smoothing his hair and feeling almost nervous. His son, Richard, was leaning a tennis racquet against the hall stand and stepping out of his trainers. He had James's hair, slightly less red, and a deeper colour to his eyes so that they verged on blue. He lacked the thin skin of the redhead and instead had Saul's skin, smooth and lightly tanned. A vision of the boy in his childhood rose up to choke James.

'You're looking well,' he said thickly.

'Am I?' Clearly Richard was spoiling for a fight.

'Your mother and I have been having a chat. She seems quite happy.'

'Fat lot of consideration you ever gave to it. Look, will you get out of my way? I want to go up and have a shower.'

'Oh, for God's sake, Richard! All right, you're angry, but it's ancient history now. It's two years since I left here.'

'And the first time I've seen you in all that time,' said Richard, giving his father a grimace that could never have been a smile.

They stood, facing each other, James blocking the way through the narrow hall. They had never touched and now they stood at a distance, as if to avoid contamination. James reached into his pocket and drew out a thick square envelope. 'Wedding invitation. Next month. I should like you to come.'

'Get stuffed, Daddy.'

'I imagined you might say that. It's a pity, I think you'd like Diana. She's a very remarkable woman. Her son's going to play the violin at the reception, his college is tipping him for stardom. You needn't bother to reply. If you want to come we'll make room for you.'

'Are you bothered it will look bad if I don't turn up? You can't leave us flat and then demand attendance when it suits you. No, I won't come, you can take that as final. Now, get out of my way.'

He tried to push past his father, but James grabbed his shoulders and held him. They stood, frozen in the contact. James thought, 'I would never have done this before Diana. She awakened me to touch.' 'I love you Richard,' he said gruffly. 'I know I haven't shown it. You're finishing university soon and I want you in the firm. Come and see me, we'll discuss it.'

Richard looked away, screwing up his mouth against emotion. 'I've got a job,' he muttered. 'I'm going to work for International Wools. I'm one of the leg men, they want to send me to South America straight after my finals.'

'There you'll be one of twenty, with me you're the heir apparent. Please, Richard, I need you.'

'No.' The boy put up a hand and grasped his father's wrist, wrenching it from his shoulder. He ran up the stairs, head bowed.

James went back to Marjorie. 'You've done a job on him, haven't you? Really turned him sour.'

'You should have visited him when it happened. He waited and waited for you.'

'I didn't know! Why didn't you tell me?'

She shrugged, with benign malevolence. 'Why did you need telling?'

On the way home he thought,'Thank God for Diana! Just thank God I've at last got someone with feelings.' When they made love she didn't lie passive beneath him, she demanded, insisted, on satisfaction. It was like a mountain that he climbed often, knowing the thrill would be there on the summit, yet sometimes hardly able to bear the effort of the climb. When they were married, things would be calmer. He looked up and saw that the car had headed unerringly into Lumb Lane.

This time he took a girl he hadn't seen before, a West Indian with a black bush of hair. She had heard of him though, she knew what he wanted – straight sex and a bit of dirty talk about other men. They did it while another couple of girls stood chatting by the wall, only mildly interested. Afterwards the girl said, 'Dangerous this sort of thing. You could get mugged. You ought to set a girl up in a flat. I know a nice place.'

James laughed. 'I bet you do. No, I like it this way. Know who I am, do you?'

She nodded. 'Everyone does.'

'If you want to get on in this world, go ask for a job at Bardsey Mills. I'll put in a good word for you.'

She made a face. 'Why d'you think I'm on the game? They don't take blacks.'

'They will if I tell 'em. Go on, give it a try.'

She got out of the car, grinning. 'You never know, I might at that. Name's Mandy.'

He started the engine. 'I'll remember, Mandy.'

Chapter Sixteen

On the day of the wedding, Rowan stood in the little back bedroom in the mill cottage and cursed. Sally, dressed in smart pink and white, sat on the bed. 'You should wear your lovely wool dress,' she urged.

'Not to this I won't,' declared Rowan. 'The dress would be spoiled forever.'

'You don't have to go,' said Sally.

Rowan sighed. When she had said that to her mother the reply had been uncompromising: 'Come or I take over the firm.'

'I haven't got anything,' she said despairingly. She would not wear her plum, that was her buying outfit and someone might spill something on it. Apart from that her wardrobe was trousers, trousers and more trousers. So, trousers it would have to be when she longed to upstage her mother and amaze James Barton by her charming and elegant appearance. Diana should have threatened her earlier.

She pulled on a pair of black velvet skintight trews. If she wore them with black high heels the bottom half was all right, but the top was extremely difficult. Sally said, 'That skinny white T-shirt and your blue silk blouse.'

'Together?' She tried them. The white top was actually sleeveless and very low cut, it had to be worn without a bra. If she wore the silk blouse with the sleeves rolled to the elbow to disguise the burn mark on the cuff from the iron – a lesson in ironing silk never subsequently forgotten – and she cinched it with Sally's gold chain belt . . . she turned to her sister.

'What do you think?'

'Smashing. Very sexy, when Joe sees that he'll rape you in the back of the van.'

'Sally! Don't be horrible. Have you done your homework?'

'No. And I'm not going to.'

Rowan knew better than to argue with her. Confronting Sally these days meant drilling through her carapace of wordly control into a seething mass of emotion. Hysterics were commonplace, but whenever Rowan steeled herself to talk to Diana about it the only suggestion was to pack her off to a psychiatrist, when anyone could see Sally wasn't mad! Rowan supposed it was inevitable, really. If you took grief and shock and impotent rage and mixed them together with adolescence, you produced an unholy cocktail.

She glanced sideways at her sister. Despite the little girl dress Diana had chosen, Sally was developing into a lovely woman. Her cascade of blonde hair, held back Alice in Wonderland style and falling over her shoulders, could not disguise two plump breasts that put Rowan's skinny figure to shame. Yet she had her mother's long legs and slender waist. Sally, at thirteen, was distinctly toothsome.

Rowan pulled her hair free of its band and bent over to brush it, trying to shake her head free of horrible thoughts. Sally's friends were all boys these days, she picked them up on the way to and from school. Sixteen year olds in leather jackets, shambling along beside Sally in her school uniform. And Sally was becoming a great deal too knowing. Rowan, who knew not very much herself, was daily fighting panic.

Bumping along in Joe's van, the girls were unusually silent. Rowan was conscious of a guilty pleasure in the outing, because it was a party and she hadn't been to one in ages. Her avowed stance of prim outrage was starting to bore her. She wanted to have fun and yet still not let James Barton think he had won her over, a difficult balancing act.

Glancing across at Joe, cheerfully whistling through his teeth and ramming the ancient gear lever up and down the box, she knew she had done right. In his smartest clothes of sharp suit and dark green button-down shirt, his hair over his collar and his nails still ineradicably black with grease, he was in himself an insult to James. The presence of Joe turned Rowan from dutiful daughter into freedom fighter, and left her at liberty to have as good a time as she chose.

Joe turned into the Town Hall car park, expertly carving up a Mercedes Sports and a Jaguar. Sally said, 'Oh, look, I remember them. They used to be Daddy's friends, fuck them.'

Joe glanced at Rowan, but she didn't meet his eye. 'I don't like to hear girls swear, Sally,' said Joe sternly.

'And who the fuck cares what you like?' retorted Sally, flinging out of the van.

Rowan caught Joe's arm. 'Don't get at her, she's in a state. I knew today was going to be bad. Mother insisted she come, I kept trying to tell her Sal wasn't up to it.'

'There's no excuse for that sort of rudeness,' complained Joe. 'She needs a clip round the ear, she does.'

Not for the first time Rowan felt the desire to hit Joe with a brick, to knock some vestige of sensitivity into his brain. Perhaps the Rugby League had knocked it out. More likely that it had never been there, which was why he was such a success at the game, mashing opponents without a qualm.

'You're getting in a state as well, aren't you?' said Joe.

Rowan grinned into his earnest face. He was a simple soul, but he tried.

They followed Sally into the building. It was the usual functional public place, more suited to planning permissions than marriage. Expensively dressed people were everywhere, half of them unknown to Rowan. James and Diana hadn't arrived.

'I hope they come,' complained one woman, her feathered hat wobbling. 'I didn't dress up like this to spend the morning in the Town Hall and get a basket meal at the local pub.'

'Where is the reception?' asked Rowan.

'Why, at the Manor, of course. And who are you, dear, a relative of James's?'

Sally, whose demure dress was somewhat at odds with her

provocative sprawling across the wooden chairs, said: 'Not yet but she soon will be. Won't it be fun to be related to the shit, Rowan?'

'Be quiet, Sally,' said Rowan levelly. As the woman moved away, Rowan asked: 'Are you determined to make a scene, Sal?'

'Yes. No. I don't know. I just hate it here, I hate all of it.'

'I know, I know.' Rowan sat down next to her and took her hand. She could feel Sally shaking, a fundamental shudder that involved her whole body. 'Do you remember when we were little and you had nightmares? I used to sing you a song, didn't I?'

'You can't sing it here,' said Sally miserably. 'What's going to happen, Rowan? Everything's so frightening and horrid.'

Rowan looked at her. 'Nothing's going to happen. We'll be fine, you and me, I won't let anything go wrong. After today we don't have to see him again.'

'I wish I was as brave as you,' said Sally. Rowan almost laughed. If Sally knew how scared she was, how she clung to the one or two constants in her life because of the security they offered, would her sister be reassured? Or would it be the shifting of one of her few rocks?

'When it's all going on, I'm going to think about the song,' she said feebly. 'You think about it too, Sal.'

There was a commotion by the door. Diana and James entered, followed by a morose-looking Andy. A rustle went through the crowd, a gentle chorus of admiration, and Joe said, 'By, she's a stunner, your ma.' Jaundiced as she was, Rowan couldn't disagree. Diana was wearing her hair swept up into a knot, and perched on the top was a ridiculous and flirty piece of green lace. Her jade silk suit had a narrow skirt and flowing jacket, worn over a pale lemon camisole. Her nipples showed through, the only provocative statement in an otherwise prudish rig. James, in a pale grey suit, white shirt and blue tie, wore an unaccustomed heavy gold bracelet. It was as if he was today celebrating more than a marriage; he was showing the world his money, his sex appeal and his power. 'This is my woman,' he was saying, 'any man here must long to have her in his bed. Here is my gold, I can even afford to wear it as jewellery, and soon you will see my magnificent, enviable home.'

They stood together, Diana and James, welcoming their friends. Andy pushed roughly past them, clattering chairs to reach his sisters. The enemy triumvirate stood shoulder to shoulder and glowered.

'You're not really going to play for them, are you?' demanded Rowan.

'Yes, I am actually,' said Andy. 'It's good practice for me. After all, music's got nothing to do with any of this.'

'Yes it has,' said Sally. 'You shouldn't do it, you're betraying Daddy.'

Andy looked away from the girls: he drew imperceptibly apart from them. 'My music's my own,' he said stolidly. 'I won't have it dragged into everything. I have to play when I'm asked, it's vital. I ought to be asked more.'

Everyone was settling down and falling silent, but defiantly Rowan kept on talking. 'Aren't you doing as well as you hoped, then?'

'Yes. No. I want more appearances, they keep saying I'm not ready. But it's them, they don't want the hassle of having me well known, they want to keep me under wraps. My career's got to start soon, I can't play to myself forever. Mother's asked a music critic from the paper to come to the reception. I'll get some publicity for my next competition.'

'Will you win?' asked Sally. He had been placed three times so far.

Andy nodded. 'This time, I must.'

The registrar cleared his throat and at last they subsided. The sunlight was falling through a dusty window, sending speckles of gold splashing across shoulders and faces. Rowan pushed herself out of her body, she sent herself soaring up into the sunshine, away from this horrible place. Her ears closed against the words being spoken, her face took on a look of distant happiness. Saul, sitting grimly by the door and amazed at himself for being there, for a scant second admired her and wondered who she was. He felt a shock of recognition.

Afterwards the throng moved like water out into the car park, trickling away towards Aspley Manor in their smart cars. The van, proclaiming its status to all who wanted to read the name on the side, blasted blue smoke over the legs of people next to it and roared vulgarly out. They were squashed in the front this time, with Andy bumming a ride.

'All right, Sal?' asked Rowan.

The girl nodded. With one of her mood swings she had backed off from the edge and retreated into little girl solemnity. 'She's all right,' Rowan told herself. 'I don't have to worry about her any more today.' She was tired of worrying, her head ached with responsibility. Surely now she could enjoy herself?

Diana and James were greeting guests as they arrived. When James saw them approaching, he put on an act for the benefit of those watching. 'Well, hello you lot! Is this the latest thing, arriving like a parcel?'

'We've been treated like parcels, we thought we'd make the point,' retorted Rowan. James could say nothing without worsening things. He glared at Rowan, a gaze of such venom that she felt herself colour. Diana drew her to one side and said softly, 'Don't you dare make a scene! And why are you dressed like some sort of pop star? And with that vulgar man, why did you bring him?'

'I like him,' said Rowan, because she did. And at that moment she admired him, standing amidst so much unaccustomed wealth in the magnificent hall of the Manor House, looking round as if speculating on how much it would fetch for scrap. Joe had no sense whatsoever of inferiority, he was right up there, tattoos and all.

Diana contented herself with a hissed, 'Just make sure he behaves!' and went back to James's side. Joe wandered off, saying loudly, 'Think we'll get a drink then, Ro?'

'Don't mind if I do,' said Sally naughtily, and followed him in search of booze. Rowan caught Andy's arm. 'You keep an eye on her, Andy! It's your turn.'

'All right,' he said vaguely. Rowan wasn't to know that he hadn't heard her, that his mind was totally involved with the pieces he was to play.

She too strolled off, aware that she was attracting stares. It was an unusual sensation, she didn't know if they were admiring or incredulous. Suppose she did look ridiculous, as Diana had said? Very tall, very thin, very flat-chested. A man came towards her carrying two champagne flutes.

'There you are, Rowan,' he said. 'I was looking for you. Here's some champagne.'

She turned a little pink, and took the glass. 'Hello, Saul.'

As she sipped, he stared at her. She looked down, trying to glance surreptitiously at him, because he was so tanned and healthy. All she could see properly from under her lids were his hands, the hairs on them gold from the sun, the fingers squared at the ends. A sudden and unexpected sensation caught at her stomach. She looked up into his face and he was staring right at her.

'You look gorgeous,' he said softly. 'Like the principal boy in a pantomime, the boy prince.'

'My mother said I looked like a pop singer,' said Rowan, trying to laugh.

'Well, so you do. I'll be your first fan, if you like.'

Rowan gulped her champagne. This man was flirting with her, and it was so, so exciting. 'I thought you'd be furious with me,' she said bravely.

'Who, me? Just because you stole our range?' He rolled his eyes in amazement. She wondered if he had drunk more than one glass of champagne. 'I did you a favour. You're the one who ought to be worried, I might call it in.'

'What do you mean?'

'I might ask for something in return, something you don't want to give. I could have lost my job for you.'

'But you didn't have to show me,' said Rowan, backing away a little. 'You know we're so small, we can't hurt Bardsey's. Anyway, what would you want?'

He laughed at her, shaking his head. 'Rowan, you are so young. Come on, let's find some more champagne, let's dance.'

There was no dancing yet, they had first to eat the food Diana had provided. Lobster and salmon, venison and beef, snails *à la grecque* and caviare, centred around an ice sculpture of a heron. 'It should have been a vulture,' said Rowan.

Saul, drinking yet another glass of champagne, said hazily, 'You're too hard on him. He's a great man in his own way. But he's a jealous man, and you and I nibble away at him. I suppose he's childish really, he has a thousand toys but can't lend any one of them, not to me, not to you, not to anyone.'

'I wonder if Mother knows that?' said Rowan, driving her sharp teeth into some really quite tender meat.

'I think he's met his match there, don't you?'

They both turned and stared across at the happy couple. Diana was bending to talk to a man who was a friend of James's, and her breasts were swinging forward into the camisole, lolling unfettered above and against the silk. The man was enjoying it but James was not, he kept trying to persuade Diana to straighten and move on. Easily, deftly, Diana kept him at bay and teased him. When at last she straightened up and moved away with James, he said something fiercely to her and she merely smiled, and lifted one scornful eyebrow.

'She's so sure of herself,' muttered Rowan. 'When I see her look like that, I hate her.'

'You might be like her one day,' said Saul.

The champagne made Rowan reply, 'I haven't got the boobs.'

He laughed and put his hand on her shoulder. 'I bet they're lovely little apples,' he said softly. 'Topped with cherries. Just what I like for a tasty mouthful.'

Rowan cast him a startled look. She moved away hurriedly. 'I'm going to the loo,' she said shortly, and went, almost running. Saul cursed. He really should not have drunk so much.

Rowan went in search of Sally and Joe. There was no trace of Sally, but since Andy was nowhere to be seen either she assumed they were together. Joe was being propositioned by a woman wearing the sort of professional make-up that only looks good in photographs. He was watching her phlegmatically, sitting on a hard wooden Elizabethan chair, her hand stroking his muscled thigh as it bulged against his trousers. He saw Rowan and stood up, discarding the woman with firm kindness, as if she were a cat.

'Hello, Ro,' he said. 'Been wondering where you got to. Fancy some air?'

The woman glared at Rowan, her face falling into grim lines. She mumbled something and began to weave an unsteady path back to the booze.

Rowan and Joe went out into the gardens. It wasn't particularly warm. 'Would you believe it,' he commented. 'That old biddy wanted me to go upstairs with her and – you know – in one of the beds. I was fair took back.'

'She looks the sort,' said Rowan.

The beautiful, windy parkland all around made her feel sad all of a sudden. A peacock, one of James's conceits, was trailing its tail over the lawn as if carrying not some beautiful appendage but a load of trouble. 'I wish I could go home,' said Rowan.

'Party's hardly started,' said Joe. 'Wonder if there's any beer?'

They went back into the house, Rowan determinedly trying to shake off her gloom. Diana was crossing the hall. 'There you are, Rowan. Come along, Andy's going to play.' She looked as strung up as if she were going to play herself. James came out of the dining-room.

'Diana! Come along, you can't desert everyone.'

'I have to see to Andy,' she said abstractedly. 'This is important for him.'

'And today is important for me,' said James, every word clipped and pointed. 'For both of us.'

But Diana seemed not to notice. 'Go on, will you, Rowan, see to things,' she murmured, and went off to find Andy.

James reached out and caught Rowan's arm. 'I'll thank you to control your sister,' he said nastily, venting his anger on Diana's daughter. He was gripping her arm to the bone.

'Stop it,' she whimpered.

'Here you, let go of her,' said Joe, and caught James's arm in turn, gripping like a vice.

'For Christ's sake!' said James incredulously, releasing Rowan. Joe slowly released his own grip. Indentations remained in the cloth of James's suit where Joe's fingers had pressed. James flexed his fingers. 'Sally is drunk as a skunk and being sick in one of the bedrooms,' he said furiously, clearly at the end of his tether. 'And your mother is fussing over the future Yehudi Menuhin. Since you, Rowan, are the only one sober and actually present, would you mind coming in and helping me get everyone through for this bloody concert!'

Rowan eyed him nervously. 'Is Sally all right?' she asked.

'Now she's being sick, yes. Before that she appeared to be trying to seduce one of my oldest friends.'

She snapped back, 'If he was a friend of yours, it was probably the other way round.'

She went into the dining-room and began to smile and usher guests through to the chairs set out in the ballroom. James stood and watched her, then glanced back at Joe, standing stolidly in the hall. 'What does she see in you?' he asked.

Joe said, 'Dunno. You got any beer?'

'In the cupboard in the kitchen, ask someone. God, what a day.' He too went to his task of guiding the guests.

Upstairs Andy was tight with nerves, snapping at his

mother every time she spoke. 'Just remember, take it steadily,' she insisted.

'Don't be stupid! It's meant to be fast. This isn't a school concert, there are critics out there.'

'Try not to think of them,' she advised.

'Of course I shall think of them! I have to remember they are there, I *want* them there.'

Diana subsided. She tried to straighten his tie and he cursed her, she smoothed his hair from his forehead and he hit her hand away. Then, he turned and picked up his violin. 'Good luck,' she said, but she might not have been in the room. His face settled into smooth, inward-looking lines. Violin and bow in one hand, he pulled his jacket down with the other and went down to play.

Diana's legs felt weak. Suppose it went wrong, suppose he did not play as she knew he could and this opportunity she had given him turned to stone? If the school was right and he wasn't ready, this was the worst thing she could have done. Somehow she couldn't face going downstairs, sitting there while people watched her watching him. She would sit on the bed here and listen.

The babble of conversation was falling away, silence was spreading through the house. The air was heavy with expectation. When it had lasted for long seconds, when she thought her nerves would break waiting for the notes, someone said, 'Why don't you go down?'

She looked up, startled. It was Saul, James's half-brother. He stood in the doorway, tall, brown, swaying slightly. 'Be quiet,' she breathed. 'I want to listen.'

Shrugging, he came into the room and sat on the bed beside her. In her tense, hyper-sensitive state she thought she could hear his heart. They were quite silent. In a matter of seconds Andy began to play.

The notes fell clear and sure and beautiful. The piece was sonorous, almost melancholy, swelling to wild joy and then drifting into tranquillity. Diana's eyes closed as she listened, and then as Andy launched himself upon the central allegro vivace, taking it at a gallop, her eyes flew open and her nails bored into the palms of her hands. Instinctively Saul's hand covered hers, they could hear each other's breathing, they sat together in mutual tension. As the piece moved to its gentle conclusion, they each let out their breath in a long sigh.

Diana said, 'Isn't he wonderful? I knew he could do it, he needs an audience to show what he can do.'

'He's brilliant,' said Saul. 'But the other day I heard someone say you could have been better. They heard you when you were at school.'

Her face relaxed into a smile. 'I was good. I still am, but James doesn't really understand.'

'James never does undertstand,' said Saul throatily.

They looked at each other. He thought how beautiful she was, how luscious, in the ripe bloom of maturity. Downstairs the violin still played, Andy was settling to a popular, merry piece he could play blindfold. 'You really excited me today,' said Saul. 'I was watching you. I thought I would die if I could just make love to you.'

'Would it be so thrilling?' asked Diana slowly. She felt as if the music had caressed her senses, liberating her.

Saul grinned. He reached out and took hold of her breast, loose within her silk top. 'You're my brother's wife. There would be nothing more thrilling. And for you too, this is your wedding day after all. You've got to keep one step ahead of James, you know.'

'Oh, I know,' said Diana. She reached out and touched Saul's crotch where his erection reared hard and tireless. 'You're very young,' she murmured. 'James gets so tired sometimes. He'll be tired tonight.'

'Well then – ' Saul got up and shut the door, turning the key in the lock. 'We'd be doing him a favour then, wouldn't we? Taking the pressure off.'

He unzipped his fly and his erection sprang free, like a blind caged beast. Diana laughed, almost hysterically. 'If you men knew what you looked like!' she said. 'At least take your trousers off.'

He had her over the end of the bed, his feet still on the floor. Either side of him spread her stockinged legs and as he thrust between them, seeing even as he struggled that she was looking at him with contained, judgmental mockery, he felt sudden sympathy for James. It was good, oh it was good and fierce and wonderful, but this was not a woman you could fail. In this one act with her a man could taste the joy of heaven and the torment of hell.

All at once she convulsed about him. He let himself go, bathed in sweat, exhausted, guilty and yet triumphant. 'Never again,' he told himself, watching her dress. James was welcome to her.

In the ballroom Andy was smiling, bowing, acknowledging the applause. He only ever looked truly relaxed, reflected Rowan, in those brief moments following a successful performance. He was tense even when he played, and that was transmitted, sometimes uncomfortably, to the audience. He was wonderfully gifted, but even now there was the sense of potential not quite realised and it had been like that since he first stood up in front of the family and played 'Three Blind Mice'.

Someone James knew, in television, was at her elbow, rather the worse for wear. 'Fantastic, wonderful,' he slurred. 'D'you play? No? Pity, you'd be a sensation, should be a model. Wish your brother was a bit more off the beam, doesn't look mad enough.' He wandered off to tell Andy that he ought to dress like a deranged monk. Rowan felt her spirits starting to rise again, reviving at the compliment like a flower after rain. Did she really look like a model? Perhaps she ought to capitalise on it and take to way-out dressing. It was bound to be more fun.

The chairs were being moved to make room for a disco. Some of the women were going to the cloakroom to repair their make-up and take off their hats, and a press photographer had appeared to snap the local celebrities. Diana came into the room. She had changed into a pale flowing kaftan. She went across to James, took hold of his upper arm in both her hands and kissed his cheek.

'Better now?' he murmured, aware that the photographer was recording the scene.

'Much,' she replied. They exchanged a look and a laugh, in a rare moment of true intimacy. Saul, watching from the doorway, sober now and hardly believing what he had done, thought, 'God, but she's a viper.' 'You poor sod, James,' he murmured.

Diana turned and caught his eye across the room. She gave him a rueful grin and then, as James began to talk business with a fellow wool baron, she drifted casually over. Curtains were being drawn and strobe disco lighting was replacing the sunny afternoon. The first record began to play, 'Love Love Me Do.'

'Why on earth did we do it?' she said softly.

'God knows. I can't really believe we did.'

She eyed him speculatively. 'Don't look so anxious, it wasn't the start of anything. It was a vulnerable moment, that's all. Nothing for you to worry about.'

Saul said, 'It was a shitty thing to do, even to James.'

She shrugged. 'I think James can take it. Oh look, there's Rowan.'

She summoned her daughter with a peremptory wave, and Rowan's face became inscrutable. Nonetheless she came over. 'Did you want something?'

'Darling, thank you for helping James. You must have some fun, I think you should dance with Saul.'

'Not to this, it's too slow. Anyway, no one else is dancing.'

'Don't be difficult.'

Diana left them. Saul said, 'I'm sorry I was rude earlier. I was drunk.'

'Aren't you any more?'

'No.'

They stood in silence. The man running the disco, getting no response with his dirgelike first record, cut it off in midstream and instead put on 'Purple Haze.'

'Good God,' said Saul. 'That's a bit wild for the middle of the afternoon.'

'Let's dance,' said Rowan, because she wouldn't when told and would when not.

'I think I'm too sober,' said Saul. Nonetheless he went out onto the floor.

Rowan was a good dancer, and she knew it. Whenever exotic movement was called for in a school play, the consensus had always been 'Ask Rowan Judge'. Long legs and arms twined and twisted, her narrow hips undulated as well as any belly dancer's. Now, with guitar music howling into the atmosphere, with champagne inside her and the lights dimmed, she let herself go. People turned to watch, and Saul, whose normal style of dancing resembled grape treading during the siesta, knew he looked a fool. There was nothing for it but to enter into the spirit of the thing. He took off his jacket and tossed it to the side and then really got down to it, feeling the sweat sticking his shirt to his back.

'That's better,' said Rowan, punctuating the music by clasping her hands together and whirling them round as if throwing the hammer.

'Good God,' said James, watching from the sidelines. 'You have to admit she's fantastic.'

'Which is more than can be said for Saul,' commented Diana. 'I would say energetic and workmanlike, but lacking in anything resembling talent. Oh, my God, look at her now. She can be really embarrassing.'

At that moment Joe came into the room. He fancied himself as a dancer and at Rugby Club dos was often asked to perform. He watched Saul's antics for a moment then sniffed, hitched up his trousers and sauntered on to the floor. 'Get off, mate,' he said sympathetically. 'I'll show you how.'

Saul, who had not realised the extreme length of 'Purple Haze', retreated to the bar. 'Right, Ro,' said Joe. 'Let's motor.'

He caught Rowan by the waist, flung her from arm to

arm, released her and did a handstand, going over on to his feet and gyrating on the floor for a moment or two before getting up. The photographer's flash gun popped and popped again, Joe let out an ear-piercing rebel yell, Diana hid her face in her hands and James stormed on to the dance floor and yelled at Rowan, 'Get that ape out of here!'

In the end Rowan drove the van home while Joe snored beside her and Sally sat by the window, green-faced and silent. She felt absolutely empty, drained of unhappiness, expectation, everything. They had attended not a beginning but an end; she was tonight shutting the door on the past.

The little mill house was in darkness. She left Joe in the van to sleep it off and helped Sally into the house and up to bed. How good it was to be home again. She went out into the yard and stood looking at the dark bulk of the mill, as inefficient and outdated a structure as anyone could wish for. Stone on stone on stone, each tough and creamy piece hacked out of the earth and placed there by hand. Bradford was full of such mills, and the labour required to build them defeated the imagination. City of stone, city of soft, soft wool. Was her mill, was wool itself, doomed to die, as the stonemasons themselves had quietly passed away? There was no place for anything that could not pay its way.

Yet the mill comforted her. Without it there would be choices and decisions to make, about herself and her future. What was going to happen to her? She was eighteen and the years ahead were like the blank pages of an exercise book, waiting to be filled. She wanted so much out of life, she wouldn't settle for half measures, not in anything! Nobody seemed to understand. There was an ache, a long slow ache deep inside that had been with her for years and only today seemed sharp and insistent. It was a longing for someone, something, that was hers and hers alone. She wanted to be loved.

Chapter Seventeen

Diana put down her violin almost roughly. It was not often that music failed her, but today it seemed not to calm her thoughts but to work against them, so that the music jangled and her head whirled and the notes tied themselves into knots that were translated into tangles in her mind. She slammed the case shut, closing her eyes for a desperate second. Perhaps a walk in the garden might help.

One of the cleaners was polishing the hall floor but Diana took no notice and left footprints on it. Normally she would take care to avoid antagonising the help, simply because they tended to leave, which was a nuisance. The woman stood in mute accusation, watching Diana's white set face.

It was cold outside and Diana had not stopped to get her coat. She didn't mind, the discomfort distracted her. Arms folded across her body she walked briskly down a gravel path and through the orchard. The apples were poor this year, it had been cold early on and killed the blossom, and then later there had been no sun to ripen the fruit. Nonetheless she picked one of the hard green knobs and gnawed it, grimacing at the taste. What on earth was she going to do?

Because the answer to that question was not going to come easily, she found her mind drifting back. Didn't it all prove she should never have left Andrew? She had killed him, as surely as if she had put a knife in his ribs, and yet it might have ended like that anyway. The business would have gone down, he was useless at it, and their marriage, their family, could never have survived bankruptcy. More to the point then was that she should never have married him, and the causes of that were lost. It might be now that she should never have married James. She was beginning to think that was the bitter truth.

Why was it that strong men always had chinks in their armour where she was concerned? It made her despise them, just a little. She had loved James most when he had blackmailed her into continuing the affair, when he had outfaced Andrew, brutally disillusioning him. He seemed different now, a middle-aged man hanging on to youth.

Last night, as on so many nights, they had gone to a nightclub with some of James's vulgar textile friends. After some wild dancing in which Diana had been almost assaulted by a man who professed to have known James for years, they had gone on to a gambling club. The croupier had been a small weary girl in a tight black dress. James flirted with her, giving her chips. Diana, not at her best and never a gambler, had bad-temperedly lost fifty pounds. In the car on the way home she and James had had one of those scratchy, nasty arguments.

'What on earth do you want to do in the evenings, damn it?' he had raged. He did not understand her essential puritanism. Left to herself she ate a light supper, practised, read and listened to music.

At least she had ensured that Andy's training was the best, and that was something for which she had cause to thank James. But the girls – well, Rowan was never easy. As for Sally, she was as wild if not wilder. Was it something in the genes perhaps? Rowan had never been so precocious, but Sally was so much prettier. Too pretty, she thought anxiously. If only James wasn't such a pig about the girls.

Annoyance sparked through her. He was a bastard sometimes, an absolute sod, and she didn't trust him. Only last week her so-called friend, Linda, whom she now remembered had shunned her when first she left home, had commented lightly, 'Donald saw your James the other day, in Lumb Lane of all places! You'll have to tell him he'll catch something.'

Diana had replied smoothly, 'Don't be silly, Linda. It's a short cut he often uses.'

'He'd stopped the car. Probably buying a paper or something. You'll have to tell him, people will talk.'

'I'm sure they wouldn't be so foolish.'

You didn't forget conversations like that. To hell with him catching something, so might she! If this other thing hadn't been on her mind she'd have challenged him straight out, and even though he denied it he would have known that she knew. The extent of her hurt surprised her. If she lost James what would she have, what would be left to her?

Her breasts were full and aching, they always were in early pregnancy. If only James liked children the whole thing would be simpler. Except – could you foist what could well be another man's child on to your husband? Wouldn't you remember every day that it lived? Again she told herself, as so many times before, it had been just once with Saul that month and many times with James. The odds were that James was the father, she had grown careless and didn't always use her diaphragm even with him. She had got out of the habit of considering pregnancy somehow, she had felt past all that sort of thing. Yet here she was again, sick and weary and aching, and she didn't want a baby, whoever's it was, she was too old for broken nights and nappies.

The decision seemed to be made then. She would make an appointment with a clinic and get herself seen to. She felt better at once and started to walk back to the house, but the logistics of a stay in a clinic rose up to haunt her. What would she say to James?

She made an appointment at the clinic for the very next morning, and set out in the car soon after James left for work. The place was familiar, it was where she attended for her smears and check-ups, she had parked in this self-same place half a dozen times at least. Then as she went in she had an overwhelming sense of unreality. She wasn't really pregnant, none of this was real, the doctor would examine her and tell her to stop imagining things. The routine of the clinic mesmerised her and it was a doctor she had seen before, young and distant. As she undressed and lay on the couch, as the doctor felt her breasts and belly and reached up inside her to feel her womb, she was inexorably reminded of those other times she had experienced this.

The doctor rinsed his hands at the basin and Diana scrambled back into her clothes. He said, 'I think about six weeks. Is that your feeling?'

'Yes,'

'And why do you want a termination, Mrs. Barton?'

'I'm too old. I have three grown-up children, I'm not up to it any more. It's not something I want to think about.'

'Well.'

She pulled her blouse straight and sat down before his desk. All the composure she normally had at her disposal seemed to desert her, she was on the verge of tears.

'Have you discussed it with your husband?' enquired the doctor.

Unwisely she said, 'No, and I'm not going to. I don't want it, he won't want it, not at his age. He doesn't like children.'

In a paternal, soothing voice, the doctor said, 'That may not be the case, Mrs. Barton. He might be thrilled to be a father in middle age, you never know. Now, it seems to me best if you go off and talk to him about it and then, if he agrees, you can both come and see me again.'

Diana stared at him, dumbfounded. 'You mean you won't do it?'

'Not without your husband's agreement.'

'You stupid, pompous sod!'

She left in a rage and it was still burning when James came home that evening. Somehow, when she saw him, it dissolved into tears. 'Oh James, I'm so glad you're home,' she wept. 'It's been such a terrible day.'

'What on earth's the matter?' He was taken aback, but

most flattered. The row earlier in the week had lingered, they had been stiff with each other. He patted her shoulder and she leaned against him, a gesture he misinterpreted. He cupped her breast and squeezed but she yelped.

'Don't do that, it hurts.'

'Does it? Why, are you ill?'

She gulped. 'Yes. Yes, I'm ill, and I've got to have an operation and you've got to agree. It's so silly but you will agree, won't you?'

James's face changed. 'What sort of operation?'

Wiping the tears with her fingers, Diana said, 'Just a silly woman's thing. It isn't important. Look, I'll get us both a drink.'

He was watching her with cool grey eyes, she could feel them boring into her, she could almost hear his brain clicking. 'Are you trying to get an abortion?' he demanded. 'Are you pregnant?'

She turned to face him. 'Yes. How did you know?'

'I'm not stupid, Diana. How far gone are you?'

'About six weeks. But it doesn't matter, I'm getting rid of it. We're too old for babies. If the doctor hadn't been such a fool I'd have been done tomorrow. He's got some ridiculous idea that you'd be delighted to have another family. Apparently middle-aged men get a kick out of parading with a pregnant belly beside them, as if they were walking around with an erection on public display.'

James said, 'He's right. I shall like it.'

It was what she least wanted to hear and yet she knew all along she had expected it. The tawny eyes opened wide with rage. 'James! It's my body, I'm the one involved! I won't have it, I absolutely refuse!'

She flung herself down on to the sofa, chewing at her fists. He went and took hold of them saying 'Diana, Diana' but she hit out at him and kicked up at his groin. 'Bitch,' he muttered and pushed her down, forcing her back on to the sofa. She resisted, silent but red-faced with anger, until suddenly he let her go. She gave a cry and lay there, breathing hard.

'You've been going with prostitutes,' she panted. 'Don't deny it, you've been seen. I've probably got some filthy disease.'

He was going to deny it. But somehow he wanted her to know. 'I go quite a bit,' he said casually. 'Tuesdays and Thursdays usually, the girls know me. You won't catch anything, I always use a rubber.'

She looked up at him. 'Oh God,' she said miserably. 'Why on earth did I leave Andrew for you?'

Later in the evening, when they were both very drunk, he said, 'The baby will save us, you know. We'll have something together.'

'Will we?' She lay slumped in a chair, her hair a tangled mass around her face. Already he could see that her waist was thickening, her breasts hanging heavily.

'I'll never go near another scrubber if you have it,' he promised her.

'What did you go for in the first place?' she demanded. 'I never said no to you.'

'Different thing,' he said. 'It's like masturbation, you don't think of the girl. It's quick, they don't care about you. Sometimes the other girls stand about, they don't even bother to watch. They'll do anything if you pay them enough.'

'How much for what I do for you?' hissed Diana.

James reached across and put his hand on her belly. He had the upper hand, he had got his own back on her and it satisfied him. 'I wouldn't do that with them. You've got to understand. You're different, I love you. I want our baby.'

She sat up and stared into his face, hating his slight smile. 'What would you do if I still got rid of it? I could, you know, if I told them what you've been doing. They'd realise what sort of man you are.'

He picked up his whisky glass and drained it. 'I'm your

sort of man,' he said. 'But you know how I'd feel about it, you know what would happen.'

'What? Tell me. Go on, say it.' She had to know that she really couldn't win. She had to know that there was no easy way out.

'I'd leave you.'

Diana felt herself go very, very cold.

Rowan drove her ancient car slowly and carefully through the dismal streets of the Leeds suburb, trying to look for the name of the firm she was visiting and avoid running over a dog, cat or child. Now that she had her own driving licence she found herself thinking far more about the journey to her customers than the customers themselves, she was exhausted by anxiety even before she arrived. Somehow the presence of Joe next to her, however drunk or disinterested he might be, had acted as a tranquilliser and without him she was suffering acute withdrawal symptoms.

When she finally drew up in a parking place, having rejected three others because they would need reversing, she had a headache and found she couldn't quite remember why she was there. It came back to her in a rush of panic. To visit Sylvex, a company she had approached before but hadn't persuaded to buy anything from her. They were one of those large, unobtrusive firms that made up vast ranges of clothing under a bewildering number of labels. Most people had something by Sylvex in their wardrobe and never knew it.

She got out of the car and locked it carefully. She was wearing a long orange skirt, orange beret, boots and a vivid green fitted jacket. The material was Judge's own, run up for her by Mr. Suzman, who was only too delighted to make something 'looking like some fun' as he described it.

Now, out in public wearing the fruits of their combined imaginations, she felt conspicuous and perhaps foolish. A girl of her height shouldn't try to stand out, she should merge into the scenery, play down her long legs, narrow waist, over-sinuous neck.

The tailor hadn't thought so. 'You look so good,' he had chuckled. 'I think you could be in a play. I like that. Now I make for you a tabard, and tight pants. Good cloth this time.'

'Our cloth,' said Rowan firmly, and then, as an afterthought, 'and it is good.'

'It is not worsted,' he retorted.

'That doesn't matter, it's still good. Please, Mr. Suzman, use my cloth and make it look good. Please.'

He gave in to her, perhaps because his fatherly kindness had been so stretched by his own girls that he had plenty over for someone else's. The final outfit had delighted them both. She had swirled out of the shop longing for an occasion to wear it.

Where had all that confidence gone? Sometimes she had it, buckets of it, and other times, times like this, it leaked away as if every bucket was a sieve.

But, you didn't need real confidence if you could fake it. Striding into the lobby, lined with well-dusted plastic palms, she announced, 'I have an appointment. Rowan Judge to see Mr. DeSande.'

She stood in the middle of the floor, swinging on her heel and looking at the clothing samples pinned to the walls all around. Men's voices approached from the hinterland of the building. One of them rang an unpleasant bell. Two men came through the swing doors into the lobby.

'Hello, James,' said Rowan bravely.

He swung round, fixing her with the twin cannon of his grey eyes. 'Good God,' he declared. 'You look like something out of a bargain basement ragbag.'

His escort, the managing director, Mr. DeSande, lifted an eyebrow. Rowan knew she must not respond in kind, it would be tactless. 'I'm sorry you don't like it, James,' she said coolly. 'It's our own cloth, I suppose that would account for it. By the way, how is Mother?'

'Haven't you spoken to her? She was going to ring you.'

'Has something happened?'

James slid his hands into his pockets. This announcement was one he could savour. 'She's pregnant,' he declared. 'Due at the end of April.'

Rowan's response was highly gratifying. The colour drained from her cheeks, she looked shocked to the core. 'Oh,' she said feebly. 'Oh dear.'

Mr. DeSande, who had been observing the exchange with some interest, said, 'My dear, can I get you something? It must be quite a surprise.'

'I'm all right, thank you,' said Rowan. But Mr. DeSande took her arm and led her to a chair. 'I am sorry,' she apologised. 'Could I have a drink of water?'

Casting James a look of deep reproach, DeSande said, 'Of course, my dear,' and went off to fetch it.

'Stop play-acting,' snapped James as soon as he was gone. 'Are you hoping for the sympathy vote?'

'Yes,' she retorted. 'And I'll get it. Mother must be mad, she knows how horrible you are to children.'

'Only other people's children.'

Rowan looked away, her thin fingers playing with the fluffy pile on her skirt. James thought, 'She really is upset, she's white as a ghost, and so thin.' From the heights of his proven potency he looked down and felt sorry for her. 'How's business?' he asked jerkily.

She glanced up. 'All right. Hard work though.'

'Damned hard work I should think, turning that mess round. Are you making much of your own stuff yet?'

She sighed. 'Not a lot, no. Most of it's contracted out.'

'Then if I were you, I'd sell that barn of a mill and get somewhere more sensible,' advised James. 'You'll never get back into proper production, you haven't the capital. And if you try, it'll break you.'

Hearing her own worst fears voiced galvanized Rowan.

She got to her feet, saying shrilly, 'That isn't true! You're always wanting to run us down, you want me to fail! You want me to come begging to you for help, you want us all to be grateful and living on handouts. The only reason you pay for Andy is because it puts him on your side. I won't give you the satisfaction!'

Mr. DeSande, entering with the glass of water, saw her take a step towards him. She reached for the glass but her hand didn't take it. For a long second she hung suspended in the air and then crumpled on to the cold marble tiles.

When James told Diana about it over dinner, she asked, 'Did you leave her there? Was she all right?'

'She was fine,' said James. 'DeSande was fussing over her like a mother hen. The thing that appals me is I'm not sure she didn't stage the whole performance, she might even have got an order out of him. Which is more than I could manage.' He grimaced thoughtfully.

'I thought you said you were making a courtesy call,' said Diana.

'That was the excuse, yes. Hello Bill, just thought I'd pop in and see how you're getting along, been a long time, and so on. The truth is we can't get orders from them and no one knows why. I bet she got something.'

Diana got up and went slowly over to the sideboard to bring the pudding. She was feeling tired tonight, although in general the pregnancy was flourishing. She stifled a yawn. 'I wish Rowan could do something else,' she said wistfully. 'She's leading a terrible life, no fun and only that ghastly Partridge man to go about with. God help us if she's sleeping with him.'

'Probably got tattoos on his balls,' said James absently. As Diana sat down again he reached out and took her hand. 'Look,' he began. 'I've been thinking. Judge's can't possibly make it as it is, they haven't the money, and Rowan's grinding herself into the floor over it. That faint wasn't put on, she'd gone green. I know she and I have been at loggerheads, but I don't hate the girl! She's got guts. Wouldn't it be best if I bought out Andy and Sally's share of Judge's and put in some investment? I'll pay a bit over the odds, to show there's no fiddle going on. When she knows I've got control, she'll sell her share too, there should be enough to buy a little business. Fashion shop or something.'

Diana put his hand to her cheek. 'That is so sweet of you,' she murmured. 'But she'll never agree!'

He shrugged. 'She doesn't have to. You do. It's time the poor girl had some life, or she'll turn into an old maid with a tacky business and nothing else. I don't want our baby growing up asking, "Why didn't you ever do anything for Rowan, Daddy?" I owe her this, and I owe it to you.'

In the candlelight Diana's eyes gleamed like vintage port. 'Sometimes you really surprise me,' she whispered. 'You make me glad about the baby, and I wasn't at all till tonight. I'm grateful to it already for making you kind to Rowan.'

'Didn't I tell you it would make all the difference?' James leaned across and brushed her soft lips with his own. He felt a great, abiding peace.

At first Rowan could make no sense of the letter. She sat trying to understand what it said, half-aware that Sally was using the kitchen shears to cut her long blonde hair into a ragged bob.

'What do you think of it?' asked Sally.

Rowan glanced up. 'It's lopsided. Go to the hairdresser. Has Mother been talking to you? About selling your share of Judge's?'

'I haven't given her the chance. She wanted to meet me in town last week but I didn't go. Is that from her?'

'No. Her solicitors.'

'She can't take me to court for not meeting her in Rackhams!' wailed Sally. Rowan said nothing so she picked up her school bag, in which she kept sweets and pop comics but never homework, and flounced out.

Joe's van roared in as Rowan went out to the mill. It was his day for taking scoured wool to be carded and spun, he had a regular contract now. She went across to talk to him. 'Joe,' she said cautiously, 'have you heard any rumours lately? About Judge's?'

'Nah.' He heaved a bale of wool aboard the van. 'Only rubbish.'

'What sort of rubbish?'

'Someone said he'd heard that Bardsey's were buying you out, but as I said, it's a family firm, they can't.'

Her face flamed. 'Not Bardsey's!' she exploded. 'She couldn't sell it to that man, not even she could do that!'

'Well, she wouldn't, would she?'

Rowan thrust the letter in his face. He stared at it, sometimes his lips moved. 'I don't understand it,' he said at length.

'Oh, give it here!' Rowan snatched it back. 'It says they want to meet me to discuss the agreed disposal of the company. I thought at first it was something left over from Dad dying, but it isn't. It's Mother. She's trying to sell out from under me, and she hasn't breathed a word. God, I hate her!'

'No you don't, Ro,' soothed Joe.

'And I hate you too!' she shrieked.

As soon as she had stopped shaking she drove out to Aspley Manor. It was nearly Christmas but the weather was still mild, the leaves hung on the trees awaiting a gale to send them flying. Rowan stared out at the park and said loudly, 'You've got all this, James Barton, why do you need poor little Judge's as well? Doesn't anything satisfy you?'

When she arrived she got out of her car and tramped round to the back door. She could see her mother, sitting at the kitchen table, still in her dressing gown. It hung open and her swollen belly, a strange protruberance on an otherwise slim figure, bulged out obscenely. As Rowan flung open the door, Diana jumped.

'Rowan! Why, you did startle me.'

'Did I?' She sat down opposite her mother, watching her with fierce green eyes. They gleamed with unshed tears.

'I've been wanting to talk to you,' said Diana awkwardly.

'I bet you have. I'm not going to let you do it, I won't!'

'Well, it's not up to you, is it?' said her mother. 'You can't stop me. I've put a lot of thought into what's best for you, all of you. I can't let you go on treating Andy and Sally's shares in the business as irrelevant, it isn't fair.'

A tremor crossed Rowan's white face. 'I'll never sell him my share,' she said bitterly.

'You might have to,' said Diana. 'Darling, at the price he's paying the others I'd be mad to refuse. I have to act in their best interests!'

'But not in mine,' said Rowan.

'It is in your best interests if you had the sense to see it! You slave away at that place nineteen hours a day, you never go anywhere, never have any fun. If you really won't sell then you can sit tight and reap the profits when James has the firm turned round.'

Rowan flared, it was like someone throwing petrol on the embers of a fire. 'I'm the one that's turning it round! That's the only reason he wants it, now it's doing well! The man's a crook, a shark, you should see that!'

'Darling, that's rubbish,' said Diana patiently.

Rowan half rose to her feet. 'You say it's rubbish. Did he tell you about the other day, about Sylvex? He couldn't get an order, not however much he grovelled. I got one. I got the biggest order we've ever had, and James Bloody Barton knows it! And the reason is that we do what he can do, but we do it cheaper and quicker and without so much paper. We do what people want. He hasn't cornered the market in business ability. He's been so busy sleeping with other men's wives and buying houses and racketing from one nightclub to another that he didn't notice what we were doing, what *I* was doing!'

'Have you heard something about James?' demanded Diana. 'If so, you've got to tell me.'

Momentarily diverted, Rowan said, 'What should I have heard? What's he done?'

Her mother swallowed. 'Well. Nothing, I shouldn't wonder. He's working very hard now I'm expecting this baby. It's changed him.'

'Oh yeah,' sneered Rowan. 'All of a sudden he's turned sweet and lovable. Don't you think it's a bit odd? Don't you think what he really wants is Judge's at a bargain price, before we start showing what we can really do? Because we're going places, Mother, we really are!'

'But at what cost?' Diana got up and came round the table, shuffling a little in her silly mules. 'Darling, you're white as a ghost, you're thin, you've got bags under your eyes. I want you to be free of all this, and to please me, because of the baby, James will set you free. I think that's sweet of him, only you can't see it.'

Rowan felt like crying. Why was it that other people always seemed to think they knew what was best for her and never took a blind bit of notice of what she said?

'You don't mind about the baby, do you, Rowan?' asked her mother, almost plaintively.

'You know I do,' said Rowan shortly. 'It's childish, but I do. It seems rather horrible somehow, and the way he gloats about it is even more horrible.'

'That's just the way you see him. In your eyes he does nothing right. Look, will you drive me into town? We'll go and see James and talk about this.'

'No,' said Rowan. 'I won't see him. And I warn you, Mother, that if you sell to him I'll never speak to you again, and I won't let Sally speak to you and I'll try my best to turn Andy against you as well. James doesn't need Judge's and I do.' She spun on her heel and flounced out, sending the door crashing back against the wall. The winter wind, at long last tinged with ice, blew gustily across the floor.

Diana drove herself to see James. These days she had a Porsche, which she did not want but James had chosen. Occasionally he would borrow it because it suited his image sometimes to be the boy racer, screaming through the park and outstripping Rolls Royces on the road into town. He now considered his own Roller very staid, an old man's car. The novelty had palled, as with so many things. Perhaps with him, everything?

The Porsche's bucket seat didn't suit her back. She wriggled uncomfortably. She wished James would get rid of the damn thing so she could get back to a neat hatchback with room for the shopping and escape being chatted up by other drivers at traffic lights. Her cool, disdainful profile framed in the window of the Porsche seemed to be irresistible.

Today was particularly troublesome. Some guy in a Japanese hotrod chased her all the way into town, grinning and making faces, and had the temerity to follow her into the multi-storey car park. It occurred to her that it might have been wiser to park at Bardsey's, but so often there wasn't a space. The man would go away if she was firm with him. She got out of the car and locked it, her wide tan coat swirling about her, concealing all trace of her pregnancy.

'You certainly do that car a favour, don't you, sweetheart?'

He was in front of her as she hurried to the exit.

'Go away,' she said distantly and tried to push past him. He caught her arm, the other hand fastening on her handbag. For the first time Diana felt scared. 'What a pretty, rich lady,' purred her attacker.

She said nothing but pulled back, holding on to the bag and staring in fixed horror into the man's grinning face. He was in no hurry, he was enjoying tormenting her, frightening her. Suddenly he jerked her forward, pushing her between two cars. He was forcing her to her knees. A short, anguished scream broke from her.

'Diana? Diana, are you all right?'

She tried to pull round, yelling, 'Saul! Saul, come quickly!' and saw that he was getting out of the Aston, a hundred yards away across three lines of cars. The man let go of her, lashing out with a punch that caught her in the belly. She fell with a painful grunt. 'Rich bitch,' said the man and left her.

She lay in a daze, not thinking. After a minute or so Saul picked her up.

'He got away down the stairs,' he told her. 'I thought I'd better come and see to you.'

'He hit me,' muttered Diana. 'I think I'm all right.'

Saul helped her to her feet. She was white and shaking, with dirt on her coat and her face. 'Er – the baby,' said Saul awkwardly. 'Do you think I'd better call an ambulance?'

'No.' she was fierce and emphatic. 'Help me to get to James. I shouldn't have parked here. I don't know why I did.'

They went down in the lift together, Saul supporting her and hating every minute of it. Diana said, 'You don't have to look so pained.'

'I'm sorry,' he said. 'Diana, there's something I've been wanting to ask you.'

The lift doors opened and they stepped out in unison. 'If it's what I think it is,' said Diana, 'then you can rest easy. It isn't yours.'

He let out his breath in relief. 'Thank God for that. It's one thing having a drunken fling, but we can do without results. And James is over the moon, full of untypical love and charity, even to me. I've been choking on guilt.'

'Poor you,' said Diana thinly.

When James saw his wife he went white. 'What in God's name happened?' he asked. Diana shook her head, fighting tears. Saul said, 'She was attacked in the car park. I got there before he could do much but I think he punched her. You'd better call a doctor.'

'I'll do better than that. We'll get the consultant gynaecologist. See to it, will you? Tell him it's an emergency. Darling, lie down at once, here on the sofa. It's all right, I'm here now.'

Diana clung to him, suddenly shaking violently. 'He was going to rape me,' she whispered. 'He was dragging me off to do it. He might have killed me!'

'But it didn't happen.' James gripped her hands hard. 'And the important thing is to look after this baby.'

'But I was so frightened!'

'Yes, yes, of course you were.' James adored her at that moment. All her hard edges had been knocked away, she was dishevelled, vulnerable and she needed him.

Saul came back into the room. 'He's coming straight over. They're bringing up some tea, I thought Diana could do with it.'

Diana struggled up into a sitting position. She would not be seen like this by Saul of all people. In a tight, high voice she said, 'James, I was coming to tell you. I don't think I can sell Judge's to you, Rowan just won't have it. She was raving at me this morning.'

'That bloody girl!' declared James. 'Take no notice, Diana, she ought to know better than to make scenes. We don't need her consent.'

'But I thought – ' began Diana.

'Darling.' James put his hands either side of her head. 'Don't think. You needn't worry, I'll see to it.'

Saul, absorbing everything about this exchange, said, 'That poor girl. There's no end to what you'll do to her, is there, James?'

'You keep your nose out of it,' snapped James. 'It's none of your business.'

'I like Rowan,' said Saul. 'She's a brave kid. Losing Judge's now, when she's done so well, it would break her heart.'

'But it's *for* Rowan,' said Diana shakily. 'To take away

some of the strain. She's having a terrible time working there!'

'She doesn't think it's terrible,' said Saul. 'If she says she wants to keep the firm, then that's probably what she means. It's not up to you to say what's good for her and it certainly isn't up to James. I'm not surprised he wants to get his hands on Judge's, they're proving quite a thorn in his side.'

'Rubbish,' said James automatically. He rested a hand on his wife's belly. 'Good Lord, Diana, it's fluttering. Can you feel it?'

'Yes. Yes, I can. Saul, do you really think Rowan should keep on wearing herself out like that? She looks so tired.'

'Then she probably needs some help. She doesn't need a takeover.'

James, unable to concentrate on what seemed to him a trivial discussion when the life, the welfare, of his unborn child was at stake, snarled: 'Diana! Lie down and rest, you're not doing yourself any good.'

'But James, if Saul thinks – ' began Diana.

'I don't care what Saul thinks,' he declared. 'Look, it isn't important. We'll let her keep the firm for now, we've got a year or two before the children get control, and she'll have it motoring by then. It might cost me a bit more but I can take it any time I want. Now lie down and rest.'

Obediently, thoughtfully, Diana lay down. So much for James's altruism then. The momentary impulse to take the strain from Rowan would not have survived an instant if he had not also wanted to get his hands on a thriving and competitive business. She had been naive, and more than that, stupid. If James owned Judge's it would benefit no one but James, and the exclusion included her. Marriage to James was not like marriage to Andrew, there was no merging of interests. She must watch out for herself, and for Andy, Rowan, all of them, because James was a hunter and they were all his prey. Perversely, the thought lessened the distance between them. When he reached out and touched her cheek she brushed her lips against his hand.

Chapter Eighteen

When Saul wandered into Judge's yard his spirits sank. It was rather worse than he had expected. But then he was used to Bardsey's fleets of wagons, efficient loading bays and neat paintwork, he was not prepared for the ramshackle air of making do that typified this relic of the nineteenth century. Set against the valley side, for half the day it was in shadow, while for the other half it basked in soft Yorkshire sun. Without light the stone was black, charmless; in the sunshine it took on the colour of old honey.

He sauntered towards the mill and was almost immediately intercepted by a young and aggressive warehouseman. 'Can I help you? Looking for Miss Judge?'

'Er – yes I was. Name of Barton. Saul Barton.'

'You come with me.'

It was rather like being put under armed escort. But then, he thought, if James had been as security conscious Rowan would never have got to see the range. Or indeed, if he had been less treacherous. He didn't regret it.

They went upstairs to Rowan's office. She was crouched over her desk, doing sums, rather like a child at school, her tongue at the corner of her mouth and pages of workings out screwed up everywhere.

'Hello, Rowan,' he said.

She looked up and went pink. 'Oh, hello, Saul. Just a minute.' She picked up her papers and put them all carefully into a folder, put the folder in a drawer and locked it.

'You can't be too careful,' said Saul pointedly.

'People are so sneaky.' She grinned at him.

The warehouseman said, 'I've still got them bales waiting,

miss, they've been waiting all week.'

Rowan looked troubled. 'Have you? It's not like Joe to let us down. Can you get on to him?'

'I thought you might want to.'

'No. You do it.'

They waited until he had left. Saul said, 'Have you fallen out with Joe Partridge?'

She shook her head. 'Not really. He's cross with me. He's only left those bales so I'll ring him, and I won't.'

She was wearing a pair of black trousers, gathered at the ankle, and over the top a straight tabard of the same black material, with appliqued green fabric roses dotted around on it. And she had had her hair cut again, into wisps that wandered about her face. She looked wistful and strange.

'I thought you were serious about him,' said Saul.

'It seems he thought that, too,' said Rowan, sighing. 'It annoyed Mother so I led him on a bit. I didn't realise he didn't know, and now he's all upset and hurt and it's my fault.'

She looked rather unhappy and all at once Saul thought of the trail of women he had left behind who had thought he was more serious than he intended. He had never hung around long enough to feel this sort of guilt, and that in itself made him feel guilty. He'd used a lot of women.

He found himself longing to ask if she had slept with Joe. He had an arousing picture in his mind of Rowan's long, thin body beneath the tattooed stockiness of the man, of her white innocence ravaged by an insensitive brute. A fierce erection was making itself felt, he hoped she couldn't see it. He sat down, unasked.

'Did you want something?' asked Rowan innocently. Her green eyes in that white face were like emeralds, he thought. How was it that she had bypassed prettiness and yet become desirable? She was nothing but skin and bone. He tried to speak but his voice croaked. 'Rowan – I wanted you to come on a trip with me.'

'Whatever do you mean?'

He wished she would stop looking at him in that gently enquiring way, he wished her little breasts would make more or less of an impression on her clothes. That pert hint of a presence disturbed him utterly. He got up, startling her, and strode over to the window, putting his back to the room. 'It's like this,' he said loudly. 'James hasn't given up on getting Judge's, he's biding his time. If you're going to keep him at bay you can't rely on your mother. In the end James can make her do anything, it's only her pregnancy keeps him from cracking the whip now. But if you can move the firm on, make a leap into the international market, he won't be able to afford to buy you out. I'm going to Japan on a selling trip. I want you to come with me.'

Rowan stared at his back. 'Is this the favour you said I owed you?' she asked stiffly.

He turned and laughed. 'No, of course not. Separate rooms, I promise. But you can't break into the overseas markets on your own, you need help and I want to help you.'

'Why?'

That was Rowan, direct and uncompromising. He crossed to her desk and sat close to her on the edge. He ran his fingers down the edge of her tabard. 'Because I like you. Because James deserves to be troubled by you. Because I often go to Japan and should love to have you to show around.'

'Who pays for the fare?' she asked, and he thought, 'God, doesn't she ever think of anything except business?'

'I'll pay half,' he promised. 'And we won't tell James what's going on, will we?'

She looked up at him. 'Ought I to trust you?' she demanded.

'To a point,' he said.

When he had gone, Rowan sat at the desk and felt shivers racking her body. That man, that strange man. From the moment he came into the room she had been conscious of heat, moving from him into her, making her aware of a deep inner fire in her belly. At the wedding reception he had called her breasts tasty mouthfuls, she hadn't forgotten.

It was all his fault that things had got out of hand with Joe. She had wanted to know if men really did put their mouths there. When Joe had started his usual late night grope she'd encouraged him to get into her T-shirt. Before she'd got used to his big, clumsy hands he was pushing her down under him, and she was cursing and hitting him and telling him to get off. The whole thing had revolted her, she felt ashamed and guilty and foolish. More than that, she felt – unsatisfied.

It had ended in a fierce and bitter row. Joe thought that after all this time she owed him 'a bit of the other', as he described it. He cared about her. He thought she cared about him. And if she said she did he would be wrongly encouraged, and if she denied it she would be lying. Joe was her friend, her good friend, and she didn't want more than that.

Was Saul Barton a friend? He was acting like one – almost. At least he was no friend of James's, she was sure there was no way he would work with James against her. He was certainly a playboy, letting money cascade into the mouths of endless women, or so she had heard. To her he seemed entirely sincere, surely she wasn't wrong about that? He was such fun; when he was around the world looked different, felt different, quite possibly was different, because he did what he wanted and took nothing at all seriously. Perhaps that included her.

He was right about James, that much was certain. And perhaps she ought to go to Japan. It was the market of the future, everybody said so. She'd never been anywhere.

Suddenly she was bubbling with excitement. It was as if a fairy godmother had waved a wand, transporting her from fluff and dust and drudgery out into the great wide world. And if Saul proved not to look after her, she was sure she could look after herself.

* * *

They were to go in January, and Rowan told no one at all. The secret bolstered her, because it was Christmas and she hated it, because everything about the season recalled how it used to be. Andrew always loved Christmas, he was silly and fun and made them all stand outside in the garden singing carols on Christmas Eve. Sometimes even a tinny rendering of 'The Holly and the Ivy' in the supermarket made Rowan blink back tears.

This year Diana was insisting on a family Christmas at Aspley Manor. Rowan had longed to refuse, but dared not do so and besides, could not face the day in the gloomy little cottage. So she, Sally and Andy all attended and sat round the festive board.

Just as she had known it would, everything about James enraged her. He sat at the head of the table exuding self-satisfaction, and however much Rowan tried to deflate him she couldn't. Diana was almost as bad, presiding over her expanding belly much as James over the turkey, as if between them they had discovered the secret of everlasting life. Determinedly Rowan concentrated on the turkey.

'That's what I like to see, a good appetite,' said James. 'Want some more, Rowan love?' She felt like a rattlesnake kept like a pet in a basket.

She waited until the pudding before dropping her bombshell. 'Mother,' she began casually, 'will it be all right if Sally stays with you after Christmas? I'm going on a selling trip.'

Everybody's spoon paused. She could feel James watching her, but she looked instead at Sally's small, pretty face. She was accusing. 'You didn't tell me you were going anywhere. Why? I'll come, I won't stay here.'

'It's business, you can't come,' said Rowan. 'You wouldn't enjoy it.'

'You don't want to tow me around with you, that's all,' said Sally. 'I won't be dumped here, not with him!' She flicked a contemptuous hand at James.

'Don't be a bore, Sal,' said Andy lazily. 'I'll be here, so he won't have just you to yell at.'

'I wouldn't have to yell at you if you would do your practising at reasonable hours,' stated James forcefully. 'That means before twelve at night and after six in the morning! Good God, can't you three even let Christmas dinner pass without a scene? Rowan, you'd better find somewhere else for Sally, I won't have Diana upset. In case you've forgotten, she is expecting our baby.'

Diana, who had listened to all this with her usual calm, said, 'Do be quiet, James. Of course Sally will come here. Rowan, where are you going?'

'A selling trip,' said Rowan.

James, who quite liked Diana to see him as over-protective, said in a milder tone, 'Do we have to be quite so secretive? You're not in the KGB yet surely?'

'You'd sell your own son if it suited you.'

To her surprise, James winced. He picked up his wine glass and drained it.

'How did you get on with Richard?' asked Diana levelly.

'As you might expect.' James's tone was icy, precluding further questions. The expensive camera, chosen by James after hours of deliberation, had gone out with him in the car that morning and had returned with him, smashed.

Rowan said, 'Please don't snoop around the mill while I'm away, James. They've been told to watch out for you.'

'I see no reason to go and look at half a dozen ancient looms and a lot of empty floorspace,' said James cuttingly. 'Diana, this pudding is excellent.'

Sally put down her spoon. 'I feel sick,' she announced.

James threw down his own spoon. 'I knew that brat would disrupt things somehow! If she wants to throw up, she can do it somewhere else. Rowan, put her in the car and take her home.'

'Darling, do you really feel ill?' asked Diana, ignoring him. 'Come and lie down upstairs.'

In the ensuing disruption Andy wandered off to watch

television and James and Rowan sat before the unfinished pudding and looked at each other.

'And a Happy Christmas to one and all,' said James.

Rowan, knowing she was to escape from them, raised her glass. 'Happy Christmas,' she said.

Rowan felt utterly filthy. She was exhausted and sweaty, hungry and yet sated with plastic airline meals. Her feet felt swollen. She longed for sleep but was too jumpy to rest. On the flight out, Saul had drunk steadily, making her more and more nervous. He had been exuberant, then sleepy, and at last vaguely amorous, sitting very close and resting his hand on her knee. She had been relieved to see him go to his own room, but now she was alone and she felt abandoned in this foreign place, amidst a sea of jabbering Japanese.

In truth, everyone in the hotel spoke English and Saul was only next door, but it wasn't the same, it wasn't home. She had longed to go, and now she longed to go back. Moving with slow deliberation she went into the bathroom and took off her clothes, then almost scalded herself on the taps. The water was nearly boiling, the room was instantly filled with steam. So much better than the lukewarm dribble at the mill cottage, she told herself, where the towels were rough and the bathroom freezing. In Tokyo it was just as cold, but everywhere was properly heated. In a technological world the Japanese had learned to work the switches.

She eased herself gently into the steaming bath. It was wonderfully soothing, she would like to stay there forever. Dimly she heard a knock on her bedroom door. She took no notice, the door was locked and they couldn't get in. Besides, it would only be the chambermaid. She closed her eyes and began to daydream, her favourite saga in which Judge's was filled once again with machinery, all of it high-tech and super-efficient. The Queen was bestowing her award for industry. 'We are proud to know that you, Rowan Judge, have single-handedly revitalised Britain's textiles,' she was announcing.

Saul's voice said, 'So there you are.'

Rowan's eyes flew open. Saul was leaning on the doorpost staring down at her naked body, obscured only by a cloud of steam and some very clear water. He looked very tall and very powerful.

'Get out,' said Rowan flatly.

'I don't think I want to,' said Saul.

'I knew you were drunk on the plane,' said Rowan. 'Go away and sober up.'

He straightened up and took a step towards the bath. In a flurry of movement Rowan pulled her knees to her chin and crouched there. He put out his hand and touched her hot, wet shoulder. 'You are so wonderfully long and smooth,' he murmured. 'Are you like that on the inside?'

'Go away,' repeated Rowan. 'I don't want you here, you're drunk and I don't like it.'

'And to think I only came to see if you were all right.'

'Well, I am.'

'And I'm not,' he said mournfully. 'Why don't I come in that bath with you?'

Rowan turned her head away. She wasn't going to look at him, she wasn't going to think of him. Rapidly, purposefully, she soaped her sponge and started washing herself with brisk, unerotic movements. Saul sighed. After a few moments she heard her bedroom door close.

In the morning, after they had both slept, Saul was apologetic. Rowan sat herself down at the breakfast table, barely glancing at him. He poured her some coffee and she sipped it, gazing into the middle distance. 'I know I made a nuisance of myself,' said Saul. 'Sorry.'

'I thought you were going to rape me,' said Rowan.

He grinned. 'Me? I think I'm a bit too soft-hearted. One squeal and I'd call the St. John's Ambulance. I can't even squash flies.'

'Do they have the St. John's Ambulance out here?' asked Rowan.

'Shouldn't think so. They're a bit bloody bloody, the Japanese, actually. They probably expect you to hobble to hospital with a broken leg. By the way, are you a virgin?'

She spread her napkin brusquely. 'Yes. But I don't think it needs treatment, thank you.'

He picked up the coffee pot and refilled her cup. 'Let me know if it does. I wouldn't hurt you for anything, Rowan.'

She was awash with heat. She couldn't look at him. All through breakfast he made sensible conversation about their visits that day and she could barely reply. Was it so odd still to be a virgin? Was the male body something she ought to experience?

They went upstairs to get their samples and their coats. Rowan sat on her bed, her hands folded in her lap. Sally was on the pill, she had found the packet in her bedside drawer when she was looking for something. There had seemed nothing she could usefully say. It was one of the lads from the brickworks. He and Sally met on the corner most Saturdays, she said they went for walks. What happened in the dark and smelly alleys? Sometimes there was brick dust on the back of her coat... Rowan imagined her pressed up against some wall. Yet if she fought her and kept her in, Sally lay in her bedroom sobbing, frighteningly out of control. To give in to Sally seemed the only way to maintain some precarious balance. And here was Rowan, so much older, supposedly so much more mature, afraid of something even her little sister understood.

The door opened. It was Saul. 'Where did you get the key?' she asked.

'From Reception,' he said. 'They think we're sleeping together, they'd be surprised if they knew we weren't.'

Rowan got up and gathered her things. The sample case was a lead weight, she had probably put in too much but it was no use wanting something in Tokyo that you had left in Bradford.

'Don't be scared,' said Saul. 'I'm not going to be horrible to you.' But it wasn't Saul she was scared of. It was herself.

They went out into a crisp, cold morning, the Japanese sun sparkling down through the winter smog. The crowds were offputting, filling the pavements, surging into and out of buildings with early-morning zeal. Rowan clung to Saul's arm to avoid losing him. 'The Tokyo beehive,' he yelled to her above the row. 'They don't sting.'

'But how can they bear it?' She and Saul towered above the Japanese, she could feel people watching her, hear those closest muttering about her. At least Saul seemed to know where he was going, and so did she in principle. They were to visit an agent who was organising their tour of potential customers. He was a man Saul had worked with before.

Saul, striding peremptorily into the road, flagged down a taxi. He had to drag Rowan out of the way as the door swung open. 'It's automatic,' she said wonderingly, and smiled dubiously at the Japanese driver. He smiled back and bowed his head and for some idiotic reason she was thrilled that even the taxi driver should be Japanese. She felt as if she was in some sort of film set and that the real world was on the other side of the buildings, or the street, or perhaps in the taxis. She kept looking for the exit.

They joined a snail's pace queue of traffic. Rowan gazed out of the window at the hordes of people. 'They're dressed just like us,' she said in disappointment.

Saul said, 'I'll take you to Akasaka one evening and you can see the geishas going to work by rickshaw. They're an odd mixture, the Japanese, they keep the old style going but a bit as if they're acting it.'

'I felt like that,' said Rowan eagerly. 'It's like being in a play.' She felt close to him suddenly, she felt that he understood.

'By the way,' said Saul. 'Don't say much at this meeting.

My agent isn't used to dealing with women, he'll only want to talk to me.'

'I can't have that! I'm here in my own right!'

He put his arm round her and gave her a squeeze. 'Darling Rowan, this is Japan. It isn't the same here, try and remember that.'

No. It wasn't the same. She allowed herself to relax a little against him.

The agent was called Yushida, but whether this was his first or second name Rowan could not establish. He bowed to her formally, putting his hands together, and after a moment's hesitation she repeated the gesture.

'How was your journey?' he asked politely. 'Do you have family at home?' Perhaps she hadn't replied properly. At any rate they were the last words he said to her until she and Saul were being ushered out. 'I am honoured to have met you,' said Yushida, repeating his bow.

'And I am less than honoured to have met him,' said Rowan sourly, once they were safe in the street. 'Will they all be like that?'

'Until you've been here a dozen times or so,' said Saul. 'And then you've got to sort of grovel. "If you'll forgive my presumption, Yushida-san, might I suggest that if it were not too inconvenient for you would it be all right if this trip I made a profit?" It's hard enough for Western men here, let alone a girl.'

'Aren't I lucky to have you looking after me?' purred Rowan. For he *had* taken care of her; after the list of Bardsey appointments he had nudged away at Rowan's side of things. They were to spend three days in Tokyo and then go on to Kyoto for two. There seemed to be nothing arranged for the last three days, though the return date for their ticket was open.

'Do we have to keep time free to go back and see people again?' asked Rowan curiously.

Saul glanced at her. 'I thought we should keep some days

available. Look, with a bit of luck these people we're going to see this afternoon will entertain us tonight. What do you want to see? Puppets, that's Bunraku, or Kabuki, or Noh? For God's sake avoid Takarazuka, it's like one of those thirties films with nothing but girls with feathers on their heads and ballgowns parading down staircases grinning. Terribly proper and terribly boring.'

'I've heard of Noh,' said Rowan. 'But I can't remember what I've heard.'

'Nobody can remember much after a Noh performance,' said Saul ruefully. 'It would be all right if it didn't go on so long. On and on and on. I learned to meditate at a Noh theatre. I recommend the puppets.'

'I don't know why you didn't say the puppets in the first place,' said Rowan. 'Why ask me when you know and I don't?'

'Don't be ratty,' said Saul. 'Or I'll take you to a Noh play.'

'If you know about Noh, say no,' retorted Rowan. 'You'd have to sit through it too, remember.' Saul chuckled.

They lunched at a cafeteria which had plastic replicas of the meals set out in the window. Rowan liked the look of none of it and what she did choose turned out to be excruciating. 'I shall starve to death,' she said miserably, watching Saul munch his way stolidly through something he said was Oyako-don and then proceed to finish her Kitsune Udon.

'We'll stop at a hamburger store,' he assured her. 'You're being very British, Rowan.'

'Only my taste buds,' she said apologetically. 'I really am trying to be cosmopolitan, I'm bowing so often I feel as if my clockwork's running down.'

'I don't suppose you eat much anyway.' He sat back and eyed her wand-like figure. She was wearing a green wool tube that clung to every bone and fleshy protuberance. It extended right down to her white boots.

'Normally I eat like a horse,' she said. 'But horses

wouldn't eat this either. Don't stare at me like that. Is the dress all right? I thought it looked a bit staid.'

He cleared his throat. 'You realise when you stand sideways I can see your pubic mound?'

Rowan's face flamed. She said, 'You're just trying to embarrass me. Stop it.'

'I would if I knew how. Oh God, Rowan, but you do turn me on.'

She kept her eyes on the table. All around people chattered away in Japanese, and a Japanese waitress came up to their table, bowed and smiled. 'She wants to clear away,' said Saul. 'Come on, love.'

She got up automatically bowing and smiling at the waitress. 'James calls me love,' she commented. 'It makes me want to savage him.'

'The difference is that I don't do it to annoy,' said Saul obliquely.

They took a taxi to an enormous shiny skyscraper. Just the look of it intimidated Rowan, and she was beginning to feel exhausted. Everything was so difficult when you understood none of the language, could read not one word of the writing and the familiar was so dangerously spiked with the oriental. She was hungry, too, because Saul had forgotten her hamburger. His presence was the one constant in a changed world. She felt a momentary panic if he went to the washroom in case something inscrutable happened to him and he didn't come back.

They fizzed up to some floor or other in a glass lift. The controls were so high-tech Rowan didn't understand them. You appeared to be able to programme the lift to call back for you.

'That really is awfully clever,' said Rowan admiringly.

'Don't be fooled by it,' said Saul. 'It's a bloody silly idea and it doesn't work. People at the top of this building can wait hours to get down because the lift's loyally visiting floors where the people long since took the stairs. The

Japanese are not that brilliant. Remember, we built the empire!'

'And they the transistor radio,' said Rowan.

'The empire didn't need batteries.'

The doors swung open and Saul stepped out. Before Rowan could follow they closed again. 'Saul! Help! Help!' she shrieked, but the lift had kidnapped her. Paralysed with fear she was swept onward and upward. Where was Saul? Where was she? How did you sound the alarm? When the doors again opened she fell out into the midst of a group of small Japanese men.

'I do beg your pardon. Do excuse me,' she burbled. They all grinned, bowed and jabbered at her. Pinning a fixed grin to her own face she blundered away from them, looking desperately for the stairs. One of the men followed her and kept on jabbering, and it was only after a few hectic moments that she realised he was actually talking English. The Japanese accent was thicker than custard.

'I want to get down,' said Rowan slowly. 'I can't find the stairs.'

He bobbed up and down, and eventually Rowan deciphered something on the lines of: 'Please, allow me to accompany you in the lift? What is your destination?'

Explaining that she didn't know was beyond her. She backed away, grinning, and he followed her, grinning and bowing, and every time she opened a door and found it wasn't the stairs, he held it for her as if she wanted to go through and she had to back away again like some demented inmate of a mental hospital. When at last she found the stairs and bolted down them he stood at the top, chattering unintelligibly and bowing.

She met Saul coming up to meet her. 'Thank God!' Rowan flung her arms round his neck in an agony of relief. 'I thought I was going to be trapped here forever with these insane Japanese.'

Saul pulled her to him, and for a minute they stood,

pressed together. Then Rowan pulled back, flushed and awkward. 'Where's your sample case?' asked Saul.

'Oh no! Oh, I can't have! I've left it in the lift!'

Saul put his fist to her head in a mock threat. 'Idiot! Don't you know you lose your life before you lose your samples? Just wait here.' He started past her back up the stairs but she followed like an apologetic puppy. They met her Japanese friend coming down, carrying the sample case.

'I could not allow the lady to be distressed,' he burbled, or something similar.

Rowan, Saul and the Japanese indulged in an orgy of bowing and grinning.

It was late when Saul and Rowan finally made it back to the hotel. They had displayed their samples, Saul had negotiated prices for both of them, and they had found themselves transported from office to restaurant, from restaurant to Bunraku, and just when they were becoming mesmerised by the brilliant half life-size puppetry they were whisked away to a club where hostesses with traditional painted faces served them formally. For Rowan it had all been too much. She was almost sobbing with weariness.

'Come on, I'll put you to bed,' said Saul as she slumped against him in the lift.

'Not that as well.' She tried to pull away from him, but he held on to her.

'It's all right, I'm not that insensitive. This is the exciting glamorous life of the salesman: aching feet, upset stomach and exhaustion.'

'My face aches,' she groaned. 'I never want to smile again.'

'More tomorrow, love,' said Saul remorselessly. 'And you've got to keep on making the sales, so get with it.'

'Brute!'

He unlocked her bedroom door and watched her fall fully clothed on to the bed. He came in after her and pulled off her boots. 'Have a bath, you'll feel better.'

'No! Go away, I'll be all right.'

'Shut up and let me baby you.'

He reached behind her head, found the zip of her dress and peeled it down from her shoulders. Rowan lay on the bed, helplessly languorous. His large brown hands touched the skin at her waist. 'My hands go right round you,' he said wonderingly.

'Do they?'

She had said she didn't want him, but now, in exhaustion, she wanted to be at his mercy. If he had made love to her now she needn't resist, she could blame it on Japan. But he didn't. Instead he put his arm beneath her knees, lifted her and swept the dress away. She lay in her underclothes, watching him beneath shadowed lids, her arms like seaweed spread about her on the bed.

He pulled the quilt across her. 'We'll stop there,' he said shakily. 'Are you all right?'

'Yes,' she murmured. 'Thank you, Saul.'

'Think nothing of it. Look, I'm going downstairs for a drink in the bar. You'll be all right, won't you?'

She felt warm and safe and cherished. 'Goodnight,' she whispered.

On the way downstairs Saul felt lightheaded. The more he was with Rowan the more attuned he became to her long-legged spiky elegance, the more he loved her directness, her moments of gauche embarrassment. His face split into an involuntary smile. How he loved looking after her. He went on down the stairs to assuage his longings with a few glasses of Japanese whisky.

The day they left Tokyo for Kyoto, Rowan felt a great sense of release. She wasn't used to the roar and bustle of a great city, and in Tokyo, that westernised bridge across two cultures, there was a filth that left a dark ring around the nostrils at the end of the day. Nonetheless when you sent your grubby white shirt to the laundry it came back spotless, beautifully folded and wrapped in plastic, with a flower nestling against the collar.

Sitting in the air-conditioned express train, watching Saul slumped easily in the seat opposite, she knew things had changed. They were comfortable with each other, unembarrassed. She didn't ask any more what they were going to do with their last three days in Japan. To ask she felt would be to spoil everything, to label emotions and intentions and put them in cardboard boxes. With Saul even the mundane seemed exciting. She could sit here on this train forever, just watching the way his long legs sprawled, the way his eyes looked out lazily from beneath his hair.

'I started too high,' she said thoughtfully. 'My first trip abroad should have been France or somewhere.'

Saul grunted. 'That would have been a mistake. In France, my sweet, if you want to get decent sales you have to visit hundreds of customers, and in Germany hundreds more. And you have to be fluent in the language. They don't have any patience with some blundering Briton who expects everyone to know English. Now in Japan no one thinks you should know the language, and look at the orders we've been getting. Worth a little trouble, don't you think?'

Rowan sighed. 'What do you think James is getting up to while I'm away?'

Saul shrugged. 'Replacing me, I shouldn't wonder.'

Rowan could tell by his tone that he meant it. She sat up. 'He wouldn't. He knows how valuable you are to the firm.'

'And I happen to think he's got it in for me just now. Well, for a while actually. And just now Diana's gunning for me as well and it isn't healthy. I can sense it in the air.'

'Mother? Whatever for?'

Saul gazed out of the window at the frosty countryside. There was a temple framed against grey-blue sky, and a tractor roaring across a field next to it. 'You know her,' he said vaguely. 'She has her moods.'

Rowan fell silent. Actually she didn't think Diana particularly moody, or at any rate not for inexplicable reasons. In general she was rather cool, infuriatingly so.

In Kyoto Saul taught Rowan how to display her samples. He sat on the bed acting the part of the customer while Rowan practised her geisha girl style of humble, deprecating modesty, putting forward each piece of cloth as if it were almost too unworthy to be noticed. 'I'm too tall for this,' she complained. 'You have to be nearer five foot and Japanese.'

'It's the smirk that counts, not the height you do it at,' said Saul. 'Anyway you can always kneel.'

'I will not!'

Diverted for the moment, Saul picked up two of Rowan's swatches, a grey flannel and a navy with red on the weft. 'These are nice,' he said. 'Did you think these up yourself?'

'Not really. There seemed a lot of that sort of stuff in the Paris fashions. I study all the magazines, you know.'

'I thought you were getting more and more way out.' He twitched the hem of her tunic, a style Rowan was very fond of. He was becoming equally fond of it; sometimes he thought she looked like his squire, young, boyish, eager to do his bidding. He liked the concept enormously.

'I'm going to have one made shorter,' she commented. 'And I shall wear tight trousers with it.'

Saul lay back on the bed. 'Take it off,' he murmured.

She glanced at him. 'I don't think – now?'

Their eyes met. He said, 'Don't you want to know where we're going?'

Rowan wrapped her long arms around herself, walling herself in protectively. 'I'll leave it to you,' she said in a small voice. 'I suppose we'll be – together?'

Saul swallowed. 'Very together. Absolutely together.'

Rowan nodded, dipping her head, half in shame. There could be no end but this.

That night they were taken to see Sumo wrestling. Rowan

found it strangely erotic, watching huge bearlike men waddling around almost naked. It wasn't that they were attractive, except in their confidence and arrogance, it was more that they were so unashamedly physical. It made her aware of her own body, her thinness as opposed to their enormous bulk, her damp skin set against the oil and sweat of their own vast chests. The Japanese next to her was bobbing up and down in excitement, she felt sorry for him. Her presence was inhibiting him terribly. Saul's leg pressed wordlessly against her own. Between them they generated a living sexual charge.

Chapter Nineteen

They had not done as much business in Kyoto. For all Rowan's assumed humility, she seemed to be too much for the provincial city. People stared at her and apologised for doing so, they treated her like an exotic species.

'They'll give you orders next time,' Saul consoled her, lending his weight to her suitcase as she tried to shut it.

'I'm not sure I shall come again,' she said. 'It's such hard work. I keep remembering how much money it's all costing, and if you don't get the orders it's terrible.'

Saul put out a finger and tapped her nose. 'Don't get down. If you get disheartened, you've had it. The one thing you've got when selling is your confidence.'

She let out a long, dismal sigh. 'But it's so hard. I tried so hard!'

'And the world's an unfair place. I remember one week I had, on my own, I ended up standing in a Spanish market-place after a week selling nothing. I couldn't bear to keep on trying, I thought I wanted to die. I sat on the edge of a fountain and got green slime on my suit, and that does not look good. But I dragged myself up to the next guy and he bought something, and suddenly I was back up there. I was making it.'

'You never seem not to be confident to me. I don't know where you get it from.'

'It helps if you don't mind making a fool of yourself.' She looked away, because they both knew how much she hated to appear ridiculous. He picked up the bags. 'Ready? We'll check out.'

Standing in the lobby while Saul settled up, Rowan let her

mind flit nervously over the immediate future. She sidled up to him. 'Where are we going?'

'On the train. Then a hire car.'

'But where to?'

He grinned, white teeth in a brown face, his fair hair falling over his forehead. He smelled faintly of booze, or mouthwash or something. 'You wait and see,' he said. 'It'll be worth it.'

A vendor on the train sold them bento, a beautifully gift-wrapped packed lunch. It was almost too lovely to open, but in the last days Rowan had lived mainly on the American-style hotel breakfasts and little else. She was unfastening the string of her box almost before Saul had paid for it, and when she took off the lid she gasped. Then she said woefully, 'I can't eat it! It's too beautiful!' Exquisite little portions of highly coloured and unidentified foods were rolled and cubed, sliced and decorated, set out with all the care of a jeweller working on a Fabergé egg. Nothing was large, nothing was ugly, it seemed criminal to spoil something so perfect.

Torn between admiration and hunger, Rowan almost moaned. But hunger won the day. She picked up a cube of what appeared to be pressed rice, decorated with a presumably edible green flower. She munched. Her face fell into lines of disappointment. 'It's horrible,' she said dismally. 'Rubbish,' said Saul and took another of the cubes. He chewed vigorously and then his jaws slowed. The food moved in a glutinous lump around his mouth. Eventually he gave a Herculean swallow and got rid of it. 'That lacked a little something,' he confessed. 'Try that dinky little pink thing.'

Rowan picked up the round pink glob and nibbled at it cautiously. 'Some fruit they very sensibly haven't tried out on the rest of the world,' she declared. 'You can have it.'

Eventually Saul consumed most of the contents of both lunchboxes, and Rowan went hungry. 'Health farms ought to send their obstinate cases here,' she muttered. 'One hundred per cent success rate, everyone beanpole thin in days.'

Saul wiped his hands on a tiny tissue from the lunchbox. 'Look,' he began, 'where we're going tonight is very Japanese. You're going to have to eat the food, you'll be ill if you go on like this.'

'Where are we going tonight?' she asked. 'Don't tease, I want to know.'

'Spoilsport. It's a Ryokan, a traditional Japanese hotel: sleep on the floor, beautifully painted paper walls, plum blossom in the gardens, perfect little flower displays. It's out of this world.'

Rowan said glumly, 'Do they do omelettes?'

Saul stared at her in outrage. He couldn't believe she was so plebeian. 'Look, Rowan, you've come half way across the world, you're experiencing a whole new culture! Why in God's name do you want an omelette?'

'Because I'm hungry!' she flared. 'Next time I come abroad I'm bringing a crate of baked beans as well as the samples, I don't see why I have to starve. I hate raw fish. I can't bear pickled octopus. And I don't care how pretty the vegetables are, if they don't taste nice I don't want to eat them!'

She fell silent, hopelessly woebegone. After a moment Saul sighed, delved into his pocket and brought out a chocolate bar. Rowan fell on it, almost gibbering with relief. She didn't stop until she had licked every last crumb off the silver paper. 'You're a saint,' she murmured to Saul. 'How many did you bring?'

'I bought two dozen this morning. Will that last you three days?'

She nodded. 'I should think so. You know, I think I'm human again. I'm not open to reason when I'm hungry.'

'So I noticed.'

After a while she said, 'Did you buy anything else this morning?'

'Like what?' He was watching her with an expression she had learned to recognise, he used it when selling. It welcomed and encouraged, but gave no clue as to his own thoughts.

'If you've only booked one room,' she said doubtfully, 'then really don't you think we ought – don't you think you ought – I'm not on the pill,' she finished bravely.

He cleared his throat. She realised he was actually rather embarrassed. 'That's all right,' he said brusquely. 'I'll take care of it.'

'I don't want anything that needs taking care of,' snapped Rowan. 'That's the whole point!' Their eyes met. Suddenly they were convulsed with laughter.

The Ryokan was set deep in the country. When they drew up in their car, wondering if they had taken a wrong turning because they could see no building, two men appeared, bowed, and ushered them towards a path. The trees, just starting to bud, stood in gentle symmetry. 'Where's the hotel?' asked Rowan.

'We must walk to it,' said Saul. 'They'll bring the luggage.'

He took her hand. Together they strolled down the path, and there was the sound of water and birds singing. It was rather cold. As they rounded a bend they saw before them a long low building, in the ancient style, with a heavily gabled roof that dipped at the eaves. Before it was a small pool and as Rowan passed she saw that it was filled with gleaming golden fish.

'Remember,' said Saul softly, 'we're entering yesterday.'

A woman in a kimono was waiting for them. Silent, but bowing and smiling, she motioned to their feet. 'Slippers,' said Saul. They stepped out of their footwear and the woman covered her mouth in giggling amazement at their huge European shoes. They each put on silken slippers. Rowan's were embroidered with birds. Still silent except for giggles the hostess slid aside a paper door and went through. Saul and Rowan padded after her.

'This is weird,' said Rowan softly. Outside they could hear the water gently falling.

'It's superb,' said Saul. 'What next, do you think?'

'Don't you know?'

He shook his head. 'I've never been to one of these either.'

Their hostess stopped at another sliding paper door and stood aside to let them pass through. They were in a lobby, the floor covered in matting. Another door stood open showing a step up to the bare interior of a tatami-covered room. The only furniture was cushions and a low table. A shelf at floor level carried a vase with a single spray of flowers. As Rowan stood there, the woman fluttering about, she had the feeling that they had stepped through a door and might not be able to step back.

Left to themselves they began to relax. There were cotton robes, yukata, which were to be worn whilst in the Ryokan, and over them a thicker gown. When Rowan peered through the shutter she could see one or two Japanese men strolling around the garden dressed in the same way. She took up her robes and looked for the bathroom.

'Saul,' she said dubiously. 'Come and look at this.'

There was no bathroom. Instead there was a cubicle and in it a ceramic bowl, set in the floor. A pair of slippers stood to one side, and there was even a flower arrangement.

'Where do we wash?' asked Rowan.

'Not in there,' said Saul. 'Do you want a bath?'

'Well – yes,' she said dubiously. She wished she could enjoy this as much as Saul appeared to. The strangeness of everything upset her slightly, she felt she could not get her bearings, and added to which the place was not warm. Draughts whistled under the doors and rattled the paper walls.

They found the bathroom down the hall, a large tiled room with taps and little wooden seats, a huge steaming tub of water in the centre. Saul's face became unreadable.

'Well?' said Rowan. 'Is this it?'

'Looks like it,' said Saul. 'But it's communal. Don't worry, I think this is the women's one.'

'I'll lock the door,' said Rowan. 'I won't be long.'

'Er, what I mean is – ' explained Saul '– everybody uses it – together.'

Rowan gaped. 'At the same time?'

'Well, I think so. It's my first time too, you know.'

Again they started to laugh. They were blundering about this stylized oriental world like a couple of elephants. A little voice broke in on them. 'Please excuse. This is not gentlemen's washplace.'

They turned to see a diminutive Japanese lady, her greying hair drawn back into a bun and spectacles on her button nose. She bowed, and automatically Rowan bowed, and while she was so doing Saul backed out of the room. 'Saul!' squeaked Rowan in a panic.

The Japanese lady advanced on her. 'I help you,' she said determinedly. 'I show you the Japanese way.'

When Rowan at last staggered back to their room she could say nothing for some minutes. She was wearing her robes and sank down on to the cushions in a flurry of fabric. 'Have some sake,' said Saul, holding out a tiny ceramic cup. 'It's hot.'

'I don't need any more heat,' said Rowan. 'She boiled me!'

'The water is hotter in Japan,' he agreed. 'You'd think it would affect fertility or something. I forgot to tell you, you're not supposed to wash in the bath, you do that before you get in.'

Rowan sniffed. 'Actually, I found out the hard way. That woman made me undress and took a scrubbing brush to me. Then she poured hot water all over me and made me get into boiling water in the bath. And she wouldn't let me get out!

After a while I lost all feeling, I think my toenails are going to drop off. By the way, she thinks we're on honeymoon.'

Saul settled down beside her. He sipped the sake and then passed her the cup. It was quite pleasant, she decided. In fact, now that she had bathed, it was all quite pleasant. The sound of water gurgling outside, the slow, formal functioning of the place, the austerity of their spotless room. With so little to distract her she found her attention focusing alarmingly on Saul. His legs were brown and covered in thick, golden hair. She could see the inside of one thigh, the muscles like ropes beneath the skin. She sipped some more sake and let out her breath in a long, wanting sigh.

Saul reached out and took the cup away from her. 'Let's put out the bedding,' he said softly.

'Suppose someone comes?' she whispered back. 'Someone might hear us.'

He took hold of her hand, pulling her gently to her feet. 'Let them hear. I agree with the Japanese lady. We're on honeymoon.'

She didn't know what to do. The heat of the bath clung to her and fused with an inner heat, her breasts felt swollen. Fluid seemed to have drained into her groin, the folds of tender flesh at the entrance to her body were heavy and engorged. Saul was laying out the bedding, unfolding it into a smooth and wrinkle-free couch. An embroidered white quilt was spread on the top. 'Will I bleed?' she asked.

He straightened and turned. 'I don't know. You look so young in that robe thing, you hardly seem old enough.'

'Then I'll take it off.' She slipped her arms out of the robe and let it fall to the floor. Saul's face became set.

'You're lovely,' he said throatily. 'Like white marble.'

'Let me see you,' whispered Rowan. Her hands fluttered above her pubic hair, she wanted to hide herself but also show him what was there. She wished she was drunk.

Saul took off his robe. Before he let it fall to the floor he held it in front of his genitals. 'It's such an ugly, brutal thing,

I can't bear to hurt you with it.'

'I want to see,' said Rowan. He let the robe fall. She stared at him, at first unable to believe that his body, so brown and firm and muscled, should come to its focus in that thing. It was blind, and wet, and thrusting. Saul would take care of her, that thing would not.

She turned away, covering herself with her hands, and he came up behind her and put his arms round her. She could feel it against her back, even now pulsing and thrusting. 'Don't be afraid, there's no need, I promise. Let me touch you, please, please!' He was kneeling, turning her towards him, burying his face in her belly, in the rough hair at its base. Disgust rose in her, it was appalling, horrible!

But, like an express train, a feeling surfaced from her primitive soul. It coursed through the fluid in her belly, it set her legs trembling so she could do no other than part them. His mouth sucked at her folds, for long, endless, but so short seconds. Rowan arched herself back from him, her thin fingers clawing at his hair, arched herself till she should have cracked.

Suddenly Saul lifted his head. 'Get on the bed,' he said urgently. 'Hurry.' He was fumbling with plastic, trying to fit a sheath. Staggering, bewildered, Rowan pulled back the quilt and lay down. She was dizzied, disorientated. And he was desperate. He came to the bed and got straight on top of her, she couldn't believe the weight of him. The thing was nudging at her. 'Spread your legs wider,' he urged. 'Wider! God, but you're tight.'

It was hurting her, at first hardly at all and then as he powered it with his haunches, more and more. She let out a cry and he covered her mouth with his, her tongue thrashed against his. She clawed at his buttocks. A sudden, sharp agony as she split. She screamed into his mouth.

He became quite still inside her. Hot blood damped her pain, it was only sore now. Lifting, he said, 'All right?'

She couldn't speak. Gradually her long, slender legs

wrapped themselves around him and they rocked together, he striving to contain himself as instinctively he sought the long thrusts that would satisfy him. She wouldn't let go, he bucked and carried her with him, and suddenly he took hold of her knees and forced them down. The first hard stroke brought a cry but he was beyond caring. Seconds later he was finished.

The quiet of the Ryokan lapped about them once again. Water, the sound of birds. Rowan said softly, 'Nothing will ever be so wonderful again.'

'Don't pretend,' whispered Saul. 'Look at the blood!'

It was everywhere. Rowan rubbed her finger on the sheet and smeared the fluid on to Saul's lips. 'I wanted to bleed, for you. You can do what you like to me, I won't ever say no! I want to please you, and I don't know how, I want you to do that again and again, all the time!'

He fell on her, mouthing her shoulders, her little apple breasts, licking the sweat from her belly. She laughed, already aware of the insistent throbbing of her womb. Why hadn't she let him do this before, why hadn't she known? 'I do love you,' she whispered. 'I do love you so.'

Time passed, measured in sighs and tears and laughter. They played a game, there in the bare little room, exploring each other from tiptoe to crown of head, remarking and caressing each fold of skin. 'I shall never get over your feet,' said Saul, cradling them in his hands. 'You have the only beautiful feet in the world.'

'They're too big,' said Rowan lazily, lying back on the futon.

'Rubbish! They're just long. Everything about you is long, long and narrow. You make me feel like a raw, badly hewn statue.'

She reached up and put her arms around his shoulders. 'Poor you, poor you! A statue turned to stone. What shall I do to turn you back to flesh and blood, to let you know and enjoy the – pleasures – of life?' She ran a long-fingered hand up his thigh.

'That's doing quite well,' he commented. 'But not well enough. A kiss in the right place is what's needed.'

'Which is the right place?' asked Rowan.

He grinned and pulled her head down. 'You can only find that by experiment. Lots and lots of experiment!'

They lay entangled together, and never wished themselves apart.

On the last night, Rowan cried. There was no need to ask why, even the lady who brought the food knew why. She came with three perfect lilies and set them on the floor. 'They remind me of my father's funeral,' wept Rowan.

'You can't think of that here, you can't think anything unpleasant.' For the first time he seemed restless. He got up and wandered about the room, which was too small for such things. Suddenly he turned. 'What clothes have you got?'

'What do you mean? I've got lots of clothes.'

'I mean something special!' He went to the cupboard that housed their suitcases and rummaged through it. At once things spilled out on to the floor, spoiling the spartan symmetry of their clutterless room.

'It's all ended,' sighed Rowan. 'Even before we go.' She got up and extracted a silk dress from the suitcase. 'This is special. I bought it for Christmas, but Aspley Manor was so cold I didn't wear it.'

Saul looked at her sad face above the folds of silk. The dress was lovely, but to him she was lovelier. In the last days her face had lost its childlike look and in its place was a glow. He felt weak with love for her. He knew that if he didn't do it now he never would, but just go on and on, like a rootless plant, feeding on others. He so wanted her, he so wanted what she could give him. He needed walls, he needed purpose. He said, 'Wear your dress and marry me. We can get it done at the Embassy in Tokyo.'

She had known he was going to ask her but not now, not yet. She shook her head, choked with tears.

'Don't say no! You can't mean no!'

'I don't mean no!' she croaked. 'I mean yes. But I'm crying!'

They were glad to go in the end. They wanted to celebrate, to shout and tell the world what had happened, but in the Ryokan all was quiet and calm and inner tranquillity. Once in the hire car they sang sea shanties and recited dirty poems, and Saul said, 'Thank God we can drink something that isn't sake. I wonder how long it takes to get married?'

'Ages, I should think,' said Rowan. 'Whatever will Mother say?'

Saul grimaced. That was something he did not intend to think about.

Chapter Twenty

They asked a professional photographer to take pictures of the wedding. They loved every one of them, from the stiff, rather embarrassed officials who had so obviously been inveigled into posing, to the prints of Saul and Rowan themselves. The photographer had shot them from below, so she was all legs in a swirling silk dress and he was as tall as a house in his good dark suit. Their faces were almost distant, the faces of strangers, caught forever in a moment of joy.

Back in cold and windy England, sleeting with rain that caused a bad skid on the way back from the airport, it was hard to remember the exuberance. Saul said, 'I thought we'd go straight to Aspley Manor and tell them. Best to get it over with.'

She nodded wearily. A thought struck her. 'Where are we going to live? I know your flat's nearer to Bardsey's but I'm not sure I ought to be away from the mill. What do we do?'

He took his eyes off the road to grin at her and the Aston wagged its tail. Rowan gripped the seat nervously. 'Calm down, will you?' he said. 'We're not going to crash. Look, I've been thinking. I know we sort of assumed I'd be working at Bardsey's and you at Judge's, but when you think about it that isn't going to work. James won't stand it for an instant, nor should he. Too damned incestuous for words. Now, I don't want you to think I'm treading on your toes but I do feel the most sensible thing would be for me to come over to Judge's. There's no doubt that you need my selling skills, is there?'

'We can't afford a full-time salesman,' said Rowan incredulously. 'It's impossible!'

'Not if you and I work the same way. Right now you take what you need out of the business, and so would I. No fixed salaries, we're both sensible. We'd be partners, running it together, because don't forget James may have chained me up on sales but it's not my only skill, ducky. I know Bardsey's inside out. Think of all that experience I can bring to your very own door.'

Rowan felt bewildered. She hadn't considered any of this. 'It isn't the same sort of thing at all,' she said feebly. 'We might not work well together.'

He gave a slight shrug. 'Always a possibility. Not very likely, is it?' He reached over and put his arm round her and she snuggled up to him, for the moment shelving her doubts. Not for a second had she considered sharing Judge's. She felt as if someone had ambushed her and demanded the donation of some vital organ.

After a few moments she said, 'Where would we live then? At the mill?'

He nodded. 'Best all round really. My flat costs an absolute bomb and I'm hardly ever in it. What's more we could have odd women turning up there for months to come, blowing in from South America or somewhere and wanting to catch up on lost time. You'd be amazed the number of times two arrive together, must be something to do with the phases of the moon. In fact, it's quite possible I married you out of pure self-defence!'

'Have you had lots of women?'

He popped a kiss on to her head. 'Lots. But have I loved lots of women? Well, there it's just one. And I love her quite a lot.'

The anxieties that had crowded in on her since the airport seemed to recede a little. She loved Saul so very much, it was as if all her emotions were sensitised. If she woke in the night she lay looking at him as he slept, adoring the blunt curve of his nose and running her fingers over the stubble of his cheek. If he ignored her or she upset him then she was utterly miserable. For him to love her even a tenth as much seemed miraculous.

Thin snow covered the drive up to the Manor. The car left black tracks in it, which were covered again within minutes. 'We can't stay long,' said Rowan. 'We'll be stuck for the night.'

He hugged her. 'Don't be scared.'

'I'm not scared of James!' she said in crisp amazement. Saul laughed.

Diana opened the door herself. With the lights behind her, and warmth spilling out of the door into the open air, she looked the essence of womanly fertility. Pregnancy softened her, blurring the outline of breast and belly, high forehead and arched nose. She was wearing a dress of soft green velvet and when she saw them she put her hand to the lace at her throat. 'Rowan darling! And Saul! Did you meet on the way here?'

Saul took Rowan's hand and stepped inside. 'Not really. More on the way out. We've been to Japan together.'

There was a slight pause before Diana closed the door with a definite click. 'Good heavens,' she said thinly. 'How interesting for you both. Won't you come through? James has a cold and is home this afternoon.' Rowan went willy nilly into the drawing room. She wished Saul would not hold her hand, it embarrassed her, it lacked dignity. 'Is Sally all right?' she asked tensely. 'She wasn't any trouble?'

'Darling, you know she was,' said Diana. 'It's all right, she's upstairs playing records or something. And I have the feeling that you are about to be just as troublesome. Aren't you, Rowan? James dear – ' She pushed through the heavy oak door. A fire was blazing and a big wing chair was pulled up to it. 'James, we have Rowan and Saul to see us. They've been away together.'

There was a sneeze. A muffled voice said, 'Oh my God!'

James peered round the edge of the chair like a tortoise looking out of its shell. His carrot hair was on end, and was nearly matched for colour by his nostrils. Clearly he had a terrible cold. 'As if I don't feel ill enough,' he said morosely. 'I knew there was something going on, I told you as much, Diana. You're looking bloody pleased with yourself, Saul. How many more secrets have you handed over in pillow talk? I suppose you took her to Japan?'

'He didn't take me anywhere,' said Rowan, dishonestly. 'I went of my own accord.'

'That sounds like the wrong half of a music hall joke,' said Saul. He grinned at James cockily, as if for once and at long last, he had the advantage.

It rattled James. 'I couldn't give a damn about your comings and goings,' he said nastily. 'Good God, Saul, it wasn't supposed to be a pleasure cruise! Is it too much to ask if you did any business?'

Saul moved to sit down on the arm of the sofa. He pulled Rowan with him, and kept her against his leg. The moment was one to savour. 'We got an awful lot done over there actually,' he said. 'Lots of orders, for Bardsey's and Judge's. And Rowan and I got married.'

Into the silence, Diana said, 'I knew she'd done something stupid. Rowan, how could you? You're barely nineteen years of age! Thank God for divorce.'

James sneezed again. He took his time blowing his nose, letting everyone worry about what he was going to say. 'I imagine you've thought of the implications for Bardsey's,' he said at last.

Saul grimaced. 'You could say that. I think that at long last you are going to have to manage without me. I had intended moving on to another company, but we've talked and the best thing is if Rowan and I run Judge's together.'

James sniffed. 'What a very convenient move for you. Do you mind being married for your business potential, Rowan?'

She ducked her head but Saul said sharply, 'Don't be so

bloody silly! Deny it as you might, James, I have acquired some few skills at Bardsey's. I can do a lot for Judge's and you're going to find it very much harder to replace me than you think.'

'I'm calling in the loan on your flat,' declared James triumphantly.

Rowan glanced at Saul, she had not known anything about this. But he only said, 'I thought you might. Put your mind at rest, we're setting up house at Judge's.'

'If you expect that firm to keep you in the manner to which you're accustomed, you'll find they can just about let you have a push-button biro!'

Rowan pulled away from Saul and went to sit down. 'Please don't squabble,' she said wearily. 'There isn't any point.'

'You realise I could still sell Andy and Sally's shares to James?' snapped Diana. She handed round glasses, adding, 'It's whisky. We need more notice for champagne.'

'I'm sure you won't sell,' said Rowan anxiously. 'Please, Mother.'

'Oh, she's a dear little girl when she wants her own way,' said James. 'I swear you don't know what you're taking on, Saul. She's a termagent.'

Diana ignored him. 'I won't sell yet, Rowan, that's all I can promise. I'll have to see how things go. When I've had the baby and things have settled down, we can talk about it.'

Rowan knew it would have to do. She felt rushed and unprepared; all she had volunteered for was marriage, not to change her entire way of life. But if having Saul meant doing just that, she would do it gladly. All the same, she felt the shifting sands of uncertainty.

Diana went to the drinks cabinet and refilled her glass, saying, 'Don't tell me not to drink, James, I need it, we all need it. You hardly know this man, Rowan! Why on earth couldn't you wait until you came home? You're not pregnant, are you?'

'No! No, I'm not.'

Saul said, 'Look, you're upsetting her. You might at least try and be pleased. You and I at least can be friends, can't we, Diana?'

'What else?' said Diana ironically.

Rowan got up and went out, she could not stand a minute more. The house was cold. Between the pockets of warmth, chill air hung lifelessly. She found Sally upstairs, crouched over an electric fire. She was dropping cotton on to the element and watching it flare.

'You'll electrocute yourself,' said Rowan.

Sally spun round. 'Rowan! At last! Why didn't you ring or something? It's been terrible here, purgatory!'

Rowan sat on the bed. 'I couldn't ring, I was in Japan. Sally, I've got married. To Saul.'

Sally gaped. 'You mean – Saul Barton? His brother?'

'Well, half-brother. Yes. We got married in Japan. They're being so odd about it downstairs, Mother especially.'

Sally turned back to the fire. 'Well, what do you expect? So I've got to stay here, have I?'

'I – I don't know. We haven't discussed it. We'll work something out and it'll be better, really it will!' Even to herself it sounded feeble.

A smile struggled on to Sally's face, but soon died. 'Will it? I hope you'll be happy, Ro, I do really. I mean, he's very nice and things. Isn't he? I don't know him very well.'

'Neither do I,' said Rowan, and then clapped a hand over her mouth. 'Isn't that stupid! Of course I know him. He's so kind, he really is.'

Sally began to giggle, the high-pitched beginnings of hysteria. 'Don't, Sal, don't!' begged Rowan. 'Let's go and tell Andy. Is he in the music room? Please!' With a gasp Sally stopped. They went to tell Andy.

Andy took it better than anyone. 'Good idea, I should think,' he said dispassionately. 'He can help you with the business.'

'I didn't think I needed help,' said Rowan. 'At least – yes, I suppose he can do things.'

'You can be so hellish patronising,' remarked her brother. 'You should give the guy a chance. By the way, do you want to hear my new piece? You can tell me if I've improved, you haven't heard me for a bit.'

Rowan shook her head. 'Not today. I'm a bit jet-lagged. I'll go and have a drink.'

'Me, too,' said Sally.

'They're not letting you drink, are they?' asked Rowan anxiously. 'You know how bad it is for you.'

'She can't stop me and neither can you,' said Sally, and there was an edge to her, a rock on which Rowan had foundered before. It was no use crossing Sally when she was in this mood.

Andy caught her arm as she went out, holding her back after Sally had gone. 'She's bound to be upset, Ro,' he murmured. 'I mean, Mum's got him, I've got my music and all of a sudden you've got this bloke. Leaves Sally a bit on her own.'

'And what do you suggest I do about it?' said Rowan tightly. 'There's not only me that has to look after everyone. And anyway I don't know how.'

Andy's bow swung idly between his fingers, it was as if he wasn't involved in all this, as if he was merely observing. 'No one else can do it,' he commented, feeling no breath of criticism.

When Rowan went downstairs, Sally wasn't there. James and Saul were drinking hard while Diana paced the room, turning her wedding ring over and over on her finger.

'There you are, Rowan!' she exclaimed. 'Are you going to stay? It's snowing heavily.'

'I don't know,' said Rowan. 'Saul, what are we going to do about Sally?'

He looked blank. 'What am I supposed to do? Give her some camels and donate her to the owner of some Asian takeaway?'

Diana said crisply, 'The point is that Sally lives with Rowan. She hates being here, she behaves terribly and causes nothing but trouble. I don't want to wish her on you two, I know how important it is to have privacy when you're first married – '

'All that screwing in front of the fire,' said James wistfully. 'My God, Diana, if they do stay tonight we'll be kept awake till dawn by creaking bedsprings!'

Rowan blushed scarlet. Saul, quite unmoved, said: 'Let's have another, James, or are you getting even stingier? Before I left they were saying you even haggle with the tarts.'

'I don't think we need to hear your vulgar tittletattle, Saul,' snarled Diana, and stormed out into the hall. Rowan followed.

Diana, arms folded over her stomach, was pacing up and down the marble flags, her expression one of irritation bordering on rage. 'Mother – ' begged Rowan.

'What?' snapped Diana.

'Mother, you're not letting Sally drink, are you?'

'I have as little control over Sally as over you it seems.' She turned on the girl, saying desperately, 'Oh God, Rowan, how do things get so tangled? What on earth possessed you to marry him?'

Taken aback, Rowan stammered, 'But I thought – you like him. You said so. You told me he was nice.'

'Did I? Well... we'll just have to see, won't we? But you're far, far too young and I never thought you'd be the one to rush off and do something like this! You know nothing about men.'

Sensing something, Rowan said slowly, 'What should I know?'

Diana said breathlessly, 'Nothing, everything! What if I told you James had been going with – women. Paying for it. I mean, what if I told you that? Even Saul, he won't be faithful to you. He could go off with a married woman or anything, even just once.'

Rowan watched her mother's white, tense face. She felt an obligation, however unwelcome, to try and comfort. 'I think James loves you, Mother,' she murmured. 'He's given up an awful lot for you, his son and everything.'

The words took a little time to make an impression. Then, stiffly, Diana smiled. 'Yes. So he has. And you're going to be wonderfully happy, aren't you, my darling? Next time you come we'll have champagne.'

The drive to the mill cottage was cold and slow, the snow falling in soft, handkerchief sized lumps against the windscreen. Rowan had insisted they left, she couldn't bear to spend the night there. Saul sat behind the wheel, despite all he had drunk. Rowan said, 'Would you mind terribly if Sally lived with us? I'd mind if it was your brother.'

'That would be James and we'd both mind.' He was silent, guiding the car smoothly through the snow. 'I'd rather we were on our own. It's a big change for us both, we're bound to make a mess of things to start with.'

Rowan nodded fiercely. 'Did I tell you I can't cook? I mean, I'm useless, I burn fish fingers.'

'Oh Christ! Well, I don't suppose it matters. I'll do the fish fingers, you put up the shelves. They threw me out of woodwork for incompetence.'

'I can't do that either,' sighed Rowan. 'Actually, I don't think there's anything I can do. Nothing at all.'

His hand came off the wheel and ran along her thigh. 'You can do the important things, love,' he murmured, and at that moment the car slid into the gutter. The back wheels churned uselessly. In the end Rowan had to drive while Saul got out and pushed. Snow heaped up under the low-slung bumpers, hampering every yard. 'Much more of this and I'll be glad to see it go,' said Saul, shivering. 'And I love this damned car.'

'Do you love it more than me?' asked Rowan, blowing on her blue fingers.

'Not at the moment, I don't. Look, it's only two hundred yards, let's leave it and walk.'

Obediently she got out. They took a case each and locked up the rest in the car. Then they started trudging. 'I wonder if one day you'll leave me in the snow and walk home,' she said.

'Only if you run out of petrol. You look frozen, lovey, and that house is going to be like an icebox. We should have stayed, you know.'

'Not with James leering.' She slipped and dropped the case. Saul picked it up and carried two, while she struggled along on her own.

'Cheer up,' he said shortly, and she tried to smile at him. At least he understood.

There were lights on in the cottage. 'Someone's there,' said Rowan in a shrill, nervous voice. 'Someone's in my house.'

Saul put down the cases, waving her quiet. He walked stealthily to the door, stood listening, and at the last moment threw it open. There was a cry and a scuffle. Rowan flew into the house. Saul and Joe Partridge were embarrassedly disentangling themselves from the wreckage of her standard lamp. The fire was lit and the little room was warm.

'I – I wasn't expecting it to be you,' said Saul diffidently.

'Lucky you caught me by surprise,' said Joe. 'I mean, I'm handy.'

'I'm sure you are.' Saul picked up three of Joe's shirt buttons and handed them back to him.

Joe said, 'I've been looking after the place for you, Ro. Had to light the fire to stop pipes freezing, you shoulda thought. Can't leave a place empty in middle of winter, not without draining system.'

Rowan twisted her hands together. 'It looks lovely, Joe. Thanks.'

Joe stood looking at Saul, waiting for him to go. For a scant second Rowan considered fleeing herself, running out into the snow and ending these dreadful interviews. The silence lengthened.

'What Rowan means,' said Saul awkwardly, 'is that she and I got married a few days ago. It was a bit unexpected. It was in Japan. And we couldn't have a nicer present than coming back to a warm house. Could we, Ro?'

'No – no,' said Rowan. She went to the fire and rubbed her hands together, not daring to look Joe in the eye. He stared at her, a sad disbelieving gaze. 'We only made up our minds out there,' Rowan burbled. 'We didn't want to wait.'

'You could've written,' said Joe. 'I mean, Ro – you make me feel a right plonker. You're not up the spout, are you?'

'My mother said that too,' said Rowan. 'But I'm not. Saul, there's some sherry in the kitchen, I think.'

'Cupboard by the stove,' said Joe glumly. 'But I'll be off, Ro. This is no place for me, not now.'

He pushed out through the door into the snowy yard, and Rowan had to pick up his jacket and rush after him. The wind stung her face, it might have been that making her eyes water. 'I'm sorry, Joe,' she murmured, pushing the jacket at him. Inexplicably, she added, 'I didn't mean it!'

'I hope you know what you do mean, Ro,' he replied. 'I hope you know what you done.'

She went back into the house. Saul was watching her. 'I didn't think he'd be so upset,' she said mournfully. 'He looked as if I'd slapped him.'

He tipped her chin up and kissed her. 'Can't be helped, love. A woman your age can't have more than one husband at a time, particularly if she can't cook. Have some sherry, I'm off for fish and chips.'

When he came back she was sleepy from warmth and hunger. The smell of food revived her. They sat before the fire and devoured the fish and chips from the paper.

'I always lose pounds of weight on a trip to Japan,' complained Saul. 'And in the States I pile it on. In France the food's good but all that wine gives me the runs and I come back needing milk and Farley's rusks, and in India it's not whether you got a bad gut but whether or not you needed hospitalising for it.'

'I like it best at home,' said Rowan comfortably.

'Coward. Give me somewhere else every time, or at least a large part of the time. Home in large doses is just bloody boring: no revolutions, no weird food, no nutters trying to jump out of the aeroplane.'

'That's what I like about it,' defended Rowan.

He turned his head to give her a deep and lingering kiss. 'My darling, we are totally incompatible.'

They slid together down on to the rug. Rowan said, 'I hate to do this. James knows we're doing it.'

'Bollocks. Oh, Rowan, if there was another plate of fish and chips I'd eat it, but failing that I'll feast on you – '

There was a knock on the door. Saul said, 'If it's Joe Partridge, I'll kill him.'

'Don't you dare touch him,' said Rowan hastily. 'He's got a conviction for savaging someone on the rugby field. They had to gather up pieces to send to hospital.'

Hastily zipping up, Saul went to the door. 'Now look here – ' he began. Then he stood there, absolutely silent. Rowan crept nervously up behind him, peering round to see who it was. Standing dismally in the snow, her bag in her hand and her face blotched with cold and tears, was Sally.

Chapter Twenty-One

Snow fell heavily during the night and by morning the mill yard was a white carpet, only pocked with the tracks of birds. The stone buildings looked magical, almost weightless. Here and there a drift of snow hung down from the gutters, like a joke, like a tipped hat on a drunk. Rowan stepped back from the window.

Saul was still fast asleep, but with new orders to set in train and the mill running itself all the time she was away, she couldn't bear to waste time sleeping. She dressed very quietly, and wondered if from now on she and Saul would have to do everything quietly. Last night they had made love as silently as criminals, in case Sally heard them through the wall. It wasn't fair, she thought miserably, it just wasn't fair.

As a gesture to Saul, and in some measure Sally who had hitch-hiked from the Manor and arrived frozen solid, Rowan lit the fire. The place smelled of fish and chips, a delectable scent last night and revolting this morning. The air freshener had run out. Someone would have to do some shopping, and it ought to be Sally, to make up for all the upset she was causing.

Stamping across to the mill, Rowan felt mean. It wasn't Sally's fault. As a little girl she had been adored and rather spoiled, because she was so pretty and bubbly and fun. Overnight someone had switched off the sunshine. Nowadays everyone thought she was a nuisance.

Rowan had forgotten to put on her boots and by the time she reached the weaving shed her shoes were full of snow. Ignoring the sensation she went rapidly round the looms.

One was standing idle, not set up. Did that mean they had finished the run of black or was there a problem? She went sniffing about the burling and mending department, checking the rolls. It looked as if the black was done, with two weeks in hand. They might be able to fill in with a few sample runs, or do a spec order on the misty blue tweed. She had a feeling that was going to sell really well. She must ask Mr. Suzman to make her a cape with purple frogging...

Her feet left wet prints on the way through to the dye-house. The little spark of optimism within her faded and died. During the night the snow had drifted in through the cracked tiles and skylights. It lay in pristine heaps amidst the squalor. Puddles of dye had leaked out of the battered vats and frozen on the floor, no two puddles the same colour. The dying took so long, it was so hard to get a match. If they didn't modernise, and they couldn't afford to modernise, what would they do?

'Hello, Miss Rowan. You're in early.'

It was the boiler-man. Wasting no time in pleasantries, she said, 'Will you look at this mess? How am I ever going to afford to make it better?'

He tramped through on his way to stoke the boiler. 'Won't seem so cruel when t'snow's cleared away. 'Sides, never thought we'd last this long so you haven't done so bad, lass, never fear.'

Her feet were freezing. Wrapping her arms around herself, she scurried back to the house. Saul was sipping tea. 'Made some for you,' he said. 'Went out and found the milkman, got bread and eggs as well. I was going to do egg on toast.'

Rowan eyed him. 'Do you think I ought to do that? I mean – '

Saul said, 'I don't think poaching an egg is going to make my balls fall off. If watching me makes you grow a beard, then all right, you do it.'

She tilted her head to one side. 'Well, who *is* going to do it? And the shopping and the cleaning and everything. Somebody's got to.'

Saul went into the kitchen and found a saucepan, sloshed some water into it and put it on the gas. Then he cut two doorsteps of bread and shoved them under the grill. 'Having lived alone for a great many years, there are a few things I can cook,' he said cheerfully. 'But I've been thinking. This is a ghastly house, needs pulling down if anything. God knows how you've escaped electrocution, the wiring's lethal. Let's move, get a flat somewhere, a big flat. Then we might at least have a bit of privacy, and if we get a housekeeper we might have some comfort as well.'

'A housekeeper?' Rowan was almost dumbfounded. 'I can't afford that! I can't afford anything! No!'

He waved a knife under her nose. 'Don't get hysterical, love! You're a working woman, you've got to have help. A cleaner then. A new flat and a cleaner.'

She swallowed. 'But this is so convenient. So close to the mill.'

'And so bloody, bloody uncomfortable.'

For a moment she saw it with his eyes. Familiarity had blinded her to the cottage's inherent nastiness, the tiny rooms, the damp, the miserably mean thinness of doors and walls and skirtings. Seventy years ago someone had built it on the cheap and it showed. 'I suppose we could get a mortgage,' she said doubtfully.

'Course we could. I'll ask around, find somewhere.'

She watched him anxiously, nibbling her lip. He wanted to spend money. He wanted to spend *her* money. All at once she was back to the time when she had to beg for money for food. She remembered the panic of it, the feeling of total helplessness. She ate her breakfast, grateful for every mouthful, saying not a word.

They went over to the mill together. As soon as all the workers had arrived she called a meeting in the canteen and introduced Saul to them. He made an attractive little speech about Judge's being a family firm, complimenting Rowan on her achievements thus far. He said they were going to expand into many overseas markets. He said that he and Rowan were going to share responsibility, that he was only too glad to relieve her of some of her heavy burden. Afterwards they went back to Rowan's office.

'Had I better come in here?' asked Saul. 'It could take another desk.'

She hardly seemed to be listening. 'What? Oh yes, fine. Look, use mine for the time being, I've got things to see to in the mill.'

'I'll come,' he said quickly. 'I've got to get the feel of things.'

But Rowan hesitated. 'Look, it's a busy day, I've been away so long. Why don't you look at the post and sort out some selling appointments? You can have my desk. Otherwise we'll both want to use it together.'

He thought of insisting. Years of selling had attuned him to the put-off and he knew at once that Rowan was feeling threatened. Instinctively, he backed off. 'OK, I'll get on here. I know you'll want to talk to everyone on your own. We'll take it gently, I won't try and get involved in everything right away.'

She beamed at him, and rushed over to kiss him. 'I knew you'd understand.'

When she'd gone he sat down in her chair, put his feet on her desk and started reading the mail. There was nothing of great interest and much that was very boring. He put the fire on, hooked the telephone towards him and started ringing round his cronies, having a chat about life and spreading the word about his marriage and his move. After a long time, when Rowan had still not returned, he sauntered across to the house, yelled at a still slumbering Sally to get up and rustled up some lunch.

Rowan appeared at twelve-thirty. 'You left the fire on in my office,' she said at once.

'What of it?' As far as Saul was concerned, it was a cold day and the fire needed to be on.

'Rowan never leaves fires or lights burning,' said Sally. 'She's paranoid.'

'I don't believe that for a minute,' said Saul. But Rowan said, 'I have to watch the bills you know! People just don't think. I mean, if you knew how much one light can cost – it isn't as if it takes much trouble, every penny saved is just so important – ' She trailed into silence. Saul was staring at her as if she had gone bonkers.

'I told you, she's a terrible Scrooge,' declared Sally, by her very presence inhibiting any sensible discussion. Kicking her chair like a child, she went on, 'Mother said to ask what you wanted for a wedding present. James said you could have anything except a new loom.'

'Right then, I'll have a card,' snapped Rowan. She sank her hands into her pockets and spent a pleasant minute blaming James for everything.

Saul went to the fridge and poured himself a glass of milk. 'Tell him we don't need his handouts.'

'I wish it was true,' said Rowan morosely. 'He never gives anything without making you want to throw it back at him. You think he does it on purpose, but thinking it makes you feel horribly ungrateful.'

'At least he's giving you a present,' said Sally. 'I think he quite likes you actually. He thinks you're tough.'

Rowan sniffed expressively.

In the afternoon she let Saul look through the sales ledger, and when he suggested one or two improvements she listened wide-eyed and then forgot about them. The next day, she was in at half-past seven and when he strolled up at around nine she managed to sidetrack him into an unnecessary and unimportant task. She seemed to be rushing around hectically, trying not to notice he was there. It was infuriating and hard to tackle: in the mill they could be overheard and at home there was Sally. Besides, everyone he spoke to seemed to assume he had married Rowan to get in at Judge's and he suspected that she was hearing the same thing. Denials got him nowhere, and anyway, there was an element of truth in it. Why else had he married her so quickly? He would have married her if she had had nothing, of that he was sure, but the haste? He had wanted out of Bardsey's and in at Judge's, because it was right for Rowan as well as himself. And because he had thought that, and because she might now be thinking it, he had to tread carefully.

Saul took her out for a drink in the evening. The snow was almost gone and they drove across dark moors, with sheep leaping out into the headlights and owls swooping low. For some reason the owls moved to the open spaces in winter, although to human eyes there was no shelter, nothing. But on winter nights they could be heard, hunting the heather, calling to each other.

The little pub was warm, smelling of beer and woodsmoke. He bought her a gin and tonic, a double whisky for himself, and said: 'Are you sorry we agreed to work together?'

'No. No, of course not.' She opened her eyes wide in pretended innocence.

Saul said, 'We can stop if you want. I'll look for a job somewhere else and you can keep playing solitaire. Do you want that?'

She swallowed visibly. 'Of course I don't. Everybody would think we'd fallen out over it, wouldn't they?'

'They'd be right.'

She clinked the ice in her drink, her face closed and defensive.

Saul said, 'You're going to have to let me have a piece of the action, Rowan. You're not playing fair.'

Still she said nothing. 'Look,' he said, 'you can't do everything yourself. I know you want to but it's physically impossible. If the firm's going to grow, you have to have help. I can help you. Between us, we can put Judge's on the map!'

The ice clinked again. At last she said, 'I didn't think you wanted Judge's. I thought you wanted me.'

'Oh Christ! I knew that was it.'

He downed his Scotch and went to the bar for another. 'Look,' he said, returning, 'if I'd wanted to marry for money I've had a dozen chances over the last few years. I married you, because you're you. I would have married you if you didn't have a bean. And Judge's isn't the be-all and end-all you think it is, sweetie! It's a little, run-down firm trying to swim in rough seas. And I can help. I'm a bloody good swimmer.'

Her face twisted. 'Everybody thinks I've been stupid.'

'Why do you care what they think? I don't. They don't count, all those people. We're the ones that matter. I love you, Rowan.'

She smiled tearfully. 'And I love you, too. I know I've been a beast, I will try harder, I promise.'

He popped a kiss on her nose. 'Then let's get things straight. I want my name on the cheques, so I can get the things I need. One of those things is a decent desk, and I need it right away.'

'You can use mine,' said Rowan fearfully. 'You don't need a new one!'

'Oh yes I do. And I always give my mother some money each month, otherwise she can't manage. That's a commitment I always made out of my salary but now of course Judge's has to see to it. Will you put my name on the cheques, Rowan?'

She ducked her head and would not look at him. He clasped his hair and said forcefully, 'Rowan, what are you afraid of? I'm not going to bankrupt you!'

'Aren't you?' She turned towards him and her great green eyes were brimming with tears. 'You don't understand! It isn't five minutes since I was so hard up there wasn't anything to eat and they were turning off the electricity! And you want a new desk and a standing order to your bloody mother and a new flat and a cleaner and God knows what else! We can't afford it, Saul.'

He drained his whisky and prepared to get another. 'I've looked at the books. It isn't can't, it's won't. You are hanging on to money as if your life depended on it. I know the firm needs capital, I know you want to get back to where you used to be, but for God's sake, you've got to live.'

He went to get more drinks, though Rowan had barely sipped hers. When he came back, she said, 'I know I'm being silly but I do so want to get everything in-house again, then we can really make it big. We'd worry James something cruel.'

Twirling his glass, Saul said, 'How about worrying James a bit less and pleasing me a bit more?'

'But I do please you! I try to, really I do. Don't I?' She looked young and frightened and vulnerable. When she looked like that, he couldn't persist.

She gave in on the cheque book and the desk and the money for his mother. He went out and bought a beautiful new sofa, in dark red leather, so that they could at last sit down in the evenings without being impaled on springs, and on the same day bought three new typewriters and retired the firm's old ones. 'Can't send out letters looking like ransom demands,' he commented. 'I can't believe anyone would go on using a typewriter that long since lost the letter A.'

Rowan went to the bathroom and sat on the loo, trying to think things out. There was no privacy anywhere any more: Saul was in her office, Sally was in the house and confusion buzzed within her head. Yet she knew there was no real problem, only her own habits. She liked working on her own, she was used to it. Saul did not know how much it cost her to push even crumbs of responsibility his way. It seemed to her that unless she watched everything, all the time, the fabric of the mill would crumble.

Sally banged on the door and yelled, 'Rowan! Are you going to be all day?' and wearily Rowan got up. Sally's intermittent attendance at school nowadays verged on the occasional, but she left in a month's time and was promising to get a job. She was going to work as a beauty consultant in a Bradford store, wearing inch thick make-up on her flawless skin and advising ladies who certainly knew a great deal more about wrinkles than she did. Rowan stared at her own face in the bathroom mirror. No wrinkles, but a wide-eyed haunted look in her great green eyes. With her large bronze hoop ear-rings she looked almost Egyptian.

She went heavily downstairs and left the bathroom to Sally. Saul was sitting at the table, scanning the newspaper.

'I thought you were in the mill,' said Rowan nervously.

'I was. I wanted to talk to you, Rowan.'

'Oh.' It was another of those 'Why won't you involve me?' talks, she could tell. When he said crisply, 'Fashion fair next week, in Germany. I'll be going off on Sunday night, OK?' she blinked in surprise and said meekly, 'Oh, all right then. Fine.'

'Is that all you can say?' He got up and came across to her, taking her by the lapels of her jacket and shaking her gently. 'Don't you want to come? It could be like Japan, selling all day and screwing all night, one endless coupling – Rowan, I could eat you!'

She turned her face up to his and they kissed. He pushed her back against the table and slid his hands beneath her clothes to feel for her breasts.

'Really! Do excuse me,' said Sally. She flounced into the room and began banging about looking for a book. Saul and Rowan disentangled themselves.

'Don't you have any tact?' demanded Saul angrily. 'We wouldn't mind a little privacy once in a while.'

Sally picked up her book. 'I know you don't really want me,' she said, ducking her head.

'But darling, we do!' declared Rowan, lying in her teeth.

She couldn't bear to see Sally look so hurt and little girl. 'Don't we, Saul?'

He sighed gustily. 'Yes. Yes, we do. It's just – Sally, you can't just barge in on us whenever you feel like it!'

'I think you should do that sort of thing in the bedroom,' she said primly.

'We've got to move,' declared Saul. 'We'll get her a studio bedroom or something but we have to move!'

They retreated to the mill. Rowan said, 'I can't come to Germany, you know. There's masses of work on and I've got an appointment with the bank manager.'

'Shouldn't I be coming to that?' said Saul.

Rowan flushed. 'Oh, I hadn't thought. I know him so well you see, and – will it be all right if I tell you all about it afterwards?'

He shrugged. 'Looks like it will have to be.'

She knew she had offended him. That night she rushed out to the shops and bought some steak and some wine, she made a salad and put candles in bottles on the table. The steak was overcooked and tough, the candles smoked, and besides, a cosy dinner for two isn't the same when there are three of you. They went to bed at half-past nine. Saul said, 'I rang an estate agent chum this afternoon. There's a penthouse flat going, with a separate bit for granny. Super new block, doorman, everything.'

Rowan groaned but Saul put his arms around her, pulling her head into the hollow of his shoulder. She said, 'Perhaps I should ask Mother to have her.'

'Perhaps you should. But I've got an option on the flat anyway. We'll have a look when I get back, OK?'

'OK.' She stretched out her legs, putting her entire length in contact with him. The hairs on his chest were soft prickles against her breasts, she wanted him to love her. But instead he said, 'Why don't you ever talk to me?'

'But I do. We're talking now.'

'I mean in the mill. As soon as there's a problem you dash

off and deal with it, you don't even tell me when it's over.'

'They just seem like – my problems.'

'Don't you mean "our" problems?'

She nodded unhappily. 'Yes. I suppose I must mean that.'

Beneath the bedclothes their legs entwined. He seemed suddenly to want to dominate. He swung on top of her, his bulk crushing her fragility in a way that made her long for him to crush her almost to death. She let out a cry as he came into her, it was repeated with every hard thrust, but just as the pinpoint of feeling within her threatened to burst, there was a knock on the door. 'Are you all right, Rowan?' called Sally. 'You're making such a noise.'

'Go to hell, Sally,' yelled Saul, and climaxed, gasping.

Rowan chewed at her fists, caught between rage and frustration. 'And we forgot the bloody rubber,' hissed Saul.

She buried her face in his neck. 'I don't think it matters. I've got a pain, I think I'm starting my period.'

He ruffled her hair.

Three days later Saul departed on his German trip. Rowan was ashamed at herself for being so relieved. No more negotiating between Sally and Saul, trying to keep them both happy; no more guilt about the mill; no compulsion to keep the house neat and tidy, or to wash her hair every day of her period because it got so greasy. Reading the paper over a messy breakfast table one morning, she said to Sally, 'Are you going to be nicer when Saul comes back? You've been really horrid lately and it isn't fair, Saul's so kind to you.'

Sally stared from beneath a blonde and shaggy fringe. 'Men are never any use,' she said bitterly. 'Even Daddy left us, he didn't care about me or you or anyone. You think they'll stop you being lonely but they don't, it doesn't last. They only love you while they're getting the best.'

Rowan swallowed. 'Saul's not like that. Please, Sally, try and understand. One day you'll find someone to love you.'

She watched her sister's sullen little face. What was going on in there? Once Sally had been so simple to understand;

compared with herself and Andy she had been an open book. But, ever since their father's death the pages had wrinkled and curled until even her everyday actions held devious and unhappy meanings.

There was nothing more pleasant, reflected Rowan, than an interview with the bank manager when the accounts looked healthy. If she had not suffered those first, frightening encounters she would never have appreciated these cosy little chats.

'You're keeping staff costs well down I see,' said Mr. Blood happily. 'An awful lot of places are letting them race away.'

'I won't give a wage rise,' said Rowan. 'We're not out of the wood yet, not by a long way. I shall need at least a hundred and fifty thousand for my new carding machine.'

Mr. Blood tapped his lip with his finger. 'That doesn't look too unreasonable. We can lend that, I think. When could you let me have some projections, Rowan dear?'

For a brief, delectable second, she closed her eyes. She had started to lose hope of ever getting the machine. 'Tomorrow,' she said breathlessly. 'I shall have to look at absolutely all the machines, to make sure we have the best, but I know what it will cost and I know what it should do. Oh, Mr. Blood, I never thought I'd manage it!'

He beamed at her, inwardly congratulating himself on supporting her so well all this time. 'I always had faith in you, Rowan Judge.'

By the end of the week she had placed the order. She met Saul off the plane at Yeadon, still bubbling with excitement. He saw her running towards him across the marble floor, her burgundy skirt billowing out around her, and he dropped his case, spread wide his arms and hugged her.

'Did you miss me, sweet? I've been longing to get home. The wide world isn't nearly so much fun as it was.'

She slid her fingers up into his hair, by the feel of it

reminding herself of delicious hours when she explored every hair he possessed. 'I missed you so much, I never stopped working. That way I didn't have to think about it. Saul, I've got some wonderful news! I've bought the new card.'

She was conscious that somehow she had said the wrong thing. His arms fell away, he picked up his case and began striding towards the exit.

'Saul! Saul, what's the matter? Aren't you pleased for me?'

'What do you want me to say?'

'Well – it's our firm, you ought to be thrilled.'

He stopped then and faced her. '*Our* firm? Are you sure you think that, Rowan? Because you don't act as if it was anything except your own personal toy. And you never did learn to share your playthings, did you?' She was threatened by tears and in a choked voice said, 'I don't understand. I only said I'd bought the card, you knew I wanted to.'

'Just bought the first one that came along, did you?' He folded his arms, not bothering to lower his voice so that people yards away could hear what they were saying.

'I researched it, naturally, as well as I could.'

'What make is this card then?'

'German. They're all German, you ought to know that.'

'I do know that. Rowan – oh God, you must see! I've been in Germany all week. I could have bought direct, we could have gone for a forward contract on the currency, we could have arranged for someone to go across and learn how to work the bloody thing! Instead you buy from a middleman who showed you a few leaflets. You're not stupid, Rowan, you just didn't want me involved.'

'That isn't true!' She began to cry now, in earnest. How did things get so twisted? She had been having such fun talking to people and studying machines, it was the culmination of years of work and he wanted to take that away from her! She tried to explain. 'It was my work that bought it. Judge's means such a lot to me, it can't be the same for you!'

'If it did, you'd soon put a stop to it, wouldn't you, Rowan?' Wearily, he picked up his case and walked on.

All the way home she tried to make it up. He drove along, completely silent, while she burbled. At last he said, 'Do shut up, Rowan.'

She choked off in mid-sentence and sat making patterns in her flesh with her long nails. When they had driven for twenty minutes in total silence, she said, 'I bet you got lots of orders,' in a falsely cheerful voice.

'Quite a few, yes. Mostly short runs.'

Her head came up. 'We do have a minimum order, you know.'

'You might, I don't. Sprats to catch mackerels. You cancel one of them and I shall tear you limb from limb.'

'And you told me you were soft-hearted,' complained Rowan, trying to sweeten him.

'Marriage certainly shows you another side to people, doesn't it?' He shot her a glittering smile. This time Rowan shut up completely.

Chapter Twenty-Two

After dinner that night, Saul went out and didn't come back. Rowan sat up until three, four o'clock, waiting and waiting. The fire went out. The clock ticked loudly. Far away across town she heard a car engine but it went away again.

At last she crept upstairs and into bed. Suppose he was dead, suppose he had left her, suppose he was even now lying injured in some gutter? She felt lost and bewildered, because love had seemed so easy when it began and now was so terribly difficult. There seemed no way in which she could go through her days without trampling on Saul's feelings, not because she wanted to but because she knew nothing of the way he felt! Vast areas of him were unknown to her, and whereas once she had relished the voyage of discovery, now she was almost too timid to put a toe in the pond. Suppose he didn't love her any more?

Next morning when he had still not returned she dragged herself to the breakfast table, loathing Sally for being there and seeing her blotched and puffy face.

'Told you,' said Sally. 'Has he gone for good?'

'If he has, I'll blame you,' said Rowan viciously. 'You want to break us up.'

Sally got up and made coffee, then took some ice out of the fridge. 'You can't go to work looking like that. Try this.'

Rowan took the offering. Sally fluctuated between child and woman with dizzying speed.

She was in her office when Saul came back. She saw his car pull into the yard and when the familiar, tall, long-legged figure got out she thought she would die with joy. She stood at the window until he went into the house, then she flew downstairs and followed him. He was slumped in a chair, eyes closed, shirt unfastened, his tie loose around his neck.

'I thought – I didn't know where you were,' gasped Rowan. She had prepared a dozen speeches in the night for just this moment and had forgotten every one of them.

His eyes opened slightly, he looked at her and then closed them again. Almost hysterical, she screamed, 'Where were you then? At least you can tell me that?'

'Why don't you make some coffee?' said Saul wearily.

Nonplussed, she went and did so. He took the mug from her and sipped it, grimacing. 'Can't you tell me where you went?' she begged, hating herself and him for her subservience.

He shrugged. 'Around. I ended up at my mother's.'

'You could have rung me! I don't even know where she lives.'

He yawned, got up and prepared to go to bed. 'It never seemed to me that you were even remotely interested. But I'll take you to see her, if you want.'

'I do want,' said Rowan, nodding firmly. 'And Saul – I am sorry, I am truly, I didn't mean anything. I'll cancel the carding machine if you like.'

He seemed hardly to be listening. Wearily, not even looking at her, he trudged up to bed.

Because of the row, Rowan fiddled about, putting the superficial things right. They went to see his mother, Mrs. Howarth, a pale, insignificant woman who gave her fruit cake with too few currants. Despite the 'Mrs' she had never married, but at old man Bardsey's suggestion had adopted a new name and pretended widowhood. It was Saul who had thrown off the false surname, insisting on Barton, on his rights.

They were all glad when it was time to go. There was a natural timidity about the woman that Rowan found difficult; she could only liken the conversation to tempting a shy rabbit with a lettuce leaf. One sharp word or gesture and all confidence was gone.

Afterwards she said to Saul, 'There you are then. She seems very nice.'

'We didn't have to go,' said Saul irritably.

'Well, you said you wanted me to,' retorted Rowan. 'What else did you want?'

She stared at him uncomprehendingly. His eyes were so brown sometimes that she could not see into them, she felt excluded from him. Only the day before two men in the dye-house had behaved absolutely stupidly, mixing two lots of cloth and turning the whole lot bottle green, and no sooner had she heard about it than she had gone down and verbally slaughtered them. Then it had turned out Saul had dealt with the matter only that morning, and she hadn't given anyone time to tell her. Since she was the one who looked a fool, why was it he who was offended? Since it was she who had been made to share, why did he behave as if he was losing out? She didn't understand and she felt angry and bewildered.

A few days later, James telephoned. 'Hello, Rowan, it's me.'

'Which me is that?' she asked, knowing perfectly well.

'The me that sends you decent wedding presents. What was it now?'

'A silver coffee set. I'm thinking of flogging it.'

'You would, you mercenary bitch! Rowan, I want you to go and see your mother. I don't know why I have to remind you, but it seems she's spawned three ungrateful brats and I have to do these things. She's feeling very low, and that's not good for her or the baby. It means an awful lot to us.'

'I'm glad to hear you are capable of human feelings, James. 'Bye.'

'Wait! Don't hang up!' His voice cracked with urgency. She waited, because his call was about more than daughterly duty. 'I just wanted to tell you that I'm suing Saul for breach of contract,' he said jovially. 'He owes me at least a year's salary and I'm going to have a crack at getting him for the use of confidential information. That should be an absolute doddle, he's bound to be using what he picked up at Bardsey's. I thought you ought to know.'

'Thank you so much, James,' she said frostily. 'I hope I can do the same for you some day.'

'Well, I don't see why he should walk all over me. By the way, a word in your ear, Rowan. Keep him on his lead. He never did understand the principle of profit, thinks he can spend it first and make it later. Don't let him bankrupt you, love.'

Rowan slammed down the receiver. How dare he say that, on the very day she saw from the statement that Saul's expenses for the German trip were over £2,000? Most of it for small orders that would bring in little or no profit. A familiar, panicky sensation began in the pit of her stomach. She visualised a barren future, her firm crippled by interest charges, dealt a death-blow by a court case and its lifeblood finally drained by extravagance.

Saul came into the room, whistling between his teeth. She didn't dare say anything to him, not until she had calmed down. He watched her forcing her arms into her jacket. 'Where are you going? Is the building on fire or what?'

She picked up her bag and stood hovering, trying to decide what to tell him. 'James rang,' she said at last. 'He wants me to go and see Mother, she's a bit low.'

'Then why the rush?'

'Saul – James is going to sue you for breach of contract. He says he can get you for passing on company secrets.'

He threw back his head and gave a bellow of laughter. 'Well, wouldn't you know! The old bastard. Hang on a minute, let's have a think.' He wagged a finger at her. 'We'll say he fired me because of our marriage. He can't prove he didn't any more than we can he did, but it looks likely. And we'll claim Judge's and Bardsey's are industries so diverse they do not compete, and his sacking me was simply further evidence of his paranoia in that direction. You never know, I might get legal aid. I've got a big enough overdraft.'

'What overdraft?' She goggled at him. 'I didn't know you had one.'

'Good God, Ro, it's only five thousand quid! Bardsey's probably owe me that in back expenses claims. I ran it up because they never settled without a six month argument.' He saw the bleak look of panic in her eyes. 'You don't have to behave as if I've revealed a criminal past,' he said incredulously.

She blushed and picked up her handbag. 'I'm not behaving like anything, I'm going to see my mother.'

'All right. I suppose I should have told you. But I realised the fuss you'd make. Good God, you look sick if I buy three bottles of wine!'

'No I don't. Or at least, I don't mean to. Look, I don't want to talk about it.'

'Well, I do. We have got to talk about it, Rowan.'

'No! I'm going to see Mother.' He put out a hand to stop her but she struck it aside, she wouldn't look at him. He could have held her easily but he couldn't bring himself to clench his fist on that long thin arm. For some reason the sound of her feet running along the corridor filled him with pain and rage. For a minute he wanted to catch her and hit her, smash that closed, watchful look. As her car pulled jerkily out of the gate he went to the cupboard and poured himself a drink.

In the last stages of pregnancy, Diana was looking bloated, tired and old. She waddled through to the sitting room and fell into a chair. 'Don't ever get pregnant,' she told Rowan. 'It goes on forever and it's boring and painful and ugly. I see James looking at me sometimes, wondering where this elephant came from.'

'Did Dad look at you like that?' asked Rowan.

'I don't know. Possibly. I doubt it. I'm too old for all this, that's the trouble. You'll probably sail through without a murmur.'

Rowan grimaced. 'No thanks. How on earth could I manage? I've far too much to do.'

'And I have far too little,' said her mother.

They looked at each other. 'You've still got your music,' ventured Rowan.

'My ankles swell when I stand up. And James only wants to go out to nightclubs, and at the very least I owe this baby more than gin and cigar smoke. He goes without me quite a lot. I remember I was every bit as bored just before I had you, and then afterwards when you screamed twenty-three hours out of the twenty-four, I would have given anything for boredom.'

'Didn't you ever like me?' demanded Rowan. 'It doesn't sound like it.'

Diana laughed. 'My darling, if I hadn't adored you I would have wrung your neck. Did James ask you to come?'

'Yes,' admitted Rowan. 'But I would have anyway. He's trying to wreck us, you know.'

'From what I gather now that Saul is with you, he thinks you're trying to wreck him. Tit for tat, darling, you can't expect anything else. Can you tell me how it's going?'

Launched on her favourite theme, Rowan gave her mother a carefully expurgated account of progress. Almost two-thirds of their cloth was woven at the mill now, and the ancillary processes were steadily being gathered back under their own roof. They were getting a well deserved reputation for quality, colour and style.

'This is Judge's own,' she boasted, picking up her cloak. She had tossed it casually across the back of her chair, taking pleasure in the generous folds of burgundy cloth. 'Can you see, we've woven in a tiny black thread? It gives the whole thing depth.'

Diana reached out her hand, and even that was puffed up by pregnancy.

'It's lovely,' she said. 'Was that Saul's idea?'

'Good heavens, no! I mean – I'm sure he'd like to get involved but – it's all a bit difficult, really.'

Thoughtfully, Diana let the fabric fall. 'Well,' she said. 'Have you made a mistake?'

'No,' said Rowan quickly. 'We're just taking some time to adjust, that's all. I didn't think it through, I didn't – he seemed different in Japan. But we're both different, it wasn't real life.'

'And what's so awful about real life?'

'Nothing! But he wants to do things his way and he doesn't understand the mill. I don't understand him. I try so hard, I cook him lovely meals and he gets up half an hour later and makes scrambled egg. I can't seem to do anything right.'

Diana's lovely head tilted to one side. 'He must have realised he was marrying a tomboy! If he didn't, he should have. Darling, weren't you surprised when he wanted to marry you all of a sudden, didn't you suspect anything? I don't say it was all avarice but James wouldn't let him get control of Bardsey's, for good reasons I might add, and he saw his chance. God, that man!'

Rowan got up. 'It's no use talking to you, I know you hate him and you'll only tell James.'

'No I won't! And I don't hate him, not exactly – I don't know him. But, darling, you know how stubborn you can be! You'll dig your heels in just for the sake of it. As far as you're concerned there's one way to do a thing and everyone else is insane. If you want to be happy in marriage, you've got to learn to – to see the other person's point of view.'

'Have you learned that?' demanded Rowan. 'As I remember it, Dad always saw *your* point of view.'

'And I see James's,' said Diana. 'You don't want a lapdog, do you? I didn't.'

Rowan swung her cape around her shoulders. She felt a sudden and unexpected urge to hug her mother, to beg her always to be there. Diana was softened by pregnancy, she seemed vulnerable. Underneath her calm Rowan sensed that she was afraid, and fear of that sort was catching. At the door she asked jerkily, 'Will it be all right? The baby?'

Understanding at once, Diana nodded. 'I'm a little old, but it isn't the first. James has hired a great man to attend me. I expect it will hurt rather a lot, but that's all. They might even do a Caesarean, in which case I won't know anything at all about it.' She smiled, and on a rare impulse reached out and hugged her daughter. They clung briefly together and then parted in mutual embarrassment.

Driving home, Rowan was consumed with anxieties. She hunted about for one she could deal with, and thought of James's law-suit. Not stopping to analyse her motives, she drove into the car park of her firm of solicitors. They were a solid, unimaginative body of men who regarded Rowan with the fascination of bullocks teased by a butterfly, and as for her, just listening to legal jargon calmed her. It gave her the feeling that everything in life could be filed under a heading, if only you could decide which one.

It seemed that dismissed or not, Saul was almost certainly in breach of contract. They could well be liable for damages. 'Mr. James Barton can build a very fair case against him,' said the solicitor cordially. 'He could claim that he was justified in dismissing your husband, or that even if he did not dismiss him, he could well have done so. The Japan trip was somewhat risqué under the circumstances. I mean, escorting a competitor and then marrying her in the firm's time – '

Rowan stood up. 'Thank you,' she said crisply. 'I don't need moralising, I can assure you. I should like you to let me have a report of the worst possible case, and also the probable outcome. Get counsel's opinion if you must.'

'Well – yes,' he said doubtfully. She swirled her burgundy cape in his face and was gone.

As expected, the interview made her feel better. She had done something, and by so doing had stilled the gremlins that came out at night and nagged her with horrid possibilities. On the way home she stopped off and bought some fish, because Saul liked it and would be pleased.

To her surprise, when she got in Saul was in the bedroom, in his shirtsleeves, fiddling with his bow tie. 'Where on earth are we going?' she asked.

He grinned at her. 'Sorry, love, you're not included. Customer entertaining, this is. We're going gambling, he insists. There'll be a big order in it, I know him of old.'

'Is it a Bardsey customer? With this thing on with James, we'll have to tread carefully.'

In a dry voice, Saul said, 'I think I know my own business, thank you, Rowan.'

Something in his tone caught her on the raw. 'Talking of your business, I've been to see the solicitor,' she said. 'I think we'd better not pay off your overdraft just yet, a few debts will look much better in court.'

He looked bemused. 'What on earth are you talking about?'

'The court case, James suing you for breach of contract. I've had a long talk with the solicitor and I've decided – '

His expression silenced her. 'Just a minute. You have decided about *my* court case? *My* overdraft? *My* affairs?'

Discomfited, she said, 'Not quite like that, of course. But with James you can't afford to hang about, not if you want to win!'

'And you do, don't you, Rowan? It means more to you than anything I can do, anything I say, Sally, your mother, even God himself. Just so long as *you* keep on winning.'

Her eyes widened angrily. 'That's not fair! Who's going to take care of things if I don't? You don't understand the mill, you just don't! I never wanted you in it, it was never my idea! Can't you see that?'

In a deadly tone, he said, 'We agreed, Rowan. We talked about it and we agreed.'

'You talked and I went along with it. I knew it was a lousy idea.'

'But then every idea that isn't yours is lousy, isn't it, love? That's one of the other things I've learned about you.'

Alight with fury, she blazed at him. 'And what else have you learned, may I ask? Do tell me while we're on the subject.'

His smile glittered. He swept his arm to encompass the bedroom, almost obscured under Rowan's habitual clutter. 'Now that you ask, I wouldn't mind it if you put the odd piece of your clothing away now and then. I wouldn't mind if you cleaned the bath after you, or washed the odd dish, or even mastered the Hoover once in a while. I am bloody sick of living my life picking up after a slut!'

'You said we'd share the work,' she screeched in outrage.

'Who the sodding hell's sharing? When it comes to the house I do it, when it comes to the mill you do it. And I've got this funny foible, Rowan dear, when I get married I prefer it to be to a woman!'

Rowan picked up a cotton wool filled china bowl from the dressing table and hurled it at him. It smashed against the wall. They both stood in silence, as cold as before they were hot.

There was a knock on the door. 'Did somebody break something?' called Sally innocently.

Saul took a deep and shuddering breath. 'Yes, someone did. But don't worry, Sally, Rowan broke it so Rowan will clear it up. Actually she's going to clear up quite a few things, and with a bit of luck we might possibly rediscover the furniture!' He flung open the door, pushed Sally hard to one side and stormed out.

Once in the car he felt calmer. Why in God's name did she have to be so bloody butch? Fighting hard, all the time, elbowing him out of the way so that she could do it her way, have it her way, all the way. And it wasn't her, or at least it wasn't all of her. Inside, beneath the fear and the insecurity and the aggression, there was soft, yielding, feminine Rowan, who needed him. He was too close to her, he thought dismally. At a distance you could see through her toughness but close up her carapace repelled. Reaching down inside the pocket of the door he found a silver hip flask and expertly uncorked it. The liquor hit his throat like hot coals, and he gasped and drank again. He felt, more and more often, that he might just have made the biggest mistake of his life.

The gambling club was one he used to visit quite often. Fringed red lights hung low over the tables and men huddled round intently. Velvet curtains muffled all sound except the high pitched click of chips, the whir of the roulette wheel and the bored voice of the girl dealing vingt-et-un. She looked tired and thin; her low-cut black dress could have done with more filling. Thank God Rowan had the sense not to wear plunge necklines, he thought, instead cultivating skin-tight jersey dresses that showed up her nipples in the cold.

He was dining so he went through to the bar, at once ordering a double Scotch. His customer hadn't arrived as yet, so he spent the time scanning the crowd. As always in Bradford it was cosmopolitan; the croupiers Italian, two or three very tall, very loud Germans speaking accented English, and a sprinkling of Asians. The ethnics were inveterate gamblers given the chance which, as with all things pleasurable, was usually denied them. The vast majority were Moslems for whom it was forbidden to drink or gamble, but the men here were presumably stretching a point. If you spend your days working twelve-hour shifts in a factory, followed by a couple of hours at the mosque, was it any wonder you fancied blueing some money on a flutter? Yet they were nervous punters, risking little.

The customer still had not arrived so he finished his drink and went through to play roulette. He got the chips in twenties, which was unusual for him, he generally chanced a fiver here or there. On the first turn of the wheel his number came up.

The croupier shrugged and smiled, and a girl dealing Black Jack rippled the cards encouragingly. They didn't mind what he won as long as he stayed long enough to give most of it back. He turned to go back to the bar to get another drink. There, in front of him, unavoidable, was James.

'And hello to you,' said James. 'Winning, I see.'

'Just a flutter. I'm waiting for someone, we're dining. Fancy a drink?'

'I'll have a Scotch. Glad to meet you actually, I wanted to talk.'

They went back into the bar and James at once settled himself at a corner table. It was early, the place was thin of people. Saul ordered two doubles and sat down. In the pinkish glow of light James looked healthier than normal. He also looked remarkably cheerful. 'You're going to have to make her sell, you know.'

Saul laughed. 'Not a cat in hell's chance! She lives and breathes the sodding firm.'

'That's what I mean. If you want any sort of life, you'll have to make her get rid of it. Diana won't sell Andy or Sally's shares unless Rowan wants to quit, so you make her. It's not long before Andy's of age, so we can't waste time. I'll give you a bloody good price, you'll be able to start something new. Something you can handle without the little woman's guiding hand. I tell you, it's your only hope.'

'Are you saying I can't handle Judge's?' Saul dribbled water into his Scotch and downed it in one. He raised his finger to the waiter for another.

'She won't let you handle Judge's,' said James. 'I admit, I'm scared of her. She's too damned good, she could go places. I've heard the way she's treating you, like the lackey. My advice to you is get her pregnant and make her sell up.'

Saul chuckled again, this time with real amusement. He looked at James's smooth, outwardly innocent face and for once in his life knew exactly what he was thinking. It was all falling into place. James, with a single call to Rowan, had planted a few seeds of suspicion. Saul was unreliable, Saul needed direction, Saul wasn't a man you could leave in charge. Besides which, Saul was going to cost her money. James knew that Rowan was paranoid about money, it was only Saul who had found it out the hard way. Having driven his wedge, James was now ready to commiserate with one half of the partnership and suggest a suitable way out. It was admirably neat.

'Is Diana enjoying her pregnancy?' he asked as a diversion.

'What? No, not one bit. But it draws their fangs, brother mine, it draws their fangs. They come over all dependent and start treating you as the protector and breadwinner. And wouldn't that be a nice change?'

'I'm surprised you're out tonight, actually. Doesn't Diana mind being left alone?'

James grunted. Oddly enough *he* minded, let alone Diana. He couldn't understand now why he had come. He knew Diana was capable of telephoning the ambulance herself but he had the horrible feeling that if he allowed her to do so, she would not forgive him. In a moment he would go home again. He couldn't relax, his mind refused to free itself of concern.

'I thought it was a bit sneaky trying to get me for breach of contract,' said Saul.

James came back to the present with a start. 'What? Oh that. You certainly asked for it and I'm taking it all the way. I've a feeling I shouldn't have told Rowan though, that girl is too sharp by half. She'll have done some damage limitation by now, I don't doubt.'

'Naturally,' said Saul. He felt a leaden sense of doom weighing him down. Why didn't he have this sharp, fencing mentality, possessed by both Rowan and James, enabling them to seize upon and devour the enemy? He was more fun, he was more witty, he could walk into a room full of squabbling people and charm them all into good humour. But he was so absolutely, totally, unmentionably bored by this continual state of war.

James said, 'That your man? Christ, another one of ours. I warn you, we're turning ourselves on our ear to see you off and we've got the muscle to do it.'

Saul got up and left him. He greeted his guest and ordered more drinks, anything to dull his senses. In a while, after a meal, they would gamble a little. Tonight he wanted to gamble a lot.

Chapter Twenty-Three

James went out to his car. He wouldn't have minded a girl tonight, but it was starting to rain and he was distinctly unhappy about Diana. Aspley Manor was a bleak, desolate sort of place in winter, he didn't like it much. The peacocks trailed about cackling like witches, leaving their infernal droppings on the doorstep. Summer was the time, with the oaks in leaf and bees buzzing in the drowsy air. He turned the car out of town and accelerated hard.

'Diana! Diana!' He was calling almost before he had opened the door. He knew something was wrong, he could feel it. The light was on in the drawing room. He burst in. She was lying on the sofa, her huge belly uppermost and her face contorted. 'For God's sake, Diana! Say something!'

Through gritted teeth she muttered, 'Contraction. Can't. Ambulance coming.'

'Sod the ambulance, I'll take you in the car! Oh, darling, I knew something was wrong.'

The contraction subsided and Diana put up a hand to push damp hair from her forehead. 'Don't panic, James. I started around six, I didn't think much would happen till at least eleven. I took ages with the others. And this is a bit – beastly.'

James leaned down and slipped his arms under her shoulders. 'Car. Quickly. This is no time for stoicism, both you and the baby could be at risk. How long since you called the ambulance?'

'Over half an hour,' grunted Diana.

'Then they've probably got lost. Right, hold on to me. We'll stop whenever we must, but let's hurry.'

They made slow progress. Every contraction drained

Diana a little more, her breath was coming in racking gasps. James had panic on a tight rein, this did not look right at all! At last she was safely in the car, as if that was all that safety asked. He sent the machine howling off into the night.

'I knew I was too old,' she muttered.

'Nonsense. You should have gone into hospital straight away, that's all. God knows what might be happening – '

'That's right, cheer me up!'

He glanced at her. The skin of her face was drawn down in lines of pain.

He said, 'Sorry. I'm anxious, that's all. I couldn't bear to lose you.'

'Suppose we lose the baby?'

At another time he would have decried her pessimism, but as the rain slashed at the windscreen and her body contorted once again, it seemed the most likely outcome. Already there was a ball of sorrow lodged in his guts. He drove harder still.

Another car was leaving the gates of the nursing home as he swung into it. The rear wing of the Mercedes slid away on the wet road, catching the other car, a Jaguar, a glancing blow. James cursed and drove on, screeching to a halt at the door. The driver of the stricken car ran up, exuding fury.

'I say! What the hell do you mean driving off like that?'

'Get out of my way, damn you! My wife's in labour, she's seriously ill.'

'I don't consider that any excuse – '

James ignored him and ran into the hospital. The man turned to Diana, sitting immobile in the car. 'I'm sorry, madam, but I really must insist – ' He was silenced by a long moan. Her head lolled against the seat. Slowly and unhappily the man withdrew, went back to his car and drove away.

Hours later James remembered him. Who on earth had he been? As far as James recalled, the Merc had made a terrible mess of his Jag. A doctor appeared in the corridor and James tensed, but the man walked past. It was at times like these you fervently wished you had never given up smoking, he thought distractedly. When would they tell him what was happening?

A nurse passed in the corridor. It was amazing the activity in this place in the middle of the night. He glanced at his watch, it showed a quarter to six. Nearly morning then. He had been there forever.

The soft footfalls of theatre boots took him by surprise. 'Mr Barton?'

'Yes. Yes.' He couldn't bear to hear and he couldn't bear not to know. The doctor smiled above his green mask, the smile of compassion or congratulation? 'She's fine,' said the doctor. 'Mother and son are doing well. A smashing baby boy.'

James hardly believed him. 'But – the baby was distressed. That's why you operated, you wouldn't even wait for the senior anaesthetist.'

'We had to hurry and we did. Another half hour and he would have been seriously damaged, I've no doubt of that at all. As it is, your wife's going to be rather pulled down for a while, but the baby's just fine. What are you going to call him?'

James didn't know. Perhaps Nicholas? 'I'll have to look at him first,' he said decisively. 'Let's see the little blighter, then.'

The baby was in the special care nursery, but in contrast to two other infants, wired up like robots, he was without impedimenta of any kind.

'You ought to be monitoring him,' said James at once. 'I'll pay for it, I want the best.'

'There's a mattress monitor,' soothed the doctor. 'Tells us if he stops breathing. Like I said, he's a healthy chap. Quite a whopper, in fact.'

To James he looked tiny. Brownish down covered the little head, he had minute slices of mother of pearl for fingernails. 'Nicholas James,' he said softly. 'Two good strong names.'

'Sounds fine to me,' said the doctor. 'Talk it over with your wife.'

James's head came up. Who did this man think he was to

patronise and advise, like some sort of schoolmaster? 'I want to see Diana,' he snapped. 'Now.'

The doctor was nonplussed. What had he done to cause that furious grey-blue stare? 'She'll be very dopy,' he prevaricated.

'Nonetheless I wish to see her. For God's sake, man, I am her husband!'

They passed down corridors full of early morning activity. Cleaners bustled past with mops and buckets, a porter pushed a trolley laden with clean linen. Even this early a florist was delivering baskets of flowers for some new arrival. James determined to demand a feast, a forest of flowers. There was a bubble of elation building within him, he couldn't stop thinking about Nicholas James. How he longed to tell Diana about him, she'd be dying to know.

Yet when he entered her room and saw her lying there, white and still, her tawny eyes mere slits beneath her lids, his heart went cold. 'Diana? Darling?'

Her head turned on the pillow and he moved to take her hand, but it was wired up to a drip. 'So tired,' she whispered. 'It hurts.'

He stroked her head, her forehead was damp and clammy. 'We've got a beautiful boy, darling, he looks wonderful. Nicholas James. Will you like that?'

'Yes.' She licked her lips and at once he reached out for a glass of water. But she didn't want it. He said, 'Better tomorrow, my angel. I'll let you sleep. You know I love you.'

Her eyes gently closed. He stood looking at her until the doctor said, 'As I told you, she had a rough time. Come again this evening, she'll be better then.'

James nodded. It shocked him to see her like this, white and bloodless, her lips bruised from her own teeth. How she must have suffered, and she hadn't wanted the child at all. Yet she had given it to him, so that he could try again, make a fresh start at fatherhood.

He had failed so badly with Richard. Ought he to ring him and tell him what had happened? Richard always found it easy to be cruel over the 'phone. The best thing would be to visit him now, in his flat, it might just be the moment to restore some semblance of a relationship. On this first day of Nicholas James's precious life, James felt an impulse of reconciliation.

Richard's flat was in an expensive suburb of Leeds, close to Roundhay Park. On summer nights he was sometimes treated to the sound of pop concerts in the park, which he liked if it was Genesis or some esoteric jazz band, but loathed if it was teenybopperish. Besides, the younger element invariably parked their heaps in front of his garage door and walked over his Ferrari when he left it outside. Not that they had to stretch their legs much; the car's dark blue shell rose a mere couple of feet from the floor and drove like an elongated skateboard, clinging to the tarmac. But, it was useless in snow and the front end tended to lift if he crested a hill at more than a hundred and ten, so he was deliberating whether to get shot of it. He was engrossed in pleasurable speculation when his father rang the bell.

'One pint, please,' yelled Richard, not bothering to stir from his designer kitchen chair. The bell rang again. Cursing, he put down his toast and shambled over to the door. He was feeling a little the worse for wear, still jetlagged after three days back and struggling with the thought of a day in the office. How nice it would be to be paid that much for not doing the job.

When he saw James his jaw momentarily sagged. They hadn't met in months, they never wrote, 'phoned or communicated in any way. 'Hello,' said James. 'Can I come in?' He pushed his way into the flat, determined to forestall any rejection.

'How did you know where I lived?' asked Richard.

Shrugging, James said, 'I make it my business to know what's important. This is all very flash and expensive. Are you enjoying the job then?'

'Yes – yes.' It wasn't entirely true. Last week he'd been in South America, buying alpaca. One moment he'd been up in the highlands, trading with peasants in flap hats chewing coca to combat altitude sickness, the next in Rio sampling the fleshpots. When he started he'd found nothing more exciting, but nowadays he was bored by the endless waits at airports, unamused by the stomach upsets and tired of the increasing preventative tablets and injections. Sometimes he almost thought it would be easier to catch the disease. But, when he got back home, there was the office and paper and not enough responsibility.

'You must be doing all right,' commented James, eyeing the original modern paintings and exquisitely simple Swedish glass ornaments.

'Bonus. I had a good year last year. And I – well, I do a little on my own account.'

James raised an eyebrow. If the firm found out Richard would be up the creek without a paddle, but the boy knew that, he was old enough. Clearly it was a risk he wanted to run.

'Dad, why are you here in bow tie and dinner jacket? You've obviously been up all night, have you been thrown out or something?'

'Not exactly, no.' James savoured the moment. His bubble of pride swelled and exploded inside him, he felt like singing. 'Diana had our baby last night,' he announced. 'Nicholas James. I thought you should be the first to know.'

Richard swallowed hard. 'I see. Congratulations. Why on earth should you think it has anything to do with me?'

'Well – it's your brother. Isn't that important to you?'

Richard turned away into the bathroom, shedding his towelling robe as he went. 'Actually no, it isn't,' he called, starting to run the shower. 'I don't think there's a lot that happens to you that is of concern to me, as a matter of fact. I thought I'd made that clear.'

James went into the kitchen and made himself some coffee. He took it to the bathroom, leaned against the open door and talked. Richard's body, dimly seen through the opaque shower screen, was covered in reddish blond hair. James wondered if Nicholas would have such hair, it was hard to tell with babies. 'I still see you as heir apparent to Bardsey's,' he yelled, above the noise of the water. 'You can't be entirely free of me. Half your credit rating is because you're my son. They know I won't let you go down.'

'Won't you? I would have thought you capable of anything,' shouted Richard. He turned off the shower and reached out for a towel. James handed one to him, monogrammed he noticed. His son certainly knew how to live the high life. Nonetheless he was lean and fit, not a surplus inch on him.

James thought ruefully of his own body, getting older whether he liked it or not. Was the boy better looking than him? Sometimes when he looked in the mirror he was shocked to see how sparse his carroty hair seemed, how much the colour was dimming.

'Why don't you come into the firm?' he asked jerkily. 'We could do with a younger view. Sometimes I think I'm getting set in my ways.'

'I heard you'd been having a few problems. Loss of market share and so on.'

'All due to Saul,' thought James ruefully. He'd known he was good, but not how good. Nowadays Bardsey's sales team was a headless lizard, unhappy and unco-ordinated. Damn the man.

'We've had the odd hiccup,' said James automatically. Then, remembering that he was trying to tempt his son, he admitted, 'We've expanded a bit too rapidly, as it happens. You need a phenomenal rate of growth when you do that. We've got a comber, a dye-house, several finishing plants, and one or two aren't doing so well. I haven't the time for them, not when Bardsey's own operation is struggling. That's why I need you.'

For a brief second James saw his son waver. Afterwards he knew that with the right word then, he could have swayed him. Like an idiot, he said the wrong thing. 'Just think, one day I might have two sons working for me!'

Richard pulled the towel round him and strode out of the room. 'Thanks, Dad, but I don't see myself as playing nursemaid to the brat. You might not be too old for fatherhood, but I'm certainly past playing games with little brother.'

'Don't be so bloody silly, Richard – you know I didn't mean –' but he wasn't sure what he had meant. He might want to give Richard all he desired, but now there was Nicholas to consider. Like it or not, Nicholas had changed things. 'At least come round and have a meal,' he demanded.

Richard sighed. 'OK, OK. Give me a ring sometime, will you?'

Just then the bedroom door opened. In it was framed an exquisitely small, exquisitely pretty Chinese girl. She was stark naked except for her hair, which fell well past her waist. One neat little breast seemed to James to wink at him through the fronds. 'Richard?' she lisped charmingly. 'I did not know we had a visitor.'

Richard glared at the girl, making it plain she was unwanted. Nonetheless he introduced her. 'Er – Lin Yu, this is my father, James Barton. Dad, this is Lin Yu.'

Still quite naked she extended her little hand. 'So pleased to meet you.'

'Me too,' said James gruffly. 'I was inviting my son to dinner– two weeks, Richard, I should be delighted if you would also come, Lin Yu.'

'How kind.' She inclined her pretty head, causing the breast to pop in and out like a puppet. Fearful for his control, James made for the door.

'I never had it so good,' he said sardonically to Richard. 'Took me years to have any fun.'

'She's a very nice girl,' said Richard weakly.

'I bet she is,' said James.

Outside he wondered where else he could go. It was still so early and the pent-up tension in him cried out for release. He thought of Rowan, and at once turned to his car. There was nothing more natural than that he should tell Diana's children personally.

As he drove he felt an almost uncontrollable urge to head

straight back to the hospital, to stare and stare at the minute scrap of life he had created. The thought of how it would be when at last the boy came home delighted him so much he found himself chuckling out loud.

There was a carrier's wagon blocking the entrance to Judge's, smart dark green with the name 'Partridge' emblazoned on the side. James grimaced. If the satellites were flourishing, what did that tell you about the planet? He parked in the street and walked in, noting that the driver was not Partridge himself, and if that wasn't uncalled for expansion he'd like to know what was. A frisson of insecurity rippled up his spine. Bardsey's was so big, how would it be if the tide was turning towards the little people, leaving people like him washed up on the sand? It was paranoia of course. Bardsey's could crush a firm like Judge's as and when it chose.

There was a light on in the cottage and he went and rapped on the peeling paint of the door. After a moment or two Rowan answered. She stood staring at him, wearing jeans and a sweatshirt, her face white and strained. There was a duster in her hand and her feet were bare.

'You don't do the cleaning, do you?' asked James. 'Why don't you get someone in?'

Rowan stood aside to let him enter. The little house was neat and sweet-smelling, but nothing could do much to redeem a dingy room dominated by one huge sofa. James looked about him distastefully. 'Good God, I shouldn't have thought Saul would put up with this. A great deal too basic for his tastes.'

'We're going to move,' said Rowan shortly. 'Has something happened? Why are you here?'

Hardly able to contain his excitement, James thrust his hands energetically into his pockets. 'Your mother's had the baby. They operated. A boy, Nicholas James.'

He watched Rowan swallow. She said, 'Oh. Oh, I'm glad. How are they both?'

'Diana's tired. But he's such a beautiful baby, quite

perfect. You forget how small they are, you know,' he added diffidently.

Suddenly Rowan warmed to him. For once he was letting down his guard and she was in no mood to stab him. 'I'll send flowers,' she promised. 'I'm – I'm really pleased for you, James.'

He nodded. 'Kind of you. Very kind. I went to tell Richard, you know, and it was almost as if he saw the baby as some kind of threat. So ridiculous when you think it's been years since Richard even acknowledged me as his father! I don't understand the boy.'

'You wouldn't,' commented Rowan drily.

She turned away and resumed polishing the table, although nothing could redeem its scratches and the marks of cups. 'It really is about time you let me buy you out,' said James. 'I'm going to insist that Sally and Andy sell their shares to me.'

Rowan's head came up. 'If Mother agrees, and I don't think she will, I'll keep my share regardless. I'll be a thorn in your flesh for ever.'

'And I shall close you down and leave you with nothing.'

'And I shall buy ten Bardsey shares, turn up at the Annual General Meeting and raise hell.'

They glared at each other. James said, 'You don't have to live like this! You could be rich!'

'I'll get rich my own way, thank you.'

Somehow the interview had degenerated into another of their squabbles. He made for the door, feeling beleaguered. He should have left things as they were, he had enough irons in that fire, but Rowan brought out the worst in him every time. 'Where's Saul?' he demanded. 'I think I should at least tell him the good news.'

'He's out' said Rowan flatly. 'Seeing a customer. Don't worry, I'll tell him.'

She stood at the door and watched him stride away, his black coat flapping with that special brand of self-importance James had made his own. The carrier's wagon was reversing out, the yard had been made for horses and was far too small for lorries, even without the Aston Martin parked erratically across one corner. It had been masked from James by the wagon. She felt light-headed from lack of sleep, first because Saul hadn't come home and then because he had. That he had driven home at all was a miracle and she had no idea where he had been. He might remember, but she doubted it.

Her guilt enveloped her, like an itching blanket. She had driven him to it, as surely as if she had poured each drink, because she had been managing and unscrupulous and inconsiderate. If she changed now, at this desperately late stage, surely she could put things right?

James drove into Bradford past the vast, empty Lister's mill that was so much an industrial dinosaur it was judged to be of historical importance.

Everyone had suggestions for it, but there was nothing nowadays that needed floor after floor of space. The mind boggled at the thought of the old days, the people employed in their thousands turning out stuff that was in demand throughout the empire. What had gone wrong? Had the men got fat and careless, had other nations simply got tired of going without? Times had changed, that was all. The men who started these mills were much like himself, they would have understood each other. But in between each driving, thriving generation there were sons who took it for granted and grandsons who frittered it away. He had seen for himself that Richard was hopelessly extravagant – smoked glass coffee tables and silk rugs – he hadn't kept an eye on him, that was the trouble. Nicholas was going to be different. James was never one to overlook a second chance.

He thought of that girl, the Chinese, Lin Yu. She was just – gorgeous. Her lack of modesty made you wonder a little, though. Was she on the game? It was hard to believe something so lovely would have to resort to that, but then everything had its price, he supposed. Did she live there or just stay over? What did she do when Richard was at work? With a sudden grin he swung the car on to the Leeds road. If Richard was still there he'd make up some tale about a date for dinner or something. One thing was certain: if Lin Yu was alone in that flat then he was not going home for breakfast.

She answered the door in a silk robe. 'Hello,' she said politely. 'Richard is at work just now.'

'Oh – oh dear, I didn't think he'd have left. May I come in and scribble him a note?'

'By all means.'

As he brushed past her, he caught the distinctive tang of sex. So, Richard had taken care of her before he left. The thought was exciting. He felt her watching him with those black, hooded eyes. 'Do you have any paper?' he asked, and she wandered about, looking.

'I don't know where he keeps it,' she confessed.

'Perhaps the bedroom,' said James and went through. Black sheets, rumpled into a knot in the centre of the bed, Lin Yu's tiny shoes, and hanging over the back of a chair, a scrap of lace that must be her knickers. He picked them up and held them out. 'You're so tiny,' he said. 'I can hardly believe you fit into these.'

She watched him for a moment. Then she began to open drawers, looking for some paper.

'You don't live here?' said James.

'Oh no. I come to Richard sometimes. I have many friends.'

'Friends?'

She straightened up. Her body was invisible within the robe but her hair, so long and black, intrigued him. He reached out and held the coarse black strands. 'Richard tells me you are very rich,' said Lin Yu. 'Do you want to be my friend?'

James swallowed hard, and let her hair fall. 'That depends. What do you charge your – friends?'

'That is not kind.' She lifted a finger and waggled it at him. 'I am so fond of Richard, I am so happy to spend time with him. He is away so much, I do not see him enough. Richard knows I have other friends who are sometimes kind to me.'

'Doesn't he mind? Knowing other men are – '

She smiled at him, revealing tiny white teeth, cat's teeth. 'But they are all so nice, my friends. I am very, very expensive.'

Lifting her skirt she stepped up on to the bed. Neatly and precisely she undid each of the tiny buttons of her robe, letting it fall about her. The long black hair concealed her almost entirely, and with a swing of her head she set it in motion, catching it in her arms and bundling it up to the crown of her head. 'See,' she said. 'Do you want me?'

Her pubic hair was oiled and curled, James put out his hand and touched it. 'I am very small inside,' she confided. 'Feel.'

He knelt on the bed and extended his finger up between her legs. A tiny, wet passageway into which his massive penis would never go. 'Why don't you undress?' she said encouragingly.

James took off his clothes. He expected her to lie down on the bed, but instead she came and stood in front of him. She was so small that his crotch came just above her waist. He pressed obscenely up between her breasts. Suddenly she put her arms around his neck. A monkey wriggle and she was climbing him, arms and legs like wire. Her fingernails dug into his skin and he cried out, and again as she lowered herself on to him. She hung from his neck, her feet off the floor, impaled on him. James started to laugh. 'You're fantastic. Doesn't it hurt you?'

'I like a big man,' she said calmly. 'You're bigger than Richard, you know that?'

He took hold of her buttocks and moved her back and forth, it was incredibly exciting. 'I've got stuff I can give you to make it better,' she murmured, her hair swinging to and fro with every stroke. 'Not here but at my home. I can make a man do it four times, each one better.' She reached out and took up an odd piece of metal from the bedside, shaped like a mushroom. James was thrusting towards climax. As the moment approached, she reached under her own leg and pressed the cold metal against the back of his testicles. He was aware of an explosion of sensation, his legs buckled and he fell forward, the girl beneath him, on to the bed.

His heart was pounding desperately. 'My God, my God,' he murmured. 'You're an expert.'

'Will you buy me a flat, Richard's father?' she asked, tickling his nose with her hair.

'Richard would know,' said James. 'I don't want to upset him that much.'

'He is always away,' purred Lin Yu. 'I tell him I save for the flat. I make sure you come when he is not there, I make it so good for you. Your wife's had a baby, she won't want a man like you bothering her. I like a big strong man, you come to me any time you like.'

James thought for a moment. It was certainly time he stopped picking up girls on the street, it was far too dangerous. And this one was something else again, even now she was licking and caressing his nipple. He rolled off her, mentally reviewing how he could secretly arrange the finance.

'You find the flat,' he instructed. 'I'll come to you there. I don't want you at the house except as Richard's girlfriend.'

'It excites you, that I am Richard's,' she said shrewdly. 'Let me excite you more.'

James lay back on the bed, spreading his legs wide and abandoning himself to utter and delicious pleasure. Her little pink tongue and catlike teeth sucked and nibbled ecstatically and as he lay there, suffused with rising heat, images flashed across his mind: Rowan's face, with her huge green eyes; Saul, Richard, both so much younger, fitter than he; Nicholas James; at the last he thought of Diana, and he pushed the thought away, because he loved Diana and she had no place here, even in his mind.

Chapter Twenty-Four

The penthouse flat was huge, light and airy. It had floor-length windows, beige fitted carpets and an astronomical rent, although they could decide to buy within a year. Rowan both loved and hated it, because it seemed to her the sort of place that sapped resolve, that spent money rather than earned it. Besides, it worried her to be so far from the mill. A mere half-hour certainly, but that was aeons in terms of involvement. On the credit side Sally had her own bedroom and sitting room, as well as a tiny kitchenette, and with two bathrooms there was no need to share.

The very first evening, Rowan and Saul sat with a bottle of wine in their very own sitting room, and listened to the faint murmur of Sally's television through the wall.

'Bliss,' sighed Rowan, sinking down in one of the chairs that had come with the flat. They had some odd items of furniture because of the terms of the tenancy, including a light oak dining room suite, uncomfortable brass bedstead and a cocktail cabinet.

'I'm trying not to say I told you so,' remarked Saul. 'This is how it should have been from the start.'

'I know, I know.' Rowan put out her hand and caught hold of Saul's fingers. She felt like a sailor who has survived a terrible storm, and while she was grateful to be alive she wasn't all that keen on setting sail again. Marriage was so much more difficult than it looked. Because you loved someone it didn't mean you knew what was best for them, or even what they thought was best for them. In marrying Saul she seemed to have learned more about being separate than being together. Holding hands with him then she made a silent resolution to be more understanding, to listen to what he had to say, to adopt his suggestions however half-baked they might seem.

'Why don't we have a baby?' said Saul.

Rowan dropped his hand and sat bolt upright in the chair. 'You don't have to do everything James does,' she squeaked. 'No!'

Saul laughed. 'All right, all right, calm down. It was just a thought. We want to have babies sometime, don't we?'

Rowan considered. It seemed to her she had only just got rid of Sally, she had no desire at all to replace her with someone even less reasoned and a great deal less independent. 'When I'm thirty,' she said. 'I can remember Sally as a baby. They're sick all the time, usually down your front. And I wouldn't be able to work.'

'No.'

Saul got up and wandered across to the stereo. He glanced through the records, finally selecting a violin concerto. It was Rachmaninoff, played with too much technique and not enough emotion.

'I wish Andy would get famous,' mused Rowan. 'Why isn't he? He can do this miles better.'

'Not in public,' said Saul.

Rowan turned to stare at him. 'What do you mean? You haven't heard him.'

'Yes, I have. On my last London trip, he was put on at the last moment in a lunchtime programme at the Festival. He – he was absolutely right, every note was there, every nuance, you couldn't fault him.'

'But?' interposed Rowan.

'But indeed. He lacked magic. He doesn't look interesting enough, he doesn't have anything new to say about the music. I went round afterwards and he was with this appalling wet girlfriend who was telling him all the things he shouldn't be hearing, like how wonderful it was. It's not that he can't do it because we both know he can. But when it comes to the big occasion he just seems to fall short somehow.'

Rowan's first instinct was to jump up and tell Saul that he knew nothing at all about it, that Andy had always been brilliant and would one day be acclaimed. After all, she and Andy had been loyal to each other for years before Saul came on the scene and such loyalties are not easily discarded. In her heart, though, she knew Saul was right. He had put his finger on something she had occasionally suspected, but never dared look at head on. Despite his brilliance and his faultless execution, Andy so often fell just a millimetre short. In practice he could reduce men to tears, but on a stage, in front of thousands, the same notes were powerless. There was no explaining it. Perhaps also there was no curing it.

'Why?' she asked.

Saul shrugged. 'I suspect self-doubt. All his life people have told him he was wonderful, even when he knew he wasn't. If he had some yardstick of criticism that he could trust, he might start to see the difference between really good and just OK. At the moment he doesn't believe his best performances and doesn't recognise his lesser ones.'

Rowan gnawed at her thumb, staring into the sterile coals of the electric fire.

'You didn't mean that about having a baby, did you?' she asked suddenly.

Saul came and sat on the arm of her chair. His hand slipped down the front of her blouse and cupped her little breast. 'You know I did.'

She arched herself against his palm. He had been so warm to her since she agreed to move. 'When I get the mill on its feet.'

He noticed the word 'I' and winced. Moving hadn't changed things. All the time she had been in the flat she had been itching to get back to the mill.

Irritation surged in him, he was damned if he was going to

resign himself to this. Whatever he did Rowan turned like a piece of iron to a magnet, back to the mill. What was it James had said? 'It draws their fangs, brother mine, it draws their fangs.'

Rowan looked up at him, his face was closed and expressionless. 'Saul?'

He glanced down at her. 'Let's go and try out that bed. If we bump up and down on it enough we might get rid of the lumps.'

They went into the bedroom, leaving the record playing. Saul put out the lights although normally he liked them on. She put her arms round his neck. Somehow he seemed apart from her, even now when they touched down the length of breast and belly and thigh. She felt him looking at her face in the dark.

'Do you love me?' he asked.

'You know I do. More than anything.'

'Well then. That's all that matters.'

She heard him fumbling in the drawer for the condom, there was the rustle of paper. She lay back and waited for him, in that half-life of heat and desire that knows no world outside itself. When at last his body came and covered her she felt warm and loved and safe.

The noise of the weaving shed was like the sea, an insidious background roar. It met you when you entered, it rang in your ears after you left, but while you were there, amongst the looms, it went unnoticed. Rowan never noticed it. For her it was built into the fabric of her life, a reassuring and comforting cacophony.

Today they were warping up a new design, a complex mixture of blue and silver and charcoal. The threads on the huge wooden balloon appeared unrelated; even after years of practice you could not look at them and know the appearance of the finished fabric. You had to wait, endlessly, while the ballooned fibres were wound on to a beam, taken bodily to the weaving shed and tied, one at a time, to the shed of a loom. Only then, with the loom itself combining warp and weft, could you see the cloth.

Rowan was impatient. Her feet hurt and it all seemed to be taking too long. What did this piece matter? Suppose after all this trouble it didn't sell? The most pressing problem of the day was the vague stain that had unaccountably appeared on the bulk order of red cloth they had ready for a manufacturer of ladies' jackets. She suspected the finishing, but feared it could be some contaminant from the wool itself. They would have to wash the cloth again and hope for the best, which in any event would be shrinkage and some loss of quality. Was it all worth the bother?

She sank her hands in her pockets and wandered out into the loading bay. Joe Partridge was there, counting lots. 'Hello, Ro. You look a bit peaked.'

'I don't feel too good actually. Perhaps I've got a bug.'

'Been looking a bit rough for a day or two, I think. Get yourself to the doctor, lass, don't hang about.'

To change the subject she put out a finger and tapped a heavy gold bracelet on his wrist. Each square link appeared to have been hacked out wholesale from some ingot. 'We're paying you too much.'

'This? Bit of image. Going up in the world, we are, Ro.'

She supposed it was true. Now they were in the penthouse they had friends in for drinks and glamorous dinner parties at which the cordon bleu daughter of a lord cooked spectactularly. They had chicken stuffed with duck and then with quail, and raspberries frozen into exquisite mounds of puree. The food looked fantastic and everyone was very impressed, but for her part Rowan always felt slightly sick.

At the weekend she had visited Diana and the baby at Aspley Manor, in the big, sunshiny nursery. Diana had decorated it in lemon yellow and white, she lay prettily on a couch while the baby slept in his cradle. Flowers were banked on every table and through the window there was a view of lawns and trees and distant hills. The whole scene, from Diana with her baby to the heart-breaking beauty of the moors, struck a chord in Rowan's soul. There was more to life than the mill. She felt like a mole coming up into daylight after a lifetime of toil, seeing the sun, but too weary to enjoy it. She didn't know what was wrong with her.

They were calling her from the weaving shed. She turned to go. 'You know, I think I will go and see the doctor. I've hardly the energy to care about anything at the moment.'

Joe looked slightly pained, somehow managing to imply that he would have taken better care of her than that Flash Harry she'd taken it into her head to marry. All he said was, 'Then you get yourself off, lass.'

But the appointment never got made. That evening she was content to let Saul drive her home, although they usually took two cars, for convenience sake. She sat wearily next to him and listened to Stevie Wonder on cassette. The energy of the man drained what little spark she had left.

'Not too good, are you?' said Saul sympathetically.

She shook her head and he chuckled. 'Tell you what, why don't we do the Paris shows next week? I can wangle tickets for most of them. Luxury hotel, wonderful food and wild fashions.'

'I don't seem to like food very much at the moment,' said Rowan. 'But I would like to go – I think.'

It was the thought of the packing that depressed her. It was as much as she could do to choose clothes for ordinary days and take them out of the wardrobe. In the back of her mind she thought how sad it was that Saul didn't realise how ill she was. Cancer seemed the most probable cause of her symptoms, and she was probably going to die. Fortunately she was too tired to feel very concerned.

Eventually Sally did the packing. At the last moment Rowan came to life and extracted a meaningless promise from her sister not to have boys in the flat, or girls that smoked, or anyone else unpleasant. Naturally enough no sooner were Rowan and Saul safely across the Channel than Sally threw a party at which two boys smoked pot, one snorted heroin and someone dropped cassis on the beige carpet. Sally spent the rest of the week trying to remove the stain and make the place look less like the scene of a singularly bloody murder.

Rowan had never been to Paris, and Saul had been there many times. He knew his way round the Metro, could summon a taxi out of nowhere, was used to the horrors of Parisian traffic. All Rowan had to do was dress each morning in something exotic and hang on to his arm while he swept her from one show to another, from Karl Lagerfeld classicism to Issey Miyake oddness. They were ushered in almost without comment while other far more important souls had their tickets queried. Everyone simply believed that Rowan was a catwalk model, rushing from one show to the next with a model's usual lack of punctuality.

She looked entirely the part. Mr. Suzman was dressing her in silk these days, or at least what passed for silk. Dresses with high necks and no shape but that imprinted by Rowan's thin frame; camisole tops so brief that it took nerve to wear them. She would stride past in tight black trousers and high heels, her little breasts bouncing behind their thin covering of green or ochre or puce and a jacket loosely hanging on the points of her shoulders. Doormen held doors for her, photographers took pictures, and afterwards shambled Saul, trying to look like her minder.

'We're going to get rumbled soon,' muttered Rowan, trying to efface herself on yet another little gilt chair in another overheated salon. 'Can they throw you out retrospectively?'

'We haven't deceived anyone,' said Saul. 'They chose to deceive themselves. Besides, if things get really tough at Judge's, I'll set you up out here. You're obviously the type.'

'Thin as a rake and tall as a Zulu,' muttered Rowan as the

first girl, who looked like a Zulu, set her elongated legs on to the catwalk.

They were there to look at style, and yet to ignore it completely. It was the feel of the thing that counted, whether it was drape or cling or swirl, or perhaps, and most unusually, cloth cut to stand off the body in planklike regimentation. What was shown here would be watered down and copied all over the world, and unless fabrics like these were in Judge's ranges there was no hope of tempting designers into the fold. If you waited for the magazines you waited too long; you became a follower in the train of the more ambitious.

The heat of the room was becoming intense. There was a constant rustle of fanned programmes and even the models' tight-skinned faces were beaded with sweat. Saul watched two girls stride aggressively in time to the heavy funk music, the woman in front applauded and flapped her programme at one and the same time. The smell of her perfume was overpowering in the heat. With no more than a gentle sigh, Rowan slid off her chair and fainted.

The French understand drama. Rowan was extracted and removed with white-coated efficiency, while all around people moved their chairs, kept one eye on the show and muttered imprecations. A woman of icy elegance commented in Spanish, 'The girl's obviously anorexic and probably on drugs,' to which Saul replied, also in Spanish, 'I'll thank you to refrain from insulting my wife!'

'*Anglais, n'est-ce pas?*' queried a matron of her daughter.

'*Japonais,*' interrupted Saul meanly, and vaulted over the last three chairs to get to the stretcher.

It took all his persuasion to make them let her go. They wanted to send her to hospital and immure her at enormous cost in a private room.

'She's perfectly all right,' insisted Saul. 'It was the heat. A doctor will come to our hotel.' He bundled the conscious, but shivering, Rowan into a taxi. She sagged against him. 'OK?' he asked.

'No. I think I'm dying. I think I've got cancer.'

'Oh. Oh, is that it?'

She began to cry. 'I'm sorry, Saul. I didn't mean to die!'

He put his arms round her and held her tight. 'You aren't going to die, sweetheart. You'll be fine soon. We'll call the doctor and get him to tell us what's wrong. Won't we?'

She nodded up at him. He felt a surge of love for his difficult, spiky girl. He would want for nothing if she would always stare at him with just that helpless trust.

'You knew, didn't you? You've known for weeks!' She sat up in the hotel bed, a curlicued affair covered in white and gold leaf. Her cheeks were bright red with rage.

'Er – let's say I suspected. I thought you must too, until this afternoon. Classic symptoms, lovey.'

'I suppose you'd know! How many illegitimate babies have you fathered, may I ask?'

'None, actually.' He lowered himself cautiously on to the end of the bed, and she kicked at him. 'Why are you so upset? It's an accident, that's all. You wanted a baby in the end, why not now?'

She put her hands in her hair and tugged it. If she didn't feel so ill she'd take revenge on him, but as it was it took all her strength to remain angry. 'I wanted to look after my mill,' she wailed. 'And it'll be all nappies and sick and rusks and no sleep! I can't bear it! I can't, I can't, I can't!'

Saul gently pulled her hands out of her hair and held them. He felt as he sometimes did when he played good poker and won, quietly triumphant. At the same time he felt sorry for poor, straightforward Rowan whom he had beguiled so easily. 'Do you really not want it? A soft pink baby, all your own. Do you really not?'

'Yes. No! Oh Saul, I don't know what I want.' She felt trapped. Her body, and fate, had trapped her. Rowan Judge, businesswoman and active member of the human race, was being shackled by her femininity. Warm, unbreakable bonds of love and need that she longed for, even while hating them. Wearily she leaned against her husband. The mistake had been in loving him, and in loving him still.

They went home the next day. The purple stain dominated the sitting room carpet like an egg-laying toad.

'What will the landlord say?' remarked Rowan. 'We'll have to buy the blessed place.'

'We can't bring a baby up here,' said Saul. 'You need a garden and a swing.'

Sally looked at them suspiciously. 'What baby?'

'One that's better behaved than you are,' snapped Rowan waspishly. 'You had a party, didn't you?'

'No,' lied Sally, and Rowan didn't have the strength to argue.

Sally sat down and began to cry, though whether because of the baby or the carpet no one knew. Saul patted her awkwardly on the shoulder, although he always avoided touching her. There was something vaguely incestuous even about shaking hands with Sally, because he couldn't deny the attraction of her small-boned prettiness. She had the habit, when they were alone together, of sitting close to him, her shoulders thrown back to emphasise her breasts. Now though she seemed entirely childlike, caught out in a prank.

'Rowan's not in the least maternal. She'll be horrid to it,' said Sally.

'Mothers always love their children,' said Saul with confidence. He was thrilled with himself, with Rowan, with the entire world. 'It's in the hormones, you can't avoid it.'

Rowan didn't believe in hormones. She fought hard against them, only to find that they had her pinned against the ropes. The canteen made bacon sandwiches for coffee break in the morning, great greasy white baps crammed full of best back, and the smell was enough to make her throw up in the potted palm. Everyone told her she'd be better soon, but in the meantime they got used to seeing her crouched on the stone stairs, white-faced and miserable, fighting to keep her breakfast down. And after lunch she nodded off at her desk, like some eighty year old.

Saul said, 'You can't go on like this. Take some time off, stay in bed. You look like a ghost.'

'A ghost with a beer gut,' said Rowan distastefully, staring down at her rapidly distending belly. It seemed to be growing awfully quickly. She resented it, fiercely; sometimes she lay in bed and wished it away, and afterwards went shopping and bought it bootees to make up. They bought a cot and baby bath, and Diana promised to give them a pram. Even before the baby arrived it was clear that big as the penthouse was, the small bedroom was nowhere near big enough for a nursery. Rowan found herself looking resentfully at Sally, wishing her anywhere but here. She could not be a parent to her sister, not when true parenthood beckoned so insistently.

Gradually, peacefully, her fingers slackened on the reins of the mill. Saul took over this and then that, leaving her free to stay in bed or go to the doctor or visit her mother.

Diana said, 'It suits you. You've stopped wearing those terrible boyish clothes.'

'Saul likes those,' said Rowan. 'Now I've got bulges everywhere.' She looked ruefully down at her odd exterior, clad in a print cotton dress with a Peter Pan collar.

'Actually, in that you look far too young,' said Diana.

Rowan wished she could have returned the compliment. Diana looked lined and ill, lying on the sofa but still looking as if she should have been in bed. The baby was in a Moses basket, swathed in a forest of white lace. Rowan stared in, for once fascinated.

'How do you know he's not dead?' she asked.

Diana levered herself up on her elbow. 'He's fine, darling, look at his lovely colour. And look, he's sucking in his sleep.'

'So he is.' Rowan gazed at the tiny lips, saw the little, wanting movements of the hands and wondered what it would be like to feed such as this, to offer her own body as sustenance. Once it had seemed unthinkable, now it had an almost lascivious charm.

'Does James still like him?' she asked. James's wild enthusiasms often waned, in her experience.

'He dotes,' said Diana. 'In fact, we're a couple of idiots. We can spend an entire evening staring at him telling each other how wonderful he is, and planning his education. We can't decide if he should be Prime Minister or merely revolutionise medical science. By the way, I've heard from Andy.'

Diana got up heavily and fetched Andy's latest letter. 'He's really unhappy at the moment. Even when he won the competition he got bad reviews. They're talking about theatricality in his playing, not enough basic worth. Technically he's brilliant, of course, but he doesn't have the right style.'

Rowan remembered Saul's assessment and grunted. 'Perhaps he needs a bit more – passion!'

'They're always saying his playing sounds Russian, and I hope they mean it as a compliment! He's the least passionate of all of you. Or perhaps he isn't. Boys don't show it as much, we don't encourage it, and then their wives complain. Do you think Andy has a girlfriend?'

Rowan nodded. 'Definitely. The appalling cellist, with the buck teeth and the long frizzy hair. He was very vague when he was up last, I think they're living together.'

'Shock, horror,' said Diana with irony. She put her hands to the sides of her head as if trying to smooth away a headache. Rowan was suddenly assailed by her beauty. That mane of tawny hair against the white bony face, the glow of her eyes, that were somehow enhanced by the shadows that surrounded them. So little of it had been passed on to either of her daughters; they inherited this and that, neither the incomparable whole. Even Sally, with her blonde prettiness, lacked her mother's structure.

And in the midst of it, Rowan had a premonition of death. She saw her mother's lovely face rotted to a skull, she saw Sally gone to dust in the ground. The ghosts of all things horrible reached out with dead fingers, plucking at her, calling to her. Air was denied, her lungs were flat and empty, not even enough for a moan. Before her mother's horrified gaze, she fainted.

Saul came to fetch her. They had called the doctor who put it down to raised blood pressure. Bed rest for at least a fortnight, no excitement, no work, nothing. In front of the others Saul was kind, but matter-of-fact. Alone in the car together, he suddenly pulled over to the side of the road and buried his head in his hands. 'Oh God! I thought something terrible had happened. I thought it was just a faint, but you were so white!'

'I'm sorry. I don't know what happened, I had a sort of dream – I thought – I don't know what I thought.'

He put his arms round her as if to ward off anything and everything. 'There's not enough of you, that's the trouble, you try and do too much on no flesh. You've got to eat more. Just stay in bed and grow that baby.'

'Yes. Yes, I will.' The dream still haunted her, she felt cold and lonely. She snuggled into her husband and he put his hand over the protrusion of her stomach. 'I love you, Rowan,' he muttered. 'I know recently you've thought I – I haven't said it. I was to blame, I rushed you, I didn't try to understand. I never stopped loving you.'

Softly, tenderly, she nestled her face into the hollow of his shoulder. It was warm and human and utterly familiar.

Almost despite himself Saul was developing an affection for Judge's. At first it had seemed entirely Rowan's creature, without frills or extravagances, pared down as puritanically as only Rowan knew how. But then you got to know people, you found out how it all came about, and things looked different. When a firm has teetered on the brink of disaster, nobody fails to take life seriously.

Now that Rowan was tucked up in bed Saul could allow a little relaxation to creep in. Joyless money-grubbing wasn't in him. If people couldn't have fun while they toiled, then where was the point? Besides, a little community spirit never went amiss. He started letting people buy lengths of cloth, heavily discounted. Then he began a snooker club, setting aside one of the large wasted rooms upstairs for use at lunchtime. It became his habit to wander round the mill, chatting to people, sometimes about work but more often about their families. One thing became very clear: most of the women working at Judge's, and there were quite a few, had children at home. Sometimes Grandma helped out; more often it was a hit and miss affair of childminders for the under fives, and for older children, a hazardous and often unsupervised few hours from leaving school to Mum getting home, sometimes not until six.

He thought about it in bed one night, lying awake while Rowan peacefully slept beside him. When finally he drifted off to sleep he found himself suddenly back in his own childhood, alone in the house while his mother cooked and cleaned for the old man. He made them live in their own house, he wouldn't have them with him. Saul was cold. They had a coal fire and his mother didn't like to leave him in the house with a fire, so he sat in his short trousers with his knees to his chin, waiting for her to come home. After a bit he got bored, and he was jolly cold. He had seen his mother light the fire lots of times, he knew exactly how. Yet somehow it wasn't easy when you did it yourself, the paper wouldn't crumple as it should. One sheet hung out of the fireplace and when he lit it, burning his fingers on the matches, it flared up, bright as the sun. In his dream he stood watching it, just as he had that day, watching the paper fall from the fire on to the rug. The same sense of fear, the same immobility, unable even to back away towards the door.

Saul sat up with a yell. Rowan, sleepily waking, said: 'Saul? What is it? Are you all right?'

He passed a hand across his face and found it wet with sweat. 'It's OK,' he said breathlessly. 'I had a dream.'

Rowan turned towards him and stroked his arm. 'What was it? You gave such a yell.'

'Well, I would! When I was six, I set the house on fire. I dreamed about that.'

'Good God!' Rowan sat right up now. 'How on earth did you do it? Were you hurt?'

'No, actually, I wasn't. My mother came back and dragged me out of the blazing room. I was just standing there, watching it. I'd been trying to light the fire. It was winter. I was cold.'

'You could have been killed! Oh, you poor darling, how could your mother let you?'

'It wasn't her fault. She was working for the old man and he didn't like me in the house at that time of day. He liked to bring people back for a drink and a kid my age didn't fit in. So she left me on my own till she got in. And the fire brigade came and put it out, and the insurance paid up, and after my mother had gone on at him for a couple of months the old man allowed me to go there after school. I just had to stay in the kitchen all the time, that's all.'

'Bloody man! James takes after him, exactly.'

As the dream lost its grip Saul leaned back against the pillows. 'He fights against being like him quite a bit, actually. The old man was a sod and a stupid one. But that sort of callousness does rub off, you know. Me first, the rest nowhere. He learned it from the old man.'

Rowan swallowed. 'Do you think I'm like that? Selfish?'

'You?' He laughed. 'You'd walk a hundred miles in bare feet to do something for someone you loved. Your mother, Sally, me, we only have to hint we need you and you're there. But – you're scared, Rowan. You're frightened of being poor, and lonely. Sometimes you think nobody can love you, and that – doesn't make you very lovable.'

She buried her face against him. 'I know, I know. Perhaps it's because mother always loved Andy best.'

'She might love him best, but that doesn't mean she doesn't love you at all. I think it's Sally gets the thin end of the wedge there, actually. If Diana could only be the least bit consistent ... one minute it's off on a fantastic holiday, look how Mummy loves you, the next it's fend for yourself, don't call me.'

'That's her all over. She gets very involved; she's either doing something or she's not. On and off like a light, that's Mother. She can be absolutely singleminded. And Sally – I try to help her, Saul, truly I do.'

He let out his breath, letting go of the dream at the same time. After a bit he said, 'I think she's coming right. Not so many boys hanging round, and she comes home more often, too. When does she start this beauty course?'

'End of the month. I wish we could be on our own though, Saul, especially when the baby comes.'

He put his arms round her. 'Perhaps she'll move in at the college. We must get some reward for being good, we don't need riches in heaven but we do need space down here.' Gently, soothingly, their legs entwined. It was comforting, and he had a vague wish for comfort, because of the dream. It haunted him.

The plan which formed in his head that night was not one he imparted to Rowan. He knew instinctively that she would balk at the cost. But, they had a huge mill, largely unused, and they were demanding quality work at less than the best rates of pay. Fringe benefits were bound to be cost-effective. So he employed two nursery nurses to run a day-long crêche and to supervise school-age children after hours. He signed a cheque for equipment, sent in decorators to transform one of the upstairs galleries and they were off.

In the first week they had ten children all day and forty after school. The babies were paid for, but the nominal charge for the older children barely covered the milk and biscuits they devoured. They were like a starving army falling on a town, intent on pillage, but Saul knew if he charged too much they would simply have to take their chance once again on the streets. The women who worked in the mill simply couldn't afford more.

Looking at the wild and exuberant children he felt an immense sympathy for their mothers. He began to see them not as workers but as needy and deserving cases; he found it harder and harder to insist on time-keeping, quality control and speed. They had to go home and cook and clean, not to mention coping with some member of the mob upstairs! He had always known at Bardsey's that they paid little or no attention to the welfare of the staff, and now at Judge's he had the chance to implement a new and worthwhile system. Naturally people would feel grateful, and gratitude would produce results. He left it at that.

His main interest, as always, was sales. Everything about it intrigued him, from the initial scent of his quarry, through the stalking, the initial flirtation or, if the mood was right, the direct attack, all the way to the final handshake with promises of devotion from all sides. Even when a potential customer was absolutely against everything right from the word go, he would talk and weave a little, trying to sense what it was that had so alienated them from salesmen. Were they too pushy? Saul was so discreet he might have been there to clean the carpet. Did they not understand the problems and difficulties of business today? He was as sympathetic and encouraging as a marriage guidance counsellor. They all fell for him, from nervous girls setting out on a career buying for chainstores, to hard-nosed men who had been in it for more years than he had had hot dinners.

But even Saul had the occasional sticker. Marcus Arnaud,

designer of fabulously chic clothes featured in all the glossies, wouldn't look at English cloth. He bought only from Italy, where they would do what you wanted, where the colours were superb, the runs as short or as long as you liked. What could a designer like him do with bolts of cloth when he only ever made perhaps two or three of something? Yet Saul wanted him, desperately; he wanted photographs of Marcus Arnaud clothes, made up in Judge's cloth, each with the distinctive MA logo, all over his office. What a seller that would be.

'Look, we did this for Marcus Arnaud, exclusive of course. We were very influenced by the Paris shows, were you able to make it this year? Marcus loves this heavy weave. But we do have this very similar and remarkably well-priced fabric you might care to look at? Absolutely right for the moment.'

Picking cherries would be arduous in comparison.

Saul went on a raid. Best suit, handmade shirt, gold cufflinks. 'Where on earth are you going?' demanded Rowan, sitting prettily up in bed and watching him dress. The doctor had extended her bed-rest to at least another week, so she had no choice but to stay in bed reading Mothercare catalogues and baby books.

'London for the day,' said Saul. 'Don't worry, I've left everything shipshape in the mill. They're finishing that blue and grey stuff you saw set up. I like it, I'm taking a sample. You've got taste, my love.' He dropped a kiss on her head.

'You only married me for my colour sense,' grumbled Rowan. 'If I hadn't been togged up in purple tunics, you'd have gone off with someone else.'

Saul grinned. Rowan had it in her to be a brilliant designer of more than just cloth. When she let herself go she was capable of real imagination. But, so often in anything except textiles, her fears kept her creeping round the corners of the room instead of striding out into its centre.

'If it looks like I'm going to be late, I'll ring you,' he said, as he was picking up his sample case.

'You're not taking much,' said Rowan doubtfully.

'Only what counts. Have a good day, love, and don't do anything. Is the doctor coming?'

She nodded. 'He said if my blood pressure hadn't gone down, I had to go into hospital.'

'He only said it to keep you in bed, silly. See you soon.'

He thought about Rowan as he drove to the station. The baby had been a godsend, exactly what they both needed. As James had said, if you wanted femininity then pregnancy was your goal. Rowan was even learning to knit! Not that he wanted her out of the firm forever; today, for instance, he could have done with someone who knew what they were doing minding the shop. Yesterday the washer had broken. A hugely tall machine in which lengths of cloth thrashed about on rollers, it served the dual purpose of cleaning the material after manufacture and fluffing up the fibres to thicken it. It had taken three hours to mend, and without anyone keeping an eye on them they had left the cloth dripping inside it. Wool did not improve with a good long soak. It was as felted as a doormat, simply because no one was thinking. He dared not tell Rowan, it would have dealt the final blow to her blood pressure. The order would go out late, there was no avoiding it.

He travelled first-class on the train, although Rowan would always travel second. It put him in the right frame of mind. He was talking to a man who thought nothing of charging three thousand pounds for a dress, so a few quid on a railway ticket and three whiskies was hardly going to count. Not that he wanted much for the cloth; it was enough for Arnaud to use Judge's own. At King's Cross, Saul stopped to buy a buttonhole, choosing instead of a rather dull carnation in red or white, a small yellow and crimson rose. Then, fortified, confident and determined, he took a taxi to Marcus Arnaud.

'Mr. Arnaud, please. Saul Barton. We're meeting for

lunch.' It was an appointment he had made with the secretary, managing to imply that they met not infrequently and that Marcus had suggested a date round about now.

'Yes – Mr. Barton – do you have a card?' The receptionist was nervous because he was good-looking and very well-dressed, not the sort of man you asked for his credentials. Clearly Arnaud had boggled at his lunch appointment and would not take kindly to being tricked by a salesman.

Saul flicked a card cursorily at the desk. Printed for just such an eventuality it was thick, very white and read in gold letters "Saul Barton – fabric" with a 'phone number. It had got him into any number of places, simply because they did not know who, where from or what for.

'We are acquainted,' said Saul, permitting a shade of irritation to colour his voice. The receptionist scuttled away nervously.

Within two minutes he was going upstairs. Marcus Arnaud was in his studio, a large light room littered with dummies and cloth and drawings. A small, thin man known only to Saul from photographs, he half-hid behind his desk. Saul thrust out a hand. 'Marcus! Good to see you after all this time. How are you? When was it? Paris?'

Arnaud waved a vague hand. 'Might well have been. I travel so much –'

'Don't we all,' agreed Saul. He was mentally trying to gauge the man's sexual standing. Was he gay or merely rather effete? Single, at his age, probably meant gay but you couldn't always be sure. 'Been to Italy recently?' he asked apparently inconsequentially. 'They're losing it, you know. Bloody government as always! I remember you telling me you'd had a bit of a problem with duty before, hadn't you?' That was a safe enough bet, everybody had that problem. 'And now of course they're talking about this tax. The government'll be out in five minutes, but the tax could be on for five years!'

'Er – which tax would that be?' Arnaud was standing transfixed while Saul unpacked his samples as casually as a man looking for his sandwiches.

'The worst. Something to do with the massive salaries the designers have been getting; they're trying to get a rake off. Half the big names are moving on, we'll see the results in a year or two no doubt. You'll have noticed it was all a bit dull at the last show.'

That year the Italians were showing all puce and dark green. 'One can always tell,' said Arnaud. 'Myself, I know what it's like to be unappreciated!' He made an extravagant bow, and they laughed together.

'I've booked a table for one o'clock,' said Saul, glancing at his watch. 'Thought I'd let you see what's new first. This is a little mill, got a fantastic girl in charge there, very innovative. I mean, when did you last see something like this from Yorkshire?' Apparently haphazard, he tossed the blue that Rowan had set up in an aesthetic heap on top of a navy flannel laid out on a table. Turning immediately away, he pulled out a large piece of glowing burgundy. When selling like this you never showed tiny squares of cloth, you gave them yards to look at. He half took out some green and black stripe, very much to Arnaud's taste if his wallpaper was anything to go by, and then put it away. 'No, you won't want the green, it's too different.'

'May I see?' Arnaud was trying to get into the case. Amazing how often that trick worked.

Reluctantly, Saul took out the green. 'As I said she's original. I'm not a designer myself, I don't have the instinct. Perhaps she's done too much with that.'

'On the contrary! It's superb! How much for this? Exclusive.'

Saul looked perturbed. 'I didn't expect to sell that one – I warn you, it's pricey.'

'Please! How much?'

In the end, after much coaxing, Saul quoted a highish

price. He was making it up, because by now Arnaud would have paid anything. He took an order for the green, the blue, and for the burgundy. Arnaud summoned a model to drape it round herself. The girl eyed Saul beneath long black lashes, walking backwards and forwards with her hips thrust out and her bottom undulating. Well, he thought, that was a come-on if ever he saw one. Before Rowan he wouldn't have hesitated.

When she had gone, Arnaud laughed. 'She likes you. Shall I give you her number?'

'Er – no thanks.' Saul grinned deprecatingly.

They lunched at a very expensive restaurant. Saul ate heartily, Arnaud picked at the food. He seemed preoccupied about something, every now and then falling silent and looking down at his plate. Suddenly, with the coffee, Saul felt the toe of a shoe gently against his shin. His blood went cold. Oh God, why on earth had he shied away from saying he was married? Only because he thought the guy was queer and he hadn't wanted to put him off – but then he hadn't wanted to turn him on, either!

In his mind's eye he saw the order crumbling and Arnaud running, screaming and outraged, away. He looked Arnaud full in his soft, rather anxious eyes.

'Marcus – I won't pretend I don't like you a lot. We only met briefly before, I didn't think you'd remember. But – you were someone I felt I had to see. There was an attraction, I won't deny it.'

Arnaud let out his breath in a long sigh. 'I didn't know, I didn't remember. God, I can be so stupid sometimes.'

'I had a few appointments in London and I thought I'd make you one of them. I knew you'd be someone I could talk to. I've got a few problems. A relationship, you know how it is. This guy – he wants more than I've got to give somehow. It's my fault, I'm the one that can't commit myself. And, you know, I really care about him.'

'So – you don't want to go out on a limb with me.' The

foot withdrew. Arnaud's eyes, naturally rather sad, Saul noticed, fell away.

'It isn't that!' Saul caught his hand, and then, as if they might have been seen, dropped it again. He allowed himself to appear confused and embarrassed.

'God, you're in a mess,' said Arnaud. 'Come back and have a drink. We'll talk a little, you need it.'

Back at the studio, they had a couple of brandies. 'Actually I'm in a steady relationship,' confided Arnaud. 'But I wouldn't say it was exclusive, and that goes for both of us. Your guy, he wants it that way, does he?'

'Oh yes. And if I do meet someone else and things get out of hand, well, I hate myself for it. Nine times out of ten I tell him and then the world falls apart. But if I don't tell him it's worse and he suspects anyway. I'm a lousy liar.'

'You're just too damned honest.' Arnaud got up, clearly wanting to close the proceedings. 'Look, you've got the order, and you know where I am. Any time you want to come and talk you're welcome. I mean, I've been there, you know?'

'Yeah. Thanks.'

They shook hands. Saul picked up his sample case and made it out into the street. His head was spinning and if he relaxed for a second he thought his stomach muscles would go into spasm. God, but that had been close! He'd nearly lost the order.

Going back on the train he allowed himself the luxury of a small chuckle, feeling mean about it. Arnaud was a nice guy. As he leaned back in his seat, worn out by the mental demands of the day, he felt a slight dimming of his spirits. Back to the mill and its problems: washers, looms, the noisy kids that enraged the men while delighting the women. It was the continual dashing from one task to the next that he hated, ten balls in the air all at once. Then he thought of Rowan. He thought of how he would tell her about the day, how much she would laugh and enjoy it. Suddenly he couldn't wait to get back.

Chapter Twenty-Five

By the time Saul reached home, Rowan had been in hospital for some hours. She remained there for weeks, emerging every now and then for a few days at home and being bundled back in as soon as her blood pressure rose, which it did almost the moment she stood up. She was bewildered, tearful and anxious. Saul soon discovered that the best thing he could do was to say nothing at all about Judge's beyond a soothing and often repeated, 'Nothing to worry about. Everything's fine.'

Lots of people visited her, since the maternity wing was attached to the main hospital and it seemed that most people at some time or another had a visit to make there. Everyone loved the maternity wing, peering in at the new babies. Only Rowan hated it. She was beginning to believe that she would never have a baby of her own, that it would die and she would be left forever with a paralysing grief.

To begin with she was in the GP wing merely for bedrest, and no one took much notice of her. As time went on and she did not improve, the size of the baby started to give cause for concern. To Rowan they seemed ridiculously anxious, because she had an enormous belly, like a mountain distending her thin body, but nonetheless they transferred her to the ward for difficult cases. The consultant came round every day and listened to her bump, feeling her increasingly podgy ankles and wrists.

'Who would have thought you'd be a problem, at your age?' he said to her. 'Not even twenty-one!'

She felt ashamed of herself for lack of reproductive skill. 'Is there going to be a problem?' she asked humbly.

He lifted his eyebrows at her impudence. 'I really couldn't say, Mother. We may induce you a little early. I shall let you know if it's advisable.'

'Thanks very much,' said Rowan morosely. This wasn't her baby any more, it was barely even her body; they were toys for the professionals to play with.

She complained to Saul. 'Honestly, the man's a clam, he won't say a thing. I don't like him one bit.'

'Does he know what he's doing?' asked Saul.

'Hard to say. I suppose we'll know afterwards. It's all rather frightening really.'

He held her hand tight. Every day, after his visit, he sat in the car and thought about the swollen, ill girl in the bed. The weight of his responsibility crushed him.

Most nights he went home to find Sally waiting up for him, with a casserole or something in the oven. He was grateful, but these days he was increasingly uncomfortable in her company. There was something about the way she behaved towards him that pushed the relationship beyond the place he intended it to be, although there was no convenient niche for brothers and sisters-in-law. Two sexual beings in a proximity closer than would have been acceptable in any other situation, and yet neither was supposed to acknowledge it.

'Look,' said Saul at last, 'you don't have to wait up for me. And you don't have to cook either, I can manage for myself.'

Sally flushed. 'You'd just have some bread or something, you wouldn't eat properly. I like to look after you. I like waiting for you to come in.'

'All the same, I'd rather you didn't.'

She turned quickly away, and he knew she was crying. All his soft-hearted sympathy reproached him. She was a vulnerable little girl.

'Please don't get upset,' he said awkwardly. 'If you really want to stay up, then I suppose it's all right. Sally, please stop crying.'

'Thank you. Thank you!' Her blue eyes, washed with tears, seemed infinitely appealing. Of the two sisters, Sally was by far the more sensual of the two, he thought. Mature breasts thrust out against her jumper, in contrast to her bitten nails. He knew, without a doubt, that they should not be here together like this. But what could he do? Sally had no one's exclusive love and the least he could do was offer her affection. Yet here was a luscious young girl alone in the house with him, and his wife locked up in hospital.

The next night Sally cooked *coq au vin*. She had dressed in a jumper with a low scooped neck, showing two inches of cleavage, and her hair was caught up on either side of her head in diamante clips.

'Are you going somewhere?' asked Saul doubtfully.

She laughed. 'Not at this time of night. I just thought it was about time you saw something more appealing than hospital nighties.'

'I find what's in that hospital nightie very appealing.'

Hoping he had quelled her, he sat down and began to eat the meal.

'Is it all right?' asked Sally, sitting opposite him and leaning forward. 'It's a new recipe and it took me ages.'

'It's all right.' All Saul's natural politeness struggled against such brusque praise. He tried not to look at Sally. In the gentle light of a table lamp she appeared luminous, her body infinitely soft, her hair a cloud around her head. He was too tired for all this. What he needed was not a precociously sexual teenager but his own solitary bed.

'Do you like me, Saul?' asked Sally.

He pushed his plate away and considered. 'Sometimes. Tonight, not a lot.'

Her cheeks flamed. 'How can you say that? I cooked you a lovely meal, I waited hours for you! Don't you even think I look pretty? I tried so hard, Saul.'

There was no tempering of the wind. He said, 'You're trying as hard as you know how. As far as I can work out you are doing your devilish best to seduce me, though why that should please you when your sister's ill and unhappy in hospital is an absolute mystery.'

Sally giggled naughtily. 'But she wouldn't know, would she? We'd have such fun. I'm quite experienced, you know, I'd make it good for you.'

'I have never been interested in the leavings of mangy tomcats, I'm afraid.'

There was a terrible silence. Sally stood up very slowly. 'You don't know what it's like,' she said. 'Nobody cares about you unless they're getting something, and with men it's the same thing every time. And you don't really love Rowan. You married her to get Judge's, and now you've got rid of her to hospital you're as pleased as a dog with two tails. The pathetic thing is that she thinks you love her. Bastard!'

He blinked. What he felt and what she thought he felt were so far apart as to be quite unrelated. 'Things aren't as sour as they look to you,' he managed. 'And nothing's that simple either – give me this and I'll give you that. You don't have to sell yourself to be liked. You're a beautiful girl. If you would just value yourself a bit more you'd start to see we don't have to be animals!'

Sally eyed him assessingly. 'You blackmail Rowan into doing what you want,' she said.

'Oh my God.' Saul put his fist to his forehead. 'Look,' he began, 'our marriage, mine and Rowan's, is our business. We don't need you standing on the sidelines giving a running commentary. To you things look one way; to us, each of us, they aren't like that at all. Your sister is – she's every bit as insecure as you, but a thousand times more determined. That isn't easy to live with.'

Seeing her opening, Sally hunched a shoulder. 'Like I said, what you need is some relaxation.' Quite suddenly Sally pulled off her top. She stood, smiling, her breasts restrained by a minuscule lace bra.

'Put that back on,' said Saul tightly.

She laughed, pulled her bra down and jiggled her breasts at him. 'You know that you want to,' she whispered, in a parody of the seductress.

Saul leaped towards her. As he caught her round the waist and upended her, Sally's triumph turned to fear. 'Stop it! Leave me alone!' she wailed, kicking and screaming like the child she was.

'I'll teach you to play your filthy games,' roared Saul, and walloped her bottom with the flat of his hand, five, six, seven times. Sally screeched and struggled, but he would not let her go. When at last he released her she collapsed sobbing on to the floor, cradling her bottom in her hands.

'I think you'd better move out,' said Saul menacingly.

She looked up at him through strands of tear-soaked hair. 'I wouldn't stay here if you paid me. Pig! I can afford my own flat, you know, I own a quarter of the firm! Then we'll see who I get to come and visit.'

He pointed a parental finger at her. 'You will go to an all-girls hostel and stay there!' he roared. 'I'll not have you setting up as a part-time tart, you'll learn some discipline for once in your life. And if a word of this reaches Rowan, you'll find out what it's like to get a real spanking. In comparison that last little effort was a few light taps!'

'Brute! Bastard!' screamed Sally, but he was gone. She took off her shoe and hurled it viciously against the closed door.

He told Rowan that Sally had left after she had been placed in the care of the hostel matron. It had been instant antagonism. The matron sensed trouble and bristled, causing Sally to salute the enemy by turning her radio on full blast.

'She'll be OK,' said Saul, reassuring himself as much as Rowan.

'Tell her to come and see me,' begged Rowan. 'I worry about her. She hasn't been for over two weeks.'

'Since she started her course. It's much easier for her now she's at the hostel, no buses.'

'Yes.' Rowan felt helpless and out of it. Nobody ever considered her any more, they made decisions and told her afterwards.

They decided to induce the birth at just over eight months. Rowan was seriously unwell, when Saul looked at her he could believe she might die. There had been a light in her that he only remembered when he saw it extinguished, as it was now, as she lay with a drip in her arm and the line of her chin quite lost in swelling.

'Not long,' he said, taking his seat beside her.

'You've had a drink. I can smell it.'

'You bet I have. Wish you could have one too, actually.'

'So do I.' She put out her free hand and he held it. They had taken her wedding ring off weeks ago, when her finger had swollen. Suddenly she started to cry.

Saul smoothed her hair, feeling so close to her, wishing he could pick her up and run far away. 'What is it, lovey? Tell me.'

'I'm so frightened. Suppose it is all wrong, suppose it isn't the right shape? They never tell us anything. I don't want to be here, they treat me like an animal.'

'I think they know what they're doing,' he said helplessly.

'We wouldn't know if they didn't.'

They watched in silence as a nurse came in and adjusted the drip, patting Rowan as she left. 'She thinks I'm a dog,' growled Rowan. 'Pat pat, all day long.'

'They treat me worse than a dog,' said Saul. 'The moment I walk in there's a swishing of curtains, as if they were shutting out some prowling wild beast. I'm beginning to feel like a convicted rapist.'

'It's all your fault, that's why. They blame the men for all this, we women had nothing to do with it.'

Saul did not reply. He knew she had had nothing to do with it.

The contractions began about twenty minutes later. Every now and then Rowan was examined to see how she was getting on, and Saul was sent out into the waiting room. He found Diana there.

'Saul, I popped in to see her and they said they'd started her off. Why so early, is she all right?'

He had hardly exchanged a word with her in the last year, he realised. 'I don't know, I think so. She's fed up, of course. It's her blood pressure, they won't leave her any longer.'

'Blasted hospitals! They will interfere so. Ask if I can go in for five minutes, I'd love to see her.'

But they were permitting no visitors except, reluctantly, the father. The consultant swept in occasionally, peered at Rowan, told her to be a good girl, and left. 'Woof woof,' she said loudly but he did not reply, merely raising his eyebrows and leaving. His expression conveyed that he had known all along that he was right about these creatures; the gravid woman was brainless.

Three hours later she was too weary for humour. So many faces, peering down at her. Another three hours, the shift changed and all the nurses were different, but the consultant was there and always, thankfully, Saul. Increase the drip, look at the foetal monitor, listen. They discussed her in huddles in the corner of the room, holding her fate in their hands and presuming their right to keep it to themselves.

As the consultant bent over her yet again, always avoiding her eyes, she demanded, 'What's the matter? Why won't you tell me?'

'Everything's going fine, Mother,' he intoned, not looking up.

'I want my husband back. Why do you keep sending him away? I want him.'

The consultant turned to speak to a nurse. 'Get Mother something to calm her please, Sister.'

'I don't want anything to calm me! I want to know what

the hell's going on, I want my husband. I want my baby!'

'Of course you do, dear.' The sister bustled up, it was her duty to protect the doctors from distraught patients. Rowan thought, 'This is a nightmare, they've trapped me here, I shall never escape.' 'I want to go home,' she wailed.

They hustled Saul back in, because Mother was getting herself in a state. 'Are they telling you anything?' she asked pathetically. 'Nobody even looks at me.'

'I think we'll hurry her up,' said the consultant, staring at the monitor, and nurses rushed to adjust the drip.

The room came and went in a recurring wave of pain. Rowan had no sensation of giving birth, the baby was being ejected from her, wrenched too early from the womb. Neither she nor the baby was ready for it. Unable to move because of the wires and tubes, she lay stranded and suffering. 'Can't you give her something?' Saul kept asking. His hands were cut by her nails where she had gripped him.

'Not long now,' intoned the consultant.

'Too many drugs don't help baby,' whispered the sister, explaining. 'They won't let it get too bad.'

'It's too bad already,' muttered Saul. He barely trusted himself to say more. The sight of Rowan lying there, agonised, almost reduced him to tears. Once, and only once, she cried out, but immediately clamped her lips shut on the pain.

'You don't have to be brave in front of me,' whispered Saul.

When she could speak, she said weakly, 'It's not you, it's them. Why don't they go away. I want to be left alone.'

Suddenly the consultant was putting on plastic gloves. 'Forceps please, sister,' he said distantly. 'Tell the husband to leave.'

'Why don't *you* tell the bloody husband?' yelled Saul. 'I'm not leaving, I'm staying here.'

But they hustled him out. 'We have to think of the baby,' said the sister accusingly, and defeated him. He stood outside the door, listening to Rowan's small choked gasps of pain.

They put her legs up in stirrups and gathered in a scrum at the end of the bed. The sister put a mask over her face and told her to breathe. She struck it away because they were suffocating her. It was torture, absolute torture. Pain, between her legs, sharp, raw, but more bearable than the other. The consultant began pulling, it was like having her innards extracted, the sister at one end holding her down, a dozen people at the other disembowelling. She closed her eyes, her teeth clenched to breaking point. She could hear the sister whispering 'All right, dear, all right, this is the worst, soon over.' When, suddenly, it stopped she didn't believe it. Seconds passed before she opened her eyes. Nobody spoke.

'It's a little girl, dear.'

'Can I see her?'

'She's had a rough time. She needs some help, they've taken her straight away to special care.'

'What's she like? Is she all right, has she got everything? She'll be all right, won't she?'

The sister looked down at the exhausted, wrecked girl on the bed. What could she say to her, now, when she had been through so much, with courage that even brought the odd kind word from the consultant? 'You've been a very brave girl, my dear.'

So the sister prevaricated. 'Baby's had a big struggle, but she has all her arms and legs. There's nothing missing at all.'

Rowan's face relaxed. Even so soon after the birth the swelling was subsiding. She looked again like a mischievous, green-eyed cat.

'We'll clean you up, and then hubby can see you,' said the sister. Rowan lay back, letting herself drift into warm half-sleep, believing that, in the end, everything had come right. She had her baby, she had her daughter.

'You've a daughter,' said the nurse to Saul. 'Your wife's fine.'

He felt a wave of joy building inside him, he tried to rush back to Rowan but the nurse blocked his path. 'The consultant wants to talk to you.'

Saul didn't know it wasn't standard procedure. He hung about in the corridor and the consultant strode towards him, stopping at the last moment as if to mention some minor point that had almost slipped his mind. 'Oh yes – baby Barton. Thought we might lose it at one point. Pity we didn't know. Down's Syndrome baby. Acute mental retardation. My advice to you is to institutionalise the child at once. Don't even see her, there isn't any point. The mothers get upset, you know. Sister will see to all the forms.'

He made to move away but Saul caught his arm. 'Say that again,' he said confusedly. 'What's the matter with it?'

The doctor raised his voice as if talking to an imbecile. 'Down's Syndrome,' he said loudly. 'The child's a mongol, a congenital idiot. You've got to put her away.'

He shook off Saul's stunned hand and rushed down the corridor. A nurse said, 'He finds these things very difficult, I'm afraid. Why don't you come and have some tea?'

But Saul blundered sightless away. He found himself in the waiting room and there, still waiting, was Diana. He stared at her in disbelief.

'What's the matter? For God's sake, tell me! Is it Rowan?'

He shook his head. He wiped his hand across his mouth in a bewildered, unconscious gesture. 'That man – the doctor – he says the baby's an idiot. We've got a little girl and she's – it's Down's Syndrome.'

Diana's face barely changed. After a few moments she took an enormous breath, and Saul realised that for long seconds she had stopped breathing. 'Poor Rowan,' she said. Her voice grated as if on coals of fire. 'And poor you. I am so, so sorry.'

Suddenly he had to talk, he couldn't keep it in a moment longer. 'Rowan won't be able to take this, I never meant it to be like this. He says we've got to put it away. I mean, why don't they just knock it on the head and be done with it? They would if they could, damn them! I don't believe it, I just don't believe it. Why to Rowan? Why to us?'

Diana took his arm. 'Sit down. Come on, sit down, people are staring. It doesn't help to get upset, Rowan will see. Do you want me to go in to her and you stay here?'

'No! The whole thing's my fault. I have to stay with her.'

'If there's anything wrong it isn't anybody's fault.'

He turned his head and looked at her. She had flung on an old mac and her hair needed washing, but still she had a raw, long-boned attraction. That he could feel it, now, horrified him, but somehow all his emotions seemed very close to the surface. There were feelings in him now that he had thought lost forever: childlike terror, grief, the rage he had felt when James had everything and he so little.

'Why did you have a perfect baby?' he asked suddenly. 'You didn't deserve it.'

She recoiled. 'God help us if we all got what we deserved.'

They came to take him to Rowan. Diana asked if she could go in and they said they would ask, but no one came to call her. She sat outside, twisting her gloves, wondering if Saul was right and she hadn't deserved Nicholas. God help her daughter. These things always broke up marriages, destroyed people. 'Dear God,' she prayed, 'if it isn't right, let it die.'

When Rowan woke Saul was sitting by the bed. 'Hi. You've been asleep for hours.'

'Have I?' She tried to ease herself up in the bed, but it hurt terribly. She lay back again. 'Have you seen her? They rushed her off and I didn't get a glimpse, but the sister said she was fine.'

'Oh. Oh, did she?' He sat there, immobile. Rowan realised that he must be at least as tired as she.

'You ought to get some sleep,' she said fondly. 'Tell me, what does she look like?'

He took a deep breath. 'She's – a sort of little, yellow Chinese rabbit.'

A vague frown creased her brow, she was so pale, so bloodless. 'Chinese? The poor little thing. Are there any horrid marks? Sometimes they get scars. From the forceps.'

'A bit of a bruise perhaps, over her ear. Nothing much to see.'

She put out her hand, astonished at how much effort the gesture required, and rested it on his sleeve. 'I'm just so relieved it came out right in the end,' she murmured. 'I can't tell you how worried I've been. When can I see her, did they say?'

'No – no, they didn't. She's still pretty sick, Ro. Incubator, oxygen, the lot.'

'I know, it looks terrible, doesn't it? I used to pop in and have a look in special care when they let me get up for a bath. They nearly all get better.'

He stared down at her happy, sleepy face. Exhaustion was dulling his senses, he couldn't think or talk coherently. The last place he wanted to be was here. Without a word he got to his feet and started to leave but Rowan called out in a high, nervous voice: 'Saul? Saul, what's the matter?'

He took two more steps before he realised he had to stop. 'Saul?' she called out again. 'What is it?'

He went back to the bed. There was no easy way of saying it. 'She's got Down's Syndrome,' he said flatly. 'Our baby's a mongol.'

Those eyes, so large and green, in Japan he had thought he could drown in them. They were like hard, impenetrable glass. 'You don't mean that,' she said.

'Yes, I do. There isn't any doubt, even I can see she isn't right. They didn't want me to see her. They want us to put her away.'

She dragged herself up, teeth gritted against the pain. 'I've got to see! Take me there, right now!'

He shook his head, screwing his eyes tight against the tears that would not subside. 'They don't want you to. They – they say the mothers get upset.'

A nurse hurried up with something in a plastic medicine cup. 'Something to soothe you,' she said, trying to tip it willy-nilly down Rowan's throat.

'Go to hell,' said Rowan, hitting it away and spilling it. 'They showed you the wrong baby, they said my baby was fine. I want my baby!'

'I'll have to call the doctor,' said the nurse in a low voice to Saul.

Totally fraught, he shouted, 'Don't be so bloody silly, woman! There isn't a pill to put this right! She's got to realise, now, that we've got the booby prize. Our baby's a – a mongol.'

He thought that if Rowan had not spilled the medicine he would have drunk it. Anything to take away the pain. He thought his head would explode from the pressure of agonised thought. A little, yellow monkey of a child that was to be thrown in the rubbish, and forgotten about.

Rowan said, 'I hurt so much. There isn't a part of me that doesn't hurt.'

Saul thought, if it's bad for me it's ten times worse for her. He took her hand and held it tight. 'We'll come through it, lovey. Tomorrow we'll know what to do.'

'Will we?' She looked at him with such lost desperation, he had to find strength enough for two. He nodded, with false decision. 'We'll work something out. By the way, your mother's here, do you want to see her?'

Rowan's fingers tensed on his. 'I don't think I can see anybody. Ever.'

'She can come back tomorrow, I suppose.'

After a while Rowan drifted into a shocked doze. Saul went to find Diana. She was pacing the corridor with a plastic cup of cold coffee in her hand.

'She won't see anyone,' he told her. 'I don't know if she really believes it yet.'

'She ought to see the child,' said Diana shortly. 'She'd see at once that it wasn't normal, she can't possibly believe something she hasn't seen. You should insist!'

'Rowan's ill in bed, the baby's hooked up in an incubator, if the hospital doesn't agree she can't see it. And they won't agree. They want it packed off to some asylum, as soon as possible.'

Diana's face constricted. 'It might be best, you know. You're both so young – '

'Perhaps it is best, I don't know. I don't like being pushed into something like this. We ought to have time to think.'

'Look.' Diana took hold of his arm and then let go again, moving her hands as if to scrub out the unacceptable gesture. 'Look, I've had four children, all normal. Not one of them has been easy to bring up. They take up time and money and energy; they take all your goodwill and then all your rage on top. If sometimes they bring people together, then more often they drive them apart. It isn't easy. The only thing that makes it worthwhile is the lovely people you hope they're going to be.

'Oh, Saul, I wasn't a natural mother and I don't think Rowan is either, but even if she was I'd still not want her to struggle with a handicapped child. This baby can't ever be anything! The chances are it will hardly know where it is, at home with you or in some institution. Send it away.'

He had been watching her without blinking. She was suddenly aware of the square strength of his face. 'I don't think we can wriggle out of our responsibility,' he said grimly. 'If you want my opinion I think you've been a bloody awful parent, mostly because you put what you wanted before your kids. You haven't given a thought to that poor, unloved little scrap that Rowan and I produced. Nobody wants her, not even her mum and dad. At least we owe her the courtesy of deciding what's in her best interests, not just in ours, or yours, or the bloody hospital's! Everybody but the baby can take care of themselves, and it seems to me that the one person who needs care is the one nobody cares about.'

'Blame me if you want,' retorted Diana. 'Blame whoever you damn well like, but don't make Rowan take that child home! It will finish you both.'

She turned on her heel and went out. Saul stood watching her mac swinging to the rhythm of her long stride, and he was conscious of wild, unreasoning hatred. He wanted it to be Diana's fault, somebody's fault! He wanted a victim that he could hit.

Exhaustion was dulling his brain. He knew if he should do anything, he should go home and sleep. Instead he went back to look at his daughter, pushing his way past the nurse and himself finding the secluded corner where his baby was starting her life as she was to live it, shut off and alone. When he saw her first he could not believe that she was so small, so wizened and so ugly. Now he saw that her skin was dry and flaking, the monkey skull covered with sparse wisps of hair. There was a tube in the child's nose but she was awake. A thin slit of blue eye seemed to watch him. All of a sudden he thought of a name.

'We'll call you Hannah,' he said.

Chapter Twenty-Six

Hannah lay motionless, a little yellow scrap of life. Strangely, although still in the incubator, she was without the tubes and monitors that characterised all the other babies there. Saul, refreshed by a sleep that had been as deep as it was unexpected, said: 'Are you trying to let her die?'

The nurse flushed uncomfortably. 'Of course not. Doctor feels she should be transferred as soon as she's fit.'

'Is she fit?' demanded Saul.

The nurse avoided his eye. 'Doctor would like to send her this afternoon. He says it will be better for your wife.'

Saul ran down the stairs to Rowan's ward. The curtains around her bed remained drawn. From behind them he could hear a considerable commotion.

'Don't you dare touch me with that thing! Don't you dare!' shrieked Rowan.

Saul raced down the ward and burst through the curtains. The sister, a nurse, the consultant and another man were all muttering soothingly while a syringe was produced from a kidney dish like some sort of evil missile.

'Stick that in her and I'll sue you!' declared Saul.

Rowan's expression changed from panicky fury to tearfulness. 'They won't let me see her,' she wailed. 'I tried to go and see and they stopped me, and they keep trying to make me sign forms!'

The consultant said irascibly, 'Good God, woman, we are trying to do what's best for you! Do you want to be saddled with a gibbering idiot all your life? If you take the brat you'll be back here begging us to take her away within six months. I warn you, you'll be too late then! My recommendation counts for something, I can tell you. I have women queuing up to get their great, over-sexed idiot sons taken away from them.'

'We have a little girl,' said Saul grimly. 'And nobody has once tried to explain what we can expect or where she might go or anything. The decision is ours, not yours!'

'I can't make a decision, I haven't even seen her,' wept Rowan.

The other man spoke up. 'As a psychiatrist, I fully understand the emotions you must be feeling . . .' he began.

'I bet you bloody don't!' said Saul.

'. . . and amongst them there is of course bewilderment. You feel you want to blame the hospital, to believe that they were in some way at fault. In reality we have a great deal of experience of this type of child and we can sincerely recommend – '

'Have you ever been to one of these homes?' demanded Rowan.

The psychiatrist paused. 'We – we do know of their excellent reputation – '

'I bet none of you've been,' she interrupted. 'Go on, tell me, is it a nice pretty house or a Victorian barn with stone floors? Is it only for babies or is everyone lumped in together? Well?'

The consultant sighed patiently. 'I am very well acquainted with St. Anselm's.'

'St Anselm's!' chorused Saul and Rowan together. It was the local lunatic asylum, from which inmates occasionally escaped out of locked wards to terrorise the neighbourhood.

'I'm going to take her home,' said Rowan hysterically, trying to swing her legs out of bed. 'I won't stay here a moment longer. You all think you know what's best for me. It's like a police state!'

'Hang on a minute, love.' Saul put a hand on her shoulder and restrained her more effectively than the sister's armlock of a moment ago. He glared at the consultant with loathing. 'I think she should be taken home in an ambulance, with our baby. And I want somebody to come and see her at home. Isn't there a nurse that calls round?'

'Oh, she can have the health visitor,' said the consultant contemptuously. 'See how much use she'll be when there's a sudden haemorrhage.'

'We'll take our chance. We'd like to go now, please.'

The consultant fixed his gaze on the psychiatrist, who advanced reluctantly into the fray. 'You will appreciate that neither of you is in any condition to make a rational choice,' he began. 'Naturally you feel bewildered and angry – '

'You said that before,' complained Rowan. 'We know how we feel. I just can't understand why you won't let us do one single thing that we say we want to do. It's not us that's mentally retarded, it's the baby!'

She flung back her head and stared round at them all. She had said it, she had admitted it out loud. Saul took her hand, she felt strong and calm and positive.

The consultant let out his breath in an angry sigh. 'Oh, very well, sister, get them sent home! It is after all they who will live to regret it.'

The medical staff filed away. On the bed, discarded, lay the committal forms. Saul said softly to Rowan, 'Is this what we really want to do?'

She allowed herself a small, rueful grin. 'I don't know. It might be. Can we do it first and see if we like it later? I just couldn't send her away, not without even a look.'

He kissed her dark, tousled head. He was so full of love and anguish that it almost hurt to breathe.

The ambulance was delayed for hours, and only when Saul prepared to remove wife and child in his car did it miraculously become available. As a concession to them, the baby was to be sent home in a portable incubator, so that she would continue in a constant temperature. When they saw the contraption wheeling towards them, both Saul and Rowan tensed.

'Let me see,' said Rowan, wrapped in blankets in a wheelchair. They were in the front hall of the hospital, much observed by everyone passing by. There could have been no less private place for a mother first to see her child and because of it Rowan set her face in an expression almost masklike. Saul pushed her towards the plastic box that contained their baby. She put out her hands and rested them on the upper dome, peering between her fingers at what lay within. At last after long minutes she withdrew her hands, folded them in her lap and looked away. They wheeled her into the ambulance.

The doors shut, the engine started, they began to move. In the dim light Saul, Rowan and their baby were together. 'Her name's Hannah,' said Saul. 'I don't want anything else, it seems right.'

Rowan looked at the plastic box. 'Hannah,' she tried. 'Hannah.'

'What do you think of her?'

She shrugged stiffly. 'I don't know. She isn't what I expected. I don't feel I know her. Saul, what do we give her to eat?'

He felt embarrassed. 'I thought – she'll suck from you, won't she?'

'I don't know if I want her to. Not if we're not keeping her.'

He knew without being told that Rowan was rigid with terror. She was frightened of Hannah, of herself, perhaps most of all of her own ignorance. Neither of them had any idea how to take care of a baby, let alone a handicapped one. What would Hannah turn into? Like most of the world, when they had witnessed mental disability they had simply walked the other way, never once exercising their minds on causes and possibilities. They were completely unfitted for this task.

When they reached home the ambulance men helped Rowan out and into the lift, then brought the incubator up too, plugging it into a socket in the flat's sitting room. It seemed out of place in the stark, bare, elegant room. The whole flat was geared to adult living.

'We're not ready,' apologised Saul feebly. 'I wasn't expecting this.'

The ambulance man cast a sage eye over the low shelves with the landlord's collection of delicate ornaments. 'Going to find it tough here,' he advised. 'My advice is to get somewhere a bit less open plan, with a garden. These kids need space.'

'Do you know anything about them?' asked Rowan, grabbing at this one solid piece of information.

'My sister's kiddie's one,' he said casually. 'Nice little chap. Got to watch for colds, weak chests they got. When I send him sommat at Christmas he writes me a letter, just a few words like, but he writes them. You wouldn't have believed that now, would you?'

Rowan's beam of relief was out of all proportion to the snippet of encouragement. Saul saw the men out and came back. 'Perhaps he's exceptional,' he said cautiously.

'And perhaps he isn't! Oh Saul, suppose they're all wrong? I mean, she won't ever be brilliant or anything, but she might be just sort of – average? They don't know how she'll turn out.'

He didn't want to depress her. Hannah was starting to mew, a sound that was more animal than baby. He said, 'Why don't we try feeding her?'

Apprehensively they extracted Hannah from her plastic box. She let out a cry and waved her arms about, not settling even when Rowan brought her inexpertly to the breast. Neither of the two main participants had a clue what to do and Saul could only offer vague advice. Rowan's breasts were sore and hard, the baby chewed on tender nipples without really sucking. After an hour, Rowan was in tears and the baby sucking its fists unhappily.

'She'll die of starvation. I don't know what to do! Why doesn't someone tell me what to do?'

There seemed to be nobody they could ask. The isolation of their position crushed them. They had foundered almost at once in thinking that they could cope with this child. If they asked for help, would they be accused of incompetence and have their baby forcibly taken away? Fear does not breed rational thought.

Saul said, 'Suppose we try her on a bottle? They must have done that in hospital.'

'Do you think so?' Rowan clutched at the suggestion. Within minutes Saul found himself racing out to find a chemist before it closed.

Bottle feeding did seem to be the answer, at first. They could pour milk quite easily from a fat teat into their lethargic infant. But it seemed to come out again just as easily, regurgitated all over everything and going up the baby's nose and making them think she was choking. The night passed in a haze of bottles and sick and anxiety. In her state of weary hysteria Rowan could not handle Hannah calmly, the slightest set-back caused her to panic and multiply disaster. They hadn't enough of anything, either disposable nappies or bottles or baby clothes or bedding. Again and again the baby fed, vomited over everything, and reduced Rowan to tears.

At two in the morning Saul sent Rowan to bed and bathed the baby. It was the only thing to do, although whether it would finish her off or not he could not know. She was so sticky and smelly and miserable, he lowered her into the sink and tenatively wiped at her stick like limbs with cotton wool.

'You're too small to eat much,' he told her. 'We won't feed you so much.'

He was reminded of rearing baby birds when he was young. There had been a sparrow, fallen from the nest just before fledging, which he had brought to adulthood. He dried the child and wrapped her in a towel, putting her, mewing, into the incubator while he made up yet another feed, this time thinning it drastically.

The flat was absolutely silent, except for the baby. He picked up the child and settled into a corner of the old sofa, feeling drained of everything except weariness. He started to feed his daughter, with painful slowness. It took over an hour to give her a very few ounces but at least this time it stayed down. Holding her like a piece of china, he lifted her back into the incubator and closed the top.

He had to go to bed, no power on earth could keep him awake longer. Saul staggered along the hall, cast off his clothes and fell between the sheets. Rowan was very warm and soft, he cuddled close to her to gain some of her heat. If only, if only it hadn't had to be like this! It could have been so wonderfully different. He fell, dreamless, into sleep.

Next day the health visitor came, Nurse Brown. She was a short, motherly soul, steeped in the practicalities of life. She scanned the little household with her bright eyes, taking in the mother's nerves, the father's exhaustion and the baby's sickliness. As a first step she unwrapped Hannah and weighed her.

'A very little chicken,' she said thoughtfully. 'I'm surprised they sent you home with her this small. If you wanted I could send you both to a nursing home for a few days, until you get sorted out.'

'No,' said Rowan shortly. 'It's only feeding that's a problem. I can't seem to feed her myself.'

Nurse Brown nodded. 'You won't, she's too weak. I want you to give her a bottle every two hours, a little amount each time, even if she seems too sleepy to take it. Let's try now.'

She watched as Rowan tried inexpertly to coax food into the baby. The teat was too big and milk flooded out and swamped the child. Rowan tried to mop up, got in a state and wailed.

'Let me,' said Saul, taking the little bundle in his big square hands. 'I got the hang of this last night.' Neatly and efficiently, he settled baby and bottle, tilting the teat only enough to let a gentle flow through.

'Very good,' said Nurse Brown, genuinely relieved. The mother was clearly too upset for competence, but the father seemed to know what he was doing. 'Can your mother come and stay, dear?' she asked Rowan.

They both insisted that no one was coming to stay. So it was up to the father to take care of this baby, it seemed.

On the way out, the nurse said quietly to Saul, 'Has she accepted the child? She seems very distressed.'

He sighed and ran his hands through his hair. 'We neither of us know what we've got, if we're honest. I think Rowan wants to believe it's all a terrible mistake.'

'That's as clear a case as I've seen, I'm afraid,' said the nurse, stomping out to her car in her sensible flat shoes. 'You've got a little girl that may be sweet, and may not. She'll certainly look different. And she'll need a lot of training, years and years of it. Nobody can tell you how much or how little she'll be able to do, Hannah's herself and that's all you can say. Take it as it comes, that's my advice.'

When he went back in Rowan said tensely, 'Did she say anything?'

He shrugged. 'She agrees with the diagnosis, that's all.'

'Huh!' Rowan got up stiffly and went to look down at Hannah. 'She isn't what they think, you know,' she said. 'They're all wrong. Perhaps she might be a bit slow, but if we paid for a good school she'd be all right. We'll have to look for a good one.'

Saul was stunned. 'You know that's silly,' he said gently. 'She can't be normal, Ro, there's no use hoping for it.'

Turning to him, her smile wavered and cracked. 'I know,' she sobbed. 'But I can't live with that, I can't bear it! I have to believe they're wrong.'

He put his arms round her and rested his cheek against her hair. In the hospital she had seemed to face it so bravely, he could not know that she had expected, and still expected, for the cup to pass away. There was a sense of utter desperation welling inside him, he felt that for the first time in his life he was in a situation that was both untenable and inescapable. It was terrifying.

A week later Diana insisted that they come round for lunch. It was to be Hannah's first outing and neither Saul nor Rowan particularly wanted to go. Nonetheless Saul knew that they should, because somehow the longer they hid the harder it was to come out at all.

The health visitor had sent the incubator back to the hospital. She felt it was unnecessary and tended to make the mother treat the child as some sort of freak. 'She's a child like any other,' she told Rowan, fruitlessly. 'You don't need to treat her like a wild animal. Take her out, let people see her.'

'I couldn't bear them to stare.' Rowan shuddered at the thought of it and the health visitor said forcefully, 'There's no point in being over-sensitive. She is what she is and you must love her for it. We can't order our babies like groceries, we have to take what comes. And I think it's about time you got out of that dressing gown, my girl, you should get up and get on. You've a life to lead.'

So Rowan dressed listlessly in one of her purple tunics, leaving the trousers underneath unbuttoned at the waist. Hannah wore some of the pretty baby clothes sent as presents before the birth. Against the pure white wool her face was like a wizened old man's. They packed bottles, nappies and changes of clothing, setting off an hour late for Aspley Manor.

Diana opened the door to them. 'We thought you weren't coming,' she said. 'My goodness, Rowan, you look so thin. Already.'

Rowan looked drawn and anxious, her face nothing but eyes.

Saul said, 'She could do with a good meal. We both could. Hannah takes so much looking after we've hardly time to eat.'

James came down the stairs, looking uncomfortable. He

shook Saul's hand and bent down to kiss Rowan on the cheek, a gesture as unprecedented as it was unwelcome. 'Nice to see you both,' he said heartily.

'There's three of us,' said Rowan in a small voice.

'Yes. So there is. Well, doesn't she look tiny!'

He and Diana peered in at the scrap of humanity lying in the basket. They were both horribly aware of the loud and healthy bawling coming from upstairs. 'I must go and see – ' said Diana vaguely, and hurried off.

'You don't have to worry about us seeing him,' said Rowan. 'We won't mind.'

But when they took her at her word and brought Nicholas into the drawing room, to sit in his baby chair and crow and bounce in healthy activity, she minded very much. Suddenly she put her hands up over her eyes. 'Oh God, why don't you take him away!' she said forcefully.

Diana got up at once and did so. James said, 'I'm sorry, Rowan. I did think it might be tactless but Diana felt – these things do take some getting used to. I didn't think you realised what you were taking on.'

Saul cleared his throat. 'I don't think we can go back now. Can we, Rowan?'

She said nothing for a long minute.

'Rowan?' hinted Saul.

'No,' she said finally. 'No, of course not. We're making the best of it, that's all.'

'But this might not be the best,' said James, speaking very loudly and heartily. 'There are a lot of places that take children of this age, small homes where they can be brought up just as if they were in a family.'

'Then why not keep her in the family?' said Saul. His face and tone were equally bleak. 'She's tiny, we don't even know her yet. Of course we're keeping her.'

'It's easy for you,' said Rowan in a low, miserable voice.

Saul got up and went over to the window. 'Any chance of

a drink, James?' he asked, and at once James got up and poured him a Scotch.

'I've dropped the breach of contract case,' he said pityingly.

'Thanks a bloody lot!' retorted Saul. 'That must be proof positive that we're social lepers. We don't need your sympathy. You go on and sue, James. We'll knock you into touch, don't you worry.'

James's expression did not alter. 'I know what a strain this must be,' he soothed.

Saul downed his whisky and went without asking to pour himself another. He glanced at his watch. 'Time to feed the baby, Rowan.'

'It always seems to be time.' She picked up the baby and started to unfasten Hannah's nappy. She glanced at James. 'How's business?'

He shrugged. 'Not bad. Better than for you at the moment, or so I hear. Well, you've both been so preoccupied things are bound to have slipped a bit. You should have let me buy you out while you had the chance.'

Rowan's eyes flicked across to Saul, then back to Hannah's thin little body. The baby kicked her short legs, bicycling with rare energy.

'She'll get cold.' Saul put down his drink, came across and fastened Hannah's clean nappy. Rowan wandered off to heat the bottle in the kitchen.

Diana had mistakenly indulged James in the kitchen, permitting him to stuff the room with custom-built units. Acres of worktop gleamed, enough for a restaurant, redeemed by the flowers, fruit and sculpture that Diana had installed en masse to redeem the place. Rowan couldn't find a pan. She opened and closed cupboards endlessly before she located one.

While she stood waiting at the hob, James came in. 'You ought to watch it, Rowan,' he said. 'I told you Saul would ruin you and he damn nigh has! It's about time you got back to work.'

She glanced at him coolly. 'I never believe anything you tell me, James.'

He came very close to her. 'Well, you should. You and I don't get on, ducky, but we understand each other. You're not suited to spending your days caring for a no-hope child. Get back to work! It's what you're best at.'

Rowan turned to him, the warm bottle clutched in her hands. She looked lovely, thought James suddenly, waif-like and strange. 'Do you know any children like her?' she asked.

He thought for a moment. 'There was a kid when I was young. Short, clumsy, with a big tongue. We used to tease him, make him repeat swear words and so on. And we'd muddle him up about his name and after a bit he'd cry. Someone would always take him home, we weren't that cruel.'

Rowan shuddered visibly. She who hated dependence for herself could not bear it for her child. To be at the mercy of others' charity, for all your days. Hateful, hateful affliction!

Diana came in, determinedly cheerful. 'Saul's waiting for that bottle, Rowan.' With Rowan safely despatched, she hissed at James, 'Do you really have to regale her with these horror stories? The least we can do is let her realise for herself how hopeless it all is.'

'I think somebody ought to tell her the truth!'

'I suppose so.' Diana wrapped her arms around herself, and then as if still not enough comforted, moved to let James hold her also. 'I'm just so glad it wasn't Nicholas. It should have been, you know, I'm the right age.'

Suddenly James was tired of all this emotion. He said petulantly, 'I don't suppose we could have something to eat, could we?'

Diana wasn't a natural cook. She had none of that generosity of spirit that creates rich pies and luscious gravies, cakes heavy with fruit and homeliness. Her meals were well-presented, adequate and somehow disappointing. Saul munched, found nothing he could directly criticise, and felt vaguely depressed. James too was nostalgically drawn to the memory of Marjorie's Sunday lunches, for which he had never thanked her at the time. Airy Yorkshire puddings and crispy roast potatoes, leeks done just so in a spicy white sauce. 'This is very good, dear,' he said to Diana.

'Thank you, James.' Diana turned to Rowan. 'Darling, I have to tell you – Andy's been offered an American tour.'

'Oh. Wonderful.'

'Yes, isn't it? They'll love him over there. If it wasn't for Nicholas, I think I'd go and see him perform. He'll be in New York, Boston, Washington and a couple of places I don't think God has even heard of. They throw those in to pad it out a bit. Carnegie Hall one day, schoolrooms the next.'

'Andy won't like being sold cheap,' said Rowan crisply. There was no one more conscious of his own worth than her brother. 'You ought to go, Mother, you could take Nicholas.'

Diana poked a fork round her plate. 'I don't know. I should so love to go, what do you think, James? Couldn't you come?'

But James had no wish to watch his wife mooning about after Andy and to spend his evenings listening to the endless banshee wailing of the violin. He would much prefer another kind of amusement: Lin Yu; some gambling; a little of the cocaine she had introduced him to, a lot of that stuff that made him come like a volcano. Much as he adored his wife and baby, he'd adore them far more when they got back. 'I can't really spare the time, darling,' he said mournfully. 'But you could go. Hire a nanny over there to help with Nicholas. Enjoy yourself.'

The phone rang and he got up automatically to answer it. The dining room was wood-panelled and the telephone was hidden obscurely in a carved box. As he reached in and extracted it, Saul and Rowan exchanged amused glances. James took everything, even panelling, to impossible lengths.

'Yes,' said James, and listened. He dangled the receiver from a disinterested hand. 'For you, Rowan. That ape who used to shamble around after you.'

'Joe?' She got up and hurried to the phone. 'Joe, what is it?' The line crackled and buzzed, but through it Rowan could hear Joe's voice, tight with adrenaline. 'Get back here, Ro. The place is blazing. The fire brigade's here but, my God, it's got hold!'

She was aware of her heart, thundering erratically. 'Not the mill, Joe. It'll be the cottages, not the mill!'

'It's like to be the whole bloody lot, Ro! I've got to go.'

The line went dead. She stood frozen for a long second and then slowly turned to the others. 'The mill's burning,' she said softly.

Chapter Twenty-Seven

The car squealed through the afternoon, tangling with day-trippers returning from the Dales and making its way aggressively down every twist and byway known to them. Rowan sat in the back holding the baby while Saul wrenched at the wheel. When they got near they could smell smoke, hanging in the windless air. At the end of the street a policeman tried to stop them but Rowan leaped from the car, Hannah still in her arms.

'Let me through. That's my mill burning, that's Judge's!'

'Not with the baby, miss,' protested the policeman, and she turned and thrust Hannah at Saul. She ran down the road like a hare, when this morning she had found it hurt to walk.

Water was everywhere, trickling over the cobbles. She had to climb past a fire engine and its fat, wormlike hoses, stuck like a cork in a bottle in the gateway. The mill had been built for another age, it handled neither lorries nor fire engines well. When she got through and could see the gaunt front of the building, she heard herself whispering, 'Oh my God, oh my God. Thank you, God.' For there was no conflagration, there was almost nothing to see, simply an outpouring of smoke from an upstairs window.

'That's the offices,' said Saul.

She glanced at him. 'What did you do with Hannah?'

'The policeman's got her. I'm going in.'

He ran forward and Rowan went after him. The warehouse was sodden, dripping with water, and when they burst into the weaving shed so was that. A fireman, huge in waders and helmet, his axe held casually in his hand, said, 'Out of here, please. Fire's upstairs, but we're containing it.'

Rowan moved protectively towards her brand new card. 'You can lose everything except this,' she said 'we've only just got it.'

'I'm sure it's insured, madam,' said the fireman disinterestedly and tried to hustle them out.

Saul stood firm, refusing to follow his wife. 'I can't see anything,' he complained. 'It smells like an inferno, but is it just the offices?'

'That and a room that seems to have been used as a nursery. It started upstairs, funnelled through in the roof space and went into the cottages. Quite a sight when it was burning properly but we've just about got it out now, sir. If you'd like to talk to the fire chief, he'll tell you everything.'

Inexorably they were pushed back into the yard. Rowan turned and stared at the row of cottages. She had assumed from Joe's words that they had survived, she didn't even bother to look. But instead of her little house there was a shell, windows empty of glass, the neat white frames black with smoke. The curtains they had not needed at the flat hung like charred rags.

'That was our home,' she said dismally.

'Not any more,' said Saul. He went and sat down on a stone path edging. He could barely think straight, this on top of everything; Hannah, Rowan and barely three hours sleep a night. He felt ill.

'Here, mate.' It was Joe Partridge, and he had a bottle. Saul put it to his lips and drank, deliberately scorching his throat. He coughed hoarsely. 'Thanks.'

'Could see you needed it. Bit of a bad do all round lately.'

'You can say that again. Can't quite take it in, really, but it looks as if the cottages are finished.'

'And the offices. By the way, they think it started in that nursery of yours. Some plonker stuck a nappy over a heater and left it turned on.'

'Oh, Christ!' He reached again for the bottle and drank.

It seemed to be having little or no effect.

He got up and stood staring at the diminishing stream of smoke coming from the offices. All his best schemes came to nothing, the baby, Rowan, even the goddammed nursery. It was as if the world was run by joyless puritans, only happy when they could see people like Saul, fun, amusing people, brought down. If you were James, gave nothing away, used love like tissue paper, betraying and deceiving at every turn, you got what you wanted. It was Saul who lost out, every time.

A long arm stole round him. It was Rowan, snuggling up against him. 'It's not so bad. The mill's still there, nothing important went.'

'I look at the work there is to do and I feel so, so tired.'

'It's not that bad. We'll get through.'

He marvelled at her because, since the baby, she had been lost and helpless. This was the old Rowan, staring clear-eyed into the future.

'What would you have done if the mill had gone?' he asked, because for himself he didn't think he would have cared.

'I'd start it again,' said Rowan, and then as he looked dubious she said fiercely, 'I would, you know! It's important, Judge's. Important to me.'

Word of the fire soon spread. That evening as they sat exhausted in the penthouse flat, the doorbell rang. It was a courier, with an expensive meal for two, a bouquet of flowers and a bottle of champagne, courtesy of some friends of Saul.

'I can't believe this,' said Rowan, confronting creamed quail and a glass of dry champagne. 'The mill almost burned down today and we're celebrating.'

'So we should be,' said Saul, raising his glass and chinking it on hers. With several pre-dinner drinks inside him, he was feeling decidedly optimistic. 'I think that the fire should get us off the hook. I didn't tell you but the bank was cutting up rough. We've got a whacking great overdraft at the moment and you know how short-sighted they are. The insurance money should calm them down a bit. The trouble is, we've expanded so damn quickly, we can't get the orders out as fast as we have to stock up to deal with them.'

'Have we expanded?' asked Rowan in surprise. She had vaguely believed that Judge's was plodding on much as before, because Saul never said anything different.

'We are in demand, my sweet,' admitted Saul. 'I've pulled orders right, left and centre. The problem is filling them.'

'Oh, Saul.'

He waggled his empty glass at her and then picked up the bottle to fill it. 'Don't you "Oh, Saul" me! Plod plod plod, that's you. We're up and running, and thanks to the fire we should run a bit faster. Now that the cottages are ruined, we can pull them down and have one hell of a lot more space.'

The champagne was going to Rowan's head, she felt light-hearted suddenly.

'Shall we get a nanny?' she asked. 'Then I can come back and take care of everything.'

'It doesn't need taking care of,' said Saul irritably. He ate a mouthful of the quail and paused. 'My God,' he said softly, 'real food. Rowan, taste it – quick. I haven't experienced this since I was last in France, it's what food's supposed to be. I'd almost forgotten such things existed.'

Rowan tasted cautiously. 'Bit rich for me.'

'Rich! To a man who lives on frozen pizzas or that appalling leather your mother thinks is roast beef, this is what life ought to be! Here, I'll have yours as well.'

Rowan ate bread while Saul devoured the goodies. When he finished, he put on a record, a quickstep. 'Come on,' he said, putting down his glass. 'Tonight we're letting our hair down.'

She giggled and pushed back some chairs. She had learned to quickstep at school and had never tried it outside a gym.

She was wearing purple pyjamas and felt drunk with champagne and weariness.

'This is turning me on,' said Saul softly. 'Who are you, lovely lady?'

She went on tiptoe to murmur in his ear. 'I am Masha, the Russian spy, and you will come to my room and tell me everything.'

'What do you want to know?' he asked throatily.

'How to get out of Birmingham on the ring road.'

Their footwork dissolved in giggles, and they went hand in hand to sit down. 'Somebody must know how to get out of Birmingham,' said Saul. 'It stands to reason.'

'He's lost his reason,' said Rowan. 'Forty times round the Bullring and we all do. He's fled the country, taking the knowledge with him.'

'And the police are even now trying to extradite him from South America,' added Saul. 'They've got forty Nazi war criminals and still Fred Bloggs eludes them. We ought to break this to the nation, they deserve to know.'

Rowan picked at the concoction they had been sent for pudding. 'Why do these people mess food up so?' she remarked.

'Darling, it's called cooking,' said Saul sardonically. 'One day you might try it.'

She made a face at him. Tomorrow would be different from today. With Hannah asleep and Saul close at hand and her mill miraculously spared, she felt suddenly overwhelmed. Perhaps things could never be as she wished them, but it was a waste of a life to pine always for what you couldn't have. When she heard the mill was burning she had thought it was the end, that she wouldn't be able to go on, and now she found that in fact they were lucky. The tide had turned for them. She had space again.

Undressing in the bedroom, she said, 'We'll get a nanny.'

Saul's head came up. It was he who was bearing the brunt of Hannah's care, he who coaxed the food down and mopped up when she was sick. Rowan couldn't do it, or more to the point, wouldn't do it. Her apparent calm hid something worryingly fundamental.

'You'll get used to her,' he said cautiously.

'Will I? Saul, I meant it. We must have someone to help.' She looked at him pleadingly.

'Do you really not want her?' he asked bluntly. 'We agreed we'd try.'

Rowan brought her knees to her chin and sat on the bed in silence. He said 'Rowan!' insistently and she said in a low, rushed voice, 'I do want to keep her. It would tear me apart not to have her. And it tears me apart to look at her every day and know what she is. I will get used to it, I know I'll get used to it, but I can't do it all at once! I'm going back to work. The mill needs me, especially now. I've got to get back to work.'

He sighed, gustily. 'You know, last time we worked together, it almost broke us up. Do you want me to leave, is that what you're saying?'

'Do you mean Judge's, or me, or both of us?'

There was the small, snuffling sound of Hannah starting to wake. No sleep for them yet, they faced another hour at least of feeding. 'I do love you, Rowan,' said Saul softly. 'You and Hannah.' He went to get the baby out of her cradle. She was such an odd little thing. As he became more accustomed to her he found he preferred her wizened little face to that of the normal variety. There was a certain crushed charm.

Rowan said, 'Judge's does need me. I can run it so well, you don't know.'

'Perhaps I do know. Perhaps that's what I don't like.'

Rowan took the baby and started the feed. Saul couldn't help but notice how often she avoided looking straight into Hannah's face, and when she did she seemed to brace herself, as if suffering a stab of pain. For himself the wound was scabbing over; Hannah was as she was and that was that. Rowan still bled.

He said, 'We'll get a nanny and split the work in Judge's. I'll do the selling. I'll have my own staff, do my own trips, have a separate office, separate brief, separate everything. We'll try it and see.'

She put down the baby and flung her arms around his neck, pressing herself into him like a cat. Despite himself she aroused him. Almost against his will he found his hands on her breasts and his knee forcing her legs apart.

'Ow! Don't, Saul. It still hurts.'

Of course it did, he was a brute. He let her go back to the baby.

They found a girl to come and help. Her name was Barbara. Young, eager and tender-hearted to a fault, she was delighted to have a baby whose needs were so great. Decidedly plump, she lived in Sally's little flatlet, an undemanding sort of girl with soft brown hair and breasts that swelled against her hand-knitted jumper. To his own incredulity Saul found himself fantasising about screwing her, and hated himself for it. The girl wasn't even particularly attractive! But he had been months without sex, and the enforced celibacy showed every sign of continuing.

Quite suddenly there was no reason why Rowan should not go back to work. On the first day she hung around the flat, upsetting Barbara. Saul had gone early, saying he had to talk to the insurers, and Rowan had been about to leave for the mill when she thought suddenly, 'I can't.' Suppose the baby forgot her? In a feeble mind there must be a very small reservoir of memory. Rowan was filled with the horror that she might be supplanted.

Barbara said, 'It's all right, Mrs. Barton. Really it is.'

Rowan hated to believe that might be true. Didn't she matter at all to the baby? She went to the cradle and peered in, watching Hannah wave her arms and legs in that odd, slow, swimming motion she had. It was heartbreaking to watch her, heartbreaking to think of her. Rowan picked up her bag and rushed out.

Gradually, as the weeks passed, a sense of order began to seep back into Rowan's life. Every day she worked at the mill and every evening rushed back to be with Hannah and Saul. She loved to watch him with the baby, a big man moved to gentleness, endlessly patient. It was Saul who taught her how to play with the child, because he was so open and unembarrassed. He would sit with Hannah on his lap, her head lolling and her eyes unfocused, and he'd puff out his cheeks into balloons, roll his eyes, gobble like a turkey, whistle like a train.

And the little girl would watch him. It was as if he conjured life out of something only half alive. When Saul played, Hannah emerged from whatever refuge she inhabited and played with him. Once, after twenty minutes of puffing and blowing and tickling, she smiled.

'Did you see that?' Even Saul couldn't believe it.

'Yes. Yes, I saw. Do you think it was wind?'

'Not a bit of it. That was a smile, a proper smile. Do it again, sweetheart, smile for Daddy.'

They waited, Saul jiggled the scrawny body between his square brown hands. The mouth opened, the skin stretched, and Hannah smiled. 'What did I tell you?' He put out his arm and pulled Rowan into his hug. She pressed her face against his chest, forcing back the tears.

They went out to the cinema to celebrate. It was some improbable adventure film with blood everywhere and car chases. After the fifth man had been horribly blasted all over the screen, Saul took Rowan's hand and led her out of the row, pushing past all the avid, popcorn-eating couples.

'Sorry – sorry – I'm blocking your view. Don't worry, it's an act of charity – no, we're not ill, but if we stay much longer we will be.'

Outside in the foyer, Rowan said, 'It wasn't that bad.'

'Yes it was. Anyway, you looked bored to tears. I want to talk about our wonderful baby, not sit and feel my brain turn to porridge. Whatever happened to the good films?'

Rowan giggled. 'Daddy said the best film ever was "Casablanca".'

'Man of insight, your dad. They don't make 'em like that any more.' He sucked in his lips, pretending great age and lost teeth.

'Stop it, you fool!' A policeman was watching them stonily, but Saul merely crouched to half his height and did his Quasimodo impersonation. 'The bells, the bells!'

Pink-faced and weak with laughter, Rowan dragged him off round the corner. He straightened up, held her and they kissed, very gently.

'I wish we could go to bed,' murmured Saul.

'Another six weeks, the doctor said.' Rowan's scar tissue had healed painfully. The hospital had removed some and restitched the wound. Saul was beginning to believe they would never touch again!

She put her hand to his cheek, trying to soothe and apologise. 'Let's walk,' she suggested.

He took her hand and squeezed it. 'Yes, let's. It's you with the sore bottom and it's me that's complaining. And on a day when Hannah smiled!'

They set off through Bradford's wide streets. Like many industrial cities, here and there great monolithic blocks of concrete stood in place of older, prettier buildings, but the Wool Exchange remained, and the steep side streets with their shops and warehouses. It was an exotic city too, peopled at night by Asian youths in billowing cotton trousers, here and there an older man shepherding his veiled womenfolk homeward. The dome of the Alhambra Theatre was like the relocation of an eastern temple, a monument to civic self-importance.

They walked hand in hand, for once taking the time to watch the world pass by. When Rowan tired, they sat by the fountain outside the Law Courts, watching the floodlights play upon the water.

'She never smiles for me,' said Rowan wistfully.

'But you never smile for her,' replied Saul.

She nodded. Sometimes the depth of her love for Hannah amazed her, but its shadow was the depth of her pain. 'Why us? Why her?' she burst out, and Saul shook his head.

'I don't know. It seems so cruel to do this to a little one. Life is everywhere: fit, healthy, lively babies. But – it seems to me it's only a tragedy if we make it one. If we love her for what she is, then we've a sweet, smiling little girl. We don't have to make her suffer because we're so greedy we want more.'

Rowan ducked her head into his chest. 'You're so much tougher than me. I'm stupid and practical. I'm always staring at the ground and you never look at it at all.'

He laughed. 'Which is why I keep falling over my feet, sweeting. Love you.'

'And I love you, so very much.'

They walked back, hand in hand, through the swirling river of people emerging from the cinema. In the car Saul played Frank Sinatra love songs on the cassette, while Rowan snuggled down into the cracked leather seats and was happy.

Chapter Twenty-Eight

There was something delicious, thought James, about the smell of a strange woman. Diana had excited him like this once. How long was it before strange became familiar, and ultimately commonplace? Two years perhaps? He had known Lin Yu just eighteen months, although of course he didn't see her all that often. If Richard was home, she would ring him at work and he would know not to call round on Wednesdays. Lately she had been ringing him quite often, he realised, although he hadn't heard a squeak from Richard. They remained, he and Richard, despite all his efforts, on terms of distant politeness.

He rolled over and nuzzled Lin Yu's flat belly. She languidly permitted it. Was he imagining a shade of impatience in her? Young and lovely girls only put up with old men for their money, he thought nastily. In one of those shifts which so alarmed people who knew him well, he lost his temper. 'What the hell's the matter with you? If you don't want to do this you can get out of the damned flat, I'm not paying to be tolerated!'

Lin Yu shrank back up the bed. 'Please, James,' she murmured. 'I think you must be very tired. I too am very tired. It has been a hard day.'

'You should have an easy day if you know I'm coming round. By the way, my wife's going on a trip. I want you to cancel everything, and I mean everything, for the next three weeks. I shall be coming here a lot.'

'But – you can't!' For the first time since he had known her she looked discomfited. Her hair was in a tangle over her shoulders, her knees poked through as angular as a child's.

'I can, my sweet,' he said with a purr.

She scrambled towards him, pressing herself against his back and caressing him with her little, sharp-fingered hands. 'But James, it is Richard! He will be here, his flat is being decorated, he will be staying here! I am so sorry, James, I will make it up to you.'

He caught her wrist and pushed it down to the bed. She followed and lay, trying to smile. 'Lin Yu,' he said softly, 'today I rang Richard's firm. He is in South Africa and has been for a month. So what was wrong with Wednesdays?'

Her only concession was a swallow. She tried to laugh. 'You have found me out, James. Good heavens.'

'Would you like to tell me about it?' She tried to wriggle out of his grasp but he gripped her narrow bones tight and she winced. 'That wasn't a request,' he added.

Physical violence frightened her a lot, her smooth saffron skin was tinged with grey. Speaking quickly, she said, 'I have a friend living with me. From Hong Kong, a good friend. He does not like you, James. He wants to marry me, and I should like to marry. So you see – ' Her voice cracked and tailed away.

He let her go and lay back, thinking. He was feeling old, but if he had seen himself then he would have felt better. There was something indestructibly youthful about James's long-boned legs and slim hips, something that not even grey hairs and a sagging belly could entirely destroy. 'Has he any money, this bloke?' he asked.

'He has a job in a supermarket. A manager.'

'Trainee manager, you mean.' James laughed at her. He knew Lin Yu's tastes were not likely to be satisfied by any modest income. It occurred to him that he had no real regard for her at all, he respected nothing except her expertise and that was odd, because he often liked the street girls, he liked their grit.

'Right,' he said at last. 'We can finish this now if you want. Out of the flat by the end of the week.'

'James! Oh, don't be so silly, James.' She began to stroke his foot, to conciliate him.

'Do you still see Richard?' he asked. It was for Richard he felt most aggrieved, because while he did not wish her to love himself, he thought she should love Richard. Although no doubt Richard also treated Lin Yu to this or that trinket, James preferred to think that their relationship was not in the least businesslike. He had a slice of Richard's girlfriend, and left the rest, complete with emotional ties, to his son.

'I see Richard sometimes,' she said cautiously. 'My friend – he does not like Richard.'

'Bit of a pain, this friend of yours,' said James. He visualised Lin Yu and her skinny little Chinese, which admittedly was a much more sensible physical match for her. 'I'm not paying for his little love nest. Look, I'll do this for you. You can keep the flat, for now. I don't want any trouble over when I want to come, though. I ring you and that's that. I come first or you're out. As for Richard, I'll not have you upsetting him. I'm having a shooting weekend while my wife's away, he can bring you. I expect you to make him accept. And I want him looking happy.'

She got off the bed and went to a little box on the dressing table. It was cocaine and she brought it over to the bed, on a beautiful glass tray. James prepared to snort the drug, but then he stopped and tapped the straw on the girl's hand. 'Tell me what you think of me. Honestly.'

For a minute he thought she was going to fob him off with a platitude but she said, 'You are a frightening man, James. You have no care for anyone.'

He thought of Diana, Richard, Nicholas. He said, 'Not true. I just don't care for you much, that's all. But I don't see why that should inconvenience anybody.'

He took up the straw, sniffed hard and felt the sharp burn in his nostrils. The high was immediate, the colours in the room leaped out at him with sudden brilliance. Lin Yu was snorting as well. As she bent he came at her from behind, breaking into her little body like a bull. The feeling of power, the subjugation of this woman, was total pleasure.

When James bought Aspley Manor he also acquired the shooting rights to a considerable area of wood and moor. The woods yielded mainly driven pheasants and a few woodcock, and the moor was grouse with a small flight pond for those who wanted to get up at dawn and freeze while waiting to pot duck. The idea of it pleased him but in reality James was a mediocre shot. He spent a fortune on shooting lessons but was too impatient to listen to what he was told. But, since the moor was keepered and had to be shot, he held weekends. This year he could get at least one out of the way without Diana recording every miss.

It was early in the season and a number of people were still away, so as a last-minute thought he included Saul. That way he felt sure there would be at least one person shooting less well than himself and he could patronise to his heart's content. Besides, he could afford to be sorry for him now, saddled with Hannah. James fingered the photograph of Nicholas he kept on his desk. He thought of the little boy's laugh, his happy chuckle. He had much to be grateful for.

On the day itself, Land Rovers and Range Rovers roared up to the house. Caterers had been called in to provide everything from drinks and bacon sandwiches to a lavish over-the-top lunch, which Diana would have stopped if she had known, since it was a trademark of the nouveau riche. So were James's guns, too new and prettily scrolled all over with pictures of deer and birds. He had once been heard advising the owner of a valuable and well-worn sidelock on how to get one more or less the same, a tale on which that venerable shooting man dined out still.

When Saul stepped out of his Aston, James at once strolled over to him.

'How are you, old fellow? I can lend you a gun if you need one.'

'That's OK, James, I've brought my own,' said Saul. James felt a flicker of annoyance because Saul ought to be a novice, he owed it to his elder brother.

They both stood and watched as Richard's latest sports car chugged up, with that ridiculous pant of a high performance engine trying to crawl.

'Ye Gods, that's a Maserati,' said Saul in wonderment. 'Do you print money for him, James?'

'It's you that's out of step, Saul, old boy,' said James. 'The rest of the family likes making money.'

Saul observed Lin Yu stepping out of the car in a short mink jacket and thigh-high leather boots worn over jeans. 'And he likes spending it, I see. Wow!'

James allowed a smile to cross his face. Lin Yu looked exquisite, her hair in a pony tail that stretched past her waist. She teetered behind Richard like a faithful dog. 'I don't know why you insisted on Lin Yu coming,' said Richard as he approached. 'She hates the outdoors.'

'Does she?' said James disinterestedly. 'Let's have a snifter or two.'

He thought that Saul had probably started already, he smelled of mouthwash. They drank brandy and the conversation got louder and more raucous. The men with dogs began to look at their watches.

'Right then, we'll be off,' said James at last, and began directing people to get in this or that car. It was a muddle because he told Lin Yu to get into a Range Rover with two exuberant Labradors and it was clear she did not like dogs.

'Oh, for God's sake,' said Richard and shoved her into the front seat of a dogless Land Rover. James felt a stab of irritation. He had made a considerable effort to give Richard a pleasant day and he wished he would appreciate it.

Up on the moor they had to walk about half a mile from the track. Lin Yu struggled in Richard's wake; her little voice calling 'Richard! Richard!' could be heard almost continuously. The keeper, a dour man who felt he deserved better things, muttered to Saul, 'Right bloody picnic this is! No decent guns, dogs half-trained and fucking Susie Wong. My poor birds don't deserve it, I don't mind telling.'

'Get me a good spot, will you?' asked Saul, *sotto voce*.

'I should think I will, sir,' said the keeper. 'You're the only chance we've got of hitting a sodding thing.'

Consequently, Saul found himself in the middle of the line. A crack clay pigeon shot, with considerable experience of live game, it amazed him that James thought him a beginner. What more proof did he need that James never exercised his brain for a moment on anyone other than himself? He leaned against the front wall of the butt, setting out his cartridges and checking his gun. The air, still tinged with summer's warmth, smelled of earth and bracken. Bilberry bushes grew amidst the heather, he could see some fat late berries. The grouse would be feeding on bilberry, they would be full of it.

He tried not to think of the grouse who, because of him, had enjoyed their last breakfast. Live shooting was wonderful, difficult and exhilarating, but he hated the birds afterwards, still warm but with sightless eyes. He wouldn't do this any more, he thought to himself. Hannah, and his awareness of her, had altered his perception. He had to consider lives other than his own which, although different, need not be worthless. If he could destroy a bird for the pleasure of it, why not Hannah, for the convenience of it? He often wondered if that was what the hospital had intended.

The birds started to come over, high and fast, difficult shots. He took the first two with a right and left, and despite a fusillade they were the only two that fell.

'Well done,' called James in an affronted voice.

Out of the corner of his eye, Saul could see Lin Yu sitting outside Richard's butt and effectively sending all the birds to the other end of the line. Presumably Richard could not see her and assumed he was getting a thin time purely from chance. He saw three birds rocketing towards that end, but they changed course abruptly and gave him another brace. The way a shot bird would fold its wings and plummet out of the sky, it caught at his soul in triumph and in ecstasy. As he reloaded, he took out his hip flask and sipped at it, smoothly swinging his gun up to meet the next wave of birds. Dimly he heard Richard cursing Lin Yu.

On most shoots they would see lunch off and get back out again, but James's feast was not designed to be eaten or digested quickly. Once back at the house, a good drive and not convenient, the guns started to sink the booze. Saul got himself a whisky.

'You certainly know what you're doing,' said James stiffly. 'I didn't know you shot.'

'I used to do quite a bit,' said Saul. 'Not since I married Rowan, though.'

'Enjoyed making us all look fools, didn't you?'

Saul laughed. 'What I enjoyed most was watching Richard suffer from that girl. Was it your idea to get her here? She's ruining his day.'

James glanced across to where Lin Yu was desperately trying to amuse Richard, although it was clear that he wanted to talk man-talk with the others. It occurred to him that since it had been his, obviously misguided, idea, he ought to help out. He went across to her.

'Why don't I show you round the house, Lin Yu? I'm sure you'll be interested.'

'Oh! Thank you, James!' She beamed at him and rested a tiny hand on his arm. Richard said, 'Good idea,' shortly, and turned away.

James and Lin Yu left the room. The babble of conversation receded to a murmur punctuated by someone's bellowing laugh. The caterers clattered in the kitchen but otherwise all was quiet. James led the way upstairs.

'Why did you make me come?' complained Lin Yu. 'He does not want it, I do not want it. I am cold. I could have spent my day with Chang instead.'

'Don't fuss,' said James. He took her into the bedroom he shared with Diana, half thinking of using the bed, but then he thought what an insult that would be to his wife. Lin Yu said breathlessly, 'Your house is so beautiful. I would give so much for a house like this.'

'You'll not get it with your Chink supermarket manager,' said James. All of a sudden he felt terribly randy. He unzipped his trousers and allowed his penis to rear up. Lin Yu let out her breath in an angry sigh.

'Take off your jacket,' he told her. Beneath the pure silk lining she was naked. Her brown nipples stood up against her pale skin. He half sat himself on the dressing table and beckoned to her. She came, putting her hands on his thighs and kneeling on Diana's low stool. His erection fitted easily into her mouth, he heard himself chuckling as her tongue lapped the tip. Every now and then she held him with her hands and took him into her throat, he turned his palms outward and rubbed her nipples. Instinctively he knew that he was arousing her. The more he rubbed the more sensually she worked on him.

Saul, finding the downstairs cloakroom occupied, came upstairs in search of another bathroom. The door to the bedroom was an inch ajar. He pushed it aside. There, her narrow back arched and her head bent, was the Chinese girl and above her black head James was grinning. In the side mirror of the dressing-table was reflected the girl's face, enraptured by the phallus she was licking. They were so absorbed they noticed nothing. As he stepped away from the door, he heard James groan ecstatically.

Only a few guns went out after lunch, Richard and Saul included. James stayed drinking with his cronies but Lin Yu trailed along after Richard. Saul found himself looking at her, recalling her face, her little breasts pressed into James's palms. He hated himself for his excitement.

For some reason the birds were flying like chickens. The

shots were easy, even though he was squiffy Saul could hardly miss. After half an hour he decided to quit, leaving half a dozen or so men still shooting. He felt in need of a quiet walk back to the cars. In fact, he thought he might walk right to the house. Mist was starting to rise in the valley. From a distance somewhere he heard a train, it was strange how sound carried on to the moor. Close at hand he heard repeated, rhythmic grunting.

He took a step towards a clump of wet bracken. The back of Richard's head appeared, and his backside pumped, up and down. Almost without knowing he crept a step nearer, until he could see the girl's sticklike legs spread wide. The muscles in his gut clamped tight, he gripped his gun hard and turned away.

All the way back to the house he thought of Lin Yu, but not really of her, only of sex. It had been months, he had never known such celibacy. All he wanted was a woman, all he would ever want again. If only, if only he could get in his car, get back to Rowan and die in her.

The impossibility of it choked him. She was still raw and torn, the blasted nanny was there, and besides, to go back to the flat was to take up the burden again. Sex was such a selfish need, it could not be allowed to take precedence over responsibility.

When he got back to the house they were all still drinking. James was well away, smoking cigars and full of self-satisfaction. 'Have a drink,' he said to Saul, waving him towards the row of bottles. 'We've been talking about you. Don here says you're building a house!'

Saul slugged down the whisky and topped himself up. 'I'm thinking about it. On the site of the old cottages. There's nearly an acre all told, even if it is an odd shape. Rowan thinks I'm insane. She thinks we'll go bust.'

'She's damn well right,' said James. 'God, you never could hang on to money.'

'It'll cost a mint,' agreed Saul. 'I want to include a

swimming pool for Hannah. Now we've got her, we ought to be closer to the mill, and there it is. The architect's keen as mustard.'

'All they're ever keen on is spending money,' declared James. He turned to encompass the whole gathering. 'Did I tell you about the alterations they wanted me to do to the combing plant? My God, it would have broken me, even me! They even dared to try and swing it on the factory inspectorate, bring in the law to convince me, but of course I knocked that into touch.'

Saul finished his whisky and drifted to the door. He had slipped the half-empty bottle into the pocket of his shooting jacket, where it rested as neatly and secretively as any poacher's bag. His head boiled and his body burned, he hadn't anyone to lend him solace. The evening air made him stagger a little as he walked to his car, but once behind the wheel he felt OK. Only when he began to drive did he realise how much he'd had. The road was coming at him in waves, there was no way he could get home in this state. He saw a wide grassy track leading off into some trees, and the vague thought came to him that he could stop up there and sleep it off. Somehow, while negotiating the ruts of past tractors, the car slithered sideways, putting one rear wheel into the ditch. He was stuck.

Saul got out and stared at the situation. Perhaps he could go back to Aspley Manor, or walk to a telephone. But why did he not for once please only himself? Chances were he'd get booked for drunken driving if he did ask for help. There was a blanket on the back seat of the car. In a moment of rare, selfish pleasure he put it round his shoulders, got back into his seat and opened the bottle of whisky.

Chapter Twenty-Nine

Rowan started to become anxious at around seven in the evening. Saul had promised to be back by then, because it was the nanny's evening off and he knew how difficult Rowan found it alone with Hannah. All the worst things seemed to happen then, all the choking and non-stop crying. But tonight things went fairly well, a feed in three-quarters of an hour and almost instant sleep. Rowan tried to clear up the flat; it was full of baby things. She nibbled on a biscuit, feeling flabby and frumpish, for although she was back to her old weight her shape had changed. Mr. Suzman wouldn't make for another six weeks, he said there was no point until her figure settled down.

She feared it was the end of the old her. She had hips now, and her breasts had taken on definition. If Saul had said he liked the new model she would have felt happier, but somehow there never seemed the time to talk personally. Sometimes she and Saul seemed so right together. That night in Bradford, just walking around, remained in her mind as perfection; but in the midst of the mill, and Hannah, and their increasingly frosty discussions about strategy, romantic time-wasting seemed irrelevant.

The plans for the new house were in a large brown folder on the television, beneath a packet of disposable nappies. Rowan extricated them and settled down to look at the house Saul wanted. A spectacular, wide-roofed bungalow, walled off from the mill, built over a half-cellar that was to be a swimming pool. Glazed doors led from the pool to a garden, intended to grow on what hadn't been earth for hundreds of years. The house itself was designed around a central conservatory, letting light through a glass floor into the pool and, so Saul insisted, trapping sunshine to warm the house.

It was perfect for Hannah. There was only one door, although the windows were all designed so an adult could swivel them, and climb through in an emergency. The pool was inaccessible from the house. The only way in was the sliding, and child-proof, doors from the garden. No stairs, no cars, even the garaging was set outside the enclosing wall. It was a house where a little, retarded child could grow up in sunshine and safety. Even taking into account that they had the site and a large amount of stone, it was costed at over a hundred and fifty thousand pounds.

Rowan chewed her knuckles. Saul was standing firm on the house. He had let her have the nanny, let her back into the firm, but on this he insisted. And on paper she supposed they could afford it, provided absolutely nothing went wrong. They had an order book that could sustain borrowing of this sort; even her carding machine now looked inevitable, whereas before it had seemed gross extravagance. But she wasn't used to believing in luck and hoping for the best, it wasn't her style. She knew, only too well, how narrow was the line between prosperity and ruin, how fickle taste could ruin a business which last month looked good. Saul talked of Bardsey's, but Bardsey's was a case in point. They had expanded into businesses that teetered on the verge of making losses, that cost the parent company time and capital. Yet when James first moved that way no one saw the problems, he had been universally applauded. If they built the house and failed, all the people who were now urging them on would nod sagely and talk about wanton extravagance.

Still, as Saul said, the house was an asset. They could sell that long before the mill, it wasn't money down the drain. Sighing, she put the plans away and looked again at her watch. A quarter past eight and still no Saul.

She rang James. 'Hello? Rowan here. I'm sorry to bother you but Saul's not back and I wondered if he'd left.'

'When I said you were to keep him on a short leash, I didn't mean choke him with it,' said James blearily. In the background there was the sound of men roaring with laughter, and he yelled to them, 'Shut up, you lot! What time did Saul leave, anyone know?' Turning back to the 'phone he said, 'About half-four he left here. He'd had a bit, though.'

'So have you,' said Rowan shortly. 'I'm coming out, he might have crashed or anything.'

In jeans and jumper, and slipping a battered leather jacket over the top, she carefully put Hannah in her travelling basket and went down to her car. She felt scared and shivery, but at least she was doing something. Saul was her rock, she needed him to lean on and his absence unnerved her.

After a crisp day, rain was starting to fall. Her headlights wavered through the drizzle and she realised that even if Saul's car passed her she wouldn't know it. This was a stupid errand, but she went anyway. In the back the baby made sucking noises in her sleep. When she stopped at traffic lights, Rowan turned and looked at her. Such a funny little face in that silly woolly bonnet; such a sweet, defenceless little girl. The wave of almost tearful love, coming from nowhere and swamping her, left Rowan gulping. Someone behind tooted, she fumbled with the gears and nearly stalled. If Saul was dead, killed in some horrible way, there was only her and Hannah, they only had each other.

Soon, though, she was at Aspley Manor, and had seen no crash, nothing. The men had persuaded the caterers to bring them a take-away. The drawing-room was littered with carrier bags and reeked of curry.

'Still not found him?' said James, lurching towards her. 'My God, but you look super! Got a pair of tits at last. Bet Saul knows what to do with those, the dirty bugger!'

'Shut up, James,' said Rowan distantly. 'I don't think Mother will like chicken curry on her Isfahan rug, but you never know.'

'Oh, bloody hell,' said James, following her eyes to where

a carton was leaking in a thick brown pool. He got out his handkerchief and bent down to try and scoop it back in. Rowan sighed meaningfully.

'Does anyone know where Saul might be?' she asked of the company in general. 'Had he had much to drink?' She thought there was no one sober enough to tell her. Men stared at her owlishly, gradually losing the party spirit and starting to feel sleepy or ill.

A tall young man squeezed past her into the room. He was carrying a bottle of wine and a corkscrew. Behind him came a tiny Chinese girl in a mink jacket, carrying a tray. Rowan thought she had never seen anyone look so viciously annoyed in all her life. The girl shot her a glance of white rage. 'Can you help me?' she asked. 'I'm looking for my husband, has he left?'

'I've no idea,' snapped Lin Yu. 'For myself I should like never to have come here, I should like to go!'

The tall man turned on her and said in exasperation, 'Then bloody go! Come on, let's both go, I didn't want the food anyway. I don't know why I let the old man persuade me to come, and I certainly don't know why *you* had to elbow your way in. Excuse me.' He tried to get past Rowan again but she held on to his arm.

'Do you know my husband? Saul Barton.'

'Er – yes, I do. I'm Richard. And you must be –'

'Rowan. Rowan Judge.' She was aware of him looking at her, making connections, remembering about Hannah. She turned away.

The three of them went out to the cars. Rowan said, 'If he's not at the flat when I get back, I'll call the police.'

'I wouldn't, if I were you,' said Richard. 'He'd had quite a bit at lunchtime, and he had a flask in the afternoon. If they find him sleeping it off in the car, that's his licence gone.'

'He could have crashed! He could be hurt!'

'You'd have heard by now.'

Lin Yu, standing by the locked Maserati, said shrilly; 'Richard! I am getting very cold standing here waiting.'

'Get stuffed,' said Richard under his breath, and Rowan stared at him. He shrugged. 'Today is the end of the road for me and her. We are what is known as ill-suited, and we know it even if Dad doesn't. He's behaving like a professional matchmaker.'

'Probably fancies her himself,' said Rowan abstractedly, and got into her car.

Richard came to the window and said, 'He might have stopped on a side road. You go ahead, you might see something. I'll keep a look-out, too.'

Rowan drove off slowly, trying to steer and look down tracks and lanes at one and the same time. The Maserati, behind her, seeing the countryside illuminated by her lights, had a better view. Suddenly there was a raucous blast from the horn, almost a donkey's bray. Rowan stamped on the brakes and Hannah woke up. Rowan left her grizzling and jumped out of the car.

'What is it?'

'I saw something up there, your lights just caught it. Probably a courting couple.'

Lin Yu leaned out of the Maserati. 'Richard! I wish to get home at once, please!'

He took no notice and started off up the grassy track. Rowan, about to go after him, remembered Hannah and picked her up out of her basket. Holding the baby tight to her, she followed Richard's dimly-seen shape. Twenty yards up the track he stopped. There was a car all right. She was almost up to it before she realised it was Saul's.

'It's stuck in the ditch,' said Richard. 'He must have left it.'

'Then where is he?' wailed Rowan. Now she was genuinely frightened; she couldn't imagine where Saul might be. Hannah was wingeing in earnest now. She ought to be fed, she ought not to be out in the night, they had weak chests, these babies. Rowan said, 'Here,' and pushed Hannah at Richard. He took hold awkwardly but she gave him no choice. When she opened the car door the internal light came on. In the weak yellow glow they saw him.

'He's dead,' squeaked Rowan. Saul's eyes were half open and turned up in his head, showing the whites. His mouth hung slack and he was sprawled in an unnatural position, half-twisted on the back seat. Hannah's crying was like a wailing cat, adding an eerie dimension to the nightmare.

'For God's sake, take this baby,' said Richard. 'He's only drunk, I think.'

'Nobody can be that drunk,' said Rowan. 'He can't be!' Nonetheless she took hold of Hannah and held her close, closer than ever before. She rocked herself and the child together.

Richard leaned in the back door and shook Saul's shoulders. He shook him hard, and harder still. 'Saul. Saul! Wake up, will you?'

Saul groaned. His eyes moved, the whites swivelled back into his skull. 'Leave me alone,' he mumbled.

'Saul, it's me,' said Rowan, trying to reach in with her free hand and touch him. 'Wake up, please, you're frightening me.'

'He's absolutely out, I'm afraid,' said Richard. He held up the empty whisky bottle. 'Must have decided to make a night of it.'

'He knew I was waiting for him. He knew I needed him.' Rowan felt frantic and tearful.

'Go and sit in your car,' said Richard. 'I'll get him to the road, we can move this in the morning.'

Richard heaved at Saul's loglike body. Once he got him out into the fresh air he seemed to revive a little, enough to groan, stagger briefly on rubber legs, and collapse. Lin Yu tripped down the track.

'Richard! I will not wait any longer.'

'Give me a hand, will you? His wife's got the baby, and she's in tears, poor girl.'

She stepped back, away from Saul. 'He's being sick. He's disgusting.'

Cursing her, Richard wiped Saul's mouth with a clump of grass and resumed his heaving and tugging. It took twenty minutes to negotiate the few yards to Rowan's car, but at least by the time they got there Saul was semi-conscious.

'Where do you live?' asked Richard. 'I'd better help you with him.'

Rowan shook her head. Her brief lapse of control was gone; she was shaken, obviously so, but in command of herself. 'We're in a flat, a penthouse. I'll get the night porter to help, you don't have to bother. Anyway, I think your girlfriend is getting upset.'

He grinned. 'That does not concern me. Are you sure you'll be all right?'

'Yes. Thank you. Thanks a lot.'

She drove off quickly. From the Maserati he heard Lin Yu's shrill voice calling 'Richard. Richard!' and he knew that he didn't care if he never heard her again as long as he lived.

Although it felt terribly late to Rowan, it was still only just eleven. One of the other flat dwellers was holding a party; people in evening dress were coming and going on the stairs and in the lift. Rowan went and whispered confidentially to the doorman.

'I'm afraid my husband's ill. I don't want to bring him through here.'

'Oh. Oh, I see, Mrs. Barton.' Rowan saw from his face that the man saw only too well. The humiliation of it made her flush. She wished she had accepted Richard's offer of help.

'If you take him round to the car park we can put him in the service lift,' said the man wearily. 'He's not being sick, is he?'

'No,' lied Rowan, and went on frantically, stupidly, 'he isn't drunk! It's 'flu, I think. Some kind of bug.'

'Is it?'

Rowan slunk away and drove round to the service entrance, amidst the dustbins and empty bottles. It seemed horribly appropriate.

Between them Rowan and the doorman hauled Saul into the lift. They propped him against the wall but he slid to the floor and sat, his legs splayed apart. He kept mumbling, and at one point said quite lucidly, 'Sorry about this. One too many after dinner.'

'Couple of bottles too many if you ask me,' said the doorman philosophically. 'Does he do this often, love?'

'Of course not! He never drinks normally. It's gone to his head.'

The man gave her a speaking look. At that moment Rowan could willingly have kicked Saul all the way down the lift shaft, she could have killed him for putting her through this shame. Hannah was crying, a truly hungry wail, and the doorman said: 'I suppose having a kiddie like that could drive you to it.'

The lift stopped and Rowan led the way along the hall to the flat. Some people raced up the stairs, round and down again, playing some idiot party game. But at last they were in the flat, at last she could hide him from the world. She gave the doorman a fiver but said no word of thanks. It enraged her to be in the same room as someone who thought Hannah was the cause of things,who wanted to put ordinary human weaknesses at her innocent door.

Later Barbara came back and together they undressed Saul and put him to bed. 'He's been working too hard,' said Barbara. She was a nice girl, kind and sensible. Rowan felt better knowing she was there.

The trouble with the hostel, thought Sally, had nothing to do with the utilitarian nature of the place, or the thin walls, or even the dragon of a matron who ruled like a tyrant queen over her subjects. It was the smell; an amorphous, institutional smell, made up of disinfectant and cabbage and the dust of a thousand impersonal corners. It was supposed to be home and yet it was impossible to mark it with the prints of one's personality.

She got off her narrow bed and went over to the dressing-table, staring at herself in the tarnished mirror. It seemed to her she saw a face that could have been anyone's. She could be anyone, she was faceless in a faceless place. Even her friends were interchangeable; one would do as well as another, to fill the emptiness. She was like a plant in a pond, roots floating aimlessly. No settled home, no settled feeling of being herself.

All her life Sally had seen herself through the eyes of others. She was as she was perceived, a merry little girl, a difficult teenager, a wanton. Since the row with Saul she hadn't known who she was. There was no one to tell her. How she wished he had loved her, taken her to bed and held her, not because of anything she felt for him but because then she would have had her place in his life. He would have owed her something, it would have been a hook to hold her to the family. Almost like being a second wife, a secret wife.

For her, the sex was always a means to an end. She didn't enjoy it particularly. She would lie in the back of a car with some guy up inside her and watch the lights against the sky. The girls here said you shouldn't do it till at least the third date, but why would they see her again if they couldn't have it? Sally always went out without her knickers and if they didn't try she felt stupid and ugly. She was only happy when they were holding her and gasping, saying, 'God, you were wonderful! I love you. I love you.' Anyone could have her, any time, and all she asked was that they liked her, just a little.

There was nothing to do on Sunday afternoons, and it was on that day that her loneliness became unbearable. The other girls were nice enough but she could tell they didn't really like her. Perhaps she was too posh, or too young, or even too generous, because she often bought things for people, even those she hardly knew. They were friendly while she was there but afterwards she was sure they laughed amongst themselves.

She got up quickly and pulled on jeans and a sweater. The ice rink was open on Sundays, she would skate round and round, she might meet someone she knew, some boy. If she bought some coffee and stood drinking it, people would think her friend was still skating. They wouldn't know she was really on her own. You could pretend, skating.

'I am so sorry. Did I hurt you?'

Sally looked up into the dark face. She had fallen heavily and felt dazed, for she had been lost in some fantasy, a mile away from the reality of a crowded ice rink. 'I wasn't looking. It was my fault,' she said jerkily.

'Not at all, I was skating too fast. Come, let me take you to the side.' He helped her up, an Asian of about middle height, with black eyes, blacker hair, and a fierce, warrior face. 'I must find your friends,' he said.

'My – my friends had to go. I was just going, I only stayed for one last round.'

'You like skating?'

She thought. 'Yes. When I'm skating, I don't have to think.'

Her jeans were wet from the ice, the air was heavy with beat music, the rink wild with ice hockey players practising. It was an odd place for meditation. 'Will your parents mind if I buy you some coffee?' asked the man.

'I don't think so,' said Sally. She dropped her eyes to the floor and waited. When he returned with two plastic cups, they stood side by side, sipping. 'I've got to go now,' she said.

'Of course.' He took her cup.

'I have to be back at my hostel. They give me tea on a Sunday.'

'You don't live at home?'

'My parents are divorced.'

He said nothing, but stayed by her side while she went and returned her skates and got her shoes. Sally felt him watching her. She was conscious of each and every movement she made, because he was conscious of it. Her feet, such little feet, slid almost sensuously into her shoes. Her blonde and silky hair, tossed aside, brushed against his face.

'I should like to take you home,' he said.

'Thank you,' said Sally gravely. 'I should like that.'

His name was Mohammed Shafir. He was born in Pakistan, but had come over to England with his parents when he was tiny. 'You see, I am English,' he said, but his language held the distinctive Asian lilt. His mother tongue was Gujerati; he spoke it at home every day of his life until he went to school.

'What do you do?' asked Sally, aware that as they walked he was punctiliously shielding her from the traffic.

He hesitated. 'I am a pattern weaver,' he said at last. 'I would like to be something better someday. But I am the eldest in my family, I could not continue my studies. I should like to be a lawyer.'

'I see.' She made as if to step off the pavement but Mohammed caught her arm. A bus swept round from the right, an inch from Sally's toes. Bradford's wide roads and infamous one-way system required constant vigilance from pedestrians. 'You must be careful,' said Mohammed.

'Thank you. Yes.'

Sally caught the bus back to the hostel and Mohammed came with her. They conversed politely, about his work, about her work, about his family, about hers. 'I'm quite rich,' said Sally suddenly. 'My sister runs a woollen mill. I own a quarter.'

Mohammed's dark eyes stared into the pale depths of her own. 'You must not say such things,' he said gently. 'I might be anybody.'

'But you're not, are you? You're Mohammed. I want to be friends with you.'

The bus jerked to a stop and some white teenage boys got on. When they saw Mohammed and Sally, they nudged each other. 'Take a look at that, then. Wog's doing all right for himself, ain't he? What's the matter, darling, couldn't you get a liquorice stick at the sweet shop?'

When they received no response, the boys went off down the bus. Mohammed said, 'I am so sorry. They have insulted you. I am embarrassed that you should have to tolerate such words.'

'It wasn't your fault. I don't know why people say such things, it's not as if we're doing anyone any harm.'

'Would you like me to go?'

Sally shook her head. 'I want us to be friends.'

At the hostel he shook hands with her formally and took the number of the hostel 'phone. 'Can I lunch with you tomorrow?' he asked. 'I work in the evenings, from seven o'clock.'

'Oh. Oh, I see. I have lunch at twelve, will that be all right?'

'You would please me very much, Sally.'

Alone in her room, she felt light-headed. She had been following the formal steps of a dance, a courtship dance. He was so gentle, so considerate, so wonderfully good-looking! There was something, too, in his very presence that affected her, some mutual charge of sexuality. He had barely touched her and yet she felt more aroused now than ever in her life. Unlike Sally, who flailed about hopelessly in a morass of indecision, Mohammed was firm and set and decided. The attraction of certainty was almost magnetic.

They met every day of that week. They never kissed, but simply held hands under the table at lunch. For the first time in her life Sally began to weave daydreams about someone, imagining what it would be like if he kissed her or held her. When she thought about his face, like something chiselled into the rock of a Maharajah's palace, she experienced shudders of desire. His skin was nothing like the pasty flesh of white men, it even smelled vaguely oriental. Driving a beat-up old station-wagon, he took her to obscure curry houses in distant parts of the city where she sat and watched his hands move as he ate.

He had Saturday nights off. The first Saturday they met at lunchtime and drove out of town, up on to the moors. There was an ice-cream van parked at the side of the road and they bought a cornet each. Mohammed wore a long pale scarf round his neck. Sally wore no knickers.

It was a beautiful day, warm and breezy. White clouds bustled across the sky, and two magpies sat on a rock and squawked at each other. There was an outcrop some distance away, topped by a few scrawny trees. 'Race you!' said Mohammed, and set off, with Sally in hopeless pursuit.

He waited for her behind a tree and jumped out, yelling 'Boo!' Sally shrieked and fell panting against him; he wrestled with her playfully and somehow she was down with Mohammed half on top of her.

'Please! No, please!' He had dreamed of this moment, longed for it, but now it had come he begged her to push him off.

'Don't you love me? Please say you do!'

She lay on the grass, her full breasts pointing up at him and tears in her lovely blue eyes. He had never seen anything so fragile and desirable, so in need of his masculinity.

'I love you more than you can understand,' he said reverently.

Her arms came up around his neck, he was tasting the dizzying sweetness of her kisses. He wasn't a virgin, he had had a woman before, a prostitute. She had been businesslike, he almost revolted. Afterwards he had hated himself but he had lived those few moments again and again since. But Sally! This! He found his hands on her breasts, reaching up under her clothes to find taut nipples. With no intention of asking for more he watched himself lifting her skirt, discovering dark blonde hair, discovering that she cried out in joy when he touched her.

'Stop me!' he begged, pulling his clothes open. But Sally lay back on the ground, waiting for him.

He was very quiet afterwards, and very gentle with her. 'What's the matter?' asked Sally nervously. 'I thought I pleased you.'

'Yes. Yes, you did. But – Sally, you have known men. You have done this before.'

'No, I haven't! No!' She saw his image of her crashing

about them both; he had been entranced by her supposed innocence and cleanliness. Flailing about for some lie that would please him, she said, 'It was my uncle! He did it to me, I couldn't stop him. He'd come to my room at night, I couldn't do anything!'

'Why could you not tell your mother, your father?'

'My father was dead! And my mother wouldn't have done anything. Don't hate me, please don't!'

She flung herself against him, weeping hysterically. He stroked her hair. 'Little bird. Sweet little bird. They take no care of you, your family. From this day, in our hearts, we are married. One day we shall be married in the eyes of the world.'

Sally's sobs choked and died. For all her days there would be Mohammed, loving her, telling her what to do. Once there had been Daddy, and after him a succession of faces, using her, discarding her. But here was Mohammed, taking Daddy's place, loving her and treasuring her. Blood thundered in her ears, she could hear his voice coming from a long way away. 'Sally! My darling, please!' Mohammed would love her forever.

On the day after James's shoot, Rowan paced the flat, taut with unexpressed rage. Saul was still sleeping it off, a loglike figure stinking of booze. Rowan felt she would burst if she didn't talk to someone.

She rang Sally to ask her to meet for lunch. The appalling matron answered and when Rowan gave Sally's name the woman said, 'Are you ringing for him then, is that your game? I told him he's not to call. I don't want him here and I've told madam that as well. She should know better, girl of her upbringing. That's the trouble nowadays. They've got no standards, drop their knickers for any monkey.'

Rowan said, 'I'm her sister. I should like to speak to Sally, please.'

'And I haven't got time to go up and down those stairs, up and down twenty times a day and what thanks do I get? I tell you –'

Rowan replaced the receiver. Either the woman had been half-mad when she took the job, or the girls had driven her to it. She decided to drive round, escaping the flat for half an hour or so. Barbara could look after Hannah.

The hostel was in a once-respectable street. In the past, girls from there had tripped in neat white blouses to office jobs in town, and the hostel rules had been only what any caring parent would expect. Nowadays it was like trying to impose the convent on a tribe of Apaches. The girls saw no reason for coming in at ten, signing in and signing out, meeting their boyfriends in the front hall under the vigilant eye of the matron. The result was a clandestine world of men in the bedrooms, drink under the stairs and a discreet but thriving drug culture. Girls in various wild and wonderful costumes drifted in and out, past the neighbouring doss houses, sleazy pubs and derelict shops.

Rowan parked in the street outside, and went in search of Sally. The place smelled of cheap disinfectant and there were notices everywhere, exhorting girls to come in at ten and refrain from washing dishes in the basins. Rowan ignored the one saying 'All visitors must report to the desk' and ran upstairs to Sally's room. She rapped on the door, calling, 'Sally! Sally, it's me.' From within came the sound of muffled voices and people scrambling furtively. Rowan waited, and after a minute knocked again.

The door opened. Sally's face appeared round it. She seemed to be holding a sheet against herself. 'Have you come to collect me? Don't come in, I'll be out in a minute, Ro.'

'Who've you got in there?' Rowan pushed the door aside and rushed in. Lying in the bed, smoking a cigarette, was an extremely good-looking young man. His hair was thick and black, he had piercing black eyes, and he was Asian.

'Oh, my God!' said Rowan.

'I told you not to come in,' said Sally.

She dropped the sheet and started to get dressed. Rowan looked from Sally's white body, even the pubic hair a dark gold, to the brown man in the bed.

'I think you should leave,' said the man.

'I think you had better go,' said Rowan. 'I don't like people who prey upon my sister.'

He stubbed his cigarette out and pulled himself up in the bed. 'I am so sorry. I did not realise who you were. My clothes, Sally.'

Obediently Sally passed them to him. Their hands touched and held for a brief second. Rowan turned her back while the man got dressed.

'Who is he, Sally?' she asked icily.

'I didn't know you wanted to be introduced. Rowan, meet Mohammed Shafir. Mohammed, this is my sister, Rowan Barton. You can turn round now, he's decent.'

'Not a word I would have used myself,' said Rowan. 'What is he doing here? What are you thinking of, Sally?'

Sally said nothing, instead brushing her hair with fierce strokes.

Mohammed took the brush from her and continued more gently. 'Your sister is right to be upset,' he soothed. 'She thinks I am taking advantage of you.'

'Well? Aren't you?' demanded Rowan.

His liquid brown eyes watched her, giving nothing away. He continued to brush and caress Sally's hair, as if it were the finest silk.

Sally said, 'I'm happy. I'm happier than I've ever been, don't make it dirty.'

'I can't make it anything. It is what it is. Oh God, I wish Mother was here.'

'She wouldn't care,' said Sally.

'That's not true.'

Rowan believed in Diana's care, but not in her expression of it. She gave everything or nothing, devoting herself to a child to the exclusion of all else, only to change seemingly overnight. There was no constant concern, no assurance of continued interest. That had been Andrew's strength, and it had died with him. She said, 'You've got to stop.'

'Why?'

'Oh, for God's sake, Sally, we can't talk in front of him!' Rowan waved a furious hand at Sally's lover.

He was one of the most good-looking men she had ever seen, with a clean, arresting face, white teeth flashing. Only as tall as Rowan herself, he was inches taller than Sally. Although he had finished brushing her hair, he continued to touch her, a gentle, almost reverent touch. 'Your sister is right,' said Mohammed. 'We must explain to her.'

'Don't tell me you were exercising,' said Rowan through her teeth.

Mohammed said, 'But of course not. We were making love.'

Rowan turned on her heel and prepared to go. 'There is absolutely no point in this. Sally can sleep with anyone she wants, I suppose it's stupid of me to want it to be special for her. I suppose you think it *is* special. You know what these people are like, Sally, he'll use you and drop you and go straight back to his people and marry someone else. And you'll be so damned miserable!'

'I understand you thinking that,' said the man. 'I want you to know you are wrong.'

They stood watching her, Sally's head on his shoulder, his arms around her waist. In contrast to the turmoil Rowan felt they were calm, almost serene, buoyed up by the love they felt for one another. It made her want to cry. 'I was going to take you to lunch,' she said gruffly. 'But I'll come next week.'

Out in the car she sat for a moment, her head on the wheel. Suddenly the door flung open and Sally leaped in beside her. There were shouts from inside the hostel, Mohammed was backing away from the matron, laughing and holding up his hands in surrender. The woman was yelling, 'You black bastard! Get out of here, get away from my girls!'

'Come on,' said Sally. 'If I don't get away, she'll throw me out.'

'The woman's appalling,' said Rowan and got out of the

car. 'Why don't you come with us, Mohammed?' she said grittily, and he looked in surprise from the matron to Rowan and back again.

'Thank you,' he said, and got in the back. The matron was left ranting on the pavement.

Rowan took them to an expensive country restaurant. Once a long, low manor house it nestled in a fold of hills. Today the mist hung there, making ghostly swirls out of trees and bushes, touching the skin like a clammy hand. There was a sense of nightmare about the day, the sort of state that results from a fever when people appear where you least expect them and voices come and go out of a miasma. In the bar Rowan ordered gin for herself, orange juice for Sally and Mohammed. She watched her sister. Never had Sally looked so calm and joyous.

'I'm so sorry that we should meet like this,' said Mohammed. 'I have often asked Sally to introduce me to her sister, she speaks a lot about you.'

'And what do you do, Mohammed?' asked Rowan.

'He's a pattern weaver in a mill,' said Sally defiantly.

Rowan realised she had been cherishing the unworthy hope that he might at least be rich, the son of a Maharajah with a fortune in rubies.

'I wish to marry your sister,' said Mohammed.

'Yes. We want to get married,' added Sally.

They sat holding hands and watching her, such bright confidence in their faces that Rowan herself felt a hundred years old. A weight of fear and suspicion descended on her. She took a long gulp of her gin and tonic, hating the man across the table, hating him for making her hate herself.

'He's the wrong colour,' she said flatly.

'Really, Rowan! Don't you think that's just a little ridiculous in this day and age?'

'Yes,' admitted Rowan. 'It ought not to make a difference. But it does and I know it does. I ask you, Sally, why is he a pattern weaver? I know exactly how much they get paid, and a man of his education and intelligence shouldn't put up with it. He wouldn't if he could get anything else,' she added softly.

'We can live on my money,' declared Sally.

'That will not be necessary. I find myself comfortably off, I can assure you,' said Mohammed stiffly.

'You wouldn't with a wife and family,' retorted Rowan. 'And even if you're prepared to live on the breadline, and I can see you are, what about your children? Smut and butter, and however sweet and pretty and clever they are, that's what they'll always be! Out on the edge, nothing nor something.'

'Like Hannah,' said Sally.

Rowan flinched. 'The worst thing about Hannah is knowing what's in store for her. What people will think, what people will say. Watching them leave cafés when we take her in, moving nervously away on trains. They will, you know, everybody does it, I've seen them. *I've* done it. But Hannah's here and I can't do anything about it. You don't have to do that to your children.'

Mohammed shifted in his seat. 'I think Sally spoke out of turn,' he said severely. 'That was a hurtful thing to say, Sally. But Mrs. Barton, Rowan, the world is changing. Perhaps one day your daughter will be loved for what she is, and our children too. We must hope for that day, and work for it. With the goodwill of our friends and families, we shall prevail. And if we do not, our children must, or their children, and beyond. Right will prevail.'

Rowan gazed at him in incomprehension. To her the present was everything, she had no conception of herself as a cog in the wheels of time, working towards a distant future. She could admire the man's philosophy, but she could not live by it. 'Shall we have lunch?' she said feebly.

Rowan wanted, desperately, to tell Sally about Saul, but with Mohammed sitting there, drinking orange juice and looking noble, she dared not. In his presence she felt slightly corrupt, for it was apparent that he was a devout Moslem. 'I shall take the faith,' said Sally.

'Oh.' Rowan's depression deepened. One of her fiercest

dislikes was for fundamentalist religions whose followers claimed, in each and every sect, that they alone had the answers. In her experience they were as misguided and baffled as everyone else, but they committed the cardinal sin of not knowing it.

'I see you do not like that,' said Mohammed seriously. 'Sally will lead the life of a Moslem woman, a good and useful life. It will bring her great happiness.'

'You don't mean – robes, and not seeing visitors and not speaking to people! You don't mean that?' Rowan couldn't believe it.

'A modest and useful life. That is what counts,' said Mohammed.

Sally reached out and took his hand, their fingers intertwining like twigs in the snow. Rowan watched her sister's face; it held an almost religious serenity. In that moment she was truly beautiful. The curve of her cheek was as soft as that of a child. Mohammed's free hand reached out and moved a strand of golden hair from the corner of her mouth and Rowan thought, 'He does love her. For him she is perfection.'

The meal over, Rowan took them back to town and said goodbye to them. They were to spend the afternoon walking together, until it was time for Mohammed to start the evening shift at the mill. 'It pays better,' he confided, as if somehow enhancing his financial credibility. Against her will Rowan liked him, although it would have been so much easier if she had not.

When they were gone, she went back to the flat, and Saul. To her relief he had showered, and was sitting in a chair,white-faced but sensible.

'Did you have lunch?' he asked.

'Yes. I didn't think you'd want any.'

He grinned. 'A fair enough guess. Sorry about last night, love. You know what James's parties are like, booze everywhere. I thought I was OK till I started back.'

'There was a bottle inside the car,' said Rowan. 'A whisky bottle.'

'Was there?' He looked genuinely surprised. 'Someone must have slung it there during the shoot, they were knocking it back all day. You didn't think I'd sat there and emptied it, did you?'

'Of course not.' Though she had thought it, perhaps even now she did think it. What was more, she was almost certain that he had sampled the hair of the dog that very day.

'Don't you think you're drinking rather a lot, Saul?' she asked with feigned lightness. 'I mean, you drink every single day, from lunchtime on.'

'My darling!' He got up and enveloped her in his arms, and even then she found herself sniffing for the booze. Toothpaste defeated her. 'I can handle it,' he whispered. 'OK, I knocked back too many last night, but when have you seen that before? Can't a bloke let his hair down once in a while? I got myself home, didn't I?'

She stared up at him. 'Don't you remember?'

'Of course I do.' But of course he didn't. She couldn't bear to tell him about it; the humiliation did not bear recall.

She pulled away and went to the window. They had a view across the roofs, like the slate backs of whales, and beyond, rising up into the purple distance, were the hills. 'Sally wants to marry an Asian,' she said dismally.

'What?'

She turned round and looked at him. That shock would be registered by everyone she told, she might as well get used to it. 'She wants to marry an Asian, Mohammed Shafir. They are terribly, terribly in love.'

'I don't give a damn! She can't. Not Sally, not pretty Sally.'

'Why not pretty Sally?' asked Rowan.

'Don't tell me you're in favour of it?' Saul went to the cupboard and took out a whisky bottle, pouring himself a small measure. 'She's so young, there'll be decent men a foot deep in a year or so. That girl undervalues herself all the time. And he won't marry her, I'll tell you that. Oh, he'll sleep with her, consider he's made a real conquest, but when it comes to it the family'll whistle up some Pakistani cousin and away he'll go.'

'That's what I said. But he says not, and – well, I believe him.'

'Don't tell me you like the bloke!'

She nodded. 'I do, actually. He's charming, absolutely charming. And as good-looking as anything, a sort of eagle of a man. The trouble is –' She folded her arms around herself and went back to the window. 'He tells Sally what to do, you see. Fetch this, carry that, don't say that, Sally – and all with such gentle authority. It's just what she needs.'

Saul started to get dressed. 'I'll have to talk to her. She's got to break it off. At her age she doesn't know enough to see where she's going. I won't have Sally turning into one of those timid rabbits of women, hiding in their houses in case they get spoken to, let alone raped. She mustn't get tangled up with all of that.'

Rowan caught his arm. 'Saul – why not?'

Their eyes met. He put out his arms and held her; she let the length of her body lie against him. 'Why not indeed?' he said softly. 'Sad, lost little Sally, if some bloke can give her some happiness, who are we to say he shouldn't? Your parents failed her, we failed her; if this guy can come along with some stability for her, then we should say, "Good on you, son, get on with it!"'

'If it fell apart, then so would she,' said Rowan.

Saul put her away from him to look into her face. 'Would you? If we fell apart? Honestly, Rowan.'

'I'd be in little pieces.'

He pushed her down on to the sofa, gently caressing her. He undid her blouse and licked her breasts, holding one in each hot hand. Rowan's nipples stood up for him, the breasts of a woman. She reached down and felt his penis, swollen to iron rigidity. Saul said, 'I'm sorry. I can't wait, it's been so long.'

She got off the sofa and wriggled out of her trousers and panties. She felt oddly cold and reluctant, although for once there was no need to fiddle with rubbers. The doctor had been only too eager to prescribe the pill and here she was, taking advantage of that much vaunted spontaneity. Yet her crotch felt dry and closed, as it had when the doctors examined it to see how her stitches had healed.

'I'll try not to hurt,' said Saul, and got on top of her. If only, if only she could open to him. Involuntarily her hands went between them, trying to lessen the thing pushing into her. She gave a little yelp of pain.

'You're too dry.' Saul got off and rummaged about, coming up with the vaseline they used for the baby. He made it a game, smearing some on her, letting her smear it on him.

'I love you,' he said, putting a dab on her nose. 'I love the way you are now.'

She lay back again and he covered her, she put her sticky hands on his back and felt his skin slide beneath them. She felt him begin the journey into her body, raking against the scars within, and she clenched her teeth not to let him know how much it hurt. He pushed himself home and the sudden, sharp agony stabbed her. She choked on a scream.

'Darling, are you all right? It's not too bad, is it?'

'No. No.' But the tears were gathering in the corners of her eyes. He said, 'I – I can't stop now. I'll be quick.'

He might not want to hurt her but suddenly he had no choice. Holding her buttocks, he started quick, determined strokes. Her finger nails scored his back, she bit the cushion to stop herself crying out. The knowledge of her pain delayed him, for dreadful seconds he couldn't come. Yet she was so wonderfully tight on him! He thrust again and she groaned, 'Stop it! You're tearing me apart!'

He thought of Lin Yu and James. At last his orgasm swept him on in an explosion of feeling.

She cried, curled up with her hands between her legs.

'I'm so sorry,' said Saul wearily. 'I thought it would be all right.'

'It should be! It's not your fault, I ought to be mended.'

He poured himself another drink. 'It can't have hurt that much.'

'I don't know. It seemed to.'

Rowan felt angry and guilty at one and the same time. He should not have insisted when she didn't want it, and yet did she not owe it to him? They had built a world, once, on this act. Between them they had created paradise. And now he was drinking whisky and she was crying and next door their baby was starting to wake and cry for a feed.

'I'd better go and help Barbara,' she said, getting stiffly off the sofa.

Saul, feeling like a heel, remarked, 'I'm going to fix up a trip this week. The continent.'

'You don't have to go just because of this,' said Rowan coldly. 'It's bound to get better.'

'All the same, I'd better go. We need some time to ourselves, I think. And it's a trip I've been meaning to do. Things should be better when we get into the house, we'll be nearer the mill for one thing.'

'That's months and months,' said Rowan.

She pulled on her clothes and went through to Hannah. It wasn't her fault it hurt to make love, yet he behaved as if she had deliberately held back. And he was going off on a trip, leaving her with the mill, the baby, and their impossible life in the flat – and after last night, when he had inflicted wounds he was too drunk even to remember. Although she tried to put it out, her anger burned.

Chapter Thirty

The sun on the window scattered jewels of light on to the bed. It was one of those rare autumn days when summer seems only yesterday and winter at least a year away. Rowan stood in her nightdress with her hands up to her eyes, blinking at the sky. 'It's a beautiful day.'

Saul looked at her. The nightdress was almost invisible against the sun. He admired this tall, straight, beautiful girl. Then she turned and started getting ready for work. He got out of bed and caught her hand.

'Let's take a day off. Let's go to Blackpool.'

'What for?'

'Nothing. Fun. Because we don't often have fun together. We can take Hannah and have rides at the fair.'

A small grin crept on to her face. 'I've never been to Blackpool. Mother always thought it was vulgar.'

'My darling girl, you've never lived!'

Barbara didn't want them to go. 'This weather won't last,' she said forcefully. 'You don't want Hannah in a damp car all day, do her no end of harm.'

It was becoming clear that the nanny did not trust the parents to take proper care of her charge. 'She wants to come too,' hissed Rowan to Saul.

'Well, she can't. This is our day out. We'll bring you some rock, Barbara.' She gave him another blanket and he added it to the pile of Arctic survival clothing already clutttering the boot.

'I promise we'll take care of her,' said Rowan as at last they were off. 'It's like playing truant from school,' she said, winding down the window and feeling the wind in her hair.

'I used to con my mother into writing me notes about trenchfoot,' said Saul. 'Then they sent me to boarding school.'

'Did you like it?'

''Course not. Nobody ever does. But they brainwash you into thinking you'd have been a vegetable if you hadn't gone, so everyone dutifully sends their sons after them.'

Rowan looked fondly at the baby in her carrycot on the back seat. At least no one was ever going to demand exam passes from that little soul. 'Did you have many friends at school?' she asked, fully expecting a tale of misery and loneliness.

Saul grinned. 'Droves of them. In the holidays I was never at home, I was touring stately homes and Italian villas. On my last report the headmaster wrote, "I should have had no hesitation in making Saul Head Boy were it not for his persistent misconception that life is one long party". And he'd never have made me Head Boy whatever I did, he only chose bores who were going into the church.'

It occurred to Rowan that Saul often presented the face that would be most acceptable to people. 'Perhaps he thought you were.'

He patted her knee. 'An astute comment, my love. I let him think I might be.'

They laughed together, and when Saul stopped for petrol he bought chocolate and four plastic windmills to stand in the open windows and twirl. Hannah blinked at the flashing shapes and Saul said, 'Let's start as we mean to go on! Vulgar as hell.'

It was the end of the season and much of the resort had already been closed down. But there were a few donkeys dozing on the beach, the sun was warm and the smell of fish and chips and rock drifted in the lazy air. Landladies sat at the water's edge in deckchairs and dabbled tired, fat feet in the wavelets. Saul put Hannah in a sling on his back and they wandered along the sands. Rowan took off her shoes and paddled, squeaking at the cold and the fronds of seaweed that tangled round her legs. Saul watched her bright, absorbed face.

'You're so pretty,' he said.

'Thank you, kind sir.' She came out and kissed his cheek, then slid a cold wet foot up his trouserleg and on to his calf.

'Good God, that's freezing! Stop it, you witch. Is this another piece of revenge?'

She looked away. 'What do you mean?'

'Nothing. Nothing to spoil the day. But – Rowan, don't you think I don't know what you feel?'

Gazing out across the blue and shining sea she said, 'At the moment I'm just happy and warm and a bit hungry. When are we going to eat these fish and chips?'

He put his arms round her waist. 'When I think you are good and ready for them. They are absolutely my last penance.'

She turned against him, her hands up at his chest. His breath on her cheek was warm and sweet-scented. 'No more squabbles,' she said softly.

They walked through the town, looking for somewhere to eat. There were pubs everywhere and Saul pretended to be a repentant sinner tempted by the devil. 'No, no! Take away this milk of Satan! I shall not even taste your cheese and onion crisps.'

'They wouldn't let you in anyway,' giggled Rowan. 'We're outcasts now, we've got a baby.'

'Oh God, yes. Doomed to walk the streets looking for a café that has a chair for Hannah and somewhere to change a nappy.'

But the cafés were full of twee oak tables and net curtains, or raucous with pop music and slippery with grease. So they bought fish and chips in the paper and ate them on a bench on the promenade, watching the open buses sail by with their cargo of blank-faced sightseers. Rowan got indigestion laughing because Saul was mimicking their conversation.

'Bit much this sea, in't it, Doris?'

'Aye, you're right there. When I said to Harry I was coming, he said he couldn't do with all that water. Sets him off, you see, at his time of life. We'd have had to stop the coach five times, and it ain't easy on them motorways. No privacy. Will I ever forget the M62 when Harry climbed down the embankment and we had to rescue him with Mildred Greerson's extra-large support hose. . . .'

They went to the fair and Saul won a goldfish and a teddy bear on the shooting gallery. Rowan went in the House of Horrors and came out giggling. 'The skeletons were painted and someone shot me with a water pistol,' she complained, brushing drops off her summer dress. She was tired now and needed a rest; so they, too, went for a ride on an open top bus and ate popcorn. Changing Hannah's nappy, Rowan said, 'She's being very good. Do you think she's happy?'

''Course she is. Because her mum and dad are happy. We're through the worst, you know.'

Rowan believed him. Going home in the car, sticky with rock and sleepy from wind and sun, she was at peace with herself. It seemed to her then that they had weathered storms the like of which would never come again.

Chapter Thirty-One

Richard paced the cold warehouse, his nostrils filled with the unmistakable odour of wool. It was piled everywhere, labelled bales cut open for the buyers to view. Like Richard they walked slowly round, sniffing, touching, making notes. It took years to assess wool properly; most of these men had served an apprenticeship as sorters, standing all day grading fleeces.

The trained eye, and perhaps even more the fingers, could detect the minute difference between sixties and sixty-fours, the tiny variation in fibre that meant absolute softness or a slightly coarser touch. Even a beginner could sort cold country wool, the rough British fleeces grown thick and hard, to distinguish rubbish carpet wool from good stuff badly presented. British farmers took no care, that was the constant complaint. They fed in-wintered sheep by throwing hay on wire racks, and as the animals fed, their fleeces were showered with grass seeds and cut stems. It was hard to get out, and because of it the price was low, which to the farmers meant even less reason to present a good fleece. They came in encrusted with muck, indelibly stained with raddle or dye, and it knocked the price on the head. Richard sniffed contemptuously at some good Hampshire Down that was nonetheless very dirty. He marked it in the list as turbary; the wool was in demand and he might be forced to bid up for it, despite the contamination.

He shivered. These big warehouses were icy cold even on a warm autumn day such as this. Thank God he was off tomorrow, to the Far East, to pick up some silk if he could, and some cashmere. He meant if possible to take up the entire Chinese cashmere stock, and hold it. The price rise would be a few months in coming, but come it would, and Richard fully intended to have some of it on his own account, as well as the firm's. No one could run a Maserati on salary alone.

A friend of his sauntered up. 'Surprised to see you here. Thought you'd given up real work.'

Richard grimaced. 'I've got the wrong name. If you want to get on in this firm, you have to be family. Otherwise they have you sniffing shitty wool for life.'

The other man laughed. 'You're doing all right. Biding your time to get back into your own little empire, I shouldn't wonder. Doesn't Daddy want you in?'

Richard said nothing, and moved on to the next lot of wool. He had been giving that possibility some serious thought lately. The fact was it was time he threw in this job and he would either have to set up on his own account altogether, which was one hell of a risk and would mean investing every penny he possessed, or go into Bardsey's. The decision was made a little easier by his lack of money. Richard spent liberally, and besides, he had taken a tumble on the currency market a few months ago. He'd taken a chance on the dollar and got it rather badly wrong.

His friend said, 'Come for a pint? I've had enough of this for a bit.'

'Yes, I'll join you,' said Richard. He was feeling rather bored with everything. The latest woman in his life had departed the previous week and he was neither sorry nor pleased. It was beginning to seem as if he was going endlessly round the same track, different faces but the same situations. Time to move on.

But the beer was good and the sandwiches better, crisp wholemeal rolls stuffed full of good cheese. Textile gossip washed around him. After a few years in the trade every meeting like this meant a further instalment in a soap opera in which you knew all the characters and most of the plots.

They were talking of Rowan Judge. 'That girl is a bloody phenomenon! There isn't a better mill, design's good, and the organisation's so tight you can hear it twanging. Have you seen the house they're building? Bradford's answer to the Pondcrosa.'

'Over-stretching themselves there, if you ask me.' Richard crunched into his roll. His feelings towards Judge's were ambivalent in the extreme. While he had to admire them, he disliked the contrast with Bardsey's. He felt increasingly protective towards that big, sprawling organisation. More and more he considered it his own.

'They've even got their cloth in the London fashion shows. Paris next, and a million Marks and Sparks copies. I mean, that's the way to do it – lean, hard and hungry.'

'She's certainly lean,' said someone, laughing. 'And I bet she's damned hard, too.'

'I don't think she's that,' said Richard, remembering the night of the shoot. 'How much is down to her husband, do you think? My Uncle Saul.'

Everyone considered. 'Quite a bit,' someone conceded. 'He's the one who takes the fliers. But she's the motor, have no doubt about that. Anyway, he's a funny bloke. I was on the 'plane with him going to Zurich, and he was slaughtered. We had to carry him off.'

'Probably so damned relieved to get away from Miss Efficiency.'

They all laughed and ordered more drinks.

Officially, Richard should have gone back to the office, but he was feeling rebellious. When he left the pub, he got in the car and headed up to the moors, intending to walk and blow away the drink. He pulled the car off the road in a lonely and desolate spot, and tramped the late-blooming heather, tasting the cold, cold wind. In the hollows the sun was warm on his face. He put up rabbits from their afternoon doze.

He felt restless and slightly depressed. He had a sense of

futility about his life, that he was grabbing and accruing for no definite purpose. He had the car, he had the flat, he could have this girl, that girl, almost any girl, it seemed, provided he spent enough money – and still it wasn't enough. He wondered if this was a mid-life crisis come rather early. More likely it was delayed adolescence, because the time when he should have been discovering himself had been largely devoted to hating his father. He seemed to have grown out of that lately. When he went back to see his mother, he too felt oppressed. It wasn't hard to understand James, and from that it was a short step to forgiveness.

Well, it was time to go and see the old man. He had fought against it long enough, and if he wasn't careful he would wait too long and find all the cake gone to Nicholas. It was a sobering thought, but Richard was finding himself capable of jealousy, even of a child of barely two. Nicholas received the adoration James had been too busy to give his first son; Nicholas had the Manor House; Nicholas the glamorous mother. He would not also get Bardsey's, not if Richard could help it.

When he got back to the car, a policeman was prowling round it, his patrol vehicle parked at an aggressive angle. 'This yours?' he demanded.

'Yes,' said Richard casually. He was used to police, of all nationalities, at least those in Britain didn't wear guns. 'I've got identification here somewhere.'

He rummaged in his pockets for his driving licence. The policeman said, 'Nice car this. Had it long?'

'Six months or so. Don't worry, it's not nicked. Yet. I had a Ferrari last, it was never at home, you blokes were always finding it next to the canal. Attracted joy-riders like bees to honey.'

'Was that yours?' asked the policeman with real interest. 'I drove that back once. Smashing car.'

'Certainly attracted a better class of criminal. They could turn off the anti-theft locks in less than a minute. This has got a siren you could hear in Italy, touch it and see what happens.'

'I just did,' said the policeman.

Richard sighed. 'Bloody thing never works. Take a good look at it, constable, you could be seeing a lot of this car. I might as well buy a sodding Mini.'

'When they nick those you don't get them back,' said the policeman cheerfully. He walked back towards his car. 'And watch the alcohol intake, won't you, sir?'

Richard stood and watched him go. He put out a casual hand to his car and the siren went off, a banshee wail that sent up a flock of birds a hundred yards away. He swore, fumbled the keys, and at last turned the switch. 'This isn't my day,' he said out loud. The omens were not good for a visit to Bardsey's, but Richard was determinedly unsuperstitious. He sent the car skimming down the hills into Bradford.

It was a while since Richard had visited Bardsey's and he was impressed. There was a fountain outside the main office block, and the doorman was fishing litter out of it with a child's tadpole net. As always the car park was full, so Richard parked across the back of his father's Rolls-Royce and went in.

The doorman shouted after him, 'Here, you can't do that! That's Mr. Barton's car!'

'I know,' said Richard casually and stepped into the lift. He'd like to be Mr. Barton here. He'd been out in the world long enough to appreciate it.

The executive corridor was hushed by thick almond-coloured carpet, with polished oak doors to every room. It had been redecorated since Richard's day in an elegant Regency stripe, and he had no hesitation in attributing that to Diana. Simply by association with her James had lost some of his harsh, aggressive style. It might have done him a lot of good personally, but as far as the business was concerned, James was in danger of losing his edge.

He rapped on James's door and went in. His father was seated at his vast desk, his long-time secretary on the other side, and neither looked as if they were enjoying the experience. Both faces lit up as Richard came into the room. 'Good God! Now what has brought you, Richard? Get him a drink, Margaret, tea, coffee, booze? Come on in, sit down. It's good to see you.'

The effusive welcome verged on the embarrassing. If there was one sure sign that his father was getting old, it was this. In his youth James had no time for emotion, he was leaving all that till later; and later had come.

Richard said, 'I'd love a cup of tea, Margaret. How is everyone, Dad? Diana, Nicholas?'

'Fine, just fine. Nicholas is a grand little chap, I can't see enough of him. I often think, you know, that I missed something when you were young. I worked all the time, never at home really. Such a shame.'

'You weren't happy though, were you? You and Mother.'

James shrugged and put his hands in his pockets. 'Possibly not, I don't know. It didn't matter then, I had my work, I was making good. It was later that things got difficult. How is your mother?'

'Fine.' Richard toyed with the gold paperknife on the desk. To his surprise, next to the pictures of Diana and Nicholas there was one of him, a recent shot, blown up from a snap in one of the trade journals. He was very touched.

Margaret came back with the tea, in an exquisite antique bone china pot. The cups were no attempt at all at a match, except for echoing one of the colours in the flower pattern on the pot. Diana's work again, bringing that touch of style into a business environment. James said hurriedly, 'I know this looks a bit odd but Diana insisted on this pot. I wanted silver, really.'

'She's got tremendous taste,' said Richard. 'You ought to let her have her say on design.'

'I suggested it. She says she leaves all that to Rowan.'

James sipped at his tea, trying not to betray his impatience. If only Richard would come into the firm, if he could see the line stretching on – Richard, Nicholas, their sons – then it was all worthwhile. Suddenly he could wait no longer. 'Are you coming in?' he demanded aggressively. 'It's here for you, waiting.'

Richard picked up a biscuit and broke it gently between his fingers. He tossed one of the pieces at his father and James caught it, like a trout taking a fly. 'I'm coming in,' he said.

They sat for a minute, saying nothing. James started to laugh. He got up, and Richard got up, they shook hands, they held on to each other's forearms, and finally, because nothing else would do, they hugged.

'This is a great day,' said James huskily. 'The greatest day.'

The telephone rang. James picked it up, barking angrily: 'I don't want any calls, I'm with my son.'

'It's urgent, sir.'

The connection clicked. James heard Diana, gulping, gasping. Even before she spoke, he was aware of terror. 'James? Come home. It's Nicholas, it's Nick. The doctor's here.'

'What is it? Diana, tell me.'

'Come home, James. You must come home.'

She hung up and James stood, still holding the receiver, staring into space. 'She says it's Nick. The doctor's there. She didn't say why.'

Their eyes met. Richard thought, 'I knew something terrible would happen today.' There was a judder of relief that it was not to him. He said, 'He must be ill. It might not be bad. Come on, Dad, I'll drive you.'

James automatically took his coat from the cupboard. They walked down the corridor, but then James started to run. The two men sprinted down the stairs, out past the fountain and into the car park. There was the feeling that if they got there quickly, if only they could get there in time, it would be all right. The Maserati, its power unleashed for once, howled mightily. The traffic parted before them, Richard pressed the throttle and the acceleration kicked them in the back. James said, 'Why haven't they taken him to hospital? If he's ill, he should be in hospital.'

'Perhaps he's not that ill.'

James bent his head. In a quick glance sideways Richard saw that his father was crying.

There was nothing lovelier than Aspley Manor that autumn day. The trees were turning, their leaves wonderfully gold and brown and purple, as yet only lightly scattered on the grass. There were cattle in the park, quietly chewing the cud as the Maserati punched a hole through the afternoon quiet. James fell out of the car almost before it had stopped, and staggered up the steps shouting, 'Diana? Diana!'

Richard followed. He carried with him a sense of doom.

Diana was in the drawing-room. She stood before the empty fireplace and her face was utterly white. She just stood there, saying nothing, her hands holding one of Nicholas's little jumpers. The doctor stood by her and as James burst in, and then Richard, he cleared his throat. They all stood, absolutely silent. 'I'm sorry,' said the doctor. 'Nicholas died shortly after lunch today.'

Diana's hands began to knead and twist the jumper, she began to cough, and only after seconds did they realise that she was crying dry, hard sobs.

James said, 'Where is he? You should be working on him, where is he?' He rushed from the room and the doctor followed, and Richard. Only Diana was left, twisting the tiny jumper, and sobbing.

He was in the bedroom, in his cot with the side down, and he bore the marks of all that they had tried to do to him. His little face, that had always been bright-eyed and happy, was empty now and bruised by the masks and tubes, bruised pointlessly. James held his hands and for the first time ever his son's little fat fingers failed to close. It smelled still of Nicholas, of nappies and talcum powder and sleep. He began to howl.

The doctor turned to Richard and said helplessly, 'He'd been dead an hour or more. There was nothing I could do.'

'But what was it? How did it happen?'

'I don't know. I just don't know.'

Downstairs they could hear Diana's harsh, gagging cries, but each sound from James came after long seconds when it seemed his misery was too great to express. For Richard it was unbearable, though he had not loved this or any child, and he knew that what he felt was a shadow of the grief of others. He would have given anything to escape from this, and he knew that so would they all. He put out his hand and held his father's shoulder, James put up his own hand to grasp it, and Richard thought of Diana with no one to comfort her. Richard turned to the doctor. 'We must get her children. She has to have them now.'

An ambulance came, and gently they coaxed James, and then Diana, away from the baby. Such a tiny bundle in such a huge van, they could almost have put him in a box, thought Richard vaguely. For some reason both James and Diana wanted to go to the hospital and they couldn't all get in the Maserati or Diana's Porsche, so he wandered round to the garage and found a little hatchback there, he didn't know whose it was. When he brought it round, Diana said, 'That's the gardener's,' but James just got in and so did she.

'I'll lead,' said the doctor, and Richard followed him, longing to turn on the radio to drown the sounds coming from the back seat. Suddenly James yelled, 'You left him! Why did you leave him alone? What in God's name happened?'

After a moment Diana said weakly, 'Nothing happened.

It was just as usual. He had his breakfast, you were there, you saw him. He didn't want his nap, he was a bit fractious, nothing much. He had his orange juice and I did music with him. He banged on his xylophone, he was so good. I took him out in the park.'

'He was ill, he must have been ill.'

'He wasn't ill! When we came back he had his lunch. He had egg and toast and some yoghurt. And because he hadn't had his sleep, I put him down. He went straight off, as good as gold. I was pleased because he'd been a bit grumpy all morning, and I wrote some letters and made some 'phone calls. I popped in to see him after about an hour, at the most an hour and twenty minutes. And – and – I couldn't wake him up.' She sounded so utterly bewildered.

James said, 'You let him get cold. I was always telling you to wrap him up more.'

She began to whimper horribly and Richard said, 'We can't know what it was, none of us can. There's no sense in blame.'

But Diana burst out, 'It's because I wanted Hannah to die! I did, I did, I wanted her to die! And now God's taken my baby away from me, he's taken my Nicholas. Do you know what, James? Shall I tell you? I hate bloody God!'

Chapter Thirty-Two

At the hospital they stood, grief-stricken, amidst the every-day business of sprains and broken legs. The GP came and shepherded them into a side room and James and Diana sat slumped in chairs, every now and then saying something that they had said before, and would say again, many, many times.

'He was so little.' 'He was so lovely.' 'I only left him for an hour, he was asleep!'

Richard asked Diana for some telephone numbers for the children, and she gave him Andy's and Sally's but couldn't find Rowan's. So Richard went out to the payphone, asking round for money when he found he only had notes and some roubles, finally getting enough to call Andy in London. He rang what seemed to be his flat and a girl answered, he could hear her calling Andy from somewhere. At last he came to the 'phone.

'Yes? What is it?'

'Look, you don't know me, I'm Richard Barton. There's been a – a tragedy. The little boy, Nicholas, he's dead.'

'Which little boy?'

Richard felt unreasoning rage. 'Your mother's son, Nicholas! She needs some help, I thought you might come.'

'Oh. Oh, I see. What do you think I might do then? Are there arrangements?'

'None that I can't see to. She's – beside herself. I think you should come.'

'But I've got a concert tomorrow night!' Richard heard the infuriated sigh, followed by the mental shifting of gears. 'I suppose I'd better come. Tell her I'm coming, tell her –

just say that. God, how I hate these things!'

'None of us is having a ball, as it happens,' said Richard shortly and hung up. 'Self-centred prick,' he thought to himself. After that it was Sally, and a murderous call to some woman who seemed to think he was trying to seduce the girl, over the 'phone, for God's sake! When he was down to his last coin Sally came, and talked to him in a young, breathy voice.

'It's kind of you to ring,' she said. 'I'll come at once. Poor little boy.'

He instinctively knew that Rowan should be there. She was after all the eldest child, though he knew her not at all except by reputation and that one odd night. He reversed the charges on a call to Judge's, and thankfully it was accepted but neither Saul nor Rowan could be found. In the end he left a message, relieved to avoid that same dreadful repetition.

When he went back, James was sitting with his sleeve rolled up.

'We're taking blood samples,' explained the nurse. 'Doctor wants to do an immediate comparison, before – well, as soon as possible. We have to know what happened, you see.'

As she went out, a policeman entered. Richard had a terrible sense of *déjà vu.* It was the same man who had looked at the Maserati that afternoon. But of course they had to make sure about Nicholas, it wasn't usual for a child to die like that. He went out of the room, to get some air, to escape for an instant. He heard the policeman say, 'There were a number of bruises on the body,' and Diana screamed, 'Oh God, he thinks I killed him! He thinks I killed my little boy!'

'Why don't you arrest us and be done with it?' yelled James violently.

The GP began to explain about the resuscitation and Diana sobbed. Richard couldn't stand any more. He walked quickly down the corridor, passing a small blonde girl and an Asian man. The girl caught at his sleeve. 'Aren't you – I'm sorry, I thought you might be Richard. I'm Sally.'

'Oh. How did you know who I was?'

'You look like James. Is Mother all right?'

Richard shook his head. 'Apparently the police have to be in on it. A shambles really, the whole thing.'

Sally hesitated, obviously unsure of what to do, and Mohammed said gently, 'You must wait, Sally, until everything is finished. We will wait here.'

Obediently the girl moved to one of the chairs and sat down. Richard sat next to them, though all he wanted was to get out of there.

Suddenly the swing doors burst open again and Saul rushed in. His tie was crooked and something about the way he walked hinted that he might be drunk. Richard got up. 'The police are in there. You can't go in yet, we have to wait.'

'Sod that! I know how this feels, God, don't I just! Everything spoiled, everything gone wrong.'

Richard hung on to him. 'Stay here, old man, you're pissed, you know you are.'

Saul hesitated. His big head swung and he blinked, trying to focus his eyes. 'I am a bit. But I had to come, I couldn't not – ' He caught sight of Mohammed and Sally. He said blearily, 'This the wog you're shacking up with, Sally? Oh, don't get all frosty, it's your life. You might have more luck with your kids – they could come out all black and white checks. Look at Hannah, we did something wrong there, didn't we? And now poor little Nick. He was a nice kid, Nick. I was jealous of him. He was just what I wanted for us.'

Mohammed got up and said seriously to Saul, 'I do not wish you to be offensive to Sally. We are to marry. I am trying to persuade my parents to accept her.'

Saul snorted with laughter. 'Don't tell me they don't approve! Good God, that's a bit bloody rich. Look at you people, coming over from some mud village in Pakistan, taking over our town, turning it into Pakistan except for the cows – and you'd introduce those if we let you – and then disapproving of us! Do you wonder you're not welcome here?'

Richard said, 'Shut up, Saul, will you? This doesn't help.'

Mohammed said, 'It doesn't matter. I'm used to this, I understand it. He's drunk, that's all.'

The policeman came out of the room and at once Sally got up to go inside. Saul said, 'Why in God's name did I come? She won't want to see me. If I'm in the same room with the woman, she twitches until I'm gone.'

Richard said, 'I thought Rowan might come.'

'She's out somewhere, I don't know where. Out all day. I wouldn't get this stewed if Rowan was there.' He looked owlish. 'She doesn't like it, you know.'

'Not bloody surprised,' said Richard. He felt no sympathy for Saul, only irritation. There was something sour about a man who waited till his wife was away to get paralysingly drunk.

Saul said, 'I can see you're another bloody puritan. They're all over the place, you know. "Lead a good clean life, lay off the booze, lay off the fags, don't shag the women or your cock'll fall off." Look at our ethnic friend here, even he can't manage all three. Can't get his hands on a black girl so he gets Sally on her back instead. Christ, I didn't mean that!

'What I mean is, old fellow –' he rested a hand on Mohammed's stiff shoulder '– you just take care of Sally. She's a good girl. Had some rotten luck, needs taking care of.' He turned and blundered away again. Richard knew he ought to stop him because he was in no state to drive, but instead he let him go.

Mohammed said, 'Don't please feel that you must stay with me. I am only waiting for Sally. I don't wish to meet her mother today, it would be wrong.'

'Yes.' Richard ran his hand over his face and through his hair. He felt exhausted, and angry at being involved. He wanted nothing so much as to go home.

James came out of the room, red-eyed, almost shrunken. Richard went to him. 'Are you OK?'

James let out his breath painfully. 'I'll be all right. The medical supremo wants to talk about something. Will you come?'

'OK.'

They went down the corridor to yet another small office. The white-coated man behind the desk barely looked at them, it was amazing how few people could. It was as if grief of such intensity hurt even those who saw it.

The doctor said, 'I know I can say nothing to console you. These deaths are rarely explained. There will be an inquest, of course. On the face of it, we would appear to have a cot death. I understand he was a little under the weather?'

'Yes – yes,' said James feebly.

'There is one unusual factor. The child's blood group is A rhesus negative, and the commonest grouping for this syndrome is O positive. Any statistical phenomenon is important in researching the causes of these appalling events.'

'My blood group's O,' said James vaguely.

'Yes, I'm aware of that. The child was adopted, I take it?'

'What?'

'When did you receive the baby, Mr. Barton? We have to investigate his natural parents, the circumstances of his birth. There may have been damage of some kind, a difficult delivery – '

'But he isn't adopted. My wife had a Caesarean section, in a nursing home!'

The doctor lifted his head fully for the first time. 'Oh, I see.' His lips moved soundlessly as he tried to recover the situation.

Richard said quickly, 'Obviously you haven't got all the facts, we'll come back and talk again when everything's clarified – ' But James dropped a heavy hand on his arm and silenced him.

'What are you saying?' he demanded.

The doctor blustered. 'Genetically, of course, the picture is rather confused, but all things considered – '

'Are you saying I'm not the father? Let me see those notes.' He lunged across the desk and grabbed at the papers. They were blood group slips and he could make no sense of them.

Richard said, 'Leave it, Dad, you're not thinking straight.'

'This pillock says I'm not Nick's father! Do you know anything about these blood groups?'

'No, nothing,' lied Richard.

'I bloody well know who's A negative,' said James wildly. 'Bloody Saul! Damn nigh cut his finger off when he was six. They had to put out an SOS for blood.'

'Mr. Barton, if you would just calm down,' said the doctor desperately. 'Of course you are the father of your child!'

James tossed the papers back on to the desk. 'I can't stand any more of this. I'm taking my wife and going home.'

Richard made as if to go out with him, then turned and went back in to the doctor. The man was sweating. He wiped the corners of his mouth with the back of his hand. Richard said in a low, vicious voice, 'You are not to let any of this come out at the inquest. Understand?'

The doctor said, 'How in God's name was I to know? It could have been artificial insemination, anything.'

'Just shut up about it, will you?'

He went out after James. He found Diana with Sally. They were sitting holding each other and crying. Across the room sat James. He was watching his wife with an odd and dangerous expression.

It was late when Rowan got back to the flat. She had been to

Harrogate, to a small but avant garde fashion show, and afterwards she and the girl designer had sat and talked. The visit had been Saul's suggestion, but when she got home he demanded, 'Where on earth have you been?'

'Harrogate,' she said in surprise. 'You told me to go.'

'Like hell I did!' He got up, staggering a little.

Rowan said, 'Is Hannah all right? I don't know why you have to drink like this when you're on your own, it's silly.'

'I've got to tell you,' he said vaguely. 'There's been an accident.'

Rowan's eyes widened in her pale face. She dropped her bag and flew into the next-door room, frightening Barbara, who was watching television, almost out of her wits. 'Is Hannah all right? Saul said there'd been an accident.'

Barbara put down her packet of crisps. 'Not to Hannah, Mrs. Barton. To Nicholas.'

'Yes,' echoed Saul. 'Nicholas. Cot death baby.'

Rowan went back into their own room and sat on the bed. She put her face in her hands and rocked to and fro. Saul said, 'It's all right, you know. It isn't Hannah.'

Rowan whispered, 'Suppose it was? I used to wish it was, in the beginning. Poor, poor Mother. And poor James. They've got so used to thinking poor us.'

Suddenly Saul picked up a shoe and hurled it across the room. 'I hate this sodding world!' he yelled.

Rowan flinched. 'I'll ring Mother now!' she muttered.

She dialled the number and James answered. He sounded brisk, too brisk.

'I'm so sorry,' said Rowan inadequately.

'Yes. Well. Lot to be sorry about, isn't there? I'll get Diana.'

'James – please, James. You were kind to me about Hannah. Thank you.'

His voice came back, cracking. 'It's easy to sympathise. Not so bloody easy to applaud, I was never good at that. And a bloody sight harder to take it on the chin, I find. Here's your mother.'

'Rowan?' Diana was hoarse with sobbing. 'Darling, Andy's here and his terrible girlfriend. I don't want them in the house, I don't want anyone.'

'Er – why don't you send them here?' asked Rowan.

'Yes. Yes, of course I will. You're always so practical, aren't you, never any emotion. You were like that when your father died, all you thought of was the mill. I wish I was as lucky as you.'

Across the room Saul lurched to a pot plant and was sick. Rowan said, 'I dare say you do, Mother. I'll come tomorrow, shall I?'

'Do you know, they thought I'd killed him? They thought I'd beaten him to death!'

'I don't suppose they did really. They have to think of these things, you know.'

'You would say that. Oh, Rowan, why was it Nicholas? Why did it happen to him?'

Swallowing down her tears, Rowan said levelly, 'I don't think we can know that. Don't forget, Mother, it's not Nick you're crying for. It's you, always you. I cried so much for Hannah till I realised that.'

'I'm sorry for what I thought about Hannah,' wailed Diana. 'I'm sorry, but it doesn't bring him back!' She dissolved into hysterical sobbing.

After a moment Andy came to the 'phone and Rowan gave him directions to the flat. In a low voice, he said, 'I can't wait to get out of here. God, Rowan, it reminds me so much of Father.'

'I'll make up a bed,' said Rowan, and hung up.

Saul was wiping his ashen face with a towel.

'You OK?' she asked bleakly.

'Yes, fine.' Saul was capable of functioning almost normally when still very drunk. It was only when he went an inch over the edge that you realised he hadn't been sober for hours. He said, 'I went to the hospital to see her... Saw Sally's Maharajah instead.'

Rowan grinned at the apt description. 'What did you think?'

'Sort of holy man in mufti, if you ask me. Very eldest son, very authoritarian. Just wish he wasn't black.'

'Well, brownish,' said Rowan. 'I don't want him to take her over, if you know what I mean.' She struggled to articulate what she felt. 'He just seems so terribly foreign!'

Saul shrugged. 'He is foreign. He just happens to live here. It doesn't make them English, whatever it says on the passport.'

He went to the cupboard and poured himself a vodka and Rowan a gin and tonic. She hardly tasted her drink. Nowadays she found herself so sensitive to Saul's intake that she barely enjoyed anything herself. Again she tried to tackle it. 'Don't you think you're drinking a bit much? It can't be doing your liver any good.'

He didn't look at her for a moment. Then he said, 'I'll cut back a bit. I had a bit too much today, I had a lunch out and that started it.'

'But it's most days.'

'Look, Rowan.' He put down his glass and took hold of her hands. 'Look. We've got Hannah, we've got the business, we've got a lot on our plates. You've got your way of dealing with it, you smother yourself in that mill like a mole digging a tunnel. I've got my way. Sometimes I overdo it and take a drop too much, but it isn't often, is it?'

She wanted to say yes, because although she rarely saw him drink she suspected, strongly, that he often did. Instead she said, 'No. But I worry about you, Saul, terribly!'

'And I worry about you, honey.'

They were talking, obliquely, about sex. The weeks clicked by and still it was torture. She trailed to and from the doctor and all he said was, 'give it time'. She was considering giving up taking the pill, there seemed little point when they never made love. Now she put her arms round his neck, planting little kisses all over his face. He responded, urgently, pushing her back with that delicious intent that used to excite her so. In the back of her mind she felt cold fear. Suppose it still hurt?

The telephone rang. Saul cursed and rolled off to lift the receiver. It was the doorman to say Andy had arrived with his girlfriend and couldn't understand why he didn't appear to be expected. Rowan put her hands to her head, feeling a headache starting to throb. She would take an aspirin and rub out the pain, and if she could rub out today also, that would surely be a blessing.

Chapter Thirty-Three

Sometimes even Rowan stood and stared at Judge's and found it hard to remember how it used to be. To Andy it was unrecognisable. The fire had been a blessing. They had at last rid themselves of old, unusable floors, the ancient boiler, even the antiquated and hard to clean canteen. In the midst of the reconstruction the mill was like a mutant, the old severe style contrasting with light, high-tech design.

'We're building a nursery,' said Rowan with pride. 'It was Saul's idea.'

'Can we afford it?' asked Andy.

The 'we' jarred on Rowan's nerves.

'Yes, just,' she admitted. 'That was what I wanted to talk to you about. I want to go public.'

'Don't be so bloody silly!'

He walked away from her, just as he had when they were small and she had hatched some fantastic and impossible plot. Andy was always the one to see the flaws; if anyone was relentless about practicalities, it was he.

'I can do it,' she said, tugging at his sleeve. 'Will you listen, Andy!'

He stopped and folded his arms. 'Rowan, I don't want to talk mills. I accept I've got to stay till the funeral, though God knows why. Mother screams every time she sees Astrid.'

'She has that effect on a lot of us,' said Rowan waspishly. 'You shouldn't have brought her. Andy, this is important!'

'I don't want to waste my time money-grubbing.'

'Thank you,' said Rowan. 'We paid you a handsome dividend last year, I might remind you.'

'Very gratefully received it was. No doubt you'll want a rake-off from my concerts in return.'

'If you made anything, I might,' snapped Rowan. But this bickering was getting them nowhere.

'Look, we can go public. Saul knows this company that's collapsing, it's got a public quotation, everything, but it's bust. We can buy it. We can change the name afterwards, but we've got our quotation. Apparently we then have to make a rights issue and get in lots of lovely money, and with it we can build our new dye-house and everything. The insurance will replace things pretty well, but we want to step up from here. Expand.'

'Who would own Judge's then? It's still me, isn't it?'

'You only have half,' countered Rowan aggressively. 'If you really must have it that way then we can arrange it so you still have control. But you've got to agree, Andy! It really is important.'

They walked on into the mill. Andy mooched round, ignoring the nods and grins of those who had known him when he was a boy. In contrast Rowan stopped and chatted here and there, exchanged the odd joke with someone, chivvied the overlooker about sweeping up. This was her world; within it she felt calm and resourceful and sane. Andy hated it. From a boy he had loathed the noise and turmoil, it was Rowan who stood entranced watching the coarse strands of wool turned into gossamer and on into thick, warm cloth. Yet Andy had been preferred, he was the boy and his it was. It would have been fairer, thought Rowan viciously, if she had been given the talent for music. At least then there would have been some semblance of justice.

This was the first time she had seen Andy alone. His girlfriend, Astrid, trailed about after him like an overfed spaniel, fighting off anyone who wanted to do anything for Andy, even so much as pass him a scone. With Diana she took it upon herself to reinterpret all Andy's conversation:

'I think what Andy means, Diana, is – ' and saying what she thought he ought to mean. It was incredible that Andy tolerated it.

Something about her brother bothered Rowan. He had never been one to show quite what he felt but now he wasn't happy.

'Are you sick of Astrid?' she asked abruptly. 'Do you want to get rid of her?'

He looked surprised. 'No, not particularly. I'm very fond of her. She's on edge, you don't see her as she really is.'

Rowan reflected what a pity it was that you could not veto the people about to be admitted to the family. Astrid at every funeral, christening, wedding, and many Christmas dinners would be almost more depressing than James. The addition of Mohammed would put the lid on it.

'Is it the music?' she asked. 'I thought you were doing OK.'

His faced twisted slightly. He had Diana's bones, theatrically prominent, slightly strange in a man but very photogenic. He said, 'Let's go up to the office. I want to talk.'

Rowan was lodging in a stripped-out anteroom while the building work was taking place. She had draped cloth round the walls, swathes of it hanging like medieval tapestry, emerald against black, against orange, against dark, vibrant blue. Like a cat she had lined her box, and like a cat she lived in it, a home-loving but still independent cat. Her hair was shaggy these days, and she wore dramatic eye make-up. 'I wanted to tell you,' said Andy awkwardly, 'You look great. I mean, really.'

'Mother doesn't think so,' said Rowan ruefully.

'Well, when did she ever? She always wanted you to dress like her, but on you it was a disaster. You looked like a runner bean in a dry year.' He waved at her skintight trousers and over-tunic. 'That's your style. Principal Boy meets Lolita.'

She said nothing, but her eyes scanned his sagging cord trousers, worn sports jacket and crumpled cravat. 'You're not getting on, are you?'

'How did you guess?' He sighed and went to the cupboard where Rowan kept the drinks, finding nothing but Perrier water and tonic. 'A temperance campaign, I see. Fewer bottles for Saul to find.'

'Don't be silly. I don't like drink in the office, that's all.'

He poured himself a Perrier and flung himself into a chair. 'If it wasn't for the money from the business, I'd be completely broke. It pays for my flat and the tours, the expenses don't nearly cover it, not for Astrid as well. I don't understand what I'm doing wrong, you see. I won the competition, everybody said I was made, but the agent couldn't arrange much because all the best venues are booked years in advance. Then somehow I didn't get off the ground when he did make the bookings. People had forgotten about me, I got bad reviews.'

'What about the American tour? Mother said that went well.'

Andy snorted. 'She would. Two big concerts at which I played one piece, the rest piddling little affairs with old ladies coming up afterwards and saying, "You were wonderful, Mr. Judge. Can you advise me about my granddaughter, she's six months old and has a wonderful talent." The whole thing was a fiasco, I was barely mentioned in the papers.'

'Oh. I see.'

Rowan went to the cabinet and poured herself a glass of water. Andy was without doubt a brilliant violinist, but his style was different. He showed to best effect in dramatic pieces, where his technical virtuosity could be given full rein, not in the worthy symphonic works for which his agent seemed intent on booking him. More to the point, perhaps disastrously, on a stage he lacked presence. In her mind's eye she pictured a revised Andy, his hair instead of drooping wearily over his collar permed into energetic curls. A soft black suit, they had just the cloth, a mile distant from ordinary men's suiting, made up in a collarless jacket and baggy, front-pleated trousers. With it he would wear a white silk shirt and a floppy bow tie.

'Stop looking at me like that,' said Andy. He felt better now he had confided in Rowan. A little honesty broke through the mists like sunshine.

'What you need is a fresh start,' said Rowan, still staring at him assessingly. 'It's a good thing you've got to stay for a bit. First stop Mr. Suzman. If I beg, he might get something together in a couple of days. Then the hairdresser, and when you're up to scratch we'll ring up the *Yorkshire Post* . . . story about the local boy made international violinist coming back at time of crisis. The television stations often pick up from there, and if we get a spot you've got to give it everything.'

Andy looked dumbfounded. 'What's local television supposed to do for me?'

'Get you noticed. If we can't sell you altogether as a concert violinist, you'll have to be everybody's favourite classicist. The concert career could follow, we'll just have to see.'

Andy watched her over the rim of his glass. Unspoken words hung in the air, both he and Rowan circled round them cautiously. 'Er – this isn't entirely free, is it, Rowan?' he said at last.

'I don't know what you mean.' She wandered about the room, touching the fabric on the walls, feeling it with a professional hand. 'I'd do it for you anyway, you know that. But Andy – I do want to go public. Please, Andy. You've got to agree.'

'If you're sending me up the wrong alley, I'll do you, Rowan.'

'Coward! You never would take a chance.' She picked up a pencil and threw it at him. He caught it and threw it straight back, catching her on the side of the head.

'Ouch! You never had any chivalry either.'

'Good God, if I had you'd have crucified me. I remember you tying me up for hours.'

'Ten minutes,' said Rowan scornfully. 'Anyway, I always saved you in the end. Didn't I?'

He grinned and acknowledged it.

For Diana the inquest passed in a blur. James was there, of course, and she asked Andy to come, though he brought the appalling Astrid with him. Richard arrived just as it was about to start. When he put his hand on James's shoulder, Diana thought her husband was going to cry. She wanted to hold hands, but somehow he evaded her grasp. There was a distance between them, she knew it was there and was too grief-stricken to cross it. When they said the name, Nicholas James Barton, she dropped her face into her gloved hands and wept.

The evidence was straightforward enough. After only an hour the coroner was pronouncing death by unspecified natural causes. 'I offer the parents my deepest sympathy,' he said in a cool voice that precluded any real emotion. 'They should not hold themselves to blame in any way.'

Outside Diana said urgently to them all, 'You see, he said it wasn't my fault. He told me that.'

'Of course it wasn't,' said Andy, and Astrid said, 'What Andy means, Mrs. Barton, is you shouldn't feel any guilt at all.'

'Oh, shut up,' flared Diana. 'Can we go home, James? I can't stand any more.'

'Can't you?' James stared at her with what seemed almost like cold hatred. Diana recoiled, saying, 'James?' and it was left to Richard to save the situation, smoothly moving between them. 'Come on, let's have a pub lunch. Coming, Andy?'

'I have to meet Rowan,' said Andy vaguely, and Diana

said, 'She's always got time for other people, it's only me she neglects,' although it was she who had refused to allow Rowan at the inquest. She might have brought Saul.

Over lunch, with Diana picking distractedly at the food and James, it appeared, barely noticing what he was eating, Diana said, 'Richard, have you seen Sally's black man?'

Richard swallowed down some tasteless steak and kidney. 'Only once. They seem happy together.'

'I can't understand it, I just cannot understand it. Her father would be so ashamed.'

James snorted. 'He was good at that sort of emotion; it was the positive things he couldn't manage. Bloody wimp, that was Andrew, and Andy takes after him.'

'Oh, do shut up,' snarled Diana. 'I wouldn't expect you to have any standards.'

'And what sort of standards do you have, may I ask? Or is that too leading a question at the moment?'

Diana stared at him uncomprehendingly. Richard said, 'I think you got the wrong end of the stick at the hospital, Dad. Why don't we talk about it after the funeral?'

James dug his fork viciously into his food. 'Perhaps we will at that.'

Rowan took Hannah to the funeral. Saul held her as Rowan, Andy and Sally stood at the graveside, watching the tiny coffin go into the earth. A spray of roses went with it, bearing the inscription 'To Darling Nick, with all Mummy's love', and few people noticed the omission of James. But at the last moment he stepped forward and almost defiantly threw in a little bunch of freesias. He bent down and picked up handfuls of earth, sending them rattling fiercely down on to the coffin. He threw more and more, until Richard took hold of him and led him away.

He allowed himself to be led through the crowd, openly weeping. As he passed Saul, he stopped. Softly, very softly, he said, 'I'm going to break you, Saul. Take my word, I am going to finish you.'

Saul said, 'You don't have to feed on this, James. You don't have to let it turn you sour.' He lifted the baby in his arms and turned her face towards him. She let out a tiny cry and he cradled her close. James spat into the earth and walked away.

At the house afterwards neither Diana nor James appeared. Saul had gone back to the penthouse with Hannah. 'Something's upset him,' he told Rowan. 'And that's a bloody silly thing to say on a day like this, but there you are. If it helps him to hate me, then so be it. It doesn't do me any harm.'

'Doesn't it?' She stood watching him, wanting to ask him not to drink. But if she asked him he would yell and do it to spite her, so it was better to say nothing. She went to the Manor alone, and talked to people she hadn't seen since her father died.

Andy came across to her, followed by the faithful Astrid. He was wearing the clothes Rowan had chosen for him, and looked like an exotic prince. 'I've been asked to the television studios,' he said, barely concealing his excitement. 'I did it!'

'Well done,' said Rowan, somewhat ironically. 'You must play, of course, even if they don't ask you to.'

'I've got a piece organised. I wondered if you'd like to hear it, actually.'

'What I think Andy means is, should he play it now?' interrupted Astrid, and Rowan gazed at her in amazement.

'This is a funeral, Astrid,' she said icily. 'We are not here for a concert performance. Andy can play it to me another time.'

She signalled to Sally to come, and made ready to leave. In the hall she could dimly hear the sound of raised voices from upstairs. She grimaced at her sister. 'Hammer and tongs. I suppose he thinks it's Mother's fault.'

'He always wants to blame someone. Let's get out of here, Ro, Mohammed's waiting for me.'

In the car the girls sat in silence, letting the weight of the day fall away from them. At last, Sally said, 'Rowan, what do you really think of Mohammed?'

'You know what I think. He's a very nice man. That doesn't mean you should marry him, Sal.'

'His family's against me, you know. They won't even see me.'

'I suppose they have the same objections as me. It will be very, very difficult, not just for you but for the children.'

'I don't think I care. I want to marry him, Rowan, more than anything in the world. I don't care if we have to live in a hovel!'

Rowan stopped the car on a double yellow line, causing a bus behind to hoot furiously. 'Look, you're not poor, Sally. Up to now, Mother's had control of your share of the firm, but if you married you would get that. We're going to go public, I've persuaded Andy to agree and we're going to do it. You're going to have an awful lot more than you ever expected. And if there's one thing I'm pretty sure about, it's that Mohammed will not like you having all that money. He seems to me to be a very proud man.'

'He is.' Sally put her thumb in her mouth and bit the side of it, a habit she had long grown out of. 'We wouldn't have to use it.'

'That would be absolutely ridiculous!'

'But his family might like me if they thought I was rich.'

Rowan put her head on the steering wheel and groaned. 'I just know this isn't right,' she said wearily. 'Good God, if you knew how hard it is to be married to someone the same as you, let alone someone different! We don't want it for you, his family don't want it for him, we can't all be bonkers!'

Sally took her hands out of her mouth and folded them

purposefully in her lap. 'I don't think you understand at all, Rowan. If I didn't have Mohammed, I wouldn't have anything. I only feel happy when he's there.'

That was a feeling Rowan remembered so well. And who was she to advise on marriage? People had to learn for themselves, and there was no saying that Sally would learn the same lessons as her sister. As Rowan well knew, happiness and misery lurked where you least expected them.

Chapter Thirty-Four

Sally was adept at sneaking in and out of the hostel unseen. To get in she loitered on the steps, occasionally withstanding the obscene suggestions of drunks on the way to the doss house. Sooner or later she would hear a gaggle of girls in the hall and in she would go, a short dash up and round the corner, and she was away.

If Mohammed was with her, it was more difficult. Then she sacrificed herself, engaging the matron in long conversations about lost letters while Mohammed sprinted up the stairs. They laughed about it afterwards, and even when he was caught he never seemed upset. 'She is so like my mother,' he told Sally, not without affection. It was one of the many things she did not understand about him, but that was part of his charm. He was different, somehow exotic. When he made love to her she was a precious vessel into which he poured himself.

On the evening of the funeral he found her packet of birth control pills. He sat on the edge of the bed, irritably lighting a cigarette, clicking his fingers for her to bring him an ashtray.

'You must stop taking these,' he said suddenly.

'But – I can't.' She felt nervous of him. When he neglected to indulge her it was like the sun going in and frost descending.

'I wish for a child. My mother will accept you when you are with child, she will take you as her daughter.'

'We ought to get married first,' said Sally doubtfully. 'Suppose she still wouldn't see me? I'd be pregnant and I'd have nothing.'

'Sally, Sally!' He turned and took her face in his hands, the forefingers roughened by work in the mill. 'I shall always take care of you. If I had a house of my own I would take you to it. For now I must persuade my father to let us come to his house, to have a room of our own. If my mother agrees, he will agree.'

'Do you think I ought to come and see them?' asked Sally nervously.

Mohammed drew on his cigarette, thinking about it. In his house there lived his parents, his three sisters and two brothers as well as an uncle and a cousin. That evening his father and uncle would be working. It might be a good time to confront the rest of them with Sally, to let them see that he had truly won a prize. He turned to her. 'Get dressed. A long skirt, trousers perhaps. Let your hair fall down, I like it so.'

Sally dressed before his watchful gaze, putting on dark tights, a long skirt and a high-necked jumper. When she began her make-up, Mohammed came up behind her and took her breasts in his hands. She let him fondle her, leaning her head back against his naked torso. She turned to lick his hot, different skin and after a moment he took her by the hand and led her to the bed. He pulled her clothes down just enough to allow himself entry, Sally knew at once that it was not one of those times when he was prepared to give her satisfaction. He pumped in silence, then ejaculated copiously. When Sally stood up, warm strings of semen hung from her. She had to wipe herself with tissues.

Mohammed washed his penis at the basin. He said, 'My mother knows we do this. You must not mind if she shows some contempt for you.'

Sally stared at him. 'I can't go! She shouldn't know about us, you shouldn't have told her!'

'I do not lie to my mother, Sally. Besides – ' he took her hands and held them, lovingly – 'I want her to know that you have only me. It is right that I should look after you.'

Nonetheless, when they walked together down the narrow street of terraced houses, some of the doors painted in violent reds and purples and yellows, she felt odd and out of place.

There were lots of children around, quiet and well-behaved all of them, watching her as if she were a zoo creature stepped outside the cage. They came to a yellow door, and Mohammed went in. Sally followed, almost sick with fright, sampling for the first time the perfumed, spicy aroma of an Asian home.

There seemed to be people everywhere: girls in saris, two young boys in silk suits. Everybody talked and not one word could Sally understand. She found herself hustled through to the kitchen. Word of her arrival had spread instantly throughout the house. Everyone crowded into the passage behind her, longing to see her meeting with Mohammed's mother.

She was small and plump. She wore glasses perched on the end of her nose and she was cooking. The room was spotlessly clean, but quite unlike anything Sally had known in a kitchen. An old gas stove stood against one wall, there was a chipped white sink and a wood table standing on a square of lino. Pots and pans hung everywhere on the walls, great metal things that would have done duty for an army, and there was an old dresser with glass-fronted cupboards crammed full of tins and foodstuffs. Overpowering everything was an astonishing smell of garlic.

'Mother, this is Sally,' said Mohammed formally in English. His mother cast a fulminating glance at Sally and then rocketed off at her son in a fusillade of Gujerati.

'How do you do?' said Sally feebly, when she paused for breath. The woman took no notice. She uttered a few more paragraphs to her son and turned back to her cooking.

A young woman stepped out of the throng in the passage and said something to her mother. She turned to Sally. 'My mother doesn't speak English. I am sorry for your welcome. I am Fadeema.'

'I thought she would be reasonable,' said Mohammed crossly. 'I am an educated man, I have found an educated wife, of good family.'

'Pah!' said his mother.

'I thought she didn't speak English,' whispered Sally nervously.

Mohammed made a face. 'She likes to think she doesn't speak English.'

He rattled away at his mother in Gujerati and Fadeema steered Sally into the front room. It was heavily decorated with flock paper, brass ornaments stood around a gas fire and there was a television showing an Asian video. A beauty was flashing dark eyes pleading with her lover. Fadeema went across and turned it off. 'You are a student? I am a student also, of medicine.'

'Oh.' Sally felt intimidated. She attended her beauty course but did only moderately well, mostly because she had no real wish to give facials and wax legs. She was discovering that the bodies of other women repelled her slightly. 'Don't you find it difficult?' she asked.

'It is difficult at home, yes,' said Fadeema. 'My parents don't approve of the men students. They've got used to it though, as long as I come straight back.'

Mohammed came back into the room, clearly upset. He said something angrily to Fadeema and she turned and smiled awkwardly at Sally. 'My mother is unwell. I am so sorry you cannot share a meal with us. Perhaps another time.' She went out, and for a moment or two Mohammed paced up and down, muttering angily.

'What did she say?' asked Sally.

'Everything. That you are a prostitute, that you will give me disease, that she will never welcome such a woman into her home, corrupting her children. She doesn't understand the English! I told her, we are in a different world, I lead a different life to my father, I cannot live as he lived. It's no use, none of it.'

Sally rubbed her arms. The very air in the room felt hostile. 'Can we go now?' she asked. 'I don't want to stay here.'

He was instantly there for her. 'Poor Sally, poor little bird. I should never have brought you. We'll go out and have some food, we don't need this rubbish!' He shouted the last words for the benefit of his mother.

Together he and Sally went into the hall. It was empty now but for a young girl solemnly skipping on the threadbare carpet, the youngest sister. With every step her plaits flew up and banged down on her back. 'And you can keep your nose out of it,' said Mohammed unnecessarily and bustled Sally into the street. The girl watched them seriously, and then stuck out her tongue at her brother's back.

All the way down the road Sally could feel eyes watching her, curtains twitching as they assessed the precise length of time she had been in the house. In these cramped streets everyone knew everyone else's business, and the scene in the house would have been of maximum interest to the entire community.

'They don't live as if they were in Britain at all,' said Mohammed viciously. 'They remain just the same, that man said it and it is true. They would live like this on the moon: the same prejudices, the same judgements.'

'What are we going to do, Mohammed?' asked Sally. She felt unutterably weary and depressed.

'I will not give up! My mother will never reject my child.'

A headache was starting to build behind her eyes. She trusted Mohammed totally, but she couldn't bear to think of her mother's face if she was pregnant and unmarrried, of Rowan's patient disappointment. They would all understand, only too well.

They had a meal at a restaurant Mohammed knew, run by men who hailed Mohammed like a long-lost brother and ignored Sally almost totally. Afterwards he took her all the way back to the hostel, although the mill where he worked was miles away and his ancient car sighed and wheezed continuously.

'I'm sorry. I'm sorry,' he said shaking his head.

'It's not your fault.'

He held her hands between his own. 'I promise it will be all right.' She nodded, and waited until he was out of sight before walking incautiously into the hostel. It was a mistake. The matron collared her.

'Him again! I've warned you, don't come crying to me when you're in the family way!'

Sally ran away up the stairs. She was tired and cold, so she got into bed and automatically reached out for the packet of pills. It wasn't there. She got out of bed and looked everywhere, but it was no use. Mohammed had taken them. Crawling back under the covers, that still smelled of his body, she chewed the side of her thumb.

Andy was to appear on the news magazine programme, in the early evening. It was intended that he give a few moments' brief chat about his career, play a tune, and the presenter could then smile, make a joke and say, 'Let's wish Andy Judge all the luck in the world on his forthcoming tour,' before going on to discuss the roadworks on the M62.

Rowan had no intention of letting it go at that. She took Andy to the mill and made him play his piece, a wild peasant dance by a wild peasant composer. He stood bad-temperedly in the warehouse and played it for her. People crept in to listen. Suddenly everyone had some reason to pass through the warehouse.

'Go away, go away all of you!' said Rowan peremptorily. 'The music's fine, Andy, but you're not.'

'It's the music I'm here for,' said Andy. 'I don't like being on show like this.'

'I think that's your trouble,' commented his sister. 'You want to perform, and when you do you're embarrassed. It holds you back.'

'Rubbish,' said Andy, and moved to put his violin away.

Rowan went up to him. 'Andy,' she said softly, 'I'm trying to help. Will you do something for me, just one thing? It's for you as well.'

'Stop trying to sweet-talk me, Rowan! I'm your brother, it doesn't work!'

'What does work then? I'll hit you if you like, there!' She clouted him hard on the shoulder. He gave a howl of rage and chased her. She ran like a hare, in and out of the hessian-bound bales of wool. Andy gave up first, unfit and out of breath.

'I win,' said Rowan. 'Stand on this bale here and play. I'm getting everyone in to listen.'

'For God's sake, no!'

She opened her eyes wide at him. 'Why not? There's no point being flamboyant in private if you can't do it in public. Nobody gets anywhere without practice.'

'But I do practise! Night and bloody day!'

She shrugged. 'Then you're practising the wrong thing. Up you get, Andy.'

He stood on the bale, feeling ridiculous, while she summoned the entire workforce. Since she had just chased them away they were a little bemused, but no one resisted. If Miss Rowan was prepared for once in a blue moon to put something before efficiency then who were they to argue? They gathered and stood grinning, looking up at Andy, an unhappy figure, standing on the bale.

'Get on with it,' called Rowan. 'Once more, with feeling!'

'Get stuffed!' said Andy morosely, and everyone cheered. He grinned at them cautiously. Then he gave an extravagant bow, and his black jacket flapped like wings. 'Ladies and gentlemen,' he declared, 'I am about to – excite you!'

Striking a pose, he put the violin to his chin and began. This time he embellished the tune, which rendered it vulgar to the purist but delighted the audience. As he played, he wandered about on his perch, filling Rowan with dread that he would fall off and break his leg, or worse, his violin. He finished with one leg hanging over space, about to take one final, disastrous step. They stayed silent while he hung there, suspended, but as soon as stepped back there was thunderous applause. People shouted 'More! More!' and they meant it.

Rowan waved them back to their work, and stood waiting for Andy to climb down. As people passed him they gripped his arm and said warmly, 'Grand stuff, lad! The old man woulda been proud of yer.'

Rowan bit the inside of her cheek. Andrew would indeed have been proud, more than for anything Rowan could have done. 'Do it like that tomorrow,' she said to Andy crisply.

'I'd get laughed out of town.'

'Don't be so damned British! If you do it dead-pan no one will remember you for a minute. You're a performer, so damn well perform.'

'Don't let her boss you about, Andy.' Saul had come in. Rowan smiled and went across to him, using the pretence of a kiss to smell his breath. There was the usual give-away, mouthwash, and his eyes had that distant look she associated with drink.

'He's got to do as he's told or he won't succeed,' said Rowan gently.

'Do as he's told, eh? Let's all do as we're told so we can get to the top of the fucking ladder. And then fall off.' He staggered abruptly and Rowan clutched his arm. She didn't look at Andy.

'What did you want?' she asked. 'I thought you were lunching out.'

'I shall not lunch – today,' said Saul.

'Have you cancelled? Do you want me to cancel for you?'

'Will you keep your pretty little nose out of – my business,' said Saul. 'Instead you can go back to the flat and pack everything. We're moving.'

'Into the house? It's not finished.'

'Finished or not, we are moving. I'm sick of the fucking flat! Do as you're told, woman.'

Suddenly, Rowan couldn't stand it. She let go of Saul's arm and fled, running to the new house. There were men working on the roof but inside was deserted. There were bare wires and half-laid floors and not a single door.

A few moments later Andy came in after her. 'What does he mean, live here?' said Rowan helplessly. 'We can't bring Hannah here.'

'He won't want to when he's sober.'

Rowan sniffed expressively.

'Is he ever sober?' asked Andy.

She sighed and wrapped her arms around herself. The rooms were huge and cold, although they would one day be beautiful. 'He doesn't drink in the mornings. The early mornings, at least not that I know of. He's – he's always been a drinker. But lately he's so much worse.'

'He's got a problem,' said Andy. 'He might not know it, but he has. You'll have to get help, love.'

'I daren't.' She fixed huge green eyes on her brother. He had never before considered soft emotions in the context of Rowan, his elder sister, but now he felt sad and protective. 'They might take Hannah away,' she said dismally. 'They could say we're not fit parents.'

Andy let out a crack of mirthless laughter. 'I don't think you need worry on that score. Kids like Hannah aren't wanted by anyone, you'd both have to be drunk all day every day before they took her. Oh, I'm sorry, love. I know that sounds brutal.'

'Yes, it does,' agreed Rowan. 'Everyone always feels they should talk straight about Hannah, when I wouldn't mind a bit of hedging. She's sitting up, you know. I bet you didn't know that.'

'No.'

They left the unfinished house. Rowan went to look for Saul, noting that his old Aston was still in the yard. Perhaps he wanted a new car, she thought wildly. When they went public she would buy him a brand new Porsche, or a Rolls-Royce if he wanted, with a personalised number plate. She would give anything for Saul to be as he used to be.

He was in burling and mending, touching the girls on the thigh and making crude jokes. Rowan thought, 'I know what it feels like to want to kill someone.' Tears were an unrelieved pain in her chest. She said, 'Saul, can you come? I want to talk to you.'

'I can come all right,' he leered, and put his arm round one of the younger, prettier women. She giggled nervously and Rowan snapped, 'I don't think they're paid enough to put up with being mauled by you, Saul.'

He came towards her, waggling his head. 'And what a nasty temper you've got today, Mrs. Barton. Nasty, nasty temper!' His hand reached out and he hit her. The blow caught her shoulder. It was so unexpected that she fell back against the wall.

Two of the women got up and stood like sentinels, worn blue overalls wrapped around their bulky bodies. 'Watch him, Miss,' said one. 'I know what the devils are like when they get like this. He'll have you in hospital, he will.'

Incredulous, Saul said, 'I've never hit her in my life! What the hell do you mean?'

'You just *did* hit me,' said Rowan. Her shoulder hurt and try as she might she was crying, in front of the women, where everyone could see. 'Come away, Saul, will you?'

'God, do you never stop giving bloody orders?' He pushed past her and down the stairs. Rowan wanted to follow but her legs felt like jelly and the women gathered round, full of unwanted sympathy.

'He's had too many, that's what it is, love. Overset him, the funeral and everything.'

'It's all right,' said Rowan desperately. 'He'll be sorry later. He isn't a violent man, normally.'

She knew there was no point in asking them not to gossip, they'd agree and gossip anyway. Gathering her composure to her like a pair of crutches, she followed Saul down the stairs. As she reached the yard she saw his car pull out of the gates, fast and erratic. 'Oh God,' she whispered. 'Oh God, Oh God, Oh God.' What was she to do if he killed himself? What if he killed someone else, a child perhaps, or crippled an old lady? If he got to the flat he would be making a scene, trying to get Barbara to drink with him, playing ridiculous games with Hannah. When he was drunk he always seemed on the verge of dropping her, but Hannah loved it, because it was Saul. The little girl adored him. When she saw him in the mornings she would crow with joy. Rowan taught her to hold a spoon and build bricks, and it was to Saul that Hannah showed off. He was her own, personal god.

It wasn't often that Rowan felt completely at a loss, but she stood in the yard then and had no idea which way to go. On every side were problems, in every place. 'We need a holiday,' she whispered to herself. 'If we could get away from here and have a holiday, everything would be all right.'

Someone was coming towards her from the mill and she couldn't face them. Almost running, she rushed to her car, and then as she was driving out she saw that it was Joe Partridge. She stopped and wound down the window.

'You all right, Ro?' he said.

'No. No, I'm not. What's going to happen, Joe? Everything seems so wrong.'

'Knew you was wrong to marry him. What's he given you but pain, that's what I'd like to know.'

'That isn't true.' She hung her head and whispered, 'I wish I wasn't here, I wish it was different.'

Joe squatted down and put his arm on the door edge. 'Chuck him out, Ro. He's a waster, him, you don't want no more to do with the bastard.'

'But I love him!' wailed Rowan in protest. 'He isn't what you think.'

'You'd do a bloody sight better with me, I can tell you,' retorted Joe. 'Wouldn't see me clouting you in public.'

She felt herself getting hot with shame. 'Does everyone know already?'

''Course they do.'

She wound up the window, excluding Joe, and drove away. He stood watching her. She wondered if she should have married him and had a safe, boring practical life. Saul had always been imagination and flair and excitement, and the reverse of the coin was this. It had to get better.

When she got back to the flat, he wasn't there. She waited until early evening, then drove around Bradford wondering where he might be. At eleven she rang the police, but no accident had been reported and when she spoke about a row they lost interest. At three she went to bed, and lay there, fitfully dozing, waiting to hear him come in, but she woke at six-thirty and he wasn't there.

She couldn't bear to go into the mill. She gave Barbara the day off and wheeled Hannah in her pram, round and round the streets. She got in the car and went out of the town, and carried the baby on to sheep-nibbled grass where she could roll and stretch in safety. 'I will give anything if he's there when I get back,' she told herself. 'I will never be unkind to him again, I shall never be rude, and I will never, never refuse sex, however much it hurts.' Weeks had passed since they last made love. She felt within herself a great desperation.

At last she went back to the flat. When she opened the bedroom door and saw Saul there, sprawled across the bed, his clothes wet and stained and his face grey and unshaven, she almost collapsed with relief. Immediately the telephone rang. It was the doorman. Before she had time to do more than say her name, he said crisply, 'I very much regret, Mrs. Barton, that the residents' committee has made a complaint. Your husband urinated in the main hallway this morning, in front of two ladies.'

'Oh God,' muttered Rowan. 'Tell them I'm sorry – he's sorry –'

'The residents feel he should be asked to leave, Mrs. Barton.'

She held the receiver in a white-knuckled hand. Suddenly she was shouting. 'And you can tell the bloody residents we wouldn't stay here if you paid us! You can all get bloody stuffed!'

Chapter Thirty-Five

They decided to go on holiday to Marbella for a month. When they returned, the house would be completed and the stockbrokers intended Judge's to be poised for the rights issue. Barbara was coming with them, to help with Hannah. They had rented a large villa with a swimming pool.

'It's about time we had some fun,' said Rowan nervously. She and Saul lived in a precarious state of mutual caution, walking around each other's sensibilities. When he recovered from his binge, he had gone out and bought her an emerald choker, fantastically beautiful and even more expensive. Rowan hated it. Every time she set eyes on it she thought of that night, that day, of her pathetic pleas to the landlord to let them stay at least until the end of the week.

On the day before their departure, Andy and Astrid took them out to dinner. Her brother looked almost more cheerful than Rowan had ever seen him, contrasting with Astrid in her dreary cotton dress, sandals and flab. She was a most depressing girl, thought Rowan unkindly.

'Did you see it then?' asked Andy.

'What? Oh, the television. No. No, I didn't.'

'Good God, I thought you at least might show some interest! I – er – I thought you should know, they've asked me to appear on a short series. Four programmes. "Andy Judge and His Musical Friends." I play and then invite one or two up-and-coming 'cellists, or pianists or something. Apparently the guy who was to head it has dropped out. I've got to pretend to be lifelong friends with people I've never met.'

Rowan stretched her face into a smile, saying, 'I'm so

pleased for you. Clever old Andy, you did it! Well, you could be going places.'

'So I could.'

Astrid munched her salad like a cow and said, 'I think Andy means that this is a real springboard, everybody will want him for concerts.'

Folding her hands, Rowan snarled, 'Astrid, why do you always tell me what Andy means? Do you know better than him? Do you think he can't speak for himself perhaps?'

'Don't be so aggressive, Rowan,' said Andy. 'You always were jealous of my girlfriends.'

'As I recall, you never had any girlfriends,' retorted Rowan.

Saul chuckled, and patted Rowan's hand. 'Sibling rivalry never dies, I see. What a charming dress, Astrid, like spring flowers.'

Astrid's cheeks went pink, clashing unfortunately with the dress. When at last they left, they could hear her saying querulously, 'She really is the most self-absorbed creature I ever met, Andy. Only ever interested in her, her, her.'

On the morning of their flight to Spain, Rowan dashed out to Aspley Manor to see her mother. After a fruitless conversation with the cleaner, she at last found Diana in one of the vast greenhouses. She was picking grapes from one of the ancient vines, standing on a ladder to reach the purple clusters and putting them into a wicker basket. Rowan stood and watched her. Diana's movements were slow and deliberate, and her hair needed washing.

'Where's James?' asked Rowan.

'I don't know. At work, I suppose. He comes home, he goes to work, we don't talk.' Diana snipped more bunches of grapes.

'What are you going to do with them all?' asked Rowan. 'Make wine or something?'

Her mother shook her head. 'Throw them away mostly. I don't want them, I don't want anything. But I like it in here.

It's warm, it doesn't remind me.' She got off her ladder and said, 'You know, I don't think James cares at all really. He says horrible things about Nicholas, and about me. I don't think he's capable of caring.'

'Actually, Mother, I think he's heartbroken.' Rowan knew it, although she hardly knew why. But she understood James, she always had.

'Well, if you like to think so,' said Diana.

Rowan longed, as so often before, to tell her mother everything. But there wasn't any point, Diana wouldn't understand. It was sex and yet it wasn't, it was Hannah and the mill and everything. Sometimes she and Saul seemed to have it right, to be on the same 'plane, going to the same place, but then, suddenly, it was different. Was it the drink that did that? Or did he drink because of it? If they got on a real 'plane, now, surely they could go back to the beginning. 'We're going on holiday,' she said.

Diana turned on her. 'Oh God, Rowan, you are so tactless! All right, go, leave me. I know people don't want to be close to me, they can't stand grief. People cross the road when they see me coming. I go into shops and tell the assistants all about it, I can see them hating me and thinking I'm mad. But go on, off on your holiday, everything a miserable mess here and you in the sun having fun.'

'You've got James, Mother,' said Rowan feebly.

Diana's face stretched into a rictus of pain and laughter. 'Oh yes! And James hates me, he does, he really hates me! And I don't know why.'

Rowan left as soon as she could.

The villa, when they finally reached it, was hot and remote. A car was essential. They had hired one at the airport and Saul drove them flat out along the main highway, renowned for its death toll. He had drunk quite a bit on the 'plane, but not enough seriously to affect him. On this road, though, with crumpled cars left rotting on the roadside and Spanish boys leaning out of station wagons, yelling challenges, Rowan and Barbara sat petrified.

As soon as they arrived, Rowan took Hannah into the bedroom and undressed her. She blew on the baby's fat tummy and made her laugh. 'This will get rid of your wheezes, won't it, sweet? No more coughs and colds for Hannah.'

The child had typically dry, flaking skin. Rowan spent pounds on creams and lotions. Ordinary children grew out of such things, and so might Hannah, eventually. Six months late sitting up, and now, at almost eighteen months, she was no bigger than babies of a year old. Patience, that was the thing. One day she would walk, one day she would say 'Mummy'.

'God, but this place is in the back of beyond,' said Saul. He went to the window and stared out at sandy hills covered in scrub.

'Peace and quiet,' said Rowan. 'We shall love it. Have you seen the pool?'

'Yes. Just wish I was in Madrid, that's all. I love Madrid.'

Rowan tried to humour him. 'Well, you could go. I mean you could, we're here for a month. You don't have to stay with us if you don't want to.'

'You want me out of the way, I suppose.'

She glanced at him quickly. He looked tired and tense. He walked around the marble floor in quick strides, his hands clenched in his pockets. She went to him and put her arms round his neck. 'I never want you out of the way. I want you to get brown and fat and happy. I want you to get well.'

'Do you think I'm ill, then? Is that it?'

'You've been working too hard.'

She put her lips along his jaw, mouthing him gently. At last he put his arms round her, he found her mouth and his tongue made sensuous coils around her own. His hands were on her cotton T-shirt, moving it up and down, finding the bones beneath her skin and tracing them gently.

'I love you,' whispered Rowan.

'Do you? Let's give Hannah to Barbara.'

Giggling naughtily, Rowan picked up the quiet girl from the bed and went to the door. 'Barbara! I'm just taking a shower. Would you have Hannah for a moment, please?'

'OK.' Barbara wandered into view, wearing a cheesecloth sundress, like a plum pudding wrapped in muslin. The baby safely removed, Rowan closed the door. She and Saul fell on the bed, laughing like children themselves.

He licked her breasts, he pushed his face into their shallow valley and left a trail with his tongue to her belly and beyond. 'I am enjoying this,' she told herself. 'I just wish I knew it wouldn't hurt.' Her mind kept filling with images of long scars raked by an iron pole, but he wasn't a cruel man, he had never been that. It was she who was cruel to deny him so.

At last he was on top of her. 'All right?' he asked.

'Yes. Go on, do it.'

'I – don't think I can.'

For a minute she didn't understand. Then she touched him. 'Oh dear,' she said dismally.

'Must be a bit tired, I think,' said Saul vaguely, and rolled off her.

Rowan tried desperately to think of something to say. Lots of men had this problem from time to time, or so she understood. But she felt so undesirable. 'We'll have to feed you champagne and oysters,' she said with forced humour. 'Get your clockwork oiled.'

'For Christ's sake, it's you that hasn't been able to for months! You don't have to make a fuss when once I can't perform.'

'I wasn't making a fuss. I didn't want you to feel bad about it, that's all.'

'I wouldn't if you weren't so intent on making a big thing of it.'

'We might have a thing but it certainly isn't big.'

When the comment popped into her mind it had been

framed as a joke, but on her lips it sounded hard and unkind.

'You bitch!' said Saul and got off the bed. He went to the suitcases and threw one open, tossing clothes right and left till he found his swimming costume. She felt calmer once his genitals were covered, nothing but a nondescript bulge with nothing asked of them.

'I didn't mean to be horrid,' she said.

'Didn't you?'

He went out of the room, and almost as an after-thought his hand closed on one of the bottles of duty-free spirits he had picked up on the 'plane. Rowan's mouth opened to object. She closed it again. There was nothing she could say.

Chapter Thirty-Six

In retrospect the first disastrous day of the holiday seemed like the last of the awful time at home. It was the end of the worst, Rowan told herself, revelling in day after day of sunshine. It suited her, she wore shorts, a bikini, she would have liked to wear nothing at all and laze round the pool nibbling salads and sipping wine. She and Saul were relaxing together, sending Barbara into town to do the shopping and playing with Hannah, discussing her toes and her eyes and her odd, blunt fingers.

'Would we mind more if we had a normal one?' asked Rowan thoughtfully.

Saul gazed at his daughter through half-closed eyes. 'Probably. We'd compare all the time and now we don't. But, this is the easy bit, it's going to get worse. It's OK to do things for a baby, not for a strapping great ten-year-old.'

Rowan wouldn't think of that; at once she rejected it. 'We might not have to do things. She can learn, she'll just be very slow. She could be independent one day.'

Saul said nothing. He regarded Rowan's optimism with suspicion, it was such a very short step to self-delusion. Live for today, he told himself, enjoy her for what she is and don't expect anything. Suddenly he felt very depressed.

'Why don't we go to bed?' said Rowan boldly. 'We've got to try sometime.'

'Not now, damn it.' He went and opened another bottle of wine. At least wine was something Rowan did not complain about, and he kept up an almost continuous consumption. 'Let's go to the beach this afternoon,' he said.

'Oh. All right.' He was bored then, with her, with her

body, with everything about her. Everything had seemed to be going so well. She blinked back tears.

White dry sand, a breeze, the sun glinting on an endless run of wavelets. Wind surfers careered across the sea, fished out by speed boats when they became exhausted and threatening swimmers when they were not.

'Think I'll have a go at that,' said Saul. It took Rowan by surprise; it was the first positively enthusiastic thing he had said since they arrived. Although she too would have liked to try, it seemed sensible to let Saul have it to himself. She put Hannah down on the sand and spread out her towel. Barbara stood hesitating, and Rowan said, 'You can go off if you like, Barbara. Do what you want.' And Barbara thankfully took off to the beach bar, and the boys.

Left alone, Rowan sat in her bikini and felt conspicuous. She was the only woman in the place with her breasts covered, people stared at her with open curiosity. Perhaps they thought she was deformed or something. Plucking up courage she took off her top and rubbed oil decisively into her skin. Her nipples stood up in fright and embarrassed her, but after ten minutes or so she relaxed. She began playing with Hannah, pouring sand from one bucket to another, putting a spade again and again into her hand.

'Hello there! I thought it was you.' She glanced up quickly, and against the sun, dulled by her sunglasses, barely recognised the man standing over her. He squatted down beside her. A tall man, with reddish hair and a sharp, aware face.

'Richard? Richard Barton?'

'Yes. Well, this is a bit of a coincidence.' She was embarrassingly conscious that she was wearing nothing but a tiny scrap of material that only just covered her pubic hair. Trying to appear casual she picked up her bikini top. 'Don't,' said Richard. 'Please. I didn't want to embarrass you.'

'I'm still putting it on. It's all right when I don't know anyone, but with you here I feel shy.'

'Then at least let me help.' He reached up her back and fastened the clasp. To fill the silence, she picked up Hannah.

'She's very good,' he said, trying to think of something positive about the child.

Rowan nodded. 'Too good. You have to stimulate her or she doesn't learn. You have to put experience in, and with normal children they absorb it naturally.'

He trickled sand from one palm to the other. 'I'm amazed at how well you take it. I mean, I don't know much about children but I don't think I could be nearly as calm, a tenth as practical.'

Her mouth twisted and she said, 'Oh no, no.'

'Oh yes! You amaze me, you're fantastic.'

She turned on him. 'That's rubbish! I'm sorry but it is. Today I'm taking it well, you can see me taking it well, I'm here, out here for all to see. What you didn't see, what no one sees, are the days I couldn't face anybody. The day I took her to the clinic and came away again because I couldn't bear to sit in there with all the other babies. I've got a nanny, you know. I have to have a nanny, I was going mad sitting indoors thinking about the future. Most of the time I don't think about it, I pretend she's all right. And people say I'm taking it well. It's an absolute load of rubbish.'

She looked away, out to the windsurfers. 'There's Saul. I didn't know he'd done it before.' He was skimming expertly over the sea, catching the wind and easily outstripping beginners all around him.

'How is he?' asked Richard.

Rowan licked her lips. 'Fine. Just fine. And why are you here, Richard? We're on holiday while they finish our house, but what about you?'

'I'm on holiday too. A bit of time off before I start at Bardsey's.'

The words dropped like lead shot into the pool of their conversation. He could sense Rowan arming herself against him, censoring what she would say.

'I'm pleased for you,' she commented. 'It's odd for James to mend fences.'

'He's had one hell of a battering recently. I never thought I'd feel sorry for him, but I do.'

'Let me tell you, it's a mistake,' snapped Rowan forcefully.

Richard moved so that he had Rowan between himself and the sea. He could seem to stare at the sea and concentrate on her. She was so long and slender, even her neck had unusual length, and her small head was balanced on top like a well-placed flower. Those green eyes too, windows that were at one moment cool and distant, at the next bright with emotion. He wondered what sort of passion she knew with that bum of a husband of hers.

'Are you happy?' he asked suddenly.

For a minute he thought she hadn't heard him. Then she put on her sunglasses again. 'You haven't the right to ask me such a question,' she said at length. 'Happiness isn't something you have or don't have, for always. It comes and goes, lots of times a day sometimes.'

'No, it doesn't. A happy person might not always be knowngly happy, but underneath, there's a layer of contentment. They're at peace with themselves.'

'Well, are you? demanded Rowan. 'Are you contented? You're rich, you've got girlfriends, I suppose. No problems.'

'Lots of problems,' said Richard. 'Or at least one big problem.'

'You're gay!' said Rowan decisively. 'Good, that should upset James.'

'Like hell I am! If you must know, I'm – emotionally dead.'

She stared at him. 'You can't be serious.'

'I am. I don't know what happened to me. When I was a teenager and Dad waltzed off with your mother, I was filled with emotions. They were spilling out right left and centre.

Hate, lust, happiness, love, I had them all. Since I've grown up I haven't got them any more. I just have pale copies. A bit of discontent. Mild dislike. A vague sensation of pleasure.'

'What about sex?' asked Rowan. 'That either is or isn't, surely.'

'There speaks an innocent.' He lounged on his side in the sand, amazed and excited by her directness. 'Sex isn't just on or off, even for men. Some orgasms are a quick spout, nothing to it, get up and go to work and some are – symphonies. Delicious, ecstatic whirls of feeling.' He was getting an erection, he saw her eyes behind the sunglasses focus on it and quickly look away.

Rowan was uncomfortably aware that her odd remark had seemed like encouragement. She began to gather up her things. 'What an expert you seem to be, quite a man of the world. I'm going to take Hannah in the water.'

'You can't, you've got to watch all the things.' He caught her hand. 'I seem to be upsetting you and I don't want to. Stay and talk to me.'

Rowan allowed herself to be pulled back on to the sand. 'I'm just in an odd sort of mood,' she apologised.

'Reaction I should think. You work too hard. And I work too hard, what are we doing in this textile business? We should get used to lying on beaches, we should do it all the time.'

'I'd get horribly, hopelessly bored in about five minutes flat.' She dropped her chin in her hands and grinned at him, and he smiled back, tanned, relaxed, his quick expression that seemed to be habitual. He kept staring at her longer than was polite. She felt herself flushing. 'Why are you looking at me like that?'

He kept his eyes fixed on her. 'You know why. Because you look so lovely. Not many women look great with no clothes on, but you're one of them.'

'You're being ridiculously flattering.' She tried to sound cool, but failed. She stretched out on the sand, looking away from him, hoping he could not tell what she was feeling. Somehow he had managed to prise the cork from the bottle of sexual interest, with him she felt uncomfortably alive. An ache was beginning in her belly, a hot and distressing pain.

'We shall go soon,' she said.

'That would be unkind. I'm alone here, I'm lonely. Give me a helping hand.'

His tone made the remark suggestive. He rolled on to his belly in the sand and she waited tensely for what he was going to say next. But again he surprised her. 'Am I right in thinking you're going public? The papers were full of it on Sunday.'

'We were here, I didn't see. I'm not going to tell you anything you can't find out for yourself.'

Richard laughed. 'I'm not my father, for Christ's sake! I haven't got it in for you.'

'If you're Bardsey's, you've got it in for us. It's sort of undeclared war, Saul meets it all the time, selling. Wherever he puts his foot a Bardsey clodhopper is sure to follow, and a nose, sniffing.'

'Don't tell me he's paranoid as well.'

'As well as what?'

They both looked up. Saul stood, wet and panting. He reached down and picked up Hannah, pressing his wet skin to her dry one. The child squirmed like an animal, a stumpy little teddy bear.

For a second or two Richard remained where he was. Then he sat up.

'Why don't you both have dinner with me tonight?' he said.

'You're not really alone, are you?' asked Rowan. 'I thought that was just a sob story.'

Richard confessed. 'I'm half alone. The lady had to go to Paris for a couple of days, I've got nothing to do till she gets back. Pathetic really.'

'Tragic.'

They laughed together and Saul's antennae, sharper than usual due to sobriety induced by cold water, homed in on the vibes. He wasn't surprised Richard was interested. When he really looked at Rowan, he felt a stab of pride. Gone was the gawky, prickly girl and in her place was a woman of assurance. A sexual woman, who needed and could handle a man's desire.

'OK,' said Saul, taking Rowan aback. 'We'll meet you about eight. I'll make it easy for you and insist Rowan puts her clothes on.'

'Spoilsport.' Richard took his leave of them, passing Barbara on her way back along the beach.

Saul said quickly, 'What did he say? Did he ask you to go to bed with him?'

Rowan laughed. 'Of course not. He's all right, like James really but with the corners knocked off.'

'I think it's you he wants to knock off.' Saul wasn't displeased. The knowledge that Rowan was desired by others was stimulating.

She dressed for the evening in a white jersey silk tube, reaching from above her breasts to above her knees. Underneath it she was of necessity naked since underclothes would have shown. As she walked the fabric moved on her, so every now and then she had to hitch it up over her breasts.

'Great,' said Saul appreciatively. 'Just great.' He had drunk quite a bit after the beach. He lounged on the bed, looking dashing in a white jacket and bow tie. Rowan had thought he might make love to her but the drink was calming him. Later, perhaps.

She picked up her bag and said, 'Shall I drive?' and Saul nodded. In the car her skirt rode up towards her crotch but he did nothing. She felt defiant. She knew she looked good tonight, she wanted some acknowledgement.

Richard gave it to her. They dined at his hotel, an exclusive and expensive alabaster palace. The ceilings seemed carved out of spun sugar, and were reflected in the dark marble floors. Instead of the heavy wood of so much of the country's furniture, there were gilded chairs and airy glass tables, everything so light and delicate that it was like fairyland. Saul slumped in one of the chairs like a man in a Wendy house, his head already turning as he looked for the next drink. Rowan clenched her teeth and sat also, aware that the waiters were fawning on her, that Richard was deliberately positioning himself opposite her knees. In consequence she crossed her legs, wondering how much he could see in the dark shadows of her skirt. Let Saul know that this man found her exciting, let him discover what sort of woman he had.

Richard said, 'I brought the papers out with me. I thought you might be interested.' He laid the quality Sundays out on the low coffee table and Rowan immediately picked them up. She scanned the columns.

'Listen, Saul, where do they get this stuff from? "Isaac Judge is about to take the biggest step of its career in buying itself a stockmarket quotation. Billed by some as a leap in the dark, it is in fact another brilliant move by the successful Bradford firm. Ably managed by one of the textile industry's few women, who rescued it from disaster only a few years ago, the company looks like being a certain growth stock." Why don't they mention you, darling? They could have said one of the industry's few married couples. Going public was entirely your idea. I mean, it was my idea, but you worked out how to do it.'

Saul put down his empty whisky glass and signalled a waiter for another. Rowan froze, unaware that her anxiety was immediately obvious to Richard.

He said smoothly, 'Let's make a night of it. Champagne for everyone. Waiter!'

Saul's next whisky was unobtrusively waved away. Rowan felt weak with gratitude, for while Saul could drink champagne all night and remain conscious, if he continued on whisky at that rate they would all suffer for it.

She said to Richard, 'How do you intend to make James let you do anything? It's awfully hard to let go, you know. When Saul first came to Judge's I almost elbowed him out of the office. I couldn't bear it!'

'What's changed?' asked Saul sardonically.

'Don't be silly, darling!' Rowan was starting to hate the evening, to wish she had never come.

Richard said, 'I think we'll work it out, as you two have, I suppose. He's very keen to get me in, I think he'll be sensible.'

Saul laughed. 'I remember when I started there. He was going to let me run things, he was going to involve me. Took me years to realise he'd never intended anything of the kind.'

'So you married me and got a firm of your own,' said Rowan crisply. 'A good move all round, if I may say so.'

Saul grinned suddenly. 'Are you determined I married for money? If you want us to believe that, you're wearing the wrong clothes.'

'She does look delectable,' agreed Richard, nodding.

A sexual charge seemed to run through all three of them. Rowan felt beads of moisture forming in the small of her back, coursing down into the crease of her backside. The two men shifted in their chairs. Saul ran his thick brown finger round the edge of his glass. Rowan's own fingers caressed the long stem of the glass she held, while Richard reached for the champagne bucket and took out the bottle. The moment was heavy with suggestion. 'We'll have some more of this,' said Richard. 'Let's go and eat.'

Throughout the meal, Rowan felt threatened by him. To begin with she was consciously exciting him, which in turn excited Saul. She was waiting until she was alone with Saul; she knew he would be hard and eager. Everything would be all right after that. But Richard seemed to be demanding something for himself. When a small band set up on the dais and started to play, Richard took Rowan's hand. 'Let's dance,' he said, and pulled her close to him. A tall, spare man, his brain clear and sharp.

They were belly to belly, she could feel him pressing against her. 'He doesn't give you any fun, does he?' whispered Richard. 'Always drunk, always miserable.'

'I don't like you,' said Rowan, almost to herself.

'I'm not surprised. I tell you that you're young, and beautiful, and shackled to a drunk who doesn't know what he's got. Look at him now, ordering a whisky to help things along. He thinks you won't see him. And when we get back he'll dance with you himself, only because I have. Watch.'

He led Rowan back to the table. The whisky had gone and Saul said, 'Right, let's dance then, Rowan.' She went out again to the floor and he clutched her to him and used her to hold himself up. He said, 'That guy really fancies you. He'd give anything to have you.'

'Don't talk like that. I want you to make love to me, don't you want to?'

He laughed. 'You needn't worry. I'll be fantastic tonight.'

At the table there was more champagne. Saul ordered brandy. Rowan said, 'I've had enough, I want to go home,' but the two men kept on drinking, keeping pace with one another. She was thirsty but there was only champagne, so she drank another glass, and then another. 'Let's go up to my room for a nightcap,' said Richard.

'We ought to go home,' said Rowan.

'We're on holiday,' said Saul. 'We can let our hair down once in a while. Don't be such a puritan, Rowan.'

So they went upstairs in the lift. The champagne was having its effect, Rowan felt warm and relaxed. She draped her arms round Saul and leaned on him, and he leaned against the wall. In the bedroom there was a huge double bed, covered in a white quilt. There was a sofa, too, and Saul slumped on it, chuckling. 'She looks gorgeous, doesn't she? Just delicious.'

'Yes.'

Richard poured them all drinks and Rowan kicked off her shoes and wandered about on the marble floor, relishing the chill on her feet. She could feel the two men watching her, she felt strung between them, dancing on a wire, on a rope of sexuality. The drink was very strong, she didn't know what it was. Richard stood in front of her. He touched her breast.

Just his fingers released a charge of electricity. The shock of it was sobering. She glanced quickly at Saul and the look on his face revolted her. 'Don't touch me!' She picked up her shoes, fitting them on as she went, but Saul sat there, watching. 'You want him to, don't you?' she said in horror. 'You want to watch!'

Richard was close behind her. He put his hands around her waist and she hit him.

'Leave her alone,' mumbled Saul. 'Rowan doesn't want to play.' He got to his feet and came swaying across. She hid behind him, sheltering from Richard, from the lascivious ideas of the men who saw her as a creature in some fantasy. If she gave a hint of acceptance they would both have her, one after the other, competing.

Richard said, 'Why do you stick with him? You are so, so lovely.'

'He's drunk,' flared Rowan. 'He doesn't know what he's doing, but you do, you know!'

'So did you,' said Richard softly. 'You wanted it.'

Saul reeled back against the wall, in a state of near coma. 'Oh God, I've been here before,' said Rowan bitterly. 'Help me get him down to the car, will you?'

'You should dump the shit in the street and leave him,' said Richard, his frustration crystallising into anger. 'He's no damn use to you.'

'He's my husband and I love him,' replied Rowan. 'He's the father of my child. He won't always be like this, he'll get better.'

Richard pushed her aside and bent to put Saul over his

shoulders. The big man groaned and mumbled, 'Don't drop me, I'm only little.' Bent under the weight, Richard staggered to the lift and threw him in.

'You don't have to half kill him,' snarled Rowan.

'He's doing worse than that to you, he's eating you alive. When he's not there you're bubbly, relaxed. You're so different, you should see yourself. With him, you're always watching.'

When the lift doors closed, she and Richard were crammed together in one corner while Saul lay sprawled across the floor. Suddenly Richard reached up under her skirt, pushed his hand between her legs and touched her. She couldn't get away. She stood immobile and waited for the lift to stop. It was barely a second but it lasted for ever.

'You're wonderful,' whispered Richard. 'I must make love to you.'

When the lift reached the ground she wriggled away from him, fell over Saul and got out of the door. Richard shouldered his burden and staggered into the car park. As he unloaded Saul into the back seat of the car, Rowan said dangerously, 'Don't you think you can do that to me again. Don't you ever think you can touch me again. I didn't believe you when you said you had no feelings but I do now. They're dead. There's nothing left in you but foul perversions.'

He came round to the driver's door, but she was in the car and locking it. He reached through the open window and took her face between his hands.

'You're sending me mad,' he said wildly. 'You're to blame, you drive me to it and then blame me.'

She struck his hand aside. He caught her wrists and they struggled hard. Then she spat at him, full in the face. They froze into a bitter tableau. He saw Rowan's eyes brimming with tears, and let her go. Jerking the car into gear, she drove furiously away.

The next day, of course, Saul was ill and seemed to

remember nothing of the night before. He blamed his malady on seafood eaten at dinner, and Rowan pretended to agree. Inside herself she carried a small furnace of rage and hurt. However many times she swam up and down the pool, it burned on.

In the afternoon she left Hannah and Saul in Barbara's care and took the car. She was going shopping, deliberately going down the coast to avoid all chance of meeting Richard. Her route took her along the main road, although she had avoided it ever since they came. Now she felt she hardly cared if she ended up mangled in some crash, it would at least stop her thinking.

The reality of wild driving, lorries belching smoke and stray dogs lying dead at the roadside, was more than she expected. After five miles she took the first exit, scuttling off down a side road in terror. A lorry had pulled in on her and shaved her bumper, sending her vehicle into a brief skid on the greasy road. The car was hot but she was cold with sweat. She took her hands off the wheel one at a time and tried to relax them. The road was narrow and dusty, a lane leading away into the hills. Clearly it did not lead to any shopping centre, but anything was preferable to the maelstrom she had left.

After half an hour Rowan found herself driving through a small, white village. A tall woman in black was driving four or five goats down the road towards her, urging them on with a long thin stick. The goats were tall and their floppy ears gave them a cute expression that Rowan found endearing. She stopped the car to let them go past. She could hear her heart beating rhythmically. Outside the open window the goats bleated and a gentle Spanish dust settled on her hair. The place smelled of heat and garlic and dung. The woman with the goats was beautiful, thought Rowan; she was like a figure from another age, a grand lady fallen on hard times.

She became aware that she was thirsty. She got out of the

car and wandered down the street, looking in at the dark houses, shuttered against the sun. There was a shop of sorts, although when she first looked into the cavernous interior after the white glare of the sun she could see little. The cool inside struck at her and made her shiver. Sacks of dates and olives stood on the floor, there were tins on the shelf and hessian-wrapped cheeses on the counter. One whole wall was taken up by giant wine barrels.

The shopkeeper, a woman, came in and murmured to her. Rowan pointed to some cheese and the woman cut some, offering also some tough-looking bread. Rowan added dates, some olives, and a tin of something like spam. The woman was gaining an idea of what this meal was to be, and she brought out tomatoes and some apricots, and finally went to the barrels. She drew off some red wine into a small glass and gave it to Rowan to taste. Rowan took it cautiously, because she had already bought some lemon pop. Besides, she had never much liked booze and nowadays she saw it as intrinsically wicked. It was a trap, well baited but lethal.

The wine was rough and sour. There was nothing in it to commend, but somehow it held all that was real about this place, about this day. To eat this food, to drink this wine, was to share the life of the countryside. The woman filled an old green bottle and stoppered it, then used a blunt pencil to do her sums on a pad.

Out in the street once again, Rowan looked for the goats but they had gone. It was so hot, the light seemed to bleach the colour from the earth, from the houses. But the sky was gentian, the shadows beneath the trees more purple than any dye. In a field of olive trees, wild poppies stained the dusty grass like blood. She went back to her car and sat in it with her eyes closed, watching the sun against her eyelids. At last she started the engine and drove slowly on, with no idea of where she headed.

Chapter Thirty-Seven

It was after seven when at last she found her way back. She was very tired and had begun to despair of ever making sense of hazy directions she received from people she passed. Somehow when she drove to the villa and saw another hire car there she was surprised by the intensity of her anger. Richard, incredibly, had dared to come here.

He was sitting by the pool, under the drifts of flowering creeper, talking to Barbara. 'Where's Saul?' asked Rowan crisply, depositing her packages amidst their cosy glasses.

Barbara raised her eyebrows expressively. 'Oh,' said Rowan. 'Much?'

'Enough.'

She went through to look, but he was asleep, sprawled on the bed, snoring. Prudently she removed all bottles, instead bringing a water jug from the kitchen. If he woke in the night and drank water, he would be so much better in the morning.

When she came back, Barbara had taken the food into the kitchen and was preparing it. The bottle of wine stood alone on the table. 'I was worried about you,' said Richard.

'Don't lie.'

He got up and went to the cabinet to find glasses. Uninvited he took the cork from the wine and poured some for both of them, and after a moment Rowan took the proffered glass. She sipped, tasting again the special flavour of the afternoon, absorbing the essence of that Spanish village. When Richard drank too, she felt as if he was sharing her thoughts, invading her privacy. For a moment she felt as if her soul was laid out for him to see.

Richard said, 'I'm sorry. That's what I came to say.'

'What exactly are you sorry for?'

He shrugged. 'You, mostly. Oh God, don't start getting furious! I mean that and I don't. We were all drunk last night, things got out of hand. Some of it was even your fault, for wearing that dress, doing what you did.'

She finished her wine and then poured herself some more. 'You got in the way between me and Saul,' she said distantly. 'We had our own situation, it didn't need you.'

All of a sudden Richard was fierce. 'What you don't realise is that there isn't a situation with him! Do you know, I've never seen him when he hasn't been drinking? It's been a steady progression, every year a little more, and now he's out of control. He isn't going to get better, Rowan. He's a bum. If you stick with him you're on the road to one hell of a lot of misery.'

She put down her glass and went over to the mirror, one of those ornate Spanish affairs hung surprisingly low on the wall. It reflected her dirty bare feet, her sandals kicked off at the door and the marks of the straps showing white in the muck. Long legs in a sweat-dampened cotton skirt, a sleeveless top sodden between her breasts. Even her hair was stuck to her head, but the dust had changed its colour to dull grey.

'Why do you want to spoil my life?' she asked wearily. 'All you want to do is sleep with me for a bit. I haven't got much now. If I did that I'd have even less.'

'You don't know what you might have,' said Richard desperately. He came and stood behind her, knowing that if he touched her, as he longed to do, she would hit him. 'He doesn't even have to know,' he said softly.

Rowan shot him a look of such contempt that he was scorched by it. 'I think you'd better go,' she said clearly, and at that moment Barbara came in with three plates on a tray. 'But I made him some food,' she said.

'He's not staying for it,' retorted Rowan. She went to the

door and held it open but Richard hesitated, knowing what he wanted to say and unable to say it in front of Barbara. Eventually he walked towards the door.

'You're being too hard on yourself,' he said to Rowan. 'There's no need for it, you must see that.'

'If you're staying in Spain, we shall go home.' She was implacable, her eyes like green glass. And yet, and yet – her legs were trembling. When they stood as close as this, the ridiculous happenings of last night were entirely explicable.

'I'll go,' he said suddenly. 'I'll meet my friend in Paris. But – I want you to know how much I admire you, how much I understand.'

She looked away from him, down at her long, bare, dirty feet. 'You don't understand the first thing about me or any woman. Go away.'

When he'd gone, Barbara tentatively offered her a plate of food. Rowan picked at it, dismally. Barbara said, 'He likes you an awful lot.'

'I imagine that's his stock in trade,' replied Rowan. She felt weary to the bone, and the expected relief at getting rid of him was slow in coming. Dismally she thought of the weeks ahead before they could go home. 'We'll have to try and stop him drinking,' she said, voicing her thoughts.

Barbara's soft mouth twisted. 'We can try. I don't suppose – I mean, there are places that do treatment.'

'Is it that bad, do you think? It isn't very often that he's as bad as this, after all.' Yet in the past months it was more and more often. She was deluding herself in thinking that the times in between were coming to be anything more than hungover interludes.

The baby started to cry and Rowan went to her. As she cuddled and soothed, she wondered was it Hannah, or her, or the mill or what? There was no point in sending him for treatment if the problem remained, if the fault was not in him but in the life she had brought him. Every time he got wildly drunk she felt angry, yes, but guilty too because if she had been different, so would he. A happy man has no need to blot out the world, she told herself, and she had brought him trouble, unhappiness – and Hannah.

That night she lay in the hot bed and listened to Saul's snoring. When at last she fell asleep in the cool of the coming dawn, it was to be wakened minutes later. Saul was climbing on top of her, silently pushing her legs apart. Still half-asleep she felt him nudging into her and there was no pain, nothing. Even pleasure had deserted her. She lay beneath him in the bed and felt unloved and unloving, used by a man who wanted to prove himself to himself. Her mind conjured up a picture of Richard. She hated him, she told herself, he would use her just as much, she was deceiving herself to think otherwise. Yet, as her husband subsided on to her, groaning with pleasure, it was the thought of Richard that gave her comfort.

For the rest of the holiday there was a distance between her and Saul, although they made love several times. Once when Saul was starting drinking before ten in the morning, Rowan asked him if he thought he needed to see a doctor. He said sarcastically, 'Darling, it isn't me that's got a problem, it's you. There's something very puritanical about your attitude to life. There isn't anything I enjoy that you don't think should be rationed.'

There seemed to be quite a bit of truth in that. She sat by the pool or at the window, gazing out over the hot landscape, trying to capture the colours in blocks of felt tip on paper. Designs for cloth seemed to multiply in her head, and she worked on them endlessly, defeating her unhappiness. On the edges of her vision Saul played with Hannah, with total patience, total commitment, drinking all day until he fell into bed unconscious at some time in the evening. Locked into a cell of loneliness, Rowan found herself thinking again and again, 'How did we come to this? Where did we go wrong?'

Chapter Thirty-Eight

Mohammed Shafir disliked his work. His metabolism rebelled against activity at night-time; he would often find himself fighting sleep when to lose concentration for even a minute might be to lose a finger or a hand. His was a mill almost entirely staffed by Asians, an apartheid that had developed almost unnoticed by the outside world. Asians mixed hardly at all with the indigenous population. They lived in their own areas, shopped at their own shops, and worked in cliques or whole factories where English was almost never heard. That, too, Mohammed disliked. He was a man of natural intelligence who could see the futility of walling himself into a ghetto. It rendered a situation tolerable, but did nothing to change it into something better.

Nonetheless, acceptance was written into the very fabric of his life. All Moslems learned it, as they learned the Koran, sitting in the mosque for hours after school, chanting screeds of Arabic. Allah must be obeyed, your father must be obeyed, wives must obey husbands, children obeyed everybody. There was a stability about such a life that was lacking in the English. It was as if lack of discipline set you free to crash into the gutter as well as soar to the stars.

But life was about change. The prophet himself had looked at the world and felt moved to transform it. Mohammed felt, in his heart, that this might be his portion also, in however humble a form. After all, he was uniquely placed to take from each system that which was of worth and put it to good use in a new and different lifestyle. Moslem values, British imagination, Moslem discipline and British freedom of thought.

His parents rejected such ideas utterly, of course. They felt that any small movement towards the people they lived beside but not amongst, meant a breach in the walls that protected them. Like the dams in Holland, the first leak would be followed by others until in the end they would all be swallowed up in a deluge of misery and godlessness. It was only through Mohammed's insistence and Fadeema's tact that his sister had been allowed to go to university. He, too, had wanted to go, but there had been no one to sponsor him, no one to stand at his side when he argued unforgivably with his father. So here he was, weaving in a mill, swaying with weariness, dreaming of Sally.

Sally. His sweet, pretty, dear, needy girl. Other men, other less educated men, would not understand her, would think she was tainted. He alone knew how much she needed him, and besides, he was realistic. A girl like Sally would not come to such as him quite unsoiled by the world. He had no illusions about his position on the ladder, the distance that separated him from a girl like Sally. But she had been sent to him, and he to her. It was up to him to rescue her from the chaos of her life, and for her to free him from his chains. In marrying Sally he would be climbing away up the ladder, taking with him the harness of his religion. They would stand together, two people that society preferred apart. Together they would reach heights that alone neither could scale.

The next morning, bone weary but past sleep, he waited for Sally outside the hostel as she left for college. She didn't at once see him and he was at liberty to admire her, small, blonde, her hair piled up on her head in an inexact knot from which tendrils fell charmingly. She wore a neat blue dress and, as always, high heels, because she always wanted to be taller. For himself he loved all that was miniature about her, from her little hands to her short round neck. In comparison he felt that Rowan was far too tall, that her height reflected the sort of woman she was. Sally was no tycoon, she would be his wife and the mother of his children.

'You look so pretty today.'

She saw him and turned, smiling. They held hands. He wouldn't kiss her in the street. He noticed her eyes were red beneath heavy make up. 'You've been crying.'

'Not really, no. Just a bit, perhaps.'

'I must take you away from that woman in there! I shall speak to her, she must not upset you like this.'

'It isn't her.' Sally spoke with deadly weariness. They walked on to the end of the street, and Mohammed remained silent, knowing she would tell him. The doss house was turning out the drunks and the headcases, the men released from mental hospitals and drifting down to the bottom of the pit. Sally sometimes gave them money, the sad, bewildered ones, but today she had no energy for others. At the end of the street, she said, 'I think I'm pregnant.'

'Oh!' He beamed with joy. At last, at last the door was opening. They could get married, no one would stop them now. 'We will go and see my father tonight,' he said enthusiastically. 'I will insist now. Then of course we shall see your sister – and your mother.' He hesitated over Diana. He disliked the woman, he thought her the cause of all Sally's troubles.

'I don't want to live with your mother,' said Sally. 'I've money, we can buy a house.'

He nodded. 'For the moment I should prefer you to stay with my mother. You can help her, she will learn to love you. It is important that you should know each other, respect each other.'

'But I should much rather we lived by ourselves,' said Sally urgently. 'We're not going to live like your parents, you said so yourself. We're going to do things differently.'

'But first they must see that we can live the old life,' advised Mohammed. 'You are tired, you must not go to work today. Come and have ice cream.'

Sick and anxious, Sally made no objection. The thought

of telling everyone weighed on her, she could imagine only too well what they would say. If only, if only she could see their way clear to a life of their own, a house of their own. It was what she wanted more than anything in the world, a great deal more than this baby. She couldn't imagine the baby, almost didn't believe in it. Yet it was there, growing inside her.

In the evening Mohammed took her again to his parents' house. He had snatched a few hours' sleep in Sally's room at the hostel, but it wasn't enough. As he led Sally through the front door, he felt weary and on edge, unfitted for the announcement he was to make. But he undertook much of his life when he was not at his best. He hardly knew what it was to be relaxed, well-fed and well-rested.

His father was watching an Asian video. It was a highly coloured romance, a tale of love and sin, about as far from anything his father had ever experienced as the moon from the sun. Mr. Shafir was a tall grizzled man with a beard and long, stained teeth. He worked in a combing plant, sweeping up because the overlooker thought him incapable of more, and he resented it.

Mohammed's uncle and his young brother were in the room too, all wearing the tunics and trousers that determinedly proclaimed them foreigners in an alien land. Sally took an unhappy, gasping breath.

'Father,' said Mohammed clearly. His father pretended not to hear. His uncle and brother looked uncomfortable. Mohammed went across to the television and turned it off. 'Forgive me, Father,' said Mohammed. 'I have brought Sally to see you. We are to marry.'

His father ignored him and told his brother in Gujerati to turn the television back on. Mohammed stopped him on the way. 'Father, Sally is to have my child,' he said.

The old man seemed to shudder slightly. He turned his head and stared at Sally. She found herself looking into eyes misted with cataracts. Then he erupted into furious Gujerati, railing at his son, getting up to hit at him with big, gnarled hands.

Sally backed out into the hall. Everyone had heard; Fadeema was there, and from the kitchen Sally could hear Mohammed's mother, weeping and wailing. In the front room Mohammed and his father shouted violently at each other, from the kitchen came the sound of smashing crockery. Fadeema said, 'Come upstairs, Sally. It wasn't fair of Mohammed to bring you to this.'

In the cramped little room upstairs that Fadeema shared with her sister, Sally said, 'He wants us to live here. I don't want to.'

Fadeema considered. 'It would be best if you could try, Sally. My mother will accept you if you are here, and help her. You see, she thinks you will steal him away and she will lose her son. And she knows Mohammed will do as he wants. They have found three girls before for him to marry and he wouldn't look at them. You see, your – condition – does make a difference.'

It was hard to believe, when downstairs the arguments raged and the crockery smashed.

Eventually an uneasy peace fell. Fadeema led Sally back downstairs to where Mohammed was confronting his parents in the front room. They stood side by side, rigid with disapproval. Mohammed's mother took one look at Sally and began to cry.

'It is agreed,' said Mohammed stiffly. 'My mother will make you welcome, Sally, when we are married. Otherwise we shall set up home elsewhere.'

Silently, Sally nodded. She was on the verge of tears.

Valley House. A gentle name for a beautiful home. When Saul and Rowan returned from holiday they weren't prepared for the progress that had been made. In place of grey plaster and bare floors there was white paint and acres of pale-green carpet. The doors and skirtings were of light wood, like a house in Scandinavia, light and clean and new. Through the huge double-glazed windows they could see nothing as yet but rubble and heaps of earth, but it was possible to imagine the elegant gardens the architect described, complete with cherry trees and lawns. Harder to visualise was that anyone would ever want to swim in the dirty, half-tiled hole that was to be the pool, but for now Rowan was too pleased with what she had to worry about what she had not.

They had no suitable furniture. The mishmash of pieces they had collected since they married would be a disaster in the clean elegance of Valley House, thought Rowan. There was a need for good wood, leather and glass, and lovely fabrics in striking patterns. Her stomach dropped at the added expense; she would never be able to spend money with the open-handedness of Saul. And she didn't like to think of Saul just at the moment.

She never seemed to act rationally where he was concerned. If she wanted to say something to anyone else, she would pick a time and phrase it as carefully as she could. But on their first evening back, camping in the house on air beds and tables out of the offices, she had said bluntly, 'I think you should see a doctor about your drinking. And Barbara agrees.'

The crime was multiplied because he was not at that moment sober. He swung round on her. He seemed very big and brown, almost leonine. Such dark brown eyes he had, so dark sometimes the pupils were invisible, and when he was drunk he could stare indefinitely without blinking. 'Brown is a frightening colour,' thought Rowan.

'Who the hell are you to discuss my habits with the hired help?'

Barbara shot a scared glance at Rowan, picked up Hannah and got out of the room. Rowan said, 'We didn't discuss you. We sort of agreed it. After all, she's the one that helps me put you to bed.'

'Don't exaggerate.' He always lived with the illusion that it was never as bad as she knew it to be. He always missed the worst bits. Even if he was conscious, he never remembered them.

'It isn't fair on me, or Hannah, or anyone,' Rowan struggled on, though she would have retreated if she could. He was pacing the vast empty room, and she crouched on an office chair, wondering if he was going to hit her. It seemed ridiculous. The Saul she knew once, the Saul she had married, couldn't even squash a fly.

He stopped and stared at her. 'You want me out, don't you? You want to pretend I'm an alcoholic so you can have your precious firm all to yourself and shack up with sodding Richard Barton.'

Her head came up. 'It was you that thought Richard Barton should join in!' she flared. 'I was the one who stopped it, but you won't remember, you were too pissed!'

'I get a bit sloshed once in a while and suddenly I'm an alcoholic.' He stopped in front of her chair, put his hands on either side of her face and pressed. 'I'm warning you, Rowan, I don't like being pushed around. I always knew you were a bossy woman. What you need is a firm hand.'

She remained quite still, feeling him pressing on the sides of her skull. At the moment it seemed as if he could crush her head with just the pressure of his big hands. She reached up, touched his wrists and he let her go. 'Won't you stop for Hannah?' she asked, finding her breath dragging through shrivelled lungs.

'Hannah wants for nothing that I can give her.' He left her suddenly, crossed the floor and wrenched open a holdall. It contained the duty-free allowance. Rowan opened her mouth to protest, then closed it again. As always when she challenged him, she succeeded only in making things worse.

For once she couldn't escape her anxieties, either in the mill or with the stockbrokers who were within days of launching the company on the stock exchange. Before they left, she was entranced by all the manipulating, but now her mind wandered in meetings and she had to be reminded of what they had agreed. To escape it all she and Barbara went furniture shopping and Rowan bought this and that, some of which she liked, and some of which would just about do.

'You'll be sorry you rushed it in the end,' said Barbara sagely, sipping coffee while she rested her substantial ankles on the crossbar of Hannah's pushchair. Barbara was getting extremely fat, she had even put on weight in Spain when to Rowan's mind it was often too hot to eat.

'I don't know what I'd do without you,' said Rowan suddenly. Barbara's sensible, kindly support was always there. She didn't gossip about Saul or Hannah, she didn't comment on the rows. 'If you left, I'd just crumble,' she added.

'Well, I'm not going to leave,' declared Barbara, with solid loyalty. 'You and Hannah need me, and he's not a bad old thing when he's sober.'

'He used to be lovely,' Rowan heard herself say. And in saying that, admitted that he wasn't any more.

Sally and Mohammed called when Rowan and Barbara were trying to arrange some of the lumpish furniture they had bought. There was a wall cabinet for the sitting-room which the man in the shop had declared was ideal for all those little knick-knacks. Rowan had no knick-knacks but thought she perhaps should acquire some, and the cabinet had concealed lighting and mirrored shelves and several other features that, now she thought about it, she intensely disliked.

'I'm going to send it back,' she said wearily to Sally. 'Barbara said I shouldn't have bought it in the first place.'

'Then why did you?' asked Sally. She had never known Rowan impulse buy in all her life.

'I suppose I was thinking about other things.'

Remembering her manners, Rowan sat them down on the

new leather Chesterfield and perched herself on one of the office chairs. 'Would you like a drink?' she asked Mohammed. 'Oh no, you don't, do you? Tea then.' She got up and went through to the kitchen, a beautiful room cleverly designed to exclude Hannah from the cooking area by means of a raised step and gate. Rowan blundered about looking for cups and milk and sugar.

'Is something the matter?' asked Sally. Not even her own preoccupation could entirely blot out her sister's air of anxious distraction.

'What? Oh, it's just the house. The firm's taking off, the house needs attention, everything. Everything.'

Mohammed said, 'We've chosen a poor time. Come, Sally, let's go.'

'Oh, please, no! I'd much rather have someone to talk to.' She tried to smile and seem less pathetic, adding, 'Saul's out, you see. Business.'

They took the tray of tea into the sitting-room and sat down again. The curtainless windows gave the feeling of sitting in a shop window, and one in the process of change at that. 'How's the course?' asked Rowan brightly.

'I'm not finishing it.' Sally took a deep breath, lifting her heavy breasts under her navy jumper. 'I'm pregnant.'

Rowan said nothing. Mohammed said urgently, 'Without this my parents would not agree to the marriage. It was necessary.'

Rowan linked her fingers together. 'I see. Well, then. Congratulations. When's the wedding?'

'It's going to be a Registry Office,' said Sally, looking anything but glad. Rowan felt a pang. She would have loved to see Sally in a puffball dress of white satin, however inappropriate. She would look enchanting, almost a child bride.

'We haven't arranged anything,' said Mohammed. 'We must speak to Sally's mother.'

'Yes.' Rowan hesitated and then said bluntly, 'Come into the kitchen, Sally, I want to talk to you alone.'

In the kitchen, Rowan hissed: 'What's the matter? Don't you want to marry him? Before, it was all you wanted.'

'Yes, of course I do,' moaned Sally, twisting her hands. 'It's just – Rowan, his parents hate me, and he wants us to live with them! With his mother.'

'But you've told him you could have a house, haven't you? We should make a lot of money this year, you'll have a lot of money. He could start a business, anything.'

'He thinks I ought to learn to get along with his mother.'

They went back into the sitting-room. Rowan said, 'She can't live with your mother, Mohammed, it wouldn't be fair.'

Rigidly polite he cast Sally a telling look and said, 'It is for me to decide for my own family, Rowan.'

'Sally is my family at the moment. If you want our blessing you'll do as Sally wishes and get a house of your own; my mother will insist on it.'

'We haven't told her yet,' said Sally dismally.

'Then I suggest we do,' said Rowan. 'Tonight.' She glared at Mohammed. How dare he exploit her sister, how dare he push her around?

'I have no respect for Sally's mother,' said Mohammed grimly.

'And I have no respect for yours,' retorted Rowan.

They marched out to the car. Both Rowan and Mohammed were buoyed up for battle, and between them Sally was crushed.

'I shall be late for work,' said Mohammed distantly. 'My pay will suffer.'

'Allow me to reimburse you,' snapped Rowan.

'I do not need charity!'

Rowan stepped on the accelerator and sent her little car rattling down the road. They could see the lights of the Manor from some distance away, she wondered briefly if they were having a party. But there was only one visiting car. A Maserati.

'Oh,' said Rowan, suddenly discomfited. 'Richard's here.'

'I don't mind,' said Sally. 'Let's get it over with, I can't bear all the hanging around.'

'This is a private matter, Sally,' said Mohammed. 'It is not for strangers to discuss it.'

Rowan rounded on him. 'How dare you tell her what she should and shouldn't do? You're the one who got her into this mess. You're after her money, you're just using Sally to get what you want!'

'It isn't like that,' said Sally miserably.

Rowan got out of the car and went to the front door. The others followed. She knocked on the door and after a while it was opened. By Richard.

He was surprised, Rowan was not. She pushed past him into the house, saying nothing. Chamber music was coming from the sitting-room and when she went in she saw James standing by the stereo. Diana was sitting on the sofa and Andy stood by the fire.

Rowan said, 'What on earth are you doing here, Andy? I thought you were in London.'

He looked embarrassed and Rowan had a cold moment of fear. They hadn't wanted her here tonight. What were they discussing?

James said, 'I see we are to be honoured by one of Sally's friends. Does he speak English, Sally?'

'Thank you, I can also read,' said Mohammed, and extended his hand. James took it, grinning. He had no racial prejudice, but he liked baiting Sally.

Diana, on the other hand, had stiffened visibly. 'What is all this about, Rowan?' she demanded, as if it were all Rowan's fault.

Sally coughed unhappily. 'We just thought – I thought – Mohammed and I are getting married. I'm pregnant.'

'Good God!'

Diana got up, marched to Mohammed, drew back her

arm and slapped him hard across the face. He stood quite still, doing nothing, saying nothing. Diana drew back her hand to strike again and Rowan said, 'Don't, Mother. There's nothing to be done but get on with it. He's a nice man, really.'

'And you are such a wonderful judge!' Diana turned on Sally, standing with her head bowed. 'How could you? I just don't know how you could!'

Mohammed spoke and his quiet voice cut across Diana's screeches. 'I shall look after Sally as well as I am able. She will live at my home and be cared for.'

'White slavery, and Sally's paying for it,' retorted Diana.

Rowan went and sat on the sofa and Andy came and sat next to her. 'Have you encouraged this?' he asked softly. 'It's insane, Rowan, you know it is.'

'It has nothing to do with me! But she's pregnant, we can't do anything.'

'She could get rid of it!'

Rowan caught his arm. 'Don't suggest it, please. Not for Sally. It wouldn't be good for her.'

James, who had been watching the action with interest, declared suddenly, 'Let's all have a drink! We can toast the happy couple and their progeny – probably come out in black and white stripes. Let's have champagne.' He went in search of bottles and glasses, Rowan thought she had never felt less like celebrating anything. She could feel Richard watching her.

James brought three bottles and uncorked them expertly. He poured for them all, refusing to take no for an answer, even from Mohammed. The man's dark skin flushed after just half a glass and Rowan knew she must stop this. She should never have brought them, it wasn't doing any good. 'Borrow my car, Andy,' she said urgently. 'Take them back. He's got to go to work, he's on the night-shift at Lester's.'

'Oh, Christ,' said Andy. 'I thought at least he'd be an accountant or something.'

Rowan grimaced and gave him her car keys. They watched Sally diffidently take Mohammed's arm as they left and the cold air met them at the door. Richard said, 'What a pretty girl she is. A doll almost.'

'She was beautiful as a child,' said Diana tightly. 'I don't think I paid her enough attention. You don't, with the third somehow. Why are you still here, Rowan? *You* could have taken them.'

She cleared her throat. 'I thought I'd better find out what you're planning to do with my firm. With Judge's.'

'I don't know why you think we should be doing anything,' said Diana rapidly. 'Besides, it's Andy firm, he is the major shareholder.'

Rowan turned on James. 'Are you trying to buy him out?'

He put up his hands. She thought how old he looked suddenly, how blotched and worn. 'It wasn't my idea.'

'Then whose?'

She turned on Richard and blazed at him. He watched her, his face closed and thoughful. She suddenly remembered how he had looked in the lift, touching her. 'You bastard!' she said softly. 'You're getting your own back. You're going to make me do what you want.'

He shrugged. 'I think you can relax. Andy won't bite. Seems to think you offer the better hope for the future. He seems to think he owes you something.'

'Well, you lot at Bardsey's wouldn't know about that sort of thing,' declared Rowan. 'Thank God Andy's got the sense to avoid you. Just thank God!'

'I would rather thank his television success,' said Diana grimly. 'He can afford to see how you do. But you're overreaching yourself, Rowan, mark my words, you'll come a cropper one of these days. That man of Sally's will have her share up for sale in no time, and then you might as well resign yourself. Andy will have absolute control.'

'Which is what you've always wanted,' said Rowan.

Diana let out her breath. 'Is it? I don't know any more.

I'm going to bed. Are you coming?' She directed her question to James, but when he shook his head she didn't seem surprised.

After she'd gone he drank another half glass of champagne. 'I'm going out,' he said suddenly. 'I'll take you home, Rowan.'

'I'll take her,' said Richard quickly, and Rowan thought, she didn't want to travel with either. But James's harsh bitterness would be harder to take. She nodded.

When they were alone, Richard made no move to go. 'You won't get my firm,' said Rowan softly.

'I agree, this time I won't. Soon, though.'

She knew she ought to insist they went but suddenly she was tired. The days were so awful now, and when she got home Saul might be there, sprawled on the bed or on the floor. Tonight she hadn't the strength to face it. She sat on the sofa and put her head back, closing her eyes.

Richard said, 'You have the most erotic neck of anyone I have ever seen. It's beautiful.'

'My mother and Sally are far more beautiful than I shall ever be,' said Rowan distantly.

'Not to me.'

She felt the sofa sink as he sat next to her. A finger traced her ear, moving the fine strands of hair out of the way. His mouth was on her neck, hot and lazily wet.

'Stop it,' she murmured. 'You know I won't put up with it.' She felt safe, unthreatened. He couldn't do anything in her mother's house, with her mother upstairs and Andy due back in forty minutes or so. But he didn't stop. His mouth slid to the hollow at the base of her throat, his fingers flicked open a button of her blouse.

'No,' she said more forcefully, pushing at him. It was hard to resist, like fighting through warm treacle. She wasn't aroused, this man hadn't the power to do it, but her limbs felt as if they were in chains. His hand reached into her blouse and took hold of her breast. He rolled her nipple between finger and thumb. She was stabbed with feeling, galvanized by it. She kicked out at him, straight at his groin.

The side of her shoe caught one of his testicles. He let out a strangled moan and fell sideways away from her. She wriggled free and stood up, her flesh burning where he had touched it. She was wearing tight trousers, her groin felt wet with urgent desire. He had nearly seduced her, a minute more and she'd have been incapable of stopping him. She couldn't have borne to stop him.

After a minute, he said thickly, 'I wish you'd get it out of your head that this is all I want from you.'

'I know it isn't,' said Rowan crisply. 'You want Judge's, but you don't mind screwing me on the side.'

'Better me than that drunken prat you married! It makes me sick to think of him on top of you, slobbering over you. Rowan, don't you understand?'

She didn't know what he meant and she didn't care. 'Will you drive me home or shall I ring for a taxi?' she demanded, and he got stiffly to his feet.

They went out to the car together. Richard held on to the bonnet, swaying, and Rowan said, 'I'd better drive.' He handed her the keys and she slid behind the wheel of the Maserati. The engine gave a throaty roar, she couldn't believe the power. Slowly down the drive at first, then up the gears. The night was brilliant with stars. Relaxing a little she let her foot weigh on the throttle and the car leaped forward, punching her in the back and devouring the road. She stamped on the brake and they spun.

Her hands froze on the wheel, the night whirled past her eyes in a rush of trees and confused space. 'Oh my God! Oh my God!' They stopped, still on the road, facing back the way they had come.

'Christ' said Richard. 'Here, let me drive.'

'No. I'll be careful this time.' She waited till her heart ceased its pounding then pulled gently away. The trick was all in gentleness, if she upset this proud beast it would savage her. A grin spread across her face. She was enjoying herself more than for weeks, years, perhaps ever.

'Will you at least slow down?' demanded Richard, almost through clenched teeth. 'We're doing ninety in a thirty mile limit.'

'Oh. I didn't realise. We got back so fast.' She slowed down carefully and began the twisting trail of roads to Judge's.

'Why do you want my mill?' she asked. 'You've got one of your own now.'

Richard laughed. 'Between you and me, it could do with some good red meat in it. Fat and flabby, that's Bardsey's. And this rights issue will bring in such a lot of lovely money. You should have thought of it.'

'I didn't think I'd have to watch Andy. And I was right.'

'So you were.'

She drew up at the mill. Buoyed up with relief at the safety of his car, Richard said, 'Let me kiss you. It doesn't have to mean anything.'

'Kisses don't mean anything, especially to men.' She leaned over to peck his cheek but he caught her shoulders and drew her to him. She had known he would. His lips were warm and slightly moist, where Saul's were always wet and whisky-tasting. The tongue that slid into her mouth now was no intruder, but a soft, gentle, intimate friend that took only what she offered, gave all that she desired. She had forgotten such kisses existed.

'Let's be friends,' whispered Richard.

'We shan't ever be lovers,' said Rowan. 'Good night, Richard.' She slipped out of the car and ran to the house, her long legs teetering a little in her heels. Richard got out and walked round to the driver's side. That girl, that maddening girl! Whenever he saw her she did this to him, upset him. She stole his calm, made him do things he didn't intend, feel what he thought he had outgrown. Feelings. He had had them once, and he had tamed them, locked them away.

Now, that bloody girl aroused desire and frustration and anger.

On the drive back to his flat, his mind strayed to Lin Yu. She had taught him a great deal about loving women; she had taken his youthful bull-at-a-gate enthusiasm and added subtlety and a precise touch. Sometimes when he found himself employing those techniques, as he had tonight, he despised his own calculation. He wanted to love, truly love, to immerse himself in a woman, lose himself and his mind and his bloody, bloody technique. He wanted to unleash his emotions for once instead of keeping them locked up in the box into which he had forced them.

But, he didn't want them out forever. They needed exercise, that was clear, but never again would he be ruled by them. Sometimes, after his father left, he had gone and hidden in the undergrowth behind the football pitch, and howled himself stupid. One afternoon someone heard him, they came looking to see who was making that terrible noise. Cold terror could still engulf him. If he had been found, there would have been no point in living, they would have crucified him.

It occurred to him for the first time that they might not. It had been Reynolds after all, a good sort of chap, he'd been a friend until Richard gave up friends and turned in on himself. If old Reynolds had given him a hand then, listened, he might never have shut himself away like this. A new and sobering thought.

Chapter Thirty-Nine

That night James's thoughts also turned to Lin Yu. He took the Rolls and drove quickly towards town, seeing again pretty little Sally and her out-of-place lover. Whose world did they think they would live in? If they were to have any chance of happiness they would have to lead a halfway-house sort of existence, a painful foot in either camp. He didn't know if either of them realised that.

Lin Yu would be alone when he visited, the boyfriend had despaired and left her. Sometimes he thought that they both focused on these times together; that despite all the odds they each provided more of what the other needed than any other facet of their lives. The relationship was clear and simple and unloving, he would have liked every one of his relationships to be like that. He couldn't bear Diana's red eyes a day longer. He hated her grief, hated, hated her! For she had hurt him so.

The familiar lump formed in his throat and he swallowed it down as he parked. Lin Yu would soothe him. She opened the door wearing a black robe embroidered with dragons and her hair was loose. James said, 'I had to come to you. I need something, I don't know what.'

She led him into the bedroom and took his clothes as he threw them down. When he was naked, he lay on the bed. She knelt and cradled him, stroking his thinning red hair. 'What is it, James? You're very upset.'

'I'm always upset. I can't get rid of it, you see, I can't stop thinking about it!'

'About your little boy? About Nicholas?'

'Yes. Yes.' He sat up and faced her, an ageing, distraught man. She didn't care for him, but he needed her cool thoughts. 'The doctor – he said I wasn't the boy's father. That I couldn't be, the blood group wasn't right. Richard said I'd misunderstood but I didn't, you know. A rhesus negative. The only bloke I know with that group is Saul, and Diana doesn't even like him!'

Lin Yu said, 'Have you spoken to her about this?'

He shook his head. 'I can't trust myself. I think I'd kill her. I wake in the night and look at her, it's almost all I can do not to strangle her there and then! Oh God, what am I going to do? I loved that boy so much, I can't bear to think it was all nothing. That he wasn't mine.'

'Poor James.'

She got off the bed and went to her little herbal cabinet, an antique bought with James's money. She made up a drink of something and gave it to him. He guzzled it desperately, longing to still the madness in his brain. 'Could it be him?' he asked the girl.

She lifted her shoulders delicately. 'Perhaps that's why she doesn't like him. She suspects. Perhaps even she does not know.'

He closed his eyes on tears. 'How could she do that to me? How could he? It all fits, you see; she wanted to get rid of it at first, she wouldn't tell me. She knew it wasn't mine. But him, him! I knew he'd take something from me in the end, whatever I did he'd get it. I kept him out of Bardsey's and look what happened. Now my wife. Now this!'

'James, listen to me, James! Listen to my hands.' She started to massage his shoulders, easing the muscles to his neck and jaw. Gradually he began to relax and she leaned against his back, letting the heat of his body get to her through her thin robe. She took satisfaction from James as and when she could, with a grim fatalism about her life. It seemed to her that James was to be her destiny, and all her struggles against it were to no avail. They were as they were to each other, locked in need and its satisfaction. It was a marriage of sorts.

* * *

Sally and Mohammed were married in a civil ceremony, attended by none of his own family and all of hers, if you excluded Andy. Diana was wildly elegant in burgundy silk, but Rowan was simply wild. She had woven some of the designs she had drawn whilst on holiday, and was wearing a dress striped in black and olive and rich green. Mr. Suzman had insisted on a white collar. She looked like a witch masquerading as Little Miss Muffet. And Saul, of course, was drunk.

To everyone's surprise, Richard appeared. James came across to him. 'I didn't think you were even invited.'

'Was it an invitation do? I thought on these occasions it was all hands to the pumps. Poor little kid.'

Somehow the object of their sympathy was not so pitiable today. She looked delectable in cream silk, with a flirty hat perched on top of her blonde bun of hair. Next to Mohammed's severe suit she looked small and fragile. They made a striking couple.

Suddenly the door opened. It was Fadeema, wearing a bright red sari. Both Mohammed and Sally beamed, and the Registrar paused while Diana went to welcome her. The Asian girl stood between Diana and James, an exotic, composed figure.

Saul whispered, 'She's wearing a nose stud.'

'Just as long as Sally doesn't have to wear one,' muttered Rowan.

She felt more and more as if Sally was being sacrificed into some other world, away from them all. Mohammed was a charming, educated man but he was taking Sally from them. She began to cry, and so did Diana, and then, to their surprise, Fadeema joined in.

When it was over, Sally and Mohammed were bubbling with relief. 'Why are you all crying?' demanded Sally. 'He's isn't dragging me off to another country!'

'We cry because you are so pretty and so brave,' said Fadeema. Sally reached out and kissed her. She felt happy when Fadeema was there; if Fadeema could always be in the house, she wouldn't mind Mohammed's mother and her hostility.

They went to Valley House for the reception. Diana eyed the cabinet, still not returned and probably never to be so. 'You have very odd taste, Rowan,' she commented.

'Bloody awful, isn't it?' said Saul. 'I told her to get shot of it. She can't get her finger out.'

'Why don't you go and sleep it off?' said James grimly. He hated to be in the same room as Saul, it was wholly offensive.

'Get stuffed,' said Saul, lurched and fell against the cabinet. One of the shelves slipped and broke.

Rowan tried not to notice. Saul was embarrassing Sally in front of her new family and he really ought to be stopped. Suddenly he went up to Fadeema, breathed fumes on her and demanded to dance.

'Come on, sweetheart, shake a leg,' he yelled.

'How much has he had?' asked James incredulously. 'He must have started last night and kept going. It isn't lunch-time yet.'

Rowan looked for help. She tugged Richard's sleeve. 'Just get him out, will you, please? He can only get worse.'

Their eyes met briefly. He nodded and went to Saul, who was trying to catch Fadeema's hands and boogy. 'Come on, old man, into the kitchen; I'm opening a bottle.' He took less than gentle hold of Saul's arm.

'I want to dance,' said Saul. 'This beautiful lady should dance.'

'There isn't any music yet.' Richard kept it determinedly jovial, masking blatant strong-arm tactics. Saul was hustled blearily away.

'I am so sorry,' said Rowan to Fadeema.

'Sally tells me he has a problem,' commented the girl. 'He is an alcoholic.'

Rowan was taken aback. 'Well, I don't think so – ' She

began, but Sally added, 'He is, Ro. You know he is.'

'It isn't any of your business,' flared Rowan. 'He isn't always like this. And anyway, he won't have any treatment.'

'That is often the way,' said Fadeema. 'Please, when he does want treatment, let me know. I have a friend who is a specialist.'

Rowan nodded silently, praying that Saul would have passed out by now. When he reached the raucous stage it was only a matter of ten minutes or so.

They lunched on an elaborate buffet ranged on tables around two walls of the dining-room.

'This house must have cost a fortune,' said James. 'Andy ought to see what's being done with his firm.'

'It wouldn't be a firm if it wasn't for me,' said Rowan. 'Why haven't you changed your car, James? You've had that Roller for a good three years.'

'I happen to like it,' he said frostily, and she raised a quizzical eyebrow.

Speaking rather loudly, Richard said, 'We're beyond status symbols, I think, Rowan. Dad's got a good business there, I'm enjoying seeing what's what.'

James said nothing and for some reason Rowan's senses twitched. Like a TB sufferer, now cured, she could recognise the disease in others almost before they caught it. Business problems were just as deadly.

The car arrived to take Sally and Mohammed back home. They were to postpone their honeymoon until Ramadan, when the mill closed, so the first night of their marriage would be spent in his father's house, in the small back bedroom off Carlisle Road. Everyone threw confetti, and Rowan picked up Hannah to encourage her to throw, too. 'Tars,' said Hannah. 'Tars.'

'Yes. Yes, darling, stars,' said Rowan. It was a proper word at last. Her first proper word, when they had begged for 'biscuit' or 'more' or 'mum' or 'dad' or 'no'. Her first word was stars.

She turned away and went back into the house, feeling at once joyful and intolerably lonely. Only Saul knew what it meant, only he would share this moment with her, and he lay snoring and insensible on a bed. Richard had followed her. 'Why did you come in? You looked as if you were going to cry.'

'Did I? Perhaps I was. It was – it was Hannah. She said "stars". Her first word. I threw the confetti and she said "stars", just like that. I know you don't understand. I mean, I know she's more than a year behind other children, but when she was born I hadn't any hope for her at all. I couldn't see anything good in her life, anything good she would bring to us. And then her first word is "stars". I just feel so – humble.'

An odd expression passed over Richard's face. He glanced quickly at Hannah, seeing nothing to hope for, nothing. 'You must love her quite a lot,' he remarked uncomfortably.

Rowan put her cheek against Hannah's. 'That seems a little word for it. When I think they wanted to send her away!'

'You never know, this might be the start of something. One word today; next week, whole conversations!'

She beamed at him. 'Yes! Yes! Saul always thinks I'm silly to hope for too much, but nobody knows what she might do. If she can say "stars", if she knows about stars – well. She could be anything.' She cradled the baby and her impossible hopes at one and the same time.

Richard thought how lovely she looked with her face glowing and her dark lashes making crescents on her cheek. Speaking with false sincerity, he said, 'I'm sure you're right,' and was rewarded with Rowan's shyest, most trusting smile. She thought he understood.

They stood together in the quiet room, amidst the debris of the party, and outside Mohammed and Sally drove away.

* * *

Judge's got its stockmarket quotation at a time when the government was trying to prove its record in encouraging business. One day the Prime Minister got up and declared, 'We have been remarkably successful in encouraging growth in manufacturing. Take textiles, for instance, one of the disaster stories of the past; now, have a look at Isaac Judge and tell me that we can't compete, tell me the industry needs mollycoddling. A dynamic company, a company going places, a British company!'

The world and his wife beat a path to the door of Isaac Judge plc. The share price doubled within a month, aided and abetted by the general stockmarket boom, and Rowan couldn't keep up with the work, the orders, the pressure on her poor, decrepit dye house. Valley House was at one and the same time a place of refuge and confusion. She would let no one through that door in the wall; it was her home, her hiding place. No one was going to use Hannah to add human interest to the story, or find Saul drunk and finally destroy him.

Although, actually, Saul was better. After the wedding he seemed to pull himself up a little, drinking nothing at all during the day and only a few whiskies in the evening. He began involving himself again in some of his pet projects, in a rather frenzied way, inviting magazines to write feature articles on the nursery, posting feeler samples to corners of the world as yet unaware of Judge's cloth. It was all hectic and tense, some of it rather pointless, but at least he wasn't drinking. Rowan found the relief exquisite.

Trophy after trophy fell their way, until one day an American company approached them, wanting to manufacture Judge's range under licence in the States. Rowan's gut feel was to reject the idea out of hand, it stank of piracy, but Saul was thoughtful. 'Big market,' he commented. 'We're running at full blast as it is, we can't possibly produce more until we modernise the dye house. And the accounts must go on computer, I've been thinking of it for ages.'

'Bardsey's have got a design computer,' said Rowan morosely, dropping her chin into her hands. 'Apparently you just press buttons and you get a pretty picture of what the design will look like – checks, tartans, you name it.'

'We could have it if you want,' said Saul, snapping a biscuit in half and munching it tensely.

'Yes. But I want better than that. Direct linking to a pattern loom or something. Anything to be better.'

He pushed back his chair and got up. 'Don't be childish.'

She watched him doubtfully. He was itching for a drink, but so far had resisted it. She said, 'Why don't you go to the States and talk to them? At the moment everybody loves us, we ought to take advantage.'

'Yeah. I might.' He didn't seem interested.

Rowan got out the atlas and the diary and began suggesting dates and additional people he could go and see to make the trip worthwhile. 'You could go on Concorde,' she tempted. 'And you could see that designer, the one who always uses our stuff. Hasn't he moved to the States? Marcus Arnaud.'

Saul grinned. 'Oh yes. Marcus. The dear boy. That does seem a long time ago. When we were young and silly, when the world was a fun place.'

Rowan reached up and caught his hand. 'It isn't so bad now, is it?'

Making an effort that was only too apparent, he said, 'No. 'Course not. I'll send a telex and get out and see them.'

Two days before he was due to leave he lunched in town with the directors of Sylvex. Rowan was invited herself but refused; it was one of those occasions when Saul would hunt best alone. She bridled when they suggested price cuts, she lost interest when they waffled on about other firms and other people. It was Saul, the expert angler, who could let his fish run and then land it with hardly a twitch on the line. So she stayed at home and prowled around her mill, and took Hannah to the nursery to sit and watch the other children for a while. Somehow she felt anxious. She couldn't settle to anything.

At half-past four he was still not back, she watched the gate, waiting to see the Aston Martin swing its long nose round the corner. Instead she saw a much newer car, Joe Partridge in his flash Japanese sports.

'You look a bit agitated, Ro,' he commented.

She ran a quizzical eye over his stocky figure, wedged into tight trousers and a jacket in an expensive but vulgar broad stripe. Money had not gone to Joe's head but to his belly. 'You should never have given up rugby,' she remarked, and poked his flab.

'I'll get it off one of these days. Came to talk business, actually.' He looked hopefully in the direction of the house but Rowan turned towards the office. Even her oldest friends were rarely admitted into her home. It was private, so much so that even her cleaning lady was old Elsie from the mill, who could be trusted not to gossip and could be paid far more than the job was worth, for old time's sake.

Nowadays Rowan and Saul inhabited a spectacular office. One wall was glass and looked out over the roofs of Bradford, while low cabinets lined the rest of the room. Saul and Rowan had desks at either end, with 'phones banked on side tables, and above the cabinets hung classic fashion photographs and swathes of Judge's cloth. Joe picked up Rowan's paper knife. It was silver.

'Haven't you got anything better to spend it on, then?'

'That was a present from an anxious supplier. It seems that when I needed help I couldn't get it, but now I don't people are showering me with goodies and offers of co-operation.'

'Well, I'm not.'

Rowan swung round on her heels and went to sit down at her desk. 'What is it then, Joe? Spit it out.'

'Bardsey's want to use me. Exclusive. They're folding their fleet, and they'll pay a third better than you.'

She sniffed. Her chin dropped into her hands and she sniffed again. 'Bugger, bugger, bugger!' she said. 'I thought we were friends.'

'We was, once upon a time. Don't think you're friends with anybody now, though. He's had an effect on you, I knew he would.'

'Life's had an effect on me,' said Rowan shortly. 'We'll increase the rates, Joe, you know that. We've dropped behind, there's been so much to do recently. But don't go.'

'I've pretty well made up my mind.'

His chubby face assumed an aggrieved expression, and she knew he was waiting to be coaxed and cajoled. And she couldn't be bothered. 'Of course you know Bardsey's are in trouble?' she said casually. 'Richard's adopting classic fire-fighting tactics, closing down expensive units and flogging what he can. I just wish I could get my hands on his dye house.'

'They look OK to me,' said Joe. 'Looks like you're jealous, just because you can't push them off their perch. Number one, they are, and you can't stomach it.'

'I won't have to for long,' she remarked and got up. 'They're going to take a tumble all of their own accord. Look, Joe, I'm sorry to rush you but there's something on my mind.'

He got up, hitching his trousers irritably. 'You'll have something on your mind if I leave you in the lurch. You don't know which side your bread's buttered, my girl. I'll let you off this time but I'm damned if I'll have you treating me like a bloody servant.'

'I don't,' objected Rowan.

'You do. You should see yourself these days. You ain't in the human race with the rest of us, you're cold as a bloody ice cube. And it's all his doing, he's done you no good at all.'

Joe stomped out and Rowan wrapped her arms around herself. It wasn't her fault that Joe wanted to be as close to her as before. It wasn't possible, she wasn't even there. She was locked away somewhere deep inside, somewhere she couldn't be hurt. She looked down into the yard, and still the Aston wasn't back. Almost five o'clock, a very long lunch indeed.

The 'phone rang and she hesitated seconds before picking it up. A voice, a man's voice, said: 'Mrs. Barton? I'm sorry to have to tell you there's been an accident.'

It was Joe who drove her to the hospital. She ran after him and banged, screaming, on the window of his car. 'I know he's killed himself. I know he's dead,' she kept saying hysterically, as Joe fished out his bright red handkerchief and gave it to her.

'They said he wasn't dead, didn't they?'

'They'd be bound to lie. They make you come first and then tell you. What am I going to do?'

Joe swung into the hospital grounds. 'Calm down, they'll think they've got a bloody lunatic on their hands! Suppose he's just broken his ankle? You'll have him buried before the plaster's dry.'

Rowan was out of the car before it had completely stopped, running frantically into the hospital. She fell against the enquiries desk. 'My husband. Saul Barton. You told me to come.'

The receptionist leafed casually through a sheaf of papers. 'Barton . . . road accident. Down the corridor, turn left.'

Rowan ran on, aware that Joe was following sedately in her wake. The casualty desk was before her. When she reached it, she couldn't ask. It might be the last moment of ignorance, after this she would have to know.

Someone looked at her. 'Yes?'

'I'm – I'm Mrs. Barton. You called me.'

'Oh yes.' A male nurse took her into a side room, but Saul wasn't there. She sat on a hard plastic chair and waited for them to tell her the worst, wondered which of all these people would do it. A young Asian doctor came in and shut the door. He took another of the chairs and sat down.

'Your husband is unconscious,' he said.

'Oh God! Oh no!'

'I believe his car crashed. Mrs. Barton, he was unconscious before the accident, he'd passed out at the wheel.'

'Is he hurt then? How bad is he?'

'He's been very lucky, he has broken his leg.'

She let the information sink in, closing her eyes against the alien world in which she found herself. 'You seem to be making a dreadful fuss for a broken leg,' she said at last.

'Mrs. Barton, your husband was driving his car with an almost lethal amount of alcohol in his bloodstream. He very nearly killed an entire bus queue, a school bus queue. He missed them by inches. And I believe he's in the habit of such excess.'

'You can't know that,' flared Rowan. 'He doesn't drink often. He'd been out to lunch with some customers, he probably wanted to take a taxi but you never can get them when you want. Something should be done about it.'

'Mrs. Barton – ' The doctor leaned forward and fixed her with his large eyes. 'Fadeema Shafir is a young lady I know well. We have an understanding. I gather that your husband has been drinking heavily for years.'

Rowan shook her head. 'Not for long, no. Not like this. Just since – well, since the baby really.' She put her hands up to hide her face, saying, 'Sorry, sorry! I don't mean to be so foolish. Are the police going to prosecute?'

'I imagine so. And I've made arrangements for your husband to be admitted to an alcohol dependency unit. He has only a small cast on his leg, he'll be able to get about on crutches in a day or so.'

Rowan got up and went to the door, fumbling with the handle. The doctor said, 'You'll want to see your husband.'

'No.' She had seen him unconscious too often, far too often. She ran down the corridor and saw Joe sitting slumped in a chair. When she stopped, her legs shook and her voice shook; she thought she might faint. 'He's all right,' she said vaguely. 'Broken leg, that's all. Let's go.'

Out in the car, she sat shivering. 'They've sent him to be dried out,' she said.

'Take them a good ten years. He'll never give it up, you know he won't.'

'I thought he had, Joe!' She pulled out his lurid handkerchief and stuffed it in her mouth to muffle the sobs. Only real drunks went to these places, only the down and outs. She had wanted him to have treatment, but now she had no faith in it. Suddenly she thought of Saul as a wino, huddled in cardboard boxes in a shop doorway in Bradford, swigging meths round a fire down by the canal. Her sobs froze into icy despair.

Chapter Forty

Visiting hours at the dependency unit were strict, between three and four in the afternoon. It was a difficult time for Rowan, the time when textile men get back from expense account lunches and get down to telephoning. She went on the first day, wearing an expensive emerald green dress and then hiding it under a heavy coat. She felt totally furtive, petrified in case she saw anyone she knew.

The unit was in large grounds, so that the inmates had miles to walk to escape and get a drink. They took heroin addicts as well, who could be distinguished by their methadone-induced spaced out expressions, in stark contrast to the morose twitching of the alcoholics. Saul was still in bed, his leg propped up. There was bruising down one side of his face and his eyes were half closed not, Rowan knew, from any injury, simply a vicious hangover.

'Hello,' she said quietly.

He looked at her from under his lids. 'Terrible headache. Must have got concussion in the accident.'

'Poor you.'

'The brakes failed, you know. I took the corner and the brakes failed. I haven't been looking after the old machine properly.'

'I wouldn't feel too sorry for it, they've carted it off to a scrapyard.'

'Shit!'

They sat in silence. Rowan looked round at the other beds, most of them empty. An old man occupied one at the end. He was badly shaved and muttered to himself, picking invisible pieces off the bedcover. 'That's a real one,' said

Saul, following the direction of her eyes. 'Doctor's a bloody Moslem. They think anyone who has a sherry is an alkie.'

'He's a friend of Fadeema's. He seemed to think you'd had rather a lot.'

'No more than the rest. You know those lunches.' He shifted in the bed and tried to ease his leg. 'How's Hannah?'

'Fine. She's trying to walk. Barbara's wonderful, you know, she spends hours helping her. She suggested something we ought to think about. Apparently they operate on Down's Syndrome children nowadays.'

'What on earth for?'

'Well – to make them look normal. Their eyes, and making their tongues smaller. Things like that.'

She had his interest now. 'Good God. Does it improve their speech or anything?'

'I don't know. But they look better, you see –'

He heaved himself painfully up in the bed. 'I've never heard anything so horrific! You will not inflict pain on Hannah just to stop her embarrassing us, I absolutely forbid it.'

'Suppose it did improve her speech?' said Rowan miserably.

'She'll speak all right. But with a bit of luck she won't ever understand enough to know what's going on.'

'I didn't really mean to do it, it was only a thought,' said Rowan, touching his hand. More softly she added, 'You don't have to be so bitter.'

'You didn't do a bloody thing to stop me being put in here, did you?'

She shrugged. 'I didn't know I could.'

'Why don't you bugger off? You got what you wanted.'

She stood up to go, there was no point in talking to him in this mood. At the last moment, she said, 'I don't know what to do about the American trip. They made an awful fuss when I said we'd cancel at such short notice.'

He looked at her painfully. 'You'll have to cancel. I'll go out later in the year.'

'I wondered if I ought to go.'

He let a pause develop. 'I imagine you intend to go and are just letting me know. OK, go. I'm sure I'll have a fun time in here being talked at and lectured. I hope you fall flat on your face.'

She grinned. 'Pig.'

'Cow.'

Saul gave a morose grunt, she responded with a moo. Rowan quickly bent down and hugged him tight. He put his hand over his eyes. 'Get out of here before I bloody cry. Go on, get out.'

She kissed his thick fair hair and left.

Rowan drove slowly back to Valley House, stretching her neck to ease the crackling tension in her muscles. Barbara was taking Hannah for a walk so she decided to waste a little time for once, and have the house to herself. When she went through the gate she saw the landscape gardeners at work again, enhancing lawns and paths with container grown trees and bushes. An illusion of maturity was being created, somewhat thin now but in a year or two no one would ever know that a scant time before, this had been wasteland.

They were erecting an arbour, to be covered with clematis and honeysuckle. Rowan stepped round the workmen, murmuring apologetically. They eyed her curiously, because nowadays everybody had heard of Rowan Judge. Somehow they hadn't expected someone so slim, so young or so diffident.

It was very quiet in the house. Rowan loved the space and the clean, uncluttered lines. She was even coming to love the nasty cabinet, simply through association. Things didn't have to be beautiful to become familiar, she reflected. From familiarity came affection, and no one cared about flaws in their own dear friends. Saul was right to ban operations on Hannah, she had been cowardly and self-seeking even to think of it.

She made a cup of tea and curled up on the sofa to drink

it.Outside she could hear the faint chatter of the men working in the garden, from the kitchen came the distant hum of the fridge. Perhaps Saul would be cured forever, this could be the day she set out on a new and happier road.

'Rowan! Rowan, are you here?'

Startled, Rowan sat up and pushed the hair out of her eyes. She had been nodding off to sleep. 'Is that you, Sally?' she called.

The girl burst into the room. She was wearing a pink short-sleeved top and a cream sari, swathed across the bulge of her pregnancy. Her hair was caught up in a bun but strands of it tumbled down around her face. Bright spots of angry colour stained her cheeks. 'There you are! At last, I've been right round the mill, in your office, everywhere. I won't have it, Rowan, I won't!'

'I was only taking five minutes off,' said Rowan fearfully.

'I don't mean that. It's her, his mother! Mrs. Bloody Shafir. Do you know what she did? I'm telling you, it's the last straw.'

Rowan got up and went through to the kitchen to put the kettle back on. Sally followed, pacing furiously, like a small enraged kitten. 'We were having chicken and beans,' she declared. 'I'm good at it, I've learned how to cook it and it comes out really well. The whole family likes it, even his father though he wouldn't dare admit it. *She'd* have a go at him. We agreed I'd make it, and she, *she,* went and put two whole chillies in while I wasn't looking! You can imagine what it was like. Everybody's eyes watering, no one eating a thing and me apologising and wondering what I'd done. You can imagine how she smirked. And then this morning I heard her telling one of her friends all about it, they thought I couldn't understand them. They talk the flaming language all day every day, they don't give a damn about it being as rude as hell to do it in front of me! So I got my own back.'

'What did you do?' asked Rowan, wide-eyed at these revelations about kitchen warfare.

'Slung half a pound of whole peppercorns into her vegetable curry. It was like eating badly shot pheasant, pellets in every mouthful. And she had the nerve to tell Mohammed to discipline me! And do you know what?'

'He told you off,' said Rowan, grinning. 'What else did you expect?'

'He should have taken my side,' wailed Sally. 'It wasn't fair! She did it to me first. I just got my own back.'

Rowan kept her own counsel, merely making another pot of tea. When it was brewed she poured two mugs and settled comfortably at the huge pine table.

'Does everyone else like you?' she asked.

Sally nodded. 'They do, quite. I like them. It's just her. If Mohammed needs something, she's there. Let me do it for you, I'll wash it, I'll cook it, I know just how you like it, my son, a mother's touch. If I go to him when he comes in she almost wrestles me out of the way. I won't fight over him. It's damned undignified.'

'I bet he's lapping it up,' said Rowan casually.

Sally considered. 'Actually, he hates it. He can't talk to either of us without the other one getting upset. He keeps saying it's going to get better.'

'Now you can talk to her, it might.'

'It just gives us a wider range of insults, that's all.'

Rowan got up and fetched some chocolate biscuits. 'You must be dying for some English food,' she said sympathetically.

Sally stared at her. 'We do have chocolate biscuits. We don't live at the North Pole. And actually the food's lovely. When you don't have three chillies in it.'

'Or a thousand peppercorns,' added Rowan. 'Well, you'll have to apologise. Then everyone will think how sweet you are and she'll be the baddy. Look at it from Mohammed's point of view – he doesn't want to break his mother's heart. She's old, she hasn't any education, she lives in this semi-purdah they seem to go in for, and she sees her son being dragged into strange, foreign ways.'

Sally put on a sad voice. 'You make her sound so little and pathetic. Poor foreign woman, set down in an alien land. If you knew the way she runs the house! She's about as pathetic and helpless as a barracuda! Everybody thinks these poor women are having a terrible time, and they're not! Great big families, loads of friends and everything happening at home or in the mosque. It's the men who have to go and work in these beastly factories, and then come home for the women to tell them what to do.'

'Does Mohammed do what his mother tells him?' asked Rowan, fascinated.

Her sister grinned. 'No. That's what annoys her.'

Rowan abondoned all thoughts of going back to work that day. She and Sally went through to the sitting room, turned on the television and watched *Blue Peter*.

'Do you remember Mother yelling at us to turn it down?' said Rowan.

'No. No, I don't. I don't remember much about home really. Sunday lunches perhaps. All the silver out and the cut glass fruit bowl. And Dad carving so terribly carefully.'

'The meat was always cold,' admitted Rowan.

'And Mother always got at him for being slow. I think he must have irritated her for years before she ran off, years and years and years.'

There was a sudden thunderous knocking on the front door. The two girls looked at each other. 'Mohammed,' said Rowan and went to let him in.

He was wearing trousers and a tunic, and was stiff with husbandly indignation. He marched past Rowan and into the sitting room. 'Sally. Home.'

She folded her hands in her lap. 'I'm visiting my sister, Mohammed. I'm sure Mother told you that.'

'My mother's taken to her bed. She thinks you have run off for good.'

'Then she must be delighted,' retorted his wife. 'She's

been trying to get rid of me ever since I moved in.'

'But you must not insult her!' yelled Mohammed desperately. 'She is my mother, Sally!'

'And I am your wife.'

Rowan stood between them, looking from one to the other as if at a tennis match. 'I do think this could have been anticipated, Mohammed,' she remarked. 'I did say you oughtn't to live in the same house.'

He shook his head, and said hurriedly, 'It's only till I get promoted! We can't afford a house yet, it isn't possible.'

'I can afford ten houses,' wailed Sally. 'And a new car, everything! You're just being stubborn.'

'I will not have people saying I married you for advancement.' Mohammed looked tortured, a proud man on the rack of duty, tempted by opportunity.

'Why not think of it as a dowry?' asked Rowan sympathetically.

He shook his head. 'If I was in my own country, possibly. Here it is looked down upon. I'm British, I have a British wife. I should not take her money.'

'So you make me miserable instead!' yelled Sally, and threw a cushion at him.

He caught it and threw it back hard. It hit her in the face. She squealed and instantly he was on his knees beside her. 'Darling, darling, are you all right? Oh, Sally, I've hurt you, forgive me!'

Sensibly Sally burst into tears, and Rowan withdrew to the kitchen until they sorted it out. She felt dismal and alone. She and Saul never had rows that ended in kisses and hugs. They were always deeply hurtful, wounding affairs that left lasting scars and were almost never resolved. Half the time Saul seemed unaware that they had had a row; he either didn't remember or found it convenient to forget.

After about twenty minutes Mohammed and Sally came looking for her. They held hands, and Sally was very tear-stained. 'We wanted to ask you something,' she began.

Rowan tried to look encouraging. 'Just don't sell your shares, Sally, or if you do, sell them to me.'

'It isn't that. We want you to give Mohammed a job in the mill.'

Rowan was dumbstruck. Yet when she considered, she couldn't see why she hadn't thought of it before. The mill was as much Sally's as her own, and Rowan's own husband worked there. 'What doing?' she asked confusedly. 'In the office or something? Management?'

'Managing the weaving shed. You don't have a proper manager at the moment, it's all you and Saul. You've said yourself you need one. Please, Rowan.'

'Well,' Rowan chewed the side of her finger. There were no Asians in her mill, or at least none in positions of any seniority. The feeling was that if you let in one, sooner or later there would be hundreds and no room for anyone else. 'Take over anything if you let 'em,' the men said. 'Look what they've done to Bradford.' Yet it was boom and bust that had changed Bradford, and all else evolved from it.

She swallowed. 'We can try,' she said. 'But it's a long way, will the old car stand it?' Mohammed's station wagon was renowned for breaking down at inopportune moments.

'We'll buy a new car,' said Sally urgently. 'We must, Mohammed, it's only fair. And I'll put up with your mother, at least until the baby's born.'

He nodded. 'All right. All right. When should I start?'

Rowan spread her hands. 'Monday, if you like. I'll be in America for ten days or so but that might be best actually. I'm not good at handing over responsibility.'

For a moment he seemed almost overcome. 'I didn't like to ask –'

'I'm sorry that you had to,' broke in Rowan. She felt all the weight of Mohammed's confusion; he felt owed a job, and yet resented any charge of profiting from Sally; he needed Sally's money, but couldn't reconcile taking it with his pride; above all he wanted to leave home, but when it came to it he knew how much hurt it would cause his family. Rowan realised suddenly that if the marriage had caused problems for Sally, they were nothing compared with those facing her husband.

In the evening she lay on the rug and played with Hannah, rolling her over and round like a little ball. Hannah threw her legs in the air and squealed, then struggled into her inaccurate crawl. 'Dad. Dad,' she said. Rowan stared at her. 'Why do you say that now when he isn't here? Not here, Hannah. Dad not here.'

The baby's face fell into a look of vacant incomprehension. Sometimes it was possible almost to see the little cogs turning fruitlessly, making no sense of the complications of life. Hannah didn't understand, Hannah might never understand. The world would go on and Hannah would blunder through it, desperately vulnerable. Sometimes, thought Rowan, it didn't hurt at all, and sometimes it stung as fiercely as on that first awful day. There was such a terrible weight of responsibility. Forever.

The Sunday before she left was a wet, blustery day. When she visited Saul she ran from the car park to the buildings through a hail of twigs and leaves, bursting through the doors pink-cheeked and breathless. Saul was waiting for her, morose on crutches.

'You don't have to look so bloody happy,' he grunted.

'Thanks a lot.'

She took off her coat and scanned the other inmates. They all looked miserable, except for one man, grinning like an idiot. 'He's going out,' said Saul, following her eyes. 'He's getting a drink, that's what he's happy about.'

'What's he been here for then?' asked Rowan. 'I mean, you're supposed to stay off it.'

He said nothing and Rowan dived into her bag and brought out the obligatory goodies; the chocolates and grapes, the books, the transistor radio. 'You look a lot better,' she commented. It wasn't true, he looked ghastly, pale and tense.

'Police came today. I'm going to be banned from driving. Very menacing, they were. If I wasn't in here they'd be putting me in prison, that sort of thing. Can't imagine how I'll manage without the car.'

'Get someone to drive you. Get a chauffeur.'

'That I don't fancy.'

They fell silent. Rowan felt his depression seeping into her. Suddenly he said, 'I know something that should amuse you. We do physical jerks, even me on crutches. This hearty woman, weighs about twenty stone, she parades in front of us in a tracksuit that could double as an army provisions store. We do knee and arm swinging, I have to swing my crutches. Me and the bloke next to me got slung out this morning for obscenity. So they sent the chaplain round and he told us we could be cured by faith in God. I asked if he could give me some personal instruction, and he got all excited till I told him I wanted to turn water into wine. Now I don't even get orange juice, it's a punishment.'

Rowan sighed. She didn't think it at all funny. 'You're supposed to be taking this seriously.'

'I haven't had a drink since I came in here, how much more serious can you get? I don't have to be treated like an infant as well.'

'Do you mean to keep off it? Do you even accept that you should?'

He met her eyes. She knew him so well, she could see straight through the insincerity. He shrugged. 'I'll moderate it a bit. Even I accept I was getting over the top. But I'll not live this life of evangelical purity, not for anyone. I'll do what I bloody like with myself.'

'That's what I thought.'

She got up to go, not even waiting to put on her coat. Saul thumped after her on his crutches and caught her arm. 'I didn't mean that the way it sounded. I love you, Rowan.'

She nodded. 'I know you do. Look, I'm off tomorrow. Ring up Barbara now and then, would you, and the mill. Keep a check on things.'

'You don't mean to say you need me for something.'

The old argument, again. She forced her arms into her coat, shaking off his attempt to help her. 'I don't want you to go like this,' he said.

'Well, you're making me! You're the one that keeps pushing it!'

He struck his fist against his forehead, hard. 'Can't you see what it's like in here! I'm strung out on wires and these bloody people come preaching and taking away the orange juice – ye gods, but people do so love to have a sinner to get at. But – oh, you go, you go, I'm no fun to be with. Be careful, lovey. And have a good time, you deserve it.'

Out in the car park she saw him watching her from the window. She waved, but he didn't wave back.

Chapter Forty-One

From the moment she set foot on United States soil, Rowan revelled in America. It was like the movies, with unexpurgated sound track and the added interest of real danger, from the cars, from the muggers, even from the malevolent customs man who searched her sample case as if every label concealed a secret hoard of drugs, or diamonds, or diseased tomatoes.

'Nice stuff,' he commented, as she struggled to close it again.

'It's my mill, it should be.'

'Don't tell me a pretty lady like you owns a textile mill?'

She became very English and very proper. 'I do indeed.'

'Gee I love that voice! Say it again: "I do indeed." It really turns me on.'

'Look, can I go now? I haven't been to America before, I don't know what to do, you see. Do I find a taxi out here, a cab?'

'You sure do.'

She escaped, breathless with anxiety. Customs men unnerved her; even when totally innocent she felt scarlet with guilt. Her sample case weighed a ton. It took her right back to Japan when she had been so terribly young, so frighteningly innocent. A woman barged in front of her and took her cab, she lost the next to an elderly gentleman and the one after that to an aggressive young man. For the next she pushed and shoved and at last got in. It smelled of air freshener, insecticide and tomato sauce.

Her hotel had been booked by the company she was to visit. When she gave her name the receptionist revealed all thirty-two teeth in a smile and summoned three porters with a lift of the eyebrows. 'Mrs. Barton. The Empress Suite. We do so hope you enjoy your stay.'

'Thank you.' Rowan was propelled to the separate, super-class elevator and whisked away to some distant floor. In her room there was a four-poster bed, two televisions, three telephones, a drinks cabinet the size of a small wardrobe, a bunch of flowers, a bottle of champagne and a complimentary silk dressing gown with a label reading 'To remember us by.' In the bathroom she found a shell-shaped tub with mini jacuzzi, four types of shampoo, enough condoms for the regiment of Welsh Guards and a foot sauna.

No sooner had she thrust bundles of notes at the porters than one of the telephones rang, identifying itself not only by a drunken warble but also a flashing light. 'Hi! Carter Finsbacher here. How was the trip?'

'Fine, fine.'

'Just to tell you we'll be picking you up about six. Wear something a little snazzy. Glad to have you with us, Ms. Judge.'

No sooner had he clicked off than she ran to her suitcase and started looking for something snazzy. She had brought neat business clothes mostly, except for one black silk dress with a scooped neckline and a short, stiff peplum. When she put it on it looked OK, but slightly lacking, although at home she always felt daring in that dress. Here it needed the sort of flashy jewellery she didn't own.

She picked up her bag with its wads of unfamiliar American money and went down to the foyer. Designer shops were clustered round the edge, plush little boxes staffed by elegant women and filled with rich goodies. From a festoon of costume jewellery she bought a very expensive silver and jade pendant, and next door she picked up a long silk scarf in an exotic green print. Safely back in her room she borrowed the hotel's collection of safety pins and made a huge green rosette out of the scarf. Pinned at her waist it echoed the pendant and, more to the point, her eyes.

Rowan scanned herself in the mirror. She was wearing her highest heels, and the heavy pendant round her neck gave her the slightly odd elegance of some African tribes. Saul had once called her a Zulu. When was that? Paris? Three, four years ago, before Hannah was born, before – everything. She let the thought go, she would not let anything spoil her mood. The telephone rang and her heart juddered in excitement. For the first time in ages, perhaps ever, she felt young, rich, at liberty in the world. A dangerous state of mind.

Carter Finsbacher turned out to be short, rather plump and apparently very confident. He had a chauffeur-driven car and made sure she understood it was his and not hired, and what is more it was the best car.

'Nothing's too much trouble for you, little lady,' he confided. 'We've got commitment and we want you to know that. We're high achievers at Bellerphon Textiles, we set our sights high and we score. This your own cloth?'

He fingered the peplum of her dress, quite impersonally. Rowan didn't mind, she was used to textile men shaking you by the hand and feeling your lapel at one and the same time. 'It's wild silk. We're exclusively into woollens, Mr. Finsbacher.'

'Call me Carter. Big market in naturals, it's the way of the future.'

'I think wool's pretty natural,' she said coolly. Then she relented. 'We do a wool and silk mix, actually. It's nice, I'll show you sometime.'

'Great, great.'

He rubbed his palms together as if they were sweating and it suddenly occurred to Rowan that Carter Finsbacher was very nervous. And, since he was alone with her and going to meet his colleagues for dinner, who presumably didn't cause this sort of twitching, she was the cause of the complaint. Inexplicably she found it rubbing off. Her own palms started to sweat.

'I am sorry my husband couldn't come,' she said distractedly. 'He always does the travelling, he knows what to do and things.'

'Leaving you at home to mind the babies,' he said jovially, and then thought it sounded derogatory and started to dig himself out. 'I didn't mean – a worthwhile job, who can say not – but a woman of your standing, I mean, with a textile mill – but bringing up the next generation –'

'I've got a nanny,' interrupted Rowan. 'Our little girl's mentally handicapped.'

Mr. Finsbacher's face stopped twitching. For the first time he looked at her as if she might be a real person. 'How about that? My boy's ten now. Down's Syndrome.'

For a second Rowan wondered if she had somehow known, because she never told people about Hannah. 'Hannah's only three,' she said breathily. 'We don't know any others. Perhaps we'll meet them when she goes to school or something. I don't know.'

Finsbacher stopped rubbing his hands together. 'You should come visit with my wife. We've got four kids, Jimmy's the third. And he's everybody's favourite brother, I'll tell you that, though he's got a temper! Boy, when he gets upset he upsets everybody. But he's a good boy mostly, a real good boy.'

'I'd like to meet him,' said Rowan awkwardly. 'Thank you.'

The restaurant was unimaginably glitzy. A canopy stretched out across the pavement and Mr. Finsbacher marched ahead, a rubber ball of a man pursued by a very tall, very elegant lady. A couple of photographers stationed by the door took flash pictures and then asked each other, 'Who the hell is that?' because this restaurant was the preserve of the rich and the well-known. Broadway stars sat next to television personalities who rubbed shoulders with film stars in town for deals. Round the periphery sat lesser mortals, there to see rather than be seen, amongst which were the men from Bellerphon Textiles.

Four large, sober-suited individuals rose to greet them. Rowan felt hopelessly vulnerable, five of them against one of her. Saul wouldn't have turned a hair. Why, oh why, wasn't Saul here? She shook hands automatically, aware that if she turned her head into the room she would be face to face with more beautiful people than ever in her life before.

When they sat down she couldn't concentrate. One of the heart-throbs of her youth was ten feet away, gazing earnestly at a woman as pale and lovely as any marble statue, and these men wanted to talk textiles! People moved around the room, greeting acquaintances. Rowan could hardly take her eyes off the scene to look at the menu. From what lay on the tables around her, the food was over-processed and done in miniature, baby vegetables next to embryo lamb chops. She ordered abstractedly.

Carter Finsbacher sat back and said, 'Well, how do you feel about our operation?'

Reluctantly, Rowan came back to the task in hand. 'I haven't seen your mill. But the figures look good and so do the samples you sent me. At Judge's we've built up a very good couture range, and while I can see why you'd want to produce it, I can't imagine selling our design skills for anything other than a lot of money. And I don't know how competitive that would make the final product.'

'Very competitive,' said one of the big grey men. 'We'd be selling under the Judge's label with the tag of English quality. We're not aiming for low prices, ma'am, our market segment is way, way up. Judge's Fine English Woollens.'

'Made in America,' said Rowan thoughtfully.

An English actor crossed her line of vision, a man so thin and haggard he seemed to have only months to live, except that he had looked like that for at least the last ten years. 'We'd have to have guarantees,' she murmured. 'I wouldn't want our name on anything scrappy.'

'We run a very tight organisation, ma'am.'

The food arrived and Rowan poked doubtfully at some

unidentifiable seafood. She might be adventurous in many spheres of her life but they did not include food. Neither was she conditioned to the American habit of serving so much of everything, nor to the profligate waste. Wand thin people picked at vast platefuls and then abandoned them. Similarly she gave up on the seafood and ate the bread and butter instead.

A couple came in and all heads turned to see if it was anyone important. The girl Rowan vaguely recognised, a singer who sometimes appeared on British television. Her escort she knew rather better.

'Good God,' she said forcibly. Horrible suspicion filled her mind and she turned bright green eyes on her hosts. 'Do you have anything to do with Bardsey's? I shall find out if you do, you may as well tell me the truth.'

Carter Finsbacher looked trapped, not because of guilt though. 'Er – Bardsey's? Would that be a British firm? I'm afraid – '

Rowan couldn't believe it. 'You must have heard of them! You've heard of us, Bardsey's were the, absolutely *the*, number one firm for years. Worsteds. They supply all the big chain stores.'

'I know them,' one of the others chimed in. 'I had a look at them when we researched your company. Their ratios are not good, not good at all. Too many loss-makers battened on to the main company. Prime meat for a take-over, I should say.'

'Would you?' Rowan sank sharp teeth into her bread, watching Richard exercise visible charm across the table. The girl tossed her hair a lot. It annoyed Rowan even at this distance.

She was well into her steak when Richard spotted her. He seemed taken aback, then threw down his napkin and came straight across.

'Rowan! What the hell are you doing here?'

She chewed and swallowed a piece of steak. 'Hello,

Richard. May I introduce Carter Finsbacher? All these gentlemen are from Bellerphon Textiles. Richard Barton, everyone.'

'Are you treading on my turf?'

She shrugged elegantly. 'I really don't know. Actually I thought you might be stamping all over mine but I'm almost – almost – sure you're not. What are you here for?'

'Er – selling, just selling. And of course it's business *and* pleasure, to some extent. I'm with the lady I met up with in Paris that time. Remember?'

'Too well.'

She looked across and met the over-made-up stare of Richard's girlfriend. Rowan inclined her head very slightly. 'Richard, dear, if you stand there all night our food will go cold. I hate to chase you away.'

He laughed. 'Don't be so damned patronising. Where's Saul?'

'He has a broken leg,' said Rowan. She fixed him with a grim stare, he could so easily destroy her. But all he said was, 'These things will happen.' He started to move away and then came back. 'Look, I want to talk to you about something, strictly business. Where are you staying?'

'I'm committed on this trip,' objected Rowan.

'British to the core, eh, Rowan? Never take a risk.' He knew she couldn't afford to seem timid in front of these textile men.

She pulled a pen and a scrappy envelope out of her purse and scribbled on it. 'Beats me why you couldn't talk business in England. I haven't time to spare, Richard, I warn you.'

'Yeah. So I gather.'

He took the slip of paper and went back to his table. Rowan watched him grimly. 'Bardsey Textiles,' said Carter Finsbacher. 'I knew him when he was a fly boy dealing in alpaca. Took a few too many risks, I thought.'

'A lot of money behind him,' remarked Rowan. 'Gives

people a lot of confidence. Not that he lacked it anyway.'

'The self-made have a sharper edge,' someone commented, and Rowan flushed. She had let them see that she found his affluent background galling. It was British of her to be embarrassed at letting her feelings show, and American of them not to feel anything of the sort.

When Finsbacher dropped her off later that evening, he said, 'Shall I pick you up around half-eight, Rowan? See round the mill early and we can go home and lunch with my wife. The kids are on vacation right now, so it'll be kind of noisy.'

She nodded. 'I'd like that. Thank you very much.'

In her room, restless from too much food and jumpy because of the changes to her internal clock, she ran a hot bath and sat in it. Richard Barton had been just as horrified to see her as she to see him. Why? What was happening at Bardsey's? The storm clouds had been gathering; just scuds on the horizon at first but darker now. She thought of the markets, of the rumours. One of the major chainstores, associated with Bardsey's over a very long time, was importing quite a bit nowadays. Had they junked Bardsey's? As a firm they had pioneered hand in glove manufacture, working so closely with their customers that designs evolved mutually rather than being summoned from one person's brain. The fault, if fault there was, could be said to be the exclusion of truly original thought.

And the wind of change was blowing through the High Street. They were abandoning dull worth for style and flair. For the moment Rowan was playing the right tune, but she had no illusions but that one day the music would change. She could be caught flat-footed. It could be that Bardsey's already had. Were they looking at big losses, trying to grab market share in the US of A to replace that lost in Britain? She didn't know, but it gave her great pleasure to suspect.

On the following day she dressed in boots, an ankle-length

black skirt and a jacket woven to look like purple and green tapestry. She had sweated blood over the design, which had proved much harder to produce than she had ever anticipated. The background purple had killed every other colour until she had chucked in some red before spinning. Only a trained eye could see it, but the effect was to lift the colour dramatically. When Carter Finsbacher saw it, he blinked.

'Now this would be hard for you,' said Rowan offhandedly. 'Our people are very innovative, they have to be.'

He cleared his throat and ushered her to the waiting limo.

As they were pulling away, Rowan saw Richard Barton leap out of a cab. 'Oh God,' she said. 'Do ask the driver to stop.'

She pushed the button to open the window and stuck her head out. 'Are you looking for me, Richard?'

He turned in surprise. 'Hello, Rowan. I was intending to join you for breakfast. Where are you going, it's hardly dawn!'

'Bellerphon Textiles. I think it's quite a way. Look, call me tonight. Better still, take me out to dinner.'

Richard's face was amused and wary. 'Why the sudden affection?' he asked. 'I don't know why, Rowan, but I feel naturally suspicious.'

'Don't be so nervous. Pick me up at seven, OK?'

'OK.' He stepped back and the car swept away from the kerb. He stood watching until it was out of sight.

Rowan had expected the American mill to be way, way ahead of Judge's. She was hanging on the coat-tails of technological advance; somehow she had believed others to be wearing the damn thing. But Bellerphon was a big, old, draughty place with notices everywhere exhorting people to wear ear plugs, smile, have fun and keep their hair tied back, and they had the same mishmash of old and new machines. Rowan saw at once that the layout was inefficient. They had inherited it. America might be young in terms of history but their textile factories had been around long enough to grow old.

'Have you had to shed much labour recently?' she asked.

'Some. Quite a bit over the last few years. We're on the upswing now.'

She nodded. The slump had hit everyone in the West, they had all quailed under the onslaught of foreign goods. She stopped at a loom weaving what looked like blue blazercloth and pointed a long finger. 'One of your warp threads has broken.' Finsbacher went red and hit the stop button. He went into a corner with the man responsible and went even redder. They continued their tour.

Rowan had not expected to be able to make up her mind quickly. Linking up with a company so far away was a leap in the dark for Judge's, and the anxiety level of the Bellerphon men showed that it was a risk for them too. Who would it benefit most? On the face of things Bellerphon, who needed a new image and a new and exciting product. But Rowan indulged her fantasies. Suppose Bellerphon, using her range, hooked just those chainstore people Richard was probably courting? Bellerphon were hungry enough to hunt night and day; they were trying to give her the impression of always playing high but this was certainly their highest yet. Finsbacher was in his mid-forties, he had been through the worst, he knew the score. If they could guarantee quality, she would play ball.

She said as much to Finsbacher as they drove out of town to his house for lunch. He looked dumbfounded. Eventually, he said, 'Don't you have to talk with your husband? With your board?'

Rowan hadn't even contemplated it. 'I do tend to run things my way,' she said vaguely. 'There won't be any objection, I assure you.'

Finsbacher shot her rather an odd look. 'Right. Right.'

His house was a modest, crowded dwelling with a huge tree in the garden. A rubber tyre and a rope ladder hung from it, the grass underneath was worn to bare earth. Rowan followed Finsbacher into the hall.

'Where is everybody?' he yelled, trying to keep his high spirits under wraps. 'I brought our guest home.'

Three unnaturally tidy young people came downstairs, the eldest about eighteen. In their wake careered a squat little boy, arms and legs everywhere and a beam on his flattened face. 'Dad! Dad!' he bellowed. 'I got a clean shirt, Dad! Look!'

He pulled his pink shirt out of his trousers and flapped the tails excitedly. One of his sisters, a girl of about fourteen, said, 'I just did you up, Jimmy!'

'I'll do it,' said Finsbacher. When he put his arms round Jimmy, the boy hugged him.

They went through to the kitchen. Margaret Finsbacher was a little taller than her husband with a smooth, unlined face. She had an air of tranquillity that seemed unaffected by the trauma of entertaining an important guest, or four children, or the large dog trying to batter its way in from outside.

'Dad! Dad!' bellowed Jimmy again. 'See my train, Dad!' He picked up two pieces of wood inexpertly nailed together.

His mother caught his hand. 'Not now, Jimmy,' she said gently. 'Visitors!'

The word had an almost magical effect. Jimmy looked abashed, folded his hands over the train and fell silent. 'Good boy,' said his mother.

They went through to the sitting room for drinks. Finsbacher was different at home, visibly more relaxed. The children made polite and intelligent conversation, with the exception of Jimmy, who sat being ludicrously good. Rowan reached in her bag for a photograph of Hannah.

'I've got a little girl like you,' she said to Jimmy. 'This is her.' He took the photograph and peered at it.

'Do you like your little girl?' he asked.

Rowan nodded. 'Lots and lots. I like you too.'

Jimmy stared again at the picture and then carefully and precisely put it in his pocket.

'I think you've lost that,' said Margaret.

Rowan shrugged. 'I've got more.'

After lunch the adults sat over coffee, watching Jimmy playing on the rope ladder. He was clumsy but careful, making each step with concentration.

'He's terribly good,' said Rowan. 'Very well behaved.'

Margaret Finsbacher nodded. 'It's a mistake to be sorry for them. Like any kid they need discipline, nice clear rules. I worry about him, I worry what's to happen when we're gone.'

'I don't think the others will let Jimmy down,' said Carter.

'But you can't rely on that,' said Rowan. 'You can't expect it.'

'Why not?' said Finsbacher. 'They all love Jimmy. I don't say they've got to live with him but they can take an interest in him and make sure he's set up right. Seems to me it's too easy to take it all on yourself.'

'I'd like to put some money aside for him,' said Margaret, watching her son hang by his arms, bicycling his short legs and roaring with laughter. Rowan thought, 'That is why Carter Finsbacher wants this deal. He needs it for Jimmy.'

She was tired when she got back to the hotel, a whole day of strangers was hard work. If she had known where Richard was staying, she would have rung up and cancelled dinner. Instead she showered and changed into a pair of silk lounging pyjamas. She had never worn them out before but there seemed no reason why she should not. They were cream with huge roses printed all over them. With a belt and high heels they looked oddly stylish. Long dangling earrings in the shape of elephants completed the picture.

The moment Richard saw them, he said, 'Taj Mahal meets Sayonara. Will you change to go to bed or just take off the earrings?'

'Don't be tedious, Richard.' He was wearing a dark suit and red tie. America's businessmen did seem to be boringly conventional in dress, she reflected, any peacock tendencies had been driven out by efficiency and seriousness. Even the women were following suit, in more ways than one. When they sat down to eat, at almost every other table were couples uniformly dressed in dark serge and white shirts.

'I don't want to look like the head waiter,' complained Rowan, aware that people were staring at her. 'It's not my fault the world's gone boring.'

'Talking of bores, how's Saul? I take it he was too smashed to make the trip?'

'He broke his leg,' said Rowan shortly. 'There's no more to it than that.'

'Except the prosecution,' retorted Richard. 'I do read the papers, love.'

She fell silent. Richard found himself studying the thin silk of her pyjama top, which was ever so slightly transparent. He could see the faint shadow of her breasts. 'Don't you ever wear a bra?' he asked.

Rowan started. 'You can't tell, can you? I don't sag or anything?'

He swallowed. 'Quite the opposite. A very pert pair.'

'Just don't get any ideas.'

The waiter came and Rowan ordered egg mayonnaise, which when it came was flavoured with garlic. Richard had mushrooms with garlic and truffles.

'I wish they'd never discovered garlic,' objected Rowan vehemently. 'All restaurants seem to think it's compulsory. Disgusting stuff.'

'Is it?' He hardly seemed to be listening.

She watched him surreptitiously. She could feel that he was angry with her, or possibly he was angry and was venting it on her. 'Bad day?' she asked.

'Could say that.' He met her eyes and she lifted her brows quizzically.

'You don't have to watch what you say,' she offered. 'I'm not going to use it in evidence against you. I think the world's big enough for Bardsey's and Judge's.'

His expression of open scepticism made her blush. 'Anyway, I know what you're doing,' she said defensively. 'One of the big chainstores put you in their pocket and against your better judgement insisted on a useless range. My guess is that the sludge brown was the final straw. If they sold half I'd be surprised. Now they've dumped you for someone more exciting, and that is terribly unfair. And you are left with empty looms and no customers. You're out here trawling.'

Richard put his elbows on the table. 'Since you know so much, I'll add a few titbits. I saw the writing on the wall months ago. Dad told me I didn't understand the business, we had a relationship with our customers, it was mutually beneficial, we mustn't do anything to upset them, et cetera. Now we have a problem, he wants to know why *I* didn't insist on doing things my way. You know what he said to me?' Rowan shook her head. 'That he didn't expect his son to be a yes-man. And it's me breaking stones over here, with the exchange rate against us and a design portfolio that's right out of step. I'm wasting my time.'

'What would you do instead?' asked Rowan.

'Rationalise.'

'You mean, sack everybody and flog off anything that's not tied down?'

'Pretty much, yes.'

Steak arrived and Rowan attacked her inch thick slab with surgeon-like precision. Across the table Richard toyed with his fork and watched her. All those confidences, she thought warily. He was trying to make her believe they were friends, when in fact he was telling her nothing she couldn't work out for herself. He had fine hands, she noticed, tanned, with long palms and mobile fingers. The uninitiated would call them musical, but if you looked at Andy's hands they were almost gnarled with exercise.

'Where's the girlfriend?' she asked. 'Aren't you serious about her?'

'Not now, no. I was once. She can't understand what's changed, we spend a lot of time arguing. I don't know what's changed really. Perhaps – I think I was settling for something that was OK instead of what was really good. I'm setting my sights a bit higher nowadays.'

'Don't be ingenuous.'

Her steak disposed of, or at least as much as she wished it to be, Rowan sat back and sipped her wine, regarding Richard with a cool stare that had in it all the personal interest of a judge at a dog show.

'Why do you pretend to be so sure of yourself?' he asked.

'I don't pretend, I am. Mostly.'

'I'd say it's almost all front. Nervous as anything. Too scared to take risks, any sort of risks. You want to drive a fast car but you don't. You want to spend money but you stop yourself. You want to have fun but you don't know how. You're a cat person, closed, independent and out of it. So sad.'

Saying it made it seem true. Rowan dropped her eyes and gulped at her wine. 'I don't mean to be anything,' she said hastily. 'I just am. I do what I want to do. Anyway, you said we'd talk business.'

He lounged back in his chair. 'I want you to buy our dye-house. Preferential price and a long-term agreement for our cloth to continue going through. Neither of us needs that capacity and you can afford it. We can't.'

'And you want jam on it! We can build one of our own for less than you'd make us pay.'

He grinned. 'We both know you couldn't. Money borrowed for months without return, the whole place disrupted while the building goes on, teething troubles, everything. This is an offer you can't refuse. A ready-made money spinner and a deal to benefit us both. Be sensible, Rowan.'

She looked at him earnestly. 'It does sound sensible. But I hate getting involved with James, it's always a mistake. For him,' she added, letting a smile slide maliciously around her mouth.

A thought struck her. 'Does he know about this?'

Richard grinned. 'Not yet.' He saw her quizzical expression and added, 'As it happens, Dad and I are about to have a fight. One hell of a fight actually. He is going to have to listen to what I say. I am damned if I'm going to be patronized and humoured and bloody well ignored.'

'Told you so,' said Rowan. 'He won't change.'

'He can either change or go bust,' snapped Richard. For a second the rage showed through, fuelled by all James's autocratic tactlessness. Abruptly, Richard came back to the present. 'Let's go on some place.' He cast down his napkin and signalled to the waiter. Caught unawares Rowan wondered why she hadn't had the sense to order a pudding. She liked puddings, they were her reason for dining out.

Once in the street, she said petulantly, 'I hadn't finished.'

'Yes, you had.' Richard waved down a cab and spoke to the driver. 'We're going to a nightclub,' he explained. 'I want to dance.'

'What about what *I* want to do?' demanded Rowan. She felt unconsidered and unappreciated. Before this Richard had always been absolutely focused on her, and here he was giving her minimal consideration.

'Don't be a wet blanket,' he said. She subsided, feeling herself on the verge of feminine acquiescence. Her own servility annoyed her.

Chapter Forty-Two

The nightclub was hot and crowded. Somewhere in the gloom a jazz trumpeter was splitting the smoky air into sharpened pieces of glass, and on the floor a girl danced. Her naked body was painted in blue and gold, her hair was sprayed gold and twisted into snaking ringlets. She lay on the floor, her legs twisted back, supporting herself on one painted arm while she clutched and dragged at nothing. There was sensuality, but also danger. As she knelt, her head thrown back and her body arched in abandoment, many of the women looked away.

When it was over, Richard said, 'Did you like that? Brilliant, isn't she?'

'I don't like that sort of thing. She seemed – evil. I know she was pretending but it was too real.'

Richard reached out and caught her wrist. The danger had excited him, as much as Rowan had been repelled. She couldn't get away, he held her easily. 'Are you frightened of desire?' he said softly. 'You're so innocent. You don't know how good it can be.'

'Let me go,' she whispered. 'I don't like you tonight.'

'You don't like me any night when I let you see what I want from you, because you want it too. You weren't cut out to be Mrs. Faithful, taking the knocks from your sodden block of a husband and opening your legs on the odd occasion when he's not too drunk or too sober. Why be that? It's not what you want.'

She felt off balance, and from that strange standpoint things didn't look normal. Saul was what Richard said, but only sometimes. Or was it always and she pretended not to notice? Time and again when she found herself thinking of Saul she switched at once to business matters. The transition was so smooth nowadays that she did it automatically. Thoughts of Saul meant bad feelings which at once called up something which made her feel safe. Business was safe, it was understandable and depended not at all on emotion. And in those moments when feelings did intrude in that world, for instance when Andy got involved, and Sally and Diana, then she felt her very foundations rocked. There ought to be something solid in the world, something quite unchanging.

'I want to go back to the hotel,' she said to Richard. Her eyes were wide and anxious, he was suddenly aware of her intense vulnerability. He let go of her wrist and took her hand instead, gently. The band was playing a soft, slow blues, a song about love and loss and loneliness.

'Dance with me,' he pleaded. 'I didn't want to frighten you. It's all right, I won't hurt you. You're safe with me.'

Hadn't Saul said that, all that time ago? She allowed herself to be led to the dancefloor. Richard put his arm round her waist, she encircled his neck. In her high heels their faces were almost level. He brushed her lips with a kiss. 'I'm sorry I scared you. I don't know why I do that to you. I get angry at you for not doing what I know we should! And I don't want to seduce you, I want it to be something you want as much as me. We'd do it together.'

The pale lids descended, hiding her sea-green eyes. 'Sometimes I want to. Sometimes some part of me wants to. But it's so selfish, such a mean thing to do.' She looked up at him. They had gone beyond pretence. 'It isn't fair to think only about us.'

'When did Saul ever think about anyone but himself?' said Richard harshly. 'He betrays you every time he takes another drink, a hundred times a day! And I need you, Rowan. It isn't as if I'll go on quite happily on my own, I can't take it like that any more. And there doesn't seem to be anyone else who'll do. I wish there was, really.'

She put her head back and stared at him. 'I don't want this to be serious, you know. I don't intend anything. That isn't what you intend really, is it?'

He had a choice between honesty and dishonesty. He chose, for once, to tell the truth. He sighed. 'If I say it's just a casual thing, you'll like me better, but I won't like me at all.'

Giving up all attempt at dancing he let her go, and they stood facing each other, not touching. The trumpet wailed and howled, and all around them people clung together. They alone stood fiercely apart. Richard said, 'I don't know why it is, but I think about you all the time. I feel angry with you for invading my head like this. You're in my dreams, bothering me. You turn me on when I've better things to do. I think you should come to bed with me because you don't owe your bum of a husband anything. And I should go to bed with you to see if I can get you out of my head! You're a bloody nuisance, Rowan.'

She turned on her heel and went back to the table, picking up her bag and heading for the door. Richard followed, and when they reached the street he found she was walking away. He hurried after her and said, 'Wait for a cab.'

'I want to walk. It's a well-lit street.' She pulled free and went on, and he hung back for a minute, admiring her, watching her pyjamas ripple against her body, her long legs stepping like a giraffe on the Serengeti Plain. Then a hand reached out of a doorway and grabbed her. Richard was running almost before she screamed. When she did it was a muffled shriek against a choking hand. No more than two seconds and Richard was looming over them in the doorway. Rowan wasn't struggling. There was a knife at her thoat.

'Let her go,' said Richard. 'Hurt her and I'll kill you.'

'Give me the money, man.' He was a Puerto Rican, smelling of urine and decay. Drugs, thought Richard, aware of Rowan's huge eyes above the grime-encrusted hand.

'Put down the knife or you get nothing,' he said. He put his hand slowly into his jacket and drew out his wallet. The man's eyes followed it like a snake following the movement of a snake charmer's pipe. 'Take the knife away,' said Richard. The knife moved, a scant three inches. Richard bent down to hand over the wallet and in the same moment kicked hard at the man's wrist. The knife clattered away, the man howled and Rowan bit the hand clamped over her face. Richard had her arm and dragged her to her feet. They ran like hares back to the lights and safety of the club.

'Bastards! Mother fuckers!' screamed the man after them.

There was a cab drawing up, Richard cut in front of the people who had ordered it and thrust Rowan inside. As they drove away the people on the pavement complained angrily, and twenty yards away a scrawny figure still stood, yelling, 'Bastards! Mother fuckers!'

They went back to Richard's hotel. He was in one of the opulent business hotels designed to be that important New York password, the good address. It was comfortable and impersonal, with Richard's briefcase on a chair and a tie draped precisely over a chair. Rowan sat down, shivering, while Richard poured them both stiff drinks.

'I want to clean my teeth,' she said suddenly. 'I can still taste him. God! It makes me feel sick.'

'Use my brush,' said Richard. 'Have a shower if you want.'

She did want. She felt dirty, as if she carried infection. What would she have done if the man had raped her? She would have wanted to kill herself.

The shower made her feel better. She ran the water scalding hot and scrubbed herself all over, even her scalp. Although she didn't lock the door, Richard remained firmly on the other side. His sensitivity surprised her, she hadn't thought him capable of it. In the aftermath of fear she felt tired, in need of warmth and reassurance. She felt, almost as never before, in need of sex, in need of harsh and primitive mating. He had aroused her from the first, she knew that now, and yet as always she'd denied her own emotions. She remembered how he had touched her in the lift and how she had lain awake for hours afterwards. Heat surged in her. Rubbing her hair dry, she wrapped herself in a towel and came out.

Richard was sitting in the chair, sipping his drink. Rowan picked up her own and sat on the bed. The towel was drooping a little around her breasts. She made as if to hitch it up – and then left it. 'Was he an addict?' she asked.

'I expect so. Emaciated little runt.'

'He made me think of Saul. The same desperation. I don't understand it.'

'I don't think there's any point in trying.'

He took off his tie and started to unbutton his shirt. For a moment she watched him, accepting what he dictated for her, letting the sure movements of his fingers tease her senses. Suddenly she thought of James. Those hands were James's hands, that certainty was absolutely his. Her imagination ran the film: James taking off his clothes, her mother lying watching in the bed. Whose bed? The bed of her childhood, the haven of warmth and love and Daddy.

'No!' Her voice came out hoarse and anguished. 'I don't want this.'

'Of course you do.' With victory so close, Richard was beyond persuasion.

'No. I won't do it, ever.'

She got up and went into the bathroom to get her clothes. Richard followed. She tried to push him away. His hands ripped aside the towel. Long white thighs. She turned away from him, bending to put on her pyjamas. He stared into the shadows in the cleft of her buttocks, he put out his hand and tried to penetrate her.

She rounded on him wildly, hitting out hard. 'Get off me, get away!' He felt her fingernails on his cheek and closed with her, holding her wrists high above her head. If only he had taken off his clothes! Jamming her between the washbasin and the bath, he pressed himself against her. She stopped struggling. He looked into eyes like green glass. 'If you rape me,' said Rowan softly, 'I shall call the police. They will put you away for years and years and years.'

He didn't move. 'This isn't rape. It's me making you do what you should.'

She almost spat with anger. 'I know what I want! And it isn't to be screwed in some hotel bathroom by some jerk who thinks he's going to impress me! Let me go, damn you, let me go!' She began to struggle again. Richard held himself against her for a few delicious seconds, and then let go of her wrists. She battered him viciously with her elbows and broke free.

He sat on the edge of the bath as she flung on her clothes. His eyes glittered dangerously. Rowan felt as if she were in the presence of a tiger that might at any moment spring. As she prepared to leave he got up and came over to her, standing between her and the door. He put his hands up under her top and held her naked breasts. In the heat of his palms they seemed to swell, to become pumpkins topped by hard stalks. Feebly she tried to push him away, making no real effort. She closed her eyes to shut him out.

'You want it and I want it,' said Richard. 'But loving scares you, because you don't know how to let go. You don't dare lose control. Get out then! Get out and don't come back.'

He opened the bedroom door and thrust her through it, slamming it after her. She stood in the bare corridor, aflame with heat, her breasts aching and her legs like jelly. Her hand went up to knock on the closed door, to beg him to let her in. At that moment all she wanted in the world was his body. There were voices of people coming up in the elevator. The cold wind of reality rushed into her mind. What was she doing here, about to fawn and beg a man to please, please fill her up? She was in pain, she was wet with desire. She thought of Saul, she thought of Hannah. Her fist fell away. Clutching her bag, she ran to the elevator, to get a cab and get back to her own room, and safety.

The next day she had an appointment with Marcus Arnaud. She felt hungover, not through drink but something very like it. If she had slept with Richard would she have woken refreshed and renewed, or as sour as this, as depressed as this? Sitting at the elaborate dressing table in her room she made up her eyes in great circles of purple, matching her neat purple suit, the shadows echoing her black blouse. The hated emerald choker, Saul's guilt present, went on too. She looked dramatic, very thin and strained.

Arnaud's salon was in a small street of discreet shops. His display window was understated to the point of emptiness, Rowan gazed at the two frocks displayed, beige on beige, and was unimpressed. Pushing the heavy glass door she entered the salon. The atmosphere was more hushed than any funeral parlour. A girl dressed in beige wool with a pure white collar looked up from a desk.

'My name's Barton,' said Rowan, her voice loud in the silent air. 'From Isaac Judge, Bradford. I have an appointment with Mr. Arnaud.'

The girl checked her list. 'I'm sorry, we were expecting a Mr. Barton.'

'My husband, Saul. A broken leg. I'm sorry, I thought my office had informed you.' Mentally she cursed Frances. It was a small slip but in these situations it only took something small to throw Rowan off balance. She was so far from home, so friendless. New York wasn't a friendly town, it gave away nothing at all. You grabbed and took, or went away empty-handed.

The girl got up to lead her to a gilded staircase. Rowan followed her upstairs, past photographs of dresses taken in such odd situations that the clothes themselves were hard to judge. She recognised blue cloth, trimmed with red, both Judge's make. A little surge of relief soothed her nerves.

Marcus Arnaud was in his studio, a small man walking nervously up and down in front of a drawing board. When she entered, he said aggressively, 'I thought it was going to be Saul. He rang personally.'

Rowan swallowed. 'He had an accident, broke his leg. He sends his apologies.'

'Can't he pick up the goddammed 'phone, can't he even do that?'

Rowan didn't understand the note of petulance. 'He's in hospital,' she said vaguely. 'I told him I'd look after everything, he isn't well.'

Arnaud stopped his pacing and looked at her. 'Who are you then? His assistant?'

'I thought they told you. I'm his wife. Rowan, Rowan Barton.'

The man's small, rather pretty mouth dropped open. He caught himself and grinned. 'Oh. Right, right, I see. Er – tell Saul I'm sorry to have missed him. He'd better make a point of looking me up when he's in town next.'

'I'm sure he will. You'd be very welcome to come and visit the mill when you're in England, Mr. Arnaud.'

'That's sweet of you, honey.' He had adopted any number of Americanisms.

Rowan began to unpack her samples, uncomfortable without really knowing why. 'Were you a model girl?' asked Arnaud.

Rowan grimaced. 'Because I'm so tall, you mean? No. I'm a millowner's daughter. And now I own the mill.'

'Just you?'

'And my husband, my brother and sister and a few thousand shareholders. But I was the one that pulled it round. Without me it would have sunk.' It was boasting but she felt she needed it. Although nothing had been said she felt criticised by this man. He seemed to be judging her.

As he looked through the cloth, his eye caught by the couple of Spanish pattern samples she had managed to squeeze in, she babbled: ‘It was Saul’s idea to sell your end of the market. I didn’t think there’d be anything in it for us, but of course there is, indirectly. Why do you have such dull dresses in your window?’

He blinked at her. ‘Everybody’s got windows like that right now.’

‘I thought the idea was to be different.’

He put down the samples. ‘You’re not a bit like Saul. A more tactful man I never met.’

She sighed unhappily. ‘Was that rude? I’m sorry. Look, I can see I’m taking your time. Suppose I pack this lot up and you see Saul when he’s better?’

He rested his hand on hers as she started to close her case. His touch was dry and slightly cold. ‘Suppose we have lunch. I’d like to talk. About you and Saul.’

Over pasta in an aggressively Italian restaurant, Arnaud said, ‘Are you happy, Rowan? In your marriage?’

She stared at him. ‘That’s not something I like to be asked, thank you. I don’t know why you asked it.’

‘Then you’re not happy. You don’t look it, you’re all strung up.’

‘I just hate travelling, that’s all!’ snapped Rowan. But to her horror she felt her eyes sting with tears. She fumbled for her handkerchief. ‘I’m sorry,’ she sniffed. ‘Oh, I might as well tell you. Saul broke his leg in a car crash, and he crashed because he was blind drunk. He’s in a clinic for alcohol dependency. For God’s sake, don’t tell everyone. Though everyone knew he was drinking, I don’t suppose I should mind now he’s being dried out.’

Arnaud poured her some wine. She topped it up with Perrier and drank.

‘You don’t know about him, do you?’ he said.

‘About who? Saul? What should I know?’

‘He’s gay.’

Rowan’s eyes, purple-painted, were caverns in her white face. ‘That’s an absolute bloody lie!’

'No, it isn't, lovey. He told me himself. He and I – we understand each other. I met him one time when he was torn up over an affair. I guess he married you soon after.'

'But – I know that's not true. He's normal, he is really!'

'Then why does he drink? He ain't happy, sweetheart. I'm only telling you because I can see things aren't working out. I've been through this with friends of mine. They get married, think they can keep it under wraps, end up leading a double life that makes them and the girl miserable. You need to know. It's the only fair way out.'

As Rowan looked at him, the world tilted on its axis. Arnaud was small, quietly dressed, only so very slightly effeminate, but in her mind he was a drag queen, his lips dripping scarlet, pouting, seducing men into nameless, unimaginable horrors. 'I don't believe you,' she said feebly.

'Not now you don't. Go home and ask him, love. He'll be relieved I told you. Tell him to come and see me. I'd like to help.'

'I bet you would!' Rowan got up and ran. The waiter picked up her sample case from where she had stashed it by the door and struggled after her. She stopped and took it from him, and then couldn't run because it weighed so heavy. That horrible, horrible man!

She caught a cab and sat hunched in the back, listening to her heart thunder against her chest. It wasn't true, there was no way it could be true. But doubts nudged at her. Why did he drink? What did he do on those trips away? What about that time in Spain when he couldn't?

Pacing the hotel room, she tried to think what to do. Her instinct was to get on the first plane home and confront Saul, demand that he confess. Suppose he denied it? He might still be lying. Oughtn't she to keep it to herself, sneak about and find some evidence? Besides, tomorrow was the final meeting with Bellerphon, she should stay for that. But she would burst if she didn't talk to someone.

She rang Richard's hotel with no expectation that he

would be in. When he answered she sat for a moment, holding the receiver in silence. 'Hello? Who is this?' Richard's irritated voice cut through her thoughts.

'It's me. Richard – something's happened. I need you.'

'Are you hurt? Is it someone at home?'

'No, no, nothing like that. I've found out something. Please come, Richard, I'm at the hotel.'

She heard him swallow. 'I've only just calmed down after last night.'

'I know, I know. But this is now and everything's different.'

'Wait there. I'll be fifteen minutes.'

When he arrived she was sitting hunched up on the edge of the bed, surrounded by luxury like a mouse on a sumptuous ship. He sat next to her and put his arm round her shoulders. She was shaking like a leaf.

'What is it? Tell me, quick.'

'It's Saul!' She put her face into his jacket and sobbed, sending rivulets of purple down her cheeks and on to his shirt. 'Oh God, look at the mess I'm making.'

'Never mind that, what the hell is it?'

'A man today – a customer – he says Saul's gay!'

Richard's mouth worked soundlessly. Suddenly he laughed. 'Bloody hell! Do you believe him?'

'It isn't funny! I don't know what I believe. He said that's why Saul drinks, that's why we don't get on. And I thought about all the trips . . . and in Spain once, he couldn't, you see. In bed with me, he couldn't!'

'Probably too pissed,' said Richard.

'Well, of course he was! And afterwards it was OK. Except it wasn't OK after Hannah was born, but it was my fault, not his! I was so sore, you see.'

Richard took out his handkerchief and wiped the purple smudges off Rowan's cheeks. 'How did this guy say he knew?'

A shudder went through her. 'I got the impression that he and Saul – that they had – done it. Together.'

'I can't see Saul going in for buggery somehow,' remarked Richard.

'Don't use that word! It's revolting! I don't mind men doing it, but not Saul, please not Saul!'

Richard had never known jealousy before, had never looked at the monster head on. Suddenly he was devoured by it. How dare she prefer that bastard, who cared nothing for her, to him? Not for one minute did he believe Saul was gay, but for that minute he intended that Rowan should believe it. 'He's probably AC DC,' he said lightly. 'A lot of men are. Don't mind who they do it with as long as they can have a change now and then. Probably had a taste of it once or twice, then got into the habit when you weren't in the mood.'

Rowan took a long shuddering breath. 'How could he?' she said softly. 'I don't think I'd care so much if it was another woman, but with that horrible, horrible man!'

'It's all right, my love, it's all right!' He was mouthing her neck, whispering to her. 'God, but you're beautiful, don't ever think you're not. See how you turn me on. There's no need to keep it for him now, is there?'

He pushed her back on the bed and she lay there, letting the tears run from the corners of her eyes. He was undressing her and she let him, submitting to anything he wished to do. Kneeling astride her he stripped off tie, jacket and shirt, then he bent and took her nipple in his mouth in a kiss. 'Oh God. Oh God, no,' she said and pushed him away. Her arousal was suddenly so great that it hurt her to be touched, her whole nervous system tingled. He paused, watching her quizzically. Calming herself with long breaths, she reached up and unzipped his trousers.

Almost desperate, Richard threw off his clothes. He knelt across her and she closed her hand on him, unable to believe that this was happening. He began to peel off her skirt and pants. She wished Saul could see her and know what she was doing! In the midst of her sorrow she shuddered with true and unwavering desire. It had been wrong before, but now it was owed her. He began to kiss and stroke her but she didn't want that. 'Just do it,' she said, and lay back for him, her legs wide. 'Please, do it to me.'

The availability of that black-haired moist opening was too much for him. He got on top of her, his erection searching blindly for long seconds before it plunged home. Rowan clung to his shoulders, her eyes wide and staring. He suddenly felt her tight on him and realised she was in orgasm. He stayed still and waited, forcing himself to hold on. When he began to move again she started to cry out, in exquisite agony. In a room far away he could hear a telephone ringing. Her nails fastened to his buttocks, driving him into her. For a minute he wanted to hurt her as much as she hurt him. He reached the peak and hung there, painfully engorged. Then he flooded into her.

She lay spreadeagled beneath him, they were bonded together with sweat. Richard rolled away, still swollen but aching now as well. He staggered into the bathroom and splashed cold water on to his face. Staring at himself in the mirror, he saw his own shocked expression. For once his excitement had been entirely matched by its release; there was no sense of let-down, only of pressure discharged. Exhausted, he barely knew what he should do.

When he went back, Rowan was curled up on her side. 'Why did you have to wait until you were angry with him?' demanded Richard. 'You should have done it for me, only for me.'

'Yes. Yes, I should.' She rolled on to her back, sprawling wantonly. 'Do it again.'

Just watching her made him stiffen. He lay down beside her and said, 'You do the work.' Slowly and langourously, she straddled him. 'Saul liked this,' she said plaintively.

'To hell with Saul!' Richard caught her round the waist, held her and turned over while still inside. When she was beneath him he thrust at her angrily. 'It's me here, not him,' he hissed. 'Was it ever this good with him?'

Had it been? At the start she had waded through inexperience, there had been none of this wild abandonment. This was, in truth, the most sensual experience of her life. Her breath was coming in gasps. 'You're the best,' she gasped. 'He couldn't do this to me, only you! Just you.'

They stayed together all day, through the evening and on into the night. Usually Richard hated sleeping close to anyone. Now he wanted to die in that huge bed. He wrapped himself round her back, aware of sensations he hadn't even known existed. If only she would forget about that bastard, be his alone. She murmured in her sleep, she murmured, 'Richard?' He dozed, knowing that when he woke she would be there.

The morning was grey and wet. They lay watching the rain splatter the window and it seemed more than enough reason not to get up. 'I fell right down into heaven,' said Rowan lazily. 'I feel so good.'

Richard picked up the 'phone and rang room service for breakfast. While they waited he amused himself tracing the vertebrae so visible beneath Rowan's smooth skin. He buried his face against her. 'You're beautiful. So lovely, so beautiful. What we did was beautiful, wasn't it?'

'Yes. Yes, it was.' She sat up and put her hands against his chest, where the hair was wiry and curled beneath her fingers like coarse wool. 'Fifty-fours,' she thought absently, 'you'd never get it to spin well.'

'What am I going to do?' she asked suddenly.

'Eat your breakfast, read the papers, go to your appointments, come back and have me love you.' He kissed her fingers.

'Suppose that man was lying?'

'Oh, for Christ's sake!' Richard flung himself back down on the bed. 'Whether he was or he wasn't makes no damned difference! Saul's a bum, always has been. Your marriage has had it, Rowan. The sooner you leave him the better.'

'And then what?' She stared at him, challenging him.

'You come to me.'

He had said more than he had intended. Richard got out of bed and went to switch on the television. He lay, changing channels, aware that she was lying absolutely silent beside him.

Suddenly Rowan grabbed his hand. 'Go back a bit. I'm sure I saw – yes! Look, it's Andy!' Instinctively she picked up the sheet and hid herself behind it, in case Andy could see her.

He was standing in some casual breakfast television studio, his violin dangling from one hand. Although his hair was immaculately blow-dried he wore a pair of patched cord jeans and a lumberjack jumper, and over the top a purple waistcoat. He looked relaxed and very handsome.

'What are you going to play for us this morning, Andy?' demanded a ferociously charming girl. 'Something bright for this rainy day. Something to send us all skipping over those puddles.'

'Anything for you, Helene.' He grinned at her and then shot a disparaging wink at the camera. 'Try this for size everyone.' Putting his violin to his chin he began to rattle off gypsy music, weaving in threads from various popular classical tunes. As he played he strolled around in a small circle, grinning into the camera now and then, sometimes closing his eyes and swaying theatrically, as if he was becoming seriously engrossed in the beauty of the music.

'The fake,' muttered Rowan. 'Fake, fake, fake.'

When it came to an end, the presenters gave whoops of delight. 'Thanks a lot, Andy, that was great. Couldn't you just listen to that forever everyone? See you tomorrow, Mr. Wonderful.'

'Look forward to it.' Andy waved his bow and wandered out of camera range.

Helene said, 'Don't forget, everyone, that Andy Judge's fabulous record is available now. I'm certainly buying quite a few as Christmas presents. Now, Jim, what's the latest on the traffic this morning?'

Richard reached out and clicked the set into silence.

Neither Richard nor Rowan said anything for a minute. Then Richard said, 'He's certainly good at it. Very natural.'

'The Pied Piper of Hamelin goes to Hollywood!' exploded Rowan. 'If Mother hears him play like that she'll stab him through the heart with a hatpin. It's rubbish music. And the worst of it is – I encouraged him! I told him to dump his classical principles and get popular. And he has!'

'Then why don't you like it?'

She sniffed. 'I don't know. He played well, didn't he? He's got that, you see, he always did have it. The ability to make you listen, make you think the piece is better than it is. But it never came across in concerts somehow, or at least not properly. I think what I mind is – well, I thought he'd get well known and then go back to being straight. But that didn't look like it, did it?'

'Very profitable though if you ask me. Going to buy the record?'

She nodded. 'Do you think he's dumped the dreadful Astrid?'

'Looks to me as if he's well in with the chrome-plated Helene. Haven't you got an address for him anywhere?'

She shook her head. 'I didn't even know he was in the States.'

Ever since Andy left to go to college he'd been the same. He reserved the right to come back into their lives from time to time, but for himself he demanded privacy. She might have resented it had she not remembered how it used to be. Andy, trying to keep his head together when they all pulled him this way and that. Andy, trying to come to terms with needing James, hating him, his bossy sister taking sides, his father crumbling. Andy, trying not to mind that another man slept with his mother. Yes, he had a lot of reasons for wanting to keep them all at arm's length.

Breakfast arrived at last. Rowan slipped into the bathroom while it was delivered, and while she was there she showered and dressed.

'Where the hell are you going?' asked Richard. He was drinking coffee and scanning the morning papers.

'I've got an appointment in half an hour.'

'So have I. But I don't mind missing it.'

'I don't think I'd better, somehow. It's this franchise thing.'

He put down the paper. 'Look, love, you don't have to feel I'm pressurising you. But I meant what I said. This should be for keeps.'

She stood looking at him, lopsided with one shoe on and one shoe off. 'What about Hannah?'

'Well – she's got a nanny and so on. If she comes in the package, then OK.'

A wry smile crossed her face. She wandered about the suite, picking up things to be put in her bag: lipstick, tissues, a comb. 'You'd be horrified if I took you up on it. Don't worry, I won't.'

'Even if he did screw that queen?'

She hesitated. 'Even if. Probably. But I don't think he did.'

'I do.'

'No, you don't, you just want me to believe it.'

Richard blinked. It was the sort of sharply intuitive comment that surprised him about Rowan. Just when he had decided she always played straight, she headed for an acute and difficult angle. He picked up the newspaper again and flicked it open to the European pages while Rowan picked at a piece of toast and drank some coffee.

The telephone rang. Richard reached out a hand for it and then paused. Rowan grimaced and picked it up. 'Yes? Oh. Hello, Mother. Whatever time is it over there? Er – no, I'm sorry I don't know where Richard is. I may be able to contact him, though. I have seen him around.' She flapped at him hard as he made to take the receiver. 'I see. Yes. That's – that's dreadful. All right, Mother, I'll make sure I find him. And I'll be home tomorrow, I promise. Love to everyone. 'Bye.'

She hung up and stood with her hand still resting on the telephone.

'What is it?' asked Richard tensely. 'Tell me!'

'An accident. Bardsey Combers. An Asian got tangled up in one of the conveyor belts. Two men tried to rescue him and one fell into the scouring pans. Impaled on the spikes that push the wool through. He's dead, the others are in intensive care. Everyone's out on strike.'

'Shit, shit, shit!' Richard sat still for a moment. Then with a roar of rage he picked up the breakfast tray and hurled it across the room. Rowan screamed as coffee and toast cascaded everywhere.

'As if I didn't tell him!' raged Richard. 'As if I didn't warn him it would happen! I told him we'd have to modernise or someone would get killed and he said we couldn't afford it. Well, can we afford this, may I ask? We're likely to be prosecuted.'

'Mother didn't say anything about that,' said Rowan, nervously picking toast off the carpet.

'Why in God's name didn't he let me do something? Wanted me in the firm all right, but as sodding decoration! What am I doing here, picking up the pieces from the mess he made, wasting time in bed with you when I should be back there, sorting out that – that shit-house!' He paced around, stark naked.

'Are you going to ring?' asked Rowan.

'What? No. I'm getting on the first plane. He's made a balls of it for the last time. This is where he moves over and lets me do it.'

'He won't let you,' said Rowan. 'I knew he wouldn't in the first place.'

Richard turned on her a look of murderous determination. His eyes were clear as water. She flinched. It was the wolf taking off his woolly disguise.

'I would just like him to try and stand in my way,' murmured Richard. 'I would just love him to try.'

Chapter Forty-Three

The huge scouring pans of Bardsey Combers were like enormous bathtubs. The wool entered from a hopper at one end, an avalanche of stinking fibre, matted with dung and straw and grease. The pan itself was filled with constantly circulating water, black with dirt at the start and becoming cleaner and cleaner as the wool progressed on its watery way. Rollers dragged the wool from one pan to another, hooking it on nine-inch metal spikes to let it drop into the next, cleaner bath. It was a hell's kitchen, full of noise and steam and condensation. The men worked half-naked, clambering over the rollers to remove jammed wool, roaring at each other above the rumble of the driers. Nothing was wasted. When the wash water was changed, they piped the greasy sludge away to extract the lanolin. Yet from this maelstrom came soft, clean, sweet-smelling wool.

Richard stood staring at the silent monoliths all around him. Water was dripping somewhere, slow and insistent. Without the swirling clouds of steam the full squalor of the place was evident, torn plastic hanging from the roof, a broken control box held together with wire. Half the problems of the combing plant stemmed from the scouring. The ancient machines were too slow and unreliable. In a rush of demand the wool backed up here and could not be pushed through.

Blinking from lack of sleep, he turned to the man next to him. 'Let's see what happened then.'

The other man swallowed. He it was who had ripped off his white coat to try and staunch the blood, and had stood helpless while it turned red, then black, and the floor all around became slippy with gore. At the time he hadn't considered it but last night, in bed, it had come back to him again and again.

'He was clearing a blockage, sir,' he explained. 'On the belt that feeds the hopper. Some fool had left some twine on a bale and it had tangled in the belt. Wasn't tied up right, you see, he didn't spot it. Not that he's the brightest lad in the world. Well, you don't want that in there, do you?'

'Get on with it,' said Richard.

'Yes, sir. Shan's his name. The man that got caught in the belt. He screamed like, his leg was caught up. Someone pushed the emergency button, but he'd been dragged almost over the hopper. Two blokes ran up straight away to get him out, his leg was a terrible mess, terrible. Couldn't move him, he was caught up, you see. And the hopper wasn't stopped. Before anyone knew, the other two had fallen in. One went straight down on the wool and got pulled out. The other bloke made a grab for the edge of the hopper, missed and went right over. He hit the roller, you see. That one there.'

Richard stared at the huge spikes. He imagined what it must be like to be impaled on them, what it must be like to try and get someone off. 'You got him off, did you?' he asked.

'I helped, sir. We all did. Stuck right through him they did. And he was conscious.'

'I know, I know. No need to give me all the details.'

'Thought you wanted to know, sir. You can see why the men are upset, like.'

Richard resisted the temptation to curse him. 'How about the original casualty?'

'Got a great lump out of his calf. He'll be OK though, won't lose his leg. Bloody lucky.'

'It was his own negligence, though. The accident was entirely his responsibility.'

'The inspector said we should have guarded the belt. He shouldn't have been able to get there, you see.'

Richard saw, only too well. His father had known the safety precautions were substandard and had chosen to do nothing about it. God knows how long it would be before the men could be cajoled back to work, or before they could begin to scour again. There would be claims too, for compensation, and prosecutions for negligence. The accident had been all over the papers. The local daily paper was using it to begin a campaign on factory safety.

He walked swiftly out of the factory and got into the Maserati. There was a small demonstration at the gate, a group of workers with placards reading 'We don't have to die for money' and 'Stop Killing Us'. Hostile faces, both brown and white, in shabby anoraks. He in his Maserati, they in their thin shoes. What possessed a man to put up with working in such a place, he wondered? He couldn't imagine a world of so little opportunity.

His father's car was in its spot in the office car park, the Mercedes. Richard parked next to it and strode past the doorman, ignoring his salute. Too impatient for the lift he went up the stairs two at a time, barged past his father's secretary and into the office.

James looked up, startled, from the papers he had been studying.

'Right,' said Richard menacingly. 'I've come to talk to you.'

'So I see,' said James. He took off the reading glasses he had lately been forced to wear and tossed them on the papers in front of him. 'Never here when you're wanted, are you?'

'It wasn't my idea to go to the States, if you remember. I've been to the combing plant. All we can do is grovel, pay up and modernise. And we've got to do it now, put out a public statement at once. If we co-operate with the factory inspectorate, they might not slam us in court.'

'You're bloody hopeful, aren't you? I'd rather sack the workforce and close down.'

Richard blinked. 'Are you serious? The shareholders would crucify you!'

'Rather that than be held to ransom by a load of lazy fools! The man should never have been on the damned conveyor! I'm not going to give in to them.'

Richard paused for a moment. His father was rattled, perhaps for the first time in his life. He hadn't been the same since Nicholas, of course. 'Time you had a holiday, Dad,' he said.

'Are you trying to tell me I'm past it?' James got to his feet, his hair flopping over his face, glaring at his son. 'If you are trying to push me on to the rubbish heap, then I think you're about twenty years too early! I'm damned if I'll stand here and let you – '

'Have you spoken to the bank?' interrupted Richard. His father's mouth worked.

'Well,' said James at last. 'I see you feel you are in rather a strong position.'

'If we don't get a recovery plan started we are going down the tubes.' Richard strove for reason. 'You've made this firm what it is. Without you there wouldn't be a Bardsey Textiles. But we must, absolutely *must,* sort ourselves out! We can't clothe the looms, we haven't in months! OK, we lost some big customers, but we've got to get back in there. Design, innovation, energy. We've been standing still, and in textiles it may look like you're staying in the same place but it's amazing how fast the scenery changes. We're in big trouble.'

'And you want me out,' retorted James.

'Not especially. I just want me in.'

'Is there a difference?'

The two men stared at each other.

'What if I don't move over?' asked James.

Richard shrugged. 'I'll quit. You know what that could do to confidence – even the boss's son doesn't like it.'

'I could say the crisis is all your fault.'

'Don't think I'm too scrupulous to go to the papers!'

James drew in his breath angrily. Suddenly he burst out, 'God damn it, it *is* your fault! You didn't bring anything to this firm, you've been an expensive luxury! All right, see what you can do. I warn you, if I can't turn it round, you haven't a cat in hell's chance! Not a chance in hell!'

He picked up his reading glasses, made as if to put them in his pocket and then snapped them between his hands. He threw the mangled pieces on the floor at Richard's feet, and with a sweep of his arm cleared the desk. An inkpot rolled on to the carpet, leaving a trail of dark blue.

'You never were any bloody use,' said James. His voice shook, almost with tears. Richard walked to James's chair and sat down.

When James got home, Diana was in the conservatory. He went to find her, which was in itself unusual. He didn't normally concern himself with her whereabouts. She was tending pot plants, wearing rubber gloves and ladling compost from a bag.

'Guess what's happened,' said James ironically.

'I can't. Not another accident?'

'Depends on the way you look at it. He's kicked me out. Richard's kicked me out.'

She put down her trowel and stared at him. 'That's impossible. He couldn't do anything unless you let him.'

He put his hands in his pockets and sat on a corner of the table, careless of the compost on his suit. 'Right prick he's turned into. Right lump of shit.'

'Don't be so vulgar, James!'

'"Don't be so vulgar, James!"' he mimicked her. 'Doesn't matter what you do so long as you do it tastefully, is that it? I used to love your taste, I actually thought it was important. Look what you've brought me. A mausoleum of a home, near bankruptcy, and a son who's prepared to kick me into the grave! He wouldn't have done it if it wasn't for you. You turned him against me.'

Diana turned her head away, her cheeks scalded by sudden tears. 'You don't need to blame me for everything,' she said thickly. 'I know I've made mistakes, some I've regretted over and over again. It wasn't all my doing! I've tried so hard, James, I've tried so hard to make up.'

He got up and went over to a tall plant standing in a huge terracotta pot. He took part of the stem in his hands, cradling it. 'He wasn't mine, was he?' he said.

Diana caught her breath. Was there any point in lying now? She put her gloved hands together, almost in prayer. 'I thought he was,' she said softly. 'There was only such a slight chance he wasn't. It was only the once, you see. And he was yours, really. Nobody else loved him as a father should.'

'You didn't care how much of a fool you made of me.'

'Don't be so bloody stupid! You need never have known. And if you minded that much, why in God's name didn't you let me get rid of him?'

He swung round on her. 'Would you have rather that? Never having had Nick at all? What about never having done it, what about some kind of fidelity?'

She almost sneered at him. 'For you to say that is downright obscene.'

Now that it was at last admitted they experienced relief. Fighting on seemed irrelevant, meaningless, they had done so much of it in the past months. Diana said, 'Will you let Richard push you out?'

James considered. 'I'll have to, for now. I've let things slide so badly these last months. I could do with a rest, perhaps. We could have a holiday. See how things look later on.'

'That's a good idea.'

All of a sudden, James put out his hand. Diana had to pull off her glove, it took seconds. She clutched at him awkwardly. 'He was such a lovely boy,' she whispered.

'He was, wasn't he? He used to laugh when he saw me,

always. Waving his little hands and laughing.'

'You see. It didn't matter, that silliness. Did it?'

For the very first time James wondered if, incredibly, it did not.

That night Richard did not return to his chilly flat until well after nine. He was hungry but there was little to eat except baked beans. He heated some up on the stove, light-headed with weariness and a strange sort of exhilaration. At last, at last! It was as if after years and years of apprenticeship he was now beginning his life.

He thought of Bardsey's, he thought of Rowan. Two twin strands making up the incomparable whole, neither his with any certainty, yet. To keep Bardsey's he had to prove himself; to keep Rowan he had to persist. She had had such a battering from life, poor love. If she wasn't as tough as they come she'd have gone under. And yet, and yet – she was so soft in love, so sweet and tender and young. He laughed at himself. All these years, all that experience, and he was hopelessly, endlessly in love.

The beans were ready. He stirred them neatly with a fork and tipped them on to a plate, putting the pan into the sink for the daily to wash. Before he ate he found pen and paper and settled down to eat and make notes. The press release was done, it should be in every paper that mattered in the morning, and there was a meeting for the combing plant workers at nine. At ten the finance director was coming in, at eleven there was a board meeting, and lunch was with the bank. The only hope, he was certain, was to strip out and sell off anything and everything peripheral to the main organisation. Rowan must take the dye-house. She needed it, she could certainly afford it, and afterwards, when she was with him, she could rent it back to him on favourable terms. A good link, Bardsey's and Judge's. He couldn't fault the old man's judgement there, he'd seen it years ago.

And that was as much as he intended to do tonight. He got

up, slung his plate in the sink too and went into the sitting room to pour himself a small glass of single malt. He reflected on alcoholism. There was something lacking about a man who used this to blank out life, he decided. Perhaps Saul was queer after all, and putting it another way, he was certainly odd. Tremendous potential and not enough grit somehow. James had walked all over him all his life, but all he had done was escape. Would it have taken much for Saul to be where Richard was now, only years earlier? Surely he could have held James to ransom. He just wasn't that sort of guy.

If Rowan was here now, what would they do? Talk, play music, relax together after a hard day. This flat was a cold place, it lacked heart, as he had lacked heart. He hadn't known how much a man could need someone else, a special someone, someone who understood. She was what he had needed all his life. Rowan.

Chapter Forty-Four

On the plane home Rowan sat in silence next to an equally taciturn businessman. The luggage rack was stuffed with presents; a leather case for Saul complete with matching calculator and pocket currency exchanger, and a new desk diary tooled and embossed to within an inch of its life. She was going to give them to him first and question him second, and she wasn't going to believe all that he said either. If he knew that she knew, he might stop – if he had ever started. Suppose he was outraged that she had suspected him even for a second? And suppose even the outrage was a defence? The whole thing was impossible, unbelievable and ridiculous. But wives always thought that, didn't they?

For Hannah she had bought a squashy doll that was programmed to say, 'Hello, Hannah, you're my friend', and an American policeman on wheels.When his hat was depressed he whizzed about making shooting noises. She wondered how many of the goodies on the plane had been bought for much the same reasons as hers.

Where was he now? In Bardsey's glossy offices or amongst the steamy scouring pans of the combing plant? Was he thinking of her? She let her mind dwell on that night, on all the shocking and shameful things they had done. He said she was beautiful and when she was with him she believed it, she loved herself. It was such a relief to be with a man who was in control of himself, instead of at the mercy of a genie in a bottle.

At Heathrow she caught the shuttle to Leeds, and took a taxi home. Jetlag was catching up with her. There was cottonwool between her ears and lead weights on her tongue, anything she had to say fell out in lumps. At least she wouldn't have to talk to Saul until tomorrow, when she would have her wits about her. 'Don't think about it,' she told herself. 'If I pretend to myself it didn't happen, I can pretend to him.' Besides, Richard was right. Saul had committed far greater crimes.

At Valley House she tried to pay off the driver in dollars and eventually wrote him a cheque. 'Can see you don't travel much,' he remarked, and Rowan felt quite offended. Her weary air of what she thought to be cosmopolitan sophistication had been the only thing holding her up. She blundered into the house, calling, 'Hannah! Barbara! It's me!'

They were in the kitchen. The room was warm and bright, there were toys scattered on the floor. There was the smell of coffee. For the first time in years Rowan felt a sense of home, and it had nothing to do with the house, nothing at all. It had all to do with the little squashed figure in denim dungarees that tugged at her heart, and always would. She looked into Hannah's blurred face and was choked by love. She watched the slow dawning of delighted recognition and she wept. Hannah put her palms against the tears and looked at them.

'Mummy's not sad,' said Rowan hastily. 'I'm just so glad to see you, Hannah.'

The baby peered anxiously over her shoulder. 'Dad,' she demanded. 'Dad.'

'She's been missing him a lot,' said Barbara matter-of-factly. 'I thought perhaps she should visit.'

'Not in there,' said Rowan. 'She might never understand, she might think he'd been in prison or something. And actually there isn't much difference.' She thought of Saul suffering his bleak punishment, while she, she –

'There's been a problem,' said Barbara. 'There's been a strike.'

'I know, at Bardsey's.'

'Actually, it was here.'

'Good God!' Rowan swung round on her, peering over Hannah's thin hair.

'At the mill, you mean? At Judge's?'

Barbara nodded. 'They won't work under him, you see. Mohammed.'

Rowan was speechless for a second. Her mouth opened and closed. 'What's happened then?' she asked at last.

'I think he's gone home. They're working again today at any rate.'

Silently Rowan handed Hannah over and went out. In the garden two men were planting bulbs but she ignored them. Nowadays things happened in her world that she knew nothing about, it gave her an odd feeling of helplessness. 'It's all out of control,' she thought, 'I can't cope with it all.' And the cotton wool inside her head seemed to smother even that simple thought.

But in the mill everything seemed normal. One of the looms was standing idle and the weaver was messing about, but the mere sight of her galvanised him into action. She prowled around, letting the noise wash into her, seeing the cloth she had designed and costed born inch by inch into the world. No one met her eye.

Suddenly she started punching stop buttons. The looms shuddered to a halt, one after the other, and the message ran round the shed until at last everything was quiet. People rubbed their hands down their clothes and took off their ear defenders. They all looked guilty as hell.

'Suppose someone tells me what's been going on?' said Rowan loudly. 'Where's Mr. Shafir?'

There was a long pause. Eventually one of the younger men said, 'He's gone home. Seemed best, like.'

'Who for, may I ask? Well?'

'For all of us,' said one of the older men. 'It weren't our fault, Miss Rowan. He didn't understand.'

Rowan looked down at his feet in their big worn shoes. On

Saturday nights he would wear black patent leather lace-ups and when each pair got tatty they were relegated to the mill. This man must have seen out a dozen pairs of shoes in her service.

'You realise we could have the Race Relations Board on us?' she remarked. 'And that's not to mention the trouble with my sister. She owns a sizable share of this company.'

'That's as may be. We couldn't be doing with him.'

'I suggest that a few of you come up to my office at once and explain.' She turned on her heel and went out. Behind her, one by one, looms began to clatter into action once again.

The office was cold, and there was a pile of opened letters on her desk 'Have you been in touch with my husband?' she asked Frances.

'I didn't think, under the circumstances –' said the woman, and Rowan snapped, 'You should have! This was important. And someone should have told me.'

Four men came in. Rowan waved them to chairs and switched on the fan heater. 'Well?' she asked, and forced her eyes to open wide enough to look at them. She would have given anything to sink into sleep, anything.

'We couldn't understand him,' said one. 'He didn't understand Judge's,' said another. 'He's been in some rubbish place where they don't care what it comes out like!'

'And he was trying to bring his bloody friends in! One vacancy we had, and there's a flood of bloody ethnics, some of them don't speak a word of bleeding English! Before you know where we were, we wouldn't have no summer holidays. We'd be closing down for bleeding Ramadan!

'He don't know how to treat Englishmen, and that's a fact, Miss Rowan. Tret like bloody slaves, we were! There was no standing for it, specially with everyone away. We're sorry it happened like this and we've made up some of the hours, but we're not having a bleeding Paki lording it over us!'

'They've taken over half Bradford as it is! When's it going to stop, that's what I want to know?'

Rowan's patience snapped. 'Oh, don't go on!' she begged. 'All right, I shouldn't have started him while I was away but nothing else seems very important. He speaks very good English, and if you couldn't understand, then you would in time.'

'Why should we have to try?' demanded one. 'It's our mill, Miss Rowan. We was here first.'

'As far as I'm concerned, it's *my* mill! I'll employ who I like. And if he didn't understand how we work then he soon would have! Couldn't you give it just a few weeks? I'm back now, I can help him settle in.'

'No!'

She sighed, feeling the cotton wool in her head turn to barbed wire. 'What was the problem with his attitude then?' she demanded. 'You might as well tell me everything. Was he rude?'

One of the men grimaced. 'To give him his due, I don't think he meant to be. He was nervous like, couldn't give an order straight. It was all, "Get away to your lunch, my man, and let's have no messing. I'm in charge!" Sounds funny now but down there it gets your goat. You see, Miss Rowan, he's just different. And they've got enough of our country, they don't need our jobs as well.'

A sharp buzz of anger at the narrowness of their view made her clench her teeth. They were a tribe, throwing stones at neighbours, convincing themselves that they were the real people, the only people who mattered. But anger was no use to her. She needed tact, gentleness.

'If it was just him,' she said softly, 'you'd get used to him, and he would to you. I promise there won't be any more, at least not without a clear decision from me, and a clear explanation why. I'm not going to throw you out of work in their favour, that's definite.'

'You won't have any choice! Once the Council finds out

we're against them, and he'd be the first to shout, you'll have to have them in. There'll be ten black faces for every job, and up in court if you don't pick one. I don't mind a curry once in a while but I'm damned if I'll have it served up in the bloody canteen every sodding day!'

'Now you're being ridiculous.' She put her hand to her head, shutting her eyes for a second. When she opened them again she saw four stubborn, closed faces. In a lot of ways, she thought, they were right. When different people came in there was no way things could stay the same. She was the one with the liberal principles,but they were the ones who had to make the adjustments. Stupidly she had put everyone into an impossible position.

She moved to the door, indicating that the meeting was over. 'I'll have to talk to Mr. Shafir,' she said distantly. 'And to my husband. I'll let you know what we decide.'

They filed out past her but the last man stopped. He said, 'We want to apologise for having an upset while you was away, Miss Rowan. You've done a lot for us, and for Judge's. The men wanted me to say they wouldn't have let you down if it wasn't important.'

She found her eyes pricking with sudden tears. She nodded, swallowed, and to her embarrassment found her cheeks wet. 'It's just jetlag,' she muttered, scrubbing at them angrily. 'Get on with you.'

She had not been back at the house more than ten minutes when there was a furious hammering on the door. Sally burst in, followed, unhappily, by Mohammed.

'How did you know I was back?' asked Rowan, who had been about to slide off to bed.

Sally, abundantly feminine in a red and gold sari, and hugely pregnant, paused for a moment. 'What? Oh, I told Frances to ring me as soon as you arrived. I take it you've sacked them?'

'Who?' Rowan was playing for time, although an aeon wouldn't be enough to restore her, she felt.

'You know perfectly well. Since you haven't, then I insist that you should. They deliberately flouted Mohammed's authority. I won't stand for it, I'm warning you, Rowan!' She stood, rigid with determination. Against her outrage, Rowan felt totally inadequate.

'What happened, Mohammed?' she yawned. 'Was there one special incident?'

He sniffed. He had a very straight nose, an uncompromising arrow striking down to his lips. She thought distractedly that he would be well suited to leading a warrior band, let alone a bunch of stroppy weavers. 'There were many incidents,' he said distantly. 'It is all the same with these uneducated men. It is race, class, everything. They don't work well, Rowan, and they did not like to be told!'

Rowan cleared her throat. 'I thought they were pretty good on the whole. What I really wanted was for someone to supervise the flow of work through the shed, because that is so important. I didn't need fifty per cent more effort or anything. Perhaps it was my fault. I didn't make myself clear.'

'They don't work hard enough,' said Mohammed.

'Perhaps not by your standards, but they do by ours. Look, I know the sort of conditions your people have to put up with. Endless shifts, the worst jobs and terrible pressure. That isn't what we're about in Judge's. Actually, for our sort of mill I'm not very generous. For your sort of mill, I imagine it looks terribly lax.'

Mohammed nodded. 'I think there should be many changes. They have far too many unearned privileges. The crêche, it is subsidised, a most expensive thing. The canteen food, again it is cheap though terrible quality. I bring my own, and even that is resented! There is smoking, and drinking on Fridays, and time spent in the lavatories that should be spent working. I did nothing that was not justified, even in this mill.'

Sally said, 'I think it's most fortunate that Mohammed came and saw what was going on, Rowan. They've been taking you for a ride and you knew nothing at all about it.'

Rowan resisted the temptation to drop her head in her hands and groan. 'But it's about getting the work out on time!' she wailed. 'That's my yardstick, that's what counts! I don't care how many fags they smoke in the loo if they get the cloth made, and made well. These people take a pride in their work, it's up to them to organise their day. Oh God! How on earth am I going to unscramble this?'

Sally moved with unaccustomed dignity to a chair and sat down. 'You can start by supporting Mohammed in his job,' she declared. 'I don't need to remind you that James has a standing offer in for my shares.'

'He couldn't afford them at the moment,' said Rowan absently. 'Look, we'll talk again tomorrow. I've got a splitting headache and I want to see Saul. He'll know what to do.'

'Oh, don't give me that!' flared Sally. 'The only thing he's any good at is getting a drink out of licensing hours. You don't have to pretend he's some sort of prop and support.'

'Sally, that is most rude to your sister,' rebuked Mohammed.

Words trembled visibly on Sally's lips. She and Mohammed exchanged fulminating glances and Rowan realised Mohammed had not intended that Sally should start making threats. He was furious with her.

'I've got to go to bed,' said Rowan miserably. 'I can't stand any more of this.'

'We are going home, Sally,' said Mohammed. 'You are not well.'

'I'm perfectly well,' muttered Sally.

She did indeed look superb. Wisps of blonde hair fell down from her bun and her pregnancy made her stand with her head held regally back to balance her belly. She was flushed with anger, and little beads of sweat stood out on her forehead.

'How long to the baby?' asked Rowan, ushering them out.

'Three weeks or so. Mother's looking forward to it enormously.'

'Is she? I thought she was dreading it!' Rowan couldn't help herself and Sally grimaced patiently. 'Not our mother. Mother. Mrs. Shafir.'

'Oh.' The thought of delivering one's infant direct into the hands of one's mother-in-law turned Rowan's stomach.

'She will help Sally with the baby,' said Mohammed.

Rowan had the sense that he was bored with the conversation, with women in general. It was only his courtesy that allowed him to put up with this feminine chit chat. He wanted Rowan to make a decision, take a firm stand! Although she wanted desperately to go to bed, she said, 'What do you do in the evening then? Do you go out?'

'Mohammed does sometimes,' said Sally thinly. 'I stay with Mother. And Fadeema.'

'Oh. I see.'

When they had gone, Rowan went into the bedroom. She dropped her clothes in a trail from door to bed and fell between the sheets, moaning to herself. Tomorrow she would be able to cope with this, tomorrow she would know what she ought to do. She stretched out her arms, feeling the delicious chill of the sheets against her skin, letting a brief shudder remind her – of what? Rowan slept.

In the car, going home, Mohammed said: 'I will not have you saying these things, Sally! Threatening your sister, demanding things!'

'Somebody had to say it. Rowan never does what she doesn't want if she can get away with it. She just digs her heels in, forever.'

'And so do you. It's time you learned to do as you are told, to obey your husband! Without that, what is there for our children? It is the basis of everything.'

Sally said stiffly, 'I know. I'm sorry. But she made me so angry!'

'Please. Allow me the anger. I know what is best.'

Sally shifted uncomfortably in her seat. 'Are you all right?' asked Mohammed.

'Backache. I don't know – I do feel odd, Mohammed.'

'We shall be home soon.'

They drove rapidly through the dark streets, past the open shops of the Asian quarter with their sacks of beans and their exotic displays of vegetables, set amidst peeling plaster and crumbling brick. By the time they reached the house, Sally was in tears. 'I shall lose the baby,' she whispered. 'It's too early.'

Mohammed leaped from the car and rushed into the house. Fadeema came out, followed by Mrs. Shafir, elbowing people aside to get to Sally. She hauled the girl out of the car and hustled her into the house. 'We shall call an ambulance,' said Fadeema calmly, while Mrs. Shafir berated her daughter-in-law for endangering her child.

The women laid her on the sofa and sent the men out. Mrs. Shafir put expert hands on Sally's belly and said something to Fadeema.

'What was that?' demanded Sally.

'She says you're having twins. Did they say at the hospital? They must have done a scan.'

Sally said nothing. Fadeema caught her shoulders. 'Have you not been going, Sally? You did go, didn't you?'

The girl shook her head. 'They were unkind. They stared at me. All the other women, Asian, white, they all stared. I was different, you see. A white girl in a sari.'

'Yes. I see.'

Fadeema got up and paced around the room. There was the sound of the ambulance siren wailing its way into the street and the men knocked on the door and yelled that it was coming. When they went out, there were faces at every door and window, women clustered around wishing the family good luck. In the ambulance Mohammed was nowhere to be seen. At Sally's side sat his mother and Fadeema.

It seemed to epitomise what had happened to her. Lying there, and again in her hospital bed, Sally kept thinking that her life was a series of rooms. In her childhood she had lived in a huge friendly room, thronged with people. One by one, unaccountably, they had all left. The room had grown cold, terribly cold, she had feared she would freeze to death inside it. But Mohammed had come in to warm her, he had taken her in his arms and lent her the heat of his body. He had taken her from that room to another, which was his own and was to be hers. Then, suddenly, he had pushed her through to another room, entirely filled with women. He visited her often, but he did not live there. He lived apart from her, in the room she had just left. She lived as the women lived, and now they were all that there was to help her.

Her mother-in-law smoothed her hair and continually twitched the blankets down to hide her modesty when the doctor came in. Fadeema sat beside her, cool and intelligent, explaining what was happening. Sally thought she wanted Mohammed but when he did come he was so clearly uncomfortable and so clearly unnecessary that she didn't mind him going. The three women were together, about their own business. It was something Sally found she could accept.

Six hours later she gave birth to twins, a boy and a girl. They were to be called Ali and Shameena.

Chapter Forty-Five

Saul stood at the window and watched his wife get out of her car, glance up and then walk determinedly towards the building. His heart gave a lurch of expectation. How lovely she looked, tall and bright and beautiful. He hadn't known how much he could miss her, a little more each day, a little more each night. It was because he was off the booze, of course. Normally he quenched emotions with a slug of something. He wished that he could now. Oh God, how he wished it!

She smiled when she saw him, her anxious look momentarily gone. 'Hi,' she said breathily. 'Hi, Hi, Hi.'

He stumped across to her. His plaster cast had been reduced by half in the last week and he was almost mobile again. When he took her in his arms there was an ever so slight resistance. 'I missed you,' he croaked, knowing that he was going to betray himself and hating himself for it. Was this what they wanted, all these do-gooders, for him to go around sobbing in public, embarrassing everyone?

'It wasn't so long, was it? You look well. Really well.'

Perhaps by external standards he did. The mirror told him that he looked years younger. He had lost weight, his hair shone, his skin no longer held that doughy, bloated look. Nobody saw beyond that, not even Rowan. Especially not Rowan.

They repaired to a private alcove. He couldn't help himself holding her hand, stroking it. 'Good trip?' he asked, desperately trying to keep himself from the edge.

She nodded, withdrawing her hand to show him the things she had bought. Like a mother, he thought, like a prison visitor. But he dutifully admired the extravagant gifts, none of which he wanted or needed or cared about. In here, in this desperate, terrible place, he was going mad! And she brought him toys to play with. He put down the case and blurted, 'I can't stand it in here. I've got to get out!'

'It is a bit hot.' Rowan chose to misunderstand him. She helped him up and they went out into the garden. Saul stumped round the paths at a furious pace.

'Did I tell you about Mohammed?' said Rowan jerkily, almost running to keep up. 'I started him as a manager in the weaving shed and all the men went on strike. They won't have him back and I don't know what to do. By the way, Sally's had twins.'

It seemed to Saul a string of total irrelevancies. 'What's that got to do with anything? What's that got to do with me?'

Rowan stopped and after a few more strides he did too. 'I wanted your advice,' she said helplessly.

He shrugged. 'Send two rattles.'

Her mouth twisted in pain and she linked her fingers together, forcing herself not to say the bitter and hurtful things that rose to her lips. Forming her words carefully, she said, 'I went to see Marcus Arnaud.'

A brief flicker of interest. 'The dear boy. Actually, he's a nice guy. You know he's gay, don't you?'

'Yes,' she said thinly. She swallowed. 'He said you were, too.'

'Yes. He would.'

She couldn't believe it. Her mouth worked. 'But – not with him! You couldn't!'

Some vague sense of her distress penetrated his self-absorption. 'What? Oh, don't be stupid! I put my foot in it with him the first time we met. He made a pass at me. So, I pretended I was gay but unavailable, saved a lot of hassle and embarrassment.'

'It didn't save *me* any embarrassment! When I went there

and said I was your wife, he took me to one side and told me I was married to a queer! I didn't know what to believe!'

'If I may say so, you look remarkably fit on it.'

Total disinterest. He neither knew nor cared what she had suffered. 'You don't give a damn, do you?' she said at last. 'You don't want to hear about America, or Sally, or my little problems. You're in here being waited on hand and foot, nothing to think about but whether to have a bath now or in an hour, and out there I've got a labour crisis and my sister threatening to sell her shares and this American thing and Richard and everything!'

'What about Richard?' asked Saul.

And what about him? She was no liar, and Saul was an expert at seeing what you least wished to reveal. 'Nothing,' she said offhandedly. 'He was in America, sniffing around my deal. It's Mohammed that's the real problem.'

'What possessed you to set him on in the first place? Didn't you think this would happen?'

'No. No, I didn't. He wanted the job, and Sally wanted him to have it, and I didn't think I had the right to refuse.'

'How very diffident of you.'

Saul moved away across the grass and sat down on a wet seat under a tree that was shedding its leaves. Rowan sat beside him, discounting the cost of having her pale green coat cleaned. He reached for her hand and gripped it again, but she couldn't return the pressure. She felt stiff with lies and the need for lies, and furiously angry. She thought he must be able to feel the residue of heat in her veins. 'What am I going to do?' she asked in clipped tones.

Saul sighed. 'Put him in the office. Find him a job, make him a job. If you try and keep him as shed manager at best they'll walk out, at worst they'll string him up. Didn't you see *Zulu*? The men at Judge's think they're at Rorke's Drift, holding out against the invading hordes. At least in the office he won't have much contact with them.'

'But he'll have contact with our suppliers, and our

customers. They can't be called models of tolerance either. Suppose he upsets them?'

'So what? About time someone upset the status quo. We can afford it. Do everyone the world of good to have people stepping out of their boxes for once. In ten years' time you might be able to get away with an Asian manager. We have to start somewhere, but God, you can be so clumsy sometimes.'

She withdrew her hand. 'I don't recall that you were in any state to help with the decision at the time. But then you never are in any state, are you? If you're not drunk then you want congratulations for being sober, and sympathy for having to stay that way, and support, and consideration, everything! When do I get some support and consideration? When?'

Both their minds swung back to when Hannah was born. Rowan ducked her head. 'That was stupid of me, I'm sorry. It's jetlag, it takes days to wear off. I didn't mean to sound so –'

'Why don't you go, Rowan? We're not doing any good here, just tearing lumps off each other. Give my regards to Sally. By the way, what colour are they?'

She tried to smile. 'A sort of delicious biscuit. And they're all crumpled and so tiny. They're in the nursery, and when I went Mrs. Shafir was sitting by them on sentry duty. She isn't nearly so fierce as Sally describes. She's small and dignified and she doesn't speak a word of English.'

He wasn't listening. She followed his eyes and saw him gazing out across a ploughed field, to the rising hills beyond. A flock of small birds rose from the field and settled again, then rose and flew in a ragged trail off into the grey distance. She didn't say goodbye. She picked up her bag and walked quickly back, her heels clicking on the path. When she looked at him to wave he was still watching the birds, watching them fly away.

* * *

Depression settled on her like a blanket. She had to go home and talk to people, all of whom would ask well-meaning questions about Saul. She should have married Joe Partridge, she thought, and together they would have built an empire. He was a simple man, wanting simple things, and Saul was the most difficult and complex person she knew. Strange that she hadn't seen any of that when she met him, but then, she had been too young to know much. Now, when she knew what she wanted, she couldn't have it!

She thought of Richard. She conjured up a picture of his face, of how he looked when he was angry, happy, loving her. What did she really owe Saul? Was she honestly intending to spend her life shackled to someone who almost seemed to hate her? Sometimes she hated him, sometimes she wanted to kill him for embarrassing her, hurting her, pointing up every single one of her inadequacies. It seemed a downward spiral into hell.

Back in her office she tried to settle down to work. Her brain fizzed restlessly. Tonight she would go and see Sally and tell her that Mohammed was to come into the offices. It was a capitulation but if Sally was upset she would offer to buy them a little house somewhere, as a gesture of good faith. The firm was awash with money at the moment, the problem was in deciding what to do with it. The dye-house, of course – unless Bardsey's was truly up for sale. She pondered the question. Bardsey's was stuffed full of little goodies that she wouldn't mind in her shopping bag.

The 'phone rang. She picked it up absently, then felt every muscle in her body go rigid. 'It's me,' said Richard.

'Hello me,' she said throatily. 'How are you?'

'Missing you. Needing you. Come to my flat, tonight.'

'I – I can't. I shouldn't. Anyway, I've got to go and see Sally. She's had twins.'

'Christ! Give her my congratulations and come along afterwards.'

'Someone might see me.'

'Wear dark glasses. Darling girl. Darling, darling girl, I can't wait!'

She giggled. 'Stop it. All right, I'll come, just this once. About nine.'

'Great.' He sounded like a snooker player who has potted his last ball. Briskly, he added, 'Must be going, lots to do. See you at nine.'

She grimaced as she replaced the receiver. Presumably on his list of tasks for the day appeared the item 'Rowan – entice to bed'. It was now ticked as completed. But then, he was a thorough man, doing things thoroughly. He knew what he wanted and he was out to get it. The thing was, so was she.

Sally's strained face relaxed only slightly when Rowan appeared at her bedside that evening. The girl was wearing a pink bedjacket, her hair cascading prettily about her shoulders. Seated firmly on one side was Mrs. Shafir, on the other Fadeema and the younger sister. At Rowan's arrival Fadeema got up and tried to persuade Mrs. Shafir to leave, but only after much furious muttering and glaring did she do so.

'Where's Mohammed?' asked Rowan when they were alone.

Sally hunched a shoulder. 'I don't know. He came for about five minutes and said he had to go. He wanted children but now he's not much interested.'

'He will be when they're home,' soothed Rowan.

'If Mother gives either of us a look-in!'

Rowan sat down and cleared her throat. 'I had a talk with Saul,' she began. 'We're going to put Mohammed in the offices. And as a gesture to both of you, I want to buy you a house. The firm will be buying it, of course, but to all intents and purposes it's yours. Choose what you like.'

Her sister's blue eyes fixed on her and beneath that clear gaze Rowan wilted. 'Paying us off. I see.'

'I can't swing it with the workers,' explained Rowan earnestly. 'I would if I could. But if I push it we'll have one of those pointless race rows, with the television cameras in and everyone dredging up their nastiest prejudices, and in the end everyone hating each other more than they did in the first place. There are no winners over these things.'

'But we're certainly the losers.'

'That's rubbish.'

They sat in silence. At length Sally said, 'I'll see what Mohammed says.'

'Good,' said Rowan, glancing at her watch. 'By the way, how are the babies?'

'Very well, I think. Mother's always here. When I go to see them I have to fight my way past her to the incubator.'

'Oh God. But there are two of them. You're going to need help.'

'She thinks Europeans have no idea how to care for children. It's going to be hell.'

Rowan lost her temper. 'Sally, all you have to do is stand up to Mohammed. Get him to move into a house of your own, there's no excuse for this sort of doormat mentality! He might think it's a good idea for wives but I think it's diabolical. And so, in your heart, do you.'

'Do I?' If Sally had ever known exactly what she thought she couldn't remember it now. 'You're so much more independent than me,' she complained. 'I wouldn't mind living there at all if I got on better with Mother. She hates me! She thinks I've made him abandon his culture, she's furious about this job with you.'

Rowan glanced at her watch again and began to gather her things.

'You're not going already, are you?' demanded Sally. 'I wanted to talk.'

'Yes, but Barbara wants to go out – Hannah – I have to go. Back tomorrow, love.' She bent and kissed her sister, rushing away before more could be said. Left alone, without visitors, without her babies, Sally began to pleat the sheet of her bed.

Never had Rowan felt so guilty. The very shadows seemed to harbour friends and acquaintances, all watching her park the car and sneak furtively away. A couple passed her, she dared not look to see if she knew them. She sneaked into the block of flats and crept up the stairs.

When Richard opened the door she fell inside. 'Hide me, quick! I'm sure someone saw me.'

'What if they did?' Richard put his hands under her coat and held her thin, warm body. 'We've got nothing to be ashamed of.'

She relaxed against him, putting her arms round his neck and opening her lips for his kiss. His tongue executed a slow and sensual dance around her mouth, she groaned with pleasure. 'You're so good at this,' she murmured. 'Did you learn it all?'

'I learned what to do, yes. But you taught me why I should do it. Come to bed, delicious girl.'

In bed they revelled in each other. He taught her how to prolong his pleasure, and at the same time made her weak with delight. In the end she begged him to stop. 'I can't take any more. There's nothing left in me.'

Richard rolled away. He was feeling fit, discharging all the adrenaline of the day. Naturally virile, he wanted her again, but later would do. He lay back on the pillow and looked at her.

'How was Saul?'

She put her hands over her eyes. 'Dreadful. The worst. That thing about Arnaud was just stupid, but he didn't care, you see, he didn't mind what I might have thought – he's so wrapped up in himself. No room for anyone but him, it seems to me.'

'He'll be back on the booze the moment he gets out. You know that, don't you?'

'Probably.' She changed the subject, pushing herself up on her elbows and rubbing her fingers through the hairs on his chest. 'Did you have your fight with James?'

'Not only had it, but won. He's letting me turn it round. Ten years ago he could have done it, but not now. We're on the brink, you see. He hasn't realised the way things have changed, the way he's changed! We're going to have to strip out some assets, it's the only hope.'

'Do you have much that's worth anything?'

'Yes, tons. Couple of places with big central offices, worth a packet. Put both on the market and as soon as one's sold we'll be back on course. But if we don't do it or they don't sell or we get some sharp lawyer in about the combing plant accident, then we're going to be iller than ever. We're putting people out of business, of course, but that's what making omelettes is all about.'

'Yes. Nothing else for it.' Rowan leaned back thoughtfully. Mistaking her quiet for arousal Richard swung on top of her. She gasped as he penetrated her, the bed shaking with his robust thrusting. 'You're so good, you're wonderful,' he murmured. Rowan, sated with sex, murmured dutifully. Her eyes gazed unwaveringly up at the ceiling.

She got into her own bed at about three in the morning. Richard had wanted her to stay, he was pushing her faster than she wanted to go. Her body smelled of him, he had taken everything she had to give. His semen, draining out of her, left tell-tale smears on the sheets. How did women having affairs cope with that, she wondered? The smell of adultery, the evidence of it, there in the marital bed. Perhaps they went swimming afterwards, or spent hours in the bath, or wore pyjamas and pretended they were having a three-week period. It was all rather disgusting.

She was offended with herself for thinking that. Nothing she did with Richard could be half as shameful as the things Saul did, on his own, swilling down yet another and another drink. Dear Richard. How little he knew his own father. James would let him have some rope, and Richard would either hang himself or end up trussed like a chicken for the pot. There was no way James was ever giving up Bardsey's. But – just supposing. Supposing while the cat was letting the mice play, someone else came in and stole the tin of pilchards? James deserved it. God knows he had tried to get Judge's often enough.

Would it be a beastly thing to do? She twitched her nose in the dark. It wasn't as if Richard had told her anything she couldn't have guessed really, or found out for herself. He'd be furious, of course. It might be the end of them. But she couldn't bear to let this go, knowing she would forever regret it! If Richard turned against her then so be it, the affair would be decided, but if he didn't – well. Who could know what the future might bring? All you could do was follow your nose and see where it led.

Lying back in her lonely bed, rather chilly in the wide expanse, she knew she ought to feel ashamed of herself. What she was contemplating was certainly betrayal. Instead there was mounting exhilaration, almost a sense that she was putting Richard to the test. Now she would see just exactly what lay beneath that tough skin! And he would know exactly what she was.

Chapter Forty-Six

TAKEOVER!!!
Banner headlines in the financial papers, with pictures of Rowan in all the popular dailies. The bid was so incredibly cheeky. Isaac Judge had enlisted the support of a food and drinks conglomerate, recruited by their stockbrokers, who were lending their considerable muscle to the assault. Bardsey's, so big and so encumbered by hangers-on, wallowed like a liner trying to turn to meet a storm. If this succeeded, so the pundits declared, the door would be open for energetic raiders throughout the business world. Already Judge's had a goodly percentage of Bardsey stock.

But Rowan herself cowered in her office, refusing calls, seeing no one. Thankfully James and Diana were in Barbados, where surely the news would take time to filter. Bardsey's share price climbed and climbed, Judge's fluctuated wildly. No one knew who was going to be left with egg on their face but somehow nobody expected it to be Rowan Judge. She had a habit of falling on her feet.

Day after day Richard called the house, the office, sometimes coming in person to hammer on the door. But she would not see him, because whatever he had to say would hurt her. While she knew she deserved it she could not bear the actual words, not from him.

After a week of reclusive living she started to venture out, visiting Sally in the little house off Carlisle Road, taking some baby clothes and a book on bringing up children she had found helpful with Hannah. The door was opened by Sally herself, red-eyed and distraught.

'You've got to stop her, Rowan,' she demanded tearfully.

'She won't let me near my babies.'

From somewhere upstairs came the sound of wailing children, accompanied by the determined soothing of Mrs. Shafir. It did not seem to be having much effect. 'They're fractious today,' explained Sally. 'She says its my fault with my new-fangled ideas. She thinks I should be ashamed to have produced a girl, and pray about it, when I produced one of each, damn it! It's more than she could do.'

'Where's Mohammed?' asked Rowan. 'It's up to him to sort out his mother.'

'Isn't he working? I mean at Judge's?'

There was an uncomfortable pause. Eventually Rowan shook her head. 'He never came. I thought he'd decided against it.'

'Oh. Oh, I see.'

Sally's hands rose and fell helplessly. Upstairs the wailing grew louder. Suddenly determined, Rowan set foot on the stairs and went to investigate.

Mrs. Shafir was sitting on a bed defiantly trying to rock two babies at once. With a deprecating smile Rowan took one and gave it to Sally. The atmosphere, which had been dense with tension, thinned a little. Out of politeness Mrs. Shafir offered Rowan the other baby, and it was accepted. Gradually, as the sobbing lessened, the occasion became social. They all went downstairs to drink tea together.

'I've suggested that Sally and Mohammed might like their own house,' said Rowan to Mrs. Shafir, speaking loudly as if it might help understanding. Mrs. Shafir said something to Sally.

'She says she does not feel it is for a wife to take a son away from his mother. It is for a son to support his ageing parents in their declining years.'

'A house quite close by,' said Rowan.

Mrs. Shafir gave a glittering smile and spoke again.

'How close can a son be to his mother's heart?' said Sally.

Rowan abandoned all attempt at persuasion. She turned to Sally.

'Suppose I buy the house and put it at your disposal? You could move in when you felt like it.'

Sally rubbed her cheek against her baby's downy head. 'I don't know. Mohammed would have to agree, I don't like to do things unless he does.'

Mrs. Shafir beamed and declaimed.

'How sweet it is for a wife to obey her husband, how true to the will of Allah!' translated Sally dolefully.

'Oh God,' muttered Rowan.

So disturbed was she by Sally's plight within the household that she was halfway down the street before she became aware of the kerb-crawling Maserati. She stared at it, flinched, and started to run towards her own car parked some yards away. In three inch heels she could only teeter helplessly. Richard jumped out of his car and grabbed her.

'Oh no you don't!'

She swallowed. 'Hello, Richard.'

'Don't you "Hello, Richard" me! I've phoned you twenty times in the last week and called round four. Never a convenient time apparently. Too busy stabbing people in the back, I suppose.'

'A very busy time,' she said feebly.

'Busy!'

She couldn't meet his eyes. 'Yes, busy.'

They said nothing and as she did not appear to be about to run away, he let her go. 'Why did you do it?' he asked softly.

She shrugged. 'Don't know really. Seemed like a good idea. It is a good idea, the best. It wasn't anything to do with us.'

'Don't give me that! As soon as my father hears about this he's going to be back on a plane and kicking me out on my arse, and who can blame him? The first thing I do for the company is lose it to the enemy! And I deserve to be kicked out, for being so stupid as to trust you.'

'You didn't tell me anything I didn't know,' she said defiantly. 'You should have realised how vulnerable you were! Anyway, James would never have let you run it for good. And I shall let you stay on, afterwards.'

'Well, thanks very much!' He stepped away from her, the better to express himself. 'She kicks me in the teeth and offers me a set of cut-price dentures! Rowan dear, shall I tell you what galls me about this whole thing? The really difficult bit?'

'What?' she asked, eyeing him warily. She felt he might at any moment hit her.

'It's that I thought I was the one who knew it all. Poor little Rowan, I thought, little inexperienced Rowan. Man of the world that I was, showing her such a good time. I thought, how nice to take care of her. Shall I tell you what I think now, Rowan dear?'

'No,' she said shortly.

'Hard lines, it comes free. I'm not at all surprised that Saul is where he is. I think if I was married to you, I'd be hitting the sauce too. You look like a woman, you sound like a woman, but underneath you're a fucking barracuda!'

She looked round for something to throw at him, but the pavement was bare of missiles. She resorted to words. 'I don't think James would winge like this,' she declared shrilly. 'But then, he always was twice the man you are. I suggest you get back pretty damn quick, Richard, because you're not tough enough to fight me. I shall own you lock, stock and conceit.'

He pointed a shaking finger. 'I'll burn the whole shooting match before I let you get your hands on it.'

'And you'll end up in gaol. That's where all stupid businessmen go, the ones who think they're clever anyway.'

'Anywhere's better than in your pocket. Or in your anything else for that matter.'

She took off her shoe and hurled it at him. It missed, so she took off the other and threw that too. He laughed, caught it and tossed it into a puddle. Rowan was left barefoot and fuming. 'That's how you're going to be at the end of this,' said Richard softly. 'And I won't lend you a penny.' He turned and went back to his car.

That night Rowan sat at home, brooding. She knew she should visit Saul, she hadn't been in days, not since the bid was launched. Presumably he read the papers so he must know about it. But she felt too ill, too miserable and sick. The row with Richard went round and round in her head, she couldn't escape from it! And she knew that all she could have said, should have said, was that she was sorry. She was so, so sorry, not for having launched the bid, but for having hurt him by it. That was life's unfairness, that you could never have anything without paying more than you felt it was worth.

Tonight the sadness would not go away. She turned on the television, watching some inexplicably boring comedy. She felt tearful and jumpy. She went and poured herself a drink, gin and tonic, a large one. After that she had another, and perhaps two more, she lost count. When she was sprawled on the sofa, glass in hand, sniffing tearfully into a handkerchief, Saul came home.

She was so drunk she wasn't at all sure he was really there. She blinked at him owlishly. He had a stick but the plaster cast was gone.

'You are pissed as a newt,' said Saul in amazement.

'I don't get drunk,' she said owlishly. 'Saul gets drunk. My husband, you know.'

'Yes, I have met him. Bit of a prat, don't you think?'

'Only when he's pissed. He's always pissed.' She got up and staggered against the television. Saul fielded her and set her upright.

'Why are you here?' she demanded. 'You've escaped.'

'Actually they were quite glad to get rid of me. I did leave a message asking that you should come and collect, but it seems it didn't get through. Eventually they found a taxi.'

'I don't take messages,' she said vaguely. 'Richard shouts at me all the time.'

'You are trying to pinch his company, sweetheart,' said Saul.

'I'm buying it. You're allowed to do that. And now he doesn't love me any more!' She subsided, wailing, against Saul's shirt front.

Unseen by her, his face went oddly stiff. Already pale from indoor living, he went paler, the colour draining away to leave dead-white skin. Gently he put up a hand and patted Rowan's heaving, drunken shoulder. 'Let's put you to bed, shall we?' he whispered hoarsely.

She rolled half-conscious into bed, weeping miserably. 'It isn't fair, it isn't fair,' she sobbed. 'Everything always goes wrong.'

'Do you want him so much then?' asked Saul. He sounded as if he was breathing broken glass. 'You can tell me. You can always tell me anything.'

'Yes. So I can. I want him more than anything.'

'More than me?' A ridiculous question. She opened a bleary eye and peered into his face. 'I'm glad you're home,' she said. 'It's jolly cold in bed by myself.'

He tucked her carefully in, switching off the light with a shaking hand. When he went back into the sitting room he headed unerringly for the drinks cupboard.

'Where's the point?' he whispered to himself, and there were tears rolling unchecked down his cheeks. 'Where's the sodding point?'

BARDSEY'S WHITE KNIGHT

Rowan swore and crumpled the paper between her hands. Then she swore again and uncrumpled it, smoothing out the rash creases. She read, 'A rescuer has at last appeared to support Bardsey Textiles against the opportunistic depradations of Isaac Judge. Associated Industries, with its huge capital base and diverse interests, should be well able to see off such an impertinent approach. Bardsey's are to be congratulated for persuading AI that they are a company worth such attention, and its shareholders are strongly recommended not to consider acceptance of the Judge offer at this stage. If the bid is to continue there will certainly be an offer of considerably greater magnitude in the near future.'

'Frances!' Rowan bawled furiously for her secretary. The woman came trotting in, flustered as always. It hadn't been like this in Mr. Andrew's day; she couldn't keep up with all this 'phoning to America and London stockbrokers and million pound deals. Besides, she suspected Rowan would have got rid of her long ago if it wasn't for Mr. Saul. He remembered her birthday and bought her bath salts at Christmas, and in return she got rid of the bottles.

'I want a meeting,' snarled Rowan morosely. 'Us, the bank, the stockbrokers and the men from General Foods. I don't care where it is but it must be today or at the latest tomorrow morning.'

'Oh – yes – very well.' Frances made incoherent notes on her pad. 'Will Mr. Saul be coming?'

'What? I shouldn't think so.' Rowan was cool and distant. She didn't know what Saul was doing and she didn't care. The moment he was out of the damned clinic he was drinking again, not even bothering to pretend to be trying. The only limiting factor was his driving ban, but he made do with taxis, and when he was drunk he wouldn't care if he was banned or not. She fully expected to end up visiting him in gaol.

A headache nagged just behind her eyes. They would have to increase the offer substantially, but it was as she had expected. The unexpected factor was the intervention of such a big company on behalf of Bardsey's. The share price would rocket. How had he done it? Richard had no track record. In comparison, hers was impeccable. 'It's because he's a man,' she murmured to herself, feeling beleaguered and feminine. There was no chivalry in the world any more.

But, takeover or no takeover, life had to go on. They had a new showroom now, where customers could see the current range set out in a clear north light. It was a room luxuriant with cloth. She went through to see what was happening to a pale misty tweed that was being considered by a major chain store for a vast range of matching skirts, jackets and trousers. If they took it she would contract out the manufacture; she wasn't turning away other business because of one monolithic order. That had been Bardsey's downfall.

The showroom was untidy. Someone had wandered in and out with a customer and given not a thought to the mess. If you didn't do it yourself nothing ever got done, raged Rowan, and began rolling up cloth and hooking drapes of fabric back on to the pinboard on the wall.

'So there you are.'

She was standing on a table, holding a length of red cloth. Saul took the other end, hopped up beside her and did the job. 'I wanted to talk to you,' he said.

'I'm busy, I'm afraid.' Rowan never wanted to talk nowadays.

'Nonetheless we're going to talk. Rowan, what do you want out of life?'

She almost laughed. 'I'm not standing on a table discussing philosophy!' she said stiffly. 'And I could ask you the same question.'

'But I'm asking you. Will you be happy when you've got Bardsey's? Will you want more and more again?'

'Possibly. I don't know.' Standing on the table, he was too close to her. Now that she and Richard had – well, made love together, she almost felt that if Saul came too near he would sense it. All her instincts were to keep him at a distance.

'Do you want a divorce, Rowan?'

She stepped back and almost fell. He caught her arm and she teetered, at last regaining her footing. 'Why do you have to follow me around saying things like that? I can't cope with that as well! There's a takeover bid on and you want to talk about divorce. You're just cross with me for not involving you.'

His face was unreadable, she couldn't tell what he was thinking. 'I'm not all that interested in what you do or don't cope with. As it happens, Rowan, *I* want a divorce. But I also want Hannah.'

She swung back her hand to hit him, but then closed her fist and put it to her lips instead, gnawing the knuckles. 'No one would give her to you. Not with your record.'

'I know. That's why I'm asking for her.'

She turned and jumped down from the table, twisting her ankle in her high heels. 'You just want to spoil everything for me!' she said hysterically. 'You want to ruin my bid, you don't really want a divorce. You couldn't cope with Hannah.' A thought occurred to her. 'And I wouldn't let you have anything out of the firm, not a penny! I built it myself, all of it!'

'Did you, Rowan? All by yourself?'

She swallowed. 'Everybody thinks it was just me. Oh, why don't you go away? You're only bothering me. I can't think about anything now.'

The door opened and Frances came in. 'What is it?' demanded Rowan.

'The meeting, Mrs. Barton. Two o'clock in Threadneedle Street, it's all arranged.'

'I shall have to get ready then.'

'Am I included in this?' asked Saul.

Rowan barely glanced at him. 'I don't think that would be wise. Under the circumstances, I suggest you keep your nose out altogether! I will do this on my own.'

She staggered out of the room, tottering on her twisted ankle. Her head hurt too, assailed by a thousand mosquitolike thoughts. She felt almost hysterical. It wasn't fair for him to say things like that, she wasn't ready! Oh God, how dare he ask for Hannah? It simply wasn't fair.

The London train was late arriving and when at last she reached the meeting she was last to arrive. Her ankle had swollen and every step was agony, but she fixed a smile on her face and struggled to appear poised and in control. General Foods were ruffled that Bardsey's were making such a fight of it.

'I thought Mr. Barton was coming,' said one man. 'I understand it was his vision that put Judge's on the map.'

'He's been ill,' said Rowan vaguely.

'Is he in support of this bid? I'd like to feel the management team is acting in concert here.'

'Obviously I wouldn't act against his wishes.' The muscles in her jaw were tight.

'We have only your word for that, Mrs. Barton. We want to assure ourselves that continuing with this bid is more than academic. We want to know we can win!'

She could think of nothing to say. She sat in the midst of all these men and felt threatened. Everyone else had brought one or two supporters, she alone was expected to do everything herself.

'I wonder if Judge's has the depth of management to succeed,' said a banker, echoing her own thoughts.

Rowan dredged up some remnants of confidence. 'I assure you we have the determination to win, and we will,' she declared. 'Don't forget my brother and sister are also shareholders in Judge's. I'm not quite alone.'

'And they do fully support the offer?'

'Of course.' It was a blatant lie. She hadn't even considered asking either of them.

As she left she had the feeling that she had escaped by the skin of her teeth. Why had those men thought it would be easy, she wondered? Everyone imagined textile companies to be lodged in the nineteenth century, but Bradford men had always been sharp, and gamblers, and they were still. Scarred by years of battling for their commercial lives, they weren't men to quit at the first crackle of gunfire. This was guerrilla warfare, with every avenue mined. As if in response to her thoughts she suddenly saw James. He was coming out of a merchant bank.

Instinctively she stepped into a doorway and hid. God help her if James was back. He looked well, no less pale than always despite the sun of Barbados, but there was about his step the old vigour and verve. 'Damn him,' thought Rowan dully. 'Damn, damn, damn him!'

At night Bradford streets were cold and in the yellow light of the street lamps greasy pavements glistened. Mohammed walked quickly, making for a cafe where he would meet his friend Fahad. Vague memories of his childhood stirred: running through dry streets with the day's heat still hanging in the air, all around the bustle of people. There it was at night that the world came to life, in the markets and the shops. In contrast with these damp evenings, it seemed like paradise.

Fahad was lounging on a plastic chair, as always surrounded by friends. But he kicked someone out of the circle to make room for Mohammed.

'Have you eaten?'

'Yes.'

Fahad offered a cigarette but Mohammed refused. He said, 'My car's broken down again. Starter motor.'

'You should talk to my uncle. He can get you parts.'

Mohammed was surprised. 'I didn't know he had anything to do with cars.'

Fahad nodded. 'Well then, doesn't that show you? He's got a garage now. Marrying that girl has put you out of touch.'

Fahad punched him playfully and Mohammed cuffed him

in return. They'd known each other a long time, but after school Fahad had gone back to Pakistan for six months and they'd lost touch. He was very successful, importing spices and rugs, and he was married to an educated Asian girl who somehow managed to combine docility with Western charm. In Fahad's household there seemed to be none of the squabbling that characterised his own home, and in Fahad's life there was none of the confusion that Mohammed felt so acutely. Fahad knew who he was and he knew what he wanted to become.

When Mohammed at last got up to leave Fahad came with him, flinging a friendly arm round his shoulders. In the street, privately, he said, 'Thought any more about what I suggested?'

Mohammed nodded. 'I don't know. I'd love to go in with you, but –' he felt foolish admitting it '– the money's my wife's.'

'So it's yours! She can't object to you bettering yourself, can she? Look, I can't wait forever. I need a partner and I want it to be you, but if it isn't you I'll find someone else. I'm importing all the time, I can't be there and here as well.'

'My wife's sister wants me in her office –'

'I keep telling you! There's no way she'll give you any responsibility. Look, don't take this wrong. I heard about what happened in the weaving shed. What makes you think it would be any different in the office? This way you can make real money, and without breaking your mother's heart. Get a little respect, for once in your life. Make a few trips back home, did I tell you I've a house there? And what are we here for if not to get on? You want to go back as somebody, don't you?'

Mohammed looked at him. Fahad was so persuasive, Mohammed envied him so much. He had a good car, a big house, a lot of respect, both here and at home. Sally's people had given him nothing. Was it not for his own kind to extend a helping hand? The English failed to understand the ties of religion and family.

The rain was falling again, and in the distance came the wail of a police siren racing to break up a fight in one of the West Indian pubs. After all, he was a father now, it was time to put away dreams and face reality.

Sally was bone weary. Despite the daytime battles over the children, at night she alone was expected to get up and see to them. Mohammed was out most evenings, talking with friends, he came in well after midnight. When she asked what they talked about, he said, 'You wouldn't understand. About Pakistan, and the life there. About the government.'

She knew nothing at all about Pakistan, she could not relate her English picture of primitive, over-crowded living with the scene the family painted, of communities and traditions and ceremonies. For Mohammed to talk about Pakistan seemed to her to make him less and less English.

One night when she had settled the twins at last and Mohammed was not as yet asleep, she asked, 'Why didn't you take the job at Judge's? It was a good job. It would have helped us.'

He grunted, she thought he was going to ignore her. Then he said, 'I used to think that was the way. To become more English, become like the English. I wasn't the first, it's been tried before. My friends, they've all tried. But I am Asian. I shall always be Asian.'

'You didn't have to lose that.'

He sat up, linking his hands round his knees. 'Fahad's made me an offer. He wants me to go into business with him, invest. I shall sell out of Judge's.'

Sally sat frozen. 'But – Rowan was going to get us a house. She promised.'

'That can wait. I visited James Barton today. He would like to buy your shares, we should have a great deal of money. I agreed that you would sell them to him.'

'To James? Mohammed, you can't! Rowan's always been

so good to us, you just can't do this!'

'She has done nothing for me. She did not even dismiss those men. You yourself said you would sell the shares.'

'Yes, but I didn't mean it.'

She went to the cradle and rocked it, although the baby inside was asleep. Little Ali, worshipped by all the family, given the best cradle, the best clothes, the most prayers. Shameena always came second. 'I don't think I want to,' she said nervously.

'I have told him, Sally. It is not for you to disagree.'

The conflict might have come then, she was never sure if she would have capitulated if it had. But a cry rang through the quiet house. 'Fadeema. Fadeema! Salleeee!'

'Mother.' Sally got up and hurried on to the landing. The parents slept downstairs on a couch in the sitting room. They could hear a muffled grunting.

Fadeema came out of her room, her long hair in two plaits on her shoulders. She hurried down, Sally and Mohammed close after her. Mother was moaning, clasping her small brown hands. On the bed her husband sprawled, his eyes turned up in his head, his breath coming after long and agonising pauses.

'Oh no. Oh no.' Fadeema and Mohammed bent over him. They pulled open his clothes, exposing his grizzled chest. Even Sally could see the convulsive spasms of the heart, the unnaturally distended rib cage. Mother let out the beginnings of a wail. Instinctively, Sally put her arms around her. They stood there, watching, while Mr. Shafir died.

He was to be embalmed and sent to Pakistan for burial. The expense was considerable. Again, Mohammed told Sally she must sell her shares. He didn't understand her reluctance. If she wouldn't sell to James, why not approach Rowan and sell to her? Sally would not.

The death of his father had changed him almost overnight. It was as if his association with her had been no more than a flirtation, a brief waltz with her culture, a show of short-lived defiance. Now he seemed different. He went to the mosque more often, for solemn prayers, and in the house when he spoke no one challenged. He was head of the family now, and Sally was in no doubt that if she sold her shares the money would not be hers, or even theirs, but the family's.

He made love to her often, even when she was longing to sleep. Now that he was in his father's place he seemed to have taken on energy and determination. Sometimes he sounded exactly like his father. Again and again he told her to sell her shares, and again and again she prevaricated. In the end she absolutely refused.

Mohammed took her upstairs into their bedroom. Moving deliberately he struck her face, on one side then the other. She screamed and fell on the bed, and he stood over her, quietly purposeful. 'I have decided to sell the shares. You will remain in your room, Sally, until you agree. Mother will take care of the children.'

'I wouldn't mind if you'd buy us a house!' she sobbed. 'But it's just to put a dead man on a plane, there's no point.'

'My father wished it. And I must go back, to see that all is done properly.'

'You didn't want my money when we married. Why do you take it now?'

'Because we have need of it. My father's honour needs it, and I need it for my business. Sally, why are you not obedient to me? I know what is best for us.'

She stared up at him through a curtain of pale hair, the marks of his hands on her cheeks. He could have beaten her far more severely, she knew, and it would only have been considered justice. In his way he loved her, and was trying to spare her pain. He wasn't a cruel man.

'We won't ever have our own house now Father's dead, will we?' she said dully.

'My mother cannot be left alone, Sally. You would not wish it. Now, will you sell the shares?'

'No.'

He turned on his heels, went out and locked the door. She sat on her own in the bedroom, separated from her children, from food, from the life of the household, a disobedient wife who must be brought to heel. He was the husband, she the wife, they weren't Mohammed and Sally any longer. If he wished, in Pakistan he could marry again, a Moslem could have up to four wives. If she agreed to leave her children behind she could be returned to her family, her marriage an unfortunate mistake. When she sacrificed her will to his she hadn't known that one day he would act against her best interests. She felt betrayed, by her own foolish trust.

Late in the evening Fadeema unlocked the door, bringing food. 'He has gone out,' she explained.

'Can I have my babies?' demanded Sally. 'He hasn't the right to keep them from me.'

Fadeema sat down. 'You must do as he says, Sally. You can't be happy if you don't.'

Sally sighed. 'I seem to be so unimportant to him. He puts Mother before me in everything! He talks to her when he won't talk to me.'

'You must understand, Sally. In our tradition we honour the parents. When I marry my friend I shall honour his mother and she will live with us. And one day Ali will have a wife and she will live with you and do the work, and perhaps then you will be kind to her. Will you?'

'Do I have to wait so long?' said Sally dismally.

Fadeema laughed. 'Not so long, no. In all families the mother rules in the end. You will have more children. Perhaps you will be pregnant before Mohammed goes away, and he will come back to see his new baby. Or babies. It could be twins again!' She wagged a finger.

Sally considered the alternatives. In this family at least she had a place, whereas in her own she had none. She was just Sally, difficult wayward girl. In the end where should her loyalty lie but with her husband, the father of her children? Who best to take care of her? And besides, if he turned against her and withdrew his love, she would be helpless and alone.

That night when Mohammed came home he found the cradles again by the bed. He stood in the doorway, framed by the landing light, looking down at his wife. 'Well, Sally?'

'You can have the shares.' She pulled back the sheet and he saw that she was naked. Still she could excite him, still in that pink and willing flesh lay dizzying temptation. He dragged off his clothes and lay down with her, and as they kissed she thought, 'In this at least I am special to him.' She must make it her world, enthral him in it, and be utterly loved.

Rowan could not believe what Sally had done to her. James held a massive tranche of her shares! She felt hopelessly, horribly threatened.

'You could have anticipated it,' said Saul brutally. 'It makes no difference to the bid, he hasn't got control. He's paid over the odds for them but if we win he'll sell them and still make money. If we lose he's got a foothold in the company.'

'I never thought she'd betray me like that.'

Saul almost laughed. 'Some might say you haven't been exactly honest lately. With anyone.'

'What do you mean?' She forced herself to meet his eyes and something about his glazed stare told her he had been drinking.

'It's no use talking to you,' she said angrily. 'You're never even sober!'

Saul came across. She thought he was going to kiss her and she put her hands up to ward him off. He caught her wrists in an iron clasp. 'God help you if I was,' he said softly, and let her go. She felt cold, although his hands had been hot. She rubbed her wrists.

He went out to walk, down the narrow street, wearing only a jumper on a wet and windy day. Imperceptibly, inch by inch, Rowan was floating out of her depth. Was he going to haul her back in, or leave it until she was way over the horizon? Back she would come, eventually, but possibly more dead than alive.

The cold was sobering him. He went into a shop and bought a mobile of clowns for Hannah. Was he going to become a Sunday father? Turning up like a bad penny to take her endlessly to the zoo? He felt the rage beginning, the murderous, burning rage. You couldn't allow anger like that out, you had to swallow it down, quieten it like the wild beast it was. In the off-licence across the road he bought half a bottle of whisky, and felt proud of himself. In days gone by it would have been at least a full bottle, and possibly two.

Rowan drove slowly up the drive to Aspley Manor. Summoned peremptorily by her mother she had considered refusing to go, but somehow she felt so isolated at the moment. The war between the companies was being conducted in the newspapers just now, with articles on both sides telling tales of the other's ineptitude. The latest scare from Bardsey was that a successful takeover would result in multiple sackings, difficult to refute since it would.

James opened the door to her. 'Well, well, well. Don't you look rapacious.'

She had dressed in black leather trousers and tight leather top. Ridiculous clothes, uncomfortable and hugely expensive, but a much needed boost to her ego. Men turned in the street and stared at her. 'I came to see Mother,' said Rowan frostily.

'We await you, my dear.' He waved an arm extravagantly towards the drawing room. Rowan's nerves jangled, James was wildly confident. When she went into the room, her cheeks flamed. Richard was there. So too was Andy.

'Oh no,' said Rowan dully. 'Not you too! Andy, you can't.'

'Did you ever think you should have consulted me?' Andy was draped theatrically over an armchair. He was wearing a cape lined with red silk.

'You look like Dracula on an off-day,' she declared.

'And you look like the star attraction at some whore-house,' murmured Richard.

She turned away, putting her hands together and pacing up and down.

'Where's Mother?' she asked jerkily. 'I think she ought to be here while you dismember me.'

They waited in silence. Rowan's heels clicked on the wooden floor each time she came to the end of the rug. She felt irrationally guilty, in trouble with everyone. It didn't seem fair.

At last Diana appeared, carrying a newspaper.

'There you are, Rowan,' she said distantly, and tossed the paper on to the coffee table.

'What's that?' asked Rowan.

'The article you wrote about Bardsey's. The part that particularly caught my attention concerned "ageing management too preoccupied with the pleasures of the flesh to pay much attention to share dividends". Exactly what did you mean, dear?'

'What it says,' flared Rowan. 'I don't have to apologise for telling the truth!'

'And how about if we wrote about your youthful management, too overburdened with an alcoholic husband and a handicapped child to be concerned with profit?'

Rowan recoiled. 'You wouldn't.'

'Why not? It's the same thing.' Andy got up and came over to her. 'You have started playing very dirty, Rowan. The time has come for me to exercise some control. We're pulling out of the bid.'

'You can't!'

For one dreadful moment she thought he too had sold out. She glanced at James, knowing that if he had control she was finished. But of course it wasn't possible. James could no longer afford it.

She swung round on Richard. 'Haven't you anything to

say? I wrote that but you wrote all that stuff about people losing jobs if we took over.'

Richard shrugged. 'True, and impersonal. You could have considered that what you were writing might hurt your mother as well as James.'

Tears pricked against her eyelids. Everybody was against her, no one saw that she had only been doing what was right, for Judge's! She turned to go and Richard caught her arm.

'You're in no state to drive. I'll take you.'

'I'm all right.' She tried to shake him off, but he wouldn't let go. In silence, watched by everyone, they went out to the car.

He drove her through the park. 'Do you remember driving my car here? You nearly crashed it.'

'I remember.'

He spun the wheel and sent her little runabout down a track leading to a copse of trees. Rowan said nothing to stop him. When they were quite concealed he turned off the engine and sat, holding the steering wheel.

'Bit of a bloody mess, isn't it.'

'My backers will want some kind of forfeit.'

'Ours want us to merge with them. Actually I wish you and I had fought it out straight, without all this backdoor stuff. I could still have beaten you.'

She grinned. 'You might. Was it really wrong to say that about James? It is true.'

'But unwise. Your mother was furious when she first read it.' He turned quite suddenly and started to kiss her.

'Don't be angry with me,' whispered Rowan. 'I can't bear it.'

He said against her neck, 'But why did you do it? I don't understand you at all.'

'I know. I know.'

He was trying to unfasten her trousers. All her misery seemed to fuse into white-hot desire. She pulled the zip down and started to wriggle out of the skin-tight leather. When they were just past her knees Richard swung on top of her, pushing Rowan down across the seats. She was kissing him, nuzzling his ears as he tried to get between her tight thighs. 'I love you,' she murmured to him. 'I do, you know.'

'Of course you do. Oh God, I can't wait!'

They lay tangled together. 'Does Saul do it to you?' asked Richard.

She shook her head. 'We're not on good terms. He's drinking.'

'Yes. You'll have to tell him about us, what we mean to do. Now this is all finished, there's no reason not to.'

'No.' She started to pull up her leather trousers, hating the very thought of telling him. 'We'd have won the bid, you know,' she said suddenly. 'Andy's so stupid, it really is absolutely the best thing for Judge's. OK, we were asset stripping but that's what you were going to do too! We'd fit well together.'

'But you are dropping it, aren't you?' Richard's face told her that he would never quite trust her again.

She sighed. 'I haven't any choice.'

At home, Saul was waiting. She stood in the doorway, the leather trousers sticking to her thighs with sour-smelling proof of her adultery.

'What's happened?' asked Saul.

Frostily she said, 'Nothing that should concern you. Andy's at Aspley Manor. He insists we pull out of the bid.'

'Christ. Oh Christ, the stupid shit!'

She flared up at him. 'I don't know why you aren't cheering! You didn't want this in the first place, you ought to be pleased.'

'Was Richard there?'

'Yes.' She went quickly through to the bathroom, started the water running and stripped off her clothes. Saul leaned on the doorpost watching her. Why should he mind? she thought viciously. Once he was prepared to give me to him.

'Do you like Richard?' asked Saul.

'That's a stupid question. We're fighting over the bid.'

'All the same, I should have thought he's your type. The hard, driving sort.'

'As opposed to the soft, drinking sort, you mean?' snarled Rowan in return.

He stood there, saying nothing. She knew without being told that he wanted to make love to her. Quickly, almost scalding herself, she got into the bath.

'It isn't fair, is it?' he said. 'You so wanted Bardsey's.'

'You're too drunk to understand,' she retorted, and started to soap her breasts. Suddenly he knelt down beside the bath, nuzzling her slippery foam-covered skin. Barely an hour before Richard had kissed that same flesh, had licked those same nipples.

'Get off me!' she squealed, and hit at her husband, catching him hard over the ear. In that instant she knew it had been a mistake. Brown eyes, like chocolate, like the depths of brown port, lit with sudden rage. He dragged her out of the bath. She squealed, trying to resist. She had never known such strength. He got her down on the mat.

'You're drunk,' she wailed, 'Barbara will hear! Please, Saul, don't!'

But he was past reason. His hands encircled her throat. Half-choked, in terror of her life, she flailed at him with wet arms. Her ears were filled with sound, she opened her mouth to beg him, beg him to stop. Her tongue croaked helplessly. He was killing her!

Suddenly he let her go. She clung to the side of the bath, dragging air into starved lungs, aware of a tumultuous pulse in her throat. Her husband, her enemy, crashed the door aside as he went out.

Chapter Forty-Seven

Saul lay in bed, watching thin sunshine make patterns on the ceiling. In the kitchen he could hear Hannah singing tunelessly while Barbara counted out loud the numbers of bricks, or dolls, or potatoes. All his love, all his longing, centred on that tuneless little voice. 'God,' he thought,'I hate all of myself except the part that loves her.'

He got up and went to wash. The bathroom showed no trace of last night, although Rowan's throat was black with fingermarks. She had slept in the spare room, and come to the bedroom only for a scarf. He had uttered not one word of apology.

When he went back to the bedroom he debated whether to have a drink now or in an hour. Usually he had no choice but to drink, his hands shook like leaves in the wind, but this morning he was cold and calm and steady. Poor Rowan, he thought, poor poor Rowan, who had to suffer him. And at the same time he wondered if he should have strangled her. Perhaps that was the way out. To kill the thing that tormented him.

Suddenly he decided what to do. He dressed quickly in a pair of shabby shooting trousers and a jumper, and went out to Rowan's car. Only after ten minutes did he remember the driving ban, and by then it was too late. He kept on, because if he got caught it would be fate and would prove that nothing could go right.

Nobody answered the bell at Aspley Manor, so he wandered round the house setting the peacocks to flight and leaving footmarks on soft lawns. A violin was playing, two violins. He looked through a window at the back of the house and saw Diana and Andy, playing together. He stood, listening.

There was something wrong with the tempo, Andy was quick where Diana was slow, and lingered sentimentally where she was strict. At the end Diana flung down her bow.

'You've turned into the sort of hack player that grinds out love songs in cheap restaurants,' she declared.

'Rubbish!' Andy carefully replaced his violin in its expensive polished case. Diana's battered box seemed a mute reminder of the difference between them.

'You ought not to let them do this to you!' said Diana. 'That record you made embarrassed me so much I couldn't listen to it.'

Andy turned on her. 'Look, Mother, when I did it your way I couldn't get a single booking some months. I'd ring up my agent and her assistant would take it, lying in her teeth. "I'm sorry, Mr. Judge, there isn't anything just now but I'll ask her to ring you." No return call, nothing. You sit, waiting, practising, and the bills come in and your shoes wear out. Now my agent rings *me,* twice a day sometimes, and *I* don't take the calls.'

'I didn't think money would ever mean so much to you,' said Diana in disgust.

'God, Mother, can't you see it isn't the money? I just cannot stand what goes with poverty: the contempt, the pity, the powerlessness! If Dad had had the money, don't you think he'd have been different? You would never have despised him as you did.'

Saul stepped forward and rapped on the window. Diana and Andy jumped, and then Diana went and threw up the sash. 'What are you doing here? How dare you snoop around my home?'

'I rang the bell. You didn't hear. I wanted to talk to Andy.'

'If it's to plead about Rowan's idiotic bid, then he doesn't want to hear. She's got a great deal too big for her boots and she cares about nothing except herself.'

'Do shut up, Mother.' Andy sat on the window ledge and swung himself out into the garden. He landed on the grass, dusted his hands and grinned. They strolled away across the park.

Saul said, 'I knew she hadn't told you about the bid. She's a fool sometimes.'

Andy shrugged. 'Always stupid about Judge's, that's Rowan. About anything she cares about, actually.'

'Yes.' Saul sighed, sinking his hands deep into his pockets. There was a hole in one of them, and Rowan would never mend it. Perhaps indeed she should not, except what was care if not an expression of love? They should care for each other, mutually. If they loved.

'Who's the woman in your life?' he asked Andy.

'American television presenter. Very glamorous, and a bit hard. She'd like to get married but on my side it isn't serious.'

'Don't you want kids?'

Andy shrugged. 'Depends. I wondered about the genes, after Hannah.'

Saul swallowed. 'Sally was OK. I think it's just the mix. Me and Rowan. We don't seem to match.'

'No. Well, I've wondered. You can cut your losses, I suppose?'

'Perhaps.'

Saul stopped and faced the other man. In the clear daylight Andy looked tired and strained, less sure of himself than he had seemed with Diana.

'You must let Rowan go ahead with her bid,' said Saul. 'I know she seems power-crazed sometimes. But she has to try. If she loses through her own efforts then she'll live with it, but this way she'll look a fool and lose the firm's money into the bargain. Besides, I don't think you've any right to stop her. She saved Judge's, all by herself.'

'Saved it, yes. But you put it up where it is today.'

Saul shook his head. 'All I'm saying is, don't do this to

her. Let her for once have what she wants.'

They walked on, past the empty stables, part of which had been converted into garages. James's Rolls-Royce had a flat tyre, and Diana's Porsche needed washing. 'You're right, you know,' said Andy suddenly. 'I'm doing what James wants. And I owe Rowan far more than I do him. She's never let me down.'

'Because she loves you.'

It was said in an odd voice, and Andy glanced quickly at the tall, leonine man beside him. But Saul's face betrayed nothing. All the same, Andy was aware of an almost overpowering sadness. 'You tell Rowan,' said Saul. 'Don't tell her you spoke to me.'

Rowan picked up the telephone. Richard's voice said, 'You bitch!'

She said breathily, 'You said you wouldn't have minded fighting it out. So I am.'

'What if I ask you to let it drop? We don't need this, Rowan, you and I don't need it.'

'It won't hurt us. Not if we really care.'

'Do you care?'

'Yes,' she whispered. 'Yes, yes, terribly. Oh Richard, I can't bear to stay here much longer! He's so awful!'

'Then drop the bloody bid and come to me!'

'I – can't.'

She hung up before more could be said, and smoothed her hands across her cheeks, trying to regain her composure. Everybody thought she was going to win this time. Since Andy's surprising capitulation Judge's, backed by their sponsors, had increased their offer for Bardsey shares. The headlines read 'Judge's Holding Its Nerve', and at meetings nowadays she was congratulated on her management style. But although they were now on her side, she knew better than to trust the City men.

The scarf around her neck was slipping and she adjusted

it. Saul kept away from her, they slept in different rooms and inhabited the house at different times. When this was over she would go and see a solicitor, she told herself, and be free of him. But at lunchtime she went to the house to see Hannah and he was there.

They didn't at first notice her and she stood outside the kitchen, watching him play trains with Hannah's food. For him and his chuffings the little girl opened and closed her mouth, and put up her arms and her sticky face for his kiss. 'Daddy's best girl,' said Saul, and rested his cheek against her hair.

'I'm glad to see you can at least have consideration for somebody,' said Rowan tartly. 'Where is Barbara?'

'I gave her the afternoon off.'

'You hadn't any right.'

'Don't be ridiculous.'

She glared at him, but he looked away. He said, 'James has gone very quiet.'

'He's leaving things to Richard,' said Rowan stiffly. 'He knows he can trust him, I suppose.'

'Not what I'd suppose at all,' said Saul. He picked up Hannah and prepared to leave the room. Rowan said quickly, 'Saul!'

'What?'

'You wouldn't – Hannah. You wouldn't take her?'

'No. No, I won't do that.'

'Thank you.' She stood alone in the kitchen, her hands pressed together as if in prayer.

BARDSEY MAN WRITES: JUDGE'S MANAGEMENT APPALLING – AND I SHOULD KNOW!!!

Diana took the paper from James and gaped at it. 'You're saying Richard wrote this?'

'Yes. Didn't think he had it in him. Tough lad, Richard.'

'Downright cruel, if you ask me!' Diana read on.

'"Married to an alcoholic, mother of a handicapped child, Rowan Judge is at the same time to be pitied and feared. A woman with so little to satisfy her in her personal life has to turn to her work. Sadly, she is best pleased when inflating her bank balance, by fair means or foul. Tragedy has pursued Rowan Judge, but we do not have to welcome it into other, more fortunate lives." You put him up to this, James!'

'All his own idea, I'm afraid.'

James went to the cupboard and poured them both a drink. He was feeling energetic and optimistic. 'I can finish her, you know,' he said suddenly. 'I can absolutely bring her down!'

'I think she's bombproof, James, even for you.' Diana was feeling irritable. She wanted to defend Rowan while at the same time thought that she deserved all she got.

'You watch,' said James. 'Just you watch.' He took her drink to her, and watched her thin fingers curl around the glass. Ageing hands, but still the most beautiful he knew.

Once again Rowan stood in Threadneedle Street. Once again ranged about her were the faces of anonymous men. Last week they had praised her, now they smiled with spurious pity. 'I don't believe it,' she said softly. 'I simply don't believe it.'

'James Barton made a very strong case,' purred the senior man from General Foods. 'When we considered the possibility of a merger with Bardsey's, we saw for ourselves the benefits.'

'Getting the goodies and leaving me out,' said Rowan flatly. 'It's betrayal!'

'No, my dear, business.'

They had summoned her down here just to humiliate her. She stood stock still and fought her urge to pick up something, anything, and throw it at them. Typically secretive, James had sneaked off to General Foods and sold himself to them, leaving Judge's without a backer, betrayed and helpless. 'What in God's name are you going to do with a textile firm?' she demanded. 'At least I wasn't going to close everything down!'

'Perhaps we can sell some parts to you?' someone suggested.

And suddenly Rowan could stand no more. She drew herself up to her full height, and glared down at them furiously. 'I never trade with thieves,' she declared.

Waiting for the lift outside, standing stabbing fruitlessly at the button, she heard them laughing.

In Bardsey's board room, across the gleaming table, Richard faced his father.

'You knew what you were doing to me. You meant to do it.'

'Don't be ridiculous, Richard! She was going to win, we had to stop her.'

'*You* had to stop her. Can't you see how stupid this is? If the worst came to the worst, Judge's and Bardsey's make a good fit together. But us and a food company? Are we going to weave fucking napkins or what?'

James strolled to the head of the table, and laid all his long length down in the great chair. 'You should have seen this way out. I waited for you to get on with it, and I could wait no longer.'

A great wave of rage surged up in Richard. 'What was this then?' he said in a low, shaking voice. 'A test of my balls? You wanted to do down not only Rowan but me as well, simply because I challenged you. I might be your son but to you that means nothing.'

'Oh, it does,' said James thoughtfully. 'Without that you wouldn't have lasted this long. It's my company, you see. Mine!'

'You bloody fool, it belongs to General Foods! See what you've got left in six months.'

James laughed. 'I won't have anything. I'm resigning. You see, my boy, I'm prepared to hand over, but I am not prepared to let you kick me out. That's what I don't think you understood.'

Richard started to pace up and down the length of the table, anything to dispel the whirlwind of feeling within him. 'I don't understand you,' he said thickly. 'We're father and son, you don't have to beat me! This isn't some primitive manhood ritual!'

'Isn't it?' James got up and stretched luxuriantly. He was wearing a silk tie, Richard noticed, and into the fabric was woven the picture of a dragon, mouth gaping wide. 'Look at it this way.' James paused before leaving the room. 'With this tie-up with General Foods we're solvent again. I can retire an extremely wealthy man. Admittedly at the end of the day there won't be much of Bardsey's left for you, but one day you'll get my money. Until then you can do what I did, and what Rowan Judge did, to her damnable credit. You can get your finger out and turn a struggling business into something that looks like success!'

Richard stood, in stunned surprise, and said nothing. After his father left he still stood, utterly frozen.

James didn't want to go home to Diana. At a moment such as this he wanted to prove himself, perhaps for the last time. He was tired of his mistress, she had served her purpose and there was nothing now she could do for him that hadn't been done before. He would pay her off, make the flat over to her, and be done with deceit – for the moment.

Lin Yu wasn't expecting him. She was wearing a cream linen tunic and her hair was caught up in a long ponytail. James noticed that her little face looked shadowed and beneath the yellow of her skin was a tinge of grey.

'Are you ill?' he asked shortly.

She shook her head. 'A little tired, that is all, James. Shall I make you a drink, tea? Cocaine perhaps.'

'Yes, I'll have a snort.'

As she bent over to prepare the drug, he thought that she looked remarkably unattractive. Even Lin Yu was growing older, he supposed, even a whore of her class could not defeat time. Perhaps she was an addict at last. For himself he had no trouble in that direction, his only addiction was power.

But the cocaine was good. Lin Yu took nothing. 'Are you on heroin or something?' demanded James.

'Of course not. I don't want anything now, though.' She started to undress, unbuttoning the tunic from her long neck down to the middle of her thighs. He wasn't getting much of an erection, which showed he was bored with her. Time to get rid of a whore when you couldn't get it up, he told himself. Why pay for what you can't enjoy.

When she was naked she wrapped her arms around herself as if cold and ran to get into the bed. James stripped off and followed her. 'I'm going to make the flat over to you,' he said, guiding her hand to his semi-erect penis. The cocaine had had a bad effect on him, and today that was annoying because it would crown everything to be able to do it. 'Give me something to stiffen me up, would you?' he said.

Lin Yu reached into the bedside drawer and drew out a small bottle of pills. James had used one twice before when he was tired; each time he had been a ram.

'Why are you giving me the flat?' asked Lin Yu.

'Because I think you've earned it, my dear,' said James easily. He lay back and waited for the pill to work, and whether it was the pill or the girl's kneading hand he was becoming hugely distended. James felt drunk and happy. 'I'm paying you off,' he remarked casually. 'We've had a good few years together, after all. You're still quite young, you'll get other blokes quite easily. You'll enjoy it, I shouldn't wonder. What you haven't taught me!'

Lin Yu said nothing. Her little face with its greyish-yellow skin gave nothing away. Moving swiftly and neatly she straddled the man and inserted him inside herself, working up and down with a smooth rhythm.

'Haven't you noticed anything, James?' she asked.

'What – what should I notice?' His eyes were half-closed, he could feel his climax gathering way, way off. She put her fingers against his shoulders, her sharp nails pricked him slightly.

'I look different.'

'Do you – oh my God, this is good. In what way different?'

'James – I'm pregnant with your child.'

He climaxed with his eyes wide open. The air whistled in and out of lungs half-paralysed with shock. The girl got off him and crouched at the edge of the bed. James pushed himself up and half-sat, gasping for breath.

'You're lying, you cow – lying!'

'You can see that I am not. I wanted this from you, James. You can't put me aside, not when I have your son! Another Nicholas. I shall call him Nicholas!'

Somehow James found himself on all fours on the bed. His penis, still enlarged, hung beneath him; beads of sweat stood out like marbles on his forehead. 'Not Nicholas – please – not Nick!'

Lin Yu, frightened at last, caught his arm. 'James? James, what is it?'

The pain in his chest was like being stabbed, worse than that. He couldn't speak to her. Dimly he stared up at the girl, his mouth working, and he thought,'If she doesn't call an ambulance, I shall die!'

Chapter Forty-Eight

Rowan could count on the fingers of one hand the times her mother had visited her at Valley House. Now Diana crouched on the sofa in the large, light sitting room, a diminished and crumpled figure. Fine strands of grey ran through the tawny hair, not unattractively. Even age in Diana was beautiful, thought Rowan ruefully. Her mother was well past fifty.

'If James is ill, Mother,' she said distantly, 'why are you here? Shouldn't you be at the hospital?'

Diana looked up at her daughter. 'He's got some floozy with him. Some whore. It was doing it with her that gave him the heart attack.'

'Oh. Oh, I see.' Rowan was shocked, and that surprised her. 'Did you know he had – women?'

Diana nodded. 'Yes, I knew. But she's – Rowan, she's beautiful! Tiny and Chinese.'

Rowan's heart rose into her throat and down to her guts. That girl of Richard's, it had to be! James would want her because she had been Richard's, he would find nothing more satisfying than that.

'I think he's going to die.' Diana's voice cracked on a sob. 'I want to kill him, but if he dies I'll wish I was dead too! What am I going to do?'

'Does anybody know he's ill? Have you told anyone?'

Diana shook her head. 'I went to the hospital, then straight here. I don't want anyone else to see him! Not with her!'

Rowan went out of the room. Barbara was out with Hannah for a walk, she could not advise. But at that moment the front door opened and Saul came in. They stared at each other uncomfortably.

'I thought you were at the mill,' said Saul.

'I was. My mother's here. Saul – ' She had to confide in somebody, anybody. 'Saul, something's happened. James has had a heart attack.'

A shadow crossed his face. 'Bad? I mean, is he still alive?'

She nodded. 'Intensive care. And he's got some girl with him! Mother rushed to the hospital and she was there. Apparently she's some sort of prostitute and James was with her when it happened.'

'Good God.'

He crossed the hall in swift strides and went into the sitting room. Diana glanced up and said in a voice like raked claws, 'Do I have to be exposed to you as well? It seems that you and James share a great many things, but at least he isn't an alcoholic!'

'Just at this moment,' said Saul drily, 'I am stone cold sober. But don't let that worry you. Look, we should be at the hospital. And someone's got to ring Richard.'

'I'll do it,' said Rowan quickly. Saul glanced at her.

'I suppose you will. Be quick, we've got to go.'

He and Diana were alone while Rowan 'phoned. Diana said, 'I wonder if he was revenging himself? All those women. Because of us.'

Saul blinked. 'What about us? One drunken screw doesn't add up to much in my opinion.'

'Except that in this case it did.' She opened her handbag, took out a powder puff and dabbed it energetically over her nose. 'It produced Nicholas. I suspected it, but only knew for sure when he – died. And James found out then, too. I thought you should know.

'Oh my God. Oh – my – God.'

Diana watched the blood draining from his face, then flooding back patchily. She was conscious of an enormous relief, of a burden handed bodily to someone else. Saul wiped a hand stiffly across his mouth.

Rowan came into the room, herself rather pink. 'Let's go,' she said airily. 'I've left a note for Barbara.'

As they drew into the hospital car park they saw Richard's Maserati howling along the road towards them. He parked and leaped out.

'Does he always come so quickly?' asked Saul bitterly, and Rowan threw him a surprised glance. He looked odd, shocked, and she couldn't believe it was only because of James. As Richard ran towards them, dishevelled and smelling uncharacteristically of booze, she felt herself sliding away from certainty into wild confusion.

'Hello,' said Rowan awkwardly.

'What's happened? Have you been in?'

'Not yet.' Diana drew in her breath, braced herself and set off for the building. The others followed, no one knowing who to walk beside. Behind Saul's back Richard put out his hand for Rowan to squeeze, and she took it.

They had to wait in the corridor while a nurse went to see what was happening. Diana went to stand at the door to the unit, her face anguished. A nurse took her into a side room to complete a form.

'Do you mind about your father?' Rowan asked Richard suddenly.

He looked down at her, as if intensely absorbed. 'Today he almost wrecked me,' he said softly, for her alone. 'He and General Foods have stripped out Bardsey's and given me a shell. Told me to copy you and make a go of it. I've no capital, nothing. But I still want him to live.'

'Then I assume you're not in his will,' said Saul, cutting brutally across the moment. He was walking up and down restively, and Richard put an arm round Rowan to draw her away from her husband.

In an instant Saul gripped Richard's shirt, hauled him towards him and head-butted his face. The younger man's nose and lip exploded in blood, it smeared obscenely over Saul's thatch of hair. 'Don't touch my wife,' said Saul softly. 'I don't like it.'

'What in God's name has got into you?' Rowan ran to Richard's aid, pressing tissues against the mashed flesh.

'It's what's not in me!' retorted Saul. 'I haven't had a drop in three days. And the net result is that I am bloody angry!' He picked up a chair and threw it viciously against the wall.

A nurse came bustling towards them. 'What is going on here?'

'Nothing,' said Saul tightly. 'At least, nothing that matters. I was just venting a little spleen on the bloke that's been fucking my wife.'

'Could you help, nurse?' asked Rowan desperately. 'He's broken his teeth.'

'We have people sick in here!' said the nurse. 'This is not the place for domestic squabbles!' Nonetheless she went to see Richard, leading him brusquely away.

'How long have you known?' asked Rowan.

Saul shrugged. 'Since you told me. It's drink, you know, love. Steer clear of it, you don't know what it might do.'

'Not – not that night you came home!'

'The very same.'

She dropped her eyes in chagrin, and suddenly he couldn't bear to look at her. He turned away, sinking his hands deep in his pockets and bowing his head.

'I didn't mean to hurt you,' said Rowan softly.

'Yes you did. Perhaps I deserved it, I don't know. Do you love him, Rowan?'

She hesitated a long time before answering. 'Yes. Yes, I do.'

She heard him take a long, shuddering breath. At last he said, 'Well. That's it then, isn't it? No point in bashing on with something that's dead, is there?'

'Was that why you – in the bathroom? The other day?'

His eyes were almost black. 'For a second I wanted to kill you. We both know what you'd been doing. And I have never been so – hurt and – and angry – in all my life. Not even James could do that to me. Only you.'

'I'm sorry.' It seemed inadequate, but she said it again. 'I'm sorry.'

Diana appeared, white-faced. 'She's still there,' she said desperately. 'The girl. They say she won't leave. I won't see him with her there, I couldn't!'

'I'll talk to her.' Saul strode through the plastic swing doors. Inside he was surrounded by glass cubicles, each crammed with machinery. In one, next to the bed, sat Lin Yu.

'Hello,' said Saul, watching her. She was composed, almost tranquil, in a soft robe of blue silk. Her hair cascaded down her back, held at the temples by flowers. She nodded her head to Saul.

'How is he?' he asked.

'The doctor says he is stable. Very sick, but no worse.'

'Good – good. Why are you here? You know his wife's outside?'

She fluttered a tiny hand towards the bed. 'But it's right for me to stay. We are much to each other. I am to bear his child.'

Because there was no chair, Saul squatted down next to the girl. He looked up into her delicate face, remembering what he had seen her do to James, what he had seen Richard do to her. This was no innocent. 'What are you hoping for?' he asked softly. 'Money?'

She watched him, trying to assess his threat to her. 'He must keep me,' she said at last. 'If not me, then his child. That's why I stay.'

'You can't trust him. You know that, don't you?'

'Yes. But in this I know he will care for me. If he lives. The child is truly his own, you see. As Nicholas was not.'

Saul let out his breath. 'What a lot you know about him,' he remarked.

'He does not love me,' acknowledged Lin Yu. 'But he will do much for his child.'

'All right.' Saul got up. 'Go away for now. I give you my word that even if James dies, I'll make sure you're taken care of. If he lives, it's up to you.'

'Why should I trust you?'

He shrugged. 'I can't imagine. I might get drunk and never think of you again. I don't think so, though.'

She got up and prepared to walk past him, out of the cubicle. Her head came barely up to his armpit. When she was next to him, she stopped. 'You are his brother, are you not? James said strange things about you. He said you were frightened of yourself.'

'What on earth do you mean?' Saul stared down at the tiny, small-boned face.

'I think you are a man of great power. But a kind man also. And all your life you have seen James using his own power to damage things, people. Your mother perhaps? Certainly you. Always you have said, "Power is not for me". But there is nothing else for you. Except drink.'

Saul let out his breath. 'I don't think anyone can know the harm he did me,' he said throatily. 'When I was a boy – I had nothing, you see. I was at his mercy.'

She touched his hands. 'Because he was frightened of you. I know James so well, I understand him. You're not a boy now and he is an old man, sick in bed.'

She moved smoothly out of the cubicle and away. Saul called out, loud in the hushed ward, 'I won't forget. I promise.' She raised one small, pointed hand.

Diana came in, and Richard, his face swollen and cut.

'She's leaving you,' said Richard thickly, as Saul went out.

'Not now, for God's sake,' said Diana. She went to the bed and took hold of James's near lifeless hand.

Saul thought, 'She's the only one of us that really cares whether he lives or dies.'

Out in the corridor, Rowan sat. Her hands were in her lap,

clasping tissues stained with Richard's blood.

'I've got something to say to you,' said Saul.

She glanced quickly up at him. 'Don't say it if it's cruel. We don't have to be cruel, do we?'

He said honestly, 'I don't know. When you ignore emotions they don't go away, you know. They turn sour and poison you, poison the air you breathe. Take James, for instance. I hate him. I've always hated him, loathed him, wanted him to suffer more horribly than anyone in the world! And underneath all that I love him too. If I don't let out the hate the love gets locked up with it, and we've done that, you and me.'

'Is that what you wanted me to know?'

'Not exactly.' He put out a finger and ran it down the parting in Rowan's dark hair. 'I fathered Nicholas. I didn't know it but I did.'

She looked up at him. Her eyes flooded with tears that did not fall.

'You – and Mother?'

'Once. Only ever once. On the day they got married. And it was because I was drunk, and because she was his, and she was willing, and when did a randy bloke who fancied himself as a stud ever turn up a chance like that? I didn't enjoy it. Or at least, I never wanted to repeat the experience. Neither did she actually, it was one of those stupid, stupid moments.'

'Did James know?'

'Not till the boy died. I can feel sorry for him, you know. Such a terrible thing for him to live with.'

Rowan said in an anguished voice, 'What about me living with it? Knowing what you did?'

'You said yourself, we don't matter any more.'

If she had indeed said that she couldn't remember when.

Richard came out of the ward and Rowan got up to go to him. He put his hands on her shoulders, daring Saul to object.

'Don't,' said Rowan, and moved away of her own accord.

Saul said, 'Is he conscious?'

'Comes and goes, I think.' Richard's voice was muffled by the swelling. 'I'm going to sue you for the dental bills, you bastard.'

Saul crossed the floor in a stride, yelling, 'Try it and I'll knock a few more down your throat!'

The aggression in him had welled up so fast that they were all taken aback. Saul turned away, clearly under the most minimal control.

'Go in and see James,' said Rowan shakily. 'Then we'll go home.'

The ward sister was becoming agitated by the toing and froing. 'One at a time, please,' she insisted, and Diana, who had been clutching James's long freckled hand, said, 'I want him to myself! Be quick all of you, then just go away!'

As she left, Saul leaned over the bed. James opened a pale eye. 'Upset,' he said weakly. 'About the girl.'

'Yes.' Saul looked down at his half-brother. A deep well of feeling seemed to open inside him. Heat, pain, love, longing, all kept too long controlled. 'You were a bastard to me, you know,' he remarked.

'Was I? Little pillock like you. Thought – thought the old man would give everything to you. He didn't like me much.'

'You were the favourite!'

'Seemed to me – he made more of you somehow. Perhaps not. Hard to tell.' He tried to chuckle. 'If I die I'll ask him.'

Saul took a deep breath. 'James – I'm sorry about Nick. I knew nothing until today. I swear I didn't know.'

It was as if he hadn't been heard. There was the soft buzz of machines and the hushing of a ventilator against another bed. James said, 'Thought you were laughing at me. Saw a doting fool, thinking he was dad.'

'You were, in everything that mattered.'

'Diana said that too. Why did you do it, Saul?'

There seemed no way to explain it all. 'I suppose – because she was beautiful.'

Softly, thoughtfully, James said, 'She was, wasn't she? I had the most beautiful wife in the world.'

Richard took Rowan into the garden. It was getting dark. They stood shivering on a little used path. 'Pack some things and come tomorrow,' he said.

'But what about Hannah? She loves her daddy, I can't take her away from him and home and everything, not all at once. It's all right, Richard, we don't have to rush!'

'You can leave her with the nanny, it wouldn't be for long. He could kill you. If he starts drinking again you're as good as dead. He's half mad now, you can see it!'

'Really!' He saw her teeth flash in a smile. 'I'm not scared of Saul. He's got a right to be angry. And I'm not leaving Hannah!'

Richard said, 'You left her quite happily to go to the States! Look, I'm not having this. I insist you come tonight, I'm having no argument.

'And I'm not arguing. But I'm not coming either.'

She began to walk back to the hospital but he caught her arm. 'Rowan – you can't start feeling sorry for him. He's a drunk, he's violent. You can't bring a child up in a home like that!'

'If it wasn't for Saul, Hannah would be in some mental home,' flared Rowan.

Richard couldn't believe his ears. 'You're unbalanced, Rowan! You said yourself it was hell! You've got no idea of the man he is, you can't stay with him.'

'I didn't say I was going to. I'm just not leaving yet.'

Richard turned square to face her. In the half-light his swollen face looked like a caricature of himself, still handsome but elongated and enlarged. 'I think you should know something,' he said in a warm, low voice. 'I wanted to keep it from you but I see now I can't. You don't know the man you married, Rowan. He – he fathered your mother's child. He slept with your mother. Nicholas was his son.'

'What a horrible thing to say.'

'I'm not lying to you, Rowan. It's true.'

'I know it's true! I just think it's foul of you to tell tales to try and persuade me. Leave me alone, Richard, I'm beginning to think it's you I don't know very well!'

'What do you mean by that?'

She glared up at him. 'That horrible article you wrote in the paper. The mess you made of the bid. James has wrecked your firm and you haven't tried to stop him. Why don't you threaten to resign and veto the merger? You can put it to the board and have it thrown out. But you gave in. You're not up to this, Richard, not by a long chalk.'

'Christ, Rowan, you don't decide about people on the basis of their business acumen! Or do you? Is that the way your mind works?'

In the dark, she clasped her hands. 'I don't know. Right now all I know is I'm going home with Saul. I'll talk to you tomorrow.'

He stood, in the half-light, and listened to her heels clacking away along the path. Everything he touched, everything he had thought solid, was turning to dust beneath his hands. Never in his life had he felt so wretched.

The night was dark and rather chilly. Confused, miserable, Rowan went into the silent mill. Saul was in the house, and Hannah, and Barbara's anxious, watchful eyes. It was better in the mill, quite alone.

Somehow, despite the thousands of times she had been there since, her mind went back to the night she had walked there, and asked Elsie for money for food. A few pounds and she had been happy; she distinctly remembered that surge of relief and joy. If only her problems could be resolved so easily today. Yet what was it her mother used to say? 'Rowan always knows what she wants to do.' If it had ever been true, it wasn't now.

Richard had been wonderful in New York. She had loved everything about him, from the reddish-haired knuckles of his toes to the soft bristle on his face in the morning. She had loved his love of her, the freedom, the delicious sense of sin! Back home, understandably, it wasn't the same. She wasn't free any more, and somehow she wasn't sure she wanted to be.

Her thoughts veered to Saul, and she put up her hands, as if physically to shut him out. Why did he hurt her so? Why was it that, with him, everything hurt so much? With him it was all extremes, and she knew instinctively that with Richard, or anyone, if it hurt at all it would be a pale shadow of this. Saul wasn't good for her, that big, strong, difficult man. She could spend a lifetime trying and never understand him.

A noise in the echoing space made her spin round. He was there, watching her. 'How long have you been here?' she asked.

'Not long.' He came towards her, his footsteps eerie on the stone floor. She had said she wasn't scared of him but here, in this lonely place, he frightened her.

Rowan took a nervous step backward. 'Don't,' he said. 'I'm past anger. I don't think – I wanted to thank you. I know how hard I've made it for you. You never let me down.'

'Yes I did. You've forgotten.'

'Have I?' He stood watching her, his hands in his pockets. Suddenly she longed to hold him, and without knowing what she was doing she went to him and put her arms round his neck. He enfolded her and they stood, hugging each other, knowing how vast was the distance between them. After a moment or two Saul realised she was crying.

He took her back to the house. A fire was burning in the hearth and Rowan went and self-consciously sat in a chair by herself. Almost as if he hadn't noticed, Saul lounged back on the sofa. He said, 'If James dies, Richard should be set up.'

She gulped. 'Depends on the will. Saul – I didn't mean that about not letting you have any of Judge's. I would, of course.'

'Why of course? You've bled for this firm, my girl, all your life! You'll never give it up.'

She went a little pink. 'We can all change, you know. Even me.'

He got up and went to the cabinet. Rowan tensed in her chair, gripping the arms, then almost collapsed when he returned with a glass and a bottle of mineral water. 'Beast.'

'Oh ye of little faith.'

'Are you off it for good?'

He shook his head. 'Not likely. Just until tomorrow. Some people get through the whole of their lives waiting for tomorrow.'

She cupped her hands and dropped her chin into them. 'It was my fault, you know. I drove you to it.'

At last she had roused him. He put down the glass with a crash. 'That is the biggest load of bloody rubbish I have ever heard! You know what drove me to it? Being nice. I'm *not* nice. The trouble is I want to be. Being nicer than James was all I ever had over him, it was my stock in trade, everyone liked me so much more than him. God, was I popular! I couldn't face you down over who ran what in this place because I couldn't not be liked. You know the best thing that ever happened to me?'

She watched him, wide-eyed. 'What?'

'Hannah! You needn't look so surprised, she was! For the first time in my life I had to look at someone and decide what was really important. It wasn't their looks, it wasn't what they could do, it wasn't how bleeding nice they were, it was something quite separate. Some essence of them. Something you could love when everything you looked for in a friend wasn't there. When I thought about her – when I was sober enough to think about her – I began to think about me.'

'I haven't thought about you in ages,' said Rowan. 'I haven't let myself.'

He turned his head away. 'I don't need to be told that.'

Picking up his drink again, he wandered over to the window. 'You'll be good for Richard,' he said. 'Sort him out. In years to come people won't remember you used to be married to someone else.'

'Will you find someone else?' asked Rowan.

'Yes, I suppose so.'

There was a long, waiting silence. The shock of it had her thoughts spinning. That he could think about, even *think* about, someone else, tonight, when everything they had ever meant to each other was coming to such an end – it almost choked her. She tried not to care, she tried to think of anything except that, but suddenly she was shaking with rage.

She said in a low, murderous voice, 'You beast! You don't give a bloody damn. You did marry me to get Judge's, and now you're going to get it and you don't care at all. All these weeks you've known about me and Richard and you haven't done a bloody thing. I hate you, Saul, I hate you because you don't love me one tiny little scrap!' She picked up the mineral water bottle and threw it at him. It sailed through the plate glass window with a crash of resounding magnitude.

In the next room Hannah started to wail and they heard Barbara rush in to her. 'It's all right, darling, your father's gone berserk, that's all.'

'It was me!' yelled Rowan back. 'And he bloody deserved it! The faithless swine!' She threw herself on the sofa and sobbed.

Saul sat down on the edge next to her and patted her back. 'Look,' he said gently, 'I thought you loved Richard. I thought you wanted to leave me and live with him.'

She pushed the hair out of her eyes and struggled to say what she felt. 'I never said I wanted to leave you! But you're all ready to pack my suitcase and wave goodbye!'

'For God's sake, Rowan! You said you loved him!' Saul's face, so dear, so utterly familiar, twisted in real anguish.

'I do love him,' she said miserably. 'But – it isn't the way I love you. It's not a real kind of thing. Not the way we are.'

'You slept with him, you told him you cared! Look, I know I deserve it but this is torture, Rowan. You can't tear me apart just for your amusement.'

'I didn't ever want to hurt you! But – oh, it was better in New York! It was like not being married, I didn't feel bad. Here it was all rather horrid really. Too much like James and my mother. Doing things for yourself, and not for anyone else.'

'Even James and Diana care about each other, after a fashion.' He put his big fingers gently on her cheeks and wiped the tears. Her eyes, wide and suddenly fiercely determined, stared up at him.

'I don't want it to be like that. I want our sort of love, the way it should have been, together and honest and Hannah knowing who her daddy is. We got it right sometimes. Didn't we?'

Saul got up, his hands thrust deep into his pockets. Rain was coming in through the broken window and next door Hannah still sobbed. 'You know I love you,' he said harshly. 'I always have. But I want life my way this time, and that might not be your way. I don't know. We can run Judge's together, but only if you let it happen. I want to expand, buy up great chunks of Bardsey's if we can get it. Diversify. Add a bit of capital to Joe Partridge's set-up and get involved in transport. And I want more kids. Lots more kids.'

Rowan swallowed. 'How many more?'

'About three for starters. We can have all the tests, it might be we have to stop at Hannah. But – Rowan, I want to try.'

Her eyes felt gritty with tears, she felt she might sob and sob forever. It was as if all the tears for years past were dammed up inside her, all her past sorrows and failures and disappointments. 'Children hurt you so,' she wept. 'You hurt me so!'

'But that isn't the most of it!' said Saul in surprise.

'But it's the part you remember.'

He went out and got a board and started to block up the window. Rowan helped him, holding the hammer and the tacks. His hands moving so purposefully twisted her stomach in desire, she was shocked at herself. How could you love one man, sleep with him, yet love and desire another?

When the job was finished, almost before it was done, she had her arms round Saul's neck, her thighs pressed into his. Furtively, to avoid alerting Barbara, they sneaked into their bedroom. Making love, wildly in the dark, Rowan held on to his shoulders and moaned; 'I love you! I love you!' But afterwards, when he said, 'Tell me you'll stay. Rowan, please!' she still said, 'I don't know.'

Chapter Forty-Nine

Before nine the next morning Richard arrived. Everyone was still in bed, Rowan answered the door in her dressing gown with Hannah on her hip. Richard came and stood in the kitchen.

'How's James?' asked Rowan awkwardly.

'Out of danger, they think. Diana's gone home anyway. She sat up with him all night.'

'Oh.'

She felt shy for some reason. The memory of Saul last night was too recent. They had made love so often, had woken barely two hours since to do it again! Like teenagers discovering it for the very first time. And here was her lover, and she felt unfaithful.

Hannah winged and she poured out cereal with one hand, then sat the child down and spooned it up for her. Saul came in, wearing only a towel round his waist.

'What the devil are you doing here? Is James dead?'

Rowan was quick to step in. 'He seems better. And Richard thought – '

'I was worried about Rowan,' said Richard.

'How bloody civil of you.' Saul walked precisely into the spot occupied by Richard, forcing him to move out of the way. Richard moved only the barest minimum.

'You're behaving like a couple of dogs,' said Rowan testily.

'I see the window got broken,' said Richard. 'Get packed, Rowan, you're not staying here another minute.'

Unwisely he reached out a hand and Saul punched it hard out of the way. 'Don't you dare touch her!'

'Will you stop it!' Rowan pushed between them. 'I broke the window.' She looked from one to the other. How she wished that Richard had never come! And yet – Saul wanted so much from her. There was no way of knowing if she could ever be strong enough. She said airily, 'I'm not going now. There's things to do. Hannah's got a busy day. There's a problem in the mill.'

Richard turned on her. 'And when do you think might be convenient, may I ask?'

She dropped her head. 'I don't know.'

Suddenly Saul laughed. 'Tell you what, Richard,' he said kindly. 'We'll ring you. When the mill's running smoothly, when Hannah's out of nappies, when Rowan's got the shopping in and the fridge stocked up. It'll take about – oh, twenty years.'

'Don't laugh at him,' said Rowan miserably. 'It isn't fair.'

'I don't think I have to consider fairness just now. I've had enough of this messing about. You're my wife, Rowan! I am not letting you go!'

In a low voice Richard said, 'It's up to you. We'd be happy together, you know we would.'

And she did know. But she looked around her messy kitchen, at her baby, at her home. Saul loved her, and no one knew more of her than he. He knew her insecurities, the raw ambition, the unattractive drive that whipped her on. Yet when she failed, when weakness and weariness beat her, he was there to comfort, never to blame.

What in turn could she give to him? Only, she saw now, what had been her gift to him since the day they met. Through all the drunkenness and doubt, she had reached into a well of love, expecting always for her bucket to come up empty. Never once had it done so. There was always more, and more again. Even if she left him now, and went with Richard to a calmer life, there would be no end of it; she and Saul could no more disentangle themselves from each other than they could from Hannah. Saul needed her more than he knew. Perhaps she needed him more than she had ever understood. Slowly she shook her head. 'No,' she said. 'No. Not now, not ever.'

Later that day Saul and Rowan left the baby with Barbara and took the tram up Shipley Glen, past the wooden cut-outs of nursery rhyme characters that Hannah might never recognise. They bought ice cream and wandered amidst the families and bored teenagers, watching a boy flying a scarlet kite high into the air. A thin mist obscured the sun.

Suddenly Rowan said, 'Poor Richard. Everything's gone wrong for him.'

Saul snorted. 'I find it difficult to feel all that sorry for him, actually. This might be the making of him, a bit of real struggle. And mark my words, in a few years' time he'll be a carbon copy of his father.'

'If that's my fault, I should die of shame,' said Rowan softly.

Yet the shame now was in feeling so terribly happy. Richard's face came back to her, white and stricken, and still here she was, holding Saul's thick hard fingers, awash with happiness. Regret tinged the edges of her vision. But if there was one thing she had learned from life it was the futility of looking back, wishing for yesterday. The lesson that Judge's had taught her was one Richard had to learn: you took what you had and made the best of it, and if you were lucky, if you were brave, the best was very good indeed.

'Do you love me, Rowan?'

She looked at him. Some of his tan was returning but his eyes held none of the laughter she loved. She put her hands up and touched his cheeks.

'With all my heart,' she said softly.

And suddenly the sun came out. Saul caught her wrist and started to run, they sprinted hectically across the rocks and rough ground. When at last they stopped and fell gasping on to the grass they looked up and saw the kite, soaring higher and higher into the brilliant summer air.

Sally sat in the plane, watching England pass beneath her. She was going to Pakistan, for a visit that might extend to years. The green expanse of Yorkshire, dotted here and there with the darker bulk of cities, set down amidst the harsh northern moors, was lost in the billows of cloud. Her whole life had been lived there, everything of concern to her had happened in that wide space. How she loved it.

Her mind drifted on, to the frightening days ahead. Yet she was safe, wrapped up in the life of her husband and his family. She was changing, becoming reconciled, acknowledging that she would pay for what she needed with her freedom. She was coming to know happiness.

Below the spread wings of the aircraft, beneath the cloud, the mills clattered on. James lay on the sofa at Aspley Manor, weak and drained. Richard, his son, struggled with the shattered remnants of Bardsey's, while across the valley Saul and Rowan rearranged their lives.

And in a small neat flat, full of silk and strange objects, a Chinese girl laboured with great difficulty. After hours of torment, almost too much for her small body, at last she gave birth. It was a daughter.